FINAL
HOUR

OTHER BOOKS AND AUDIO PRODUCTS
BY JESSICA DRAPER AND RICHARD D. DRAPER:

Seventh Seal

Rising Storm

FINAL

THE DRAMATIC CONCLUSION TO THE SEVENTH SEAL EPIC

HOUR

JESSICA DRAPER
RICHARD D. DRAPER

Covenant

Covenant Communications, Inc.

Cover image (world) © Digital Vision/Getty Images; (digital highlight) Photodisc Green/Getty Images

Cover design copyrighted 2004 by Covenant Communications, Inc.

Published by Covenant Communications, Inc.
American Fork, Utah

Printed in Canada
First Printing: October 2004

10 09 08 07 06 05 04   10 9 8 7 6 5 4 3 2 1

ISBN 1-59156-638-X

And I will shew wonders in the heavens and in the earth,
blood, and fire, and palm trees of smoke. (Joel 2:30)

CHAPTER 1

"Star light, star bright, first star I see tonight . . ." The nursery rhyme dwindled into silence. Lucrezia Callatta stared up into the night sky beyond the wind-rustled awning, watching as a single star detached itself from the cosmic backdrop and arced earthward in a long streak of white fire. She sighed, looking down at the diary in her hand, its screen a glowing square in the darkness of her family's tent. It wasn't the first star she saw tonight. Besides, all the falling stars in the world wouldn't bring Porter back, or make the crowded but orderly camp feel any more like home.

Or more real, for that matter. If anybody had told her last year that by midsummer she'd be sitting in a growing tent city laid out on the old city plan of Nauvoo while the world outside crashed down around everybody's ears, she would never have believed it. But that's what had happened.

"What are you still doing up?" Donna asked, settling beside Lucrezia. "It's like two in the morning! That's way too late for star-gazing—you've got school tomorrow, remember."

"School tomorrow." Lucrezia rolled her eyes. "Like that matters." It did, according to her mother, Carmen, who felt that learning was always important. Besides, Carmen would add with a scheming smile, school keeps kids busy and out of everybody's hair. *Thanks, Mom,* Lucrezia thought. She gestured toward the sky. "Besides, this is educational. Looks like we're getting a meteorite shower."

"Meteor shower," Donna corrected, leaning forward to watch the stars. "They're bits of rock, dust, or ice, sometimes left over from the tails of comets, and some of it's just free-floating stuff left over from the solar system's formation. The correct terminology is *meteoroids* before they fall, *meteors* when they do, and *meteorites* if they survive long enough to hit the ground. Not many of them do—most just burn up in the atmosphere. In fact, every thirty seconds a tiny meteor crashes into the sky and burns up about seventy miles up. Some of them get closer, but a lot of times they explode in the air, like bombs, and don't leave pieces. A big one can leave a crater with a peak in the middle and ripples in the ground outside. But that's rare—like once every ten thousand years. Mainly, it's just little stuff. We don't see most of them."

"Thanks, professor." Lucrezia added another eye roll to underline her total lack of interest in that information. In Lucrezia's jaundiced little-sister opinion, Donna always had a streak of know-it-all, and it had just gotten worse since she'd become a teacher in one of the many schools the Mormon refugees had set up in the growing camps around the Nauvoo Temple. Another streak of light, this one tinged with gold, drew her eyes forward again.

Donna spun away into the dark tent again, only to reemerge with a camera, which she trained at the natural fireworks display above them as a half dozen more stars shook loose and hurtled toward the earth. "This will be great to show the kids tomorrow! Mom!" she called back into the tent. "Dad! You've got to come see this!"

Carmen and Tony, who had already heard most of the conversation through the canvas walls of their makeshift home, finally gave up any pretense of sleeping through their daughters' late-night chatter. "Dragging me out of bed to see a bunch of falling stars, huh?" Tony growled, trying to sound uninterested.

"Think of it as an excuse to sit under the stars with your arm around me," Carmen suggested, laughing.

Tony grinned, wrapping her robe around her. "Hey, I'm there!"

"Is this amazing or what?" Donna asked, her eye never budging from the camera's viewfinder as she moved slightly aside to accommodate her parents—and Gianni, who trailed out with his blanket cape to flop into Carmen's lap. "The kids in my class are going to love seeing this!"

"Maybe you can show them a meteor rock up close—or one of those craters you were talking about." Lucrezia got to her feet, her eyes wide as the half dozen falling stars grew to a full dozen, then doubled again. The streaks of their tails grew larger, trailing wide swaths of brilliance across the darkness, the fiery pinpoints growing larger as they hurtled closer. "It looks like they're landing out in the hills outside town!"

* * *

Ping.

The metallic noise barely registered above the humming, clicking noise of the scanners in the Earth Sciences pod of the International Space Station. It blended in with the tiny, tinny noises of distant gunshots in the background of Clara Cortez's report on the war in Ohalajishi. On the news feed from the earth far below, the chaos engulfing central Africa was still spreading, despite the efforts of the United States and United Nations to stem the bloody tide. Rebels, refugees, government troops, and peacekeepers ran, collided, and fought all over the continent, leaving only a few oases of security. Channel 8's on-scene reporter had followed a small band of refugees to one such place, a huge plantation in what had once been the Ivory Coast, where he stood under the overhanging branches of huge, lush trees, his eyes wide and weary as he described the massacres he'd witnessed on the long road the refugees had taken. Behind him, almost hidden in the vegetation beside the gates, a discreet sign identified the site as a cooperative farm owned by The Church of Jesus Christ of Latter-day Saints.

James Hideyoshi, tectonic specialist aboard the International Space Station, glanced up from the concentric color bands of a real-time topographic map of Big Sister, the emerging volcano in Oregon state, and frowned at the news footage on the screen. "This kind of thing almost makes me glad we're stuck up here," Hideyoshi muttered, shuddering. He pushed away the rest of the thought, trying to fill his mind with the data pouring in from the ground installation Becker had set up on the unstable slopes of the evolving mountain. Thinking about the volcano looming ever larger over the northwestern United States was preferable to thinking about the isolation closing in upon the small crew orbiting the wild skies of the earth.

It had been four months since the last shuttle arrived, fighting its way through the churning atmosphere to bring emergency supplies to the ISS crew. Tolliver, the astrobiologist, had talked her way onto the shuttle for its return trip, begging them to take her back to her kids before it was too late. Her colleagues watched from the station and from ground control, horrified and helpless, as the winds of a massive storm easily swatted the shuttle out of the sky, sending it flaming through the clouds in a flash of brilliant fragments. Captain Nakima had broken the shocked silence that followed with a dry announcement over the station's intercom: "Memo to crew: shore leave is cancelled until further notice." They'd laughed, the black humor of it temporarily easing the corrosive anxiety that filled the station as pervasively as the faint, chemical smell of recycled air. Ivana Mir kept a list of the punishments she'd like to inflict on the "genius" who decided to add a piña colada fragrance to the air filters; the list got longer and more baroque every day.

Another, louder *ping* caught Hideyoshi's ear, finally drawing his attention away from the incoming data. He looked at the news feed, but the noise didn't fit with the announcement that the war in west Africa, combined with weather-related difficulties in the shipping industry, would badly disrupt the world's supply of chocolate (a weeping gourmand decried the injustice of the dwindling supply of "heritage" cocoa blends for his award-winning recipes). A rattling noise, almost like heavy raindrops on a tin roof, brought the tectonic specialist to full attention. Muting the volume on the newscast, he listened intently. Sure enough, another series of pings and rattling came through the station's walls. Its thin, metal and plastic walls. The noise didn't soothe, the way the sound of rain on the roof used to. Instead, it sent a chill rush of adrenaline down his spine. Rain couldn't bash right through the roof—and let all the air out of the house when it did.

Hideyoshi took a deep breath, refocusing on the rainbow display on his monitor. No use worrying about something he couldn't do anything about. Besides, it's not like small collisions didn't happen frequently. Space dust, tiny meteoroids, bits of junk from other missions, and other objects hit the space station all the time; its outer skin was pocked with tiny craters from collisions with sand-sized objects. He had seen them personally, when the continued absence of specialized maintenance personnel forced the science staff into space suits to assist the flight crew with repairs. Larger projectiles, however, posed a real danger if they got through the station's protective sweeper screens. And from the pinging noises, it sounded like some definitely had.

A louder bang, like a soccer ball hitting the wall, made Hideyoshi flinch, and the sudden tightening of his fingers entered a line of completely bogus data into Becker's simulation. "Shoot!" *That sounded bigger than a loose screw.*

The intercom bell sounded through another surge of the pattering noise, followed by Captain Nakima's deep voice. "Attention. As you all know by now, something's knocking on the door. Don't worry, it's not the Big Bad Wolf. Dr. Kirmisse tells me we're experiencing what is not technically termed a meteor shower. Whatever they call it, there's no need to panic. The station is now at yellow alert. Everybody get into your suits and stay in your labs. Kirmisse will fill in the details while you're fighting with your fasteners."

The insistent chime of a yellow alert sounded over the groans of the dozen station inhabitants, followed by the slow drawl of the station's resident astrophysicist. His deliberate way of speaking had always belied his intense interest in scanning the skies for near-earth objects, or NEOs, massive asteroids a kilometer or larger in diameter. Now, a tremor underlay the astrophysicist's soft Georgia accent.

Kirmisse's face on the intercom monitor looked strained as well, slick with sweat that he wiped away with a shaking hand. "We've entered the path of a previously unmapped swarm of meteoroids. Initial analysis suggests that they are rocky and metallic in composition, rather than icy, indicating that they are not debris from a comet on a periodic orbit." Another loud bang made him flinch, along with everyone else. Hideyoshi muttered a litany of comically sanitized curses aloud, silently praying for protection for all of them as he tightened the microfiber fasteners on his environment suit.

"The incoming bodies are big enough that the station's sweepers aren't catching them all, as you can see," the astrophysicist continued, swallowing visibly as he sent the data on meteoroid composition, headings, and velocity to everyone's data screens. It formed a slice of virtual space, with the station and incoming projectiles lit up as glowing outlines. Kirmisse stared at his own monitor, watching the multiplying points of light flicker like fireflies. The display glittered in his wide eyes as well. "The meteoroids could damage the station— puncture the outer hull and cause a section to decompress—"

"In which event, follow standard emergency procedures, as we've drilled," Nakima broke in, as Kirmisse's voice began to rise. "How long before we get out of range?" Nakima continued.

Kirmisse took a breath, his voice steadying. "The station will leave the immediate vicinity of the swarm in fifteen minutes." The simulated space station on the screen moved away from the flock of red marks indicating the largest of the incoming meteoroids. The red dots kept coming, however, with larger ones inexorably approaching from the far edge of the virtual projection. A long cone, its point tapering off into the distance, intersected the station's orbit and spotlighted a wide swath of the earth below. The lighted area slowly traveled across land and sea as the planet rotated, a spotlight on the stage where the meteorites would make their debut. The astrophysicist steadied his voice even further, its slow drawl sounding not so much calm as almost dead. "The swarm itself will continue to intersect the earth's orbit for several hours before the first wave subsides."

"First wave?" Mir's question echoed the other crew members' thoughts. Her section of the intercom screen showed that she'd struggled into her space suit, speaking as she pulled on the silvery gloves.

"Yes. This is simply the first wave. Observations indicate three more waves containing bodies of significant size," Kirmisse affirmed, still with an odd deadness in his voice. He hadn't begun to pull on his space suit, wearing only his coveralls as he floated before the camera and his own chattering readouts.

"Looks like they're going to hit on the night side too. Gonna be quite the show for the groundhogs," Mir said, drawing laughs from several others.

Hideyoshi's own smile faded as he realized that tears had joined the sweat on the astrophysicist's face.

"And in the third wave," he continued, "are the largest bodies yet, including two true NEOs: one measuring fifty kilometers, the other over sixty. They are also on a collision course with the earth. I calculate a 90 to 95 percent probability that they will intersect the earth's orbit and enter the atmosphere at acute angles and extreme velocity. They will strike the surface with a force equivalent to the explosion of dozens of massive nuclear bombs, precipitating thousands of tons of dust and water into the air, causing worldwide extinctions."

His voice had dropped almost to a whisper as he finished, his head bowed. The months of staring into the endless darkness from the isolated station and the horror of the pictures of devastation in his mind rose in a black wave inside him.

Stunned silence greeted his prediction. He looked up, the tears in his eyes shining in the stark overhead lights. "And there is nothing we can do about it. Absolutely nothing. I am so sorry. Tell them all that I am so sorry." In another moment, he disappeared from the screen.

On the monitors, a huge, ruby-colored spot of light floated gently down the cone of light. It touched the green grid of the earth and disappeared in a burst of white radiance. In the frozen silence, the pinging of the monster's tiny outriders sounded like gunshots.

"Kirmisse!" Nakima's voice roared over the intercom, as the corridor camera caught the astrophysicist floating swiftly and purposefully toward the empty shuttle bay. "Get back to your station! Everyone else, stay put!" A second later, the camera recorded the captain flying down the same corridor, swinging hand over hand after his insubordinate crew member.

A reverberating crash tore through the station, the yellow alert changed instantly to red, and the louder, lower tones of the automated voice alarm sounded over the captain's furious swearing. "Warning. Airlock open. Warning. Impact damage in storage compartment C. Warning. Airlock open. Warning. Decompression in storage compartment C," the automated warning system chanted, handling two emergency scenarios at once. Heavy doors swung into place, locking off the decompressing storage area, isolating the damage from the meteor storm's parting strike.

The outer airlock door, on the other hand, swung closed automatically, resealing the shuttle bay behind Dr. Kirmisse. The astrophysicist's glazed eyes turned toward the pearl-streaked sapphire of the earth, the tears freezing on his face as he began the long fall toward his doomed birthplace.

"Guess he finally found his NEO," Mir muttered. This time, nobody laughed.

Hideyoshi closed his eyes, whispering a prayer for Kirmisse—and inspiration for all of them. "What can we do? There must be something."

"Like blast them out of the sky with all the missiles we've got in storage?" Nakima leaned his forehead against his hand, his knuckles tightening on the handhold.

"Like find out if 90 to 95 percent is the same as 100?" Hideyoshi asked.

Nakima straightened abruptly. Time to implement the philosophy that had served him well through military duty, astronaut training, and innumerable clashes with bureaucracy: when in doubt, start giving orders. "All right, if we can't stop it, we'll convince ourselves that it's not going to hit us. Mir, turn your sensors over—time to look at clouds made of rock instead of water. Wong, heat up the comm. We've got to tell them something down on the ground, even if we don't have definitive data yet. Main thing is preventing a panic. Hideyoshi, dig into Kirmisse's computer and make that simulation dance. In six hours, I want to know exactly what's going to hit us and when!"

Another crash reverberated through the plastic and metal hull as a fist-sized space rock bounced off the side of the station. Its cousins dove past the station, following Dr. Kirmisse into the atmosphere. In the thickening darkness, the space-born rocks began to glow with friction heat, red first, then yellow, until they blazed with brilliant white light, growing tails that flared across the dark sky and reflected in sparkling shards on the surface of the black waves of the Pacific Ocean.

* * *

Far below, an orange glow flashed momentarily, the dim light unnaturally bright in the darkness. For a split second, the wavering firelight silhouetted a small figure in the ragged opening of a camouflaged door. The door shut, concealing the entrance to the low, dank room beneath the ramshackle warehouse slowly surrendering to tropical decay on the far end of the sweeping seaport. Diamonds smuggled from Africa had graced its stone shelves in the smugglers' heyday. At the moment, however, the only glitter came from the guttering candle flames reflecting in the wide eyes of the people packed into the cramped space.

The underground room belonged to the family of Felipe Aquino, a rough-and-tumble merchant who ran his own small-scale shipping business out of the low-rent end of Manila's busy port. The hidden chamber beneath the Aquinos' legitimate warehouse had been built centuries ago as a pirates' den and smugglers' hideaway, filled in more prosperous times with raw opium, stolen cargoes of everything from ancient silks to ultramodern electronics, and a dizzying variety of contraband luxuries bound for equally discreet warehouses in other ports all over the Pacific Rim. The early Aquinos were profiteers, pirates haunting the dangerous waters around the inviting sweep of Manila Bay—and successful profiteers at that. Lately, however, the Aquinos' checkered inheritance showed more in their propensity for wicked laughs than actual larceny. While they took a perverse pride in their pirate heritage, the last three generations of Aquinos lived their lives according to the dictates of the faith that Grandmother Aquino had found on her knees in the great cathedral many years before. As a young widow, Great-grandmother Aquino had prayed seventy rosaries to the Virgin, asking clemency for the late Grandfather Aquino's soul and begging for solace at his passing. As she made her slow way down the broad steps, she had staggered—and found herself in the arms of a startled young man in a white shirt, tie, and name tag bearing the unlikely first name of Elder. Four of her sons took that name as well, bringing the word of eternal mercy to living souls and extending the blessings of sealing to the dead (including their own piratical ancestors). The Aquinos left the Catholic Church for The Church of Jesus Christ of Latter-day Saints, and in the years that followed they brought hundreds of others with them. The Virgin, as Great-grandmother Aquino observed, her eyes sparkling, had quite a sense of humor.

So did Felipe Aquino, though at the moment he was far too tense to laugh. He moved swiftly to the hidden door, closing it firmly after his son slipped into their bolt-hole, and flashed a reassuring smile to the small group of weary, frightened Mormon refugees huddled in the musty cavern. Brother Light tolerated no opposition to his growing religious empire; he had declared the Mormons anathema early on, then proclaimed open season on Catholics with the burning of Archbishop

Corazon in the square before the cathedral. Muslims soon felt the weight of his Hands, as the black-clad, red-masked enforcers and the mobs of angry, hungry, fanatically dedicated Children of Light offered a simple choice to everyone in their path: proclaim allegiance to the One God and the Prophet, or die. At first, many Mormons had taken the second option, giving their lives in defense of their souls, before the word had come at last to the faithful Saints from the Savior Himself after His coming to Adam-ondi-Ahman: leave the world, gather to Zion. Since then, the Aquino family had smuggled over a hundred of their fellow Saints, and a large number of faithful Catholics and Muslims as well, from the grasping Hands of the Prophet.

For the ten people staring out of the darkness at young José Aquino and his father, the way to Zion ironically led through a smugglers' lair. The most recent shipment of human cargo had hidden in the Aquinos' underground smugglers' cache for nearly twelve hours, since the white-robed mob of the Children of Light burst into the small Mormon chapel in a poor neighborhood by Manila's crowded docks. Led by a heavily armed Hand (a group of five of Brother Light's vicious soldiers), the attackers waved torches and knives, screaming their vows to destroy the infidels who denied the Unity of the One and the authority of their Prophet—as well as the mob's right to confiscate anything that caught their eyes. A few of the ward members died in that attack, sacrificing themselves in a desperate rear-guard fight that let the others escape. The rest of the congregation ran literally for their lives, scattering through the back alleys of the ports, desperately seeking any possible way to reach the safety of the nearest temple and the accompanying pockets of Zion. The Aquinos' multitude of cousins swept up this group, bringing them to the underground safe house. Now, they needed safe passage through the dangerous streets of Manila to the temple community in Quezon City.

Unfortunately, the Aquinos' success hadn't gone unnoticed. The Hands of the Prophet didn't know who repeatedly snatched their prey, or exactly where their victims hid, but after repeated frustrations, they had deduced the section of the docks into which the targeted infidels disappeared—and from which they inexplicably vanished. Thus, two Hands of red-masked assassins stalked the alleys and piers of the low-rent port district above the old pirates' cave.

Inconvenient for the latest generation of Aquino smugglers—but not insurmountable.

Felipe Aquino glanced around at his latest shipment of human cargo, exchanged a quick, reassuring smile with Paz, his imperturbable wife, then turned his attention to the young son who had volunteered to go scouting. "Well, what news?"

The boy swallowed hard, willing his voice not to crack as he looked at his father. "They're coming this way—two Hands and a mob of white robes, pounding on all the warehouse doors. They're yelling that they're going to start burning things down next if somebody doesn't tell them where we're hiding." The older man's confidence reinforced José's courage; he returned the smile with a defiant lift of his chin. "That's not so many. They don't know about the back door, and they don't have a boat. I made sure Uncle Marco has ours ready. We can get past them on the water if we can get to the dock."

"When we get to the dock," Paz corrected gently, giving the child in her arms a hug.

Felipe nodded briskly. "Just two Hands? Twice as many would be no match for the will of our Father. All right, we'll go out the back door, and run for the dock. It's not so far. Just follow us, and keep moving." He thumped an older man's shoulder encouragingly. "You gave up smoking, Ismael; now we'll all run and not be weary."

Offering a hand to a mother carrying a baby tinier than the one Paz held, he brought the group of refugees into a circle for prayer. "Our Father, give wings to our feet and blind the eyes of our enemies. We seek to serve Thee, and Thy Son, in whose name we seek thy aid. Amen."

Thirty seconds later, the orange light flicked out, and the ten refugees slipped through the camouflaged door under the warehouse. Felipe's hand went automatically to the knife in its sheath at his side, loosening it enough for a quick draw—just in case. Two more Aquino cousins, Fernando and Hernán, emerged from the darkness to flank their small flock as the entire group moved swiftly through the garbage-strewn shadows in the backs of the warehouses toward the long pier and Uncle Marco's waiting motorboat. Back-lit eyes glowed at them from atop piles of rotting crates, the occasional hiss warning them away from a particularly choice piece of feline territory. Scurrying noises preceded them, as the wharf rats in the drifts of trash scuttled out of the way of the humans' feet. Much louder, the noises of running, crashing, and shouting came from the marginally better lit lane in front of the warehouses, covering their hurried march—and reminding them of the need for both stealth and speed.

Felipe came up short at the corner of the next tumbledown warehouse, peering cautiously around the buckling sheet-metal panels. José slipped up beside his father, his heart beating fast, his eyes wide with excitement as much as fear. The pier, a pale line against the dark waves, stretched away to the left, the waiting boat a semivisible smear beside it. "There it is!" José whispered. "Uncle Marco's there; he just doesn't have any lights on, to fool them. Let's go!"

"Not yet!" His father's alert catch stopped the boy from bolting into the street. A few seconds later, a knot of white-robed Children of Light ran down the wider street between them and their getaway vehicle, their torches throwing wildly dancing shadows across the faces of the rickety buildings. The torchlight also illuminated the frightened face of a half-drunk dock worker, staring in terror at the tall, red-masked man who held him by the throat in a carelessly vicious grip.

"Where are the Mormons?" the assassin demanded. He sounded almost bored, as if he'd asked that question a hundred times that night and fully expected to ask it a hundred more.

The sailor choked incoherently against the pressure on his windpipe, pawing ineffectually at the arm that held him on the tips of his toes against the dented wall. Gasping and stumbling nearly to his knees as the leader of the Hand released his grip, he managed to cough out, "I don't know. I—"

The rest of his denial, explanation, or excuse was cut short by a wave-edged knife. Without pausing to watch him fall, the leader of the Hand moved forward, his eyes under the crimson mask restlessly scanning for another informant, the knife dripping and gleaming darkly in the torchlight of several lesser disciples who stood by in their ghostly white robes. They flowed respectfully around their leader, one pausing to spit on the still-twitching body of the dead man, and ran down the street. From that direction, a larger, brighter glow slowly grew as the frustrated mob set fire to a warehouse whose owner, confident in the bribes he'd already paid to Brother Light's financial representatives, had made the mistake of telling them where they could put their questions and to keep their paws off him. He didn't protest the basic unfairness of their shaking him down for protection money and failing to honor their side of the bargain—or feel the pain of watching his hard-won merchandise looted or destroyed—because he was dead before they tossed him into the blaze.

Felipe ducked back, pulling a much paler José with him, as the leader of the Hand, still as an obsidian pillar in the dusk, paused as if listening to some nearly silent sound under the cacophony all around them. With serpentine smoothness, a red-veiled face turned slowly in Felipe's direction. As surely as if he were a hunting dog catching the scent of prey, the assassin moved toward the alleyway, the long blade held at the ready. Coming around the corner of the building in a low crouch, he saw a flash of pale shirt in the alley's darkness in front of him and instantly lunged—not forward but sideways. The knife hit, bit deep.

With a startled exclamation as he felt the wet chill of the blade against his ribs, Hernán twisted frantically away. His shirt ripped away from the knife, leaving it embedded in the corrugated-metal wall behind him. The assassin wrenched his weapon loose, slashing it around in a lethal circle. Fernando, who had leapt forward to help his brother, leapt backward again, the knife slicing the air inches from his throat.

At the sight of Fernando's backward movement, Felipe leapt backward as well, crowding the others back along the alley. They turned to run back the way they had come. Paz, bringing up the rear with a young mother, shouted a warning. "Not this way! More of them coming!"

The noise of clawed feet preceded the sudden appearance of two other members of the Hand, as rats scattered away from the assassins who burst out of a side door further down the alley. The red-masked assassin in front of them laughed, the sound wicked and chilling, as he lunged again, this time at José. The point of the knife scored across Felipe's bicep as he half shoved, half threw his son away from the blade. He whirled away, dodging the killer's practiced backhand slash, and came up with his own knife ready. The sizzling hiss of the wave-edged blade as he deflected it tore at his nerves; he forced himself to concentrate on keeping the metal away from his skin, looking for any opening in the fanatic assassin's guard. Two passes were enough to prove that Felipe's knife-fighting skills, adequate for discouraging the brawlers and mobbers that made up most of the Children of Light's strike forces, wouldn't defend him against the expert killer in front of him.

Or those behind, closing in on the little group of refugees. Ismael grabbed a length of bent rebar from the mess against the warehouse wall and pushed to the back of the surrounded Saints. Paz pulled the other women and children into the center of the alley, deflecting Fernando to Ismael's side and sweeping up the children, ready to fly the moment Felipe and Hernán defeated the assassin (and they must defeat him, she prayed). The two other men and one young woman followed his example, holding their makeshift weapons between the advancing members of the Hand and the rest of the refugees. The pair drew their own knives, the curved edges flashing.

Another cobra-fast strike, and another long rent appeared in Felipe's shirt, high across his chest. He managed to deflect the worst of the blow but couldn't escape altogether. The cut across his arm had begun to burn, bleeding freely, and his breath came in rapid gasps as the panic had begun to build. The Hand leader's jeering laughter sounded again as he blocked Hernán's desperate thrust, kicking the young man hard in the knee, sending him sprawling. Felipe lashed out to prevent the killer from following Hernán down, but as his blade slid away from its target, he knew the fight wouldn't last much longer. He had to get these people past this madman and down the pier to Marco's boat! "Please, God," he whispered, "help us!"

José, whose sudden plunge into the stack of crates had dislodged a feral tomcat perching on top of the pile, fought his way out of the collapse. In a moment of wild inspiration, he seized both the moment and the cat, hurling it with all his strength. The yowling, spitting ball of fur and claws instantly hit the assassin's red veil, knocking him off balance, twisting the cloth around his eyes. Felipe drove forward, plunging his knife into the man's chest and pausing only long enough to shove the mortally wounded killer aside. Hernán, lurching to his feet, added a hard blow, knocking the soldier into the pile of broken crates that José had vacated.

"Run!" Felipe shouted. "To the boat! Now!"

Paz, seizing the opening, ran forward, pulling the baby-burdened women and younger children with her. José caught Hernán's arm, helping his cousin limp as rapidly as possible despite his wounded leg. Ismael, flailing hard at the two remaining assassins, covered their retreat, until Fernando almost picked him up and carried him down the pier. Felipe counted them off, at last falling in behind them, hurrying them on like a sheepdog herding a flock of amazingly obedient sheep. Marco, waving and pointing frantically from the deck of his battered-looking boat, shouted a warning.

Felipe shot a wild glance over his shoulder, to see what looked at first like a solid wall of black-spotted, luridly flame-tinged white rushing toward him. It resolved into dozens of white-robed Children of Light, the members of the Hand standing out starkly black in the hellish light of the burning warehouses. A freezing chill replaced the heat of panic as he saw not two but three assassins emerge from the mouth of the alley he had just left. The robe of the leader gaped away from his chest, revealing a bleeding wound. His veil had fallen away as well, his badly scratched face still distorted in an unnatural, heedless grin.

"For the One! The Prophet! The Lord of the earth!" he shouted, blood trickling from his lips as he leveled his knife at the retreating Saints.

With a roar, the mob charged, overtaking Felipe. As the noise of his feet drummed hollowly on the ancient wood of the pier, Felipe knew that they would never make the boat in time. He stared toward it, seeing Paz so close and yet so far, the boat's lights beckoning.

Suddenly one of those lights seemed to grow larger, more bright and brilliant than the others, outlining the boat's highest mast poles. A low whine, like the distant sound of a train, deepened to a thunderous whistle. A fireball as big as a man's head skimmed over Felipe and slammed into the ground right in front of the pier. Dirt and stone fountained up, the heavy boom of the impact shaking both wood and earth. Felipe, feeling the shockwave of it almost as a physical push in the boat's direction, pounded on, grabbing Hernán's arm and moving his nephew and José toward the boat. Paz had already boarded, only now looking back as she helped the others in, waving frantically for Felipe to hurry.

Behind them, the front line of the Children of Light came to an abrupt halt, staring at the smoking hole. For a moment, crackling silence filled the hot night. Then the wounded assassin, staggering as the manic spirit possessing him fought a losing battle with the dying body, lurched to the fore. "Kill them," he ordered, his eyes glowing in the dying fire of the crater.

The others took up the cry, "Kill them! Kill them!"

Once again, the mob surged forward, pouring around the wounded man. Over their shouts, the low whine bore in again, louder and longer. The leader looked into the sky, to see four more stars screaming down toward him. With a laugh and a defiant curse, he raised his arms to the heavens. The second meteor blasted him into flaming pieces; the others crashed into the tightly packed mass of Children of Light, killing, burning, wounding. The barrage destroyed the pier, steaming into the sea as Marco pulled his rocking craft in a tight circle, arrowing through the rain of fire toward the north, the mouth of the river, and the temple in Quezon City. Not a single fireball singed the boat. Behind them, however, warehouses exploded under the barrage of heavenly artillery as hunters became prey, scrambling blindly, burrowing under the broken rubble for protection from the violent sky.

* * *

Dear Chisom,

    This day both joy and sorrow fill our hearts. Sorrow because your mother and I will not be seeing you for a while. When you decided to extend your mission in the new Republic of South China, our desire to see you was swallowed up in delight because you had decided to accept the Lord's call. The wait, however, only serves to whet our appetites for the time when we will see you again. We have missed you much and ached to have you close again. Thus, knowing that you will be unable to come home for yet a little while longer causes us sorrow.

    Joy because you have once again chosen to serve your God, albeit under different circumstances. I am pleased that, due to your language and personal skills, the Brethren have asked you to stay and work for the Church. I am sure you will enjoy it. I certainly do. Yes, I too find it interesting that you will be doing about the same thing there that I do here. As you know, I enjoy doing public relations work, as taxing as it gets at times. I'm sure you will find it fascinating too and, as a perk, you get to be close to the leaders of the area and see what's going on from the inside.

The fact that you have decided to stay means that you missed the window of good weather during which the Church pulled all its younger missionaries home. As a result, even though you will have vacation time, you may be stuck there for a while. We only hope our separation will not last very long. Still, it does not look like conditions will get better anytime soon. In fact, according to prophecy, conditions will, believe it or not, get worse.

Since the Lamb has thrown His protective power around Zion, the wrath of God has been fully unleashed against the nations of the earth. Little did we realize how nasty nature would become. I should have known better. The scriptures clearly describe today, with the seas heaving themselves beyond their bounds, hailstorms wracking the planet, pollutions covering many lands, and a desolating sickness haunting the streets of many cities. Few planes now risk the hostile skies, and few ships cross the raging oceans. I'm so glad the Church's satellite system lets us keep in contact with one another! It is working exceptionally, some would say miraculously, well.

As I watch world events, I see another prophecy being fulfilled. This one is mentioned six times in the scriptures, suggesting its importance and impact. Using Doctrine and Covenants 34 as a sample, we learn that not long before the Second Coming, "the stars shall refuse their shining, and some shall fall, and great destructions await the wicked."

Though all the storms have scrubbed the atmosphere so that the moon no longer looks like blood, here in Independence, we don't see it or the stars often. Clear days and nights have become unusual. After years of devastating drought and boiling sun, it seems that all the rain pent up in the heavens has descended at once. The clouds break only occasionally, giving us but brief glimpses of the sky. How well did John say, "The fourth angel sounded, and the third part of the sun was smitten, and the third part of the moon, and the third part of the stars; so as the third part of them was darkened." I dare say, we don't see them much more than a third of the time. And when we do, some of the "stars" are indeed falling and causing sudden destruction wherever they hit.

It is not the falling stars I fear the most, however. The scriptures tell of something worse. Two prophecies lie in the not-too-distant future. The first comes from the second chapter of the writings of Joel. He saw that the last days would be full of both great and terrible things. Among the wonderful events would be a downpouring of the spirit of revelation upon God's faithful children both within and without the Church. We have been delighted at the large number of good people who are gathering to us, because they have been touched by the Spirit.

Joel, to our sorrow, saw something more. He saw the earth savaged by "blood, and fire, and pillars of smoke." What concerns me is that Joel did not use the usual Hebrew word for pillar (ʾammood) but teemarah, *the word suggesting date palm trees. Thus, Joel saw the time when something that looks like palm trees made of smoke and fire would torch the lands.*

The second prophecy comes from John's writings. Thus far, we have felt the brunt of the first four of the Revelator's trumpet blasts, and I wish that were the end, but John heard an angel lament, "Woe, woe, woe, to the inhabiters of the earth by reason of the other voices of the trumpet of the three angels, which are yet to sound!" The first of those three trumpet blasts signals the gathering of the armies of Satan and the second, the devil's unleashing them upon the world. We here at Independence fear the first (or fourth) of those trumpets has, indeed, sounded. The armies of evil seem to be gathering. Watch, my son, for it will not be long after that when the earth shall see unbelievable devastation ending in Armageddon. Then will destruction come upon the wicked.

Be righteous and strong. Help out every way you can.
With love,
Your father,
Chinedu

* * *

Pillars of smoke rose toward the stars, illuminated by the ground-based lightning of blue and red strobes. A deep, almost subliminal purr rumbled beneath the ecstatic chanting of the crowd. Dancers swirled across the stage in intricate arabesques, costumed in glitter and gauzy veils that revealed more than they hid. Brother Light stepped forward as the strobes came on full, the lightning blast of light shimmering as it reflected from his white robe. He gazed at his crying disciples, huge monitors at the back of the platform reflecting his hypnotic eyes as he raised his arms high. The swaying, stomping throng roared its adoration. The Hands of the Prophet, assembled in long lines of black menace along the sides of the speaker's stage, drew their flashing knives in salute and defiance.

"Forces gather against the Truth, against the disciples of the One God. They seek to destroy us, to deny what is rightfully ours, to oppress and exploit us." His voice flowed from the speakers, easily overcoming the noise of the crowd, yet seeming soft and personal as it infused itself into the minds of all who heard it. "They will not succeed. We call on the Unity, the power of the One, and in that power no one and nothing can stand against us!"

A steady, hypnotic beat grew out of the rumbling thunder filling the stands, the rhythm of the chant rising. Lightning blasted out of the sky, haloing Brother Light in a coruscating globe. He stood relaxed within the ravening storm of energy, smiling serenely as more lightning bolts screamed out of the sky, striking harmlessly into the glowing shield around the Prophet. With a wave of his hand, he dismissed the screaming electrical storm; it vanished instantly, leaving luridly colored afterimages dancing in the spectators' eyes.

With a subterranean rumble that shook the arena, fire erupted from beneath Brother Light's feet, the flames rising hungrily around him. His flowing white cloak belled in the hot wind, its edges igniting. Flames raced through the fabric, burning toward his shoulders. A gasp burst from the watchers, fear rippling through the stands. All sound stopped, the crackle of flames loud in the shocked silence. With a laugh that filled the arena, Brother Light swirled the cloak away, throwing it into the air, where it disintegrated in a cloud of sparks. The fire around him surged, only to flare harmlessly away as he walked through it, unsinged. With a clash of blades, the Hands struck their knives against each other as the chest-thumping beat rose again, in time with the thunderous chant that senior acolytes cued in the vast crowd.

Shining in the focus of the spotlights, Brother Light opened his arms wide, the screens magnifying his jubilant face and brilliant eyes as the beat and chant rose to a euphoric crescendo. "No power on earth, above, or below, can overcome the power of the One!"

A final, thunderous shout of acclamation filled the arena, rising to the skies and shaking the ground. Then the scene went black.

"Nice," Monk admitted, leaning back in his chair.

"So glad you liked it." On the screen wall in front of Monk's control console, Rashi Janjalani's face replaced the recorded devotional. Bright light poured through the car window behind him, throwing the luxurious vehicle's interior into shadow and giving glimpses of the thronged streets of Bangkok as the limousine purred past crowds of scarf-waving Children of Light. He'd made this call directly to Monk himself, transmitting the footage over the phone to Channel 8's chief producer as a sample of what he'd presented to the board as part of an exclusive broadcasting deal.

In the tight-focus shot of a handheld Vid comm, Janjalani—Brother Light, as he presented himself to his legions of devoted disciples and the rest of the world—didn't come across as the all-powerful messiah that the recording presented. In fact, the self-proclaimed prophet's face would be entirely forgettable if not for his remarkable eyes and captivating voice. What the guy had, Monk decided, was presence. It all came down to one thing: star quality. And star quality meant people would watch him no matter what he did. And that meant ratings, if they played it right. So the board had kicked it downstairs (or, more accurately, upstairs, given Monk's location at the top of Channel 8's primary office tower) for an expert opinion on whether Janjalani's content would sell their advertisers' products and services to a worldwide audience.

"I liked it—as a magic show," Monk corrected skeptically, stretching before settling into his habitual slouch, ready for the serious negotiation. "Special effects and dancing girls make for good programming, but don't expect us to fall for your prophet act—or promote it. Channel 8 isn't in the business of religious proselyting."

Brother Light laughed easily and sincerely. "Mr. Monk, I would hardly expect you to fall for anything, and I have no trouble admitting that everything you just saw could be done with gelignite, subsonic generators, and electromagnets to dazzle a bunch of uncritical primitives so unlike your sophisticated American and European audiences. But doesn't the promise—or threat—of divine retribution make for a better story?"

Monk glanced at Kim, his ever-present assistant, and raised his eyebrows. The guy wasn't going to come over all holy on him, which made things much more promising. Kim raised her eyebrows back, then returned her attention to the board, expertly managing the flow of images, data, and sound that made up Channel 8's worldwide, multichannel, continuous broadcast.

"As for proselytizing," Brother Light continued, still smiling, "Channel 8 already spreads the message of the One." The limousine came to a smooth halt; the black figure of a member of one of the Hands opened the door and bowed deeply as his Prophet left the car. Sepphira, as always, fell into place a few steps behind her former husband.

"Oh, yeah?" Monk scanned the data on the estimated numbers of members of the Children of Light. The map lit on his secondary screen, red spreading from the Philippines throughout Southeast Asia, staining the edges of Australia, stretching into China, flooding India, crimsoning the east coasts of Africa, lapping at the heart of the Muslim world. Not bad, especially since Channel 8's hold on those areas wasn't as strong as it could be. If Janjalani could deliver that many eyeballs . . .

"Certainly," Brother Light nodded to an obsequious figure in an ornamented white robe, who gestured for a pair of young women to open an ornate temple door. "Your broadcasts promote love, prosperity, freedom, and pleasure—all of the teachings of the One. As you can see for yourself."

Through the Vid comm's transmission Monk caught a glimpse of the incense-hazed interior of the building, with a short line of saffron-robed monks kneeling on the colorfully inlaid floor, their bald heads bowed. Before he could discern whether their hands were tied behind them, the scene disappeared. A riotous rainbow of flowers bloomed on Monk's screen, blazes of color in the hands of smiling, singing women and children. A parade of flower-laden horses moved through the crowd, Brother Light in the center of a group of people carrying the banners of the One God. Intercut with shots of happy, well-fed, worshipful Children of Light came images of the unenlightened ground down in poverty by the hard heel of government, clergy, and uncaring rich. Janjalani's compelling voice overlay the images, calling for the destruction of evil so its hoarded wealth could be shared among the deserving true believers.

"Not exactly pushing for an ascetic lifestyle, are you?" Monk asked, watching the succession of luxurious palaces, shimmering fabrics, elaborate feasts, and invitingly smiling beauties illustrating the treasures that rightfully belonged to the devoted followers of the One.

"Oh, certainly not," Brother Light dismissed that idea with contempt. "Asceticism is the great lie that traditional religions promote, telling us to deny ourselves pleasures for the good of our souls—only so they can keep the cream for themselves. Christ, Buddha, Mohammed, all the great prophets promised paradise to their followers. Then grasping priests twisted their teachings, corrupted the old accounts, saying that paradise came only after death, persuading the vast masses of common people to give up their hopes of ease and prosperity in this life for an easy afterlife. Any rational person can easily see through that fallacy. The One God is loving, beneficent. Why would such a being withhold and forbid the best things the world has to offer?"

The guy sounds like a commercial for every product on the ad list—and an effective one, too, Monk thought. A muffled cry came through over Brother Light's voice and then a faint voice growling a question or an order, followed by another hoarse howl. "What are you doing there?" Monk asked.

"Punishing an obstinate abbot who sent his monks to preach lies against the Unity of the One God. My loyal Hands are cutting off those monks' fingers and toes to emphasize the seriousness of his mistake—and theirs for listening to him." Brother Light's smile came through clearly in his tone.

"Don't kid like that." Monk shuddered. He didn't mind showing violence, but he didn't like it getting too close—even over the phone.

"So sorry," Brother Light apologized, but with a slight mocking edge. "I shouldn't joke about such things—especially when your own reporters seem eager to spread rumors about me and my loyal disciples. That's one of the reasons I approached your superiors, Mr. Monk. I want Channel 8 to tell the world the truth about me and my peace-loving, innocent Children, to refute the lies of our enemies."

"You sure you need us to do that? As I recall, some of those Hands of yours tried to stop a few rumors themselves by trying to kill Anne O'Neal," Monk informed him.

"Oh, I hope Ms. O'Neal didn't take that personally," Brother Light exclaimed. "That unfortunate incident was merely a misunderstanding—a few loyal but ignorant men misunderstood my concern and took matters into their own hands." Under his semiapology, Monk thought he heard another muffled whimper. "Still, you will acknowledge that Anne's report was quite critical of me," Brother Light continued. "Perhaps she deserved a little jolt, just to keep her on the right track. Besides, I imagine it gave your ratings numbers quite the spike—a live feed of their dramatic escape?"

Monk glanced at Kim again, but he didn't need her confirming nod. He vividly remembered the numbers climbing as Leon managed to keep his camera on during the wild race through Manila's waterways.

"Really, Mr. Monk, you may as well admit that Channel 8 wants to be the One media source," Brother Light said persuasively. "And for that, you can certainly use me."

"As much as you use us?" Monk asked.

"Oh, if not more!" Brother Light laughed. "Do tell your Board to accept my offer. And keep your receiver open. I have some amazing footage for you. None can stand against the One God—on penalty of death by fire from the sky!" He clicked off the connection, nodding to Sepphira to send the producer their images of the meteor shower that destroyed a large section of the Manila docks.

Rising easily to his feet, he walked over to gaze into the steady eyes of the elderly abbot lying trussed on the temple floor. The young monks, their arms and legs covered in blood, had passed out from pain, shock, and blood loss. He poked one with a careless foot. "You made the wrong choice, and these fools have paid for it. Do you understand that now, Excellency?"

"I understand," the old man answered, with his own serene smile. "I understand that you, who call yourself Light, spread darkness. You will learn the error of your choice."

At the flick of Brother Light's finger, the nearest red-masked assassin flashed his long knife, silencing the old man's insolence and ending his life.

"Finish the carrion too," Brother Light growled, unsatisfied and uneasy at the abbot's serene departure; it felt like the man had escaped him somehow. "And throw them out where others can see them. For their own sake, they had better learn more than these did, or I'll call down fire from the sky to blast them and their beehive temples!" His psychotic self-confidence returning, he strode out, completely unconcerned about the scatter of bloody spots marking his white robes.

Sepphira caught the hem of his sleeve as he settled once more into the soft leather seat of the limousine. Dabbing carefully at the spots with the water-soaked corner of her blue scarf, she said, "The meteors hit our own people, Rashi. The ones you sent to find those Mormons that escaped."

He slapped her, then surrendered his sleeve again. Eyes stinging with tears, she continued her practiced spot removal.

"That doesn't matter," he said, gazing out the window at the cheering throngs. "We have the video, and it shows what we want it to show. Mr. Monk will pass it along. It isn't the truth that matters; it's what people believe. And belief is the real power in the world."

"Can it let you call meteors from the sky?" she asked, quietly persistent as she tried to guard him against the one power that could bring him down—himself.

This time he laughed, stroking her reddened cheek. "No—but you can tell me when they will fall, and no one will be able to tell the difference. Especially not those self-satisfied fools credulously watching Channel 8's propaganda. We have the South and the East. It's time to turn our faces to the West."

Sepphira shivered, refusing to glance at the far corner of the car, but sickly aware of the shadow that lounged and grinned there. "Before we finish the Mormons here?" she asked.

"We will finish the Mormons in their den," he assured her. "Their stronghold in Quezon City will fall when we destroy the viper's nest in America. The Mormons—and the rest of those fools who call themselves Christians—will feel the weight of my Hands, and the world will see that their god is powerless to save them. Then they will bow before the One."

"And his Prophet," Sepphira whispered. The demons' laughter rustled in her mind, ghost voices sarcastically whispering, "All hail the Prophet!"

CHAPTER 2

The soft voices from the cargo compartment immediately stilled as Brother Neruda downshifted, bringing the truck to a jolting halt beside the makeshift checkpoint on the winding mountain road. What the sawhorse barricades lacked in sturdiness, the rifles in the guards' hands more than made up for.

Back roads didn't get the sharp-looking government troops or sophisticated depots that appeared on the main streets; the neatly dressed military regulars in the city itself were there partly for security but mostly for show, to intimidate nervous citizens and reassure international observers. Johann Brindermann, General Garza's right-hand man and the expert in organizing occupied territories, detailed the irregular troops of Garza's black-ops guerilla army to watch the back door, confident that they would shoot anyone who looked suspicious—or failed to come up with an adequate explanation of their presence on the road.

"Halt!" the guard in the middle of the road ordered, slouching forward with his rifle slung over his shoulder. He looked careless, but it would take only a single motion to bring the barrel of the gun to bear. His two companions, sitting in the guard shack beside the jury-rigged barrier, left their card game and stood behind him, ready to raise the barrier—or blast out the tires of the truck.

Mercury glanced discreetly out the window, trying to look casual as he crouched on the floor beside the driver's seat in the stripped-down cab. (The passenger's seat had disappeared during another supply run—Neruda joked about people being nervous to sit in a seat already peppered with bullet holes.) Mercury traded a look with Tomás, Neruda's son, who grinned.

Smuggling operations were nothing new to Tomás; since General Garza first ordered El Jaguar's guerillas to terrorize Chile two years ago in the guise of revolutionaries, the Neruda family had used their small fleet of delivery trucks to spy on the supposed rebels under cover of delivering the supplies they demanded in return for sparing the villages that agreed to send provisions. The supply trains had taken these back ways, originally to avoid Major Zamora's anti-rebel strike force, now to hide the volume of ammunition, weapons, and rations Garza's army plundered from the lands under his control. Neruda had negotiated the safety of his family and village early on, acceding to El Jaguar's demands that he use his trucks to supply the rebels. True to his word, he delivered the provisions the rebels ordered, but he also sent coded messages through the Mormon underground and most recently made his deliveries with "added value" extras the rebels definitely did not request—locator devices that revealed the rebels' convoys to Zamora's listening posts. The bugs had helped Zamora deal a nasty blow to El Jaguar and capture proof that the supposed rebel leader got his orders from the General, but winning a few jungle battles hadn't won the war.

Since the treacherous vice president had conspired with Garza to become president and begun to round up all potential enemies, the Nerudas' deliveries had expanded to include living, breathing cargo. Among (and, in the kids' case, inside) the crates in the back huddled four families, men and women with prices on their heads for their involvement in "antigovernment activities" and, primarily, for being known as incorruptible Mormons. All over Chile, Mormons (and those Catholics whose priests protested the coup) found themselves the targets for reprisals, forced to deny their faith and loyalties or run. Most chose to run, following the directive of President Smith to gather to the Zion communities around the Church's temples. Some made the trip on their own; others needed some extra help—like the passengers in the back, the families of military officers in the Second Command district north of Santiago who earned Aguilera's enmity by working with Zamora's forces and opposing the former vice president's machinations. When Garza's men rolled in under the new president's order, they had gone underground, refusing to assist their new masters and declaring their allegiance to a free Chile. Now, they depended on a smiling, open-faced trucker and his two young roustabouts to get them through the conqueror's lines into what the General thought of as the Mormon prison camp around the Santiago Temple.

Looking casual didn't come easily to Mercury. He and Tomás had accompanied Neruda to add color to his story of hauling supplies to one of Garza's depots—and to provide additional firepower if worse came to worst. Mercury's hand settled on the stock of the gun concealed in a compartment under the truck's floorboards. The less the border guards knew about the gun—and the camera snugged in beside it—the better.

"What you got back there?" the guard asked, glancing into the cab. He grinned at Mercury and Tomás. "Besides a couple soft mama's boys who oughta be in the army."

"Ah, you wouldn't want these two in the army," Neruda snorted, grinning back. "You'd spend all your time telling them not to drop the grenades."

Mercury and Tomás (their healthy teenage-male egos pricked despite the danger of the situation) looked insulted, which made the guard laugh. Neruda laughed too. "I'm trying to get some use out of them, loading and unloading these supplies for Herr Brindermann. I'd hire more competent help, but they're my sister's kids, and you know how it is."

"Family," the guard nodded sympathetically. "Yeah, I got a sister too—kept nagging me to get her boy into the army. Got the manifest list? The paper pushers gotta have their fix."

"Right here." Neruda handed over the clipboard and its load of grubby, curly-edged papers. "So, what happened with your nephew? Did you get him a spot in the General's troop?"

"Sure did." The man shrugged, giving the topmost paper a cursory glance. "Idiot walked over a mine outside Quito."

"Too bad," Neruda said philosophically. "Army work doesn't have a lot of long-term security."

"Looks all in order." The guard found the pair of colorful bills clipped under the form at the top of the pile; they disappeared into the inside pocket of his dirty camouflage jacket. Handing the clipboard back, he grinned again. "No, but it has other benefits. How about you pop the tailgate for a closer inspection?"

Mercury glared at the man. Neruda had paid the bribe, and now the pig wanted to skim a few crates off the truck? He moved slightly, but Neruda's hand landed on his shoulder, squeezing warningly. The other two moved closer with their own greedy grins.

"You don't mind us taking a look, to make sure the manifest's accurate, do you, Pops?" the sentry asked. "Probably got a couple more crates than you should have. Who knows? Maybe the civilian suppliers got confused, slipped you an extra case of wine."

Neruda laughed. "More like they tried to short me one, Captain. There's nothing in the back you want to see, and nothing you'd enjoy drinking."

An odd shiver ran through the split-second pause. Mercury felt the hair along his arms rise. The guard seemed to feel it too, shaking his head as if to dislodge a mosquito. His companions looked distinctly uneasy, glancing into the trees, at the sky—anywhere but at the rust-spotted vehicle in front of the barrier. The captain took a step toward the truck, hesitated, looked at Neruda's open, guileless face again, and gestured irritably toward the other two sentries. "Yeah, probably short. Better make sure you have a flaming good explanation for that when you hit quartermaster camp, or you'll get the difference in hot lead."

"Life's bad when they start issuing guns to bureaucrats," Neruda agreed. Flicking a nonchalant wave to the sentries, he drove the overloaded truck past the raised barriers and into the wet, green jungle.

The voices from the back started up again, first sighing in relief, then raised in a sincere prayer of thanks. Mercury echoed the sigh, then smacked Neruda's leg enthusiastically. "Man, that was amazing—what kind of Jedi mind trick did you play on those bozos? You didn't wave your hand!"

"The original mind trick," Neruda told him, laughing. "They just got hit with a dose of the real Force."

"What?" Mercury asked, amazed—and intrigued. Was Neruda serious? Could he learn to use it? That would impress Dove—and his father too.

"Conscience," Neruda said simply. "They know jacking things out of the truck is wrong, and they got a dose of guilt about it."

Mercury stared at him. "Guilt? Conscience? These guys don't have consciences!"

"So imagine how much it startled them when they got hit with guilt out of a clear, blue sky," Tomás suggested, then glanced at the actual sky through the window. "Well, the cloudy, gray sky, anyway."

"Conscience," Mercury repeated again.

"Yes. Holy Father keeps His children safe when it fulfills His purposes, and sometimes that means a miracle or two." Neruda skimmed around a huge sinkhole, then sped up as the road leveled, bumping through the thickening curtain of rain. "He's pouring His spirit out on the earth now—and that means bad guys feel it just as much as good guys. They just don't like it. It's what's keeping Serrey's security forces out of our little slices of Zion. He's there, kid—God's wherever the Saints are now. When the thugs come close, they feel all the sins they've committed, and they don't want to come any closer."

Mercury saw Tomás nod, then looked toward the back of the truck and the miraculously delivered people huddling together. A slow, wondering smile spread across his face. "Conscience attacks."

* * *

"Sandoval, man, I don't think we oughta be doing this." Barra hesitated, half in and half out of the broken back window, glancing longingly back at the quiet alley behind him. At the corner, he imagined he could see a glint from the spot where they'd hidden their comms—just in case somebody unsympathetic decided to check their location, Sandoval said.

His companion dismissed that comment with an irritated wave of his weapon. "Shut up, Barra. You want a share or not? Gonna stand around outside all day for scratch? Well, I'm worth more than that, and I'm getting it right now." Sandoval strode into the silent house, his running commentary trailing behind him, growing dimmer as he moved away. The General didn't pay them enough, and wasn't loot part of the deal? Everybody else, getting rich stripping the pickings off dead villages, cargo transports, even government buildings now, and what do they end up with? Sentry duty outside some old officer's house. Probably a dead old officer's house, or the officer got smart and disappeared up north as fast as he could carry his moneybags. Everybody knew that the Chilean Army practically stripped the banks bare right before President Aguilera took over—where else did the reserve money go? This wasn't wrong—it was stealing from thieves. Now, the thieves better have something worth stealing back, or he'd have to bust the place up . . .

Barra sighed and hauled himself into the neglected kitchen. Though only sixteen years old, Sandoval had big ideas, always complaining about how everybody was getting the cream but him, full of justifications for whatever he wanted to do next. This time, the kid had decided that pulling sentry duty on Major Zamora's house was a clear invitation to help himself to a good-service bonus. Why else would Serrey have assigned only the two of them to guard the place? Barra didn't know why Jorge A. G. Serrey, special security chief whom General Garza appointed to assist President Aguilera in his security efforts, did anything—and after standing stiffly to attention while Serrey looked him over with flat, glittering eyes, he'd decided he didn't want to know. The hard glint of afternoon light on a rack of kitchen knives reminded him of Serrey's cold gaze and made him shudder.

A kind of Zen neglect permeated the major's home, its few furnishings of good quality but definitely not luxurious, the rooms notable for their complete lack of jewels, artwork, expensive rugs, and other easily transportable, valuable goods. Sandoval's voice came into focus again as Barra left the kitchen for the neat, strangely bare front room; he watched his fellow sentry stalk through the entryway and into the small study under the stairs. He'd found something he liked, judging by the glossy leather jacket covering his grubby, guerilla-issue T-shirt. "So where's the . . ." His comment trailed off, then faded into an exclamation. "Whoa, look at this! This I could use!"

This, Barra saw as he loomed in the doorway of the office, was a sleek computer/communications console. He didn't know much about computers, but he figured it had to be pretty good, judging by the glint in Sandoval's eyes. (Sandoval tended to know a lot about anything he could sell.) As Sandoval played with the expensive terminal, the line of tiny, flashing status lights, winking hypnotically in green, yellow, and red, caught his attention. He watched the shining contraption with superstitious dread. The lights seemed to watch him back, reacting to his presence like the glowing eyes of an awakened watchdog. The thought sent a sick shiver along his nerves.

Computers could watch you, couldn't they? That's how the captain (and the General behind him) always knew where they were, how far they'd strayed from their posts. The shiver grew, leaping from his nerves to larger muscles. "Sandoval, maybe you shouldn't play with that," the big man began.

His objection trailed off under the contemptuous stare Sandoval shot him. "You saying I don't know what I'm doing? Think I don't know how to check out a computer? Think I'm as stupid as you are?"

"No," Barra muttered, watching his underage fellow soldier turn back to the screen and flick through a bewildering array of images and boxes. He knew he wasn't bright—but he also knew that sometimes being bright just made you a better target. A click and buzz from the computer, a sound like an open phone line, made up his mind for him, breaking the momentary hesitation. He quietly retreated, slipping through the broken window and back into the alley, where he picked up the locators Sandoval had ordered him to hide so the captain wouldn't know they'd gone into the house. He began walking slowly around the property, resuming their interrupted sentry run, relieved; now the captain couldn't punish him for deserting his post. And maybe he could still score some of Sandoval's profit by pointing out that he'd provided cover for the kid's looting spree. Maybe he could point it out by holding Sandoval upside down by the ankles and shaking it out of him. The thought made him feel better, and he continued his rounds with a slight smile on his wide, beefy face, confident that he was fulfilling the duty that the captain said Señor Serrey had specifically chosen him to do.

Inside the house, Sandoval turned to tell Barra that he'd managed to open a Net connection on the computer, proving both its capabilities and his own electronic prowess. When he realized that Barra was gone, he snorted, realizing that the big lug had chickened out and gone back to the street. He turned back to the terminal, poking around in its electronic memory for useful and profitable information. He knew just enough about computers, and most other dangerous things, to get himself in trouble. His problem wasn't a total lack of intelligence; it was overestimating the intelligence he had.

The reason Serrey appointed two semicompetent sentries to a semiobvious security operation around Major Zamora's home was quite simple: he had far better security arrangements in place and wanted a pair of obvious idiots visible on the beat to trick Zamora into assuming the house had no other guards. It was a long shot, but in Serrey's experience, leaving a door open for an opponent's stupidity often paid off.

A long way off another set of lights blinked on, wavered, then glowed steadily. A low tone sounded through a set of stacked speakers that could do major structural damage to most buildings. In her ceiling-suspended control hammock, Medea stirred, rubbing a yawn off her face. The scene that blinked onto the wall-sized screen bank in front of her blew the sleep from her eyes. Two figures appeared there, drastically foreshortened in the broadcast of the camera hidden above the computer console in Zamora's home. The picture blurred faintly, a flurry of electronic snow sifting through the atmospheric effects of volcanic dust and roiling sunspot storms. It was clear enough for her to see an older, larger man and a younger one, more a kid. She glanced at the two identification photographs embedded in the display. No, the bigger one didn't look like the elusive Major Zamora. The kid's picture was about five years old, which made it a more difficult match, but this kid looked the right age, had the same build as the spec sheet Serrey had sent.

Medea grinned, then swung free to launch a padded lead ball across the command center to bounce off the shoulder of another sleeping cracker. He grunted a complaint and rolled upright in his own harness. "The mice just arrived in our trap," she announced. "Get Serrey on vox—and tell him to transfer the money if he wants to see the pretty pictures."

Minutes later, Medea's bank account had grown by several thousand points, and Serrey himself gazed at the grainy transmission, watching the image of a teenage boy at the computer. The boy's hair was long, and the amateur logo of his American street gang glinted from his jacket. "And so the little boy surfaces at last," he whispered. "Hasn't your dear papa taught you to stay away from home when you're in trouble with the law?" He raised his voice, directing a sharp question at the communications tech hunched in the observation seat in the co-opted security headquarters. Serrey had taken over Señor Olivares's private office, with all its surveillance equipment and personnel. He'd been disappointed that it wasn't more high tech and powerful. "Any sign of Major Zamora?"

Barra's comm beeped, startling him as he paced around the front of the house. He fumbled for the delicate unit, bringing it to one of his cauliflower ears. "Barra here," he said, his deep voice tentative.

"Sentry report," the voice on the other end demanded crisply. The tech listened to Barra's fumbling response as the big sentry, terrified of being busted for not keeping Sandoval out of the house, assured him that all was well, quiet, nobody around, both of them were just completing another circuit. He wondered if the computer could hear him sweating as he lied.

"No sign of anyone, according to the men at the scene," the tech informed Serrey, after hanging up on the mumbling soldier. "Both sentries are still at their posts; the idiots never noticed anybody sneaking in the back way. The major may be there, out of sight."

Serrey considered that, watching the boy on-screen, flipping through the other views that Medea's team provided of the house's interior. "No. He's not there. Looks like little Michael Angel's gone off on his own again. Maybe he can't find his papa. You'd think he'd learn from last time."

"Should I dispatch a security team to apprehend them?" the tech asked, his hand halfway to the call box.

"No. The boy means nothing to us alive." A thin smile flicked over Serrey's heavy-lidded face. Ernesto's heavy, unintelligent features flashed through his memory—not out of affection for the departed, but out of fury at having been thwarted. Ernesto had died without completing the mission Serrey had assigned, leaving the Zamora brat breathing, and by association leaving a bloody stain on Serrey's honor and reputation. How convenient that the boy's impulsive stupidity gave him another chance to prove his ruthless efficiency. "We promised Major Zamora that his son would suffer if he failed to obey orders. He ignored us—and managed to plant bodyguards to save Michael's life once. He probably believes we have forgotten. I want to make sure that the major knows how wrong he is."

With a casual gesture, he flicked open the channel to Medea's Net-pirate lair. Medea's flame-topped face appeared more clearly beside the spy cam's grainier picture. "I want to close the trap. Send me the arming codes," he ordered.

On the illicit feed, Sandoval got up and started poking around the back of the console, trying to figure out how to detach and disassemble it. He startled visibly as he spotted a glint from the ceiling-mounted camera above the screen. Brushing his long hair out of his eyes for a better look, he caught the top of the desk, pulling himself up toward the tiny lens. The fish-eye lens distorted his face.

Medea's hand hovered over a control barely visible to Serrey in the corner of the monitor. "You sure, Señor Jorge? There ain't no Undo on this one."

"I am sure," Serrey told her coolly, watching the boy on the screen back down, then think better of it and climb back up to disconnect the electronic eye. The numbers glowed on his screen. "Goodbye, Michael Angel. Your papa will miss you—for a little while." He pressed the final button with a cool smile.

The camera Sandoval reached for exploded, smashing the young man back into the room. The blast wave blew through the house, blasting into and through the front wall. The wall collapsed, the wreckage falling over Barra, as charges planted throughout the house went off in blinding succession. Major Zamora's house—and the overconfident, larcenous, and unlucky Sandoval—disappeared in a cloud of smoke, flame, and flying debris.

* * *

The small crew cleaning char marks and patching bullet holes in the long stone wall surrounding the Santiago Temple grounds waved at the line of heavily laden, dusty workers trudging into the Mormons' refugee camp. Brother Neruda, leading the ragtag parade, winked at the cleanup squad's supervisor. The man adjusted his cap, casually looked over Neruda's porters, and nodded. A moment later, the refugee officers and their families disappeared into the crowded but orderly settlement, taken into other families and welcomed to safety. Mercury grinned at Tomás, shot him a victory sign, and headed toward the basement of the maintenance building, where Olivares and his father had set up their command center/hideout. When he realized how long the trip had taken, his casual stroll changed to a flat-out run. He'd gone with the Nerudas on the spur of the moment; he hadn't asked his father for permission, and if Zamora realized he'd left the temple community, he'd be late for his own funeral.

Mercury hadn't been there the night that Serrey's security forces did the damage to the walls. He and his father had still been in deep hiding, moving from one temporary safe house to another thanks to Señor Olivares's well-organized network of bolt-holes. As chief of intelligence for President Quintana and assigned to monitor both the military and civilian administrations to prevent corruption, Señor Olivares had ferreted out a half dozen conspiracies, underground cells, and smugglers' rings—and not only exposed their plans and arrested them, but co-opted their hideouts and equipment. He advised both the Molinas and Major Zamora to disappear rather than join their fellow Saints at the Santiago Temple; it was, after all, the first place Serrey would look for them.

Since Garza's rise to power through a series of well-orchestrated rebellions, coups, and "police actions" on behalf of beleaguered states, the General's troops and the national armies of the countries the General corrupted and collected one by one had standing orders to search, question, and if necessary detain anyone "suspicious." That included virtually all Mormons and most upstanding believers of other faiths as well. Garza distrusted Mormons because he couldn't easily bribe or intimidate them; their integrity kept them from collaborating with his schemes, and their faith let them face death calmly. He considered it fortunate that they had elected to contain themselves, gathering into self-made ghettos and staying quiet as the conquerors consolidated their hold.

Serrey, however, wanted to impress Garza and establish himself as a force to be reckoned with as chief of security under President Aguilera. His elite guard fanned out through the larger cities in a series of raids, arrests, and violent demonstrations. One squad, led by Serrey himself, had appeared outside the gates of the Santiago Temple two days after President Quintana's assassination and issued an ultimatum: the Mormons would surrender the traitor Major Zamora and the so-called Apostle and fugitive Molina by sundown, or face execution.

That evening, the president of the temple and de facto mayor of the refugee community, along with three other Mormons, had met Serrey's death squad at the appointed time. The temple president walked into the line of gun sights with dignity and informed the security chief that Elder Molina and Major Zamora were not within the walls but that the Saints would do all in their power to aid and assist the two to promote the cause of God against evil. They declared their faith in their Heavenly Father and Savior and stated that they would do nothing against the dictates of their consciences.

Immediately, all four fell, dead of gunshot wounds. Incendiary bombs crashed against the wall, and other fires began inside the walls, devouring makeshift shelters and meager possessions before hurriedly formed teams managed to put them out. The soldiers moved closer to the walls, then hesitated; uneasiness ran through their nerves like an electric current, whispering warnings of danger behind those innocuous stones and lack of obvious resistance. Guilt and fear seeped through them, instilled by the sight of the lovely white building in the distance. The captain glanced at his leader, wondering if Serrey would order them to charge—and wondering what would happen if they did. They didn't find out; Brindermann had issued strict orders that the "coalition forces" were to exercise utmost discretion in dealing with the civilian populace. As long as the eyes of the world (through Channel 8's correspondents, primarily) watched the General's movements, any necessary "suppression of insurgent elements" must be done in the old tradition of disappearing enemies, not gunning them down in public. Serrey didn't agree with such caution, but he knew better than to blatantly defy Brindermann's orders.

Thus, the barrage continued for just a few minutes. Walking forward to stand over the bodies of the martyrs, Serrey lazily smiled at the watchers on the wall. A ripple of revulsion spread through his slight frame, a silent threat to the reptilian coldness deep inside his soul. Anger sharpened his drawl. "Faith will not save you from me. Remember what happened tonight when I ask you again." With that, he walked defiantly away from the wall. His confidence grew as he withdrew; he was sure that he had frightened the Mormons and that fear would crack their solidarity. And once they cracked, he would sweep Zamora, Molina, and the rest of them up like so many pieces of a shattered wall.

Three days later, the wall still held firm, and the population inside had grown. So had the pressure on the leaders of the former resistance movement. Inside the completely nondescript maintenance building, Major Zamora paced, looking at the monitors only at the far end of each circuit, fury and anxiety keeping him on his feet, a silent prayer alternating with white-hot thoughts of exactly what he'd do if his suspicions proved correct. "If that boy isn't dead, I'm going to kill him!" he finally burst out.

The screens, set up in makeshift metal racks alongside the original satellite, computer, and communications equipment for the temple complex, showed a blazing ruin, dust still drifting on the breeze, fire-fighters keeping the fire from spreading to neighboring houses. In a chair in front of the monitors, Señor Olivares watched the scene steadily. He glanced at the major and smiled wryly. The intelligence reports they gathered from open-circuit communications between the security forces at the scene suggested that Serrey destroyed the Zamoras' house because he had reliable intelligence that Michael Angel had come home.

Other monitors displayed statistics, reports, and video from all over Chile (and into Peru and Ecuador), gathering all the available data feeds Olivares had managed to reestablish since his precipitous departure from the central-intelligence office. It wasn't as complete as he would like; not only had many of his agents been flushed out and killed when President Aguilera took power, but others had gone over to the new administration, taking their access codes and knowledge with them. He'd stitched together a patchwork of informants and communication streams from the remaining loyalists—and from the surprisingly organized Mormon infrastructure that Elder Molina commanded. If he had known how extensive their organization and communications systems were before, he would've been deeply suspicious of The Church of Jesus Christ of Latter-day Saints. As it was, he was just glad they were on the same side of the revolution. Of course, at the moment they both seemed to be on the wrong side, but he had no intention of meekly submitting to Aguilera—or to the puppet president's master, General Garza—and the Mormons, in his calculations, appeared to be the best allies for banishing the foreign conqueror and restoring a free, democratic, and stable Chile. Olivares would not see the national security for which he had worked like a demon his entire adult life disappear in a wave of corruption and chaos.

The door opened, and Mercury ran in, out of breath. "Señor Olivares," he began, "the General has set up the same kind of . . ." His voice trailed off as he caught sight of his father.

"We thought you were dead," Zamora told him, striding over to grab his son by the shoulders. He spun him around to face the monitor showing the sad remains of their home. "This report came in that Serrey had demolished our house because his spies had spotted you there. And when we tried to find you—"

"I was out with Señor Neruda, picking up the officers you sent him to rescue and checking out the General's communication system," Mercury protested, staring at the destruction. "I didn't go near our house!"

"No, you just slipped away without permission—you could've been recognized and killed, or captured, questioned—tortured for information!" Parental worry and anger had completely cracked Zamora's famous cool. "I would've expected more of Neruda—and you. Haven't you learned anything? You slipped away like that, and Elder Callatta died for it. Who else needs to die before you start remembering how serious this situation is?"

"I remember Elder Callatta better than you do!" Mercury snapped back, swallowing hard against the sting of his father's rebuke and of the tears in his eyes. It hurt, though he knew that the harsh words came from his father's concern for him. Why couldn't they just love each other without all the strain and strangeness? He wanted so much for his father to be proud of him, but he also resented the emotional distance and wary distrust between them. He'd been a jerk kid when his mother died, acting out and causing problems at school and in the neighborhood, but his father hadn't handled it well either, disappearing into his work, then sending him to live with Aunt Anabel when he pushed it too far. He'd learned a lot in New Mexico—not what Major Zamora had intended, but a lot. Including how much he wanted and needed his father's approval.

Mercury met Zamora's eyes, forcing himself to speak calmly. "I also remember Dove Nakai, and the Santos, and Elder Molina—and you. I am sorry. I should've asked you, told you what I thought, but—" He stopped. No excuses. Dove didn't make excuses; he wouldn't either. "I know the situation is serious. It's deadly serious, and I want to do everything I can to stop the General, just like you. I know better than to go off on my own, or walk into any more traps. That's why I went with Brother Neruda instead of on my own. And I found evidence of a nasty trap the General's men are building." He stopped, silently pleading with his father to understand, to forgive him, and to listen to him.

"Go on," the major said, the heat showing only in his eyes. Angry as he was, he had to admit that the boy had handled himself well, giving a coherent explanation of what he'd done and why. Even if Zamora didn't agree with Mercury's tactics, he'd earned the right to be heard. "Finish telling Señor Olivares what you risked your life to find out."

Mercury swallowed hard, suppressing an Amexican curse at his luck and nodding crisply. "Yes, sir. General Garza has set up the same communication network here as his troops use up north. It's a private, encoded transmission system, with booster relays all over the General's territories. Data and voice." He offered the small camera to the former security chief, who took it and plugged it in, reviewing the images of angular towers sprouted from the camp Garza's forces used outside the city and from the roof of La Moneda as well. Despite the worry about his father's reaction, Mercury grinned. "The best thing is, we've figured out how to hack into it. They're using a signal bounce from a couple of satellites and the International Space Station, and there's a corporate network that uses the same kind of system, and if you double-echo the codes, you can eavesdrop on anything they're sending. We—the Santos—did it a couple of times, caught their raiders totally—"

"It has more than that," Señor Olivares interrupted, as the door opened again, revealing Elder Molina. "This system has broadcasting and guidance capabilities. Intelligence reports say that General Garza has made a deal with the Americans to get high-tech, guided missiles and that he's also bought nuclear warheads to mount on them."

"That sounds dire," Elder Molina observed, taking a seat and waving Major Zamora to another chair.

Señor Olivares nodded at the Apostle. "It is. From his base in Bogotá, Garza can use the high-tech weapons to begin his move into Mexico—and then probably to the United States itself."

"Treacherous to the last." Zamora shot Olivares a narrow look. "Did you put Mercury up to this little spying trip?"

Overriding Mercury's indignant protest, Olivares mildly said, "Michael Angel is the one most familiar with Garza's communication network since he's hacked into it before. And he may need to do it again, if we expect to stop Garza and Brindermann from extending their empire to all of North and South America."

"More to the point," Zamora said, rising to pace again, "we've got to do something to keep Brindermann's bulldog Serrey from deciding to just start shooting Mormons wholesale." He gestured toward the wall, where a series of photographs were tacked to the edges of an oversized map. The map showed Chile largest, with the rest of South America in various sizes; a tide of bloody crimson marked Garza's territories, while the scattered Mormon outposts were colored in green. The photos showed five men, some with their families, smiling or gazing soberly outward. Zamora had put the pictures up to remind himself—and the rest of the commanders—of the people they'd already lost. Looking at them, Zamora's voice sharpened. "The weasel has already ordered Mormons summarily shot, just to remind the rest of us that he's serious! What will he do next if we don't stop him?"

"He will do only what the Lord permits him to do," Elder Molina said. His serene expression didn't waver under the major's hot stare. "The Lord permits the Saints to suffer so the wicked can condemn themselves. Have faith, Manuel."

"Faith." Zamora's stare didn't waver either, though he did moderate his tone; he felt sick to think that the entire March Revolution, all the effort, all the nation building they had done, could disappear in the smoke from a madman's guns, vanishing with nothing to show for it. "Does that mean they—we—all have to die just to put more blood on Garza's hands?"

"Señor Serrey could come no closer to us than he did," Elder Molina said confidently. "While I would neither second-guess our Lord nor refuse to submit to His will, I do not believe that we are meant to die or go down to defeat at the hands of Serrey or his masters. We may be in bad straits, but the Lord won't altogether abandon His people as long as they don't abandon Him—and we haven't."

The Apostle gestured toward the emerald patches on the maps. "All over South America, Mormons are gathering at the temple sites, obeying our prophet, staying true to the faith even under the direst of circumstances."

"Mormons started running for the temples early on," Olivares pointed out, leaning back to regard both Zamora and Molina, a speculative look in his eyes. "Fortunately, it appears that Brindermann and Garza view this as a positive development. Voluntary isolation saves them the effort of gathering up your fellow believers to put them in ghettos—and they've been surprisingly biddable." With a flick of his wrist, he called up a database on the central monitor. Pictures, statistics, degrees, and personal data of all types scrolled over the screen. "What may work to our advantage is that members of your church also represent the primary reservoir of technical and organizational ability in Chile."

"And most other countries," Zamora added, looking at the personal records and at the man who'd collected them. "How does that help us?"

Olivares permitted himself a small smile. "I am surprised, Major, that your much-vaunted tactical mind hasn't yet grasped it. Think: the General is bent on conquering, but he has no talent for ruling. Outside the small elite corps and Herr Brindermann's executives, he has no administrative staff. His guerillas are thugs and drug runners who have no idea how to put together a real community—which is exactly what the Mormons are famous for. Brindermann especially needs dependable people to run his master's captive empire. He has more strings in his hands than he can weave without competent help."

"Which is exactly how we can turn the situation to our advantage," Elder Molina said, leaning back with a broad smile. "The Lord does work in mysterious ways!"

"So we propose a bargain, Mormons agreeing to help administrate the conquered areas in return for immunity and safety?" Zamora considered that idea, nodding slowly. "It would work—we could put saboteurs inside every communication and command center in Garza's operation."

"With their families as hostages to provide cover and camouflage for the agents, helping the invaders to see them as good and loyal workers," Olivares finished the thought, then raised an eyebrow as both Zamoras and Elder Molina stared at him, incipient protests in their eyes. "Remember, Brindermann—and Serrey—believe they can smash the temple communities at will. You, on the other hand, believe that your people are safe behind these walls. Do you not?"

"Time to decide what you believe," Mercury quoted, his voice almost a whisper.

"We do," Zamora said firmly. He lightly touched Mercury's shoulder.

Elder Molina simply smiled, confident and proud of his younger brethren.

Olivares nodded. "So be it, then. I shall send the message through the intelligence network to all of our listening posts in Chile."

"We need to get the word out to all the outposts in South and Central America," Elder Molina corrected. "And we have our own communications network. I am sure that our Brother Neruda is ready to go on another supply run—with more than beef and beans to distribute."

"Neruda's supply runs and a bunch of strangely cooperative Mormons will look suspicious with hostages." Zamora shook his head. "Will the General believe that everybody will roll over so quickly? We fought him tooth and claw before he got here. And he knows we're out here. Serrey's looking for us—Santa Maria, he blew up my house!"

"There's no way Garza would fall for it," Mercury said flatly. "They're too paranoid to decide there's not a counterrevolution going on somewhere."

Olivares's smile disappeared. "Do you propose to try to defeat General Garza, El Jaguar, and President Aguilera's entire Chilean Army?"

"No." Zamora shot him a grin. "I'm surprised that your excellent tactical mind hasn't grasped the problem and solution, Señor Olivares. We can't fight Garza's troops directly—we'd never win a full-out war against those thugs and guerillas. We'll have people on the inside, by infiltrating everything, acting as administrators, techs, and so on. Fine. But Garza expects armed resistance, and we're going to give it to him."

"Oh? Who is 'we'?" Olivares said it, but Elder Molina looked interested as well.

"You and whose army?" Mercury muttered, but an echo of his father's smile spread across his face too. "How about Zamora's army?"

The major nodded. "Exactly. We've gathered loyal officers from all commands—and I've still got most of my command staff. Captain Guerra knows most of the junior lieutenants and noncoms. We can put together our own band of guerillas, specially chosen from among the Mormon officers and soldiers in several countries." He stroked his chin thoughtfully, looking at the monitor showing the constant feed from Channel 8, where Rosa del Torres narrated a summary of recent events for viewers who had been living under Martian rocks for the last year. "Garza created El Jaguar as a rebel, then changed his story to say that I was the true rebel all along—that I arranged President Quintana's assassination. Why not live up to my reputation?"

"What an excellent idea. I shall put all my files and agents at your disposal. For now, I shall leave you to assemble your strike teams. Good evening." Olivares got to his feet, stretching slightly, then walked to the door. He trusted the Mormons—Elder Molina had won his grudging respect, and he had always had a high opinion of Major Zamora's abilities—but he maintained his own concealed lair outside Zion's borders. His conscience wouldn't let him stay within the precincts of the temple community for long. He paused at the door, and his face remained utterly serious as he added, "Do make sure you grow a mustache fit for a bandit chieftain."

* * *

"Are you going to grow that mustache?" Mercury asked his father later that night, as they watched Neruda's deceptively rickety-looking trucks trundle off into the jungle rain. He didn't wait for an answer, following up the facetious question with another, more serious one. "I want to do something real, Papa, something that makes a difference. Do you think Captain Guerra could find a place for me in his crew?" He didn't look at his father.

Zamora gently rubbed his son's back, surprising both of them. "Anybody can carry a gun and run through the mud," he said gently. Mercury's shoulder slumped under his hand; his fingers tightened on the boy's arm. Boy—or young man? There was muscle under that sleeve now, and Mercury was almost as tall as he was. The missed years loomed in his heart and mind; he dismissed them. No time to deal with emotional baggage now. "Michael, you've got other skills that we need."

"I'm not afraid to face a gun," Mercury assured him. "With the Santos—"

"Are you brave enough to face Serrey's enforcers over a keyboard instead of a rifle?" Zamora asked, interrupting another story about

Dove Nakai and his vigilantes. "We need someone on the inside, and you've already hacked into Garza's communication systems once before. Could you do it again?"

Mercury, his eyes wide, opened his mouth to exclaim, Yes!—then stopped, his face sobering as he gave the thought due consideration. "I think so. But it would have to be from the inside this time."

Zamora nodded approvingly at the cautious assessment. "You can be a real asset to us—as long as you take orders and tell us what your plans are before you implement them." He tapped his son's head warningly. "You want to be a soldier, son? That means following orders—no more going off on your own."

"All right," Mercury agreed, giving his father a long look. "As long as you'll listen to me too."

"Any smart commander listens to his men," Zamora assured him.

"Are you a smart commander?" Mercury shot back, grinning.

Zamora smacked his shoulder reprovingly, but smiled. "Getting smarter all the time. Which is a good thing. A dumb rebel is a dead rebel."

CHAPTER 3

"What we got here is a dead rebel," the uniformed peace officer said confidently. Behind him, the ruins of Zamora's house still smoldered, thin trails of vapor rising into the morning sky. The firefighters had successfully prevented the blaze from spreading to the neighboring buildings, but they hadn't made any effort to save the house; with the front and side walls completely blown out and the roof collapsed, it was well beyond saving.

Rosa del Torres frowned at the wreckage and the smug paramilitary officer. "This is the home of Major Manuel Rafaelo Rivera Zamora, the former commander of Chile's antiterror squad. Major Zamora was implicated in the assassination of President Quintana; he was seen leaving the scene and hasn't surfaced since. Unconfirmed reports say that he perished in the blast. Can you confirm those reports?"

The sergeant looked nervous. "Señor Serrey, chief of domestic security, told us to direct all inquiries to his office. You'll have to ask them."

"Thank you, Sergeant." Rosa turned to the camera, cutting the man out of the picture (if he wouldn't give her what she wanted, she wouldn't put him on television; for a camera junkie like her, it was the ultimate punishment). "While the officers on the scene have no specific information about what happened here, exclusive sources close to the Department of Domestic Security tell me that at least two rebel operatives died here last night while attempting to create a bomb."

Footage of the new president waving and smiling at his inauguration underscored her next statement. "President Aguilera may have been the terrorists' target this time, especially since one of the rebels has been identified as the son of the officer turned probable traitor, Major Zamora."

This time, Zamora's stern face appeared beside Rosa's, then an old picture of Mercury as a broadly smiling ten-year-old. A bloody *X* appeared over Mercury's picture, and Zamora's grew to occupy half the screen. "President Aguilera's government is offering a generous bounty for information leading to the capture of the major himself."

"Security for our citizens is the paramount concern for me and my entire administration," President Aguilera declared as he posed for a cheering crowd on the plaza in front of La Moneda.

Behind him, two sets of bodyguards watched the crowd and the president—his own men, under the command of his handpicked bulldog General Fresno, and Garza's security detail, to make sure that the newly inaugurated president remembered to obey his master in Bogotá. "I assure you that all efforts are being made to locate, arrest, and bring these traitors to trial. If anyone has information about their whereabouts, I urge them to contact the Department of Domestic Security. Helpful citizens will earn their country's deepest gratitude."

"So far, over a thousand people have called in tips, and it seems likely that the wanted men will be in custody soon, as General Garza fulfills his promise to assist Chile in overcoming the rebel threat that has hung over the country." Rosa's live shot replaced Aguilera's photo op, a running list of names and faces scrolling beneath her, each with the specific dollar amount of the reward.

If Rosa was cynical enough to realize it, or resented the game she played a part in, it didn't show in her face as she said, "From Santiago, this is Rosa del Torres for Channel 8. Back to you, Clara."

Clara Cortez, Channel 8's anchor, never heard Rosa's report—neither did anyone outside South America. Stringers filed reports all over the world, and their local producers requested airtime. The sign-offs were strictly for the viewers' benefit, creating the illusion that omnipresent Channel 8 cared about their minor local matters. In reality, only the most ratings-friendly bits made the cut to Monk's roster; everything else, if it aired at all, aired only locally. Rosa would do anything to have a worldwide, live audience, but despite all her digging for sensational stories, she had never cracked the ratings ceiling.

So, completely unaware of Rosa's summary or the official confirmation of Mercury's obituary, Clara looked up as Monk, from his control booth, sent her the cue signal.

"Big announcement time, Clara. Sell it, but not too big. We need 'em scared enough to stick to the screen, not hide under their beds," the producer ordered. "Unless they've got monitors in their rooms."

Obediently, Clara gazed steadily into the dark lens of the camera, her dark eyes wide and concerned. "Moving on to breaking science news, we have a follow-up on a previous report that has caused widespread panic in many parts of the country. A troubling statement from highly placed, confidential sources in the International Space Administration confirms that one of our worst nightmares may have come true. A huge asteroid, a 'near-earth object' or NEO, a 'planet killer' like the one that destroyed the dinosaurs, is heading directly for the earth."

A recording of panicked crowds thronging grocery stores and home supply centers appeared beside Clara, rapid-fire images of desperate people trying to buy their way out of certain death—or do a little looting among the abandoned shops.

"Civil authorities assure us that there is no reason to panic and that the reports are officially unconfirmed," Clara noted, her expression carefully calculated to raise her audience's anxiety levels just enough to make them want more information. "But, if a major asteroid did collide with the earth, the consequences would be devastating. According to reports from Dr. Kirmisse on the International Space Station, the impact of an asteroid one hundred meters in diameter is the equivalent of one hundred megatons of TNT, as powerful as the largest thermonuclear bombs."

Computer simulations of extraterrestrial missiles hitting the earth's surface sprang to life on the screen, illustrating the consequences of larger and larger space rocks blazing through the atmosphere to crash into the ground or explode in the air. "Initial reports from the International Space Station indicate a pair of incoming asteroids, one sixty kilometers across, the other eighty," Clara continued, the size of the asteroids having grown several kilometers from Dr. Kirmisse's observations to the prompt screen.

The graphics changed, including not just massive rocks from space sending ripples through the simulated insides of a virtual planet, but spreading earthquake waves that tilted and toppled houses, malls, and skyscrapers, all of it underscoring Clara's words. "Expert analysis indicates that direct hits by both asteroids could trigger an extinction-level event, or ELE. The explosions could throw enough dust into the air to cause the equivalent of a nuclear winter, blocking out the sun and making temperatures plunge all over the world, which is the kind of weather disruption that probably killed the dinosaurs."

On screen, virtual dinosaurs died of cold and starvation, then gave way to the stereotypically disheveled figures of a pair of professional astronomers, identified as the resident experts at the Royal Observatory in London. "Channel 8 contacted astronomers from the Royal Observatory in London to comment on the initial reports from the International Space Station," Clara introduced.

The royal astronomers politely disagreed with everything from the size and number of the asteroids to the consequences of a direct hit—without downplaying the danger. "Really, Clara," the senior astronomer lilted, "the most catastrophic scenario would be if one of these large bodies impacted on a fault line or active volcano. A direct hit on the emerging volcano in the American Northwest, for example, could send earthquakes down the entire coastline, with potentially devastating effects for the entire western seaboard." The graphics showed a long strip of coast from Baja California to San Francisco shiver and peel away to disappear into the ocean in a cloud of beautifully rendered steam.

At this point, the junior astronomer, newer to broadcast stardom than his mentor and nursing a streak of British black humor, interjected, "Time to invest in that beachfront property in Arizona!"

More talking heads appeared, and Monk expertly controlled the tone through Clara and the precise timing and juxtaposition of images and information, making sure they didn't go too far with either pessimistic or optimistic possibilities. Too much optimism, and the viewers would decide to turn to a game show; too much pessimism, and Channel 8 would lose the audience to dust bunnies or street riots. The viewing public had an extremely short attention span; the story of huge asteroids hurtling toward the earth, like coverage of the continual wars in Ohalajishi and Kharagizstan, interested them only as long as there was something new to report.

At the right moment, Kim ran the Breaking News banner and theme music as a panel of government advisors appeared to reassure everybody that things were fine and there was no need to worry. "In fact, the best thing to do," said Secretary Garlick, chief of Homeland Security, "is to keep up your normal life. Let us worry about national security—your security. That's what you hired us for. Go to work, go out for the evening, catch a movie—and remember that astronomers come out with this kind of wacky prediction once every few years. NEOs are nothing new. Chicken Little has shouted that the sky is falling for a long time—and it's never come true yet." The ads for survival shelters and reserved places in guaranteed sheltered communities scrolled across the screen, undercutting Garlick's reassurances.

* * *

"Well, I guess that shows one thing for sure. Even the end of the world isn't a reason to stop taking advantage of the gullible to line your pockets," Hideyoshi muttered, watching the advertisements for asteroid-proof basement additions and thinking about the latest flurry of asteroid-strike simulations—simulations that looked familiar indeed. He glanced at his tectonic-imaging computer, with its intricate models of the Big Sister volcano, and then over at Mir, hunched over a read-out from one of the station's outward-facing sensors instead of her usual high-altitude weather eyes. "I wonder how the story about the NEOs got out so fast, with detailed simulations."

"Maybe Kirmisse dropped them a note while he dropped himself," the climatologist suggested. Under the weight of Hideyoshi's stare, however, she finally sighed, swirling to face her colleague. "All right, Jamie, stop giving me the hairy eyeball. Yeah, I told them. And I used your computer to guess what would happen if one of our space babies hit your precious volcano."

"What might possibly happen if one of them did." Hideyoshi shook his head. "Ivana, we don't know—and you don't know enough about the volcano sim to give it the right parameters. What you did was scare the pants off a whole bunch of people who don't know any better."

"Oh, did I scare the groundhogs? If they had a brain in their heads, they'd wait for official confirmation and hard data and not go running around bleating like sheep!" Her face hardened, her hand slashing out to point to the monitor. "Why not scare them? The weather's gone to pieces, the ground's coughing its guts out all around them, there are crazies shooting each other all over the world, but it takes a couple of big space rocks to get them to sit up and take notice. If I have to know I'm going to die up here, why shouldn't they worry that they're going to die down there too?"

Mir caught herself on a handhold as the violent gesture sent her into a zero-gravity spin. "How you can be so blue-streaking happy when we're stuck up here in this poor excuse for a hamster cage? Don't you ever get tired of putting a good face on everything, Mormon boy? Like you have anything to be happy about." She hovered there, every nerve tensed, holding back a wave of fear with a hot wall of anger. "Like any of us do."

Hideyoshi smiled slightly, well aware that he depended on a shield of faith to hold back that same fear—and that it, just like Ivana's anger, wavered occasionally. "Right now, being happy is beside the point, Ivana. So is being mad at the world, just because they're not breathing recycled air."

"It's not the recycled *air* I mind," she muttered, staring into Kirmisse's telescope again.

"Whatever," Hideyoshi snuggled up to the data projections of the trajectories for each rock in the oncoming swarm. Hundreds of tiny lights filled the screen, escorting a few larger ones like a school of fish around a family of whales. More to himself than to her, he added, "It'll work out. God's in charge. Whatever happens, things will come out right."

* * *

Dear Chisom,

I was pleased to get your last Vid, and I appreciate the pictures. You have a real knack with the Vidcam, and Adaure was very pleased with the 3-D images you were able to catch. She has rearranged the living room so she can display them. What do you think about that? A proud mother, right?

On another note, I too find that the threat of the asteroid strikes has caused a lot of attention but little repentance. The Brethren have assured us we have nothing to fear from the big ones. I'm sure that some of the smaller ones will cause quite a bit of damage for those outside God's protection. Just such destructions have been prophesied. Both the New Testament and Doctrine and Covenants tell us the "stars" will fall, as I wrote you already, but they are not the sign of the end of the earth.

I agree that public relations work can be difficult. I, too, am amazed at the lengths our detractors go to discredit us. What I have discovered, and you will too, is that it must be more discouraging for them than for us. The harder they work and the more they spend, the more the Church grows. I will admit that we have not yet had to battle Brother Light's people, as you have. I fear he will have his day in the sun and prove to be a strong and effective antagonist. Like so many other items, God showed John the Revelator Brother Light and his ilk. The Lord used the image of a lamb with two horns that was able to do wonders that astonished people, causing them to worship the dragon. But do not worry, my son; nothing will successfully stand against the true Lamb and His kingdom.

Even now, those in Zion and her stakes are feeling God's protection. The Lord promised Joseph Smith that Zion would be safe for "the glory of the Lord shall be there, and the terror of the Lord also shall be there, insomuch that the wicked will not come unto it" (D&C 45:67). The scripture has been proven true over and over. Our enemies will not come against us. It is not because the glory of the Lord can be seen as much as because it can be felt. That is the wonder of it. Our little towns and bigger cities seem normal to those looking on, but when anyone not prepared tries to enter, they feel God's power. It doesn't consume them, but reaches into the depth of their souls, stripping away all those rationalizations, justifications, and excuses they have used to live more or less comfortably with sin. Their consciences feel the full weight of their transgressions and crimes. It hits them like hellfire, and even the toughest cannot abide it for more than a few seconds. As a result, they run.

The power is less severe on those who are not outright wicked. These less-than-pure souls can endure our society for a while, but they eventually withdraw.

Should conditions get bad enough in South China that the Saints have to gather, that area will experience this protecting power as well. I suspect you will also see something else that pleases me much. It is not just the Saints who come under this power. There are many people of pure enough heart that they can enter into the joy and protection of Zion.

What concerns me are those who won't come all the way in. You see, we have satellite communities growing up near a number of our centers. Their inhabitants are not willing to be righteous enough to dwell among us, but they want to get away from the chaos and horror growing in the world. They hope that the ripples of Zion will protect them while they continue to live less than pure lives. Most do not seem to understand that now is the time for commitment. We do work among them and find some success, but many, though decent enough people, are too hard to touch. In Revelation, God warned the lukewarm that He would spew them from His mouth. For that reason, I fear for these people. They, like so many others, bask in a false security. To their sorrow, I fear, destruction will find them.

This potential causes me pain, but I must focus on all the good that is happening, and fortunately there is much. Our PR efforts have proven quite effective. In spite of the problems at Lake Creek, where bigoted anti-Mormons and hotheaded Saints almost caused a civil war, governmental agencies here in the U.S., Canada, and Mexico are, so far, treating us fairly and see us as a stabilizing influence. I am pleased. We are watching Garlick and his cadre, however, and doing what we can to thwart his efforts. We are fortunate to have a number of allies.

We look forward to getting your next Vid and finding out more about how the Church is faring in the Far East. With this transmission, I am sending you some of the PR materials that we have found effective. I hope they can be translated and transculturated for your purposes. Let me know what you think.

In the meantime, know this: the world should fear sin, not asteroids. As tough as conditions are, all will come out right.

I am proud of you.
With love,
Your father,
Chinedu

* * *

"Will this all come out right?" Tommy Gibbs leaned against the gilded lectern, gazing out at the crowd packing the stadium seats. Some, caught up in their own world of prayers, whispered or shouted pleas to the Almighty; others, captivated by the man at the center of the vast space, swayed to the rhythm of the evangelist's practiced flow of words. "'Will it come out all right, Brother Gibbs?' they ask. Everywhere I go, I hear the same questions, from men, from women, from little children. And do you know what I say to them? Do you know what I say when I look into their eyes, full of pain and confusion and uncertainty?"

He straightened, his handsome face full of photogenic regret. "I have to look deep in their eyes and tell them that I don't know." A gasp rippled through the crowd, a sound of mingled shock and anticipation. "I have to tell them I don't know, because it all depends on them. It all depends on them, because only Jesus can make it come out all right—and only they can accept Jesus, take the healing power of the King of Kings and Lord of heaven into their lives. Only they— only you—can take that hand, that beautiful, wounded hand, that He holds out to you. He wants to save you, brothers and sisters. He wants to save you from the dangers lurking all around you."

Pointing dramatically skyward, he raised his voice. "Do you think that an asteroid is the biggest danger you're facing? I'm here to tell you that there's a deeper danger lurking all around you, everywhere you go, every day. The Apostle Paul saw the real enemy, lurking in every shadow, setting snares and traps for your feet. Lord Jesus himself warned us that the devil never rests, always weaving his ropes, waiting to weave them around your necks and lead you down to his dominion of pain forever. The real danger to your souls isn't coming from outer space—the real danger is right here on the earth, in the blandishments and lies of the prince of darkness."

Shouts of agreement, pleas for deliverance from devilish snares, and snatches of song rose all around Gibbs. He raised his own voice commandingly. "But the King of Light is sending His own warning, clear as the sun in the sky. The asteroids we hear about on the news, the same asteroids that have baffled the military, the space agencies, and all the world's wisdom, are messages from Jesus Christ Himself. With this flaming ball of unearthly fire, our God is sending a sign to members of the church of the devil, giving them warning, giving the wicked one last chance to repent. The rent has come due, brothers and sisters. This world belongs to the meek, and Jesus is serving sinners an eviction notice!"

The choir on the side of the stage began to hum, clap, and sway, adding an underlay of excitement to the preacher's rhetoric. Gibbs didn't sway; he gestured eloquently as he continued, "When the asteroids hit, the good, the righteous, the people who forsook the devil and took the hand of Lord Jesus will be raised to heaven in glory, while the wicked burn in the worldwide conflagration, as the earth melts with fervent heat and the elements run together, all the impurities burned away in a burst of celestial fire."

The audience exploded with amens and hallelujahs. Several women, overcome with fear and relief, fainted into the arms of their companions. All over the stadium, arms waved in the air, hands clasped, and people closed their eyes in fervent prayers for their own salvation.

"Just think of it," Gibbs's voice dropped, the speakers amplifying his near whisper over the noise of the crowd. "Millions, billions, of people who never knew Lord Jesus, who never trusted Him enough to take His hand, who would not let Him gather them under His wings as a chicken gathers her chicks—all of them left to burn in the pillars of fire and smoke that will erupt from heaven and earth when the asteroids come, when God unleashes His wrath and fury upon the rebellious." He paused, as the horrific image built in the minds of his listeners.

"Do we want that to happen? Do we want to watch the ignorant and faithless melt with fervent heat?" Gibbs disregarded the few affirmative shouts that met that question. Compassion filled his face and voice. "Of course not! We want all of our brothers and sisters, the benighted and ignorant ones, to be saved in the bosom of Abraham. So pray with me, pray to a loving God that He will avert the disaster, that He will create faith in the hearts of the worldly, that He will pour His love down and cast Satan out of the hearts of the people, so the disaster can pass them by. Pray with me, pray for the mercy of the Lord Jesus on all the world!"

As the preacher bowed his head, the choir burst into song, echoing the words of his prayer. The entire audience rose, repeating the words, adding their own supplications. Gibbs ended his prayer with a resounding "Amen!" and raised his head once more, flashing an angelic smile to the crowd as he stepped away from the pulpit. The choir leader took his place, leading them in singing a hymn as the star strode backstage in a swirl of royal blue and gold-trimmed robes. The softer light of the stage's wings replaced the harsh spotlight glare. Gibbs flicked out a handkerchief, dabbing at the sheen of sweat on his forehead.

"I'd say never let 'em see you sweat, but they love it when you do," Michael Romanoff told him. The producer/organizer of Gibbs's evangelical empire waved an impatient hand at one of the bevy of adoring minions who converged on Gibbs. "Go get the reverend a drink, honey." Romanoff turned back to his boss (and meal ticket), grinning. "And they're loving this—as do all the viewers at home. Lots more eyeballs tonight, Tommy—and lots more money pouring in."

Gibbs gave him a weary look. The reverend did the preaching, the public appearances, the faith building; Romanoff handled the empire building, managing all of the mundane financial and publicity details. He did it exceptionally well, too, building what he saw as the Tommy Gibbs brand into a national (and someday, he dreamed, international) powerhouse. His job description combined competition, schmoozing, politics, and a generous splash of P. T. Barnum, which suited Romanoff's temperament and personality just perfectly—and let Tommy Gibbs focus on all the teaching and preaching, healing and inspiring, floating above the sordid exchange of empty promises and filthy lucre that fueled the evangelist's juggernaut. Strains of singing and clapping drifted backstage.

Romanoff flourished his ever-present computer, tapping from screen to screen as he ran down the current state of the business. "We've completely beat out the Bower Family evangelist empire. Congratulations, Tommy, you're the undisputed king of the revivals all over the South and Southeast, and we're gathering lost sheep all over the West too. East Coast's still heathen land, but we may pick up a few more bodies with the asteroid coming and the economy going to—"

"No progress in the Midwest?" Gibbs interrupted, giving Romanoff a silent, raised-eyebrow warning to watch his language. The adoring throng of lower-level functionaries surrounding them would be shocked and appalled to hear Romanoff using language more suited to a Hollywood producer, which he had been, than a pious missionary.

"Jersey, gone straight to Jersey," Romanoff finished. "The Midwest is a mix; our bottom line out there isn't anywhere near the bottom. We've got more than enough to build the revival chapels and call centers in Biloxi and Terre Haute." His grin faded slightly as he admitted, "But the big surge is slowing down out West. Our push against the Mormons bottomed out with the big problem in Lake Creek; nobody likes sending the National Guard out to shoot civilians. Would you believe they've dug up the old Kent State thing? Some people have no sense of proportion." He shook his head, then shrugged off the setback from the bad publicity. "But we may be able to pick it up there, if we put in a little extra sauce. There are several local groups who'd love to sponsor a revival and have you come to speak about the Mormon problem. Reverend Lebaron's called several times."

"Samuel Lebaron," Gibbs closed his eyes, rubbed a hand across his forehead. The man had led his Millennium Brotherhood in an outright war against the Mormons; they'd shot back, which led to the National Guard driving them out of Lake Creek, Illinois, to the larger settlement at Nauvoo. However, Gibbs wasn't ready to lend his name or prestige to vigilante violence. Opening his eyes, he fixed his producer with a stern look. "I told you, Michael, I'm not going to deal with that man. Stop returning his calls—and tell him to stop calling. Mormons aren't evil; they're misguided. We don't want them to die in their sins; we want to save them from the hell their devilish cult is leading them into."

"Right." Romanoff nodded and made a note on his screen to tell Lebaron to cool it—for now—and get back to him when the numbers looked better. "Speaking of cults, though, we've got big competition on the coasts from that crazy Janjalani character and the Light Children."

"Children of Light," Gibbs corrected. He smiled as he accepted a cold glass of water from the girl Romanoff had sent to fetch it. She looked flushed, staring at him with bright, intent eyes. He didn't think much of that; he'd become accustomed to the worshipful stares of any number of women, young, old, and in between.

"Yeah, whatever," Romanoff shrugged off the correction. "Bunch of heathens. Saw on a Netcast the other day that Janjalani has like thirty kids on the way, practically his own harem. And telling everybody they don't have to feel guilty about stealing everything they can get their hands on if it's from unbelievers. No wonder the liberal crowd likes him, huh?" His mischievous grin returned as he showed Gibbs the headline of a Channel 8 report warning about the danger "fundamentalist Christians" posed to the ailing democratic process. "They sure don't like you. But that's all to the good; the more they yap about your being anti-choice and homophobic, the more donations we get from the ones who don't like them. So we get a payoff both ways."

A headset-wearing tech caught Gibbs's eye and gave him the high sign. "Two minutes."

Gibbs nodded, submitting himself to the attention of a makeup specialist who expertly combed his hair and applied a little more powder to keep the sweat and shine down.

Romanoff stepped back, giving the pros room to work. He watched Gibbs's preparations with a mixture of parental pride and sheer avarice. "Looking good—downright angelic. I'd pay big bucks to get into heaven with you before the world goes boom. Genius idea, by the way, praying for the asteroids to pass."

"Why?" Gibbs glanced at him, removing the tissue from his shoulders. "Are you worried about the state of your soul? Not completely confident that you'll be caught up in the Rapture?"

"Nah." The thought had never crossed Romanoff's mind; he was a heathen through and through, though he was a useful one. "This way, you're right either way. The big rock goes by without hitting us, it's because Tommy prayed it away, which is a huge boost; it hits, and nobody's around to care." He became aware of the stares ranging from shocked to furious leveled on him from the devout worshippers standing nearby, and hastily added, "That is, all the good guys'll be up in heaven, safe as the mint, and the rest can go ahead and barbecue."

Tommy sighed. "Mike, you're a cynic. Haven't you got any faith at all?"

"Sure I do!" Romanoff did; he had plenty of faith in the numbers, and in people's desire to buy their way out of trouble. Did he believe that the Rapture was coming? Not enough to stop paying insurance premiums, unlike many of Gibbs's audience.

"That's good," Gibbs assured him, knowing full well that Romanoff would believe whatever Gibbs wanted him to—as long as Gibbs was convincing to the paying audience. The producer liked to tell people not to be fooled by the Russian name; he was a capitalist to the bone.

Romanoff's mercenary attitude almost troubled Gibbs, but he'd been in the business long enough to know that it came with the territory. Gibbs kept him on because nobody could get bookings and arrange publicity like Romanoff. Without his heathen producer, he'd still be the pastor of an affluent but small church, without the nationwide fame and the unsurpassed platform it gave him to spread his message. And if looking out at the huge crowd exhilarated him, giving him the performer's high he loved more than any other sensation he'd ever felt, the fact that he was spreading the good word of Christ more than salved the few pricks at his conscience. He was in the business of saving souls, after all, he thought to himself, taking one last, long sip from the glass, and if that yielded emotional and material rewards, well, the scriptures promised joy to those who lost themselves in Christ, and the laborer was worthy of his hire. Gibbs wasn't a greedy man, and certainly not a bad one; unlike so many fallen evangelists, he had successfully resisted the temptations and allure of the world's wealth.

Its admiration, on the other hand, had proved far more seductive. As a newly commissioned reverend building his small congregation, Gibbs learned that what the people wanted to hear was that Jesus would take care of them, reassuring promises of a salvation within their grasp; they wanted to know that the devil was responsible for most, if not all, of the evil in the world and in their own hearts and that they had no need to feel guilty if they simply tried to live a "Christian" life. If he wanted people to listen to him, and he wanted that more than anything else, Gibbs had to tell them what they wanted to hear. Thus, if he preached doctrines he didn't himself believe, it was only for the good of the simple souls who needed black-and-white certainties. He spoke eloquently of the Rapture but no more believed that God would dramatically snatch up the righteous than he believed he could fly under his own power. However, if the promise of being swept to heaven prompted his listeners to live more ethical, moral, Christlike lives, he felt no qualms about using it. His ends were noble; his means were good, if not perfectly honest; and he truly loved humanity, especially when they so generously and adoringly loved him back.

Gibbs closed his eyes as he mentally prepared to take the stage again for the second-set encore. A sharp flash of foreboding hit him, his eyes opening as if he'd heard a shouted warning. Through the clear bottom of the glass, he saw a strange glint, as the intense girl who had brought the water moved. A silver pistol glittered in her hand, swinging up from her pocket to point at his chest. Dreamlike, the world seemed to slow. Gibbs stepped sideways, tossing the glass toward the girl's feverish face. She fired but flinched at the recoil of the gun. The shot went wide, punching a pair of holes in the wide sleeve of Gibbs's blue robe and shattering a standby spotlight behind him; the stand tipped and fell with a resounding crash. The girl herself went down in the same moment, borne to the ground by Gibbs's security men.

As she fell, she screamed, "You lied! You said Mama would get better, that she didn't need her medicines if she had faith! She sent all her money, all her savings. You promised Jesus would heal her! And now she's dead, she's dead!" The heavy weight of the bodyguards smothered her cries; they hastily pulled her to her feet and hustled her out to the police covering the event.

They left chaos in their wake, confused people shouting, running, cowering under or behind anything that looked like cover in a firefight. The noise of the gunshot reached the choir performing onstage; their harmonies and descants dribbled into disorganized notes, then into silence. An overexcited assistant ran onto the stage, whispering the dire news to the choir leader, whose eyes widened with alarm. He raced to the lectern as questions began to spread through the vast audience, thousands wondering what had happened. "It's awful—an enemy of Jesus has tried to assassinate Tommy—Reverend Gibbs!"

The crowd began to roil, shouts, cries, and screams bursting from all sides. Hearing the pandemonium, Gibbs disentangled himself from Romanoff's grip. "I'm fine, Mike. I'm not hurt. But if I don't get out there, someone else may be."

"Are you sure?" Romanoff asked, blinking.

Gibbs smiled, shaken but strangely exhilarated, "I'm sure I'm fine—and I'm sure these people need to hear what I have to say."

The commotion only grew when Gibbs himself swept out of the wings and caught the choir director's shoulder, then gently removed himself from the man's anxious embrace. Stepping to the lectern, he spread his hands, calling for attention, asking for calm. The shrieks of dismay turned to shouts of joy and hallelujahs, and then into a spreading, hungry silence.

"Brothers and sisters, as you see, I'm just fine." Looking out at the audience, he raised his arm, showing the bullet holes in his sleeve. "The bullet, like the fiery darts of the adversary, missed its mark." He paused, allowing the eruption of cheers to subside slightly. "And I have none other than the Lord Almighty to thank. Without His timely warning, I would not be standing here in front of you now! As He has stretched forth His mighty arm to preserve me so I may serve Him, so He will preserve all who surrender their lives to Him."

Raising both arms, his voice ringing through the stadium, he called, "Pray with me now, a prayer of thanks, a prayer of supplication that King Jesus will always protect His faithful people, thwarting the arm of evil, be it demon-influenced men and women or the blind malice of the asteroids hurtling toward the earth!"

The audience rose as one, swaying, singing, and praying to the Good Shepherd to protect His faithful flock against all evil.

A few hours later, Tommy Gibbs's face glowed on screens all over the world, as Anne O'Neal reported the news of his miraculous survival and triumphant prayer to the world on Channel 8. Romanoff's men had sedated the girl responsible for the attack and whisked her off to a private hospital funded by one of the many charities that Reverend Gibbs sponsored. Her sudden disappearance let him spin the reason for her attack (thwarted admiration, low-level schizophrenia, and unfortunate family incident). Of course, rumors of the girl's accusations did leak out, but they were so mixed with other theories that in the lack of concrete information, they blended into the general confusion of motive and countermotive. "What does stand out, Clara," Anne summarized, "is that Tommy Gibbs has survived a dramatic attempt on his life, and he credits his escape to a timely heavenly warning." After she signed off, a battery of skeptical commentators dismissed his "claims of divine intervention," but their disdain couldn't disguise the shining belief in his face—and the faces of the people who loved him.

* * *

In a shadowy, luxurious apartment half a world away, the blue flicker of the screen failed to illuminate the indistinct shapes that swirled and mouthed threats at the hated name Gibbs invoked so easily. The light glinted and reflected in Brother Light's dark eyes as he glanced at Sepphira. His ex-wife sat huddled on a cushion, as near to him as he would permit her to come, her own eyes flickering toward the corners of the room. The spaces that drew her gaze looked empty to him, but he knew that she could see the spirits that gathered there, the spirits whose diabolical information and advice had proved so useful to him.

"Sepphira." His remarkable voice, low and gentle, instantly caught her attention. He stroked her hair, and she leaned longingly into the touch, resenting the distance between them but too weak and too much in love with him to break the bond completely. "What do our friends say about that claim? That their dying god will always protect his people?"

She swallowed, fear and hate rising in her chest for the shadows that haunted her days and nights, but she answered the question. She always answered his questions. "They say the American reverend is not so faithful as he believes. They say that the sheep who flock to him believe in him, not in their god, and that he leads them astray." Her voice dropped and she shivered. "They say they are hungry, Rashi."

"Are they?" He leaned back, his hand dropping away from her hair, leaving her to huddle alone again. "We shall find a way to feed them. We gave them Archbishop Corazon and Apostle Stacey for appetizers. Reverend Gibbs will make an excellent first course." He smiled slowly, looking at the broadcast image of Tommy Gibbs—a rival and, if correctly used, a powerful tool. How many would turn to the One God when they saw that their own god could do nothing to protect his chosen servant?

CHAPTER 4

Tommy Gibbs's handsome, smiling face beamed out of the console screen next to the running script of standard soothing responses for telephone psychics. The evangelist wasn't part of the company-sponsored program, but Sally Mae Loftus fervently believed that her psychic gifts came directly from divine inspiration. And because letting her do her own thing kept them on the line at least as long as any other option, the managers let it go; they didn't know that she often called the most needy or troubled clients on her own time from home—or that she prayed over everyone who called her.

At the moment, she was trying to convince one of her clients not to spend the rest of the week hiding under her bed. Between the reports of approaching asteroids and the clean-water shortage that hit most of the South after yet another triple hit of tropical storms, Gladys had decided that life in the dark with the dust bunnies was preferable to dealing with the harsh light of reality.

"Oh, honey, you can't just stay under there." Sally Mae's soft, sweet voice lilted into the phone, in response to Gladys's somewhat muffled complaints. "No, you've got to come out. The future's going to get brighter. It really is. I promise. I'm not seeing any disasters in your future, just light."

She sighed at Gladys's tart response as she speared through the cellophane of a snack-cake package with one of her elaborately fili-greed nails. The sweet things were getting more expensive every time the guys refilled the vending machine, and with all the reports of food shortages and sugar rationing on the news, she almost felt guilty about tearing into another one, but she needed the carbohydrate high—and the emotional boost. "No, I don't mean light like nuclear explosions from the asteroids. I mean real light, honey, divine light." Glancing at the portrait of Reverend Gibbs for inspiration and moral support, she shifted from psychic precognitor to spiritual counselor. "Gladys, there's just one way to ensure your future, make sure you can step into the light I'm seeing. You just need to get right with God, and you'll be taken up before the end of the world. If you'll just do that, honey, if you'll just pray and accept Lord Jesus, He'll sweep you right up in His loving arms, away from the fires and trouble."

Jenna, one of the other telephone psychics working in the boiler-room call center, bored with the Net broadcast of Virginia Diamante's latest single, flung down her headset. She'd overheard Sally Mae's advice to Gladys, and she shoved back from her tiny cubicle, leveling a glare at her. "He will, huh? Jesus is just going to sweep all the lame-brain prayer junkies up to heaven while the rest of us turn into crispy critters?"

Sally Mae looked at her cubicle neighbor, waving her glitter-tipped fingers for quiet and patience. She didn't get either, as a few of the other psychics sniggered. "Just a second, Gladys—I gotta think about this. You just keep on praying." Tapping the Hold button with one nail, she pushed her own chair out. "Jenna, I was just—"

"You were just doing what you always do," Jenna interrupted. "You were coming off all righteous, all precious about how wonderful your Lord Jesus is and how great it's going to be when the clock runs out at the end of the world and all of us nasty sinners get what's coming to us."

"I'm just telling the truth," Sally Mae protested. "Jesus is all that can save us—"

"All that can save you, maybe." Jenna detached her ID card and with a flourish disconnected her console. A heady sense of freedom surged through her, the kind of rush a suicide feels just after jumping off the twentieth-story balcony, before the reality of the street below hits her. "Well, if the Christians are getting taken up and the rest of us get to stay down here and burn, I'm partying now, before the end of happy hour. If life's that short, it's for sure too short to spend doing this!"

A sprinkle of applause and laughter greeted that declaration, shouts of agreement coming from cubicles. The chatter dwindled immediately, however, as a supervisor hustled up the narrow aisle. He came to a halt in front of Jenna, giving her a management-approved quelling stare combined with the body language that the trainers told him showed empathy and toughness.

"Is there a problem here, Jenna? What's going on?" he asked in a discreet half-whisper, not waiting for an answer before plowing on. "Remember, all our private conversations have to take place in the break room, so our clients don't hear noise in the background during their one-on-one consultations."

"Sit down and shut up or I'll get a write-up? Because if the suckers on the lines hear a call center instead of a little gypsy tent with a crystal ball, they won't believe in us anymore?" Jenna demanded, her voice rising. "Well, guess what? They shouldn't! You heard that, caller? We're lying!" She threw her ID tag at the stunned supervisor. "And I'm through lying for you!"

Cheers drowned the rest of her invectives, and the roar got louder as Jenna flipped an eloquent finger at the surveillance camera, swept her bottle of Bliss into her little leather purse, and flounced out. Several other operators followed, with or without the sign language, frightened or angry enough to throw away the thin security the job offered to cash in their chips and party before the end of the world.

Sally Mae tuned out the supervisor's frantic orders and looked at the lights on her board. Each one represented a client who needed help, advice, reassurance—and salvation. "Please, Sweet Jesus, show me what they need to know," she whispered, "and give me the strength to tell them."

Another click and she rejoined Gladys in the dusty darkness under the bed in the back room. "Gladys, you still there, honey? Sorry 'bout that—let's talk about you, honey, and what it'll take to get you out from under that bed. Shall I ask the angels what they see for you?"

Gladys eagerly agreed with that idea; she'd called hoping for supernatural reassurance, and angels were as dependable as any other type of spirit guide her psychic chose to use.

Sally Mae closed her eyes, praying as she usually did for inspiration to reach out and touch the heart of her client. Most of the time, the answer came out of her own down-to-earth common sense and from the caller's own words. This time, however, Sally Mae had barely begun her prayer when a blast of light and noise hit the inside of her head. Visions of chickens flying backward against a black-green sky accompanied a pandemonium of howling alarms and the growing sound of a freight train. Dread grew with it, a wordless warning to run, to hide, to do anything to escape the danger screaming down on her. Her eyes flew open, and she grabbed the edge of her desk to keep from falling over in her chair.

"Gladys!" she yelped, the deep roar ringing in her ears. "Gladys, you have to get out of there right now. Get out from under your bed, honey, 'cause there's a train coming!"

The improbability of a freight train plowing into Gladys's trailer didn't hit either of them until the urgency in Sally Mae's voice had pulled the woman from under the bed, out of the door, and into the yard, where the wind swirled wildly around her, groaning in the branches of the trees lining the road. "But Sally Mae, there's no train tracks 'round here," Gladys protested.

Sally Mae blinked, taking a deep breath to steady herself. The immediate panic had subsided, but the conviction that Gladys should get out of there persisted. Had she actually had a vision? Was she psychic, or had the Lord finally decided to give her a direct answer? The question boggled her mind, but she didn't waste time thinking about abstracts. "I don't either, honey, but I think you'd better—"

Then the sirens started. The howling whoop of the tornado warning sounded in the distance. Gladys didn't wait for Sally Mae to finish her sentence; she knew all about tornadoes' affinity for trailer parks. By the time the twister ripped through the neighborhood, uprooting and planting a tree right into her bedroom, she was long gone, huddling in a tornado shelter with everyone else lucky enough to get the warning in time.

That tornado died away after drawing a curving, randomly dotted swath of destruction through southern Missouri. Its cousins, boiling out of the turbulence in the sky, touched down in ones and twos, sweeping the length and breadth of Tornado Alley in an unstoppable march.

Long, twisting cones of whirling air touched down from the sky in unpredictable patterns, the clouds above them seeming to boil out of the empty skies as if some malevolent force summoned them. To Lucrezia Callatta, leaning on her hoe and staring toward the black wall of cloud speeding toward the field where she and a group of other teenagers had spent the morning weeding in the vast community garden, the emerging funnels looked like a monster's searching tentacles. Spikes of lightning flashed to the ground.

"Wind speeds in tornadoes have been measured at over two hundred miles an hour," Lucrezia's friend Jelisaveta Sarkesian said, the sight of the tornadoes bringing all the trivia she knew about tornadoes to her mind—and therefore her mouth. "With the bigger ones, the center of the cone is completely still, like the eye of a hurricane, only a lot smaller and drier, and the air pressure drops to almost half of normal. It's like being on top of Everest, only not as cold, of course—"

"Fascinating," Sister Shaw interrupted, catching the talkative girl's arm and motioning to the rest of the kids. "But let's not just stand here discussing it, okay? Get moving—back to the vans, everybody!" As one of the supervisors for the work group, she wasn't about to have the whole lot of them sucked into Oz on her watch.

Sister Shaw had volunteered for garden duty this morning as a break from working in Nauvoo's overburdened hospital, thinking that a morning of hard but peaceful work would do her nerves some good. More people came asking for help than she would have believed they could handle, problems ranging from accidental injuries to chronic conditions to life-threatening diseases to colds.

The ones that worried her, however, showed symptoms of massive allergy attacks for no reason the medical personnel could pin down at first. They didn't seem to have anything contagious, but their immune systems had gone into overdrive. Giving one patient medicine to bring down the fever, she and another nurse had looked at each other with a sudden realization and asked the woman if she'd had her shots. Indeed, she had—she'd taken the highly touted AllSafe shot a little over a year ago. They'd made her as comfortable as they could, and hurried to catch the head resident. She listened, agreed, and said that another doctor had come to the same conclusion about another patient. The question now was what to do about it. Giving the patients the AllSafe booster would keep them alive, but it wouldn't solve the problem—a problem that would get bigger as more people poured into the temple communities and camps around them. After doctors, nurses, and city administrators discussed the problem—with input from the temple president and advice from Church headquarters in Independence—

the decision came down to a waiting game. They would just have to handle it as best they could with the limited supply of booster shots they had and hope that the research going on in Salt Lake City would come up with a solution. So Sister Shaw had plenty on her mind when they set out for what she'd hoped would be a physically strenuous but mentally easy afternoon of pulling weeds and motivating teenagers. And now this!

With all four supervisors herding and shouting orders, the weed-removal crew reluctantly abandoned the long garden rows for the vans. Staying in the fields had become interesting. Lucrezia piled into the van slightly ahead of the rest, managing to secure a spot on the van's backseat where she could watch the developing storm out the back window.

"Tornadoes form out of vortex winds in the upper atmosphere, where hot and cold columns of air rise through layers of other warm and cool columns of air, and the convection currents start getting mixed up and wind around each other. Like the bubbles in oatmeal, only not so thick, of course. More like boiling water, only boiling water going down the drain," Jelisaveta continued, slipping into the seat beside Lucrezia.

April Shaw joined them, leaving the driving to her mother, and all three girls stared as one long, gray funnel stretched downward toward the green hills. It touched, lightly, as if seeking a firm purchase on the ground, lifted momentarily, then touched again. This time it held, the swirling column going dark as it sucked up leaves, dirt, and anything else not firmly anchored to the ground. In another minute, it had enough power to pull up small bushes from their anchoring, and the winds grew stronger. The vans rocked in the veering gusts.

Lucrezia, who'd tuned out Jelisaveta's nervous babble (sometimes she was as bad as Donna, though with Jelisaveta it was more like listening to a random idea generator than a middle school science lecture), turned her head when April exclaimed, "Look! Another one, over there!"

Off to the left of the road, a second funnel had descended, this one not hesitating at all as it poured down from the clouds to rake its claws against the ground. It swirled in place, as if getting its bearings, then began to move, pacing the two vans as they sped along the road.

Growing larger as they watched, this tornado ran into a small shed on an abandoned farm across the road. The owners had refused to sell the land to the Church but couldn't make a living on the farm anyway; they'd joined Lebaron's Millennium Brotherhood and lost two sons to the reverend's misguided crusade before giving up and moving south. The storm's dusty foot swept over the little building; a few seconds later, a scatter of dirty white boards appeared far above, mere splinters spinning in the dark air of the funnel.

"Here comes the other one too," Lucrezia shouted, to make herself heard over the noise of the van—and the lower, bone-shaking roar of the storm outside. The funnel behind them sped up, wracking the line of trees that bordered the road. It had grown wider as well as faster, filling Lucrezia's view.

"What happens if they catch us?" April whispered, her dark eyes wide with imagined consequences.

Both drivers hit the accelerators, driving the vans forward as fast as the heavy and heavily laden vehicles could go. Gradually, they pulled ahead of the two funnels, coming over a hill to see the outskirts of Nauvoo town spread before them. Tent flaps and awnings billowed in the rising wind. People moved to shelters as word of the approaching tornadoes efficiently spread through the temporary neighborhood that had grown up around the temple, a branch of Zion grafted into the Illinois farmland. The storm loomed before the flimsy but orderly settlement and the town in its center, poised to blow the entire city into a mess of rags, splinters, and shattered brick. Its two arms reached out, swirling closer to each other.

"What happens if they run into each other?" Lucrezia overrode her friend's frightening question with a possibly more reassuring one. "Do they cancel out?"

Even Jelisaveta didn't know the answer to that one—until the two huge funnels swept around each other in a twisting, swirling dance, tighter and tighter. With a roar that shook the road beneath the van, and a spray of lightning that flashed through the clouds and over the ground, the tornadoes wrapped around each other and merged into one huge, black wall that completely covered the road and stretched into the fields and trees on either side. Rain scattered out of the sky, then hail plunged down like bullets made of ice. The windshield starred and cracked in front of Sister Shaw, as a shower of actual stones fell around them, leaving dents on the van's hood and roof. She had to swerve violently to miss a battered, green-velvet sofa that fell out of the sky to land upright in the middle of the road.

"You know you're close to the storm when you start seeing debris dropping out of the sky," Jelisaveta observed, watching the unlucky sofa dwindle in the distance—and get swept up once more by the wild winds.

"Maybe it'll miss us," April said optimistically, watching the storm roaring across the fields toward them.

The massive tornado, towering from the ground to the clouds, roared forward toward the defenseless town—and then stopped. The entire black funnel shuddered, lost coherence, and fell apart, like a dust devil hitting a wall. Winds, freed from their spiral prison, whirred away in every direction. Leaves, branches, entire trees, terrified birds, a tractor, and tons of dust, left in the softened air with nothing to support them, promptly fell to the ground. With a last crackle of lightning and a distant growl of thunder like the parting curse of a foiled villain, the clouds drew up and spread out, becoming once more merely distant pillows of steam in the sky.

"Yes!" Lucrezia shouted, bouncing on the seat as the van came to a halt in the parking lot of the stake's jerry-rigged garage.

"Peace, be still," Jelisaveta sang.

The other kids in the van took up the hymn as well—and so did the adults at impromptu gatherings all over Nauvoo, as the Saints offered prayers of praise and thanks for the divine power that saved them from the storm. Others didn't sing, but they did gather as word of the Mormons' amazing luck spread all over the world. Outside Nauvoo and the other stakes of Zion, more refugee camps began to grow, as weary, frightened people converged on the Saints' temple communities, drawn by the hope of safety and peace. With the world falling to pieces, miracles sounded pretty good.

* * *

"Well, I don't know if we can exactly call it a miracle, but it's pretty d—darn amazing." Cal Weathers grinned broadly at his implied profanity and clicked on the exclusive Channel 8 footage. In the shaky, grainy eye of a handheld camera, the massive tornado blew forward, crashed into an invisible barrier, and disintegrated, then did it again in slow-motion play-by-play. "There it is, folks, live from Illinois. Category 4 twister blows up, way outside the usual range, and then it goes just six miles before it completely falls apart—guess they just don't make tornadoes like they used to, huh?"

Weathers tapped his map, illustrated with animated tornadoes. "But if quality's dropped, Clara, quantity's certainly up. It's been an unusually active tornado season—again—with damages in the hundreds of millions of dollars. Between the inland storms and the hurricanes that have messed up everybody's travel plans, we haven't had normal weather in three years. And, according to our projections and exclusive information from Ivana Mir, the weather specialist on board the International Space Station, the weather's just going to get wilder."

"Maybe you'd better work with the National Weather Service to redefine 'normal'! Thanks, Cal." Clara dismissed the weather man with a smile and turned to the next story. The less said about the amazing event at Nauvoo, the better; Monk had decided that weather curiosities were worth reporting, but the Mormons were still anathema to the board, thanks to deep-pocket sponsorship deals from outfits that had no love for the Church (the Children of Light and MedaGen chief among them).

"And maybe the twisters will blow us all away before the asteroids get here," the anchorwoman continued. "In addition to weather predictions, the research team on the International Space Station is reporting that they are still tracking the meteor swarm and the two largest NEOs. This despite the unfortunate loss of Dr. Stanislaw Kirmisse, the station's resident astrophysicist, who died in an accident during a spacewalk just after he detected the meteors. The International Space Agency is repeating its statement that the trajectory of the meteor swarm will bring them close to the earth but that they are not certain that the largest objects will hit the planet."

Clara accepted the report soberly—but not too seriously. Monk wanted viewers to be half reassured by the official statements and ready to feel superior to the idiots who overreacted to the threat. "Others, however, aren't so optimistic. People all over the world are reacting to the possibility of a worldwide disaster, which has brought out the hedonistic streak in some—and the survivalist streak in others. But maybe we won't have to survive Armageddon," Clara suggested, "if we've been living right."

Several well-known evangelists' faces appeared beside her, Tommy Gibbs's most prominent among them. "Fundamentalist Christians are declaring that the end of the world is coming and that the Rapture is imminent. Others are proposing a different solution," Clara voiced over images of sign-waving, shouting protesters. "A protest movement camped outside the Capitol in Washington, D.C., and in other capitals all over Europe is demanding that governments do something about the NEOs."

Secretary Garlick treated the press conference and video audience to an amiable smile. "Be assured that we're doing everything possible to prepare for contingencies. Federal and state agencies are preparing disaster plans, and we urge everyone to remain calm and carry on your normal lives. Don't let all the hype scare you. Remember that so far, our data is inconclusive—the biggest meteors may not hit the earth after all."

* * *

"Quick, change the channel," Donna ordered, running into the Callatta family's tent. "Check out the satellite channel!"

"Why?" Lucrezia looked sideways at her sister. She'd tuned their tiny portable console to Channel 8 for the tornado coverage and stayed for the freak show, even if Carmen had made her close her eyes when the blue crazies came on. Carmen distrusted the media news and kept an eagle eye on the screen as they watched the news updates. Lucrezia didn't resent her mother's do-it-yourself censorship. Just as well—the sight of a bunch of naked hippies covered with blue paint would probably put her off her lunch.

Carmen looked at Donna too, but much more tolerantly, then turned her attention back to dishing Gianni's soup and her phone conversation with Dr. Meredith Galen. "Looks like we've got breaking news here," she told her friend Merry over the phone connection to Salt Lake City. She turned her attention back to Donna. "Yes, why?"

"Because the Church's news network is up, finally." Donna reached over and changed the channel herself. The Church's private satellite stream, beamed through the International Space Station, reached Zion communities all over the world—and those communities had the capability to broadcast in return as needed. For the first time, however, the instantaneous communication system would play a different role from its original purpose of sending specific meetings or events over a closed circuit. A new picture appeared, with a smiling man gesturing to a tall, tropical tree loaded with ripe fruit as he explained the techniques his stake had used to cultivate their orchard.

"Orchard reports?" Lucrezia asked, rolling her eyes. "Oh, please—boring!"

"Sounds like we're up and running on the communications network," Carmen told Merry. In an aside to her kids, she said, "Your dad designed that logo," pointing to the lower of the two station marks that identified the broadcast as coming through Nauvoo's transmitter. The other mark said it originated in the Hawaiian Islands. The logos and the ID codes behind them were part of the security system that ensured no pirate broadcasters could take advantage of the Church's communication system.

"They'll have interesting things on later—one of the other teachers said they might broadcast a Seraph concert," Donna assured her little sister. "But what's important is that now we'll get accurate reports of what's going on all over the world, instead of just what Channel 8 or any other broadcaster want us to see."

One of the first reports the Saints saw came from President Smith, who appeared on the Church's internal broadcast system that night. In stark contrast to Channel 8's carefully orchestrated emotional manipulation, the prophet's gentle smile and voice calmed and reassured the watchers as much as his words did. "My dear brothers and sisters, I assure you that our Heavenly Father and His Beloved Son are in charge, and They are leading this Church in the way we need to go. The events of the last few weeks are amazing. We are living in the most anticipated time in the history of the world—excepting only, perhaps, the first coming of the Savior. As you know, some of you all too well, these days are also tumultuous, and many of you may be frightened by the events you see in the outside world, from wars and rumors of wars to reports that asteroids may strike the earth."

President Smith's face reflected his absolute certainty. "I can assure you that there is no need to fear. The earth will not be destroyed by the asteroids—I have that on good authority." That earned a laugh from his audience. He smiled, then said seriously, "Have faith, and trust you are being led by a divine hand. I especially address those in South America, Africa, and China, who find themselves in chaotic political and military situations. No matter what happens outside the borders of the temple communities, Zion is utterly safe from the depredations of evil people and the adversary who drives them. Let the Lord protect you, and He will guide you in what to do. For all of us, the best strategy is to keep your eyes open, your ears tuned to the Brethren, and your shoulders to the wheel."

He smiled, enthusiasm and excitement shining in his face. "We're all pioneers in a new world today. Do not waste time in worry—you'll have enough to do just doing the Lord's work! We still have the opportunity—no, the responsibility and sacred calling—to bring as many of our brothers and sisters to Zion's fold as will listen and heed the call. We want all to have the chance to stand in the glorious light of the Savior's presence. So keep striving, continue to be faithful, because it's not over yet. There is much that is wonderful yet to come!"

Wonderful events yet to come excited everyone in the temple communities. Men, women, and children pitched in to work in the gardens and farms, provide services in town, and reach out to others as their leaders directed. The idea of having to keep working, on the other hand, definitely didn't appeal to all the citizens of Zion.

"Oh, please, Miss Callatta, not more homework!" Donna's junior high students groaned as she wrote yet another set of basic science experiments and accompanying lab exercises on the chalkboard.

Conditions weren't ideal, and classes were crowded, but schools were among the first priorities for the town council in their planning sessions to handle the huge influx of people who nearly swamped Nauvoo. With careful organization and a lot of inspiration, they organized several schools for all ages, and classes ran five days a week. The town council recruited teachers as well—and Donna persuaded them to give her a chance. With an experienced educator as a mentor, she taught four junior high science classes in the mornings, then studied for her own teaching certification in the afternoons. She'd never worked so hard and found she truly enjoyed it.

"Come on, look what's going on!" Sean Shaw pleaded. He was the little brother of Lucrezia's friend April and was as loud and hyperactive as his sister was quiet and sensible. "It's the last days, for crying out loud. It's nuts that we're still in school." His classmates nodded and shouted agreement.

Donna grinned at them, completely unsympathetic as she leaned casually against the corner of the desk. "Sorry, guys. Even the end of the world isn't going to get you out of your homework."

"What use is this stuff, anyway?" Sean persisted, flicking his fingers disdainfully at the assignment on the board. "It's not like we're going to need it. Who needs to know chemistry now?"

"You do," Donna said, her tone catching their attention, despite their adolescent attention spans. She stood, flinging her hands out to include the entire class. "All of you do! Why do you need to know chemistry—or math, or Spanish, or anything else you're learning in school? Think about it. How many of you are still alive?"

A ripple of giggles swept the class, but they all admitted to breathing on a regular basis.

Donna nodded. "Okay, so you're all alive. How many of you are hungry?" She acknowledged their emphatic answers to that question, since their class was right before lunch, and continued, "Which means somebody's got to provide food for you. Which means somebody's got to know how to grow fruit, vegetables, and grains, to take care of farm animals for meat and milk. And then somebody's got to know how to get them ready for you to eat. And both of those people have to know chemistry to do it—and botany, and biology. That's not mentioning the doctors and nurses taking care of you when you get hurt or sick, and what do they need to know to make medicines?"

"Science!" shouted several of the kids.

"Science," Sean reluctantly agreed.

"Boom!" Donna brought her hands together in a loud clap. "There's my justification, class. You have to learn chemistry and science because you still need it to take care of yourselves—and other people. And we're going to have to take care of other people, not just ourselves."

Moving to the world map tacked to the wall, she tapped the broad stretch of savanna in East Africa, then swept her hand up to northern China, across the wide expanse of the seas. "You know that right now people all over the world are starving because they can't grow the food they need. The Church is helping, establishing big farms and orchards to produce local crops for the temple communities, and they've got hospitals and libraries and schools that can handle everybody who's fled to Zion. But someday we're going to need to take care of everybody in the world."

"But what about the Second Coming?" Sean asked, not giving up until the last straw of argument disappeared from his fingers. "Isn't everything going to get changed then?"

"Things are going to change, but they're not going to change that much," Donna cautioned. "Remember, the earth will still be here, and there will still be living people here. We don't know exactly what that'll be like, but we do know that Joseph Smith said that we'd live to the age of a tree—which is a long time—and that it would be hundreds of years before Judgment Day. We've still got the Millennium to live through, which means plenty of exciting things to do and learn. When everybody's working for Jesus, there's no room for slackers in the kingdom." She grinned at them. "And that's why you need to do your homework."

The bell rang, and she stepped out of the path of the stampede, calling, "Remember to clean up after you do the experiments—I don't want any mothers complaining about vinegar and baking soda all over."

"Isn't the Judgment going to happen pretty soon?" One of the other kids, a quiet, intense boy, poked Sean's shoulder. "And who's Joseph Smith?"

Sean looked at him, surprised. "Don't you know? Where you from?" It occurred to him that he hadn't seen this kid before. "What's your name, anyway?"

"Everest," the other boy said, adding, "yeah, like the mountain. Dad's into extreme sports. We're from Chicago." A hint of defiance showed in his face. "And we're not Mormons. We're Catholic. We're just here because it's—well, Dad said it would be safer."

"Oh." Sean blinked. He'd heard his mother talking about the non-members who'd started coming to the temple communities, but he'd never met one. Still, if Everest was here, it must mean he was okay, right? All the bad guys got stopped at the border. He looked at the other boy with interest. "So, you want to know who Joseph Smith was?"

"Sounds like you better tell me—if I'm staying here, I better know the lingo," Everest sighed.

Everest's family had come to Zion, as his father said, seeking safety—and they had found it. Membership in the community didn't depend on membership in The Church of Jesus Christ of Latter-day Saints; it depended on a person's spiritual status and willingness to abide by the rules. In fact, some members of the Church found themselves unable to stay in the community for long. The Spirit was so strong that those with guilty consciences soon had to either confess and repent or leave because they couldn't stand the internal pressure. The divine power that descended on the communities not only protected them from outside threats, dire and violent in many parts of the world, but internal threats—factions, cliques, dissensions—as well. People still had different opinions, of course, and different ideas and interpretations of just about any situation or question, but all had to approach the tasks at hand with a good heart—or have to face their own consciences. A broken heart and a contrite spirit, plus a willingness to pitch in and dedicate time and talents to keeping the community going and, in the case of members of the Church, to building the kingdom, were the only entrance fee or rent payment required.

Many who came to the stakes of Zion, however, couldn't or wouldn't pay it. Outside the boundaries of the towns and farms, at the perimeter where the Lord's protection descended over the Saints, other camps began to grow. The people who gathered there hoped to take advantage of the Mormons' "luck" in avoiding natural disasters, thinking that staying downwind of the temple communities would somehow shield them from the worst of the winds, droughts, floods, and earthquakes. They still clung to habits or mindsets that they wouldn't let go: their addictions to drugs, drinking, gambling, lying, anger, materialism, lust, or pride made them extremely uncomfortable inside the boundaries of Zion. They couldn't stand the spiritual light, so they hovered in the shadows at its edges.

The refugees' camps, while not as organized as the communities they surrounded, were surprisingly quiet and orderly. Part of the credit for the overall peacefulness belonged to the Mormon security/hospitality agents, always kind, attentive, and firm about the rules, who offered advice and assistance to any who wanted to take it. They spread through the refugee camps, calling anyone who would listen to come to Zion. The primary reason for the prevalence of law and order, however, came from the invisible but undeniable glow of righteous power spreading from the dedicated people in Zion itself. Some misguided but enterprising types attempted to set up saloons, brothels, and drug sales to cater to the Gentiles in the outer camps, but they never lasted long. The brothel disaster exemplified the way it worked. Instead of a crowd ranting against immorality or enforcers coming down to break the place up, a group of grandmotherly sisters moved themselves and their knitting to a row of chairs outside the makeshift bawdy house. Few johns had the determination to walk into a brothel under the gaze of women who looked like their mothers, or at least the ideal version of what their mothers might have looked like. The women smiled and waved to them, calling out maternal admonitions: "You don't want to go in there, do you, dear?" "There are so many better ways to spend your time." "You need to find a nice girl and settle down." "What would your wife think?" That same motherly charm worked on the muscle boys the madam sent out to "reason" with the women; under the ladies' limpid stares—and the spiritual weight of the angels behind them—the bullies couldn't do more than shuffle and mutter. They left. Several of the girls, bored and tired of being cooped up, wandered out as well and started talking with the knitters. Expecting icy disapproval, they found warm concern, understanding, and offers of help and encouragement to mend their lives. The brothel closed permanently within a week. The saloons and drug parlors, catering to more literal addictions, lasted slightly longer, but eventually folded as well.

"The Mormons ran us out!" A furious man, his truck still piled with his stock of liquors, waved his arms as Anne O'Neal interviewed him at a town several miles from Nauvoo.

Channel 8's popular religion specialist had come back to Illinois for a follow-up story on Governor Kerr's decision to pull the National Guard out of the conflict with the Mormons. As the story spread, with Leon's pictures showing exactly what happened, the idea of fully armed National Guard troops pursuing a caravan of family cars and minivans looked increasingly like a governmental overreaction. Even more disconcerting, many of the National Guardsmen themselves had either refused to carry on the pursuit or joined their former prey, pleading with their superior officers for leniency.

Finally, in an exclusive interview with Anne, the governor rescinded the warrant he had issued against the Church. "The National Guard successfully rounded up the terrorists among the Mormons, and we have determined that the ringleaders responsible for the devastation in Lake Creek were killed in the fighting they started," he stated, as pictures of Jack DuPris, J. H. Smith, and Smith's three sons let the viewers know who the government had settled on as scapegoats. Governor Kerr forced a politician's smooth smile and added, "As long as the Mormons behave themselves, the state of Illinois has no problem with them."

The state of Illinois officially had no problem with Reverend Samuel Lebaron and his Millennium Brotherhood either. However, when Lebaron attempted to see the governor after the battle in Lake Creek, he found himself not only denied an audience, but told to disappear before the state's attorney general decided to conduct a grand-jury hearing with Lebaron as the star. His violent followers' actions had embarrassed the governor, and now the whole thing was going to go away. Kerr had a political career to safeguard, and consorting with wild-eyed fanatics didn't fit the image he wanted to project. He wanted the whole episode over, now.

It didn't look as if the Mormon controversy in the Midwest would fade anytime soon, however, especially not as long as stories about the Mormons' antics drew eyeballs and ratings to Channel 8. Indignant individuals lined up to tell Anne their sob stories outside Nauvoo, angry and grumbling about the Mormons' intolerance and bigotry in forcing them out of their potentially lucrative businesses. As she pressed for details, though, none of them could cite actual cases where the Mormons had issued eviction notices—and the tales of Mormon enforcers wrecking tents, dumping alcohol, and burning marijuana stocks always happened to someone else, a friend of an acquaintance's brother, or some equally vague and untraceable person in a different community.

"The Mormons ran themselves out because nobody wanted them around," Leon summarized, wrapping up his camera equipment. The overcast sky failed to subdue his eye-searing tropical shirt. "And now everybody wants to follow them, and they get mad because they can't live in Mormon neighborhoods. These people just can't win for losing."

Anne gazed across at the quietly bustling town beyond the ragged fringes of refugee tents. She'd seen the National Guard convoy come to a sudden halt as if it had hit an invisible shield, seen soldiers crying as their consciences seared them, felt for herself the strange emotional attraction/repulsion that surrounded the Mormons' haven. She couldn't explain it; she'd abandoned belief in miracles long ago, after she graduated from Catholic school and rationally embraced the "real world," but she couldn't deny that something was there. Something that protected the Mormons, and something that they wanted to share.

"Actually," she said, glancing at her cameraman, "I think they're through losing. It will be interesting to see what happens—here and everywhere else."

"You think they're going to start fighting back, like they did in Lake Creek?" Leon asked, frowning.

Anne shook her head. "No, I don't think they'll have to." She shot him a smile, hiding the illogical conviction growing in her mind beneath her light tone. "I think somebody else is going to do that for them."

* * *

"Trust in the Lord to protect your families, and do what you are called on to do." The word from Elder Molina spread through the Mormon communities in Chile, then into neighboring countries under General Garza's iron fist. The message carried the added weight of the First Presidency's signatures and well wishes. "Offer no resistance; do your work well. Help the occupiers see you as harmless. Remember Limhi's people, whose burdens the Lord lightened and whose captivity He ended in His own time. Be patient, keep the faith, and all will be well."

Obedient to the Apostle's counsel, and the prophet's command through him, faithful Saints offered their services to Brindermann's bureaucracy, returning to their administrative and technical jobs. The wobbling infrastructure steadied; the power came on and stayed on, the phone lines cleared, the schools ran on schedule, the torturous process of identifying and registering citizens for the occupier's security services smoothed out. Civilians, knowing they could trust the Mormon officials to deal honestly with them, cooperated in return, grudgingly going back to work in the farms and factories that Garza needed to supply his army and ambitious plans. Brindermann, watching the neat efficiency and strict honesty of the Mormon workers who refused bribes and opportunities to divert goods to the thriving black market, decided to allow them to keep working but set spies to watch them and arranged to station the General's most vicious bands of guerillas in easy striking distance of their temples to ensure their continued good behavior.

The chief administrator had other problems to worry about. The military resistance he and the General expected had materialized with a vengeance. Reports from Serrey's security net said that Major Zamora had reappeared in the mountains outside Santiago with his own group of rebel guerillas. They had attacked an army camp in the night, blowing up the generators and destroying the communications tent. They'd also left an arm patch from the major's antiterror squad as an explanation—and a challenge.

"So, the major proves us right," Garza reflected, gazing at the belated report from the affected camp. "How convenient that he has chosen to live up to the reputation our ambitious Señorita Del Torres is building for him."

"No casualties," El Jaguar noted, standing beside the General to read the report.

He was the original rebel leader Garza had sent into Chile to destabilize the region and put pressure on the late President Quintana's government to accept Garza's assistance in dealing with the rebel insurgents. After Vice President Aguilera's men assassinated President Quintana and blamed Zamora for it, El Jaguar's group immediately capitulated, declaring themselves loyal citizens and pledging allegiance to General Garza and promising to help President Aguilera hunt down the evil Major Zamora and his followers. None of these official stories matched up; there were plenty of loose threads for the curious or skeptical to pull. However, when the loose threads had armed men and certain execution on the other end, few were willing to pull them—especially when in other countries, powerful people preferred to accept Garza as an agent of stability in the notorious instability of Latin American politics.

Which left Zamora to pursue what Garza saw as a quixotic, hopeless fight against superior forces and tactics—though he took the potential threat seriously. He read the report once more, then set it aside. "No casualties—not even the sentries, who he put to sleep with tranquilizers on blow darts. He did that because he wanted to show us what he could do."

"Who did he intend to impress?" Brindermann asked. "He must know that we would not publicize this report."

"No, but armies run on rumors more than boot leather," Garza said. "He wants our men to spread the word for him, the story getting more elaborate with each telling, to worry the men into thinking they are fighting a mountain ghost. Which is why we are going to catch him and show everyone just how we reward rebellion."

His raptor eyes turned to El Jaguar, who responded with a feline smile. "Go get me Zamora."

"My pleasure, sir." The guerilla leader saluted and strode out of the tent.

CHAPTER 5

"This is not as fun as I thought it would be," grumbled Mercury, snuffing as a stream of rain ran over his face. "This keeps up, all my makeup's going to wash off."

Zamora just grinned, scanning the nearest two curves of the twisting mountain road with a pair of heat-sensitive binoculars. From his perch on the high bank that bordered the muddy track on the uphill side, he had a clear view up the road for three curves before the mist and rain helped the thick trees hide the rest of it. The road cut through the foliage and dirt, the bordering banks slowly fading as the road hit harder, rockier soil. "Then keep your head down, so nobody sees your face and blows it off."

"Who are we hiding from again?" Mercury looked at the road too. "They said they got away clean."

"Better safe than sorry," his father replied, "with our old friend the cat looking for us."

"You could beat him any day of the week and twice on Sundays, if you had the force to do it," Mercury said, then stopped talking before Zamora had to tell him to.

Zamora had organized the resistance, and done it remarkably quickly; he had to distract El Jaguar, keep him busy until the silent infiltration had a chance to firmly root itself in the General's organization. That in itself wasn't difficult; El Jaguar had arrived in Santiago from the General's headquarters in Bogotá and broadcast his intention to turn every possible hiding place inside out to outwit Zamora—and prove himself worthy of Garza's favor. Brindermann vetoed his intention to begin with the Mormons huddled around their temple, because they were invaluable in administering the occupied territories. It also helped that the Mormons in all the countries under Garza's thumb prayed that the Lord would soften the hearts of their captors; perhaps divine influence emphasized Brindermann's hatred of chaos, and his appreciation of the Mormons in lessening it.

That meant a guerilla war between El Jaguar's troops and Zamora's men. Hiding in the mountains from El Jaguar's forces did not pose a problem for Zamora's determined force; they easily disappeared into the mists from their mobile camps. No, the problem Zamora faced was manpower and weapons. Their numbers increased as the officers and soldiers who took cover after Garza's invasion made their way to Olivares's agents, who spread the word that Zamora was recruiting and vetted the applicants. Zamora laid out the curriculum, and they trained under the experienced eyes of Guerra and the other officers of the antiterror squad. With their determination to fight for their country and families, the new rebel forces were growing into a disciplined, skilled army.

Part of the training concentrated on the ability to move swiftly and invisibly through any environment (mountain, jungle, desert, and city streets)—and that had brought a small strike team out into the rain, looking for a group of Saints slipping through the jungle with information or equipment in defiance of Brindermann's curfews and travel restrictions. Word that the agent who had infiltrated Garza's primary communication network had completed his mission and was coming back to report had brought the major and his son into the underbrush as the sunset glinted in the few small breaks in the clouds.

Mercury hunkered down in the undergrowth around their hiding place and snuffed again, watching a beetle navigate the twig in front of his face. Sitting in the rain definitely wasn't his idea of an exciting mission deep into enemy territory. The bug trundled along, feelers flicking, beads of rain on its jewel-colored carapace. As it drew near the junction of the branch, a sticky rope of tongue latched onto its head. The beetle flew through the air and disappeared into the jaws of a green-spotted lizard concealed among the leaves. With an almost audible snap, the lizard's scaly lips closed. "And thank you, Mother Nature, for that wonderful object lesson," Mercury muttered.

Around him, the members of the strike team did their own communing with nature or their thoughts until Zamora whistled. They sprang to attention, watching as four men appeared around a curve in the twisting road. They darted right and left occasionally, but the banks were still too high for easy climbing—and they seemed to value speed more than concealment.

"They're running, straight out, not using cover." Mercury could see them without the field glasses as they rounded the last bend and hit the short straightaway where the rescue squad lay in wait.

"Which means they know cover's not going to do them any good in a couple of minutes." Zamora slid to his feet, whistling another signal. Instantly, the strike team moved through the wet leaves, slithering closer to their overlook perch, guns at the ready, sighting up the road past the escapees. Zamora slid down the bank to the road and sprinted to the other side, climbing up the lower bank there, just at the next curve. Mercury followed his father, running across the muddy road and up the short incline to disappear into the bushes on the far side.

The runners dashed around the last curve, starting down the straight length where Zamora's men waited. One ducked, lurching to the side. A second later, the crack of a gunshot hit their ears. All four began to weave, making themselves as difficult to hit as possible while still running. At the curve, another set of men appeared, these dressed in camouflage and carrying rifles. The one in the lead stopped and sighted down the road; the last of the running men jerked and cried out, a sudden bloom of crimson on his sleeve. As he stumbled, two of his companions turned to grab him by the arms, pulling him forward. Their pursuers shouted gleefully and ran forward. A bullet cracked against a tree trunk over the heads of their prey, sending a heavy shower of water, and assorted wildlife, gushing down. Behind the downpour, the refugees hit the curve—and promptly disappeared, as Zamora and Mercury reached out and grabbed them, pulling them into the over-hanging bushes. They spun, using up the inertia of their run, and crashed to the mold-covered ground.

"What the—" the wounded man began, then got a look at Zamora. He choked on the exclamation, then said urgently, "Major! They're following us! You've got to—" He didn't get to finish that sentence either.

A barrage of gunfire erupted from the far bank as the pursuers reached the middle of the straight stretch and ran into the rebels' ambush. Zamora glanced out through the leaves, then turned back to the shivering men they'd rescued. "They're not following you anymore, Señor Ascencio. What happened? We had word that you'd gotten away clear, with no tails."

Mercury followed his father's gaze and saw several khaki-covered lumps in the muddy road and the squad members sliding down from concealment to make sure the men were dead. He swallowed hard, telling himself that death shouldn't bother him—he wanted to be a soldier, didn't he? So why should it make him sick to see people die? They were scum, Garza's thugs; they deserved everything they got and more. Dove didn't hesitate to kill if he had to, and neither did Mercury's father. Despite his macho inner monologue, he felt grateful that he didn't have to check the bodies for signs of life, or decide what to do if he detected any, and drag them out of the road. His papa believed in treating enemy casualties with the decency due any human being, which meant pulling them out of the road at least. He turned his attention back to the men they'd originally come to escort but had ended up rescuing. The blood soaking Ascencio's sleeve caught his eye; he dug into his light backpack for the small field-medic kit, which he handed to his father.

"I did," the man sighed, wincing as Zamora felt over his injured arm and began bandaging it. "I left Bogotá clean. I got all the way into Peru, no problem. Slipped onto the black-market trade trail, just like your man Neruda marked on the map. And then we ran into a pair of trucks coming up the road—trucks with the General's insignia on them. The banks were too high to climb, and we couldn't run, or they'd know something was up. We—ouch—tried to bluff it out, but these guys acted suspicious, yelling for our papers, wanting to know which outfit we'd deserted from. The whole lot of them jumped out— two drivers and two guards for each truck—and we decided to run for it, figuring they couldn't turn the trucks around on the narrow road, and we'd outdistance them. None of us thought they'd come after us—maybe file a report, send in a recon team later. We figured they didn't know who we were, so they'd leave us alone."

"But they chased you on foot instead," Zamora said thoughtfully, finishing the temporary dressing with a firm pull that earned a gasp from Ascencio. "You got away clean, so your cover hasn't been blown yet, so they didn't know to look for you. Which means they had something to hide." He rose, nodding to the man who came to a stop in front of him and snapped a military salute. "Report."

"Eight of them," the squad leader said. "All dead. All wearing the insignia of Garza's troops, not Chilean Army collaborators."

"Let's go see what the General's own troops were smuggling along the back trails instead of over the main roads with the rest of the supplies going to Bogotá." Zamora looked down at Ascencio with a slight smile. "Your bad luck may turn out to be good for us. Stay here—and stay down." He looked at Mercury. "Call base camp, encoded channel, tell them we've got Señor Ascencio and we'll be back as soon as we look at what got him shot."

Mercury opened his mouth to protest, say that he wasn't a child to be left behind, claim he could handle a gun and himself in a fight—then caught his father's look. Did he want to be a soldier? Did a soldier question his superior officer's orders? "Yes, sir," he said, adding a salute to show he meant it.

Zamora did no more than nod and return the salute before walking off with the squad leader, but the approval in his eyes said all that he didn't. He'd brought Mercury along on this mission because he'd expected it to go smoothly, a simple rendezvous and pickup job, a taste of responsibility with enough rain to dampen the boy's enthusiasm and give him a dose of reality, but no danger and certainly no violence. It had turned into something much more serious—and possibly much more useful. He ran up the road, fast but cautious, alert for any sound in the regular forest cacophony. Around the fourth turn in the road, two dun-colored trucks sat, their wheels slowly sinking into the muddy ground. Zamora and his men approached cautiously, under cover, climbing up into the trees on the high banks, but nothing moved. Dropping from an overhanging branch onto the roof of one truck, Zamora leapt to the cab, then landed kneeling on the windshield, gun pointing at the empty seats. The other men, surrounding the trucks, blasted the locks off the back doors, then called "clear" from their positions as well—no one lurked inside the cargo spaces either.

What did lurk there earned a low whistle from the squad leader and a grim smile from Zamora. Long, narrow cases filled the shelves packed into the space, labeled boxes of expensive ammunition, state-of-the-art firearms, rocket-propelled grenade launchers, heat-seeking rockets, and other perfectly engineered pieces of bright and shiny mayhem. Exactly what they needed most. The biggest problem the insurgents faced wasn't a lack of willing recruits—it was obtaining enough arms to stand against Garza's thugs. Zamora's men didn't fear battle, and many of them didn't fear death, but they didn't want to throw their lives away uselessly either. They'd already seen how little hoes and pitchforks could do against El Jaguar's guerillas. The men and women infiltrating Brindermann's supply and administration system could eventually channel the weapons and ammunition they needed to them, but at the moment all shipments of quality supplies and matériel in the region were headed for Bogotá to supply the General's main army.

"So this is what they try to slip along the back ways," Zamora said. "Perhaps to supply El Jaguar's war against us? Or to bait us?" The silent buzz of the comm unit around his neck brought him back to the present. Clicking on the encrypted channel, he heard Mercury's voice. "Chatter says more cats are coming—can't hear what they say, but we're picking up radio transmissions."

"Major!" One of his men ran to the back of the truck. "The radio in the lead truck is squawking—they want a reply. Something about getting their flat fixed, then they got suspicious."

"Get up here with your sheep," Zamora ordered Mercury. "And tell Ascencio he'd better have Neruda's map on him."

He did have the map, secure in his front breast pocket—still readable despite the blood spatters and rain. Neruda's secondary route, the one smugglers used, lay a half mile behind them. Unfortunately, so did the rest of Garza's oncoming convoy, the companions to the soldiers whose trucks they'd hijacked. The rebels jumped into the trucks, the best drivers on the squad backing the heavy vehicles at top speed through the sharp curves of the road. One hit a protruding root with a back tire and slewed dangerously, its tall, boxy cargo space overbalanced and beginning to tip. Mercury and the other two rebels riding in the back flung themselves against the tilting wall, praying fervently if incoherently; with a squeal, the tire broke loose and landed hard, flattening its human cargo but failing to jar the well-secured munitions loose. The truck righted itself and kept going, following its mate in a sharp backward turn around a tall boulder half hidden in a mass of creeper and tree trunks.

"Full stop, all silent!" hissed Zamora into the comm.

The trucks' engines turned off, their rumble dying away. For a long moment, the only sounds were of birds and animals chattering about the sudden intrusion of a pair of huge, metal monsters into their neighborhood. A growl cut through the chatter, growing louder as the rest of the General's convoy charged up the muddy road. The noise of the other two engines blended with a low roar of thunder, and the rain blasted down, reducing visibility to mere feet and pounding the muddy track clear of any signs of the rebels' passage. Garza's trucks passed within feet of Zamora's vehicles, but did not slow. As soon as the sounds of their engines faded away, the two AWOL trucks bumped down the smugglers' trail, following the route Brother Neruda had given to Ascencio to aid his escape. Trees closed around them, impenetrably thick underbrush rose in front of them, a tangled and thorny dead end—until Zamora's men used Neruda's directions and moved the entire barrier aside, then replaced it after they drove through. It took just a moment for the birds to go back to their songs.

Far up the track, the rest of Garza's convoy drew even with their comrades, relaxing against trees on the lower bank of the road.

"Hey, what are you doing, sleeping on the job?" yelled the lead driver, rolling down his window. "You're so hot to get to camp that you couldn't wait for us to change a tire, but you can take a break for a nap?"

"Where's the trucks?" snapped the officer in charge, grasping the most important part of the scene, or its absence. He kicked the door open, jumping out with his gun ready, shouting orders for half the men to cover the banks, and half to guard the cargo. They swarmed out behind, rifles pointing into the thick greenery above them. Advancing on the nearest motionless soldier, the officer stopped, watching a large beetle drop off a limb and land on the man's shoulder—right above the hole in the breast pocket of the soggy uniform. He stepped forward, flicking off the cap that covered the soldier's face. The man's dead eyes stared back at him as he vigorously cursed Zamora, the rebels, and his own bad luck.

"Looks like we got two choices," the chatty driver observed, pale under the deep tan on his face. "We can keep going, get to camp, tell El Jaguar we lost two trucks to Zamora, and maybe get shot for it. Or we can turn around, go back to base, and hope the General's in a lenient mood."

Half of the troop had already come to that conclusion and made their own decisions. By the time the officer decided that half of a shipment and definite news of Zamora's activity in this area outweighed the loss of two trucks and ordered his men back to their vehicles, only half of them returned to their places. That half had been under the officer's direct gaze, investigating the dead men. The occasional muddy footprint was all that remained of the ones who'd stayed behind to guard the cargo. The officer swore again, and kept swearing as the remaining two trucks made their slow way to El Jaguar's headquarters outside Santiago.

* * *

Zamora stifled a swearword of his own as he looked closely at a long, heavy container lying on the tailgate of their stolen truck. The label proclaimed that it contained four automatic rifles with laser sights and all the trimmings; the tiny, glowing light on the electronic lock said that no one would touch those rifles until he entered the correct key code. Every one of those surprisingly sturdy boxes, whether it contained guns, ammunition, bombs, or more exotic weapons, had one of the nasty little metal locks.

The major turned a glower on Ascencio. "What is this?"

Ascencio, his arm now professionally bandaged by the camp medic, looked it over with a true technophile's interest in all gadgets. "I think it's a booby-trap lock. I saw a couple of mentions of them while I was setting up the back door in the computer system, in a folder of recent inventory orders. Caught my eye, because it had 'keepsakes' on the payment entries."

"These don't look like keepsakes to me," Mercury snorted.

"Really? Why not? You can't see one of these on your grandma's mantle?" Ascencio felt enough better (or was in enough pain) to be sarcastic. He caught Zamora's eye and moderated his tone. "It's from Keepsakes Ltd. It's an American outfit with a factory out in Santa Lucia, just up the coast from Santiago. They're a security company, specialize in safes with more aggressive features than the usual wall box."

"Like what?" the major asked, trading a glance with Captain Guerra. They could guess.

Ascencio looked closely at the box, gingerly touching the lid, hinges, and lock. "See here? They're wired. We try to open them without the code, they'll destroy themselves and whatever's in them. Big explosion—definitely takes out the contents, and maybe the person trying to take it. Keepsakes calls it their jealous-lover feature."

"If I can't have you, no one can?" Guerra guessed.

Zamora shook his head, waving away immaterial things like advertising slogans. "How well does it work?"

"Really well," Ascencio said, looking warily from Zamora to Guerra, who exchanged a glance that said their thought processes had taken the same road to the same conclusion.

"Better not try it on one of the grenade boxes," Mercury advised.

"Never would've thought of that for myself. Thanks for the safety tip, junior." The captain grinned and thumped his shoulder hard enough to make him stagger.

It took only seconds for two of his squad to pick out a high-tech crate whose label said it contained laser-targeting equipment and place it in a clear space well away from the rebels' camouflaged tents. An interested audience gathered; the old soldiers couldn't help but make a couple of verbal wagers. Guerra drew his sidearm, taking a bead on the tiny light flickering on the Keepsakes lock.

"Fire when ready, Captain," Zamora ordered.

The bullet hit the lock straight on, shattering the light into molecule-sized splinters. A split second later, a brilliant burst outlined the seam around the case, and it shattered into much larger but no more useful slivers. The delicate laser equipment shattered as well—the bits that didn't melt into fused chunks of metal, glass, and plastic.

"Heat and explosive force. Not bad." A few moments later, as the debris settled, Guerra poked the smoldering remains with his boot. He looked from the ruins to Ascencio.

So did Zamora. "So how do we crack them? What are the codes?"

"I didn't stop to look more closely," Ascencio admitted. "I kind of had other things on my mind at the time—like putting a sub-admin password into their accounting subroutine. I would've gone back to dig around if some kind of network snoop hadn't come up on the connection. Whatever security system they've got going, it's fast. I got out before it caught me, but I couldn't finish fixing a portal for outside access. Lucky they missed my back door." He shuddered, thinking about the close call. They knew something had happened, even if they didn't know exactly what or who. It had been a close call, though; the next day, everyone in his work group found their passwords had expired. "I figured they'd blow my cover pretty soon, so I took off."

"You got any geek tricks up your sleeve, kid?" Guerra poked Mercury, who swatted at him.

"Keepsakes Ltd." Zamora looked at the slick finish of the rifle box, then at the computer spy. He appreciated the importance of technology to any modern battle strategy, and knew that electronic intelligence was absolutely vital, but he preferred to use weapons he could touch—and fire at enemies he could see. Creeping around a virtual maze pursued by phantom monsters sounded like a nightmare, or a game. The programmer's scatter-shot method of reporting added to the brusqueness that came from his low-level uneasiness with the entire mission. "Anything else catch your attention while you did your electronic carpentry work?"

That earned him a grin from Mercury, who'd developed a competitive dislike of the older hacker. Sure, the guy was good, but he struck Mercury as overcautious. The fact that a bullet had creased him both added and subtracted points from Ascencio's overall score; he'd taken it well, but he'd not been fast enough to avoid it in the first place. Everybody knew that a real Net crawler was as good on a skateboard as he was on a keyboard.

Ascencio grinned too, wearily. "Yes, sir. That's what you and Señor Olivares sent me for, right?" He rummaged in his pocket and handed Zamora a glittering data disc. "The details are on this. The short version is that it looks like Garza's getting a big shipment of cutting-edge war toys from the United States. Looks like he's made a deal with one of the government contractors."

"Or with the government itself." Señor Olivares joined the conversation with his usual smoothness.

Mercury started slightly and turned to look at him. Zamora just nodded a silent greeting—he'd seen the spymaster coming. Never being taken by surprise was a point of pride with the major.

"But I am sure that an analysis of the data you obtained will tell us more about exactly who the General has seduced this time," Olivares continued, holding out his hand. Zamora gave him the disc. He looked at it, like a jeweler assessing a rough gem's potential value, and tucked it away in his jacket pocket. "If you have finished with Señor Ascencio, Major, I will finish his debriefing after he has had some rest."

Zamora nodded, then held up one finger. "Just one thing. You said you set up a back door. Could we use it to get the codes to these boxes?"

"Absolutely, if you were slick while you explored the system. The back door gives administrator access, even to encrypted files. Turns out the chief accountant rigged his own little back door when he programmed the financial apps, probably so he could do some skimming, maybe get into some possibly valuable information to sell. That's what let me in. If the system designer hadn't left it, and I hadn't read about a million lines of code to pick up the clues for it, I wouldn't have been able to build on it. Convenient for us, if not him. He never got a chance to use it before they knocked him off so he wouldn't give away the secrets of the system he created. Guess white-collar crime doesn't pay all the time." Ascencio shrugged, then winced as the motion jarred his arm.

"So how do we get to their system to use this back door?" Zamora persisted. He didn't bother to tell Ascencio that he'd found the clues because God wanted him to, but that seemed more likely than the guy coming up with it on his own, when Brindermann's own software warriors had missed it. The guy was Catholic and could take a saint's intervention a lot better than the idea of an earthly prophet intervening in his spy mission. Elder Molina had added the hacker to his prayers, and Elder Molina tended to get what he asked for.

"Well, that's the thing," Ascencio said, looking half angry, half embarrassed. "Like I said, I couldn't set up the remote access key, with that Net spy closing in. So the door's there, but you've got to log on to the system before you can use it."

"You'd have to be physically at one of the General's consoles, with a legitimate user account already set up," Mercury clarified. "Basically, you'd have to be at the house. Then you could use the backdoor key. It's not like wire fraud; it's more like breaking and entering."

"Meaning that one of our agents would have to walk into the command center in Bogotá and ask for permission to use their computers?" Zamora asked, his jaw clenching with frustration.

"Well, yes, kind of—not that blatantly, of course," Ascencio admitted. "Like I said, I didn't have time before they figured out what I was doing."

Olivares's mild voice carried the sting of a whiplash. "Then you have created a tool we cannot use. A door we cannot approach is useless to us."

"Maybe it's not," Mercury said thoughtfully.

"No living creature's going to make it past their security screen, especially after they blew my cover," Ascencio said flatly.

"How about a ghost?" Mercury looked at his papa. "They already think I'm dead. It's been all over the news. Serrey himself had to verify it to keep the General from coming down on him for blowing up the house."

"Just because Serrey verified it doesn't mean he believes it," Zamora pointed out.

Mercury had his argument ready. "But he's never met me either. They've got an old picture from Aunt Anabel's. I cut my hair, stand up straight, act like a sheeplike Mormon programmer, who's going to link me with that wannabe punk kid Major Zamora sent up north?" He watched the speculation in Olivares's eyes, the hesitation in Zamora's, and went in for the kill. "Besides, we don't have to send me to Bogotá. Brindermann's efficient—he's got to use the same accounting system throughout the network, to make sure nobody's shorting the bills or skimming. Right?"

Ascencio blinked at being the center of three intense stares. "Sure, yeah. Should be accessible anywhere on the network—*if* you have a legitimate account."

"Which I could. You know they've already put out the call for anybody who can help them get things stabilized, run their communications and computer systems," Mercury reminded them. "So I show up, network admin certification in hand, and I'm in."

"As a junior-level tech," Olivares said.

"Yeah, but a junior-level tech with access. Plus, I can jack into their comm system like I did up north. We'll be able to listen to whatever orders Garza's sending down here." This time, Mercury concentrated on his papa. "I know I can do it. And if I can't, I promise I'll get out without tripping any alarms." He ignored Ascencio's snort at that claim.

Zamora didn't—but he couldn't refute it either. He'd watched Mercury help set up the computer systems in the rebels' own mobile command centers as they moved from camp to camp to avoid El Jaguar's strikes.

"His age could be in our favor," Olivares said, "making Brindermann's agents less likely to suspect him of more advanced skills. And, if I may point this out, Major, we do not have much time. We have to use that back door before Brindermann's network spies discover it. Which they undoubtedly will."

His age is one of the reasons I don't want him to go, Zamora thought. But he hadn't been much older when he joined the first stirrings of what eventually became the March Revolution. He looked at his son, forcing himself to see the current reality instead of the bright-eyed five-year-old happily jabbering about his mastery of some arcane intricacy of a child's computer game. The boy—young man, now—didn't look so terribly young anymore. He'd handled himself among the gangs in Amexica, and he had come home more disciplined and focused. If this boy weren't his son, would he hesitate? No. The command officer side of his brain knew he could trust Mercury, both to keep the mission secret and to perform the computer espionage Olivares's man had set up. He couldn't deny the quiet confidence that grew in him, whether it was inspiration or just rational argument. Was it any safer for the kid hanging around the guerillas' jungle camps with El Jaguar's men searching for them? He couldn't contribute as much to the resistance as a noncombatant communications specialist as he could in the infiltration force—and this assignment might keep him out of the line of fire. Where's the place the authorities would last look for an escaped convict? Under the warden's bed.

"You can't go in alone," Zamora said at last.

Mercury hesitated, keeping down the wave of excitement. Might be premature. "Does that mean I can go?"

With a silent prayer for the protection of confident teenagers and guidance for worried fathers, Zamora nodded. "With a handpicked team. If Elder Molina feels good about it—and Señor Olivares."

The spymaster smiled slightly, amused at his belated inclusion. He didn't understand the Mormons' total faith in their leaders' and their own revelations, but it seemed to work for them well enough to let them go with it—while making his own backup arrangements, of course. "Thank you, Major. There are several older men among your

Mormons, experienced programmers, who we can send in as cover for this one and a couple of other young assistants. They can draw the occupiers' suspicions away from the real threat."

Zamora nodded, pushing away the last flickers of reluctance, and turned a stern eye on his son. "This is serious, Michael Angel. Deadly serious. Remember, this is not a game. You will have your own and others' lives in your hands. Can you do this? Are you willing to take on the responsibility?"

Mercury stifled a whoop—that would completely wreck the serious, soldierly image he needed to keep up now—but he couldn't do anything about the grin that spread across his face as he snapped off a salute. "Yes, sir!"

* * *

"I know a kid who'd love to get his hands on this stuff." Dove Nakai leaned over to look at the four palm-sized monitors around the larger one, five computer channels going at once, every one monitoring a different part of the Church's vast communication system. Pictures, abstract patterns, and lines of data chased each other across the screens. Dove knew they represented an amazing amount of information, and Mercury would be able to read it like a neon sign, but it was all digital Greek to him.

The kid who currently had his hands on the stuff laughed manically, flexing his fingers. "Oh, you ain't seen nothing yet, my Native American friend. We got big medicine here." The light from the screen winked off his anachronistically thick glasses.

"That was totally culturally insensitive, Maynard," the other programmer in the cavelike lair pointed out, her voice patient. She'd been trying to train him in social graces for a while and hadn't made much headway.

The boy—well, probably technically over twenty-one and therefore a man, but he struck Dove as a brilliant child prodigy who never grew up—looked at Dove closely, as if he were trying to detect any sign of offense.

Dove just grinned. "Dazzle me with your magic, Great White Father."

He got a grin in return, and the magic show started in earnest as Socks gave him the grand tour of the amazingly complex and far-reaching network linking Church sites all over the world with communication and data.

Merry had parked Dove with them to keep him entertained (and, he suspected, out of trouble) while she reported the latest results from Section 89 to Elder Nabil and some of the other Brethren. He obediently followed Jonathan Crow to an elevator, down more floors than he expected, and wound up in the sub-basement. Instead of boilers and maintenance closets, they arrived at a sturdy-looking door with a retina-scan security lock.

Jonathan's eyes passed the test with flying colors, and the lock clicked open. He smiled at Dove. "We don't need this, not with all that's happened lately, but nobody's got around to changing it, and I think Maynard likes it. It probably makes him feel like some kind of superhero."

The big, dim room behind the door contained more computer hardware than Dove had seen outside of science fiction movies—and two computer jockeys. Jonathan waved to both of them, and told Dove they'd answer his questions and to have fun, before he headed back upstairs. One of the techs looked up as soon as the door opened, smiled manically as he waved to Jonathan, and introduced himself as Socks.

The young woman didn't pause in her rapid-fire coding or turn in her chair as she said, "Don't fall for it. He's Maynard Stockton. Socks is his Net name. He thinks it's cute. I'm Juliet Faux—and before he tells you, it's Fox on the Net. His taste in literature never matured either."

"Don't mind her. She's still upset because Anna Karenina died in the end." Socks shrugged off his colleague's derisive snort at that comment.

Both remarks went over Dove's head, but he did get the idea that both Fox and Socks were communications specialists for the Church, connected to the Church's worldwide network from their lair deep beneath the Church Office Building in Salt Lake City. Fox took her job seriously, and dressed the part, in a subdued suit and severe hairstyle. Socks's cyberpunk-infused imagination, on the other hand, painted them as a pair of Net rangers on the wild virtual frontier, and the only thing wilder than the colors on his superhero tie were the curls standing out from his scalp. Dove figured they must not get on each other's nerves as much as they pretended to, or somebody would've wound up dead by now.

Wound up dead. The thought distracted him from Socks's enthusiastic detailing of every terabyte of instant-access memory and data streaming. The programmer's high-speed chatter faded into the background; Dove's own heartbeat sounded loud in his ears. He could've wound up dead—maybe he should've. He shoved away that thought—and the thought of the AllSafe still lurking in his system. It itched in his mind, despite Merry's assurance that taking the vaccine wasn't a sin.

He could picture Merry giving him a patient look as she listened to his breathing, checking to make sure the damage to his lungs was healing well, and repeated her argument for the millionth time. "The Church issued the warning because MedaGen lied about AllSafe. They created a vaccine that would kill people if those people didn't pay MedaGen again for the temporary antidote—and paid again, and again. You took it because it was the only way to stop the nasty virus Slick infected you with. Can you please remember that?"

She'd also warned him against trying to scrub out the AllSafe under his skin while he showered, giving him a remonstrative look. "We don't need a Lady Macbeth episode around here." Her expression softened as she rubbed his shoulder. "It will be okay. We just have to have faith." He suspected that she was trying to reassure herself too—but if anybody could break the AllSafe code, Dr. Meredith Galen could. Dove, always looking for role models, thoroughly admired both Merry and Elder Nabil, the doctor for her brilliance and compassion, the Apostle—well, because he was an Apostle.

"Hello? Earth to Tonto?" A thrown data disc bounced off Socks's head. He rubbed the spot and modified his attempt to regain Dove's attention. "Earth to Samuel the Lamanite?"

Fox groaned, rolling her eyes. "Can't you just use his name, for crying out loud?"

Dove smiled at her. "He couldn't pronounce it." The justified grin on Socks's face disappeared as Dove's fingers dug deep into his white-guy Afro and pulled him as far back as his ergonomic chair would tilt. His wide eyes stared into Dove's from a distance of three inches as Dove said gently, "So just call me Dove, all right?"

The chair snapped back upright as Dove released his grip. Socks snapped upright too, staring at Dove.

For a moment, Dove wondered if he'd miscalculated, offended the computer specialist.

Then Socks grinned hugely. "Whoa, that was smooth! You did the voice, just like in *Noir City!*"

"Online game," Fox supplied, correctly guessing that Dove wasn't into virtual reality.

Dove let that go; he wasn't into games, and he wasn't interested in them either. "Sorry for the fadeout back there. What were you saying?"

Socks regarded him with sincere puzzlement. How could anyone not find the intricacies of a world—no, galaxy!—class computer system absolutely fascinating?

"How about we cut the talk about processor speeds and bandwidth and show him what this rig can do?" Fox suggested.

"What can it do?" Dove asked, jumping at the chance to escape the other programmer's endless recitation of technical specs.

"It can provide live feeds of a full audio-video presentation in a hundred and three languages simultaneously," she said casually, "but you have to know how hard that is to be impressed. How about this— we can link to every Church system in the entire world, from headquarters at Independence to Johannesburg and back, and we never have to rely on anybody's lines or transmitters but our own. Nobody can shut us down without deploying a full-on scrambler, and that would affect only the local site."

Seeing that the strategic implications of that fact had caught Dove's attention, she launched into a practical demonstration of the encryption system that ensured security for all Church broadcasts. It was impressive, with a cool factor high enough to interest Dove despite his user-level acquaintance with computers. Thanks to Fox's brilliant coding, anyone could see the primary broadcast, which carried the Church's television signal, but nobody without a hard-coded Church terminal could intercept or send data on the secondary channels. She wouldn't admit it, but having the admiring attention of such an exotic creature as Dove tickled both her vanity and curiosity.

"So the only non-Church part of the system is the International Space Station," Dove summarized, after watching elegant graphics

illustrate the available data paths with cleverly animated bugs representing hackers as the system detected attempts to break through the
security codes. "Doesn't that leave the hub of the system out of
your—the Church's—control?"

"Ah, you'd think that, my young friend." Socks leaned back in his
chair, tossing a cheese curl into the air to drop into his mouth. Through
the crunchy crumbs, he said, "We've got an agent there." Shooting
Fox a neon-orange grin, he added, "Or maybe I should say angel?"

"The station is out of our control, but we could get around it if
we needed to; without it, we'd just have to boost the power on our
transmitters, and we couldn't wide-broadcast like we do now. The
signal would go through the secondary satellites, straight to receivers
in the temple communities," Fox corrected, ostentatiously ignoring
Socks as she explained to Dove. "James Hideyoshi, the tectonic
specialist on the ISS, is a member of the Church. He jumped through
the bureaucratic hoops and got Captain Nakima to give permission
for us to use the station as a primary relay point. That lets us contact
as wide an audience as Channel 8—all they have to do is turn to the
right frequency."

"Hey, you want to see?" Socks sat up, brushing orange dust into
his tie in an attempt to get it off. It blended quite well with Magma
Man's flaming aura. Fingers already flying, he summoned the direct
link to the International Space Station. The connection signal chimed.
"Hideyoshi's our mole in the Space Agency mountain, sending the
Brethren the straight scoop, no matter what the official line is, making
sure that the Saints know what's going on, no matter what Channel 8,
Homeland Security, or anyone else wants to tell us."

"It's okay," Fox hastened to add, more because the idea of Hideyoshi
doing anything illegal bothered her than because she thought it might
bother Dove, which it didn't; Dove took a broad view of the laws of
men. "Nothing on the ISS is classified—that's the whole point of it
being a civilian, multinational effort. Sure, sometimes the scientists,
and especially Captain Nakima, report their findings to the Space Agency
first, and may not make information public if it's uncertain or unproved,
but they don't just hide what they discover behind some "Top Secret"
stamp. If the military or governments could keep the information
secret, the whole thing would be useless. James—Hideyoshi—is

just—" She stopped abruptly as the subject of her defense appeared on screen.

"Hideyoshi here. What's up, Salt Lake?" The tectonic specialist looked weary, Dove noticed, which didn't surprise him—and he was sporting a shiner, which did.

It surprised Fox too. She leaned closer to the pickup, concern warming her cool expression. "Juliet here. James, what happened?"

"We've got the fourth data set coming in now, and the composition of the swarm's coming clearer," Hideyoshi said, running a hand through his rumpled, waving hair. His voice sounded automatic; he'd switched unconsciously into official-report mode, assuming she wanted an update on the incoming asteroids. Everybody else did. "We're confident that we know the path of the swarm itself, but with every high-resolution reading we take, the gravitational forces get more complex, which makes it harder to predict the exact path of any single meteor—"

"I mean to your eye," Fox broke in gently. "We're not worried about the asteroids."

That brought a wry grin to Hideyoshi's face. "You're the only ones who aren't. We're getting forty calls a day, wanting the latest estimates—and a hundred more just wanting reassurance or tips for surviving an ELE. One woman wanted to know if we could send a meteor to Manchester, because her ex-husband lives there. Captain Nakima and Mr. Wong have had their hands and ears full."

"So they took out their frustration on you?" Juliet persisted.

Dove looked at her, then at Socks, who winked at him. So the cool MIT grad wasn't so cool where a certain space-going scientist was concerned. He grinned.

Hideyoshi sighed, gently touching the bruise. "No, Ivana did. I tried to tell her that the asteroids wouldn't destroy the earth, and when she asked why, I told her the prophet said so. She didn't take it well; she cussed me out and told me she'd pound some reality into my head so she wouldn't have to hear any more of my religious baloney. She's terrified that she's going to die up here, and she's—well, having a hard time, like the rest of us. I don't think she meant to hit me, but it's tough to judge angles and velocities in zero gravity—especially when you don't have any experience with null-grav boxing. So I got a black eye, and she's in a royal sulk in her bunk, because the captain came down hard on her. Can't blame him; we've all been feeling stressed lately . . ." His voice trailed off into an apologetic shrug.

Dove figured he didn't want to complain—or maybe show weakness in front of Fox.

"Anyway, I'd better get back to asteroid observing and data crunching," Hideyoshi said. "Too bad there's no way to get as tight a reading on space rocks as InSAR can on Earth rocks. Maybe we could convince Becker to get out there on one of the bigger ones—" He grinned at the thought of the geologist taking measurements of the geologic stresses on a heavenly body about to smash into the earth.

"He'd love that," Fox laughed. She sobered, her voice warmer as she said, "Take care, James."

Dove missed the tectonic specialist's reply because Socks leaned over and said in a stage whisper, "She's been over her head for him ever since we got the direct connection for Elder Nabil a couple of months ago. All the while she's got me sitting right here! I tell you, there's no accounting for taste."

"Or lack of it," Fox riposted, giving his tie a disdainful look. She turned to Dove. "What did you think?"

"I think you've got a date, if he ever comes back down here," Dove told her, grinning.

She gave him a disgusted look this time. "Oh, not you too. Don't start with me!"

"Because you're already taken, and I wouldn't have a snowball's chance?" Dove asked, then raised his hands, warding off her comeback. "Okay, sorry. Sorry! Seriously, that's cool. So now everybody in the Church knows the asteroids aren't going to hit us, thanks to the prophet's using this system to tell them. Nice. Is this how he's going to manage field communications when the war starts?"

"War?" This time both programmers stared at him.

"Yeah, the war." Dove looked back at them, raising his eyebrows. "You know, when the Saints finally rise up and start kicking some unrighteous butt? Christ's here; it's time for the bad guys to feel a real burn. Like the Book of Mormon says, the unrighteous will never inherit this land, and the people here have definitely fallen off the righteousness wagon. Look at Garlick—and Channel 8, and MedaGen. Time to throw them out—like a young lion among the sheep and the rest."

"Kicking unrighteous butt," Socks repeated, a wild grin spreading over his face. He caught Fox's big-sister look and added, "In a spiritual sense, of course."

"Of course," she nodded, making his joke a serious statement, then turned to Dove. "So if you were in a real holy war, just how would you fight Satan's minions?"

A wide variety of weapons flickered through Dove's head, from rocket launchers to holy water. Bullets and bombs had worked well against Slick, but taking on Garza himself would require a lot more finesse—and heavier armaments, not to mention antidotes and guards against biological weapons. "Very carefully," he finally said, not knowing quite how to answer that one without a lot more thought.

"Well, at least you've got that part right," Fox laughed. "If you want to fight Satan, the best way to do it is to get people to reject him as their master and turn to Christ. They win, God wins, Satan loses. And that's the plan from here on out. They're already getting things going upstairs for the next big push."

"Whoa, I'm impressed," Socks declared. "I didn't think you knew so much."

She sat back, shaking her head at his complete obliviousness. "You'd know more too, if you paid attention to anything outside a computer screen. People have been coming in all day, by special invitation. Louise—the new assistant in Elder Nabil's office—"

"I've paid attention to her, and she's not on a computer screen," Socks said, waggling his eyebrows.

"She's noticed. But you might want to rethink your strategy of sending joke viruses as the way to her heart," Fox informed him. She turned her attention back to Dove. "Anyway, Louise says Connie, the head secretary, got a bunch of notices from Sister Nguyen in Independence to make sure the visitors are expected. And they're all couples too, which usually means a big calling." She glanced at the ceiling, as if she could see through the tons of concrete, steel, and nice carpeting to the Apostle's office. "Louise didn't tell me what's up—Connie didn't tell her—but there are big things going on upstairs."

* * *

Dear Chisom,

I am pleased that in spite of the wild weather, the work is progressing in your area. I'm also pleased to confirm the rumors that you will be receiving additional assistance soon. Presidents Smith and Rojas have prepared us for this momentous day. They are now calling the missionaries who will take the gospel into all the world for the last time. The scriptures refer to these as the 144,000. Before you ask, let me make a point. Don't take the number literally. John used the number in a symbolic sense. It was meant to signify the purity, fullness, and power under which and with which those called will serve. You may wonder how I arrive at this. John is using numbers as a riddle. Anciently, many people did this. The practice was called gematria, and many became quite skilled at it. You can figure out the riddle if you know the qualitative (not the quantitative) value of numbers. Here's how we derive the meaning behind the symbol of 144,000. Three represents the Godhead, 4 represents the earth. Multiplying one by the other, we get 12. That symbolizes the power of the God on the earth, or in other words, the priesthood. Multiplying any number by itself adds the idea of fullness or completeness to its meaning. So 12 times 12, or 144, represents the fullness of the priesthood. Multiplying a number by a thousand adds the idea of perfection. Therefore, 144,000 represents the full and perfected priestly power God is bestowing upon those who are now being called to the ministry.

What all this means is that John was not telling us that God will call exactly 144,000 men, but rather those called (almost always couples) will have a fullness of priesthood authority. Also, you will not see twelve thousand called from each tribe, as John symbolically states. According to Doctrine and Covenants 77, the figure of the tribes represents nations and tongues. Therefore, these special missionaries are being called from all lands and languages. I'm sure, however, that all tribes will be represented (including Dan, whom John left out). Using the Church's satellite system, the First Presidency has instructed the Apostles and Area Authority Seventy in the various parts of the world whom to call. Some of my people have nicknamed them the Gatherers.

Again, using our satellite system, President Marquis, acting in an expanded role for a First Counselor in the First Presidency, has had the responsibility of instructing these missionaries. With nearly instant two-way communication, the program has gone well. He has stressed to them that their job is to bring all who will come into the Church of the Firstborn, thus the title "Gatherers." What is exciting is that, as it says in the Doctrine and Covenants, they are being ordained "by the angels to whom is given power over the nations of the earth." Can you imagine that? But now that Zion has been established, angels are becoming much more directly involved in the ministry. I'll tell you more about that later. For now, the power that these angels are bestowing upon the missionaries is "to save life and to destroy." Thus, they are not unlike Nephi, the son of Helaman, to whom God said, "I will make thee mighty in word and in deed," which included smiting the "earth with famine, and with pestilence, and destruction." That included the power to "seal on earth" and in heaven (Helaman 10:5–7). These missionaries are being entrusted with those same powers. They will be a force never before reckoned with, and I feel sorrow for the man or woman or army who tries to stand in their way.

The ministry of the Gatherers is going to be something, Chisom. They are the precursors of the destroying angels John saw in Revelation 7. Time now presses. The historical atmosphere is charged with portent. From here out, God will more and more openly make bare His holy arm. The direct manifestation of His power will be the final wedge driving people to or away from Him. All who find humility, even if compelled, will discover the Gatherers waiting and eager to help them to salvation temporally and spiritually. Those who will not be humbled will, as John tells us, curse God and die.

Please keep us informed about what is happening in the Far East. We shall do the same for the West. I will be excited to hear more about your new job and how events develop over there.

With love,
Your father,
Chinedu

* * *

"Welcome—thank you for coming. If you'll come with me, I'll take you upstairs." Jonathan Crow smiled at the latest pair of new recruits, as Elder Nabil called them, and led the way to the elevator. He'd made the trip ten times today, accompanying a wide array of people: farmers, lawyers, scientists, fishermen, factory workers, doctors, bus drivers, teachers. What they all had in common—besides a faint air of nervous excitement that came with being summoned to an appointment with an Apostle—was the intangible aura they radiated, a confidence and compassion that came from deep, abiding, and definitely active faith.

This couple, Brother and Sister Valados, Jonathan knew from a previous encounter. "It's good to see you in person, Sister Valados," he said, smiling. The elevator doors whispered closed behind them, and the mirrored mahogany box rose slowly toward Elder Nabil's office.

She smiled back. "Nice to put a face with a name, isn't it?"

"It sure is," Brother Valados agreed. "How is that Meredith Galen, anyway? And that cute little girl."

"Who must be getting big by now," Sister Valados noted. "I know that my own grandchildren are just growing like weeds."

"They're both fine," Jonathan assured them. "Missy is indeed growing like a precocious weed. My wife, Tasha, often babysits her during the day. Sister Galen is working with Section 89, a medical firm here in town."

"Finding a solution to that AllSafe problem," Brother Valados nodded approvingly. "It's about time. The media is trying to keep it quiet, but there's a lot of trouble with that AllSafe vaccine of theirs, and it's only going to get worse from here, as all those poor dupes who took it start getting sick."

"She'll find it," Sister Valados said confidently.

"And here we are." The doors opened, and Jonathan handed the couple over to Connie, who was standing near the doors. She led them to Elder Nabil's office.

Another couple was just leaving, a pair of young, outdoorsy types who smiled as they passed, as if they shared a bond with the older couple. The sparkle in their eyes, an air of thrumming excitement about them, caught Sister Valados's attention; she watched them go, wondering what had happened to them—and what would happen to her and her husband. She didn't have to wait long to find out.

"Welcome, and thank you for coming," Elder Nabil greeted them with his usual warmth in his low, melodiously accented voice. "Please, sit down." He turned to the other two people in the room. "May I introduce Mia and George Valados?"

Surprised, Brother and Sister Valados turned their attention to the strangers.

Amazingly, the strangers overshadowed the charismatic Apostle. At first glance, they seemed like a normal couple, unremarkable, but a certain light in their eyes, a grace in their movements, and the utter attentiveness of their gaze made them different and distinctive. They were subtly larger than life, but instead of sucking all the air out of the room, they seemed to pump oxygen in; being with them didn't squelch or overwhelm, but inspired confidence and optimism as if through sheer radiant energy.

"I would like you to meet John and Mary Stevenson," Elder Nabil said.

They both smiled, and the man stepped forward, extending his hand, first to Sister Valados, then to her husband. "So good to meet you—we have heard so much good of you, from so many people. Your service has truly been well given and gratefully received." His voice, lighter than Elder Nabil's but with a musical tone that made it a pleasure to listen to, also had a lilting accent; but, in contrast to the Apostle's, his pronunciation sounded less foreign than faintly antique.

"Thank you, sir," Brother Valados said, instinctively adding the honorific and nodding politely toward the woman. "Ma'am."

She laughed, the sound like golden bells and sunlight. "Please, we are all servants here, on the errands of our Lord. Just call us John and Mary."

"And we are here to set you apart, if you accept the calling I have the privilege of extending," Elder Nabil told them. "You have been chosen, through revelation and divine favor, to act as the servants of Christ in bringing the gospel to His children in these closing days of the earth's telestial history—if you choose to accept His seal and commission." With that, he opened the scriptures, reading from Revelation 7: "And I heard the number of them which were sealed: and there were sealed an hundred and forty and four thousand of all the tribes of the children of Israel. . . . After this I beheld, and, lo, a great multitude, which no man could number, of all nations, and kindreds, and people, and tongues, stood before the throne, and before the Lamb, clothed with white robes, and palms in their hands; . . . These are they which came out of great tribulation, and have washed their robes, and made them white in the blood of the Lamb. Therefore are they before the throne of God, and serve him day and night in his temple: and he that sitteth on the throne shall dwell among them. They shall hunger no more, neither thirst any more; neither shall the sun light on them, nor any heat. For the Lamb which is in the midst of the throne shall feed them, and shall lead them unto living fountains of waters: and God shall wipe away all the tears from their eyes."

The Apostle looked up from the pages, the words still echoing powerfully, as the Spirit testified of the wonderful promises the Revelator recorded. "Mia, George, we extend a call to you to join the ranks of the one hundred and forty and four thousand servants whom the Lord calls out of every nation, kindred, and tongue to serve Him, His temples, and His children. This calling will not be easy and may involve some physical risk, because it will take you out of the confines of Zion and into the lone and dreary world, seeking His lost sheep. Know, however, that your labors, diligently undertaken with prayer and fasting, will bring you great joy. Inspiration will guide you to desperate but desiring souls. You will be saviors on Mount Zion." He met their eyes, finding the solemnity and opportunity of the call reflected there.

John leaned forward, his eyes brilliant. "George Valados, will you accept this call to serve the Lord, to dedicate your time, talents, possessions, and life to His cause?"

Brother Valados glanced at his wife's face, and confidently met the eyes of the angel. "Yes, I will."

"Mia Valados, will you also accept this call to serve the Lord, to dedicate your time, talents, possessions, and life to His cause?" John asked her.

She smiled. "I certainly will."

With that, Elder Nabil assisted as John set each of them apart, blessing them with the faith and inspiration they would need as they carried God's word into the world, to gather the last harvest before the fields burned with divine fire. The Spirit poured into them, an intense awareness of God's goodness, power—and, most incredibly, personal, individual, fatherly love for each of them as His children. Sister Valados hugged Mary, both laughing through the tears in their eyes.

She was still dabbing at her tears as she and her husband left Elder Nabil's office with their specific assignment and the warm good wishes of their fellow servants. Another young couple waited with Connie, apprehensive and excited. Sister Valados smiled at them and caught the younger woman's hands. "Oh, my dear, how wonderful that you are here!" With a bright smile, she took her husband's hand and joined Jonathan Crow at the elevator, ready to go out and do the Lord's work.

All over the world, the same scene played out, with individual variations, of course, as prophets and apostles selected the husband-wife teams divinely selected and called, to gather up the people who would not "raise a sword against his neighbor." Angels came to every temple community to call and set them apart for the great, final work. In Quezon City, Felipe and Paz Aquino accepted the call to continue gathering the scattered members of the Church of the Lamb wherever they were. In Santiago, the Nerudas joined the ranks of the Lord's last missionary force, traveling the smugglers' paths not only to collect intelligence for the resistance, but to spread the word among the teachable in Chile and Peru, bringing them into Zion and "assisting the work of the Kingdom."

CHAPTER 6

"Is Senator Howard W. Garlick, already the powerful secretary of Homeland Security, trying to build his own kingdom?" asked Darren McInnes, host and star of Channel 8's popular political talk show *Sunday Morning*. Behind him flashed images of the senator presiding over political rallies, terrorist busts, committee hearings, and celebrity fundraisers. "With the backing of powerful lobbyists, corporations, and governmental agencies, some critics say that the secretary wields more power and influence than the White House—and that he uses his power for his own purposes." A clip of Senator Holly Cox appeared, along with a variety of other anti-Garlick protesters.

Monk made sure the clips caught the most fringe elements of the vocal opposition, the political equivalents of the Flat Earth Society; the public loved politician-bashing programs, but Channel 8 was one of the powerful corporations that Garlick took good care to keep contented with government contracts and backing. The screen crawl listed electronic poll results showing Garlick's approval ratings in real time.

"The secretary claims that he has only fulfilled his responsibility as secretary to ensure security for all citizens. Tune in to the *Sunday Morning* special report, when we investigate the allegations and counterclaims," Darren announced, as the logo for the special report glowed from the backdrop.

"Sounds interesting. Thanks, Darren." Clara Cortez smiled at the Oscar-winning host, but the smile disappeared as she continued, "If Garlick is building a kingdom, it's not a peaceful one, despite his best efforts. He announced today that subversive elements, including extremists in this country, are responsible for the shipping disruptions and the violence that followed in many cities this week." The secretary appeared, standing in front of a smoke-blackened storefront as he assured a worried crowd that the "economic terrorists" who inspired "anarchist forces" to smash store windows would be apprehended soon.

"We certainly hope so," Clara said, shifting into a flirtatious smile. "With the mall out of commission and EDS trucks sidelined by weather delays, how will fashionistas get the week's hottest looks? How can we dress like Virginia Diamante when we can't buy her signature line? What do you think, Garrett?"

"Where there's a will, there's a way, Clara," Garrett de Long, Channel 8's entertainment reporter, said brightly. "But word on the street is that Virginia Diamante is just on the verge of being so five-minutes-ago. She's about to be out-hotted by the latest celebrity sensations, fourteen-year-old twins Charity and Chastity."

In his control room, Monk watched the ratings numbers rise. "Nothing like a little steam to add some warmth to a cold economic forecast." Monk made his living selling dreams to people who wanted to forget the much less glamorous reality they lived in. Fortunately for Channel 8 and its tireless advertisers, many of them wanted to believe the lie so much that they ignored the truth as long as they possibly could. AllSafe ads still ran alongside Darren's promotion for the exposé on Garlick.

* * *

"Is this what I'm paying them for?" Howard W. Garlick shouted, glaring at the console screen as he searched for the elusive remote. "Exposés about how I'm using the power that the people handed to me? Questions about how I carry out investigations?"

His secretary, used to the senator's imperial rages and secure in the knowledge that she was indispensable, didn't glance up from her typing. She pointed to the remote, lurking in the deep leather chair where the senator had flung it.

Garlick flicked off the set with a snort of annoyance, shrugging off his secretary's reminder that Channel 8 had sent the report to the senator's office for approval. He gazed into the office mirror, pulling his shoulders back as if posing for a commemorative portrait. He was always at his best in front of a camera or an audience, when the flights of his own rhetoric could sweep away the doubts that made his temper flare in private. Lately, the doubts had multiplied, just when his road to glory should have lain clear and obstacle free in front of him. He'd bribed, blackmailed, and bought his way into the Office of Homeland Security. He should have only had to consolidate his already tight hold on the reins of power.

Power, after all, was the entire point of the exercise. Garlick had most of the money he needed to secure that power. He had several states in his pocket and the financial backing of wealthy "businessmen" like Caesar Augosto (the most powerful Mafia boss the East Coast had seen in decades, who officially worked as an "executive" for a profitable company), General Garza (who had agreed to pay handsomely to "field test" the latest weapons designs from United States defense contractors), and Abbott and Zelik of MedaGen (who owed him for finagling FDA drug approvals).

A billboard glinted in the distance, featuring a tantalizing photo of Virginia Diamante, urging the public to visit the company's customer-service page for the latest information about AllSafe—and the rest of their breakthrough product lines. He could cover the AllSafe problem with government money and buy everybody booster shots. Of course, there were always a few flies in the ointment. His staff was already doing its best to squelch the crowing of skeptics, like those blasted Mormons. He'd put them in their place too; using Channel 8 to paint them as domestic terrorists would inflame already negative public opinion, especially after the fiasco in Lake Creek.

The political rivals posed a more thorny problem. Senator Cox opposed him on the Health and Security Bill, and she'd unsheathed what claws she had to block his next moves. He and MedaGen spent a large amount of time and money to paint her as a member of a fringe cult. Convenient that his primary enemy was a Mormon for other reasons too—her ideals had kept her from allying with his other Senate enemies because she wouldn't offer the usual quid pro quos under the table. However, she might find an issue to bring them together against him, and he would do anything necessary to preserve his power.

He also had to convince the public that he could handle security under pressure. The economy and law were both unraveling. Channel 8 had already made ratings hay with footage from a riot at a discount store, showing desperate patrons literally fighting for the last few bags of sugar to stock their asteroid shelters. If he couldn't get this under control, Garlick's situation would be as desperate as that of the people protesting in the streets.

* * *

"There's people desperate enough to pay that much for a couple bags of the stuff? You gotta be kidding," muttered one of the masked figures slipping between the shadows cast by the shipping yard's brilliant spotlights. His gaze drifted from one dripping train car to another, his eyes rolling more than strictly necessary to express his disdain for what he clearly viewed as a goofball errand, wandering around a train yard in the rain escorting a couple of old-boy civilians.

"Travell's got the buyers lined up, with the gelt ready. So shut up and keep moving," the raiders' leader whispered back, adding a heavy thump on the shoulder to the order.

Any other editorial comments about the potential profits from this particular expedition were lost in the crunch of steel-toed boots on gravel. The noise made shutting up pretty much beside the point as they stepped over the tracks and sidled around yet another nondescript, graffiti-covered boxcar. So did the sudden eruption of yells from the guards waiting inside the lookout post camouflaged as a refrigerated shipping crate attached to the boxcar. They shoved the heavy doors open and charged out at Travell's men, half of them hitting the ground and spreading out in two deadly arcs, the other half shooting from the cover of their metal gunner's nest. The first volley from the cleverly concealed defenders put an early—and permanent—end to the complainer's bad night, and the unspoken opinions of two of his buddies.

What Travell's soldiers lacked in finesse and stealth, however, they made up in firepower and unadulterated nastiness. The leader roared a battle cry and lobbed a couple of thermal grenades into the train car. A blast of flame roared back at him, converting the bogus refrigerator car into a literal oven. The guards inside abruptly lost interest in the proceedings; their more fortunate fellows hit gravel, rolling to get away from the flames. So did the attackers, because the fire didn't care who it crisped. The standoff became a running firefight, a dozen more men running from the nether parts of the yard to join in on either side as the battle rolled past the cargo containers and toward the center of the yard.

The guards, racing ahead of the raiders, formed a defensive ring around the armored container the shipyard's black-marketeer owner used as a private bank. They hit their places in perfect, practiced order, whirling to stare outward, eyes and gun muzzles glinting. To their amazement, however, their pursuers had disappeared; the lightning-harsh railroad landscape around the oversized cash box lay black, white, and empty.

"What the—" growled the guard's chief as the expected attack on the gold reserves utterly failed to materialize.

The phone in his hand squawked, his boss demanding to know what was going on. They shared a long moment of total puzzlement, when the distant rumble of train engines answered the question for them. By the time they readjusted their strategy and their location, they reached the smoldering remains of the faux refrigerator car only to see it—and the cargo containers attached to it—pulling heavily away down a supposedly closed track.

"They're taking the train!" shouted one observant, if not too bright, guard. "Those stupid bounders are taking the train!"

Through the tiny, smoked windows of the accelerating cab, they could just catch a glimpse of a retired engineer at the controls.

"Not stupid," said the security chief, as he realized what the point of the raid had been. "Not stupid—too freaking smart." He looked at the phone, not wanting to tell his boss that the raiders had left the cash—and taken something a lot more valuable.

* * *

A thin stream of white powder sparkled in the lights around the glittering, lava-rock pool as Travell Capshaw, self-appointed emperor of the West Coast drug lords, slowly let it fall from his hand into the open sack. He looked up at the battered, bloodstained raiding party and grinned. "Mama would be proud—her little boy's selling real sugar!"

His henchmen laughed obediently, and also obediently disappeared to supervise the lowest rung of the gang's hangers-on and wannabes as they unloaded the rest of the stolen cargo into a much safer location than a railroad depot.

Capshaw smiled as he tallied the street price of the goods he'd just hijacked. With shortages becoming more common in big cities, people would pay top dollar for liquor, cigarettes, and chocolate—and eventually for flour, sugar, and salt. Water looked like a good bet too, with salinity levels going up and dependable supplies going down. He'd just expand his drug operation and his empire to include other product lines. Making alliances had helped at first; a few hits here and there on behalf of Garlick and deals with Abbott of MedaGen to distribute new drugs on the street had come in handy, but he didn't need them anymore. He had most of California tied up, politicians in his pocket, law enforcement paid off or intimidated, and the potential for profit looked better all the time. The noise of a phone insistently ringing on a private frequency interrupted his glowing dreams.

"What?" he growled.

"You've pushed it too far, Capshaw," Secretary Garlick bellowed. "Cool down the blatant warlordism, or you'll pay for it."

"Senator, I already paid for it," Capshaw reminded him.

Garlick overrode him, ranting about Capshaw's men in a shoot-out in downtown L.A. last week, with Clara Cortez herself frowning about the "lawlessness of our inner cities." And now Garlick was feeling the heat.

The gangster interrupted, "As I said, I paid you plenty for it, and now I'm calling in my investment. Be nice, and I'll send you some sugar."

"Sugar!" Garlick sputtered. Capshaw's ability to cause general mayhem and distress was useful during Garlick's campaign for Homeland Security, but having it continue on Garlick's watch had not been part of the original plan. Now, with people acting crazy under the meteor threat, the AllSafe side effects, domestic and foreign terrorist threats, and Capshaw's blatant raids, everybody expected Homeland Security— him—to do something about it. "I don't need sugar—I need law and order down there or I'll have your head on a plate! You got where you are through my good graces, using my influence to keep the DEA off your back—"

Capshaw's laugh interrupted the senator's rant. "And baby, I be so thanking grateful for that. But the ol' DEA, they pretty much backed off little Travell now. Look like I'm not needing the big senator's big help no more."

"Drop the ghetto act, Capshaw, and drop your delusions while you're at it." Garlick regained his composure. "You have free run because I say you do. And I can rescind the order."

"Just try it, and see what happens," Capshaw taunted. "What you got up your sleeve, Howard? You going to set your pet Caesar Augustus on me, bring in the Mob to punish us? We both know the federal government is falling apart. It's every state for itself. In fact, I made myself a little arrangement with Tip Buchanan—you know, the governor of California? He might join up with that delicious Senator Cox and get your Homeland Security post recalled. Gotta go, Howard. See you at the polls!"

Garlick threw his phone and glowered out the window at the smoky skyline of Washington. If Capshaw didn't come back into line, he would set Augosto loose. That would wipe the grin off the punk's face. A gang war in California would also give the bloodhounds at Channel 8 something else to sniff around. No—better do it legitimately, use the Homeland Security soldiers for something he could flash in Darren McInnes's face, and watch those poll numbers and the power they represented start climbing again.

CHAPTER 7

"Look! It's the asteroid!" A little girl pointed through the window, where a brilliant ball of fire punched through the low-hanging clouds and streaked across the dark sky.

Her mother glanced up, watching as several more flaming space rocks followed, streaking down to disappear behind the uneven skyline of tenements and warehouses. As she looked, a long streak of flame rose from a rickety roof to meet the fire from the sky. She shuddered, then caught her daughter's hand and turned back to her hurried packing. "That's a bunch of meteors, not the asteroid. Ashie, we don't have time for stargazing."

Ashie sighed, hoisting her own small pack with its load of clothes, drinks, and snacks—and necessities, of course. As she tucked a doll into the outside pocket, she muttered, "I wish it was the asteroid, so it would land on Bruce and those guys so they'd stop bugging us. When's Daddy coming back?"

"As soon as he's got the bus tickets." *Please, let him get the bus tickets,* she thought, tightly folding clothes to tuck between bags of trail mix and bottles of water. *Please let the buses still be running.* Since Dale refused to join Bruce's vigilante war against the gang trashing their neighborhood, they'd become the enemy themselves. Trusting the police had turned out to be a mistake, they both realized now; instead of defending them from Spider's original gang, the cops had let Bruce take care of the problem, and now Bruce was the problem. He'd gone from resenting Spider's demands for "protection" money to demanding it himself. Dale wouldn't pay him, any more than he'd paid Spider, and when Bruce's right-hand man, Trent, broke up old

Mr. Schwab's bakery, Dale was the only one in the neighborhood who'd stood up to them. He held off Trent until Mr. Schwab's sons got there (good thing the old man had them on speed dial), but they'd taken their dad with them afterward, leaving the ruined bakery empty. They'd done the right thing, but that meant one less friend in the neighborhood— and this time, there was nobody else to stand with Dale against Bruce.

The door opened, startling both of them. "Natalie?" Dale stood there, pressing his hand against his jaw. When he moved it, both hand and cheek shone red.

She lurched to her feet, her eyes wide as she rushed over to him. "Dale, what happened?"

"Daddy!" Ashie got there first, wrapping her arms around his leg. The blood worried her, but she felt a surge of pride at her daddy fighting the bad guys. She had no doubt at all that he'd won. "Need a Band-Aid?"

"No, baby. Well, I've got good news and bad news," he said with a wry smile, hugging them both. "The bike's toast." That was an understatement; his primary mode of transportation lay in four pieces about a block away. Fortunately, all that bike riding had paid off when he had to sprint the last few yards home. "Bruce just had Trent tenderize me a little, as a warning, a demonstration of what they would do if we don't either come up with the money for the 'condo association fees' or join Bruce's army. According to Trent, if we don't, they'll give me an extreme makeover—and confiscate the apartment."

"Condo association. Extreme makeover. What a crock! Why's Trent always trying to talk like a movie tough guy?" Natalie snorted, dabbing at his cut lip with one of the diapers she'd been packing. Focusing on the idiocy of the situation kept the panic down momentarily. She shoved away the memory of Bruce shouting that he'd make an example of Dale to prove how serious he was about his perverted version of a neighborhood-watch program to anybody who doubted it. "What's the good news?"

"That is the good news. The bad news is that the buses aren't running anymore. Greyhound's finally thrown in the towel." He caught her hand gently as she gasped, her face going white. "I'm sorry, sweetheart. They're right behind me, all liquored up and ready to do something stupid."

On the couch, the baby let out a warning mewl, promising an ear-shattering sequel if nobody picked him up immediately. The sound shook Natalie out of her momentary paralysis. She gathered the baby into her arms automatically, her eyes never leaving Dale's. They couldn't stay, couldn't pay, and wouldn't join Bruce's private army of thugs—and they had nobody to help them. "What are we going to do?"

"We're going to get out—" A crash prevented the rest of Dale's answer—but provided at least a partial one of its own. The window hit the floor in shards around a brick.

A chorus of shouts from the street, most of them lame threats and heavy laughter, came through the jagged gap in the glass. Trent stepped forward; the perspective from the window made his already thick neck look nonexistent. "Oops! Look what we did to Dale's nice window! Come on down, before we have to take the damage out of your hide."

"By going down the fire escape," Dale finished, taking the baby from Natalie and swinging his own and Natalie's backpacks onto his shoulder.

Natalie caught Ashie, who was staring at the mess on the floor with a deeply offended expression, and gently pushed her toward the bathroom and the back window. "Get your backpack, baby. We've got to go."

Behind them, another brick demolished the other front room window. They skinned out the small back window, Dale lifting Ashie onto the rusty metal trapdoor. Shouts came from around the building, dimmer but still heart-stoppingly close. Other windows opened, as the apartment dwellers who had already sworn allegiance to Bruce turned out to join the chase. Most stayed shut, though, as the timid and apathetic pretended they heard nothing. For most of them, it didn't pay to get involved in other people's troubles. Heavy thumps on the locked front door testified that Trent's thugs had confederates in the hallway.

The fire escape ladder rattled down, landing on the next story's balcony with a metallic clang. Dale handed the baby to Natalie and swung down the ladder almost before it stopped moving. Natalie tossed Ashie's backpack down to him, then helped Ashie over the side.

Ashie, looking down at the ladder and feeling her parents' stressed urgency, showed a flash of emergency thinking and called, "Daddy, catch me!" She waited for his "Okay!" before she let go. He caught her and put her down in a corner of the small platform. Raising his hands toward Natalie and the baby, he called in a stage whisper, "Drop him down!"

Whispering a soft prayer of her own, Natalie bent over the rail, stretching as far as she could before she let go of the baby sack. He landed safely in his father's arms. Dale handed him to Ashie, who bravely took the weight. Then he loosed the guards on the next section of the ladder as Natalie came down the first. Again, the clanking rattle sounded, but this time the ladder stopped a good six feet above the surface of the access way between the buildings.

Dale climbed down the ladder and dropped the last few feet, landing in a puddle that he swung Ashie clear of when she jumped. Once again, Natalie dropped the baby and swung around herself— only to flinch as a half-brick clattered off the ladder by her shoulder. She didn't bother to look over—she knew she'd see Trent and the other goons rounding the corner of the alley—and concentrated on hustling down as quickly as she could. Dale caught her around the waist as she ran out of ladder and went into momentary free fall, helping her land outside the puddle. He handed her the baby, snatched up Ashie and the backpacks, and followed Natalie at a dead run toward the far end of the alley. Dale wasn't sure what they'd do once they got to the other street; his informal but decidedly sincere prayer for divine assistance kept the beat of his rapid footsteps—"Help us! Help us!"—Natalie, rushing ahead of her husband, didn't have the mental breath for any more but "Please!"

The splashing and swearing behind them came closer, overtaking the heavily burdened parents. They reached the mouth of the alley and kept running across the parking and playground square between the tenements. Ashie, looking over her daddy's shoulder, saw the bad guys snarling like a pack of wolves, swinging baseball bats and golf clubs threateningly as they reached the alley's end. Their triumphant sneers morphed into stares of sheer puzzlement, however, as a huge shape of metal and glass roared between them and their prey.

Dale looked over his shoulder too, hearing the noise of a heavy engine over Ashie's exclamation of "Daddy! The bus!"

Sure enough, a midsized metro bus, all gleaming steel and glinting windows, had pulled to a hissing, whistling stop between the fleeing family and the thugs. The sign over the front glowed blue and white in the gloom: Zion Express. The bus door opened, and a smiling woman leaned out, motioning to them. "Come on, kids! Can't make the bus wait all day. We got a schedule to keep."

Natalie's reflexes just let her brain yammer away about the total incongruity of a bus appearing in a place where no bus ever ran, right in time to rescue them; she instantly whirled and ran back toward the door. Dale screeched to a halt, the backpacks whipping around to thump into his ribs and Ashie's legs, and executed a sharp turn without sacrificing much speed. His feet hit the stairs at the same time as Trent's baseball bat hit the driver's side of the bus with a clang.

"Can't be having that, now," the driver remonstrated, his deep voice rumbling over the noise of the engine. He leaned out of his window, and something in his eyes and presence stopped one thug midswing. "You got a choice, boys—you can come with us and behave, or you can stay here and do what comes naturally."

They stared at him, then at each other. One or two glanced at the bus, feeling a twinge of warning and promise from the tattered remains of their consciences. Trent's glares brought a quick end to any thoughts of deserting, however. He turned the same glare on the driver and spat a vicious obscenity. Both the glare and the muscle-powered swing of the bat bounced harmlessly off as Trent tried to hit the driver, rebounding so hard that the big man dropped the bat, holding his hands.

"So be it," the driver intoned. The window swished closed, and the bus lumbered forward, picking up speed as it rolled unstoppably away from the open-mouthed bullies.

"Zion?" Natalie gasped, catching her breath and looking at the woman still standing at the closed doors. The baby, joggled into silence with all the running, caught his breath too and began to wail in earnest, telling the other passengers (a strange assortment, old and young, ragged and fashionable, but all returning her stare pleasantly) just how he felt about being so rudely awakened and trotted cross-country.

The woman turned from the window, her sorrowful expression lightening to the bright smile that seemed to belong on her face. "Oh, that's just George's sense of humor. I'm Mia Valados—and that name right there just tells you all you need to know about George's funny ways. He was a bus driver for nearly forty years before he retired, and he says he just couldn't go on a run without a destination on the sign."

George glanced back, his eyes sparkling. "Now, Mia, of course we need a sign—else how would people know where we're going?"

"Well, I didn't say I disagreed, did I?" She laughed and held out her arms. "Now, give me that baby to calm down for a minute, and you give your husband and daughter a big old hug. You're all safe now, honey."

"So we're not going to Zion?" Dale asked, gathering a willing Natalie up in his arms.

Mia looked surprised, then smiled again. "Oh, sure we are! I didn't mean that wasn't true. You asked for help, you believed you'd get it, and you surely did."

"Look! Is that the asteroid?" Ashie asked, pointing out the wide side window as another streak of fire hurtled down from the sky. Behind them, the superheated rock crashed through the corner of a building, smashing into the ground at Trent's feet and throwing him several feet into the air. Several more followed. They weren't *the* asteroid, but they certainly wreaked havoc on Bruce's property values—and his goons.

* * *

"The meteor strikes damaged buildings and roads from the southwestern United States into Brazil," Clara Cortez announced. Beside her, footage of the craters and debris left in the meteorites' wake alternated with dramatic video of the strikes themselves, often caught with amateur, handheld cameras that recorded the strikes complete with the shouts and exclamations of the witnesses.

"Despite official announcements from the Office of Homeland Security and other agencies urging the public to remain calm, the strikes have caused panics in several areas," she continued. The screen transposed clips of Garlick calling for calm with shots of crowds running blindly away from the otherworldly destruction—some pausing to smash store windows for a bit of impromptu looting on the way—while fires sprang up from the impact sites. Sirens wailed in the distance.

"The financial estimates of damages from the meteor strikes are still modest, compared to the federal funds requested for cleanup after the hurricanes and tornadoes that have devastated many parts of the country, but experts are issuing dire predictions for future damages." Graphs appeared next to Clara, comparing the meteorite damage to the storm damage, and then extrapolating the rising curve based on several scenarios. The highlighted line illustrated the maximum damage if the predictions of a massive asteroid strike came true. Of course, it disregarded the fact that if the massive strike occurred as the doom-sayers predicted, the federal government would hardly be in a position to release emergency-management funds.

"In the face of Nature seemingly bent on taking revenge for years of abuse," Clara observed, "the Crusaders for Jesus report record-breaking attendance at public prayer meetings, where the Reverend Tommy Gibbs leads prayers calling for God to turn divine wrath away from true believers." The image of Clara melted into video of praying, swaying, crying people at one of Tommy Gibbs's revivals—and then to others in the white robes of the Children of Light waving flowers and singing around large images of Brother Light. "Evangelical Christians aren't the only ones picking up new believers, however. Tune in tonight, when Anne O'Neal, Channel 8's religion specialist, examines the exponential growth of alternative religions since the announcement of the meteor threat in her special report, 'Newfound Devotion or Deathbed Repentance?'" Clara smiled to reassure Channel 8's viewers that she found either idea equally preposterous.

* * *

"Which do you think it is?" Johann Brindermann asked, his own tone as level and unreadable as ever. "Is the meteorite that hit our supply depot in Panama a divine threat or a mere coincidence?"

General Garza glanced over his shoulder, then back at the monitor in his command headquarters. "Looks like our northern friends are nervous." He motioned his second in command to follow him as he left the tent, then pointed toward the clouds. "Does God threaten us, Johann? Does He threaten *me?*" His hands came down defiantly spread, claiming the ground from heaven. "Does He want to blast us? Let Him try! He will need many more meteors if He expects to cripple our operations."

"Perhaps he has them," Brindermann commented. He'd caught the capital *H* in Garza's speech, and it amused his cold, cynical heart. He'd never had any use for religion of any sort, unless he could use it to help enforce the order he craved, when all the wars and confusion would stop, flattened under the iron hand of the ultimate totalitarian state. And then the General and his brutes would serve no useful purpose . . .

Garza grinned at the German, showing his teeth. He'd caught the small *h*—and the cold disdain in the man's eyes. Brindermann knew nothing of passion, glory, destiny—or loyalty—but he had his uses, and eventually the systems he created would run without him. "Maybe He does. Let Him use them! After the storm, you will press a button, and my supply depots and command centers will rise from the galactic dust. We will be the lords of all the earth, with none to oppose us."

"Speaking of which." Brindermann glanced at the tiny screen in his hand. "You requested a report of the opposition—the earthly opposition. Our agents are progressing in rounding up antirevolutionaries in the occupied territories. Informers report that Major Zamora has gathered only a few malcontents."

Garza moved forward to meet the jeep braking beside the command tent. "And now we shall see how well others' efforts to put down the elusive major are coming."

The jeep's passenger jumped out, returning the salute. "General."

"El Jaguar." Garza rolled the *r*, his smile mocking. "How goes the pacification of our newly conquered province of Chile? Have you rounded up the last of the resistance and kindly but firmly showed them the error of their ways?"

"As kindly as you would, sir—the last of the regular army regiments has sworn their allegiance to you." El Jaguar's return smile faded into a frustrated scowl. "Major Zamora, the black coyote, is the last one causing us any difficulty. I am disappointed to report that he consistently eludes our patrols."

Garza looked speculatively at his favorite, one of his hands playing lightly along the flap of the holstered pistol at his side. "I suggest you alleviate your disappointment—and mine—by finding and killing the major."

The sound of another engine drew his attention to the helicopter pad and the slender figure who slid out of the aircraft. "And if you have to use Serrey as bait, so be it—the man miscalculated badly by killing Zamora's son instead of using him to manipulate his father. Which I suspect is what Serrey is coming to justify right now."

Jorge A. G. Serrey jumped down from the helicopter. The assassin's smooth face looked as calm and careless as ever, his lazy expression almost hiding the sociopathic glitter in his eyes. He dialed his usual arrogance down several notches; he'd come to defend himself as well as relay a communiqué from Aguilera.

"So you think you killed young Michael Zamora," Garza said. He leaned back in his chair, regarding Serrey through wisps of cigar smoke.

"I know I did," Serrey corrected slowly. "Medea, the chief cracker whom Herr Brindermann recommended, confirmed the identification from surveillance footage. The boy in Zamora's house was the right age, the right size, and wore that ridiculous American gang logo."

"DNA match?" Brindermann inquired.

Serrey glanced at him. "No DNA match. Even if there were usable DNA in the mess the thermal charges left, we have no sample from the younger Zamora—and it seems that the elder Zamora's service records and files have mysteriously gone missing."

"How did that happen under the watch of a supposedly expert security specialist?" Brindermann asked. "And how did it happen, despite all orders to the contrary, that Michael Angel wound up dead instead of securely jailed?"

"I suspect that Dr. Yazna Vasquez could best answer the first question. She had full access to all personnel medical files and is known as being—close—to Major Zamora." Serrey tossed off the implication of the doctor's romantic involvement with a sneer. "As for the second, I can only say that your cyber agent Medea had the codes that armed and detonated the trap." He addressed his statement not to Brindermann but to Garza.

Which she sent to you, Brindermann thought, *and you both erased the record of the transaction, she to cover the bribe you paid her, you to cover your tracks when the General called you on the carpet.*

Serrey finished with the last support for his action. "No matter what she did with the records, she eliminated one Zamora, which will only improve our chances of eliminating the other." He shot a smug look at El Jaguar along with the poke at the guerilla's failure to bring in the major. "We destroyed his home and killed his son, proving that we are stronger. A defeat like that will eat into his gut and his pride. He will have to prove his manhood by attacking. And everyone is vulnerable when he attacks."

Garza, however, had a better idea of his enemy's character. "A mistake, Jorge. Lazy thinking. I expect better of a man entrusted with state security.

"You have forgotten the most elementary of strategic principles," the General went on. "If you had not acted so rashly, and sent a squad to apprehend Michael instead of blowing him into burned fragments, Zamora might have put himself in your grasp trying to rescue his son—or volunteering to turn himself in to free the boy."

Garza turned his palm down, preventing Serrey's hot reply, and glanced at El Jaguar. "What say we give you enough rope to hang yourself, Jorge? Both of you try to run Zamora to earth—and I'll let the one who does capture him use the other for target practice."

Dismissed, the two left, casting wary eyes on each other. The General always got excellent results from instigating decidedly unfriendly competitions.

"Enough rope to hang both of them," Brindermann noted. "Serrey is a sociopath and probably psychotic as well."

"Of a surety," Garza agreed easily. "But you must admit that such people are useful."

"As long as you don't let them get behind you." Brindermann cracked a hint of a smile. "But I agree—they perform admirably when given assignments suitable to their . . . talents."

* * *

"So what special talent do you think you've got, boy?" The sergeant's small, vicious eyes bored into Mercury's from about three inches' distance—much closer than necessary to make it quite clear that the man had eaten something with garlic for lunch. "You think you have the guts to survive in General Garza's army?"

Mercury choked down a half dozen smart-aleck answers to that (such as admitting that his own gut had no chance of equaling the sergeant's impressive buildup of table muscle), and said only, "Yes, sir." He said it with feeling, though, and loud enough to penetrate the noncom's triple-thick skull.

"You got the mouth on you—wonder if you know how to use it." With an evil grin, the sergeant thumped an electronic pad containing the rudimentary enlistment forms into Mercury's chest hard enough to make him gasp for breath, though only when the sergeant had passed on to the next victim in line. Raul Flisfisch didn't manage to yell as loudly as Mercury had and earned a larger dose of the sergeant's crude sense of humor.

Behind the two young men, the line of would-be recruits stretched across the makeshift registration office in the former headquarters of Major Zamora's antiterror squad (a particularly nice touch suggested by Serrey), out the door, and three-quarters of the way around the plaza. Hopeful cadets and glum conscripts fidgeted and slouched along, waiting their turn to endure a sergeant's preliminary review. After that, the primary qualification for joining the new Chilean Cooperative Army came down to the ability to read and fill out a digital form with their names, ages, useful skills or training, and next of kin, for "record-keeping" purposes—and for reminding the conscripts that they had more than their own skins on the line. After that, they got their regiment assignments, received the arm band with the General's insignia that substituted for a uniform, and collected a small advance on their first paycheck. Most of them used it to get heartily drunk.

They had plenty to forget. In forty-eight hours after newly appointed President Aguilera gratefully accepted General Garza's "generous offer of assistance against the depredations of El Jaguar's vicious terrorists," the General's forces had rolled into Santiago. An entire division, fresh from putting down the resistance in Peru, poured across Chile's borders in a river of heavy armor, mobile guns, and dusty black and khaki uniforms. In their wake came Brindermann's overseers, bureaucrats armed with clipboards, curfew restrictions, census surveys, matériel requisition lists—and the ruthlessness to have their security forces shoot anyone who stepped out of line. Previously enlisted forces helped themselves to anything that the bureaucrats hadn't nailed down. Citizens who resisted the "assisting" forces' military requisition of their property learned the error of their ways; those who survived put up no more resistance to resupplying the troops. Rosa del Torres's breathless report on the miraculous arrival of the saviors of Chile somehow missed capturing the bloodied but defiant face of Señora Ulloa, glaring from her battered garden—or the others like her, too old or harmless to kill, but not to beat down.

The citizens who weren't too old or harmless had a stark choice: support Garza's troops or join them, and the surest way to escape their depredations was to join them. The Mormons, following Elder Molina's directives, presented themselves for technical and administrative duty. Others signed on in hopes of joining the conquerors and sharing the spoils, or because the alternative for themselves and their families was too horrible to contemplate. And a few, also on the word of the Apostle, signed names other than their own on the enrollment forms to infiltrate the enemy's camp and destroy it from within.

Mercury, Raul, and a handful of other young men followed the drift of newly commissioned cannon fodder into a smoky, crowded cantina. Taking an unoccupied table in the middle of the human whirlpool, they nursed mugs of warm cider and tossed a few chipped dice across the battered surface to cover a strategizing session. Mercury led the discussion by virtue of his father's military commission, his personal combat experience during his stint with the Santos, and the heat from the guilt he'd been marinating in since Giovanni's death. As much as Major Zamora worried about sending his son into the lion's den (more like jackals, Mercury had pointed out), he couldn't argue with their need to establish a communications base—and Mercury was one of their best candidates. From his stint with the Santos, he'd learned how to break into Garza's communication system from the outside, and though he'd ditched school to play in the computer lab, it had proved more an asset than a disadvantage. That morning, Major Zamora had hugged his son tight, and ordered, not told, him to come back alive and successful. Mercury had promised, through tears he wouldn't let fall, that he would make his father proud this time.

Now, he glanced around as his coconspirators, all reasonably acquainted with computer systems, and all ready to act as Brindermann's eyes and ears in snooping out any untoward activity among the Mormon system administrators. "Aim for the weak spots in the system, the databases and communications. Get in as deep as possible—but remember that we're strictly juniors. Nobody tells the grunts anything."

"Some of the grunts have guns," Raul pointed out tightly. His family had run as soon as they got Elder Molina's message; they now huddled inside the safety of the temple's walls. He and several other abruptly released missionaries had elected to go back into the city, melting into the swirling chaos of the desperate and dispossessed. They didn't have the keys and power of the specially chosen, like Señor and Señora Neruda, but they could subtly spread the word among those willing to leave the world for Zion at this late date. President Reyes, despite his private misgivings, followed Elder Molina's advice, blessing each one of the antiguerillas before sending them out to do what they could to fight the darkness spreading across the land. "And we'll need all the guns we can get if we're going to fight them."

"Oh, we'll fight them," Mercury assured him, his eyes blazing as he threw the dice hard enough to crack an empty cider bottle. Raul ducked, catching the ricocheting cube. "We'll fight them like the disease they spread—from the inside out, snipping their nerves before they realize they're infected."

Raul and the two other former missionaries, though older, ended up deferring to him because he had an unnerving dose of the same easy command his father showed—and they didn't have any better ideas.

Thus, the group of them reported to the communications HQ the next morning, directed to the designated examination room by a sharp-faced bureaucrat after he read the technical and computer experience from their applications. After a surprisingly precise technical and aptitude test (Brindermann excelled at leveraging available resources), they were brought before Brindermann to receive their assignments.

"It appears that you have had training in networking communications," the tall man behind the desk told them, his voice cool and German accented. "Are you familiar with System XX.1?"

"Yes, sir," Raul said immediately; he still had a lingering habit of missionary spit and polish. The others nodded, more or less directly, one accentuating his nerdiness by shifting unrhythmically from foot to foot. They met the executive officer's approval; his eyes swept past them and landed with a virtually audible click on Mercury.

Mercury knew that he looked younger than the other guys and that his self-inflicted haircut—to alter his appearance from the long-haired kid who'd come back from Amexica—and his adopted glasses made him look not so much like the Ugly Duckling as the Geeky Chicken. He decided to play it young, brash, and determined, so he gazed back at the man, not quite steady enough to come across as insolent, shifty enough to look basically honest, cocky as a green bull rider. "I've played with it, sir. Mainly, my training's been in MUDs— old-fashioned multiplayer games, some of the new VR, a bit of satellite linking. Not much formal training. But that's all bunk anyway—you want real stuff, you get a cracker like me."

The man considered him, sizing him up, taking in the haystack hair, the thick lenses, the slumped, gig jockey posture. "You've been to the United States?"

"No, sir. But I've played Yanks online, and regular military guys too, in the flight sims," Mercury told him, an impish grin breaking through his nervous expression. "Smoked 'em all, too."

Standing slowly and moving around the desk, the bureaucrat loomed over Mercury, leaning close enough that the boy could see the silver flecks in his gray eyes. "You are too young to join the army; you lied on your recruiting form, but you have skills we need in this back-water to maintain military communications—and if you fail, you will be shot. You wanted to join the army, and now the appropriate penal-ties will apply if you fail to perform as you have promised. Do you understand?"

Raul, who had blanched nearly white when Brindermann accused Mercury of lying, convinced that they were all blown, gradually started to breathe again.

"I understand," Mercury said, dropping his eyes not out of fear, but to keep Garza's lieutenant from seeing the hate in them.

It didn't work—but Brindermann didn't care. Able techs were in short supply; most of them were Mormons whose church paid to educate and train them, and they had proven difficult to recruit until their Apostle capitulated. He still distrusted them. This boy, with his air of virtual street urchin, could prove to be as able a cracker as he claimed he was—and as an assistant network engineer would be a valuable spy, a check on whatever treachery the Mormon adminis-trators might plan. The German didn't have time to waste here, with Dr. Twilley's experiment to supervise in Colombia, Chile to organize, and the prison camps in Peru to purge.

"Very well." Brindermann stepped back, looking at all of them. "You will be expected to assist the administration team—and to watch them carefully for any signs of sabotage. For every report you file, you will receive a bonus, depending on the value of the information." He made a notation on Mercury's recruitment file, "Watch closely, and kill if necessary," and sent the newly commissioned junior techs on their way.

Four hours later, Mercury sat at a blinking console, establishing a satellite connection from Santiago to Bogotá. The supervisor, a junior officer with more attitude than technical skill, exchanged a few words with his opposite number, to test the connection, then ordered their lowliest tech to debug the system. Mercury grumbled, as expected—debugging, after all, was grunt work, beneath a truly experienced cracker. He growled as the officer smacked the back of his head but obediently knelt to remove a maintenance panel when the man laid a hand on the butt of his gun. The supervisor impugned his courage and ancestry, then strode off, laughing. One of the real administrators, a former Young Men's advisor, caught Mercury's eye and grinned behind the officer's back.

Mercury returned the smile and laughed too, but silently, as he checked his console to monitor the repairs he'd made. Across the bottom of the screen ran a series of dots and dashes, a testing pattern many members of the online gaming community used. In this case, they sparkled out over General Garza's communications network, fed into a public-use satellite he'd co-opted—and printed themselves across a receiver deep inside a basement engineering room in Salt Lake City.

"He got in!" Socks came right out of his chair, dancing in excitement. "Elder Molina got somebody in!"

Elder Nabil had raced to the techs' lair the moment Fox had called him with news of an encoded signal. It looked as if Elder Molina's agents had successfully infiltrated General Garza's network. "Who are we talking to?" he asked. "Can we trust him?"

"Or her," Fox pointed out.

Socks shrugged it off. "I don't know his real name—he goes by Mercury. I've met him online before." He avoided Fox's remonstrative look; he knew she didn't approve of his spending time on cracker message boards, but he figured it went along with knowing the enemy—

and it was entertaining too. Still, a little guilt may have prompted him to add, "He's one of ours—one of Dove's, one of those crazy Santos Soldados. I think we can trust him, sir."

Elder Nabil read over the transcript of the brief, cryptic message again: "Molinas safe. Saints gathered at Zion. Others coming. Awaiting further revelation and word. Christ lives!" A smile spread over his face. "So, now we have an agent on the inside, thanks to divine inspiration and help. Yes, He does live." His voice rose triumphantly. "He lives, and He rules!"

Fox shoved Socks's chair over when her cave mate snorted, "He rules!" and laughed at the pun that the current situation made out of the archaic slang phrase.

"He certainly rules in Zion," Fox said quietly, giving Socks a hand up off the floor. The soft chime of another incoming message, this one from the Apostle presiding over the temple communities in Malaysia, caught her attention. She dropped Socks to open the missive.

The pictures that spilled over the console's viewer completely overshadowed the text, "Thirty gathered to Zion this day, but more lost in Jakarta." The transmission showed pillars of fire and smoke rising from the melting shells of downtown office buildings belonging to companies that had drawn Brother Light's wrath. Explosives, carried under the robes of starry-eyed, willing martyrs on every level of the skyscrapers, had almost completely destroyed the buildings and their unfortunate (and willfully ignorant in disregarding the Apostle's warning) occupants. At the bottom of the photos, tiny white and black dots resolved into the Children of Light and Hands of the Prophet dispatching anyone who escaped the fires.

"It's other places that I'm worried about," Fox finished her thought.

Elder Nabil nodded, his handsome face solemn. "The Gatherers are at work. Now, we must pray that those of good heart listen and come away with them."

CHAPTER 8

"Where have all the Mormons gone?" Anne O'Neal asked. A light breeze stirred her hair; Leon knew exactly how to frame a shot to capitalize on the girl-next-door attractiveness that helped make Anne a popular reporter and ensure his lucrative position as her cameraman/partner. "For a worldwide church so high profile that it has drawn fire from corporate interests," MedaGen's logo flashed across the screen, "to government regulators," Garlick's Old Testament scowl appeared, "to fellow religionists," the crowd at one of Tommy Gibbs's Crusaders for Jesus revivals roared and morphed into a parade of the Children of Light, "its millions of actual members are surprisingly difficult to find." Now, footage from the burned-out neighborhood of Lake Creek, Illinois, appeared, the broken windows of empty houses bearing silent testimony of their owners' absence.

"While some superstitious sorts might blame the much-touted Rapture for the Mormons' sudden disappearance," the reporter smiled slightly as she suggested that, well aware of the instant denial such an idea would elicit from Tommy Gibbs's fervent followers (Monk, behind his lights and numbers, rolled his eyes at the provocation but didn't call her on it; a little controversy never hurt ratings), "the actual explanation seems much more ordinary." She stepped aside, and Leon panned the camera over the scene behind her.

In the distance, a cluster of simple but elegant buildings stood in the midst of a neat pattern of gridline streets lined with homes that gave way to semipermanent shelters that in turn gave way to family-sized tents. Then, after a space of clear, mown field grass that looked almost like a green moat, or a thin strip of demilitarized zone, the tents and campers started again, more haphazard and dilapidated this time.

"The Mormons, acting on a message from their earthly prophet, have gathered into communities all over the world, often leaving most of their property behind." Anne gestured, indicating the white-glowing building in the center of the bustling, makeshift city. "Here in Nebraska, and in most other areas, these new settlements have grown up around the church's temples. But the question that lingers is why? Why has this church, once famous for its dedication to spreading itself and its missionaries all over the globe, pulled its members into tightly guarded communities? There seem to be many opinions on that question."

The calm, luminous face of President Smith appeared, addressing the members of the Church from its headquarters in Independence. "I have called you to relay a revelation. The time has come to gather to Zion. Come home, let Him gather you under His wings. Prepare for the great and wonderful day of the Lord."

The editing that stitched together his sentences was so smooth that only a practiced eye could have detected it. To Anne's credit, the quotes did convey the substance of the prophet's call to the Saints. She did not use the full clip of the speech that had gone out on the Church's private, secure satellite network; in fact, she'd fought long and hard to use as much as she did. The argument that everybody was interested in divine revelation, whether or not they believed it, finally won Monk over. Besides, Anne pointed out, if they wanted to address the question of why the Mormons had packed up and left, they couldn't do better than getting it from the horse's mouth, so to speak. Still, the producer insisted that the program include counterpoints for "balance"—and to dramatize the report.

"Them Mormons are trying to take over, since the government's not doing a thing to stop them," a heavily bearded, ball-capped man growled. "That temple they put up was bad enough—now we got 'em all over the place, sticking on their own farm, not giving a rat's butt about the rest of us out here."

"It's so they can do, like human sacrifices and stuff, and nobody would know," a teenage girl suggested, twisting a piece of hair around her finger as her friends giggled and played to the camera.

"We see this kind of extreme millennialism in periods of global stress," intoned a tweedy professor. "In the face of the possibility of asteroids destroying the world, their leaders are exercising their power over their gullible followers, declaring the end of the world as a way of exerting control over the uncontrollable." She shook her head. "We will probably see a mass suicide next, just as we did in Waco, Guyana, and St. Petersburg."

"Whether we accept the Mormons' belief in revelation or a more dire explanation," Anne said, reappearing on-screen, "it seems that plenty of other people are lining up to drink the church's Kool-Aid."

Archival tapes showed desperate people flocking to Church communities all over the world: ragged and hungry refugees stumbling out of the African jungles, well-dressed urbanites fleeing European cities, frightened noncombatants fleeing Chinese civil wars, unemployed (if not homeless) Americans looking for a safe place to bring their families. Some waved at the camera, but most pushed on without acknowledging the news crew, oblivious to anything but their need to come as close to Zion as possible.

"Most of the new arrivals end up in the camps outside the Mormon communities, setting up tents, or just laying out bedrolls under the cloudy sky," Anne noted. "Most of them have only basic shelter, in the wild weather, but they all believe they are safer here than they would be anywhere else."

The haphazardly organized lanes of the refugee communities replaced the lines of new arrivals, singles, groups, and families settled on the patches they'd staked out as their new but frighteningly temporary homes. Again, some smiled, but others gazed blankly ahead, or filled the long hours playing cards, listening to crackling radio broadcasts, or talking to other Gentiles, as some of the refugees called themselves. The campsites looked reasonably clean but indefinably shabby; a few scraps of litter dotted the ground, and elderly vehicles playing the role of shelters gave the settlement the vague air of a junkyard or run-down trailer park. The camera zoomed in on one of the wheeled metal huts and the small family leaning out of the open doors.

"Cameron, his girlfriend Joyce, and their son Trace left Milwaukee a month ago, and after a couple of weeks of aimless driving, wound up here, just outside the Mormon community of Hillview, Nebraska," Anne's voice narrated over the scene.

"Yeah, it's pretty thin," the young, long-haired man admitted, hitching his baby son further up on his shoulder. "But it's better than getting burned up in a terrorist bombing, right? Or having the militia come shooting us 'cause we don't have a flag on our car. Between one side and the other, we just had to get out."

"Why didn't you move into town?" Anne asked from off-camera.

Cameron looked away, sniffing slightly. "Well, you know, it just didn't fit—we're kind of free spirits, and they're kind of tight over there . . ." His voice trailed off; Joyce, sitting on the front seat of the car with her feet dangling, looked away from the camera too, smoking one of her carefully hoarded cigarettes, her fingers tracing the rose-vine tattoo on her arm.

"They wouldn't let you in?" Anne persisted gently.

A frown crossed Cameron's face. "They're pretty tight," he said again.

"No." Joyce looked up. "It's not them. We just didn't feel—comfortable in there. They'd let us come if we wanted to. Sister Adele keeps coming out to visit us, but it just doesn't feel real good." She stopped, shook her head, and took a breath. "No, it's that I don't feel real good. And I gotta be good to get in there." Her son squeaked happily, drawing her gaze. Her shoulders straightened; she looked at him and smiled wistfully. "And maybe I will, you know? Maybe I can." This time her gaze went to Cameron. "Maybe we can."

He looked away. The camera followed his eyes, panning over the disorganized sprawl of the refugee camp out to where the neat grid of Hillview began. The archive footage morphed into the current report, moving to show Anne against the panorama of green hills. "And that's the theme we hear from everyone we talk to in Gentile Town. The Mormons are good neighbors, visiting the refugee camps with encouraging words and emergency supplies. But they don't supply any more than the bare necessities—which has many people upset."

"They have enough food to feed half the county for weeks—and they won't give anything but a bag of crackers and a bottle of shampoo!" exclaimed an angry woman, identified in the crawl as a regional officer of the United Way. "We've asked and asked for help, and all we get is excuses. We've got people here who are in real trouble, people whose homes disappeared in the tornadoes, and they have nowhere to turn!"

"The government of Illinois has informally called on the Mormon Church to open its granaries and storehouses and deliver their contents for the public good," Governor Kerr announced. The crawl at the bottom of the screen invited viewers to register their opinions of the governor, the Mormons, and the odds on the next Mavericks-Wizards game. He stared grimly out at the frustrated, shouting crowd ringing the reporters attending the press conference. "So far, they have refused. We are now considering making that request formal and backing it up with police action, if necessary, to enforce the Homeland Security anti-hoarding laws."

"The same request—and much stronger demands—has come from individuals, organizations, and governments not just in the United States but all over the world," Anne summarized. "And in every case, the response is exactly the same. Mormon Area Authorities, and the church's Apostles assigned to broad areas of the world, regretfully but firmly decline. But what can they say to justify that refusal in the face of the economic, social, criminal, and weather chaos that has thrown so many people into serious straits?"

The sober but compassionate face of President Richard Rojas appeared, the soberly elegant furniture of his Independence office in the background. The Associate President looked compassionate but firm as he said, "The Bridegroom had arrived, and those without oil could not buy any from those who had wisely conserved it against His coming." He shook his head, holding up a hand to forestall Anne's question. "Please, Anne, you need to understand, it's not that we don't care. We do! Everyone who is willing to become part of Zion, to take His yoke upon them, to forsake the world, has a place in the community. Unfortunately, while some people eagerly accept, giving up the world for Christ's kingdom, the more hardened refuse to accept what they cannot take for themselves; some do all they can to prevent others from joining the Saints. They would rather starve—and force others to starve—than take on His yoke. We wish everyone would. We pray for all our brothers and sisters to come to Christ, but we cannot help them if they will not be helped."

"The Church's stance has not made them popular," Anne observed, back in the Nebraska field. "In fact, it has earned them vitriolic condemnation, withdrawal of official recognition, threats of governmental oversight, and incipient lawsuits."

"The Mormons are deliberately hoarding food, clothing, and medical supplies in the face of horrifying deprivation!" shouted a furious priest, his white collar bobbing as he flailed his arms.

"Any organization that contributes to the further destabilization of this society must be brought under control, strictly regulated, in the defense of the rule of law," Garlick pronounced over the lectern, the seal of the Office of Homeland Security glinting behind him. "And if the Mormons present that kind of threat—when they present that kind of threat—yes, they should come under the strict administration the Office of Homeland Security can provide."

"They can't keep us out of an American community in an American state!" a protester shouted, as his fellow activists waved their signs outside a courthouse. "We'll sue!"

"Of course, others have a different story to tell," Anne noted, keeping up her reputation for journalistic integrity. "One is Reverend Teresa Burns, once the pastor of Unity Lutheran Church in Lake Creek, Illinois. She and some of her congregation moved into Nauvoo a few weeks ago."

Reverend Burns appeared on the screen. "Anyone can come in, if you truly love the Lord," she assured the viewers, "not just Mormons, so the proposed lawsuits are ridiculous."

"It will be interesting to see whether the threatened lawsuits are more effective than the rash of outright attacks in changing the Church's mind—or dissuading outsiders from joining the communities or the refugee camps growing up around them." The camera returned to Anne. "The violent attacks have been completely ineffective, for a variety of strange reasons, from sudden attacks of conscience among knife-wielding mobsters to malfunctioning guns and bombs. Zion, through what the Mormons describe as miraculous means, is safe."

"It was like the storm hit a wall," said a wide-eyed teenage boy, his hands showing the effects of Zion's protective field on a massive tornado.

"These two meth heads came running up, yelling and shooting, like total psychos," a woman whispered, shuddering at the memory. "A couple of the Mormons came out, and the guys just kind of dropped, fell over like somebody cut their strings. One of them started crying."

"It doesn't look safe," an elderly man admitted, patting the rusty roof of a battered pickup. "But 'round here, it's all I need. Stay downwind of the Mormons, and nothing can get to me, floods or wind or nothing."

"And apparently staying inside the borders of Zion is safer still—whatever the actual explanation for these seemingly miraculous events." Anne walked slowly down the country road, motioning toward the distant town, as lights bloomed along its streets in the gathering dusk. "So Mormons are gathering into these communities from all over the world. Best estimates, some provided by the Church itself, say that about half of the worldwide membership is still outside the actual temple communities. Wherever possible, though, they are gathering in their own neighborhoods—especially in war-torn areas such as China and South America."

Anne didn't include the anecdotal reports she'd gathered that suggested that the individual neighborhoods were also under divine protection. She wasn't sure how she felt about the idea; sure, the nuns at the parochial school told her that praying to the right one of the vast pantheon of saints would provide heavenly assistance to good girls, but they also wore linen wimples and heavy wool habits in the middle of summer, which always made her suspect that their brains were overheated. She couldn't quite apply the same flippant attitude to President Rojas; the charismatic, intelligent religious leader impressed her as a completely rational person. A completely rational person who believed in a personal, active, and apparently talkative God. President Rojas had told her to be careful when she went to interview Rashi Janjalani—and, as his warning indicated, she had nearly run into trouble with Brother Light's infamous Hands of the Prophet.

"All the Mormons haven't disappeared into their safe houses, however." Anne threw off the disconcerting memory, continuing her report. "In fact, there are still Mormons out there, including high-profile individuals active in many areas, including politics. The most visible is Senator Holly Cox, who still carries out her quixotic crusade to rein in Howard Garlick's rampaging power grab for Homeland Security."

Senator Cox appeared, addressing the Senate Judiciary Committee, grilling representatives from the FDA about AllSafe's apparently overlooked side effects. "Of course, many of the senator's enemies wish she had retreated to the Mormons' sanctuaries with the rest of them. She made the establishment's hit list shortly after her election, a conservative disappointment to politicians and special-interest groups who threw their support behind her, expecting her to break the Mormon mold, defying the patriarchy to run for high political office. Instead, she has emerged as a staunch advocate for fiscal conservatism, media restraint, and religious freedom." Clips of anti-Cox ads flashed under Anne's brief summary, funded through Garlick's campaign war chest, several political action committees whose causes (legalized abortion, pornography, and drug use) she opposed, and corporate interests who found her opposition of corporate political power annoying and potentially dangerous.

"Politics isn't the only area where Mormons can still be found," Anne noted. "All over the world, they're spreading a message of reassurance and divine assistance despite seemingly overwhelming evidence. Even stranger, their message seems to have sparked rumors of miraculous escapes, angel sightings, and other odd occurrences all over the world, from phantom buses appearing in the American Midwest to scoop up potential victims of gang violence to a bulletproof man guiding refugees to safety in the Ivory Coast. It's the stuff of urban legends—or the Mormons have discovered a hitherto unheard-of weapon in the missionary arsenal. Whatever the case, the Church and its representatives, especially the newly minted special missionaries, are carrying on that missionary work despite political, social, religious, and natural obstacles. In the words of President Rojas, they issue an open invitation: 'Come to Zion, and share in all we have.' In the second part of this special report, we'll investigate just exactly what they mean by coming to Zion and ask experts about the kind of social and psychological pressures that keep so many Gentiles on the outskirts of the Mormons' millennial society. In the meantime, though, the Mormons carry on their quiet crusade through all opposition, blithely disregarding reports of potential asteroid disaster while asserting that the real end of the world—and the Second Coming of Jesus Christ—is imminent." She gestured toward the soft lights of Hillview glowing in the distance. "However the world ends, it's clear that the Mormons will be ready for it. The question is, will the rest of us? This is Anne O'Neal, with a Channel 8 special report."

* * *

Dear Chisom,

I'm pleased that the PR materials I sent you have promise for your area. I have felt the power of the Spirit working upon my committee. Through its power, we have seen ways to effectively get our message out in spite of sophisticated and widespread opposition. For reasons I do not fully understand, Channel 8 runs hard-hitting anti-Mormon ads. The irony is that their religion reporter, Anne O'Neal, seems balanced, perhaps favorable to the Church. She and I are meeting tomorrow in the satellite community to the east. She is interested in some of the material we have produced and wants to know how we go about doing it. It should prove a pleasant meeting and interesting to try to explain to a nonmember the workings of the Holy Spirit.

Which reminds me, a news sequence I saw proves once again that in spite of all the terrible things that are going on, most people are not repenting. I am almost stunned by this. With all that is happening, people continue to live as though nothing is out of the ordinary. Their stupidity and hardness is almost beyond me. Fortunately, I have the scriptures that help me understand what is going on. John saw that in the last days, in spite of the plagues, many "repented not of the works of their hands, that they should not worship devils, and idols of gold, and silver, and brass, and stone, and of wood" and repented not "of their murders, nor of their sorceries, nor of their fornication, nor of their thefts" (Revelation 9:20–21). And why? Because Babylon simply has too great a hold on them. They feel that the present conditions are just for the moment and with enough wealth, nothing can hurt them. All they have to do is ride out the storm and all will be well. How horribly and blindly foolish!

Our people confirm your experience. Brother Light's emissaries continue to have success in southern China. The truth of the matter is, he is also being successful in western South China, Taiwan, and India. His church is becoming massive and a force to be feared. Unfortunately, governments and institutions honor and empower him. They will rue the day. In the meantime, I'm sorry his people are making trouble for the Saints in your area. Fear not; the Lord is with His people. Reports from the Philippines tell us that nearly all of the Saints are now outside of his grasp. So far the Church in the West has not come up against him. He has not personally or actively proselytized here in the U.S. Even so, he already has an impressive following. I wonder what will happen if he ever graces the West with his presence.

For the moment, we are less concerned about him than with General Garza, who has a death grip on Central and South America. He is not the avowed enemy of the Saints that Light is, but he would turn on us in an instant if he felt threatened. Fortunately, most of the Saints in his area have been able to gather to the Zion communities. Also, the Lord is not leaving the south to his control. A large number of Gatherers are being called and empowered from that area.

What does concern us about Garza is that his hungry eyes look north, and I fear there is much trouble for the U.S. ahead. I'm not sure how this is going to play out, but at least the Saints are secure.

I am sorry I do not have time to tell you more, but work presses. I have much to do helping the Church put its best foot forward. Don't hesitate to share your successes with us. My team as well as the Brethren will enjoy hearing about it. In the meantime, I think we are ready for anything.

With love,
Your father,
Chinedu

* * *

"Now, Johann, we are ready for anything and anyone." General Garza surveyed the scene with deep satisfaction as a small army of workers, under the sharp eyes of his elite forces, unloaded an impressive shipment of vehicles, crates, and machinery from a fleet of heavy transports. The delivery represented the last of the initial shipment of weapons, sensors, drones, smart bombs, and vehicles arriving from Secretary Garlick. The man had exchanged pieces of his country's most bleeding-edge technology in return for a senator's ransom, believing he could give automated weapons to the General while secretly keeping the backdoor codes that would let him remotely disable them if Garza proved a threat. Naive. "As soon as your electron lovers have finished with them."

Brindermann nodded, motioning his chief technician forward toward the warehouse where the most important of these revolutionary weapons would rest until Garza decided to deploy them.

The woman, her red hair ablaze in the relentless sun, nodded in return, motioning for her motley-looking crew to follow her, eyeing their prey hungrily, unlimbering their connection cables and packet clamps. Medea and her Ten Tribes coterie of crackers and Net rangers had come to the Bogotá headquarters in person for the truly staggering fee the German offered for her services (the veiled threat didn't hurt either). The thought of what Brindermann wanted them to do made her smile in anticipation as she surveyed the challenge.

Long, silvery shapes settled into mesh cradles, their metallic sheen dulled to radar-repelling matte finish. The Americans called their metallic ancestors UCAVs, "unmanned combat air vehicles." These made the originals look as clumsy and half-formed as dusty Neanderthal skulls. The new weapons, dubbed Velociraptors (a pun on "velocity" and "raptor," or bird of prey, wrapped in metallic carnivore hide) took computer-aided combat to new, lethal levels. The artificially intelligent planes could handle flight in adverse weather conditions, over land or sea, accomplishing carrier landings and dogfights at higher speeds and with sharper maneuvers than humans could tolerate. Of course, the Americans, ever cautious, had built in safety precautions as well: the planes still required a human using the secure communication channel to order them to drop their bombs or fire their weapons. That limitation and the invisible leash that still tied the Velociraptors to their American creators were what Garza expected Brindermann's team of byte jockeys to overcome.

"Can they do it?" Garza asked, raising an eyebrow as he looked over the eccentric, weedy-looking Net rangers.

"They can do it," Brindermann said flatly. "They are the premier crackers in the world at the moment—and they have connections to Garlick's organization. They'll reprogram the fail-safes and disable the Americans' override codes. And then our people will double-check their work, to ensure that they've added no fail-safes or override codes of their own."

"Trust no one." Garza turned away, Brindermann falling into step beside him. "And if they somehow fail, I have no doubt that you will find someone else who won't—the Pentagon has as many greedy men in its employ as does the Senate."

In the cool confines of his headquarters, Garza touched the glowing screen that showed the map of the next phase of his campaign of world conquest. It sprang to life, the topographical rendering of the Western Hemisphere rippling into focus. Battle lines, tactical trajectories, agents, depots, and supply trails slashed across it, revealing the broad battle plan. "We will not fail. The Americans' AI weapons and biological agents, and the nuclear weapons from our Eastern European friends, will decimate the population centers, high-tech defenses, and morale of the United States. Our armies will sweep over the borders left undefended by the northerners' adventures in Ohalajishi and Kharagizstan."

"And all that lies in your way is the chaotic swamp of Mexico," Brindermann reminded him.

Garza tapped the hot-green skulls that marked targets for biological annihilation. "The bandits and American border gangs will be dead long before our forces arrive." A frown crossed his face. That phase of the operation was not going as smoothly as expected.

"Time to pay Dr. Twilley a visit?" Brindermann asked.

"Indeed," Garza said. "The doctor's progress on his Pacifica vaccine has not lived up to his superiors' promises."

* * *

At the moment, an equally grim expression creased Dr. Twilley's forehead. He glared through the glass into the triple-shielded experiment cell, watching a moaning man on a steel-and-plastic cot. The low groans stopped only when a spasm of coughing ripped through his chest and ended with a line of blood running down his chin to stain the thin hospital gown he wore. Twilley glanced at the man's inoculation record and turned his glare on the white-coated assistant beside him. "Did your team make a mistake in the dosage?" he demanded.

"No, sir," the man said.

"Then you used the wrong antivirus," Twilley stated. He thrust the digital clipboard back at the man. "Recruit another group of volunteers and run it again—but this time, make sure you use the human variant, not the simian one!"

Twilley strode off, his heels clicking on the hard floor like the thoughts that clicked through his mind. Coming up with the disease virus itself had been almost laughably easy—working with Gregor Christoff on the Corinth team that produced AllSafe gave him plenty of practice in splicing together vicious pathogens. Mr. Abbott had given him the assignment to create the ultimate biological weapon for a share of the phenomenal payment General Garza offered. The challenge and glory of being the first man in history who perfected a biological analog of matter and antimatter, however, motivated the scientist far more than money.

He paused by another observation window, watching a white-coated woman offering slices of banana to a bright-eyed howler monkey. The monkey, inoculated with the simian variant of the vaccine, showed absolutely no ill effects, despite daily exposures to the monkey version of the virus. It seized the banana bit, chirping happily and making kissy faces at the assistant.

"Cute. But aren't you supposed to be killing them, rather than keeping them as pets?" Brindermann's voice—a voice Twilley hated almost as much as he hated that idiot monkey—broke the scientist's furious concentration.

"The monkey or the girl?" The second voice brought Twilley around. General Garza himself stood there, his expression deceptively mild as he gazed at the scene through the window.

"Both—unless the girl is another volunteer in the inoculation experiment?" Brindermann made it a question, forcing Twilley to explain.

"The monkey is a subject in the inoculation experiment," Twilley informed them, his voice as featureless as his hatchet face. "It has successfully resisted the effects of the plague, with no additional side effects, for eight days—"

"So the monkey version of your Pacifica vaccine works," Garza interrupted. "Judging by what we saw on our way in, so do the ones for mouse, rat, and dog. Humans haven't been so lucky."

"The program is in its early stages as yet, but shows some promising results. If we had—" Twilley's explanation ended in a squeak, as the General caught him by the front of his coat and slammed him against the unyielding smoothness of the glass.

"If you had what? More time? More money?" Garza asked. "Is that what your MedaGen masters want? Have they told you to drag your feet, trying to increase their fee? Do they think I am a stupid caudillo, to fall for such delaying tactics?"

"No," Twilley managed, glaring into Garza's dark eyes.

"Well then," Garza stepped back, "so it's just that you can't do what I've asked, not that you won't. As you know, however, I need the vaccine now. Thus, I am willing to try to help you for two weeks longer before I give you a more useful assignment—perhaps as one of the lab animals. What do you need to assure that will not happen?"

"The experiment would progress much more quickly if I had competent assistance, instead of having to work with these half-trained morons." Twilley cast a poisonous look at his assistant. "They are useless at complicated analysis and all but basic gene splicing and recombination."

"Oh, is that all?" Garza shrugged. "Johann, get the good doctor competent help by tomorrow night. I am called away—a visit to the president of Mexico. When I return in a week, I expect to see you so confident that you take a dose of the vaccine yourself." When Twilley blanched, he simply smiled. "I see we understand each other. Good luck, Dr. Twilley."

Twilley watched him go, striding down the sterile hallway, Death temporarily departing. "I need someone with expertise in virology and epidemiology," he said, fastening on the one sure road to continued survival—and potential glory. "Someone experienced, well known. If your General hasn't killed everyone with more than a fourth-grade education, that is. I will send you a list of potentially acceptable South or Central American candidates in an hour."

Brindermann eyed the MedaGen researcher with unconcealed distaste. "And I will provide the candidate acceptable to me. Go back to work, Twilley. And tell Mr. Abbott that if you fail, he will lose his money too." He followed the General's way out, as the scientist's face blanched paler at the thought of coming between Abbott and the money for which he'd been willing to betray his own country.

The tiny screen in Brindermann's hand scrolled through known geneticists—and one name caught his eye. Yazna Kremmer Santia Vasquez, the doctor who worked with Major Zamora, the one who isolated and identified the semieffective virus Garza used on El Jaguar's rebels in Chile. She was Serrey's recommendation, and a Mormon to boot. Dr. Vasquez would be immune to MedaGen's bribery, and as long as they held her coreligionists hostage in easily bombed locations, they had leverage to force her to cooperate. And perhaps, if word spread that Vasquez was held in Garza's clutches, the brave major would be inspired to attempt a rescue. They had lost one Zamora; he had no intention of letting another slip through their fingers.

* * *

"And we just slip right through the good old virus protection— like this," Mercury said, entering the administrator's password into the watchdog program.

"Is that going to work?" Raul asked, staring at the cyber map that spread out on the screen.

"Yeah, it's going to work. It already has," Mercury assured him. The virtual Cerberus sat back and wagged its tail as Mercury set up a new user account with full privileges in the central trunk of the far-branching computer network. "It's pitiful how many of these guys forget that virus scans have total administrator control and don't bother to change their factory-setting passwords. The top dogs might be smart, and they might have official policies about security, but when it gets down to the techs sitting up all night installing the systems, getting it done fast feels more important than hiding a back door you figure nobody's going to look for anyway."

The two junior techs hunkered close to the screen as Mercury flicked through the wealth of electronic information at his fingertips. Each sparkling node of the galaxy pattern represented a functional group. Accounting, supplies, communications—and tactical. "Hmm. That one's new."

"Hey! Byte rat! Quit lazing around over there and help set up this backup rack!" Señor Colón called out. He was a current senior Net tech, former Young Men advisor, and unofficial and circumspect watchdog of the boys' discreet surveillance. To reinforce the coded warning, he tossed a foam ball at Raul's head.

A second later, the door opened and one of the security officers wandered in, casting a suspicious eye around at the smooth boxes and blinking lights of the communications data center.

Raul stood. "Yes, sir," he barked back, walking around the central console between the officer and Mercury—who blanked the network screen, replacing it with an innocuous and extremely boring-looking communication diagnostics readout. The officer glanced over at Mercury, who sprawled in his chair stifling a yawn, the picture of high-tech ennui, and turned his attention to Raul and Señor Colón. He didn't have the vaguest idea about how to configure server hardware, but watching these two fiddle with wires, shiny boxes, and ridiculously tiny clamps was more interesting than trying to make sense of the esoteric patterns of data slipping over the screens of the rest of the consoles.

Mercury glanced over, making sure the real watchdog was distracted, and brought up a secondary window. Tactical—he'd never seen that one before. What did they have that would take network calculation power to run? The fact that he couldn't gain total access after several minutes' gentle probing made him more curious. From the look of things, somebody had set up a locked-box sector in the network, which suggested that they were hiding access codes or password files that they didn't want anybody else to get to—not even other administrators. A smooth, featureless, impervious shipping container flashed across Mercury's memory, pulling a speculative smile across his face. The virtual lockbox would be the ideal place to hide the codes for all those boxes from Keepsakes Ltd.—especially with Major Zamora hijacking shipments and their crews, which made giving the codes to the drivers impractical. *So you set up a new node on the network and use the General's secure communications system to send the codes to the depots instead,* Mercury thought. *Not bad. As long as you don't have any security termites in your system. Which you do. Now.*

A termite, however, had better be smarter than the anteaters who patrolled the yard. Mercury stared at the screen and considered tactics. Okay, he'd assume that somebody was going to notice he'd gotten in; the enemy's arrogance had let him slip by their defenses, so he'd better not fall into the same trap himself. He didn't want them suspecting a byte rat in Santiago, which meant he needed to toss them another bone. Who'd want to get into Garza's system? He grinned. Who wouldn't? No, the real question was, who could? The CTR ring on his hand, a half-sarcastic going-away gift from Calvin, caught his eye. CTR—CIA. Keep the transmissions in English, use American-standard encryption, and on first glance, any footprints they found from him would look a lot like tracks left by a foreign spy. They'd go nuts, trying to plug an outside leak, and if he kept a sharp eye out for anticracker measures, he'd have enough warning to avoid their Yankee sniffers. That worked. Now, what were those IEEE standards again?

In another couple of minutes, as long as it took Señor Colón to thoroughly bore the sentry, who left for more interesting conversation with the pretty security receptionist down the hall, Mercury had implemented his impersonation of an American intelligence agent and discovered two more interesting facts: the tactical area contained another, more tightly guarded stack of files, along with a set of codes for the high-security lockboxes; and the area had its own communications node, encrypted separately from the rest of General Garza's communications system. That made him itch with curiosity—and a shiver of foreboding, remembering the reports that Garza might have conned the Americans into giving him smart hardware. Heavy AI weapons would require that kind of high security plus computational power—and a secured communications system. However, the code stack obstinately refused to crumble under his first attack; its anteater came swiftly and threatening when he tried to use the antivirus administrator's permissions to slide past it.

He broke off reluctantly. He couldn't afford to let the Net ghosts that nearly caught Ascencio scoop him up; besides, he'd just put on his CIA mask and didn't want to have to drop it so quickly. He turned his attention to the secondary communications channel. It used sausage-factory encryption (pig in one end, sausage out the other, no way to go backwards) that prevented him from unscrambling the content. If he couldn't read the messages flashing along the line, though, he could get enough access to send his own messages along with it. Hmm. Interesting. He couldn't understand a conversation over this circuit, or stop anybody else from talking, but he could add his own comments to the conversation. Or maybe invite some-body else to join the party line . . .

* * *

"With this thing, anybody can join the party," Socks said happily, waving at the map glowing on his console screen. "And we can track them in real time while they play the game. It's a combo of GPS and satellite cameras—no kidding, those puppies can get resolution down to a foot square—better, if you can get into the military-only lenses, but we don't have permission to do that. Even without it, though, these glasses can look right down and tell you if you're going bald, judging from the albedo rating off the top of your head."

"Albedo?" Dove asked. He didn't think that term had to do with technology, but he couldn't decipher about half of what Socks jabbered about. In fact, he suspected that the computer tech made most of the jargon up, because he couldn't be bothered to use the usual English/computer lingo word. Not that Dove held that against him. The gangs he and Benny had grown up in did the same thing, though in their case they skipped correct grammar or vocabulary due to drunkenness rather than impatience. Still, hanging out in the cave gave him a sense of big things happening, with the reports from temple communities and tales of the Gatherers filtering through the digital readouts and Vids. Merry let him out of Section 89 every afternoon (after he'd done the chores he'd assigned himself, mainly to feel useful and keep from going stir-crazy), and more often than not, he wound up in the communications cave.

"Percentage of reflected light from a surface," Socks explained offhandedly. "It's a lot higher than you'd think. Moon's got the same albedo as an asphalt parking lot, and look at how bright it is."

"And they're using satellites to diagnose baldness?" Dove asked. Given that the most common use of subdermal nanotechnology was animated tattoos, his question was only half facetious.

"It's not that they do, it's that they could," the hacker informed him. "If they wanted to."

"More important to you than me," Dove observed, leaning over to check the albedo of the hacker's scalp. He grinned as he caught the soft snort from Fox. "If you ever got outside for the sky eyes to see the glint."

Socks just rolled his eyes. "And thanks for that, Tonto. I'll check in with you if I need an amateur opinion. Not that I'd need to ask you—with this network, I can talk to anybody that has satellite wireless." A soft, musical chime interrupted his enthusiastic explanation. He grinned, tapping the screen, where a tiny angel icon appeared. "Speaking of which, here we've got an example—encoded, confidential report from Johannesburg, winging its way through heaven on the wings of electrons."

"Instead of angels?" Dove asked. The tiny angel glittered, the identifying symbol of the Johannesburg temple community glowing behind it, proving it was from the Area Authority there.

"Well, it's the same thing—if you substitute *electrons* for *angels* in that old question about how many angels can dance on the head of a pin, you can figure it out. If you know the metallic composition of the pin," Socks explained irrelevantly, out of habit reaching to open the message.

"Marked eyes-only for the Brethren," Fox reminded him. So did another, not so soft noise that sounded like a bitterly offended monkey. She half smiled, shaking her head in amused resignation as she expertly redirected the message to its proper destination upstairs. "How many times are you going to try to open these things before you give up and just forward them to Elder Nabil like you're supposed to?"

Socks shrugged, only half repentantly. "Hey, just testing the security. Can't be too careful, checking for cracks in the encryption, right? Making sure nobody but authorized individuals can sneak a look at privileged communications—including me." Fox just rolled her eyes.

"What's that one?" Dove asked, pointing at the second icon that appeared in the Messages window. It also represented a golden human figure, this one a discreetly naked man carrying a ribbon-wrapped wand, wearing winged sandals—and a pair of late-model sunglasses.

"Why, lookee there—it's one of your folks sending up a smoke signal, Chingachgook." Socks tapped the message, which opened into the active window. "That's Mercury from down Santiago way, wanting to parley."

"Mercury!" Dove leaned forward, interested and curious. "Can we answer?"

"Sure can," Socks assured him. "We've got worldwide communication, right through the ISS and the Church's satellites to all points of the globe. What do you want to say?"

"Tell him he could use some more clothes," Dove suggested.

Socks sniggered, his fingers already flying. "Will do, Chief." He sent an acknowledgment, "Hey, messenger boy—cover up! Nobody needs to see that!" under the Santos' armed-angel logo, and added Dove's personal online chop at the end: a dove with an olive branch in its beak and a .45 in its claws.

"Dove?!?" Mercury's exclamation sprawled across the screen in rainbow letters that pulsated with his happy surprise. "What you doing there, man? You okay? They let you out of sickbay well, or just to die with some dignity? Still coughing up a lung every couple minutes?"

That settled the flicker of suspicion that had crossed Dove's mind, wondering if someone was spoofing Mercury's identity, exchanging messages with Fox and Socks who didn't know him. Somewhat naively, but with a touching degree of humility, Dove didn't think that the General would care enough about him personally to have an agent bone up on his health status. Dove grabbed Socks by the shoulders and took advantage of the wheeled chair to spin him away from the console. Ignoring the hacker's squawks of protest, Dove removed the data inputs too and took over himself.

"Healthy enough to kick your tail, wing boy," he shot back. "Dr. Galen shot me full of devil juice to stop the mondo TB, and now she's looking for a cure for both of them. Don't worry about me—you've got enough to worry about. You shamed the Santos yet?"

"Gone over to the enemy," Mercury admitted, but his icon sprouted a sudden toothy grin. "And you're toast if I'm caught—special-agent CIA spy named Salvatore playing mole, phreaking through the lines." A multicolored diagram flashed across the screen as well, a schematic showing his virtual address deep in the General's communication network.

Fox said, "Elder Molina sent him to hack into the invaders' comm system."

It didn't surprise Dove that an Apostle would know how to put Mercury's off-brand talents to use. "Border rat to digital parasite— you're coming up in the world," he sent. Changing the display to a scriptural Gothic, he added, "Do not use my name in vain. Do well, good and faithful servant."

"Thanks, boss." A flicker at the edge of the screen caught Mercury's attention. His electronic tripwire, an alarm to alert him if the Net ghosts appeared in his connection, blinked swiftly. Somebody else had just opened a communications channel alongside the one he wasn't supposed to be using. In the high-security system, the two virtual lines didn't overlap—but he didn't feel secure enough to risk discovery if they had a watchdog too. And, from the sophisticated nets, traps, and locks he'd sniffed out, especially in this tactical area, he figured they would. Their tracks ran all through the network, and he'd narrowly avoided running into them just like Ascencio had. Fortunately, he knew they existed, so he'd set his own countermeasures, not to trap them, but to warn him if they looked his way. So far, he'd escaped detection, and when he was detected, with any luck they'd go haring off north to catch themselves a Virginia farm boy. "Oops—gotta go. This just turned into a party line, and the neighbors ain't friendly."

"Buen' suerte, messenger," Dove sent, watching as the connection disappeared. The mental picture of Mercury in the middle of Garza's snake pit, on top of the latest news bulletin from Calvin detailing the goings-on as the Santos continued to face off Garza's agents in Amexica and the encoded messages winging from one temple community to another, touched off a long-simmering reaction. Dove had never dealt well with boredom or inactivity—and certainly not when his knight-errant honor shouted that he should get out and set things right. He hadn't coughed in a week, other than that incident at breakfast yesterday—but Merry had said something funny right as he'd taken a sip of milk, so that didn't count. Besides, Merry said he'd healed from the damage Slick's disease had wreaked on his lungs. Only an unaccustomed uncertainty about the role he should play had kept him quiet and, in his opinion, immobile this long. But if Elder Molina had a job for Mercury, surely Elder Nabil could find a way to use Dove. The thought of kicking around Salt Lake doing nothing became acutely unbearable. He stood up, replaced Socks in front of the console, and headed for the door.

"Hey, Chief, where you going?" Socks called.

Dove stopped at the door, glancing back at the tech. "To fight the General," he said flatly. "I've been lazing around here way too long."

The determination on Dove's face inspired Socks too. Watching the world flash by his screens usually satisfied him, but Dove's Western-hero aura was contagious. Every geek dreams of being a superhero, and Socks was a geek to the core of his being. The tech stood up, ready to follow the Santos' leader into battle. "The General better watch out! Can I help?"

After a moment's hesitation, Dove gave Socks a narrow look, taking in the pale complexion, rumpled white shirt, cartoon tie, and intellectual physique, then grinned. "Sure. Work up a tracker thing I can take with me, and we'll see how good that satellite spy eye of yours is. With you watching over our shoulders—over our heads—we'll be that much harder to ambush." He smiled at Fox, adding, "Every soldier could do with an angel on his side."

She returned the smile and nodded consent.

"Sure!" Socks saluted. "You got it, Chief!"

Dove returned the salute and disappeared out the door. He had calls to make, strategies to figure out, a cyber-assisted campaign to plan—and another lady to persuade.

CHAPTER 9

"What would it take to persuade you to keep your pretty nose out of bear traps?" Garza looked down at the disheveled but still defiant Rosa del Torres and hooked his thumbs into his gun belt. "You have an inconvenient way of showing up uninvited, señorita."

The reporter, kneeling with her arms around one of the poles supporting the sunshade outside the General's headquarters, lifted her cuffed hands in a shrug, easing her shoulders and affecting nonchalance. "Just trying to find out about the man everyone's wondering about. What his plans are, what motivates him—what the real story is behind the amazing rise of a mercenary leader nobody had heard of three years ago."

"So you come slinking out here to find the real story." Garza caught her conniving stare in one darker.

"The people have the right to know." She shoved away the thought that he might not respect her press immunity—unlike Major Zamora, who had only growled at her intrusions and the inevitable bad publicity that resulted, and unlike El Jaguar, who'd welcomed her interviews to advance his cause.

Garza looked thoughtful, glancing over her head at the tall, fair German whose disinterested expression conveyed bored contempt. "Do the people have a right to know?" he asked.

Brindermann made a show of consulting the readout on the tiny screen in his hand. "Not under the current conditions of martial law. And not under the drafted Pan-American Constitution under consideration either."

"So where does that leave you?" Garza asked Channel 8's third-tier local stringer. When she didn't answer immediately, he filled in the answer for her—as he unfastened the cuffs. "In an enviable and advantageous position, if you are as clever about opportunities as you are about getting around sentries."

"Oh?" Rosa rubbed her wrists.

"Oh, yes." Garza offered a hand. "Please, señorita, we can't have you kneeling before me. What would people think?"

She stood, all business. "What opportunities are you talking about? An interview?" She'd tried to get an interview with General Garza for months; if this ploy worked, creeping into camp and getting tied up would pay off handsomely.

"An exclusive interview." He opened the door of his olive-drab headquarters, gesturing her inside. "The most exclusive interview, and the biggest story of the century." He and Brindermann followed her into the electronic cave. "How would you like to be the one to announce that for the first time in history, one man has conquered all of South and Central America, extinguishing every rebel and terrorist force on the continent, uniting all this vast territory under one democratic, stable, and prosperous government?"

"That would be quite an announcement," she admitted. Nobody had announced that the chronically war-torn regions had a new leader. That would deserve a prominent spot on Channel 8's daily events wrap-up.

"It would," Garza agreed. "Especially if you made it while standing beside me on the steps of what will be the Pan-American Capitol here in Bogotá—and then used your unparalleled interviewing skills to pry that 'real story' out of me in person."

"Live?" she breathed. An interview like that one wouldn't just get her a spot on the wrap-up—it would get her a spot on the prime-time lineup, a direct line to Clara Cortez and Channel 8's entire five billion viewers! She sat down in the other chair.

"Live," Garza agreed, watching the hook set tight. "I've watched your work for quite a while, señorita, and you have impressed me." Her hunger for fame and influence caught his attention as much as her dogged determination to be at the center of every breaking story. "It's finally time for us to appear together, after having cooperated so effectively already."

"Cooperated?" Rosa focused on the General, her journalist's brain riffling through facts, shaking them into a plausible story, seeing possible connections that she hadn't before. "El Jaguar contacting me to explain his reasons for opposing the Chilean government—and to let me know where the next attack had happened, before the antiterror squad got there. The documents that didn't quite confirm the rumors that the rebels were part of a plot inside the government, with Señor Olivares and Major Zamora running it. Interview invitations with Vice President Aguilera to discuss the dire threat to the administration and his hopes that President Quintana would call in the General's assistance. And that anonymous tip, telling me to show up at La Moneda at just the right time to catch Zamora running from the Quintana assassination." She examined the new pattern. "You arranged it all, didn't you? El Jaguar was working for you—and Aguilera." After a split second's hesitation, the last piece clicked into place. "Zamora didn't assassinate Quintana, did he?"

"No," Garza agreed. "But does it matter? The major is a rebel now, working against the revolutionary government of all Latin America. And you have the golden opportunity to stand before the world as the voice of that government. What do you want, Rosa? Convoluted facts no one wants to hear, or the chance to rise from lowly stringer for Channel 8 to press secretary for the president of the United States of South and Central America?"

Rosa's love of journalism ran a distant second to her love of the hot light of fame, so she nodded briskly and said, "I'll need a staff—and another cameraman. Your sentries broke the arms of the one I brought. Get me a phone, and I'll arrange the live shot. I've got a couple of contacts at Channel 8 who'll be interested."

"We'll provide them with interesting information," Garza promised. "Of course, as press secretary you will relay only the information you should."

A cynically impatient smile flicked across Rosa's face. "Don't worry, General. I know better than to bite the hand that feeds me." *Until someone else offers a better treat,* she added silently.

The best treat in the world, however, came in the form of a glowing cube of crimson atop a satellite camera, as Rosa delivered a breathless update from the steps of the antique building already undergoing a spectacular facelift in downtown Bogotá, the new capital of a new United States. "In a dramatic address today, the military hero General

Andrea Garza announced his ascension to the office of president of the newly created United States of Central and South America." Intertwined with Rosa's narration of the General's unprecedented triumph, inspiring clips showed Garza's elite troops parading through the city to the joy of flower-tossing civilians, the General reassuring and inspiring cheering citizens, the leaders of the opposition party acknowledging their defeat and Garza's generous granting of seats in the parliament (the better to keep his enemies near), and the peaceful streets where terrorists had so recently ruled.

The only negative note came with the last few moments of the report, as Rosa regretfully noted that not all was perfect in this democratic paradise. "Unfortunately, not all the news is good. To the disappointment and grief of Chileans, the man they had hailed as a hero is now revealed as a traitor. Investigations conducted at President Aguilera's request have revealed that Major Manuel Rafaelo Rivera Zamora, former chief of Chile's antiterror task force and confidant of the late President Quintana, was none other than El Jaguar himself."

The pictures proved it, fuzzy but damning video of a running firefight between Garza's Chilean forces and a shadowy commando gang ended with close-ups of the red jaguar emblem on the sleeves of dead men the captions identified as members of the antiterror squad. "This is Rosa del Torres, live from Bogotá."

In the Channel 8 studio, Clara smiled and said, "Exciting times in South America! Thank you, Rosa del Torres." Her smile faded several watts as she turned to the camera. "Other news isn't so exciting. While the latest data from the International Space Station doesn't confirm that the NEOs hurtling toward the earth will cause an ELE, or extinction-level event, they can't confirm that the asteroids will miss either. Channel 8 has obtained a clip of a confidential report from the International Space Station to Mission Control."

The scene behind her switched to a computer animation of the swarm of asteroids, solid masses for the ones with visual confirmation, transparent blobs for those whose existence was still theoretical. They spun and tumbled in complex patterns, fuzzing in and out of resolution as the mathematics hit incomplete data points.

Beside the graphic, a static-wreathed image of Captain Nakima appeared in the bootleg copy of the update report. Lights blinked and winked behind him, the bridge of the ISS clattering with electronic activity. His broad, blunt face didn't hide irritation well in the face of repeated, frantic inquiries and his own inability to give the answer he wanted to deliver. "No, we cannot give exact trajectories for the NEOs—or any of their baby cousins, either."

He gestured toward one readout, where the detailed version of the animation attempted to keep up with the real-time movements of the asteroid swarm. "Turns out that Newtonian physics can get pretty complicated with that many bodies on an unprecedented trajectory. The minute anybody can tell me they can predict the exact movement of a couple hundred space rocks coming around the sun where no space rocks should've been, they can take over, and we'll all know what's going to happen." Rubbing one hand over his face wearily, Nakima sighed. "We're doing the best we can. Hideyoshi's modified the InSAR system to focus its lasers on the swarm, and we're feeding the movement data through Mir's weather-modeling program, using nonterminal equations—"

The broadcast cut off there, sparing the viewers from hearing the rest of the captain's technically detailed explanations—and sparing Channel 8 from the inevitable ratings drop-off that always happened when people on-screen started talking about complicated numbers.

"Expert astronomers on the ground haven't made any more progress on tracking the asteroids due to what one researcher called the worst atmospheric conditions in recorded history," Clara announced. "Ground-based telescopes cannot pierce the combination of clouds and volcanic haze in the sky, and the supercharged atmosphere also interferes with the radio telescopes. What data they can pick up is sent to the Space Station for further analysis—"

Suddenly the picture dissolved into a thousand other sparkles as a massive wave of sunspot activity fragmented Channel 8's broadcast band. The emergency alert hit Monk's screens immediately—satellite connection lost. "Get my signal back!" Monk roared. "What the blue-streaking Hades are we paying people for? Where are my anti-magnetic satellites? We ordered a fail-safe system when we coughed up the billion and a half to finance that shuttle launch!"

"The ISS guys are kind of preoccupied at the moment," offered a junior producer, from the relative safety of the news floor. Channel 8 had funded the mission that deployed a swarm of tiny, self-powered satellites capable of generating their own magnetic fields to protect transmissions from cosmic interruption, but they required occasional tuning—especially when the magnetic activity burst into levels that threw the aurora borealis into the sky as far south as San Francisco. Reception had been less than ideal and growing steadily worse for months, but this was the first time the entire network had experienced a complete broadcast blackout.

"They think they're the only ones with problems?" Monk wasn't in a mood for empathy or rational consideration of the relative weights and values of the situation. The idea of an asteroid ending life on the planet mattered far less in his personal scheme of things than the tragedy of dead air. "Get those monkeys turned on *now!*" His fury finally motivated Channel 8's broadcast techs to recalibrate the anti-static mechanisms.

"Three. Two. And we're in," Monk announced.

"We're back and we apologize for the unforeseen interruption to everyone in the markets that lost Channel 8 there for a minute. That's the joy of live television," Clara quipped. "Due to unprecedented levels of sunspot activity—not asteroid collisions—we're having some difficulty with a few of our relay servers. But according to secretary of Homeland Security Howard W. Garlick, we've got more to worry about than celestial collisions."

Garlick appeared, urging the "brave people of the United States" to "stand fast against both celestial and domestic threats." Monk watched the senator's rant with only half his attention. The viewer poll running beside the senator's speech showed his popularity falling. Monk gestured to Kim. "Cut the senator short. He's not paying us enough to lose audiences."

Kim nodded, feeding Clara the next cue. Immediately, Anne's segment on the Mormon temple communities rolled along Channel 8's broadcast.

Monk watched, satisfied, as the ratings lights steadied, then slowly began to climb. Mormons were always good for freak-show appeal, especially with Secretary Garlick fulminating against them to take the heat off his failed Homeland Security policies. A mudfight between Homeland Security and the Mormons would be good for a couple weeks' headlines, especially from a "secular vs. sacred" slant as the asteroid hurtled toward them all.

"That's the real secret to broadcast news," Monk informed Kim. "You gotta play both sides against the middle, and always look for the next big thing. Even if you have to make some of it up." He grinned. "But you never heard me say that."

Kim just gave him a sideways look and cued up the next segment—Garrett's nightly interview/gossip show, prominently featuring Virginia's oversold charms. When tornadoes, riots, and assassinations didn't catch eyeballs, sex still sold, especially to people determined to party, drink, and dance away what might turn out to be their last week on the planet.

* * *

Missy danced around the office, flailing wildly around in a preschool imitation of a whirling dervish. She ran into the back of Merry's chair with every third turn, using the hard plastic back as an impromptu tom-tom as she improvised both words and melody: "Dance, dance, dance!"

"Okay, okay!" Merry laughed, throwing her hands up and grabbing Missy's. They danced in a circle until they were both too dizzy to stand, and fell in a giggling heap on the floor. The giggles subsided altogether too soon, however, as Merry craned her neck to look up at the monitor where yet another simulation ran, using investigatory evolution to extend the basic idea of a possible AllSafe antidote. This one showed some promise—but so had the last three, before they petered out to nothing in the end. Well, not to nothing; one of their treatments showed promise as a general anti-allergy medicine, calming an overactive immune system without shutting it off. But coming so close and then having to start over frustrated her to no end, when AllSafe's dire consequences hung over the heads of millions of people whose only mistake had been trusting their government's recommendations—and MedaGen's false-faced promises. Exposing the company's lies had prevented millions of others from taking the lethal vaccine, but it hadn't saved everyone, not everyone in the Church—some of whom had realized their error too late and repentantly come into the fold carrying latent death in their veins. She had picked up the pieces of her husband Chris's work after he died in a stupid accident that Merry didn't let herself think about often. It did not take her too long to find definite proof of MedaGen's lies. That fact had forced her out of her home, with MedaGen's goons in pursuit, until the charity of strangers—no, the unselfish charity of brothers and sisters—had brought her here to Section 89. In this privately funded medical research lab, the Church—most directly through Elder Nabil—both protected her and helped her try to find a cure for the man-made plague Chris had found and she had exposed to all who would listen. She'd worked like a madwoman for months now, one step forward and two steps back, while Missy played with Tasha Crow's kids, begged for the chance to accompany her mother to the lab, and got bigger every day.

Oh, Chris, how's this for irony? she thought. Her mother, Sidney, would undoubtedly tell her that there was something unhealthy about the constant internal conversation she carried on with her late husband, but he still felt so near, so real—and "talking" to him helped her think things through and stave off the loss and loneliness that some-times threatened to well up and stop her heart completely. *I gave up my medical career to raise our baby and complained that I felt my brain was turning to mush, and now somebody else is raising her while I wish I had nothing more complicated on my mind than remembering the cast of* Nephi's Neighborhood*!*

Missy looked up at her mother, then at the whirling patterns on the screen, and finally at the picture of her father next to the console. He smiled at her, as he always did; she smiled back, showing him she was a brave, good girl. Sometimes being brave got tough, though, even for a girl who was on the four side of three. "Mamamam, are we going to see Dadadad?"

The question pulled Merry out of her reverie. "Surely we will, sweetie. We're a forever family. Remember? We're sealed, you and me and Daddy, and we will be together forever."

"After we die," Missy clarified, with the stark logic of the young. "Are we going to die soon? When that star falls out of the sky and burns everything up?"

"Star?" For just a moment, the question caught Merry completely unprepared; stars whirled in her mind's eye, brilliant against the black sky, then flashing into long, fiery streaks like something out of a science fiction film. Reality caught up quickly. "The asteroid. Is that what you're talking about?" She hugged Missy tightly as the little girl nodded. "Oh, sweetheart, no, we're not all going to die because a star falls and burns everything up."

"Really?" Missy sighed, cuddling into Merry's arms. She felt more disappointed than reassured; seeing her daddy's smile in person sounded good indeed.

"Really." Elder Nabil's deep, musical voice echoed her word with warm certainty. Both Galen girls turned to see him standing in the lab doorway, as dapper and smiling as ever. Missy ran right over and flung her arms out for a hug, which he affectionately delivered.

Merry smiled, hiding her inward cringe at her daughter's forwardness. If Elder Nabil didn't mind—even enjoyed Missy's enthusiastic greetings—she shouldn't, but it still struck her as shockingly informal behavior toward an Apostle of the Lord.

"Why not?" Missy demanded. "How do you know?"

He set her back down and ruffled her hair. "Because Jesus told us so. The asteroid isn't going to burn up the world, and we shouldn't worry about it. He'll take care of us, and things will happen as He wants them to—even if He doesn't tell us exactly how yet. We simply need to trust Him." His eyes twinkled at Merry, as Missy nodded sagely. She always agreed with Elder Nabil, even when she didn't understand all of what he said. "Whatever He's got planned, we know what we are supposed to do: help the general population as well as gather all who will come to safety in the Zion outposts."

Walking into the lab, bending his tall frame slightly to peer at the colorful patterns on the console screen, he added, "Which is exactly what my dear Brother Ojukwu has told me to say when anyone asks me about the Church's mission in these eventful times. And it brings us to my visit to two of my favorite ladies. How is the help for the general population coming along this day?"

"We're making progress. Slowly. As Kendall—Dr. Learner—says, we've found a half dozen ways that don't work." Merry sighed. "I wish I could tell you more."

He touched her shoulder lightly, his expression sympathetic. "Corinne—Dr. De la Guardia—said much the same thing when I passed her on the way in. She says you spend too much time here."

"It's not all that much time," Merry protested—and gave Missy a remonstrative look when the little girl snorted in disbelief. She'd definitely inherited that little tactic from Chris, whose sweet nature hid a tart streak of sarcasm. She bumped Missy with her knee, then gave her a one-handed squeeze, acknowledging the justice of the wordless accusation as she explained, "Okay, maybe it is a lot of time. I'm just trying to find a crack, get an edge that we can use to pry it open. This is the toughest assignment I've ever faced, pounding away at this thing!"

Irritated at the self-pitying sound of that explanation, she shook her head and smiled wryly. "Seriously, we have made progress. We've stabilized our human guinea pigs, and we know SemiSafe can at least control AllSafe's full ravages by binding to the altered DNA that AllSafe inserts into the genetic chain, but it's just another booster agent, not a real solution. The AllSafe changes are still there, just kept mute for as long as the SemiSafe lasts. The tough part is finding exactly the right combination of factors to let us snip out the AllSafe and let the patient's own gene heal together again, so it produces the regular immune cells."

"Hmm. A difficult proposition, but not an impossible one, I think. SemiSafe," Elder Nabil grinned. "That sounds like our young Nakai."

Merry grinned back. Dove had a way with words (and she had threatened him with death if he ever used some of them in front of Missy). "Yes, that's him. He's doing well, too—so well that he's making us all crazy. He's a real help around the lab, but he's got cabin fever something fierce. Especially after yesterday, when he spoke with one of his Santos friends over the Net. He wants to get going again on his crusade against General Garza."

"He may get his wish, if conditions do not change," Elder Nabil said. He shook off the thoughts that crossed his mind and focused on Merry again. "We all have work to do, furthering the Lord's plans. And through all your disappointments, you keep working too, Dr. Galen. You are doing well. Even when you do not see it."

"I'm frustrated with this, with the time it's taking, with how much I'm gone—I feel like I should be doing more!" Merry burst out. "If only Chris—" Her voice broke, and she fell silent.

Once again, the Apostle touched her shoulder, this time reassuringly. "You are doing what you should do, just as Chris is. Both of you are playing your parts in a larger effort, the fullness of which we can't see right now, but you're both saving souls." He waited until her chin rose, then nodded at her, exuding bracing confidence. "And others in the Church are also working to help their brothers and sisters. I am off to speak to some of them now, farmers who have the assignment of feeding the people in the face of food shortages caused by the horrendous weather, breakdown of shipping, and mindless violence. They, like you, will prevail, because of their faith in the strong arm of the Lord. He is always there to lean on, Meredith. For all of us who want to do good."

Merry watched him leave, both she and Missy returning his parting wave. She glanced at the computer screen, then at Missy, who looked up at her expectantly. "You hungry, sweetie? How about we go solve our own food shortage at Taco Joe's?"

"Yes!" Missy crowed. "No more food shortage for us!" She danced down the hall, singing again.

* * *

"So, now people have other singles stuck in their heads instead of yours. Do you think it has anything to do with your age?" Garrett asked MedaGen's starlet and spokesmodel. Virginia's latest album had utterly failed to crack the top-ten chart, and Garrett couldn't resist rubbing it in.

Virginia glared at Garrett from beneath her frosted eyelashes, then tried a pout and a toss of her impossibly luxurious hair. Impossible for anyone who didn't have a personal beauty consultant and a virtually unlimited cosmetic budget, that is. "It's a serious album for serious times," she informed him. "These songs are personal—they explore deeply emotional themes. Bubblegum pop isn't where I'm at anymore."

"Maybe you could say this album is more *mature*? Be careful, sweetie—you might outgrow your niche," Garrett warned. "As a real veteran, you might have some valuable words of wisdom for tomorrow's stars. Have you met Charity and Chastity?" The sinuous beat of the twins' dance-house hit accompanied them out. They made Virginia look overripe—and they knew it. The staged catfight lasted to the next commercial for AllSafe.

* * *

"Oh, please!" Hideyoshi snorted, peering at the ground-side transmission screen in annoyed disbelief. "Do we have to watch this garbage?"

"Wong says Channel 8's on the same broadcast frequency as ground comms—as long as we can watch this, we know we've still got contact with the ground, making sure the satellites' auxiliary radio signals are blocking the solar interference through all the ion storms," Mir pointed out. So far, Wong's careful shepherding had kept the deployment of tiny radio satellites around the major communication lines open—and they instantly heard about any glitches.

Hideyoshi sighed. "Why do they air this garbage?"

"Well, because regular guys like looking at bimbos," Mir pointed out, looking up from her own readouts. "If it irritates you so much, turn the sound off." Mir sighed, slapping the side of her readout in frustration. "I just wish I could get back to Earth to ignore it all in person!" The readout settled, drawing probability lines that swept over, under, around, and through the earth's orbit—and the earth itself. She glared at them, as if by sheer force of will she could make them resolve themselves into a definite answer. "Come on, you little goombahs, tell me nothing's going to happen to my planet before I get back to it. I don't want to die up here!" A pleading, tense note crept into her voice. Her nerves, already strained by the additional months of space-station duty, had definitely begun to fray.

"Ivana, everything's going to work out," Hideyoshi reminded her for the tenth time that day. He couldn't explain his conviction; he would admit that he had no rational basis for the calm that he felt (though he didn't agree with Captain Nakima that it was probably a sign of shock or incipient emotional breakdown). "We'll be on the far side of the earth when the storm comes, not out in front where the asteroids are."

She ignored that reassurance, as usual. "But then, what does it matter whether anybody lives or dies—here or there? If the asteroids hit, it just means that in a couple million years the descendants of today's cockroaches will discover our desiccated mummies floating around in a miserable plastic-and-tin can in space, instead of descendants of humans doing it."

Hideyoshi grabbed a stabilizer handle for security and stretched across to pat her shoulder sympathetically. "Don't worry—the station's orbit will have decayed long before that."

That got her attention. "Oh, great—so we'll get to hit the planet after all, if the asteroids don't."

"Hey, don't you want to go home?" he asked, grinning, then dodged as she aimed a fast swat at his head. She spun slowly around, catching herself on the edge of her console; he reoriented back to his own work space. "How about we just concentrate on figuring out whether we have to worry about it at all?"

"Do they give Mormons optimism shots, or is it that inbreeding causes mental illness?" Mir asked.

He just grinned at that. "We're close on this one, I can feel it."

The computer, with all its brain power, needed precise information to run its simulated universe, mapping real-world events to their logical outcomes. Gathering that data—and teaching the computer how to interpret it—had been the challenge they'd thrown themselves into, trying to solve the puzzle that everyone on the earth had such a vital stake in. As the readouts from his redeployed InSAR lasers— combined with data from the station's astronomy, weather, and communications satellites—spread over the screens, Hideyoshi's grin faded slowly into an expression of wonderment.

"We're very, very close," he whispered. "In fact, I think we're there." Slowly, afraid to break the electronic enchantment unfolding in the depths of the 3-D display, he touched the comm button.

Mir looked over, and the readout reflected in her widening eyes as Hideyoshi said, "Captain, it looks like we've got a stable configuration."

Nakima, his face as wearily wrinkled as his ship suit, oozed around in his sleeping cocoon so he could see his own screen. The display showed the asteroid cluster, the individual rocks spinning around each other in dizzying patterns. Now, however, none of them disappeared through critical portions of their orbits; their intricate movements defied the eye, but the computer captured it all. "Run the sim," the captain ordered.

"Already started," Wong responded from the comm suite.

In the black virtual space, the glowing swarm fell around the sun, moving through the star's heavy magnetic fields and solar winds, rolling along the gravity wells of the planets toward the earth and its moon. The earth rolled slowly in its own orbit as well, displaced twenty-four hours in time, the moon rotating around its own center of gravity. The invaders drew closer, drawn down a gravity slope that pulled the individual bodies closer to each other, bounced some off others, crashed several into the barren lunar surface and even more into the atmosphere of the blue and white planet below. A cascade of impacts changed the configuration of the swarm, smaller rocks crashing into larger ones, narrowing the front of the wave, widening the sides. The two largest asteroids, Kirmisse's NEOs, moved through the debris, demolishing their smaller companions but changing course slightly as well.

Then the moon, progressing slowly on its inevitable path, loomed out of the haze of smaller grains, standing like a silver shield between the storm and the earth. One NEO swung ponderously aside as gravity slingshotted it around, grazing the moon and sending a spray of dust and rock from both bodies sparkling into the sunlight. The other, slightly behind its sister, slammed into the moon sideways. Mare Imbrium disappeared in a cold explosion, rocks rending and cracking as lunar rocks launched themselves into orbit. The blast wave spread across the moon's surface, millions of asteroid fragments pocking the dark surface of the ancient lava flows with new craters. Starburst rays of canyons formed around the primary impact crater; the entire moon shuddered as the force of the blow sent ripples of rending force into its core. On the far side, a spray of rock burst out, a reverse crater like an exit wound. Below the stricken satellite, brilliant trails lit the atmosphere of the earth, marking the paths of the asteroids, now mixed with moon rock, that fell toward the planet. Clouds swirled, oceans heaved, molten rock and dust fountained up from the impact sites—but the planet passed through the cloud of space debris without suffering the most devastating blows.

"One of the two big NEOs will hit the moon; the other will miss the earth along with most of its companions," Wong summarized, his voice amazingly cool in its comm-officer precision. "Most observers will see a disturbance on the moon, but that's all."

"Too bad," Mir joked. "They're missing a whale of a show."

"They'll get a bigger show," Hideyoshi corrected, replaying the last few seconds of the sim showing that hundreds of small objects would strike the earth, many large enough to do damage. He tried to envision the kind of devastation those brief flashes of light and swirls of cloud represented in human terms.

"Earth Saved!" the breaking-news headline on Channel 8's crawl screamed moments later, as Wong relayed the news—with the supporting data, and the important caveat that many smaller bodies would strike the planet—to the International Space Agency's headquarters, and it spread from there like the aftershocks of an asteroid strike. Channel 8's Net and radio outlets picked up the scoop, as did news agencies all over the world. Most repeated the inaccurate but exciting theme of Monk's headline, as if the worst asteroid disaster had been averted, rather than shown to be destined not to happen.

Far below the International Space Station, relief rippled outward in concentric waves from screens and radios. Jubilant crowds filled squares and streets. Three days later, Tommy Gibbs appeared before the record-breaking crowd in Houston's AstroDome to lead the multitude in a prayer of thanks for catastrophe averted. Brother Light, speaking to a vast congregation in Old Delhi, promised that the One God would still send fire from heaven down on the unbelievers and enemies of Unity. Wong's warning went out as well, prompting the sensible and careful to watch the skies carefully; this event would be the world's most amazing fireworks show, but also a dangerous and potentially devastating space storm.

As the storm arrived, the first volley ripped through the clouds and haze, wrapping the earth in cascades of brilliant falling stars, so many that it looked as if heaven itself were under an evacuation order. Most of these, the smaller pieces pushed ahead of the primary swarm, burned up in the atmosphere, leaving no trace but streaks of light. Through breaks in the clouds, amateur and professional astronomers watched in amazement as the unseen NEO crashed into the moon, wreaking havoc on the dead surface. Then the havoc began on the earth.

Two days later, larger rocks, not devastatingly huge chunks of protoplanet but significant boulders in their own right, followed the first cascade through the atmosphere. These had too much mass for atmospheric friction to melt and strip away in clouds of molten vapor. Instead, they screamed through the air, heating to blue-white fireballs. The less dense objects exploded violently high above the ground.

Others, slightly more dense, nearly reached the ground before violently annihilating themselves. A trio of these meteors, screaming through the air above London, exploded above Hyde Park, evaporating the decorative lake and laying the stately trees out in concentric circles, their broken branches pointing away from the blast zone. A ten-meter chunk of space debris narrowly missed land, striking into the Atlantic with the force of an atomic bomb, sending huge waves crashing nearly to the top of the famous White Cliffs of Dover. Gouts of steam, columns of smoke, and clouds of dust rose into the atmosphere, already murky from volcanic ash, darkening the wounded moon and dimming the asteroids' eye-searing light.

"Reports pour in from all over the world of asteroids—pardon, now meteorites—crashing to the ground," Clara Cortez breathlessly announced. "The most dramatic meteor shower in recorded history has ended, with unprecedented damage to property and a rising number of casualties. Fortunately, and amazingly, most of the meteorites struck in a wide path across the Atlantic Ocean. Coastal regions in the UK, Europe, and the Americas report damage from tsunamis raised by the impacts."

She could barely keep up with the dramatic video streams, live feeds from Channel 8's local reporters in a swath from Iceland to Colombia. The remains of a fishing boat, its masts outlined in the flames that spread from its meteor-destroyed engine, glowed against the dark sea. Fires rose from craters between high-rise buildings in Boston—and one gleaming office tower sported a dramatic hole punched right through its upper floors, as if a gigantic bullet had perforated the entire structure. A rain of fish fell across the eastern coast of Mexico as an especially violent impact deep in the ocean threw not only water but aquatic animals high into the sky. New Orleans lost its levees not in a flood but in an explosion equivalent to the bomb that leveled Hiroshima, loosing a towering column of steam into the sky—and a rolling tide that swamped the city and filled the newly created crater. Unprecedented waves crashed into Haitian shores, carrying the tattered remains of boats—and avid, or insane, surfers.

"After a night of devastating stellar violence," Clara summarized, after twelve hours of continually breaking news, "it seems that the storm is at last dying down. While the observers on the International

Space Station, which survived the shower intact, say that we will continue to see smaller meteors for several weeks, especially from the damage to the moon, the worst has finally passed. While some recriminations are already beginning to fly—a group of senior senators accuses Homeland Security Secretary Garlick of failing to adequately prepare the East Coast for potential meteor damage—the overall mood is wildly enthusiastic."

CHAPTER 10

"Praise the Lord, all are safe here," Elder Molina sent word through the Church's satellite network. Other reports came in from the temple communities around the globe, in some cases equally dramatic as the ones saturating the commercial news channels, but always more practical. While the world outside breathed a collective sigh, got drunk, looted, burned, and found other extreme ways of expressing their relief at the asteroids' passing, the Mormons quietly went about their business, following the prophet's directive to gather in all who would listen to the message. Of course, it helped that the asteroids' warning pass didn't surprise them at all. Those who had paid attention to statements from Presidents Smith and Rojas hadn't wasted time either worrying about or denying the possibility of an extinction-level event; instead, they redoubled their efforts to be ready to assist their late-arriving brothers and sisters, even in the face of extreme and ever more organized hostility.

"The final readings have come down from the International Space Station," observed Miu Ling, one of the chief operators of a Church-owned pirate radio and Net station broadcasting reliable news as well as the gospel message to a wide swath of South China. She waved the opalescent disc over her head at the other airwave buccaneer in the control room before plugging it into the console. The screen lit, showing the initial simulation of the meteor shower, then the corrected data from actual observation of the impact patterns.

"Well done," Huang Chi approved with a grin, noting that 90 percent of the station's simulation matched reality.

The images that followed sobered both of them, as they watched brief but telling reports of the devastation that the commercial news outlets had omitted. For Channel 8 and its sponsors, selling expensive champagne for victory parties and celebrating a narrow escape for the wealthy elites of the world had higher priority than relaying the plight of Dutch city dwellers whose streets flooded when the heavy waves from the ocean-centered explosions overwhelmed the dikes, or the frantic firefighting efforts of peasants in the dry Spanish plains of La Mancha, or the stream of refugees displaced when a series of impacts had torn up fishing villages on Mexico's eastern coast. Still, the messages relayed along the Church's secure, and, to Wong's amazement, static-free satellite channels brought hope and reassurance: all over the world, the Saints had escaped the ravages of the firestorm.

"Looks like that puts the lie to Lord Xi Xian's claim that the asteroids have obliterated the West, proving his claim to the mandate of heaven," Ling noted, pulling on her headphones.

"And Brother Light's promise to have the asteroids wipe out the non-Unified and make the world into a paradise for the Children of Light," agreed Chi. His grin returned. "Let's tell them all about it, shall we?"

The word spread invisibly through the ether, Ling's crisp tones accompanying the words and images to radios and computers in their broadcast area, picked up by other pirate stations all over the vast continent. The stations spread accurate news not only of the outside world, but of events inside China's vast borders as well, countering propaganda from the beleaguered government in Beijing and its sworn enemies in the far-flung provinces. As always, the news brief melded into the call for all who believed to come to Zion, out of the wicked and dangerous world, away from the warlords and wolves preying on those outside the walls of divine protection.

Of course, the Mormons' station hardly dominated the airwaves; anyone with a transmitter and power to run it could offer his own version of reality to anyone who would listen. Both Lord Xi Xian and General Huang-ti used broadcasts to call the faithful to their banners and issue threats against the traitors and collaborators who refused to join them; the embattled government did the same, adding its own fulminations against "anti-revolutionaries" who sought to subvert the "people's republic." Buddhist monks using the venerable Todai-ji temple in Japan added their own political/religious messages, as did the Children of Light from their base in Thailand. A myriad of other competing voices whispered and shouted through the radios and television sets still functioning, all advancing their own agendas and denouncing others' words. Sometimes, however, denouncements simply didn't go far enough—especially when the wrong words reached too many eager, interested ears. The Mormons' simple but uncomfortably effective programs definitely fell into that category.

Hence, ten black-clad, red-masked figures slipped around the gray walls of the nondescript building where Ling and Chi sent the news of the asteroids' actual impact out to hungry listeners. The place itself was a former foundry, standing on the outskirts of a battered, semi-industrial town whose lingering population was made up almost entirely of Mormon converts. Security was nonexistent; the Hands of the Prophet easily bashed through the large doors and raced through the main room, empty but for the hulks of long-cold smelting equipment, to the control room in the executive offices on the second floor.

Ling looked up at the flash of movement through the glass surrounding the supervisors' offices and sprang to her feet, raising her hands as if to hold them off with merely her ten slender fingers and the fire in her eyes.

Chi saw the red-masked men try the door, and calmly finished his sentence before they smashed through the window. "Here is the message of President Richard Rojas, prophet of the Lord and Associate President of The Church of Jesus Christ of Latter-day Saints." He touched the Transmit button, shoved his chair away from the console, and rose to take Ling's hand as bullets roared toward the two radio operators.

Glass smashed, bits of electronic equipment flew, smoke poured from the consoles, lead pellets screamed through air and machinery alike. The machine-gun fire wreaked havoc on the delicate equipment, converting intricate circuitry into meaningless masses of broken, sparking junk. The Hands screamed invocations and battle cries, invoking the name of their master and prophet to overcome the infidels' own Master and the words of His prophet, screaming threats and death to all those who defied the words of Brother Light.

Through the billows of smoke and sprays of sharp-edged, glittering fragments, Chi and Ling emerged unscathed. One of the assassins, raising his rifle, cursed them in the name of the One God and opened fire. Bullets thudded out of the barrel in a torrential stream, cutting across walls and control boards, sending the chairs skidding and flipping backwards.

The would-be assassins fell back in astonishment as Chi stepped forward out of the smoke and debris, raising one hand as he said, "You and your dark master cannot stop the work of the Lord, or His servants."

Darkness filled the room as a third Hand, racing around the building from the outside, destroyed the station's generator. And in that darkness, the voice of President Rojas spoke on, declaring the Savior's love for all His children in China and all of Asia, promising His protection to all those who believed in His name, and calling them home to Zion.

"How can it be?" said one of the Hands. "How can it be?" he repeated and fled in terror.

* * *

A different message beamed out at the same time, half a world away. "It is not yet time to go home," Tommy Gibbs announced to the vast audience behind the cameras and microphones clustered in front of him. "Your faith has found favor with the true Ruler of the universe. King Jesus has heard your plea, and He has granted a stay, a reprieve from what looked to unbelievers like certain death! Your faithful prayers and righteous offerings have averted the disaster that seemed to hover over us all. It looks like He's given us a wake-up call, brothers and sisters, telling us we need to get on with the business of building up His kingdom."

The evangelist smiled. "Now, some of you may be disappointed that the Rapture isn't going to happen yet. But don't get too down about it. It's still coming; the signs are still out there that our Lord and God is making His vacation travel plans. For now, though, it looks like there's still plenty of time for us to get out there and do some good in the world—and enjoy the good life He's provided for us."

"Gotta love these guys," Mir laughed, taking one last sip from her celebratory and last bottle of carefully hoarded booze. "The world ends, they're right because they warned the sinners. The world doesn't end, they're still right, because they prayed it away. Where can I get a gig like that?"

"You've got a gig like that, Ivana—you're a meteorologist. You can be wrong every day for a month, and people still tune in to get the forecast," Hideyoshi pointed out breathlessly.

The breathlessness wasn't due to any particular enthusiasm for weather or forecasting; he had used bungee cords to fasten himself to the treadmill in the tiny workout room and was trying to work off the tension of the last few weeks by simulating a brisk run on the earth. Other station personnel were celebrating or blowing off steam in other ways; Wong, exhausted, had fallen dead asleep floating above the comms console; a couple of others had joined Mir in getting drunk. Hideyoshi didn't understand the impulse to kill brain cells as a way of celebrating, and he felt way too wired to sleep—hence the workout. The exercise regimen did help him feel more centered, even if it didn't completely make up for the lack of gravity, but it appealed to him more than spending time in the centrifuge or the vibration chamber that used high-frequency pulses to fool his body into thinking it needed to manufacture more bone and muscle cells. He preferred to sweat out his frustrations and nervous energy.

Mir idly and somewhat tipsily flicked a towel at one floating globe of evidence that Hideyoshi's efforts had at least that much effect. "Yuck, Jimmy. What is it with you and mucking the place up?"

Hideyoshi slowed, mopping his face with another towel before using it to snatch back the rest of the floating perspiration drops. "Do you some good to sweat some too. It sure beats losing the ability to walk when we get back. They're going to be carrying you off the shuttle when it finally gets here."

She stretched and shrugged. "If we get back, I'm hiring the biggest, brawniest, most beautiful man I can find to carry me anywhere I want to go. I'll celebrate my miraculous return by having him—"

An alarm buzzer sounded, interrupting both Hideyoshi's workout and, much to his relief, Mir's incipient description of her plans for her personal pack mule. He unhooked the bungee cords so quickly that the recoil flipped him halfway across the small room. Catching the handholds along the short corridor, he acknowledged Nakima's blasphemy-blackened demand to know what was going on with a quick, "Getting there, sir."

"I thought we were done with the rotted alarms," Mir groaned, pulling herself after him.

"What the—?" The numbers scrolling across Hideyoshi's lone earth-oriented scanner cut off the tectonic specialist's own remark. Line after line burned red in the display tank, the topographic data showing a massive upsurge in the Three Sisters area of Oregon. As if asteroids weren't enough, for crying out loud! As he watched the computer's report, a strong conviction settled into his mind—and gut. "Captain, looks like we've got major tectonic action downstairs. I'm seeing deep, powerful lava flows and InSAR movement all along the entire Pacific fault line. Looks like the Big Sister is going to earn her name any minute now. I can't pinpoint exact indicators right now, but it's going to blow—and it's going to be a big one."

The recurrent blast of profanity Hideyoshi expected didn't materialize. After a silence just long enough for the fleeting worry of a stroke to cross the tectonic specialist's mind, Nakima said slowly, "Patch it up, with the computer's interpretation and your own, then send word to the guys on the ground. I'll notify the bureaucracy."

"Yes, sir." Hideyoshi's fingers flew over the relays. The full communication hit the transmitter at the same time as a distant ringing came through another communications channel, this one directed at a small geology research camp deep in the overactive Oregon mountains.

"Hey, Jim!" Andre Becker's grin blinked on in the monitor. "Man, you spacemen know how to put on a show! Most of it was over by the time it got our way—just some fireworks left over from the Atlantic seaboard—but wow! Gotta hand it to you on that one. Nice predicting!" The geologist's broad smile faded as he processed the grim expression on his collaborator and friend's face.

"Got another prediction for you, Beck—and you're not going to like this one." Hideyoshi sent the data as he spoke, watching the screen reflect in Becker's eyes as the data cascaded across it. "You're going to have to pack up and get out of there—right now."

"Big Sister, all right—but this is only about a quarter of the sensors," Becker protested. "We can't pack up and leave on a quarter of the sensor data! We just set up deep-vent samplers, and the robot crawler's ready to go."

"We redeployed the rest of the sensors to watch the asteroids," Hideyoshi reminded him impatiently. "This is enough to base a solid warning on, and you know it. Send word to the emergency authorities, and get off that mountain before you get toasted!"

"I'll tell Portland and Seattle and all points in between," Becker agreed, "but if it's heating up, we should stay here, monitor events—"

"It is, and you definitely should not," Hideyoshi assured him. "Andre, listen to me. Have I ever led you wrong? You've got about six hours to get you and everybody you can grab to safety. Get to Portland—" He hesitated for a split second, testing the burn in his stomach against what he was about to say to his good-hearted but definitely unreligious friend, then plowed on when the soul-deep urgency won. "Get to the temple community in Portland. Dump the cigarettes on the way. And then stay there. Please!"

Becker looked at Hideyoshi's stressed, distorted face in the monitor, skepticism whispering dismissive reassurances in his mental ears. Balancing the scientific hardheadedness that argued for staying to double-check the crippled InSAR readings (and possibly making a breakthrough discovery that would send his career into the geology stratosphere—so to speak), the memory of what he'd seen in the Judean desert bloomed in his mind. All the water they released from previously unknown aquifers, millions of gallons of the stuff bursting out of the ground and blasting its way toward the Red Sea—that water didn't go down the hastily built channels all by itself. Sure, he'd laid out the plans and guided the crews and done all he could to guide the flood, but he knew enough about water—and about the rock under it—to know that he hadn't witnessed a strictly natural consequence of blowing the side off a mountain to deliver a river.

Glancing up at the newly active volcanic peaks above him, blackened with new, slowly cooling magma flows and coated with fine, gray dust, he knew the skeptical side had lost. "All right, we'll try it. But if you've scared me off this mountain and I lose a month's work for nothing, James, I'll take it out of your hide."

"I'll hold still," Hideyoshi promised. "Get out of there, Andre. And take everybody you can."

"Me and whose army?" Becker groused—but the second he flicked off the comm, he yelled for his grad students to pack up and use those phones of theirs for something useful for a change.

Between the geologists' efforts and Captain Nakima's forceful reminder to a functionary at Homeland Security that Garlick couldn't afford to waste the goodwill he'd inexplicably built up with the asteroid's near miss by ignoring a potentially devastating volcanic eruption right on the edge of the homeland, an all-points warning went out for the area only an hour later. The message gave the obedient, watchful, and paranoid enough warning to clear a vast patch of Oregon wilderness. Only those too ignorant, stubborn, despairing, or heedless to act on the warning stayed close enough to personally witness the largest volcanic explosion in recorded United States history. They didn't survive to add their observations to the rest of history.

The massive dome Becker had christened the Big Sister, a complex upwelling of geologic fury that united and activated the magma plumbing of three ancient volcanoes under tremendous subterranean pressures, surged violently skyward as the moon rose, copper colored already from the ash of previous eruptions. Mountains of ash, geysers of superheated rock, and clouds of volatile steam replaced miles of forested wilderness, towns, and roads. A column of smoke and fire hurled itself into the atmosphere, reaching nearly stratospheric heights before it leveled out and began to flatten, sheets of ash and choking vapor spreading in all directions like the canopy of a dark, nightmarish palm tree. Missiles of half-melted rock blew into the sky and crashed down miles away, starting fires that raged through canyons and across flatlands. Floods of sluggish, liquid stone ran down ravines and road-ways, forming delicate sprays, pillows, and tidal patterns of super-heated minerals. Far above, the ash, superheated and only slowly cooling as it billowed forward, filled the already particle-contaminated air. For miles, the incredible temperatures of the thick air flash-cooked everything in its path, converting animals, trees, and people into gray statues. It surged forward in banks and clouds, burying resort towns at the far edge of the volcanic zones and moving on to coat everything in its expanding path with clinging, astringent dust.

The sky-high bank of ash and thick air, blocking the light of the rising sun in a charcoal haze, rose like a tidal wave above Portland, poised to break over the city in a choking storm. It grew, piling up against the morning breeze, and then collapsed, falling in on itself in a wide crescent around the community surrounding the Portland Temple. Flakes of ash, as light as snowflakes, fell gently on the refugee camp around the outpost of Zion—and on Andre Becker, who stood wide-eyed, contemplating the sudden disappearance of the massive column of smoke and fire that should've come this far without noticing the sea wind.

He stared at his instruments, relaying data on equally huge explosions along fault lines stretching far out into the Pacific, down the mountain chains into Wyoming, across the unstable thermal beds of Yellowstone. Everywhere the disturbance went, pillars of smoke, steam, and fire sprang from the ground. The tale of vast upheaval played for several minutes, before the interference from the huge, heated clouds of electrically charged particles completely wiped out the transmission.

"Andre? Becker? Where are you? You okay?" Hideyoshi's voice came through the static, the ISS transmission caught and passed along the Church's network.

Becker found his voice, coughed to clear the dust and shock out of it, and managed to reply, "Yeah, Jim, I'm here, in Portland. I'm okay."

"Oh, good." Hideyoshi sat back in relief. "I'm glad. I was worried about you."

The geologist swallowed. "Man, you're the one I'm worried about."

"Why?" Hideyoshi asked, surprised.

"There's going to be a lot of upset people around here, wanting to know why we didn't stop it—or give them a few months' warning—and you're going to have to explain it to them." An incredulous grin cracked the thin coat of ash on Becker's face. "Plus, you're going to have to explain to God how I managed to escape!"

"Those with ears to hear," Hideyoshi shot back, grinning himself at the next thought. "Better grab a missionary, Andre—you're going to have some things to explain to Him yourself!" Laughing at Becker's groan, he added, "Just remember, He's a forgiving guy. Like he says, though your sins be as scarlet, they'll be white as wool."

"Too bad the weather's not going to clear up so easily," Becker muttered—but he didn't argue.

* * *

"The primary geological effects of the volcanic explosion are over," Hideyoshi explained down the link to Cal Weathers, Channel 8's chief meteorologist. "But the climatic effects are just beginning. Dr. Mir can explain what to expect."

"The ash will spread through upper-level winds and darken the sunlight," Mir said, sending her computer models of the eruption's probable effects down the visual line. "That, combined with the pollution, will have a devastating effect on crops in the northwestern U.S. and Canada, and could spread as far as China and Siberia on the transpolar winds. Unfortunately, we'll be living with the aftereffects of Big Sister's tantrum for years."

Cal, grasping for a way to lighten that news with morning-show happy talk, finally replied, "Thank you for that explanation, Dr. Mir. And I have to say, you don't look or sound like a stereotypical scientist. Your English is excellent."

Mir gave him a look that froze him right through the studio lights despite the miles between them. "Oh, yeah. It's tough learning English when you grow up in San José." With that, she broke the connection, leaving him stranded in stupidity and dead air.

"Think we hit the wrong time with her?" Monk asked Kim.

"More like the wrong year," Anne answered. "She's been stuck on that space station for months. Is it any wonder she's lost all patience?"

"So long as she's up there and I don't have to deal with her." Monk glanced over at the religion specialist standing in the control room's door and raised his eyebrows. "But look who's here. Do I have to deal with you?"

"I'd think you have enough to deal with at the moment, with the Northwest practically blown back into the dinosaur ages." Anne came into the producer's screen-lit lair, pointing at the ratings and demographic charts. Most of the northwestern United States had joined portions of England, France, and Spain as shadowy spots on the surface of the viewing world.

Monk looked at the dark patches, tapped his chin thoughtfully, and shrugged. "That's marketing's problem." He transferred the tap to the ratings monitor. "This is my problem. As long as I make sure that all the TV sets still operating stay on Channel 8, I'm happy—and so is the board. And that's the trick. Cal's just not packing them in like he used to." Casting a speculative glance at Anne, he added, "Don't suppose you're interested in being a weather bunny?"

That earned a wry laugh, equal parts disbelief and amazement at the producer's one-track mind. "Oh, I think I'll stick with religion.

I don't completely understand belief, but I'll never understand weather systems."

"Well, it was worth a shot." Monk sat forward again, gesturing to Kim, who offered a printout. "Looks like your dedication—so to speak—has earned you another big trip. The board wants you in the air to India, covering Brother Light's latest move."

"I wouldn't get near enough to Rashi Janjalani to . . ." The thought made her shudder. "I wouldn't get near him. He's completely psychotic! If I'm braving the wild skies, I'll go to Africa to cover the Christian renaissance there. That's about religion, not a South Asian power grab."

Monk considered the angles. Getting Anne to West Africa also got her that much closer to Brother Light's territory; once she was out in the field, it would be a lot easier to order her over to Asia anyway. He'd long since learned that manipulation worked a lot better than confrontation. "The Mormons, huh? Yeah, they tell you all kinds of things. So did Janjalani—for different reasons, but he still did. Looks to me like you've got an in with both sides." His narrowed eyes gave way to a sly smile. "It'd be interesting if you could arrange a little interaction for sweeps—like getting Brother Light and President Rojas to debate each other. Maybe throw Tommy Gibbs in there, just for fun."

Anne shuddered at the mental image that thought invoked. She didn't mind Tommy Gibbs—he seemed well-meaning enough—but the memory of Brother Light's smooth but perfectly sharpened malice made her skin crawl. "There is no way Richard Rojas would ever consent to that." She didn't explain that somehow she just knew that Rojas had already made the public statements he felt appropriate and wouldn't bother to bandy words with someone like Janjalani, who cared nothing for truth and less for his own people—or that she wouldn't arrange it even if it were a possibility. She couldn't offer anything but gut feeling, and flatly refusing a theoretical request from Monk wouldn't work to her advantage. "I'm not a diplomat, Monk. You hired me to cover the religion beat, and that's what I'm going to do. I report the news; I don't create it—or stage-manage it."

Her tone irritated Monk. He'd picked her off the roster of some obscure, little local station and given her a slot at Channel 8 that other reporters would kill to get—and now she got all righteous with him? She'd soaked up way too much holier-than-thou attitude from the religious fanatics he sent her out to interview. "How do you make a living as an investigative reporter with your eyes tight shut? Word to the wise, Anne: you may not have the religion beat if you keep favoring the Mormons. You disobeyed a standing memo, leaking that Mormon broadcast. If it hadn't worked, the board would've had your head on a plate. News is more than news—it's business. And when it comes to business, Channel 8 demands results."

"I report things the way I see them," Anne said calmly. The thought of joining the aimless mobs on the street without the safety net Channel 8 and its money provided chilled her to the bone. She rationalized backing down by thinking that she could do more good within the system. "I felt the public had a right to know what President Smith said, rather than feeding them speculation. And, as you yourself said, it worked. People want to know, and I can get the stories they're looking for. And the Mormons know they can trust me—and they still have screens that work."

Monk couldn't argue with that. Still, he warned, "You just better be sure that your journalistic ethics don't get in the way of putting ratings on the board or money in the advertising budget. Now get out of here. You and that flower-shirted nut cameraman of yours have a plane to catch. If the flight hasn't been cancelled again."

* * *

"All scheduled flights to the American Northwest have been cancelled due to extreme weather conditions—and pending cleanup of the volcanic ash covering the Seattle-Tacoma, Portland, and other regional airports," Clara said from the news floor. "Flight control on the East Coast reports day-long delays and cancellations as well, as the remnants of Tropical Storms Xenia and Yvette blast the country from Texas to New York. In fact, with all the cancellations, it looks like a good time for our travel expert to be on vacation. We just hope you get back all right, Teresa!" In the crawl along the bottom of the screen, airlines advertised desperate conditional-bargain-fare rates just in case the weather settled down; immediately following, Armstrong Associates' Insta-Suit Service offered online lawsuit filing for all those frustrated, stranded travelers.

Shots of storm-wracked docks replaced the airport maps and empty runways. "The extreme weather conditions have also disrupted overseas shipping for many areas," Clara noted. "Businesses report dire losses all over the world, due to shortages of materials and manufactured goods on one hand and surpluses of raw materials on the other. In the few areas where businesses manage to conduct business as usual, retailers report heavy losses; it seems that consumer confidence is at an all-time low."

Frustrated, aimless people wandered in a street scene, looking for work or simply staring off into space as their still-employed peers bustled by, trying not to make eye contact. The ever-present ads scrolled beside the images; the not-so-subtle message was, "You're better off than the losers who don't have jobs—and here's the way to show it!"

"While the United States is better off than many areas of the world, consumers have a lot to worry about here as well," Clara observed. "The unprecedented storms boiling up from the Gulf have killed crops and shut down shipping lanes and disrupted air travel. That same weather, along with acts of sabotage and an already overstressed power grid, has resulted in rolling blackouts throughout the East and West Coasts." Dramatic footage of tornadoes, high seas, and volcanic eruptions said more than Clara's intentionally mild words conveyed. "In a statement from Homeland Security, Secretary Garlick extended congratulations to the courageous workers who have kept local power grids online, keeping their neighborhood lights on. 'If we all do our part, the lights will never go out on this great country!'"

Only Anne—and a few observant viewers—realized that over half the communities in the heartwarming montage of well-lit roads, peaceful houses, bustling country stores, and green farmlands that accompanied his speech were from Mormon temple communities. Only Kim knew exactly where the images had come from—and she also knew that the last thing Monk wanted to show was the inner-city and poor-rural desolation that made the United States look uncomfortably like the second- and third-world countries whose dire images accompanied the first part of Clara's report.

* * *

Mr. Abbott, MedaGen's CEO, leaned back in his leather chair, hands behind his head, watching worried MedaGen executives and lawyers shout at each other. As Ms. Zelik, the COO, came in, the sound of his open hands hitting the glassy black surface of the conference table cut through the noise. All eyes turned toward him. "Well, boys and girls, what say we all sit down and figure out how to remove the pain from our collective neck?"

He continued when they settled. "So, to summarize, patients who haven't been smart enough to get their AllSafe booster shots are dying of massive allergy attacks. Which means lawsuits are cropping up against MedaGen left and right. We're all highly upset. Have I missed anything important?"

"Just the protesters who shut down our Saint Louis office with firebombs," Humphrey suggested. "And the ones inside our parking garage at the moment."

"And the federal grand jury," muttered Frieze, MedaGen's chief counsel. He'd already spent two uncomfortable weeks in Washington, D.C., testifying before a federal grand jury. "Luckily, the lawsuits have a thin legal basis—as the grand-jury investigators have finally begun to admit. Everyone who got an AllSafe vaccination signed a fully legal consent form stating that they realized that AllSafe might require boosters and are therefore on record as accepting the possibility—and indemnifying MedaGen of any damages resulting from the patients' own negligence in failing to obtain said booster, so long as it is readily available. Which it is, and we have ample proof of the fact."

"So legally, if they're sick, it's their own fault." Abbott nodded. "That takes care of legal. Frieze, you handle Armstrong Associates and their nuisance suits. Now, how do we get the public back to buying our product—and the boosters? Errol?"

Marketing director Errol Humphrey waved casually at the images glowing under the table surface. "We're keeping up the ad campaigns for the booster, but Virginia's losing her luster. When you've shown it all, you don't have anything else to show. So we're going with plan B, reminding everybody that we're their best hope for healthy kids growing up in a dangerous world."

"Very nice," Abbott approved. "I like the guilt angle. Okay, time to apologize for unspecified people's incompetence, promise to help the FDA be more responsible, and show a lot of happy kids running around. All right, boys and girls, get out there and make me proud— your jobs are depending on it!"

"Dodging blame for the booster will put a lot of pressure on Garlick," Zelik reminded Abbott as the last lieutenant and lawyer left. "We may lose our strongest advocate in the government, if he folds under the pressure. The polls haven't been kind lately."

"He won't fold, because he can't afford to," Abbot said confidently, snipping and lighting a cigar. "And if he does, we've got Garza on our side."

"As long as Twilley's doing well with Pacifica," Zelik commented.

CHAPTER 11

Secretary Garlick, hurrying to a press conference to answer the latest allegations from the class-action lawsuits, waved off the FBI agent trying to warn him about a possible outbreak of bioterror, based on reports from their South American informants. "It's that stupid AllSafe inoculation, Ettinger."

"But, sir, there's no indication that AllSafe would do what we're seeing in New Mexico—" Ettinger persisted, trying to hand Garlick the report.

That earned him a glare from the secretary. "You earned a promotion from the FBI for being smart about those meth runners in Wisconsin," he said. "Don't give me any reason to think you're stupid now. It's AllSafe—we're up to our necks in a lawsuit that says it's AllSafe!"

Ettinger was smart—but his kind of intelligence was suited better to investigation and finding answers than recognizing and negotiating the politically charged atmosphere of the Homeland Security hierarchy. They'd promoted him to give themselves a public-relations boost after he'd helped expose the collusion between meth cooks, gunrunners, and some religious fanatics in the Midwest; they didn't bargain that he would take the promotion and his new duties seriously. "They're lawyers, not doctors. I've got medical reports from all over the West."

Garlick grabbed the report and threw it hard at the recycle bin, pausing only to stab a finger into the former FBI agent's chest. "It's AllSafe. That blasted lawsuit says it's AllSafe, I say it's AllSafe, you say it's AllSafe. Now go do something useful about that idiot Travell Capshaw!"

On the screen over his shoulder, the Channel 8 news update caught Ettinger's attention. If the senator wouldn't listen to the warnings about

General Garza's possible involvement in bioterror, maybe someone else would.

* * *

"The blame game heats up as the death toll rises," Clara announced over footage of doctors, policemen, medical executives, and politicians all pointing fingers at each other. "Adding to the panic are reports that the Office of Homeland Security may have information about a possible outbreak of man-made plague along our southern border. A report leaked from the Office of Homeland Security reveals that field agents had reported suspicious deaths, but the reports were not acted upon at the time."

"Do we have the source of the leak yet?" Monk asked Kim, watching the roster of commentators eager to grab some of the limelight from the political fat crackling merrily in the fire. "They're going to sacrifice somebody over this; you can just see it in Garlick's eyes." Reading over the report his assistant sent to his console, the producer's smile widened. A photo of Ettinger appeared in the electronic packet, as did copies of several medical reports about the plague. "Looks like somebody's eager-beaver ethics got out ahead of protecting the secretary's tail. Did I say that hiring FBI field agents for office personnel would bite them, or did I say it?"

In the dark cave of his control room, Monk appreciated the ratings boost from breaking the exclusive report; nothing like a spreading outbreak of invisible but dramatically nasty bugs to glue people to their sets for updates and health tips from experts. Well satisfied with the world's events, the producer sat back to orchestrate just the right amount of hysteria.

* * *

Dear Chisom,

I'm feeling down today. I hope you don't mind if I lean on your shoulder a bit. My job has certain requirements that bring me stress. One is that I have to keep up on the news. The other is that I have to keep up on what our enemies are saying about us.

Fortunately, the two sometimes overlap, saving me time. Neither brings me pleasure. Do you find that to be the case where you are? It upsets me that the news continues to focus primarily on what the producers think will sell advertising space. Consequently, they show the worst. The worst, however, is so awful that I can hardly bear it.

One sickening reality that the news brought home tonight is that some ugly prophecies are being fulfilled. Pictures were shown of areas where, due to war and other preventable horrors, plague has broken out. In Africa, South America, Indonesia, and other places, plagues run rampant. Some sections of the U.S. have not been spared. The irony is that here, the agents of the disease are not the result of Mother Nature gone mad but of human beings corrupted by pride and greed. As Merry Galen warned, AllSafe has proven to be anything but safe. Now many are learning the hard way what it means to ignore the warning of a righteous woman and the Lord's prophets.

The clips on the news have given visual images and testimony to the words in Doctrine and Covenants 29, where the Lord warned that "because of the wickedness of the world, . . . I will take vengeance upon the wicked, for they will not repent." He promised He will "send forth flies upon the face of the earth, which shall take hold of the inhabitants thereof, and shall eat their flesh, and shall cause maggots to come in upon them; and their tongues shall be stayed that they shall not utter against me; and their flesh shall fall from off their bones, and their eyes from their sockets; and it shall come to pass that the beasts of the forest and the fowls of the air shall devour them up." Oh, how I wish these words were just a metaphor, but the news proves their reality. The images I saw have upset my stomach, and my anguish has, I fear, spilled over into this letter. The Lord clearly warned us that when the generation of the Gentiles comes to a close, we shall "see an overflowing scourge; for a desolating sickness shall cover the land." Well, here it is.

So, using you as a vent for my disgust and outrage, let me say that what torments my soul is that some of these diseases have been human engineered. We are seeing an outbreak in the States of a bacterial infection that Church sources hint is man-made. We'll have to wait to see if that idea is confirmed. I hope not. I cannot imagine people so cold and obscenely wicked that they would make such germs. One thing I have learned, however, is that there are people out there who would do deeds uglier than most of us can imagine. How long can such a world stand? I know the answer—not much longer. And all I can say is, "Thank the Lord." Every hour in our temples and homes, the Saints pray for this nightmare to end. I delight in knowing our prayers will make a difference. How do I know? The Revelator saw this period and noted that in heaven an angel "came and stood at the altar, having a golden censer; and there was given unto him much incense, that he should offer it with the prayers of all saints upon the golden altar which was before the throne. And the smoke of the incense, which came with the prayers of the saints, ascended up before God out of the angel's hand." What was the result? God moved to end the wickedness and destruction.

The Saints are now free from the dangers of the spiritual and physical horrors, but we still feel for those who are not, and their sorrow, fear, and terror pains us. For that reason, we figuratively keep our gates open day and night, inviting all who do not want to live in such a world to find peace with us. It breaks my heart that so many would rather die in this man-made hell than live in our earthly heaven. I fear this letter is much too gloomy. I'm sorry about that. I hope my blowing off steam does not cause you undue distress. It does feel good to talk about this even if I can't do anything about it. At least that will spare your mother from getting the whole dose.

By the way, she's grown even more wonderful since you left. I am so blessed she is mine. She has a calming effect on me that I need so much during this time of trial.

Speaking of that, now that you are no longer a missionary, you need to be planning for the future. You never mention any social life in your Vids. I know you are busy, but I hope you are taking time to relax and maybe do some dating.

One more item before I sign off. I am pleased that in your region of the world, at least, peace seems to prevail for the present.

I understand that the Church has begun a farm in your area. If it goes like the others, it should be producing well. Though not all our farms escape local problems, most are not hit as hard and some flourish. The result is that, overall, the Church farms continue to yield good crops and our canneries are busy and storehouses full. Another result is that it often drives our enemies into a fury because we thrive.

Well, I better sign off now, while I'm feeling better and before I start venting about other problems. Please know that Adaure and I are pleased with you and delight in your service to the kingdom. Just keep working.

With love,
Your father,
Chinedu

* * *

"Who's doing this to me?" Garlick shouted, waving an anonymous letter. The writer threatened in no uncertain terms that Garlick had deeply disappointed his party with his handling of the AllSafe crisis and would pay the price for his bungling. "Ms. Lincoln! Where the great blazes did this thing come from?"

"Someone in the Senate," his secretary said.

"What?" he blinked.

"It's from someone in the Senate," she repeated. "I noticed as I laid out your mail that it was written on the cloakroom stationery."

"Of course it is," he finally growled, stomping back into his office. Anonymous letters on top of dire news reports. He shook his head, muttering to himself, "If this keeps up, Holly Cox will eat us alive."

* * *

"I'm not interested in eating Garlick alive," protested Senator Holly Cox, member of the Judiciary Committee and consistent anti-Garlick crusader. "I'm not interested in eating him dead. I'm not interested in any sort of political cannibalism, of Howard Garlick or anyone else. I just want the man stopped! Senator White, we can't let him continue like this. He's building Homeland Security into his own private kingdom, trampling civil liberties on the way, and he's utterly blind to the threats the president was manipulated into hiring him to prevent!"

She visibly trembled in place with intensity and focused energy; she also took personal responsibility and political integrity to nosebleed levels. She was as straight as a ruler among corkscrews—and nobody could play her either. Still, the opportunity to channel all that energy to his ends was undeniably tempting.

"William, please. Let's not stand on ceremony, Holly. We're colleagues here." Senator William White, longtime personal and political enemy of Howard W. Garlick, wheezed a sigh. "You want him stopped," White repeated judiciously. "What would you do to stop him?"

"Is this the part where I say 'anything at all,' like the idiot ingénue, so you can leer and say '*Anything?*'" Cox rolled her eyes. "William, let's please not play melodrama. Despite our differences, this is serious. Howard's getting close to overturning the establishment clause, exerting state control over religion as well as doing away with protections against search and seizure. All the while, we're losing the battle against crime and terrorism on every front, the president has withdrawn into some kind of denial fugue, and citizens and judges are so frightened that they'll agree to anything to stop the violence."

"So how do you propose to rectify the situation?" White inquired.

"I propose to have him investigated, convicted of malfeasance, and thrown out," Cox returned. "The reason I'm here is that an effort like that will take heavy political pressure. I have a couple of allies, but not enough. If we join forces, we'll be able to get the votes we need."

White found the offer tempting—and the fact that she made it herself, without hesitation or game playing, confirmed the rumors that she had solid reasons and proof for opposition to Garlick. She wanted to protect the Constitution, motherhood, apple pie, and the American way.

"Maybe we could, maybe we couldn't," he cautioned. "And while I don't deny I'd love to nail that polecat's hide to a wall, we need a real smoking gun to go against him and his posse."

"Nice accent there." Cox looked at him, a hint of a smile playing around the corners of her mouth. "Oh, please, William—you've never seen a polecat."

"Doesn't mean I can't call our friend Howard one," White pointed out placidly.

"True. And we can call Garlick all the names we want without pushing him one step out the door." Cox tilted her palm screen toward him. "Look. With the AllSafe implosion and the West Coast crime spree all coming together, Howard's poll numbers are falling to their lowest levels ever. We don't need a smoking gun when we've got a loaded one."

White gently pushed her hand away. "To use another rural saying, Holly, don't teach your granddad to suck eggs." He stood up from the deep armchair with an ease that belied his old-man act. "Yeah, his poll numbers are falling and MedaGen's stock is going down. They won't be able to help him if we make our move at the right time. He's looking vulnerable to the public too. He promised security; he hasn't delivered."

"Even if there's nothing he can do about earthquakes, volcanoes, and storms," Cox noted.

"That kind of knee-jerk honesty will sink your political career, Miss Holly," White warned her, with a twinkle. "Or might, if being a weasel were the only way to get ahead in the game. Speaking of which, some Homeland Security underlings have been squeaking."

"Oh?" she asked. It didn't surprise her; Homeland Security had come under heavy fire, and it looked like Garlick had decided to shift blame for the buried bioterror reports onto anyone else.

"Sure enough." White leaned against the edge of his desk. "Seems that to help get their tails out of a sling, Howard's minions have been making visits to some of our colleagues. The most senior of them haven't exactly come out and said it, but there are hints that they know things that could help them—for a price."

"And will they pay?" Cox asked.

"Turns out they will. Ol' Howard's in for a rough ride." He extended a hand, which she took, sealing the temporary alliance. "How does it feel, Holly? You've gone and made a deal with the devil."

"If you were the devil, William, there wouldn't be a deal," she assured him. "I hope we can work together again—on the side of the angels."

The first ads hit the air before she finished the commute home to her Georgetown apartment, where her husband greeted her with a hug, a kiss, and an order to set the table while she told him about her day.

* * *

"Just ask yourself: Do I feel more secure now?" asked the announcer, over images of bullet holes, bloody ambulance gurneys, and fresh graves with Garlick's snarling face superimposed over them all. "Homeland Security needs more than big talk—it needs big results."

"And so starts the next big story," Monk observed, directing Kim to cue up Garlick's equally substanceless but more vitriolic electronic riposte. With both sides running attack ads, the war looked to be a profitable one for Channel 8—the media equivalent of a cheerfully bipartisan arms dealer.

"Has the Office of Homeland Security forgotten about providing homeland security?" Darren McInnes asked portentously. "Several members of the Senate have come forward to say yes. My guest today, Senator Holly Cox, is a well-known opponent of Howard W. Garlick, secretary of Homeland Security. After months of being the lone voice in the wilderness, it appears that you finally have support from some of your fellow senators. To what do you attribute this surprising turnaround?"

"I don't see it as surprising," Cox said. "Secretary Garlick has used Homeland Security to enhance his own political power at the expense of the most basic American liberties while conspicuously failing to promote a safe environment for his fellow citizens. It's no wonder that other leaders are finally holding him accountable. The only unfortunate aspect is that they gave him so much rope to hang himself."

"The problem with her is that she's way too nice," Lucrezia Callatta declared, looking up from preparing lunches for the day. She gestured at the screen as Senator Cox admitted that Homeland Security couldn't have foreseen the exact moment that the Big Sister volcano erupted, and praised the local authorities who expedited the evacuation. "She's giving them points instead of coming out all claws and teeth."

"Shows she's one of ours." Tony wrestled Gianni into his sweater, maneuvering the sleeve around the toy car that the kid wouldn't let go of. Gianni watched the process, interested to see how his daddy would overcome that obstacle. "She's got to be fair and honest—unlike a lot of those guys."

"She's going to get creamed," Lucrezia sighed, with all the cynicism of her fifteen years.

"She's going to win," Carmen said firmly. "She's got the Lord behind her. So we can let her do it without armchair quarterbacking her left and right." Flicking off the set, she added, "And we've got better things to do than watch outside news shows. Get moving; time to go earn your keep." She bustled and kissed them out the door, snatching up Gianni and walking the other direction with Donna, toward the school where both of them herded little kids on weekends while the bigger kids worked with the grown-ups.

Lucrezia put her headphones on as Brother Sarkesian and Bishop Newstead joined them, and the conversation turned to wire gauges and the best strategies for setting up the solar collectors for the new street of houses they were building. She hummed to the end of the Seraph song playing on the Church's radio broadcast as she watched the green fields flow by the van windows, then half listened to the ads while she scanned the sky, only partially cloudy today, as the wind shifted to blow the smoke and ash west instead of east. In her ears, expertly crafted spots called for people to repent, to care for their families, to stay honest, to live good lives, to have hope and faith. The messages, along with the comedy routines, news updates, and music, beamed out of every Church settlement across the airwaves to anyone who would tune in—and completely amazed the secular stations with their popularity. A couple of the big broadcasting conglomerates, Channel 8's radio and Net division included, had tried to shut them down by petitioning the FCC, but the Church had met all the licensing requirements. Now they were trying to use Homeland Security to stop the broadcasts as anti-American—which efforts Senator Cox was fighting to stop.

The thought of a little Church-run radio station making international media monsters nervous brought a smug grin to Lucrezia's face. If they had anything interesting to say, they wouldn't have to worry about losing listeners to the Mormons, who provided entertaining, informative programs—and a big dose of positive propaganda about living a good life and getting out of the mess the world was in by coming to Zion. If Nauvoo was any indication, it was working too. The whole town was buzzing; more people were arriving every day, settling into temporary shelters while they waited for a more permanent place. All the Zion towns used the same basic patterns, she knew from the broadcasts. New neighborhoods with gridded streets grew between stretches of farmland, with the necessary businesses, factories, water stations, and solar power plants nearby. Independent of outside power and supplies, designed for sustainable, environmentally friendly growth, the plans for the new Mormon settlements had risen to the challenge of providing for an unprecedented influx of new, and often destitute, residents. Setting it all up, however, entailed more work than Lucrezia had ever imagined.

Thus, on a Saturday morning after a long week in school, she set her lunch bag down beside her father's and went to work helping to build more houses for the newcomers. And, at long last, for her own family; their ward area had finally made it to the top of the list for a real neighborhood. She looked at the raw boards and dangling wires with a swell of proprietary pride, glad to be pounding nails instead of tending kids like Donna. As Tony said, though, the division of responsibilities worked because people had different tastes and preferences. Donna would rather herd a bunch of hyperactive ten-year-olds through a science experiment; Lucrezia would rather take the chance of permanently maiming her thumbnail with a hammer. It all got done in the end.

The amazing thing was that it did work. Lucrezia glanced around at the bustling work crew, sharing a quick grin with Imre Sarkesian as he went by with a large roll of electrical wire. They'd talked about Karl Marx in history class, about what went wrong with the ideal of "from every man according to his ability, to every man according to his need," and why it would work in Zion. After the teacher, with a smile, corrected the concept to "every person," the class had reached a consensus that a society like that could succeed only when it had the right leaders, and when everybody honestly looked out for others, not just for themselves, and did whatever they needed to do just because it needed doing, not for their own enrichment. Come Monday, Tony would be back at the computer too, programming the eye-catching interfaces for the Church's Net sites, part of the drive to educate current members and put the word out to people who hadn't heard the gospel yet; Donna would be pounding science into the heads of reluctant junior high students; Carmen and Gianni would be helping out at the preschool, training up proto-kindergarteners. Weekends, everybody pitched in with the extra work that needed doing to take care of hundreds, and, internationally, thousands of immigrants, everybody doing what they could to keep the entire thing rolling along, whether or not they'd done that kind of thing in their lives before. Which is how a former software multimillionaire like Rob Sarkesian ended up grimy and whistling while he put up drywall next to Everest's dad, who used to be a surf bum and extreme-sports athlete.

The Church had an amazing ability to use everybody's talents, known or unknown, to their best advantage. Merry Galen, for example, was working a couple thousand miles away in a lab in Salt Lake City trying to figure out how to keep people from dying from AllSafe allergies. The thought of her mother's friend led to memories of her daughter Missy—and Merry's husband, Chris, who'd started the whole campaign against AllSafe when he ran into some suspicious files in MedaGen's network. He'd died in a car crash that turned out to be just a stupid accident, even if Carmen still suspected that MedaGen would've liked to bump him off. His easy smile, ruffled hair, and the way he treated Merry like his one true love made it easy for Lucrezia to develop a massive crush on him; she still had a hard time believing he was dead.

Teenage fatalism kicked in with the next thought: *But that's how all the guys I like seem to end up.* Memories of Porter Smith, with his own sweet smile, brought a lump to her throat. She took a deep breath, taking comfort in Carmen's confident assurance that Porter would be all right; he had been doing what he thought was right, obeying his parents, even if that meant following his crazy father into a war zone. But she didn't want to think about that right now. As if proving her right, the hammer glanced off the staple and smacked into her hand. Sucking her smarting finger, she glared at the recalcitrant bit of metal before pounding it securely, and carefully, into place.

"Fulfill the measure of your creation, you obstinate thing," she commanded, co-opting Tony's phrase. *So what will I end up doing?* she wondered, stapling the last length of wire up the side of a stud and running its end into the socket box. *What's the measure of my creation? What do you do when the world's ended but not gone away?*

"You're going to make a great electrician at this rate." Tony rubbed her back, looking over the wiring job.

She grinned. "Maybe that'll be my calling in life. I'd better be good at it, at the rate people are gathering!"

* * *

The image of green leaves fluttering in a gentle breeze caught Ettinger's eye. He stared for a second at the screen attached to the stall door as the peaceful scene replaced the customary ads for the latest hot brand of intoxicant. He thought about the leaf ad's message of hope and peace as he assembled the gun he'd smuggled through the Imperial Club's previously compromised security system.

Ettinger wiped his forehead on the sleeve of his garish jacket, careful not to smudge the fake tattoos around his eyes. He muttered an expletive of his own, a general statement of his reaction to being busted down to foot soldier on an operation he'd helped plan. Garlick made sure he knew why he'd been reassigned from Homeland Security to "give front-line assistance" to the FBI's West Coast antiterror unit too; saving lives was no excuse for releasing Homeland Security reports on the bioterror threats to hospitals, even if Homeland Security had decided to ignore them. Calling him a Boy Scout just added insult to injury.

Moving his head to peer between the door and frame, he checked the occupants of the black and neon room in the long mirror. His target—the seven-foot bruiser—wore the insignia of Travell Capshaw's inner circle. "Bigfoot's moving back," he said into the microphone tucked into the choker around his neck.

"Daddy's in place," the answering voice whispered through his earring, which meant that Capshaw had settled into his usual downstage pit in the exclusive Hollywood nightspot.

The gangster's brazen confidence made Ettinger's teeth grind. When a federal prosecutor pressed racketeering and tax evasion charges, Capshaw's crew shot up an IRS office in broad daylight, daring the authorities to come after them. Capshaw even gave a TV interview about it. "The feds gonna come down here, they gotta be ready to play. We just keeping it local."

It had just stopped being local. After a delay that Ettinger didn't want to speculate about, Homeland Security finally authorized putting a stop to Capshaw's reign of terror. If the governor of California wouldn't step in, the FBI would. A soft hum from the agent's earring gave the signal that the stepping in would begin now.

Ettinger burst out of the stall door, dodging around psychedelically dressed patrons in the rest room, and plunged into the main room. A dozen other FBI agents—bartenders, waiters, and patrons—threw off stealth mode, pulling out their weapons. The ring converged on Travell Capshaw and his crew. The plan Ettinger had worked out said that the three female agents schmoozing the gangster and his buddies should hit the entire posse with knockout gas and get out of the way so the rest of the detachment could round up the escapees and truss the sleepers for delivery to a federal prison. Somebody had changed the plans.

Smoke plumes rose from the VIP pit, but it was tear gas, not knockout vapor. Shots and screams drowned in the roar of the sound system as the club's inhabitants realized that their opium den had morphed into a war zone. Capshaw's giant bodyguard reared up out of the fog, letting loose with a barrage from the illegal machine pistol tucked like a toy into his huge hand. Showers of sparks erupted and the lights went out. Darkness descended, the noise of curses, crashes, and heavy thuds painting a vivid picture of chaos between amber flashes of emergency lighting.

"What's going on? Capture, not kill!" Ettinger screamed into his comm, shoving panicked civilians to the ground to get them out of the line of fire. "Crawl—fast, toward that exit," he ordered, smacking them on their way before demanding again, "Ettinger here—this wasn't in the plan! Capture, not kill! What the Hades is going on?" He got no answer, and in another second, he didn't need one.

Capshaw, a gun in each hand, shouted that they would never take the King of California alive. One of the undercover agents, abandoning her pose as a waitress, tried to grab Capshaw's wrist and got a bullet in the face. Grabbing her as she fell, he used her body as a shield, muscling his way toward the exit. Around him, the remaining gangsters got organized, taking cover as best they could around the perimeter. The agents redoubled their fire to pin them down. Through the stinging haze of tear gas and smoke from the burning curtains, Capshaw's big bodyguard spotted a gap in the attackers' line and shouted for his boss to go that way. Capshaw flung the dead agent away and dove for the opening—only to meet a bouncing ball of metal coming through the same gap.

"Grenade!" Ettinger shouted. He'd seen the little package too, and knew what it meant. He and the two agents nearest him ran for the doors, shoving the terrified mob ahead of them.

The flash of the explosion reflected from an intricate pattern of sequins embedded in the dress of the woman in front of him, and then the blast wave hit, throwing the FBI agent into her—and a table into him. *So this is what Garlick meant by doing something useful about Capshaw,* he thought, before he fell into the spinning vortex filling his head.

* * *

"They're bringing him out in pieces," a soot-streaked EMT informed the camera. "Him and about sixty others, civilians mostly." Behind him, crews combed through the smoking shell of the Imperial Club, retrieving what remained and what evidence they could find in the mess.

"And so ends the reign of the self-proclaimed King of California, Travell Capshaw," Clara intoned. "Will the fall of the King topple other rulers as well?"

"Tell you this, Tip Buchanan backed the wrong horse this time," a grinning FBI director opined to the camera.

"He sure did," chuckled Howard Garlick, watching the broadcast from the comfort of his plush office. The right man at the right time with the right bomb, and his erstwhile allies got carried out in body bags, with very few gangsters captured alive. The secretary smiled and raised his glass to the screen.

* * *

The scowl on Caesar Augosto's face, on the other hand, was anything but happy.

"Woo, would you look at that?" crowed Johnny Mack, gleefully punching Smokey's shoulder. "Man, did I tell you that uppity punk'd get a faceful of lead, or what? Got your education now, didn't you, Travell? That'll show you!"

"Yes, that will show the uppity punk." Augosto rose, cutting off his bodyguard's jubilation. "But it'll show us too." He gazed out the window at the exquisite view of his rose garden.

"What'll it show us?" Johnny Mack asked, several mental paces behind.

"It'll show us that Garlick isn't to be trusted." Augosto turned his glare from the roses to Johnny Mack and the looming bulk of Smokey behind him. "Get the spooks on his trail. I want them looking closely at the senator."

"Sure, boss," Smokey agreed. "But why?"

"Because the next time the secretary of Homeland Security needs a big bust, it just might be us he chooses to show the world his power," Augosto explained patiently. Smokey made up for his slow processor with lightning-fast reflexes and unquestioning loyalty.

"Not cool." Johnny Mack scowled as the full implication struck home.

"No," Augosto agreed. "Definitely not cool."

He left the office, his two bodyguards falling in behind him, kissed his impatiently waiting wife's cheek, and climbed into the limousine waiting to take them to Tommy Gibbs's blockbuster revival. Mrs. Augosto had embarked on yet another quest to save his soul. He'd humor her— and use the two hours and his electronic organizer to set the gears on the machine that would destroy Garlick if he so much as hinted that he intended to raise a hand to Augosto's empire.

* * *

"The Empire of Light, as some commentators call the ever-expanding religion of the Unity of the One God, whose adherents are known simply as the Children of Light, made a dramatic march into the heart of the Bible Belt today." Anne O'Neal read the teleprompter's copy with a straight face, hiding her distaste for the subject as well as the hyperactive style. She narrated the report from a hotel room in Atlanta, stuck in the city while the rain poured down and the winds howled out the remnant of the thirtieth tropical storm this season.

Under her voice, images of the gathering of white-robed Children of Light appeared. Nothing about the scene itself was unusual: the white robes, the dancing, the flower petals strewn before a gilded image of the Prophet, the black cloaks and red masks of the Hands of the Prophet standing silent guard around the ceremony of devotions. No, the truly groundbreaking element of the video was where the Children of Light held their rally. Atlanta, Georgia, had never seen such an event.

"No one expected such a large crowd to appear here in conservative Atlanta on a 'day of celebration' decreed by the self-proclaimed Prophet," she noted. "With this event, Atlanta joins the growing number of American cities hosting the rave-style sacramental services of the Children of Light. Will this trend continue? Tune in to Channel 8's special report, 'Spreading the Light: Unity in America.'"

"And we're out," Leon said, as the red light atop his camera died.

"Not a minute too soon." Anne paced over to the window, gazing out at the soggy, green and gray airport beyond the hotel's grounds. "Thinking about those Hands in the same city—it makes my skin crawl."

The cameraman nodded sympathetically. "Don't let it crawl too far. One of my buddies in air traffic control said there's a good chance the weather will break and we'll be out of here tonight, winging our way to Africa, a long way from Rashi Janjalani and his homies."

"I hope so," Anne shivered slightly. "I just can't shake this feeling that I'm going to run into him again."

"Maybe," Leon shrugged noncommittally. He caught her arm as she passed, giving her a reassuring look. "But if we do, we'll give him a run for his money. There might be a sucker born every minute, and ol' Rashi may be ready to take him, but we're not suckers." He sighed, flipping the feed line on the camera from record to transmit. "Even if it sometimes feels like we're the only ones left."

They weren't the only ones—just part of a shrinking minority of people who didn't buy the vague, permissive, glamorous teachings of the One Prophet. New York's Central Park, Chicago's Wrigley Field, San Francisco's Candlestick Park, Houston's Astrodome, and Hollywood Boulevard made perfect stages for Brother Light's recruiting campaigns, American backdrops for the Prophet's worldwide broadcasts—commercials for the radical new faith that converted its founding scriptures to motion pictures and created miracles out of special effects. It worked just as well as the other media campaigns—and the media loved Brother Light, because he always made for excellent copy. Even his refusal to set foot in the nation falling in love with him only made Rashi Janjalani more popular. Would-be groupies formed fan clubs on the Net and in neighborhoods; pilgrims seized breaks in the worldwide storms to travel to Manila, New Delhi, Singapore, and anywhere else they thought Brother Light might be; celebrities dim and brilliant declared themselves one with the Unity.

As much inspiration and devotion as Brother Light inspired in the new-age types all over the West, he provoked more intensely morbid fascination in Christian, Muslim, and other religious leaders.

"Any path that leads away from our Lord Jesus Christ is a path to certain damnation," Tommy Gibbs declared, his eyes dark with warning. "Rashi Janjalani is no different than that other diabolical being who called himself a son of the morning—Lucifer himself. All Christians, all good-hearted folk everywhere, must turn away from him as they would turn away from a devil in hooves and horns. Do not tempt the Lord thy God by following this false shepherd, this ravening wolf!" Raising his hands dramatically, he intoned, "Get thee behind me, Satan!"

"Extremes of all kinds disturb harmony," a bald, serenely confident Buddhist abbot said, gently adjusting his saffron robe over one bare shoulder. "Only by transcending struggle can we be truly free."

"By his presence in the great and holy city of Kandahar, the infidel has insulted Allah's chosen messenger," intoned Mullah Ahman Akbar. The cleric's deep frown drew his bushy eyebrows down almost to meet his long sideburns and beard. "We declare a fatwa, a jihad in the name of the one true God and His prophet against all those who call themselves the Children of Light!"

Brother Light, a sad smile on his face under those remarkable eyes, said, "Opposing the Unity places one outside the protection of the One God, in the darkness beyond the Light. And demons lurk in that darkness." He gazed deeply into the camera over the French correspondent's shoulder. His hand, below the view of the lens, gestured to one side, the rings on his fingers sparkling.

Sepphira glanced aside at the demon, who nodded its blob of a head and smiled, the illusion of red embers glowing in the nightmare slit of its mouth. Her desperate need for Rashi's approval drowned thoughts of escape or protest. She threw her head back, a low wail beginning deep in her throat. As she opened her mouth, the wraith swept in, filling her chest and lungs. Her eyes blanked, the ebony irises disappearing under her bruised eyelids. "Mullah Akbar will die," she whispered, her voice deepened to a smoky roar. "The One God reigns! The God of this world will repay!" A convulsion jerked through her, sending her to the floor. She fought against the evil inside her, clawing at her throat, helpless whimpers choking the demon laughter. Crashing to the floor, she rolled helplessly, a bundle of blue cloths wrapped around a rack of trembling bones.

Two of Brother Light's black-robed bodyguards sprang forward, catching Sepphira's bloodstained hands, picking her up. A medic, hastily summoned, stabbed a silver needle into the woman's leg. The anesthetic spread through her body, removing the demon's control. It spread out of her in a dark puddle, oozing back into the air, gnashing its flame teeth.

Three days later, Mullah Akbar burned to death in his mosque, despite his disciples' ready guns and paranoid vigilance. The proud, vitriolic cleric, his eyes turned outward to face threats from the infidel, never foresaw that the hand of his trusted deputy would close the mosque doors and bar them from the outside, never realized that Brother Light had promised power and control to the man who stood in Akbar's shadow in return for his silence and cooperation. The demons never made a mistake when they whispered the names of those who lusted for gold, burned with envy, harbored secret grudges; with phantom laughter, they showed Sepphira the mental levers Rashi should pull, the emotional buttons to push to arm and detonate a human weapon. The Hands of the Prophet, waiting the signal their master told them to watch for, materialized out of the night, silent as the shadows that filled their eyes. They lit the fires that transformed the graceful, ancient structure into an oven, melting back into the rapidly melting darkness as pillars of flame rose like prayers to heaven. The next day, Mullah Akbar's beloved disciple took his predecessor's place in the hearts of the devoted disciples—and within a week, lay dead in the street, the victim of what commentators dully termed a "sectarian struggle." Brother Light had prophesied his demise too.

In fact, Brother Light's uncanny ability to prophesy murders, disasters, and destructions of all kinds, from mullahs assassinated to mothers and babies caught in crossfire battles between Hindus and

Muslims, drew attention from nervous and worshipful watchers all over the world. Though some, Anne O'Neal prominent among them, speculated that the Prophet's "prophecies" of convenient uprisings weren't so much divine revelations as previews of his own plans for his enemies, no one could pin the blame on the Children of Light and their leader. While the deaths of the mullahs in Kandahar raised suspicions about the exact tools the One God had used to bring the sect's detractors low, the most gimlet-eyed observer could find no way to connect Brother Light or his followers to the assassination of Tip Buchanan—which he prophesied just minutes before a drug runner's henchmen used a rocket-propelled grenade to destroy the governor's motorcade as it moved through downtown Sacramento in the early afternoon.

"There is no god on this earth greater than the One God; no others can withstand the ultimate will of the Unity. In the Unity, all time is one, all space is one," Janjalani said calmly, answering the interviewer's questions easily. "From the perspective of omniscience, the universe holds no secrets. One simply tunes into the mind of that universe, and all truth reveals itself."

Especially if one were willing to help those predictions along with a judicious nudge here, a bribe there. In the cold light of logic, the predictions involved a heavy dose of common sense (with Travell Capshaw gone, Buchanan had no one to defend him against other ambitious criminals) and an adept hand at manipulation. What logic could not handle, however, lay locked behind Sepphira's pleading eyes: the shadows always knew the evil lurking in men's hearts, and what plans incubated there.

* * *

Dear Chisom,

I am sorry I have not corresponded with you for a few weeks. Work has taken me away, but I understand from your mother that you know what I'm talking about since you missed sending us a transmission or two due to your own press of work. And it does press, does it not? I can't promise I will do any better. My solace is that I know Adaure keeps you abreast of family matters.

I am pleased that your area remains stable and that the Lord's work is going forward. I wish I could say the same for all the world. Some places are in utter chaos, but, thankfully, the Saints are largely secure. I delight that the Lord prepared us for this day. Not many days ago, President Smith shared a thought-provoking and encouraging insight with my staff. He related the story of Moses bringing the children of Israel into the desert, where they ran out of water. Some feared and many bellyached. Their complaints came to Moses. In response, he prayed to the Lord, who directed the camp to water. To their disgust, the spring was "bitter," meaning they could not drink it. Their complaints rang with more furor than before. Again Moses prayed and in response, the Lord showed him a tree not far off. He told Moses to have the people cut down the branches of the tree and steep them in the water. The people did so and the water became sweet.

President Smith pointed out that the cure was a tree—a tree, not a bush, a shrub, or a bunch of weeds, but a fully grown tree. He then asked when and how it got there. His point was that years before Israel needed it, the Lord set forces to work to get the right tree in the right place at the right time. So, too, the prophet said, it was with the communities of Zion. A long time ago, the Lord started getting His centers ready. The prophets built temples all over the earth and set apart other places of safety. The result is that now when times have become most bitter, these places offer refuge and sweetness. In every area, places of refuge exist close enough for the Saints to get to, albeit in some instances at great sacrifice. Even so, they can get there. The number of Gatherers grows ever larger, and the work of those already called is beginning to bear fruit and their power manifest.

I am sorry to hear that Brother Light's people are creating problems for the Saints over there. Brother Light's sensational antics have been having their effect over here too. They have helped him win disciples from former faithful Christians, Muslims, and Jews. Of course, we should not be surprised by this, Chisom. Jesus warned us that in the last days, "There shall also arise false Christs, and false prophets, and shall show great signs and wonders, insomuch, that, if possible, they shall deceive the very elect" (JS—M 1:22). What you need to understand is that the Lord's words do not mean that the less elect will be deceived. The word very, *in this case, means "truly" or "actually." Thus the Lord is saying that those who are the elect will pay little heed to the false leaders and counterfeit signs of the last days. We are finding that to be true. Church members and other righteous souls are not enticed by the works of Berother Light or impressed by his theatrics. His One God will find no worshippers among us. Do not worry. You will find the same to be true over there. Yes, there needs to be yet a little weeding. Janjalani is helping gather the tares to be burned, while the Lamb gathers the wheat into the security of the storehouses. We have nothing to fear. We know what the Lord is planning.*

Much love,
Your father,
Chinedu

* * *

"I want to know what he's planning! He is not going to fool me!" Howard Garlick emphasized his furious order by pounding his desk.

"Don't worry, Mr. Secretary. I'll get an answer out of Mr. Abbott." Caesar Augosto broke the connection, frowning at the group of indecently dressed young women outside a bank's gilded storefront, calling seductively out to passing cars. Society's values had definitely declined. When he controlled this territory, he'd make sure those prostitutes got cleared off the streets and into the brothels where they belonged. With Capshaw gone, Augosto would sponsor a new governor, add his organizational muscle to quell the chaos, and get the state back on its feet—so it could take its place as one of the jewels of the most impressive criminal empire the American continent had ever seen.

"Hey, don't you worry neither, sir," said Johnny Mack, eyeing the darkly glittering tower of MedaGen's San Diego headquarters looming before them. "Either one of 'em sneezes your way, he's dead. Nobody betrays the firm."

"If they sneeze in our direction, take care that you don't breathe, or you might be dead too," Augosto told him. To Augosto, the building looked like a negative-image cathedral, the temple of those who played god with arrogant pride and careless malice. No wonder Garlick distrusted his MedaGen ally—Augosto distrusted both Abbott and Garlick.

The Mob boss's distaste and watchfulness sharpened as they entered the biomedical firm's plush reception area. A vacantly beautiful assistant escorted them to Abbott's office. Abbott himself rose from his luxurious chair, coming around the glossy expanse of desk with an equally glossy smile and offering his hand. "Mr. Augosto—Caesar. So good to see you. What brings you to San Diego?"

Augosto pointedly ignored the hand, taking a seat on the leather couch with its commanding view of the window wall. A bank of clouds built and roiled on the far horizon, gray with ash and heavy with rain. "Paying my respects at Tip Buchanan's funeral. We had business."

"Indeed," Abbott said. He glared at Johnny Mack, who settled one hip against the corner of the desk. "So, what business were you and Tip Buchanan into together? Drugs? Money laundering? Gambling? Protection rackets?"

"What business are you in, Abbott?" Augosto shot back. "Extending your bioterror portfolio? Spreading plague viruses around the Southwest?"

"It's a vaccine. And we are certainly not dabbling in that kind of virus," Abbott lied easily.

"That kind of virus." Augosto threw the phrase back. "What kind do you dabble in, then? The kind you used on those poor slobs in Houston? I don't like terrorists—or people who sell weapons to them. I'm a good American, and so are my boys."

Johnny Mack flicked his butterfly knife in a sparkling arc.

"It would be a shame for somebody to destroy the country," Abbott intoned, "before you and the Mob can rob it blind. Chaos is bad for business, isn't it?"

"You wanna say that again, germ boy?" Johnny Mack snarled, uncoiling to hold his blade against Abbott's throat.

"You want to watch your tone," Augosto observed. "Johnny's a patriotic boy. He gets excited." After a moment, Augosto nodded.

With a disappointed sigh, Johnny let Abbott go. Augosto continued, "You would also do well to tread carefully. Some of your friends are getting nervous about you. Some of your enemies already were. So watch yourself."

"Oh, we do," Abbott assured him. He gestured as the door opened. "In fact, we have Ms. Zelik to watch things for us."

Zelik glanced from Smokey, who had never left his watchful post beside the entryway, to Johnny Mack, then to Augosto. They didn't exchange nods as the three men left the office.

"Oh!" The look Virginia gave Augosto as he narrowly avoided running into her was as hot as Zelik's had been cold. "Why, Caesar— how wonderful to see you again," she purred, stepping close. "It doesn't look like you're having a wonderful day. Whatever's got you so upset?"

"Your boss is a plague dog," he said, moving to avoid her. "You'd better be careful you don't catch anything from him."

She stepped in front of him again and giggled. "Oh, don't you worry about me catching anything from him. Even if we didn't have AllSafe! Mr. Abbott isn't my lover—or my owner. In fact, I'm a free agent— and I'm more than willing to entertain offers now."

Augosto had no use for cheap broads. However, this one lived in the viper's nest, and rumor said she might part with valuable information if properly encouraged. He nodded politely. "You keep in touch, Miss Diamante. Especially if you've got something interesting to say."

Virginia gave him a little wave as the elevator doors closed.

"How nice to hear that you consider yourself a free agent." The sound of Zelik's ice-queen voice brought Virginia spinning around.

"Well, only in the romantic sense," Virginia said hastily.

Zelik tapped her watch with one diamond-hard nail. "Don't you have a photo shoot to do? The last one of the campaign, I understand."

"Yes, I do." Virginia seized the opening and pushed the elevator button. She couldn't help giving Zelik a glance under her eyelashes as the door opened. "It's a lot of fun, all those people fussing over you. It's too bad you won't get the chance."

"I'll get other chances," Zelik hissed to the closed doors.

Augosto's lack of interest worried Virginia much more than Zelik's hostility. "What's wrong, Julian?" she demanded of her assistant in her dressing room. "Zelik's been hovering around me like a smug zombie all day today. And Abbott won't return my calls. And that dreamy Augosto didn't light up when I gave him the full-on brush!"

"Then he's dead," Julian said, tackling the most ego-hurting element first.

"He doesn't look dead," Virginia pouted, throwing her shoes in Julian's direction.

Julian caught one and picked the other up, glancing darkly at Virginia, who was looking for more things to throw. "Well, since you're in a mood already, I might as well tell you that I saw Charity and Chastity in Studio 2 this morning, doing their own photo shoot for the AllSafe booster."

Virginia froze momentarily. "Those little—" The vivid and inventively obscene description of her rivals trailed after her as she ran from the room toward Studio 2.

Julian, racing after her, thought it a miracle that the wood paneling didn't blister.

The bulbs in the light rack did crack, however, as Virginia burst into the studio and heaved over the heavy stand. She followed that with a light meter and a barrage of cushions, shrieking threats, and insults. Charity and Chastity scrambled to put as much distance between themselves and MedaGen's senior spokeswoman as possible. Electricians, photographers, assistants, makeup artists, and other minions scattered, familiar with Virginia's rages. The fits usually ended when she wore herself out enough for Julian to get a couple of tabs of Bliss into her and put her to bed. This time, however, salvation came from an unexpected source.

Three burly security guards rushed in. One came in from behind in a low crouch and picked Virginia up. With the other two deflecting her flailing arms and kicking feet, and all three ignoring her shrieks, they hauled her out. Julian, almost as surprised as Virginia, ran after them, barely making it into the elevator as the doors closed.

By the time the elevator doors opened in front of Abbott's office, Virginia had gone limp, breathing deeply in her version of "meditation." When the guards stepped out of the elevator, she asked, demurely, to be put down. "I'm much better now."

Reluctantly, her captor released his grip, swinging her down to her feet. The guards stayed close, however, as they went into Abbott's office.

Abbott frowned. "Virginia, you've been tossing things around again. It is just this type of outburst that has forced us to replace you as spokesmodel for our AllSafe booster campaign."

"Replaced?" Virginia gasped.

"Why, yes," Abbott said. "Didn't you get the memo?"

Memo? They were replacing *her*? Virginia's street-fighter side reasserted itself through the shock. "Fine," she spat. "It's your funeral! I'll just go to BritPharm."

"Sorry, sweetheart," Abbott shook his head. "You've still got six months on your contract here before you can work for anybody else. And, unfortunately, we just won't be able to use you. Your ratings numbers aren't what they used to be. You know how it is—we've got to think of the brand."

"What about *my* brand?" Panic rose through her confidence. "I can't disappear for a half year!"

"That's not our problem," Zelik said with a malicious smile. "You should've thought of that before basing your career on your fading looks."

Virginia snarled wordlessly and lashed out, leaving a reddening welt across Zelik's face before security caught her arms again.

Zelik treated her to a sub-zero glare. "You will pay for that."

"Now, now, ladies, let's not have a catfight right here in my office," Abbott broke in.

"Let me go," Virginia ordered, shrugging away from the guards' grip. She swept them with an imperious stare and stalked to the elevator. Julian fell in behind her, closing the doors to Abbott's office.

Virginia's queenly composure lasted until the elevator door closed; then she sobbed as she clung to Julian's shoulder. Under her assistant's murmured reassurances, Virginia's ironclad self-interest reasserted itself. They'd fired her. She needed to salvage her career—and she needed to make Abbott and Zelik suffer for what they'd done to her.

* * *

"I simply want to make sure Meredith Galen suffers for what she did," Zelik said, the hard glitter of hate in her eyes as she gazed at the underling across the desk.

Breaking the eye lock with Zelik, Humphrey reached across the desk, straightening the pen holder on the blotter. His outward nonchalance hid the rapid whirring of his finely tuned weasel brain. Unfortunately, he'd achieved his promotion to the second-tier executive suite just as the floor sagged out from under it. MedaGen's stock prices, and thus his own personal worth as the company's indentured servant, had fallen right through that floor. He had absolutely no intention of following the debris to the basement or of sacrificing himself for this icicle woman.

"You let her go, Errol. And then you let that Callatta creature escape. You didn't have a lot of margin for error in the first place, and you've definitely crossed the line."

"Does a personal grudge have any place in high-stakes biomedical business?" Humphrey asked. "I ruined their credit, didn't I? Tony Callatta was unemployable. There wasn't a bank in the world that would give them credit. Their daycare business had gone bust. The little lady narrowly avoided a rough-up from a bunch of would-be carjackers by not stopping when they rear-ended her. Their neighbors were on the verge of handing in a petition to evict them as illegal aliens. Their house had more liens against it than the IRS could dream up. If they'd stayed around just one more day, they would've got their car impounded. And DCFS was all set to snatch away those darling little cherubs of theirs to a reeducation camp in the Klondike. Pardon me while I indulge in the wicked laugh of an almost-undefeated villain."

He issued a perfunctory cackle, then shrugged. "So just as the mousetrap was poised to slam shut on our family of religious-fanatic rats, they scampered away as if on the wings of angels. So, it was my fault they pulled a bunk off to Mormon Fort Knox before I could tighten the noose? I did everything I could think of—and a lot more than anybody else came up with. I burned a cross on their blasted lawn!"

"Clearly, you should've burned a lot more." Zelik shook her head.

Humphrey looked at her incredulously. "I'm a project manager, Ms. Zelik, not an assassin!"

"You couldn't manage this project," she pointed out. "You should have apprehended the Callattas immediately, before they left for Noveau or whatever the place is."

He countered, "You're the one who said not to do anything extreme, because it would look suspicious. And, as it happens, you were right—with Garlick's lifeboat leaking like a sieve, your instincts proved exactly correct on that score."

"So the Callattas are out of our hands. The real threat is that Meredith Anthony—Meredith *Galen*—" Zelik spat the name, "has taken vital portions of our corporate property and gone to ground somewhere—"

"She's in Salt Lake City, Utah, at an outfit called Section 89," Humphrey corrected.

"Knowing that hardly makes me feel better. Eliminating the threat would. I want Meredith Galen punished—something that might happen to other people around here if they don't prove themselves worthy of continuing employment." Zelik turned from the window to look at Humphrey.

He summoned a smile from the reserves of strength that he never applied to the right causes. "Oh, but that's the one upside of slavery. You own me, which means you can't let me starve. Kind of like it being illegal to mistreat a pet. I'm a dependent. MedaGen's my family—why, you and Abbott are like my parents."

Zelik suppressed a shudder. "You had better do a lot better, Errol, or you'll find yourself busted down to cleaning crew."

"Janitorial? And waste a guy who can pull us out of the hole we're in?" He shot her a calculating look. "How's Dr. Twilley's project coming?"

Zelik shrugged. "Not as well as Abbott had hoped—he can't find the human antidote, so Garza's threatening to use him as a guinea pig. Abbott is getting nervous about that too, but he's not going to pin me with that one. It will be interesting to see what happens to Abbott if this project falls through; he already has the board breathing down his neck about the stock drop."

"Which he tried to pin on you too," Humphrey reminded her. "And failed. So now he's on the front line of the firing squad. Couldn't happen to a nicer guy."

Raking Humphrey with a disdainful look to remind him that no one disrespects a top MedaGen executive but another top-level MedaGen executive, she snapped, "All kinds of things can happen to nice guys, Errol. You're not exactly safe yourself. Impress us all with the next marketing campaign—and get to Meredith Galen. You have a month, while we're stuck in D.C. straightening out the grand-jury fiasco, to find a way to stop her before she puts out a real antidote to AllSafe that will crash MedaGen stock."

Humphrey blinked, "You think Merry could do that? She's a nice kid, seemed smart enough, but I always thought her husband, Chris, was the brains—"

Zelik interrupted. "Yes, *Merry* can do it. Both of them were brighter than they acted."

"Yeah, I guess you're right," Humphrey conceded. "They must be smarter than they looked. Hey, they fooled the omniscient Ms. Zelik, didn't they?"

That earned him a glare. "Yes, and she fooled you too. Never forget that, because I won't. Four weeks."

"And shall I deliver her liver and lungs to you in a jeweled box, my queen?" Humphrey muttered after the door closed behind her.

* * *

"And now Leroy's got a couple of boxes in the backseat of his car, stacked on the floor so you can't quite see them through the window. They look like cigar boxes, and I think he's taken up smoking. Oh, he says he wouldn't do something so dangerous, but some days I just don't know . . ." The client's voice whined on in Sally Mae's ear, complaining about her son's latest escapades.

The noise faded into the memory of pleading and screaming in the nightmare she couldn't escape last night. Terrified people huddled in the cracked landscape beneath the blackened sky, drowned in rivers of filthy water, burned in white-hot blasts from volcanic vents, and, crying for lost family and friends, pleaded for help. Hoofbeats sounded, and she whirled to squint through the light rising from the western horizon, hoping that the cavalry had arrived. It had, but as the four figures pounded nearer, panic rose choking in her throat. The four riders swept over the burned, parched, flooded earth, not to save it but to strike its death blow. Laughter roared from them as they cut down all in their path, and another voice answered from the ground, crying out triumphantly. Despair and horror filled Sally Mae, the conviction that no one and nothing could save her or anyone else. Every time she woke, trying to shake off the feeling of doom by reassuring herself of the mundane reality of her little apartment, she'd fallen right back into the barren plane of the dream. The only thing that kept her from dissolving into complete hopelessness was the gleam on the eastern horizon, the whispered hint of immanence.

Sally Mae shook her head, trying to clear the leftover vision. The immediate images receded, but the feeling of deep dread, and the incipient hope associated with it, persisted. So did the uneasiness in Sally Mae's stomach. She'd always cared about her clients, always prayed for them, always felt that the "psychic" side of the business was a little white lie, a tiny bit of imaginary grease to make it easier for strangers to confide in her and accept her heartfelt advice. Since the day she'd mentally "seen" the tornado right before it demolished Gladys's house, however, she couldn't escape the growing conviction of something else going on—or Someone else trying to speak to her, mostly through dreams, but sometimes during the day as well, in flashes of nightmare intuition. She knew about Marie's baby running for the backyard pool; she saw the shotgun Mickey's boyfriend bought to punish his girlfriend for talking to another man. She'd always believed in prayer, but she'd never thought much about revelation.

Her eyes strayed to the vividly colored picture of Jesus as the Good Shepherd that decorated her workstation. *Lord Jesus, have You decided to start talking to me, after all the years I've been talking to you?* she silently asked. The figure's brilliant blue eyes shone back at her. Did the sparkle in them come from the paper or from the inside of her head?

"Lizzie," Sally Mae finally said, giving up on her inner argument about saying something about the vision. She broke through the tale of woe that the woman on the phone had spun for the last fifteen minutes. "Lizzie, honey, I understand. But you got to open your eyes. Leroy's been lying to you all along; you keep telling me that. I don't think it's smoking he's into—well, not smoking tobacco, anyway— and with that much, he's selling it, not just using it. It's time you stopped turning a blind eye to what that boy's doing. We just don't have that much longer to put things right!"

Lizzie, taken aback by Sally Mae's unaccustomed directness, lost the threads of her complaint. Usually, Sally Mae sympathized with her stories of Leroy's insolence and inconsiderate behavior, drawled soothing and intentionally vague assurances that the future looked brighter, then led her in a prayer for patience and understanding. And that was just the way Lizzie liked it. "I couldn't do that! Search his car or go into his room without permission," she exclaimed, seizing on the easiest part of what Sally Mae advised her to do. "He's a child, but children do have a right to privacy!"

"He's not a child, sweetie." Sally Mae used the endearment belatedly, to soften the impatient edge of concern in her voice. "He's a grown man—an immature one, maybe, but a grown man. And if you don't step in, he's going to get hurt, or hurt somebody else."

"How do you know that?" Lizzie asked. She never asked questions like that when Sally Mae told her what she wanted to hear.

"Remember, I'm a psychic," Sally Mae offered, trying to keep her answer light. It didn't work; she just wasn't cut out for denying the Holy Spirit when it struck. "Oh, Lizzie, I just think that Lord Jesus has a message for you, and He's just not going to let me rest until I tell you! Leroy's in trouble, and you've got a chance to help him, if you'll just put your trust in Jesus and do what He tells you to do."

Stunned silence fell on the far side of the line, the sound of guilt warring with pride and laziness. "I feel that remark is completely inappropriate," Lizzie finally said. "I'm disappointed in you, Sally Mae. I didn't call for religious fanaticism—or hearing that I'm to blame for Leroy's behavior problems. He's got a learning disability, and he's just going through a difficult stage right now, with the economy low and—"

"He's going to get killed, or he's going to kill himself," Sally Mae interrupted the same old justifications with the urgency that rose like the toxic dust from the superheated desert of her dream. "Lizzie, please—the Holy Spirit helped you see those boxes to help you save your son! If you'll just—"

"I am not listening to this!" Lizzie interrupted her disappointingly pushy counselor this time. "In fact, I'm sorry, but I'm going to have to put a word in with your supervisor, Sally Mae. I think your religious fanaticism has gotten completely out of control!"

"But Lizzie, you just have to—" Sally Mae sighed as the connection went dead. No, it didn't go dead; the blinking light on the edge of her console let her know that Lizzie hadn't broken the connection—she'd just transferred it directly to the call supervisor's line. The rest of her board went dark, all incoming calls instantly routed to other psychics while her manager evaluated the situation.

Mama Lenora's Psychic Angels took no chances with its corporate image. Dissatisfied customers stopped paying exorbitant fees, and dissatisfied customers contacted Armstrong Associates and used their Insta-Suit service to file a complaint with the courts alleging fraudulent business practices. If AA collected enough complaints to make it look like a potentially profitable enterprise, they'd empty their kennel of legal pit bulls. At the end of the dogfight, the complainants might not get more than the satisfaction of knowing that they'd put the treacherous phone psychics out of business, but AA would have made enough in legal fees to buy high-class kibble for a few more months.

A few seconds later, another button lit up—the one summoning Sally Mae to Ethan's office, the one room in the cubicle warren with actual walls and a door, since employees reprimanded in front of their coworkers could also file suit for embarrassment, libel, or emotional abuse. She whispered a quick prayer for merciful intervention and made the long trek to the office, trying not to notice the other psychics' knowing looks.

The interview with the manager didn't go well—especially when she admitted she'd had another vision of the Four Horsemen of the Apocalypse, with General Garza as War and Brother Light as a lamb with tiny horns on his forehead leading a flock of human sheep into the mouth of a dragon; and beyond them all, an angel standing far to the east, his beautiful face sorrowful as he poured fire and vapor into the air. Behind him, a faint wash of ruddy gold stained the greenish black of the roiling sky.

Her supervisor's curt response was to tell her she'd been reading the Bible too much, and telling him about seeing the tornado before it hit Gladys didn't help matters. She stood, trying to get through to him. "And I've had other visions—horrible ones, but with a little hint of joy too, the good Lord holding out His hands to call us to a safe haven. How can I not tell people that? How can I not share the warning? It is the end times, even if the asteroids didn't hit us, and Jesus is coming back. We've got to be ready when He does! I know He's been trying to tell me something." Tears welled up in her eyes. "I just think that Jesus has something to say, and for whatever reason, He wants me to help Him say it."

"Well, He may, but you're not going to keep doing it on work time," the manager ordered.

Sally Mae looked him in the eye, stacking her thread of security—her tiny apartment and supply of sweets on one side, Jesus' incongruously bright blue eyes on the other. With a regretful sigh, she realized which end of the scale weighed more. "I'm sorry, but I can't stop trying to lead people to Jesus."

The supervisor looked at her and then shrugged. "All right, Sally, if that's the way you want to play it." With a snort, he pressed the button on his phone that called security, then extended a hand. "You're as bad as that Mormon nut we had to get rid of. Hand over your badge, and wait for security to get here to help you clear out your desk—especially that kitschy picture."

"It's Sally Mae," she corrected, after months of saying nothing. Keeping her chin up, she detached the employee ID from its lariat around her neck and put it in his hand. She kept her chin up as she stuffed her personal effects into her oversized handbag and walked out of the building between two burly security guards, ignoring the sniggers and sarcastic comments.

Her chin did quiver later, however, as she huddled on her flowered couch. The screen light gleamed off the picture she'd propped up on the side table, bathing the Good Shepherd in a blue glow. It went out abruptly, as the poorer neighborhoods briefly lost the energy tug-of-war with the big businesses downtown. "Oh, Lord Jesus, what do You want me to do?" she asked aloud in the darkness, the capital letters in the pronouns coming easily. "I've been doing what You asked, trying to tell everybody that the last days are here, and they need to be ready for You to sweep them up in Your loving arms. But nobody believes me. Please, if You want me to spread Your word, please guide me to someone who'll believe me!" She closed her eyes tightly as she prayed.

* * *

". . . looking for someone to believe." Sally Mae's eyes flew open as her outdated TV sprang to life again.

The dignified, ministerial face of Tommy Gibbs filled the screen, his royal-blue robe sparkling under its gold trim as he leaned into the spotlight over the podium. "Now, some of you all look around in this world as the end times come, and along with all the trouble, all the terror, all the sadness, all the sin, you see people out there, people trying to do good. Now, these may be people who aren't in your churches, people who aren't joining the crusades, people who aren't Christians, and you say, 'Reverend Gibbs, what about my Jewish friend? What about my Muslim neighbor? What about my Mormon coworker? They're good folks. They're trying to do good. Doesn't Jesus love them?'"

He paused, smiling reassuringly, then grew sober. He gestured emphatically, pointing to the sky and out to the audience. "And I tell you, of course Jesus loves them. He loves them and gave Himself for them. But unless they follow your example and accept Him as their personal Savior, there's nothing He can do. If they don't choose Him, they choose the path of hell. So speak to your friend, your neighbor, your coworker. Remind them that the end times are upon us! Witness to them of the redeeming grace of our Savior! Open their eyes to the danger they're in—the mortal danger from the spiritual poison of Satan's teachings! Call them to come up to Christ, to join King Jesus in the clouds with you and all righteous believers before the world suffers its final cleansing from all evil!"

Sally Mae watched and listened raptly, convinced that the Savior had given her an answer to her heartfelt prayer—not in the preacher's words, though she believed them with all her heart, but in the crawl across the bottom of the screen. Along with the customary pleas for donations to spread the work of the gospel to heathen lands to hasten the Second Coming, advertisements for Tommy Gibbs's published recordings and books, fundraising announcements for political causes, and other miscellaneous programs Michael Romanoff implemented to transform Gibbs's charisma into cash, an announcement caught Sally Mae's eye and lifted her heart. "Angels Wanted: Support the kingdom as a phone consultant for the Crusaders of Jesus." In customary brief style, the notice explained that Tommy Gibbs's ministry was looking for telephone consultants to help them spread the gospel over the network lines to the world, and, of course, gather donations from the faithful. Telephone representative experience a must.

She dialed the number before the last of the words disappeared from the screen.

* * *

The phone rang in the darkened office. Humphrey, silhouetted in the light from the console screen, picked up the receiver with a brisk, "Marketing, Humphrey."

A pre-recorded message began, just as he had arranged, a business-like conversation issuing from the desk speaker, providing a phone-log alibi. Humphrey rolled his chair back, putting himself in a camera angle that made it look like he took off his suit jacket to get comfort-able, but didn't show the janitor's jacket he wore in its place. He shuffled out of his shoes, propping them upright against the glossy brochure boxes. To a casual observer of the overhead cam, it would look like he'd kicked back with his feet on the desk to take the phone call.

Camouflage complete, he slithered below desk level and out of the cameras' sight. Getting to the door unseen would've been impos-sible with all this maneuvering if he didn't have backup from the night-shift security tech. Sean was the guy who had given Meredith Galen deep-level security access on Zelik's orders; she'd kept him on so he wouldn't spill the origin of the order. Humphrey had used the episode as a lever to open a conversation with the tech—and found out that in return for a staggering amount of virtual platinum, Sean was willing to forget to put the third camera on the replacement/repair list when it stopped transmitting due to a fatal overdose of cola. The kid was good at editing video footage too, erasing inconvenient images, like Humphrey out for a little corporate espionage. Moving up to director of marketing soothed his wounded pride but did nothing to erase his abiding hatred of his masters or satisfy the fierce ambition that got him into his current contract predicament. He was determined to find a lever, a crack in Zelik's and Abbott's defenses, that he could use to vault himself ahead. In a way, he had Merry Galen to thank for giving him the kick that got him moving again—he owed her for the costume idea too as he played janitor all the way to Abbott's breakfast nook/conference room.

The lingering smell of coffee permeated the room. Humphrey polished the table, topped off the shine on the wall panels—and engaged the catch to the CEO's private office, the one place in MedaGen's headquarters where Abbott made sure that Zelik had installed no cameras. Humphrey stood, unobserved, in Abbott's sanctum sanctorum. He tapped a skeleton code into the console. The code bypassed the retina-scan security on the console, a back door built in on the chance that the scanner itself would malfunction. It came from Sean too, though the junior tech didn't realize that Humphrey had looked over his shoulder when Zelik called to demand access to whatever Abbott was hiding from her. Ninety percent of serendipity came from being prepared to take advantage of it.

Humphrey checked Abbott's personal files, scanning for anything he could use to blackmail Abbott, embarrass Zelik, or just sell outright. None of Abbott's files seemed to have anything to do with the rumored Western bioterror or other major scandal, however, and the clock was ticking. With a growl, he downloaded the most likely looking files. As he backed out of the system, Zelik's name on a shared sector caught his attention. As the contents scrolled past, Humphrey realized it didn't contain information about Zelik, but information *for* her, the latest reports on a shared project. Pacifica. The name appeared in the last few memos Whittier had sent, before the previous marketing director committed suicide by shooting himself in the chest. Several times. Humphrey shrugged off a moment of doubt about the fatal project and ordered the console to copy the files to a randomly generated admin account. Then he wiped down the console one more time, logged out, and slithered back to his own office.

Three hours and a fight with a surprisingly sticky encryption program later, the first streaks of dawn lit the sky and picked Humphrey's intent face out of the dusk inside the marketing director's office. It did nothing to warm the strained, hollow-eyed face of Dr. Twilley, staring from the monitor.

". . . the additional funding request, attached as per your request, will enable us to build two more isolation rooms to run the protocols at double speed. This is necessary, given the unscientific impatience of the sponsors of this project. Pacifica protocols 101b and 143a have shown some promise in promoting immune resistance to the base antigen. Despite the lack of proper assistance, I believe I am close to attaining the goal. The clients have promised me the help of a local researcher, Dr. Vasquez, but I doubt she will have the necessary skills and knowledge to make a positive contribution to the project. I again request that you send competent lab assistants from company headquarters."

Humphrey rubbed his eyes. Just one more attachment to this transmission, and he could dump the lot. He wasn't interested in Abbott's executive research projects; he couldn't sell something MedaGen was going to profit by anyway. He'd been suspicious when it looked like the project hadn't been approved by the board, but it looked like Abbott had just made an end run around the board again to get a project going. When the last attachment opened, however, he snapped to full attention. Twilley's note said merely, "Interesting scenery outside the lab."

"Interesting," Humphrey whispered, staring at the locked Keepsakes Ltd. crates, the gleaming metal shapes of weapons, the dull finish of what had to be a whole flock of cutting-edge military drone planes. And around them swarmed men in jungle fatigues, techs in greasy coveralls—and officers wearing the black uniforms and shoulder patches of General Garza's United States of South America. Pacifica wasn't another AllSafe; it was a bioweapon, one with a special antidote. Which meant the enemies weren't Americans or Europeans, who had AllSafe to guard them, but natives who hadn't been vaccinated. Looked like the last holdouts in General Garza's new empire were in for a nasty winter, even if the General was saving the hardware for somebody else.

The next thought made Humphrey's eyes glow with avarice: those high-tech weapons didn't come from MedaGen's labs or factories. They came straight from the Pentagon's private stash. He wasn't exactly a weapons aficionado, but he knew enough to recognize major military hardware when he saw it. There was no way that the military would send their pride and joy in bang babies down to a megalomaniac South American dictator. This meant that Garlick had managed to sneak the stuff out the back door, probably in return for cash to help him fight off Holly Cox. Humphrey realized that he'd found a break big enough to get his contract voided, make a pile of cash, and retire to some nice island to ride out the crash.

Now, he just needed a buyer for the information. The files disappeared into his personal PDA as he scanned through his list of acquaintances to find the right connection. The name Galen caught his eye, still in place out of a sentimental attachment to someone who'd given Zelik and Abbott a black eye. A strange thought crossed his mind: what if he handed the information over to Senator Cox out of the goodness of his heart and accepted her protection as a whistle-blower? He shook his head, "Good try, Galen, but I'm not falling for that altruistic thing. Look where it got you!"

* * *

"There you are! Got you!" Merry exclaimed, parting the hanging branches of the weeping willow tree on the edge of Grandma Galen's backyard.

Missy squealed and laughed, running away across the summer lawn to hide again.

Chris, his smile dappled with leaf shadows, feinted left, then grabbed Merry, squeezing her tight. "Now who's got who?" he asked as he bent to kiss her.

"Whom," Merry corrected teasingly, returning the kiss. She closed her eyes tightly, his scent, taste, and touch filling her senses. Desperate need, hunger, and fear rose behind the familiar, beloved sensations, darkness lurking beneath the sun lights on the inside of her eyelids. "No!" she cried as she felt him let go.

"Let's see if you can find us again," he said, as if he hadn't heard. He slipped out of her grasp as if her hands could grip no better than the fingerless mitts of a rag doll.

Opening her eyes, she lunged after him, but the lawn seemed to stretch on forever, impossible distances of green fading into blue sky and then into the black depths of eternity beyond. Chris ran into the emerald vastness, calling back to her, overtaking Missy and kissing the top of her shining head as he passed her, calling playfully back to Merry. He didn't see the shadow detach itself from the blackness beyond the blue, the horrible blot that appeared in the warm summer day. The grass tangled around Merry's feet like seaweed, slowing her wild run, holding her back despite her frantic efforts. She clawed at the turf, trying to gain traction with her hands, shouting wordless, frantic warnings at Chris to watch out, to move, to come back.

Missy, watching with wide eyes from her car seat, waved her tiny hands and shouted, "Dadadad!"

Chris looked back, his smile shaded with apology, his mobile face compassionate. He stretched his hands out toward them. "I love you," he said, his voice husky. "I always—"

The scream of burning brakes and tortured metal cut off his words, and the lid of a glass coffin silenced his last ragged breath. The coffin lowered away into the dark ground under the green grass, a pale amber light glowing from Chris's bones as he slowly drifted away from her, the darkness swallowing the gleam like deep water.

"But families are forever!" Missy protested. She wavered, shifting between four years old and two, tiny infant and almost kindergartener, then older still, becoming a poised young woman whose face shone with the same sunlight glow. "Families are forever," she said again, and the last word, *forever*, echoed over and over in Merry's ears as Missy ran into the dark, joyfully disappearing to join her father, leaving Merry alone as their two lights receded into unimaginable distance.

"Please, come back!" Merry called out, panic and loneliness rising to choke her. "Please! I don't know the way yet! I can't keep up!" She stumbled forward, slipping on the unseen ground beneath her feet, reaching toward the two lights so far beyond.

Figures loomed out of the darkness, reaching for her in turn. Men, women, children coalesced from the black mist, blocking her path, surrounding her. She recoiled on seeing their drawn, pale faces; they clustered around her, hollow-eyed and gaunt, racked with deep coughs, skeletal fingers plucking her sleeves as they demanded in choked voices, "Help us! Cure us!"

"Get away!" Merry gasped, brushing at the grasping hands, trying to find a way through the tattered mob. "Chris! Missy! Please! Wait for me!"

An opening, a break in the human wall, appeared; she dove toward it, breaking out of the circle. Across the gulf, the clear lights that were Chris and Missy glowed invitingly, but Merry's headlong run slowed and finally stopped. She looked down at the child beside her, a girl only Missy's age, holding a doll who coughed along with her mistress, the tiny sound making the original cough that much more pitiable.

"It'll be okay," Merry said, tears rising in her throat to choke her voice. She couldn't go on. She knew, as clearly as if the words had appeared before her eyes, that she couldn't leave them; she had to stay here and make them well, even if it meant being alone. The tears broke free as she turned away, blurring the bright colors of the DNA helixes glowing in her hands. She spread the jeweled strands over the gray skin of the people around her, touching each one in turn, watching their lifeless complexions gradually glow with new color, flesh bloom over their bones under her cold, shaking fingers.

And her fingers weren't cold anymore; they steadied as Chris's hands covered hers. He held her from behind, his presence melting into her, giving her strength, helping her, part of her forever. "You always knew the way," he whispered. "You always will."

A persistent ringing slowly grew, shattering the dark, sending the brilliant DNA jewels flying everywhere. Black went to gray, then to the hard white of fluorescent lights shining through the door into the lab's crash site, as Corinne referred to the supply closet they'd squeezed a small couch into for emergency naps. Merry raised her head, looking at her watch, then realized the ringing came from her phone, not the alarm. Which hadn't gone off. Rats. She'd slept an hour longer than she meant to. So much for attempting to make a power nap make up for the last week's late nights.

Sitting up and rubbing a yawn off her face with one hand, she dug out the phone and clicked it on with the other. "I'm sorry, Tasha—the simulations are running long. I was going to call—"

"And who is Tasha?" asked the all-too-familiar voice on the other end of the connection.

It was her mother. Double rats. Big Norway rats. Aloud, Merry said, "Hi, Sidney. Tasha's a friend. She's tending Missy for me. How did you get this number?"

"What a question," Sidney protested. "I haven't heard from you in months, and the first thing you ask is how I got your number?"

"You haven't heard from me because we've both been busy," Merry sighed. She'd been busy trying to find a cure for AllSafe; her mother had been busy traveling the country promoting her favorite causes (which Corinne, in her usual amusingly hyperbolic way, characterized as abortion as birth control, lesbian marriage, and the death penalty for anyone convicted of sexual harassment). "And, if you haven't noticed, I'm not exactly popular with certain people right now. I ask out of security concerns."

"The receptionist there transferred me over," Sidney finally explained. "I am your mother, after all."

Sister Lavine, bless her heart, Merry thought. Sidney must've put on her good-mother act with a vengeance to get past the receptionist's usually impeccable baloney detector.

"It's not like any of us are safe," Sidney continued, a pitiful tremble underlying her voice. For someone who always preached feminine strength and decried stereotypical female weaknesses, Sidney was an absolute master of the "damsel in distress" act. "You're such a scientist, always buried in your lab. You don't know what it's like out here. The flight from Los Angeles hit such a pocket of turbulence that the pilot had to dive for a thousand feet before we leveled off again. We were so close to the desert that I swear I saw a prairie dog looking back at me! And L.A. is a mess, just testosterone running rampant everywhere. Brainwashed women fawning over that horrible misogynist Rashi Janjalani, or running around like lemmings after Tommy Gibbs—"

"Sidney," Merry interrupted firmly. "I'm sorry you had a frightening flight, but there's nothing I can do about the nutty people in L.A. I do need to get over to pick up Missy, though. So what can I do for you?"

"You can let me stay with you." Sidney's words came out in a rush. "Just for a while, just until things calm down. I'm sure it won't be more than a week or two. I don't feel safe in my apartment, and the road's so crazy—"

Stay with me. You want to stay with me. The words rose in Merry's head as a scream. *You want to stay with me, because it's safe here and you're frightened. Your fanatic daughter is in the one safe place on the earth, and now you decide you need me for more than proof that raising a daughter without stereotypical socializations and far from the influence of icky men works just fine—you don't have to spend time with her personally, as long as you've got a hired nanny to look after her. You wouldn't come to Chris's funeral, you wouldn't help with Missy when I needed you, and now you want to stay with me!* Bitterness welled up, a whole fountain of sharp words, cutting remarks she wanted to fling through the phone like knives. What came out, however, showed either the deep sickness of a codependent relationship, which Sidney would instantly assume, or the progress Merry had made in forgiving her mother. "Certainly you can stay with us. Where are you now?"

"I'm at the airport," Sidney said, her voice taking on an unaccountable edge of irritation for someone who'd just gotten her way without a fight. "I'm right here at the Salt Lake City airport."

"Oh." Merry blinked. For some reason, she'd assumed Sidney was in Las Vegas. "All right, then. Just grab a cab, and come on out to

Section 89. The driver should know where that is—they'll be glad to have somebody coming in who already has family in the area. You've probably noticed how many people are pouring in, and a lot of them don't come in with anything but the clothes on their backs. I'll let Tasha know you're coming, and we'll go get Missy."

"I don't think you understand," Sidney said. "You need to come get me and take me to wherever you're staying. I assume you're not staying in the city."

"Actually, I am," Merry said, puzzled. "Why wouldn't I be?"

"They let you?" Sidney demanded. "They won't let me out of the airport!"

It took several more minutes until Merry had the whole picture: Sidney arrived at the airport, tried to leave to drop in on Merry, but literally couldn't do it. Every attempt she made to exit the building brought a swell of what she called "panic," and she couldn't go any further. Furious, she blamed airport security, the police officers on duty at the airport, the blasted Mormons in general, and finally Merry in particular, for her inability to enter the Zion community of Salt Lake.

"It's not a rule, it's not a law, and it's not discrimination," Merry finally shouted, exasperated. "It's your own guilty conscience! You've spent your entire life fighting against a lot of important truths, and now it's catching up to you! You can't come in because God is here, and you can't stand feeling His spirit all around you!"

"That is just nonsense!" Sidney shouted back. "It's not superstitious blather, it's a subtle, vicious campaign of mental intimidation and brainwashing—probably using subsonic frequencies. You get me out of here right now, out to where the rest of you are, or—"

"Or what?" Merry demanded. "Or you'll put God in time-out?"

"You'll see," Sidney said tightly. "You and your religious-fanatic Mormon friends and everyone else in the world. Discrimination like this is intolerable." And, as usual, yet another mother-daughter conversation ended with the cold click of a snapped connection.

Merry leaned her head against the back of the couch. "Oh, no. What is she going to do?"

CHAPTER 12

"Armstrong Associates reports that a group of aggrieved citizens has filed suit against The Church of Jesus Christ of Latter-day Saints, known as the Mormons, demanding that the Church open access to the so-called Zion communities," Anne O'Neal reported, from London, a stop on her way to Africa. "The suit alleges discrimination on the basis of religious belief, which is illegal under federal law."

"Discrimination like this is intolerable!" Sidney shouted, making the most of her photo op. Other participants in the suit waved signs and fists around her. Even if she was stuck out in the world with the natural disasters and human lemmings, she'd at least found yet another way to get herself on TV.

"It's un-Christian of them, hoarding all the wealth, taking good land and food away from honest, hard-working folks in this country," Reverend Samuel Lebaron growled. "They oughta be sharing, and the government oughta make sure they do! They can't keep people out of safety like they're doing. It's downright un-American!" The reverend, after the disastrous defeat of his Millennial Brotherhood in Lake Creek, Illinois, had found himself on the sharp end of Governor Kerr's disapproval with no backup; he was attempting to rebuild his career by joining the suit to force open the doors of the Church he once declared he would burn out like the cancer it was. He also didn't seem to see the irony in the situation.

"Representatives from the Church say that they have done nothing to refuse anyone access to the communities," Anne continued. "They maintain that the discomfort some people feel in Zion is the natural reaction of a sinner to the presence of the Divine. And if that's the case, Armstrong Associates has quite a challenge coming."

"I am sincerely sorry that some people have decided to try to sue their way into heaven." With a well-hidden sigh, President Rojas observed, "But as far as I know, God doesn't answer to any earthly court. Everyone is welcome in Zion—in fact, we plead with everyone who will listen to come and partake of the peace we have—but to do that, to feel comfortable here, they have to live Zion lives, or they simply can't stand to stay. It has nothing to do with organized persecution or 'bouncers,' as the suit suggests. The Church doesn't have police; the people leave of their own accord."

"Of course, some don't go far," Anne noted. "The growing number of refugee camps springing up around the Church's Zion communities testifies to that. Unfortunately for the people caught between Zion and the outside world, it looks like the divide between heaven and earth is not only as wide as it ever was, but getting wider all the time. This is Anne O'Neal for Channel 8 News."

"Look at them down there," Leon commented after the recording light on the top of his camera flashed off. Gazing through the viewfinder at the Zion community spreading out from the London Temple, he gestured with his free hand. "Busy as little ants and bees, zip, zip, bustling here and there, just working away. For an outfit that thinks the world's coming to an end, they're sure not taking a day off. If that was me, I'd be kicked back in an easy chair, waiting in comfort for the Big Man to make his grand entrance!"

"Just goes to show you're not a Mormon," Anne told him, smiling at the mental picture of Leon, his Hawaiian shirt much worse for wear, kicked back in a battered recliner, drink in one hand, snack bag in the other, watching the horizon for Jesus to burst on the scene. The Second Coming, however, was unlikely to find Leon in a recliner. In his own way, the cameraman kept as busy as the Mormons he used the camera to zoom in on. "One of their symbols is the bee. That's why you get so many beehives carved into buildings in Salt Lake and Independence. They claim that the name *deseret* means 'bee' in—"

"What's that guy doing?" The sudden urgency of Leon's question had nothing to do with Anne's background explanation. The cameraman had come to full alert, focusing tightly on the scene at the edge of the refugee camp around Zion. His instincts, honed by years of photojournalism, guided the hand that flicked on the recording mode. The red light glowed again.

Anne shaded her eyes, trying to see through the perennially misty English air. Figures wandered, somewhat aimlessly, near the border of the makeshift settlement around the Mormons' perfectly organized community, appearing and disappearing in the collection of tents, trailers, and lean-tos. Following the invisible trajectory of Leon's camera, she made out one figure, a heavy backpack bulking out his silhouette, marching purposefully through the patchwork of claimed territory. The way he moved drew her eye once she knew which direction to look; he paid no attention to the carpet of blankets, jerry-rigged fences, and other marks that delimited each family's "home" as he headed straight into the camp, ignoring the shouted imprecations and shaken fists of the residents in whose "yards" he trespassed. As she scanned the wider scene, she saw another man and then another several yards off, likewise burdened, doing the same relentless power march forward.

"Leon, look—there's two more." She pointed.

He widened his view field to take in all three as they arrived at the strangely obvious border that separated the inhabitants of Zion from the people who wanted the protective cover without the personal commitment. The men staggered as if they'd hit a wall; one fell to the ground and rolled away before gathering himself to his feet again. Instead of backing away, however, they pushed forward again, battling against the heavy spiritual current pushing them away. When they reached the limits of their endurance, maybe thirty or forty feet inside the invisible barrier but a hundred yards from the outskirts of the Zion community, they stopped. Through the zoom lens on the camera, Leon captured the glint of what looked like a phone in one of their hands. He held it to his head, nodded once, and threw it to the ground.

The thought struck both of the watching journalists at the same time, but Anne was the one who started to say, "It looks like they're going to—"

They did. Three dull explosions tore through the misty air, sending shreds of cloth, blood, bone, dirt, rocks, and deadly clouds of ball bearings, nails, and other makeshift metal projectiles flying outward in all directions. Three columns of flame rose where the single-minded men had ended their suicide mission and their lives. The noise of the blasts reached Anne and Leon before the chunks of airborne debris hit the tops of their arcs and descended. The screaming started almost immediately, but by that time, Anne and Leon had slipped into journalist mode. Anne slipped on her mic as Leon framed her against the chaos behind them.

"The scene is chaotic," Anne said unnecessarily. "Just outside of the Mormon community in London, three men, apparently suicide bombers, have blown themselves up. The damage seems to be extensive, as few of the shelters here were constructed of anything more substantial than sheet metal." After a few minutes, the two moved down the slight rise into the camp itself, Anne continuing her commentary as Leon filmed the aftermath. All around her, Leon's camera caught panicked refugees running in all directions. Crying children, shouting men, and screaming women ran past. Closer to the site of one of the explosions, others carried the bloody wounded away, as silent figures appeared amid the wreck of ruined shelters on the ground. Leon zoomed in on one tiny body, half invisible under the crumpled metal shell of a small tow trailer that looked as if a giant fist had hit its side. Leon swore under his breath, looking frantically around the camera's viewfinder. A pair of men, dressed in the distinctive uniforms of EMTs, crossed the journalists' path, and Leon caught one of them by the arm. "Over there—a kid under that silver trailer, near the right side. She's still alive."

"Got it, guv," the EMT said instantly, and sheered off to the rescue.

His partner, in an upper-crust accent that offered a startling contrast to the first man's Cockney, gently spread his arms to herd the camera-man and reporter away. "Please stay back. There may be danger lingering yet—if this is the same group we've run into before—"

Another series of explosions, smaller than the first three but coming in rapid-fire sequence, finished his explanation for him. Along the path of the three suicides, smaller bombs went off. These packed incendiary material instead of shrapnel; fires blossomed among the refugees' possessions. One tiny black cap, looking like a hockey puck, morphed into a ball of fire just ten feet from where they stood. The heat of the chemically fed fire nearly singed Anne's hair. She yelped, jumping away, pulling Leon after her.

"It's them, all right," sighed the King's English EMT. "Are you all right, miss?" he asked solicitously. When she assured him she was—merely startled and shaken—he nodded and renewed his warning that she and her companion "record this little incident from a safer distance."

"And get out of your way." Anne added the subtext he didn't say aloud. He gave her a smile and nodded. She considered protesting, but she was a religion reporter, not a war correspondent; they could see just as well from a distance that didn't impede lifesaving efforts. Guiding Leon, who walked backwards in order to continue recording the scene, she retreated out of the direct impact zone—but no further.

Other EMTs, along with an army of jumpsuit-wearing men and women whose only formal identification was a glittering Angel Moroni badge, poured out of Zion, restoring order, comforting the wounded, retrieving the dead, and locating unexploded munitions. Leon recorded it all from their perch just outside of the swirling activity. It looked like an anthill someone had stirred with a stick, Anne thought. His footage included the successful retrieval of the little girl who'd been caught under her trailer. Somehow, in the hands of the angel-sporting, Cockney EMT, she came away with only a few bruises and a gash across her forehead. Others, however, didn't fare so well. It took some time before the municipal services, small and belated, and Church rescue crews coordinated reports and announced official casualties: fourteen people were dead and over thirty more badly injured. And Anne had a report of three other such attacks.

Two hours later, queasy and angry, they arrived at Heathrow Airport.

"Why hadn't we heard about this before?" Anne demanded, waving the tiny screen at Leon. "Look at this! Three more—another suicide bombing in Korea, and two episodes of somebody firing rocket-propelled grenades and small arms into the refugee camps around the temple in Quezon City!"

"Do you have to ask? It all comes down to who's got the most to gain by shooting up the Mormons." Leon glanced at the video screens above the ticket counters, then stared, mental wheels turning.

"It's not the IRA, like that idiot BBC reporter kept saying. It's the people behind these other attacks. Monk says that with all the suicide bombings and loose RPGs out there, nobody cares about three more. But he got that squirrelly tone in his voice, the one he does when he wishes you'd just shut up and let him get back to his ratings bars, which means the board's probably put the kibosh on the story from the local stringers and any follow-up I might want to . . ." Anne followed his gaze, her voice trailing off as the news registered.

On Leon's screen, Brother Light beamed down on a procession of Children of Light, as Clara told the world that an invading army of white-robed fanatics had taken over the sacred Muslim shrines at Mecca. These, however, did not follow Muhammad's creed; they broke down the Three Pillars, ripped the coverings from the Kaaba, and proclaimed their One God as the only true avatar of Allah. Furious Muslims all over the world declared their intention of ridding the entire Arabian Peninsula of the defiling infidel presence—and the government of Qatar fell to a coup led by more of Brother Light's devotees, who promised to lead the converted to ultimate victory in the name of Unity.

"He's out to prove his is the only possible god." Anne looked at the remarkable eyes of Rashi Janjalani as he declared victory from his throne in the desecrated cathedral of Manila, a message beamed from halfway around the world to chill the hearts of unbelievers and call the faithful to the banner of the One God.

"Even if he has to kill his own people to do it," Leon finished. He picked up his camera bag and slung it over his shoulder as the preter-naturally calm voice of the flight announcer read off their number, then glanced at Anne. "This time tomorrow, we're going to be within about a thousand miles of him too, right there in the Ivory Coast on the edge of Zion with about a million Children of Light running around the continent. You ready to get between him and the Mormons again?"

"I don't think there are that many in Africa—the numbers are inflated to make him look good, because he's paid for a lot of adver-tising." Anne swung her own bag onto her shoulder, and fixed a steady glare at the smiling man accepting the adoration of flower-throwing throngs on the screens. It felt strange, almost as if she were looking at a live shot of Hitler or Mao or Stalin or Ajulu, a mass murderer in the making. The memory of his touch, his expressive and disdainful voice in her ear, made her shudder—and steam inside with fury and determination. Their narrow escape from the murderous Hands of the Prophet came vividly into her memory. "Yeah, I'm ready to get between him and the Mormons, now that I know I can't get away from the nut. No matter how much he's paid Monk, I'm going to make sure everybody knows he's using deluded fanatics to attack people who just want to be safe from the insanity all around them."

"That's my spunky girl reporter," Leon approved, punching her shoulder lightly. He accepted her returning punch, then observed,

"Good thing he's a religious fascist. This way, nobody can say you're stepping over the line."

"No, but he definitely has," Anne growled, earning a raised eyebrow from the airline attendant who took her ticket and compared her current glower to the pleasant smile on her passport holograph.

* * *

The brilliant line of fire glowed against the black basalt of the floor. As Rashi Janjalani easily stepped across it, the flames from the white-hot coals beneath licked up around him but failed to ignite the trailing skirts of his silk robes. "So the faithful fly through the flames of death unharmed," he intoned. "Your faith will give you the wings and will of dragons, fill you with the omnipotent power of the true God of this earth."

The double line of black-robed men bowed their crimson heads, chanting the mantra of the One God in time to the flash and flare of the flames. Their eyes glittered behind the masks, fastened on the man who promised to lead them to victory. With a roar, the Hands finished the mantra and rose to their feet, swords sweeping out to point to the blackened ceiling of the ancient building. As one voice, they promised their lives, blood, and souls to the Prophet of the One God in return for wealth and power. And then, one by one, they came forward to kneel before him, feel the weight of his hands on their masked heads, and receive the blessing that imbued them with superhuman strength to carry out their tasks of destruction.

Sepphira, ghosting along behind the intricate screens that shielded the blasphemous ordinations from the eyes of the non-elect, watched the recruitment with her knuckles pressed hard to her mouth to stifle the screams that rose in her chest. Only she saw the black shadows that flew from the darkness between the flames to burrow like parasites into the bodies of the men under their leader's hands. The men shook, moaning as the demon sank its spirit claws deep into their souls; when the convulsions ended, they rose, blank-eyed and hard-faced, to take their places with the other berserkers.

"And so it shall be with all who resist the power of the One God." Brother Light raised his hands, not in a blessing but in a final, irrevocable curse as the fire blazed up before the possessed Hands. "They will burn in the fire of divine wrath."

A tongue of that fire outlined the black robe of the figure standing on the wall of Quezon City, a fire that devoured the huts that had sheltered refugees from the monsoon rains and typhoon winds that ripped through the Philippines. Nothing could save them now, however, as the Hands of the Prophet poured through the outlying settlements of those who held to the world. The crackle of rifles and sharp stutter of machine guns punctuated the roar of the flames, providing a hard, aching beat to the chant of the attackers. The man who stood on the walls of Zion, his hands raised in curses, roared blasphemous threats down from the alabaster slabs. His gun hung empty from his shoulder, its lead pellets spent uselessly against the group of Saints who stood within the walls, their faces calm but sorrowful. The demon's fury glowed in his eyes, fighting with all the energy of its infernal pride to push through the barrier that the one true God had drawn between His sheep and the ravening wolves of the adversary. All along the wall, other shapes mounted to the top of the fortifications, adding their hoarse voices to the chorus of hate and fear.

As one, three of those sheep stepped forward, raising their own hands as they hurled a countercharge against the infernal forces. "In the holy name of the Son of God, and by the power of His priesthood, we command you to depart and trouble us no more."

For an instant, the roar of the flames seemed to still, as silence as deep as eternity fell over the outpost of Zion. Then a scream, louder than any human voice could produce, broke the silence, issuing from the bleeding throats of the possessed berserkers. The sound rose higher and higher, shrieking into nothingness. The figures on the walls dropped, as if abruptly unstrung; they landed outside and lay, already half-burned and smoking from the violence of the demons' departure. From inside the city, another sound rose, hundreds of voices blending in a harmony that healed the rent heavens, as the Saints sang praises to the Shepherd who delivered them.

"Jesus has saved us again," one of the Twelve whispered.

"But there's nothing He—or we—can do for those outside," Felipe Aquino replied, wiping the tears from his face as he prayed for the souls whose stubborn addiction to sin left them outside in the inferno.

* * *

Dear Chisom,

We were delighted with your last Vid and once again enjoyed the 3-D images you were able to capture. I couldn't help but notice that there were a fair number of a lovely, tall, young woman, some with you standing next to her. Is there anything going on over there that you have not yet mentioned? Are the pictures a subtle hint? Have you been keeping yourself busy with matters other than your PR work and Church callings that you haven't bothered to mention in your Vids? Hmm?

I am pleased that you are enjoying your PR work and more that it is having success in spite of the work of Brother Light's people. I see that you have found out for yourself that one of the blessings of our job is being close to the Brethren. I am not surprised that you are now meeting regularly with Elder Hung to discuss PR matters. I meet with President Rojas about twice a month now, and more often when circumstances dictate.

Normally, I would meet with one of the Twelve, but with them scattered over much of the world, the First Presidency is having to pick up a lot of the load. Thank goodness we have the Seventy who, though many are assigned throughout the world, still have a strong base here and help pull the load. Thank goodness, too, for the Church's satellite system. By that means the Quorum of the Twelve can still meet regularly with the First Presidency and stay in contact with Church headquarters in spite of the wild conditions in the world. They continue to have their Thursday morning meetings in the temple, albeit a bit modified since they are not all in the same temple. Technology is wonderful.

On another note, you may have heard that there have been a number of failed attacks against our Zion communities. We do have reports that out of these attempts, most of our enemies have determined not to come against us any more. In D&C 45, the Lord told us that the wicked would not come up against Zion because the terror of the Lord would be there. And it is.

There is one amusing item I will share with you. That many people get uncomfortable near Zion while others can't abide getting *close has not gone unnoticed. This protection is the clearest sign yet of God's increasing and ever more direct involvement in history. The phenomenon has caused quite a stir, because it is hard for people to ignore, and many don't, in spite of Channel 8's attempt to discredit it. I would think, therefore, that people would come to us for an explanation. I find it a bit amusing, if frustrating, that they don't. Instead, the speculators are having a field day trying to determine what is causing it. What they come up with is at least entertaining.*

For example, those who see the Church as technologically advanced insist that we have some kind of psychic dissonance generator that disturbs the brain waves of people we don't want around. Others have posited the possibility that we have invented some kind of force field. Still others, more far out, insist that we have teamed up with aliens (connected, by means they don't explain, with the asteroids) who have surrounded our cities with protective beams. I might add as an aside that this group is further away and yet closer to the truth than the others, depending on how you look at it. Those of the National Enquirer *crowd postulate that, through evolution, the Mormons have developed some kind of telepathic power that they are using on outsiders. A sophisticated 3-D Vid has been circulating that shows President Rojas, not with horns, but with antennae.*

Much less amusing is the view of our detractors who insist that the phenomenon is a display of satanic power. The Mormons have, they say, accepted full partnership with the prince of darkness and he is now protecting them. The latter is laughable only in the sense that some of those who have been interviewed describe their experience in trying to get into Zion as being burned by hellfire in the mind.

These speculations remind me of a somewhat parallel Book of Mormon event. Samuel the Lamanite told the Nephites that God would give them a sign announcing the birth of the Messiah—a day and a night and a day with no intervening darkness, accompanied by the appearance of a new star. From what I can tell, when the sign came, there was not a Nephite or Lamanite who did not see it and marvel.

One would think that such a sign would have converted many, but "from this time forth there began to be lyings sent forth among the people, by Satan, to harden their hearts, to the intent that they might not believe in those signs and wonders" (3 Nephi 1:22). Amazingly it worked, not because Satan's lies were all that good but because the people grabbed at anything that helped them explain away what happened.

The Revelator, in his symbolic way, depicted this period when the devil's lies would run rampant. He says he saw "three unclean spirits like frogs come out of the mouth of the dragon [Satan], and out of the mouth of the beast [institutions and governments], and out of the mouth of the false prophet [philosophical and false theological systems]." In chapter 16, he explained that "they are the spirits of devils, working miracles, which go forth unto the kings of the earth." And what is their purpose? "To gather them to the battle of that great day of God Almighty." Notice that the lies are not directed at the righteous, but at the wicked. The irony here is that Satan is deceiving his own people. And why? To keep them moving steadily toward destruction.

I hope that, by now, the fact he is marching his own people into ruin does not surprise you. As I have mentioned before, Satan is in this thing for misery. He thrives on pain and terror and horror. His insatiable hunger drives him to destroy his own for the delicious savor, even if momentary, of unimaginable agony. As Korihor learned to his sorrow and death, the devil will not support his own.

I glory in the fact that God does support His own. Not only that, but He is still buying us a little time to get the work done. Reports are coming in from the local and area leaders as well as the Gatherers that in many places people are gathering to us. It is a good thing that the cooperative Church farms are doing so well so that we have food for those who are coming in. In that regard, the needs of the times also mean we are able to keep people employed. In all, to paraphrase Dickens: It is the worst of times and the best of times.

While we still have time, let us labor in the Lord's cause. And if you just happened to tell us a bit about the young woman we *saw with you in your pictures, your mother and I would be most interested.*

> *With love,*
> *Your father,*
> *Chinedu*

* * *

"You proved your medical investigative skills working with the treacherous Major Zamora," Serrey noted, opening the jeep door. The doctor slipped out, refusing his assistance. "Consider this just the beginning of the consequences of competence."

"He's not a traitor, and you know it," Dr. Yazna Vasquez snapped back. As chief of security for the Chilean territory of Garza's United States of South America, he helped cook up the story of Zamora's secret life as a terrorist and his role in the assassination of President Quintana. She realized that the statement just made her sound like the ingénue in a bad melodrama, but she didn't care.

He knew that too, and a sardonic smile crossed his indolent face as he took her arm. His fingers only tightened when she moved to shrug him off.

She snapped her mouth shut and clenched her jaw, forcing her arm to relax, to give Serrey no more satisfaction by reacting to him. Instead of fighting the situation, she turned her attention outward, focusing on taking in the details of this section of General Garza's command camp. Early that morning, the official demand came to Santiago: the General required the instant presence of Yazna Vasquez as part of the Mormons' labor levy. After a short but heartening interview with Elder Molina, Vasquez obediently reported for conscript duty. Now, after a plane ride bumpier than any she could remember, she found herself in the heart of the enemy's citadel, walking across the graveled driveway toward a long, low building on the outskirts of the General's camp outside of Bogotá. The buildings themselves looked hastily but sturdily constructed of actual walls with the sheen of sealant washed over them rather than the ubiquitous reinforced tents. Long pipes hugging the beams, tightly closed windows, and double doors defied the jungle heat and told her that the building had a self-contained air-conditioning system. That fit with the bits and pieces of intelligence that Brother Neruda and other rebel operatives had gathered, rumors that Garza's next-generation weapons included a more refined variation of the bioengineered sickness his guerillas had already used in Peru and other especially resistant areas.

They paused at the door, where a pair of hard-eyed guards, much different from the semitrained thugs who'd whistled at her on the walk over, examined the papers Serrey presented. One hung a tag around her neck, bright orange as a warning of her conscript status.

"Walk softly, Yazna," Serrey told her conversationally as they passed between the sentries, through a second airlock-style portal, and into the hallway beyond. At the far end, a huddle of white-coated people gazed through a window set in the wall. The soft whisperings of their conversation reached Vasquez; the words sounded rapid, intense, but she couldn't hear what they said.

"That badge tells the guards that they can shoot you if you make them nervous," Serrey's words came through with perfect clarity. When she touched the tag, he smiled again, enjoying the fear he imagined she felt. She hid it well, but not completely. "But don't take it off, or they'll shoot you without waiting to get nervous. Very important work here, confidential. You won't leave this building until your work here is done, and you will speak to no one outside. If you so much as show your pretty face in the doorway, you won't have time to explain before someone shoots a hole in it. The General and Herr Brindermann do not want anyone to spoil the surprise they're brewing for their enemies. See those coffins waiting in the storeroom there?"

She had; the half-open door of the room closest to the entrance gave her a glimpse of a row of light metal and plastic coffins, stacked and ready. A sheaf of biohazard stickers lay on the table just inside the door.

"The only way you will leave this place is in one of those coffins, unless you cooperate," Serrey told her. "And you will not like what happens to you before they lay your bones in one of those boxes." He gently stroked her hair, exerting pressure on her neck to bring her to a stop beside a sealed door and the frosted window beside it. With a firm twist, he turned her face to the glass, at the same time pressing a button in the frame.

The opaque glass cleared instantly, revealing a tiny room divided into two cages—human-sized cages. In each wire-mesh enclosure, a naked, battered human figure thrashed, tied to a gruesomely stained cot. Their moans and thick, bubbling coughs came through the tiny speaker that activated when the viewing port opened. Vasquez's expert diagnostic mind detected the symptoms of advanced pulmonary hemorrhage, nerve damage, and mental deterioration without examining the subjects closely.

"Juan and Carlos. They served in El Jaguar's troop, before they let your Major Zamora slip through their fingers. The General promoted them to assist the campaign against the rebels more . . . directly, by trying out the vaccine against the prototype of his rebel-killer virus," Serrey whispered in her ear, too close to her, his hand still on the back of her neck. "As you can see, the vaccine lost the match this round. They've been dying for two days now, and they're finally getting quieter. When the pain first began, they could speak, screaming curses before they turned to pleading, but the virus causes what the doctors here call 'rapid-onset dementia' as well as physical deterioration, so they didn't make sense for long. Isn't it funny, how the prayers we learn as children, the nonsense syllables the priests pound into our heads, are the last things to go when the mind turns to mush?"

Vasquez barely heard him, staring horrified at the two men as they convulsed, muttered, cried, coughed, and slowly died, locked in wire cages. The idea of bioweapons hurt her heart; though she did most of her best work as a medical examiner and investigator rather than as a healer, she had trained as a doctor, and the thought of physicians deliberately creating diseases to kill sickened her. The visible proof sent a hard jag of nausea into her stomach. She swallowed hard, fighting the physical reaction and the fear that threatened to overwhelm her. Not fear of the disease—horrible as it was—but deep terror of the evil that would do such a thing, consciously and carelessly. Serrey's sadistic interest in watching the slow murder marked him as a monster, but a monster who recognized the value of life. The cold calculation of the mind that ordered human beings tortured to death from inside out as part of an experiment completely defied her imagination.

"And here is the good doctor whose handiwork we are admiring," the security chief announced, loosening but not releasing his grip.

Dragging her gaze away from the window and the two poor creatures within the cages (no matter what they did, no matter what threat they posed to Manuel—Major Zamora—no one deserved such a death), Vasquez looked up. She didn't quite expect to see a demon in human form, and after an initial mental scattering as her mind correlated the mundane reality of the man with the enormity of the crime beyond the window, her eyes locked hard and tight on the tall researcher in the white coat who strode up the hallway.

"This is an impossible situation. Substandard equipment, substandard research conditions, undependable power supplies, untrained or half-trained assistance, impossible scheduling demands—" He rattled off the litany of complaints as if incessant repetition had made it as much a part of him as the rhythm of his breathing. Coming to a stop a few feet from Vasquez and Serrey, waving his clipboard vaguely in their direction, he seemed to see them as the authors of his problems—if he saw them at all.

"Dr. Twilley, from up north." Serrey carelessly cut across the trail of complaints, waving a hand toward the doctor and shoving the clipboard hard against Twilley's thin chest. "Shut up, Twilley. Here's help for you." He shoved Vasquez forward too, almost dangling her by the scruff of her neck in front of the American scientist.

That broke Twilley's preoccupation. He swept Vasquez with a cold look, as if she were a barely qualified job applicant come to beg a position on his staff. Touching a button on the clipboard, he scanned the resulting information and fixed her again with that gimlet glare. "Yazna Vasquez?" he asked.

"Dr. Vasquez," she responded crisply as she rattled off her precise medical credentials—then repeated them in English when Twilley just stared at her. She did not extend a hand. Instead, she returned his stare steadily and thought a heartfelt, silent prayer for guidance in just exactly how to foil every last tiny piece of this creature's plans. She had waited behind the walls in Santiago, treating the Saints injured as they infiltrated Brindermann's work crews, doing what she could to unravel the virus she and Zamora had found in the bodies of El Jaguar's rebels, praying for Manuel and Michael Angel—and half hoping that she, too, would be called to the front lines against the black-hearted General. Now her opportunity had come, and though the immediate suffering and horror frightened and chilled her almost to tears, it also strengthened the steel in her spine.

Twilley nodded at last. "We speak English in the lab," he informed her. The scowl on his ascetic face deepened. "It is impossible to get good help in this part of the world. Watch the lab techs carefully; they are lazy and undependable at best, unconscionably careless at the worst. Sometimes, I believe that they are deliberately sabotaging the work, which is not only treacherous but criminally stupid, given the penalties for incompetence—"

"Do have fun, Yazna," Serrey breathed into her ear, his hand stroking her neck. She caught it, giving him a look full of frozen poison. It only provoked one of those lazy smiles and a flash in his flat, glittering eyes. "I'll come visit later—to make sure you don't get lonely with just that querulous old man for company."

"Please, neglect your duties for me," she whispered back, flicking her fingers at another mercifully opaque isolation-room window. "Maybe we'll get you in as a guest." She kept her voice level as she said it, despite the bile that rose in her throat at the actual thought. Without a backward glance at Serrey, she followed Dr. Twilley down the hall, deeper into the bowels of his top-secret medical hell.

It didn't take Vasquez long to ascertain the current situation: apart from Juan and Carlos, no other subjects currently suffered through the results of a vaccine failure, because the team was between protocols. Twilley tossed off fragmentary explanations of the equipment and procedures, leaving her to put the puzzle pieces together to figure out what protocols, serums, and viruses had proven useful or failed; his ego seemed to drive him to browbeat his team for failures while simultaneously withholding vital information, preventing them from succeeding so he maintained his preeminent place as chief researcher.

The ostensible reason for Twilley's current rage showed in his repeated assertion that they had fallen behind because he couldn't find or keep "competent assistants" to fill out the research team. "You Mormons are supposed to cooperate now," he muttered darkly, looking at her over the sleek bulk of an imported gene sequencer.

"Indeed," Vasquez replied noncommittally, adding, "so here I am. What do you want me to do?" when his eyes narrowed suspiciously.

"Find out why the antigen receptors in Protocol 39a have mutated," he snapped. "Check the length of the telomeres. And then run another correlation between A, D, and S proteins in the envelopes of the original virus strain. Make sure the samples aren't cross-contaminated with later strains. I want the results tomorrow."

And any one of those tasks could take weeks to complete properly. Vasquez didn't bother to argue; she simply nodded, turned on her heels, and collected the two techs he had reluctantly assigned to her. As they repaired to the far end of the lab, Twilley shouted after them, "Remember—we speak English in the lab!"

She spoke English as she directed her assistants to lay out the recent experiments for her, bending her investigative skills to uncover not the reason for the receptor mutation but for the entire enterprise, while she set the techs to the most likely successful of the tasks Twilley assigned. After a long day and longer night, she sat back from her concept map and ran her hands through her hair. Absentmindedly repinning the long coil back up into its frayed twist, she looked at the situation she had laid out, built from Twilley's few hints and the hard data in the lab's computer logs.

Twilley had come to Bogotá on loan from MedaGen to develop a devastating, fast-spreading virus for Garza to use against the next targets of his war machine. Mexico had the favorite spot in the lab pool. Designing and perfecting vicious infections had proved stunningly easy; the General had personally commended Twilley on his success in creating revolutionary new ways to kill people. He also, however, demanded that Twilley find a fail-safe way to inoculate Garza's troops against the custom-designed plague—and there lay the rub. The first-generation antidotes that Colombian scientists produced for the General's original wave of biological attacks kept El Jaguar's men and others from succumbing to the poisons in their system, but they worked only in the short term and required frequent doses of the antidote to keep the disease symptoms in check. Twilley's attempts to find a more permanent virus/vaccine solution had gone badly. Combinations that worked well in animals didn't work in humans, and the already unstable viruses mutated altogether too quickly for easy containment and control. At practically every step, they discovered another version of a potentially lethal infection, but every step took them further from a cure.

Presenting a vast array of potential toxins utterly failed to distract or appease Garza, who demanded that his own troops not get sick with the toxins they deployed, and who also demanded faster results.

The heat made Dr. Twilley break out in a sweat, since Brindermann decreed that the punishment for slacking would be employment as a guinea pig.

The pile of data gave Vasquez far more motivation than she needed. Thoughtfully tapping her stylus against her lips, she reviewed her initial design for another experiment, one that might help isolate some of the mutation factors and bring a vaccine slightly closer to reality. It contained little actual bioengineering, because the precise details of DNA manipulation lay outside her experience and training. The other scientists here, despite Twilley's low opinion of them, had the technical and genetic expertise to deal with the intricacies of the viruses' undead metabolisms; what she could contribute came with her hardheaded, logical approach to the problem, her experience with the military mind, and her acquaintance with disease vectors. She had no qualms about dedicating her entire attention to finding a cure for the vicious bugs Twilley had produced, though she knew she could not participate in or condone the forced human trials he and his masters were using. Right now, however, there was one thing she had to do before she could throw herself into the search.

Glancing at the thin, gray light oozing through the frosted glass of the laboratory office, she rose from her chair, stretched hugely, and moved through the equipment-stuffed room. Time to begin fulfilling the call that brought her here. The disc in her pocket already contained all the basic data she had downloaded from Twilley's isolated system, compressed and encrypted, ready for other minds to analyze. Gliding into the huge cold room, she plucked samples of each of the promising protocol viruses from their foam coffins and tucked them into a padded sample case. She slipped the disc in last, snugging it between the soft foam and the hard shell of the lid, and snapped it closed. Tucking the case under her arm, she left the cold room and walked into the long corridor, nodding to the yawning lab tech on duty outside the lab room. The motions came easily, as if her hands and feet knew exactly what to do.

As she neared the airlock doors at the front of the building, however, the smooth certainty wrinkled and faded. Of course she had full freedom of movement inside the lab; why prevent an inmate from having full run of her jail cell? The sentry's shadow against the outer pane of the double doors darkened the vague hint of dawn outside. One door, one way out, guarded. The insubstantial weight of the box under her arm seemed to increase, pulling at her. She had to get the information out, sabotage the General's plan by giving the data to someone who could find a cure even if (she faced the thought squarely) she failed and succumbed to the disease herself.

"Oh, Holy Father, what should I do?" she whispered. "Please help me." She didn't know what she expected, but hearing an indefinable, inaudible voice reply, "Go out the door and down to the loading dock," definitely wasn't it.

Just walk out? Just go out the door, with the sentry standing right there? she mentally yelped, staring at the dark silhouette on the frosted glass. The rational, logical, scientific side of her mind rebelled, protesting the sheer stupidity of the idea. So did the side that definitely did not want to end a promising medical career in a hail of lead shot. Still, the force of the feeling pushed against the fear and disbelief. Did she believe in God? Did she believe in revelation, in miracles? Did she believe in Christ and His awareness of her? If she did, didn't it necessarily follow that what she felt was valid? She believed in germ theory, so she washed her hands. She believed in the justice and divine support of the Saints, so she came here on Elder Molina's orders. She had seen amazing things with her own eyes, the hand of a God who could stop that psychopath Serrey from ordering a division of troops or an air strike to level the Santiago Temple. Could that same God clear her a path to save a few more of His children from dying in their sins? A wash of calm reassurance poured into her, along with a wordless push, telling her to go now, and hurry—but don't run.

"Santa Maria," she said, taking comfort in the memory of the blue-robed Virgin who had so captured her imagination as a child, "if you could say yes to an angel, I can say yes to a voice. And if I get shot, you can tell me why I should have said no."

Trying to silence the running commentary in her mind, Vasquez walked forward. A heavy rumble, partly muffled by the airtight door, sent her scurrying back, flattening her back against the door of the first examination room. Its latch clicked, opening under her hand. She slipped in, keeping the door from closing all the way, and looked through the crack. The airlock doors opened inward and locked in place. Predawn light filtered in, along with the sound of men's voices.

"Too early for a delivery," one grumbled, and she saw a sentry back in through the open portal, guiding a cart with a large, heavy shipping package balanced on it. One of the wheels juddered and spun, knocking the cart slightly off balance and making the sentry swear.

The other sentry and two uniformed deliverymen helped him wrestle the heavy thing across the sill, then caught it again as it threatened to tip its load off the other side. "This thing's going to crash before we get it back to the lab," one of the deliverymen complained. "You guys have to help us haul it back."

"We shouldn't leave the door," the second sentry protested.

"What, you afraid a lab rat's going to escape?" jeered his partner. "You heard the doc—they finished killing their stiffs last night." He pointed outside, where two sealed coffins waited beside the door for the cleanup crew to take away for proper disposal. "Nobody's infected right now. And the techs aren't going anywhere. They miss roll call, we round 'em up, and they're the next sacrifices on the altar of science."

"If this thing breaks, it's all our heads," added the deliveryman. "All the way from the States."

"The doc's always saying he needs bigger equipment," the hesitant sentry quipped, earning a general laugh. With a shrug, he joined the effort to herd the recalcitrant cart and its precious load down the corridor.

With many disparaging remarks about the cart's descent from a broken-down truck and a desperate donkey, they passed by the doorway where Vasquez watched with wide eyes. None so much as looked up as the cart went by—or as the doctor slipped out of the room, through the doors, and onto the gravel roads of Garza's headquarters.

Looking around, trying not to look like an escaped prisoner, she felt a light touch inside her head and walked briskly in the direction it indicated—the same direction the soldier had pointed when he commented about the stiffs, to the right around the building. A few uniformed soldiers stood beside the other tents across the wide delivery area, or walked slowly past the lab in the pale light, but none paid any attention to an official-looking woman purposefully walking past. The one who did react only stirred enough to give her a desultory wolf whistle, simply out of habit when his groggy brain realized that a female had walked by. Ignoring him with the ease of long practice, she turned the corner of the long lab building and saw the two coffins lying on the ground, tightly sealed, marked with a brilliantly colored biohazard sticker and a note specifying that the contents were destined for the high-pressure incinerator, not merely the dump. The lab's workers had dumped them right beside the huge trash containers just behind the mess hall. Just beyond the coffins and dumpsters, a group of dusty, battered trucks off-loaded produce at the back of the mess hall, while a crew loaded garbage into another large hauler.

So she'd made it to the loading area behind the lab. Now what? The coffins drew her eye, the memory of their contents increasing the feeling of urgency that made the packet in her pocket feel heavier than lead weights. One of the burly figures lounging on a bench as he supervised the unloading caught her eye. Her heart beat faster, from hope this time rather than fear. She had heard that Brindermann assigned the Mormons all the necessary but undesirable tasks that someone had to do, and do consistently, but that no one wanted to. It made sense that list would include garbage disposal—especially when the garbage included the highly toxic, highly secret results of Twilley's experiments. Mormons would follow the orders on the coffins; others might open them out of curiosity or dump them somewhere instead of making sure they were completely destroyed. So this is what Neruda meant, complaining about Elder Molina's assignment reducing him from entrepreneur shipper to rag-and-bone man.

Altering her trajectory slightly, she glided up to pass behind him, dropping the box and its precious cargo behind the bench. "Special delivery, Brother Neruda. Get this to Dr. Joseph Gee in Arizona," she said, keeping her voice low. Dr. Joe had handled the first samples from Slick and his men; he was the best person she could think of to receive the next shipment. Plus, he had a network of associates, including Meredith Galen, who could add their expertise to finding the cure for Garza's killer disease. She hesitated, looking at the first coffin as Neruda's men lifted it into their flatbed truck, remembering Serrey's threat. So she would only leave the lab in a coffin, eh? "And if you ever see a coffin with two biohazard stickers on it—two, not just one—be sure you open it before you put it in the incinerator."

"Got it," Neruda responded, watching out of the corner of his eye as Vasquez walked on without pausing and turned around the far corner of the mess tent. *Good luck, señora doctor,* he thought. *You are a brave lady in a jaguar's den.* A few minutes later, when the officious military bureaucrat strode over and thrust the sheaf of forms in his face to countersign, Neruda rose and picked up the package, tucking it into his coat. It rested innocuously between Tomás Neruda's feet on the road north to the border, then, after a little palm greasing, joined a private collector's special stash of Mayan artifacts bound for Arizona.

Vasquez, trusting that matters were now in Neruda's hands (and God's), forced herself not to run as she returned to the lab. Breathing a sigh of relief as she rounded the last corner, she slipped into the still-open airlock to join the lab techs crowded around the new machinery— and narrowly avoided an accident when the top of the heavy crate the deliverymen were unpacking under Dr. Twilley's brusque orders toppled off the counter and nearly hit her. Anyone noticing the relief on her face probably put it down to her narrow avoidance of a potentially broken foot. Nobody heard her sincere, silent prayer of thanks— or her wholehearted agreement with the feeling that she'd probably used up her ration of miracles for a good, long time. She'd definitely have to tell Manuel Zamora that he wasn't the only one pulling daring raids and miraculous escapes.

* * *

"There they are," Guerra reported from the raiders' forward position, his voice whispering into Zamora's ears through the tight-band comm that let the rebels exchange communications through a private channel. Leveraging the Church's satellite-broadcast system to let them listen in on Garza's troops while keeping their own exchanges secret had proved surprisingly simple, once they had their agents in place throughout Brindermann's command and control network. "Ten minutes for outriders to pass. Fifteen for main convoy. Twenty minutes for the rearguard. Five-minute window before the hornets get back to the nest."

"Acknowledged." Zamora passed the word to the half dozen men ranged behind him along the road to Bogotá. The team came to attention immediately, rousing from their catnap sleep to full predator alert. They abandoned their positions on the ground, springing up into the overhanging boughs, climbing high into the swaying maze of the forest canopy. Through the heavy tree trunks and emerald tendrils of the jungle, the puddles on the supply road glinted in the evening sunlight as a heavy whine grew in the distance, deepening as it drew closer.

Heavy tires splashed through the potholes, sending glittering droplets flying high. Around the leading vehicle with its mounted guns, men on stripped-down motorcycles swarmed, armed not only with the heavy rifles in scabbards by their knees, but with laser-enhanced goggles tuned to analyze and highlight any possible target in the green confusion around them. The men didn't look up into the branches this time; they would next time. Unpredictably, one of the riders would pull his rifle and send a stream of bullets into the undergrowth, forcibly clearing the way against a possible ambush. Zamora's rebel raids had shown the foolishness of depending solely on the protection of broken terrain and little-known roads to guard the convoys of weapons and matériel that flowed into Bogotá, and Brindermann was nothing if not a quick study.

This convoy moved at a good clip, however, its commander's confidence growing as it neared the primary depot. It had traveled far out of rebel territory without more than a single, minor incident back in Quito, and its commander had understandably relaxed. No rebels had ever raided this close to the General's headquarters before.

Which is exactly why, five minutes after the sweepers passed, two dozen camouflaged rebels dropped from the trees onto the tops of the slower-moving transport trucks. Zamora and his men struck the leading edge of the convoy while Guerra's team took the tail end, precisely picking off the soldiers guarding the supplies.

Ignoring the furious, cursing driver of the lead truck, Zamora pumped two rounds through the windshield, killing the backup driver and guard in the cab. Slipping over the hood to balance on the fender and holding onto the front of the grille of the still-moving truck, Zamora pulled a grenade from its place on the belt across his chest and pulled the pin, showing it to the driver before popping the hood. The man, redoubling his curses, hit the brakes as hard as he could and bailed out the door, rolling through the mud and into the thick vegetation at the side of the road. Zamora tucked the grenade behind the truck's manifold and leapt away from the vehicle himself. It trundled on a few more feet, then rushed forward as the second truck hit it from behind before its cab disappeared in an expanding globe of flame. At the back end of the convoy, a similar explosion marked Guerra's success. Instantly, the rebels converged on the middle two trucks, pausing only to discourage the few surviving soldiers with a handful of well-placed shots. The trucks' doors opened, revealing a cargo of sleek, metallic crates, each with the Keepsakes Ltd. logo emblazoned across the code pad of the lock.

"Now we find out if skipping school pays off," Guerra said, crouching beside Zamora, rifle at the ready.

Zamora just grunted, keying in the code that Mercury had sent. He'd found the codes while trolling through Garza's computer network to set up their communications and had passed along the data, "just in case you get a chance to try them out." On that chance, Zamora had planned this raid to include enough time to test the codes. If they worked, the rebels could steal the weapons that Garza intended to use on them; if not, they could still blow the entire convoy to slag and make El Jaguar look like an incompetent idiot by allowing the rebels to strike so close to home. The codes ticked in, the lock considered its options, Zamora and Guerra sweat bullets—and the light turned green. With a melodic click, the crate's top popped open a centimeter or so. With a triumphant shout, Guerra pulled the first tricked-out weapon from its tray. Its laser sight threw a ruby dot against the stained canvas truck cover.

"Staying in school pays off too," Zamora said dryly, but he couldn't quite hide a smile. *Very good, Michael Angel.* "Now, as my son would say for reasons that escape me, let's blow this popsicle stand."

He started the process himself, tapping a random sequence onto the keypad of the nearest Keepsakes crate. Guerra and the other rebels did the same with the rest of the trucks' contents. The oncoming drone of the second security squad rose over the insistent beeping and soft-voiced demands from the crates that they enter the correct codes or press the Abort buttons. Running from the automotive time bombs, Zamora paused just long enough to toss a salute at the driver of the truck he'd disabled. The man flinched back into the leaves, expecting a deadly accurate shot to follow. Instead, he nearly got decapitated by a flying truck seat, as the Keepsakes security locks detonated in rapid sequence. The oncoming riders slewed around frantically as pieces of flaming debris rained down around them, trying to negotiate a road blocked with broken metal hulks. A gleaming lock, its Keepsakes logo still intact, bounced off the hood of the rearguard truck.

* * *

The silver fragment glittered in Brindermann's hands. "The crates did not malfunction. These locks were purposefully set to self-detonate." He turned his cool gaze on El Jaguar, who glared back.

"So the rebels successfully destroyed an entire shipment of weapons, practically on my doorstep. This does not speak well of our efforts to quell the opposition," Garza summarized, taking the broken lock from Brindermann and weighing it thoughtfully in one hand before hurling it at El Jaguar's head.

The guerilla leader ducked but caught the potentially lethal chunk of metal. His fist closed around it as if to crush it into powder; the sharp edges dug into his hand. "Zamora," he hissed. No blasphemy could contain more hate than he poured into that name. Raising his hand, he noticed the dark drops of blood welling between his fingers. His teeth showed in a snarl. "By my blood, I will kill him myself and bring you his head!" he swore.

"You'd better." Garza's flat statement punctured the dramatic moment. "Or you'll find yourself on the receiving end of Dr. Twilley's latest experiment."

"A pitiful end to such a—dramatic career," Brindermann noted, dangling the implied insult in the face of the General's fading favorite.

CHAPTER 13

"It's not an insult, you know." Humphrey leaned against the doorway of the plush office that had once belonged to Virginia Diamante. It was more of a dressing room than a proper office; Virginia visited MedaGen only for photo shoots in the company's private 3-D studios. Even those few visits had filled the room with a kaleidoscopic mess of bric-a-brac.

"Wasn't it?" Julian asked uninterestedly, piling bits of the collection into bags. "What was it then?"

"Just business," Humphrey assured the redheaded assistant, stepping into the room. "Nothing personal. It's all a matter of what sells at the moment. It's all just a matter of money in the end."

"Virginia doesn't see it that way," Julian told him. "She's taking it very, very personally."

"Well, maybe what she needs is somebody to talk to her, show her that this isn't the end of the world," Humphrey offered. "I think she'll soon see that there are possible advantages in every situation, if you know someone to show you where to look. I could do that for her."

"She would very much like to show Mr. Abbott his mistake in dumping her," Julian replied, "before she could dump him."

"If she'll meet me for dinner—say at the Three Lilies, tonight at eight o'clock," Humphrey suggested, "I could give her some information that would make it a lot easier to torpedo Abbott's ship before it had a chance to come in."

"I'll pass the message along," Julian smiled politely.

Humphrey shrugged for the benefit of the watchful electronic eyes and walked away, adjusting the lay of his lapels. He made the restaurant reservation from a subordinate's personal phone.

At 8:00 P.M., he sat against the silk hangings of the restaurant, scanning the early crowd for any face he recognized, thinking about possibilities. He hoped that the information on the disc in his pocket would put a substantial dent in Mr. Abbott's golden armor. Eliminating Abbott might eventually open further opportunities for him in MedaGen's command structure—if he decided to stay. For now, grabbing as much cash as he could carry sounded like the best plan. Virginia's star might be sinking, but she was still loaded.

And she still knew how to make an entrance. As she drifted into the room, a rustle of recognition passed between the tables; everyone knew Virginia Diamante, even if they didn't like her music, or her media-saturating advertisements. Humphrey watched her undulate toward him in the wake of the maître d', Julian pacing unobtrusively behind as always. He rose to hold Virginia's chair for her.

She settled into it and treated him to her slow, suggestive smile. "Well, Mr. Humphrey, at least you know how to dress." He looked professional without flash, like an accountant or a low-level lawyer, certainly not a social acquaintance or romantic interest, but someone she'd do business with. "Julian tells me that you have an interesting proposition for me."

"I do," Humphrey agreed. "What would you say to the chance to put a spoke in Abbott's wheels? Proof that he and Ms. Zelik have over-stepped their bounds in a way that MedaGen can't ignore?" Watching the calculating light in her eyes, he laid out the skeleton of what he'd found: Twilley working on a top-secret, private project; high-tech weapons appearing in the Colombian jungle; the possibility that Garlick had allies mixed up in something a lot more serious than political intrigue, if not actively participating in it himself.

"Remember Herr Brindermann, that cold German who brushed you off a few months ago?" Humphrey wrapped up his bait in the ingredient guaranteed to snare her—bruised ego. "Turns out he's working for General Garza. He's second in command, as a matter of fact. And now Garza's working with Abbott. Clearly, Brindermann got what he wanted when he visited the office. Even if that was just bioweapons, not you."

That earned him a cat-eyed glare, but she took the bait—and the hook. "Like they say, you should be careful what you want," she observed, calculations clicking behind her perfectly lovely face.

"What you wish for," Julian corrected.

Virginia poked her assistant's shoulder. "What I wish for." Visions of what she wished for filled her head: Abbott defeated, Zelik brought down and her nose rubbed in Virginia's superiority, everyone worshipping Virginia.

But how would she make that happen? Information alone didn't help her at all; she had no idea how to use it. The patrician face of Caesar Augosto crossed her mind, along with the garish American flag tattooed across the neck of his obnoxious bodyguard. Augosto would know what to do with this information—and he'd care, too, that Abbott and Zelik sold MedaGen's services to a foreigner, a threat to the United States. He'd appreciate her, too, finally look at her, realize how much he needed her and wanted her. He would also raise her out of the fickle entertainment business to her rightful place as the empress of a real empire. He could buy her all the media companies in the world, and she could hire and fire people like Abbott whenever the whim struck her. No one could escape her then! She could almost feel the heat of the spotlight, the glare of the light in her eyes. Security, wealth, worship—everything she wanted.

Her gaze fixed on the glitter of the disc in Humphrey's hand. "How much?" she asked, motioning for Julian to give her the credit card.

"Oh, not much for you," Humphrey said. "In fact, you could consider this just the first payment in a long, profitable association. Kind of a subscription to Abbott and Zelik's Greatest Hits."

Virginia smiled at the quip, watching as Julian made the transaction. The moment the disc rested in her hand, her nails closed over it like claws and she stood. "We'll see about that—but we'll first be interested in giving this album a test listen." She kissed his forehead. "Good night, Errol."

"Just remember." Humphrey caught her face between his hands and gave her a stern look. "I don't know anything about this. If anybody asks, you got the pictures from somebody else. If you bring up my name, I'll deny it—and I won't give you the option on the next little land mine I uncover."

Virginia rolled her eyes. "I know, I know. Don't worry so much. It'll make wrinkles." She patted his face. "You just leave the thinking to me."

* * *

"So what are you thinking?" Julian asked, settling beside Virginia in her limousine. The car drove forward, humming through streets emptied by fears of plague and gangs.

"I'm going to tell Augosto about Zelik and Abbott's selling bioweapons to Garza," she said.

"That's a way to go," Julian said. The thought of drawing the Mob boss's attention threw up more red flags than a stadium full of referees; getting involved with the Mob would blow the career they'd built on Julian's songs and Virginia's exhibitionism. "On second thought, it might be more effective to blow the whistle on Garlick—hit Abbott and Zelik where it hurts, blowing their official government sponsor. Just think about it—once Garlick's gone and can't defend them, we'll be there to watch them twist in the wind, utterly ruined. Then you'll tell them that you're the one who trashed their careers."

She giggled, appreciating the thought. "So, who's listening for a whistle on Garlick?"

"How about that senator, the one who's always after Garlick—Holly Cox?" Julian suggested.

"Perfect. We women have to stick together, after all," Virginia agreed.

"Right," her assistant agreed. "But we've got to be careful on this one. You don't want to answer questions about those pictures. Errol's not going to admit he gave them to you."

"I know—he said that," Virginia snapped. "So we have one of my fans send it to the senator—but just a couple pictures first, and a hint about where to look for more. They're so smart, they can do some digging too."

"And then, if they're not getting it fast enough, we send a few more," Julian completed the thought. Using a go-between to send the images anonymously would work; so would keeping some information back, something to offer in return for safety, just in case Abbott or Zelik did manage to figure out that Virginia had anything to do with the leak.

"And that's my good Julian, always so obedient." She handed over the disc. "Take care of it. And Augosto's in town, so call his boy and make a reservation at Malena's—he likes Italian."

Julian hid a shudder. "I don't think it's a good idea to get involved with the Mob."

"Of course you don't, because you are way too practical, for a songwriter," Virginia teased, watching Julian send the tattletale message through a network of groupies.

* * *

"Senator, you need to see this!" called Charles, the young man who manned, as the senator noted with a sparkle in her eye, the receptionist's office of Senator Cox, staring at the screen as a message appeared— "Is the barn door open?"—along with a pair of pictures showing men in jungle camouflage and distinctive arm patches working on a sleek, matte-black drone in a high-ceilinged hangar.

"More spam?" Senator Cox said wearily, coming into the office from the conference room and yet another meeting with Senator White. They'd almost convinced Senator Benyanny to join them, but the senior senators, and their noncommittal, mostly anonymous allies, claimed they still needed more ammunition before they started their campaign to bring down the secretary.

"Not exactly, but the pictures are pretty revealing," her assistant said, turning the console screen toward her so she could see and read it too.

"Revealing," Senator Cox repeated as she scanned the rest of the message, feeling her heart rate increase. "Just a little roasted-Garlick appetizer," it said. "If you like this, you should ask the secretary for the full recipe."

"Oh, I've always been a fan of roasted garlic," Senator Cox said, already dialing a voice connection as she forwarded the message. "William, we just got a whole crateful of ammunition."

A low chuckle greeted her statement. "And here I thought we'd have to load our own rounds. Got a little divine intervention working for you there, Holly?"

"Maybe," she replied, "but it's more likely a double-cross from the other side. Evil is usually its own worst enemy, William."

"There's always exceptions," Senator White said slowly, gazing at the pictures—and at the portrait of Howard Garlick that he kept on his desk to motivate him, right there next to a snapshot of Holly Cox's honest smile, which reminded him of the tack he should take in dealing with an altogether too honest woman. The kind of personal attention those pictures represented had made William White the most respected, and feared, man in the Senate for many years. "In this case, evil's worst enemy is us."

* * *

"You're hindering the work of the deceiver in bringing souls to Christ Jesus, Miss Loftus." Michael Romanoff looked up from the personnel report and treated the nervous, sweet-looking woman standing in front of his desk to a bright smile. He waved a perfectly manicured hand. "Please, sit down. You're not in any trouble. Completely the opposite, in fact! It's Sally, isn't it?"

"Sally Mae, thank you very much, sir," she replied, settling gingerly on the edge of the soft, beautifully embroidered cushion of the visitors' chair. The producer's office, with its understated elegance and the obvious costliness of everything from furniture to carpet to curtains, would have made her nervous in any case, but the fact that the office belonged to the man second only to Tommy Gibbs himself in the Crusaders for Jesus operation put a sheen of holiness over everything in the room.

"Sally Mae, right." Romanoff's smile brightened a couple of watts. He appreciated deference; it usually marked a malleable personality, and knowing how to mold malleable personalities had furnished this office, and the more luxurious country home he didn't spend nearly enough time in. "Well, as I said, you've done an absolutely amazing job as a phone agent for us. When I look at this call sheet of yours, I'm just amazed."

He had reason to be; Sally Mae's three-week stint as a phone representative gathering donations for the Crusaders had broken all records—calculating in the fact that she worked overtime every day, and then voluntarily, without complaint or requests for time and a half.

She blushed, but met his eyes directly, her own eyes bright with sincerity. "Oh, Mr. Romanoff, it's because I just know, deep in my heart, that this is where Jesus wants me to be. He's put me in the right place to help Him gather His sheep into the fold, right in the bosom of Abraham where they belong!"

"Well, you're definitely getting that message out," Romanoff agreed, trading the call sheet for another document and picking up the stylus for her to affix her signature. He'd heard plenty of enthusiastic endorsements of Tommy Gibbs's ministry—usually before rather than after people worked in the call center—but he decided to keep her in mind if he needed a positive blurb or, with that cute Southern accent, a voice-over for an ad.

"Oh, thank heavens for that!" Sally Mae rushed on, before he could change the subject to what he saw as the more important, rational, business-oriented reason for meeting with her. "It's just so important for us to do what we're doing, encouraging our brothers and sisters to join the cause, gathering all their resources to defeat Satan and win their place in heaven. When I can feel that another person has opened their eyes to the light of sweet Jesus, I just know that they're saved, ready to fly up to the dear Lord's arms in the Rapture!"

Romanoff blinked, automatically offering a tissue as she dabbed delicately at her tears. Sincere tears. If only that kind of enthusiasm were as contagious as asteroid fever, he'd never need to hustle for a gig again in his life! "Well, Sally Mae, I just wish we could capture whatever it is you've got and bottle it!" he exclaimed. "Which is why I want to offer you a promotion, from the call center to the public relations arm. You'll still be working on the phone part of the time—bringing people to the light of sweet Jesus—but you'll have a chance to spread that enthusiasm to the volunteers who work our venues too. Inspire them with some of that bright faith of yours."

"Really?" Sally Mae breathed. "Me? At the actual revivals? In the same place as Reverend Gibbs?"

"Well, in the same convention halls, helping organize and motivate the many, many people who work so hard to make the revivals such a success," Romanoff temporized gently. "You won't have to come backstage, or worry about the technical aspects of the show. Leave that to the pro team. But I'm sure that Reverend Gibbs will deeply appreciate your enthusiasm and efforts, even behind the scenes."

"Oh, I'm just fine with behind the scenes," Sally Mae hastened to assure him, blushing again in embarrassment that he might think she wanted to put herself forward. Still, the thought of the chance to be there, in the same space as Tommy Gibbs, sent an excited shiver through her. "I'm just happy to serve, any way I can."

"Wonderful." Romanoff extended the document, indicating where she should sign. "You said on your application that you'd be willing to travel, right?"

"Oh, yes." Sally Mae carefully wrote her looping, feminine signature on the line.

"Wonderful," Romanoff said again, clicking a button to log her signature into the database along with her promotion—and security clearances. "You'll need to be on the bus to Atlanta tonight. Sorry about the short notice. Can you make sure you'll be there?"

"To Atlanta? To the nationwide Call to Christ program?" Sally Mae nearly squeaked. She'd been selling tickets to that event all week, and now she'd be there herself!

"That's the one," Romanoff agreed. He practically had to catch her as she sprang out of her chair, ready to run home to pack that instant. He untangled his hand from her enthusiastic shaking and sent her off to his secretary for the necessary itinerary and preparation list. He sat back down in his office, amazed. No wonder she could gather donations like a vacuum cleaner! Those floor hands in Atlanta were about to get a taste of Hurricane Sally. He smiled smugly. And she didn't ask about a raise.

* * *

"It's my first time as a—floor supervisor," Sally Mae paused to double-check her job description in the information packet spread over her ample lap, and smiled at her seatmate. "And at the nationwide Call to Christ too! I just feel so blessed!"

"You're going to feel tired too if you don't get some sleep," advised the other woman, a veteran of many revivals whose genuine devotion to the cause didn't make her giddy. Sally Mae's boundless enthusiasm would almost be cute, if it weren't so tiring. "You just lean your head back there and nap, and we'll be there in no time."

"Oh, I hope I don't disturb you, but I'm too excited to sleep," Sally Mae said, hoping for a little more conversation, maybe a story of an actual encounter with Reverend Gibbs, but her companion had already reclined her seat and pulled her sleep mask over her eyes.

With a sigh, she read through the packet again. Her duties, as Romanoff had said, consisted primarily of monitoring the ticket takers, ushers, and other floor representatives, reminding them to project Christlike love and make sure that nobody got in without a ticket or out without paying a donation. Clicking the reader shut, she looked out the window into the darkness of the freeway rushing past. A burned-out car on the side of the road, the sad shell of it flashing by almost too quickly to see, sent a trickle of worry across her nerves, but a quick prayer banished thoughts of bandits. She was doing the Lord's work, and He would protect her. Doing the Lord's work. The thought lulled her to sleep at last.

* * *

"Sally Mae," Reverend Gibbs's voice startled her. She looked up from the long swatches of silk she was carefully folding, to see the evangelist standing right in front of her. Smiling, she rose, taking his offered hands.

"Thank you so much for your assistance in this great work of the end times," he told her. "Look at all the souls we have to save before Judgment Day."

She followed his gesture, seeing an endless line of men, women, and children, stretching out into the darkness of the vast convention hall. The sheer number daunted her, but she took courage from the light in Tommy Gibbs's face and the smooth softness of the cloth in her hands. "I'm ready, sir," she said.

He smiled and swept up the cloths she had so carefully folded, appearing at the far side of the stage in his beautiful blue robes, the gilded trim gleaming in the lights. The choir began to sing, clapping and swaying. The line moved forward, each person stopping beside Sally for directions through the door that would guide them to Reverend Gibbs. She pointed each one to the door, setting their feet on the correct path.

In the distance, a white light gleamed through the darkness, a light in the shape of a glowing man, hands outstretched as if he were holding out his hands in loving invitation. A long, narrow road led from the spot where Sally stood, past the podium, and along the edge of the cliff toward the Savior's city on the hill. The people she guided walked to the podium, where Tommy Gibbs preached God's unconditional love and gently tied one of the cloths around their eyes.

"But sir," Sally began, running forward as the blindfolded people wandered, oblivious, into the darkness. "But sir! They can't see!"

"They must walk by faith," Tommy Gibbs assured her. "Faith will lead them to the Rapture."

Sally found the lengths of silk in her own hands, watching as if from a distance as she wrapped the white bandages around the supplicants' eyes, unable to find her voice or stop her hands. She could only gaze in silent, open-mouthed horror as they strayed from the silver road, falling off the cliffs, wandering into the black wolves' dens that dotted the mountains, completely unable to see the true fold or the true Shepherd.

"Oh, Lord Jesus!" she finally managed to cry, the plea ripped from her throat. She woke, gasping, staring into the darkness. A single light, glowing from an isolated farmhouse in the dark, gleamed back at her. She could almost see the form of the Savior in the glow. It swept past, faded in the distance as she breathed deeply, praying for solace from the nightmare the devil had sent to torment and turn her from her appointed task. Slowly, like reluctant mist, the tendrils of the nightmare finally dissolved as she rationalized it away.

* * *

One after another, the dark blots swung loose and disappeared, detaching from the strings of pearls in the ladderlike matrix and melting into the variegated blue of the blurred background. Dove watched breathing shallowly, as scan after scan showed exactly the same thing: the AllSafe dissolving away in his blood, new DNA strands replacing the genetic alterations that primed his immune system to such a pitch that it would attack his own tissues without regular boosters to stop the process.

Merry watched too, amazed and almost reluctant, after so much effort and so many false roads, to trust the story her eyes, and the readouts, and the simulations, and the sixteen other blood samples, told her. She'd hoped that the last tweak Kendall had made to SemiSafe would give it the last tiny adjustment it needed to bind to the same spot on the gene that AllSafe exploited—and it had worked! Now their tiny swatch of reengineered DNA didn't merely bind to the AllSafe, rendering it temporarily impotent, but replaced it so the body could manufacture less powerful but ultimately more dependable white blood cells.

The rest of the team kept a close eye on the monitor as well, as it spun out its final conclusion that Dove Nakai was officially free of the AllSafe alteration. Corinne de la Guardia, the post-doc research fellow whose dreams of "making a difference" were coming true in front of her eyes, had no trouble accepting reality. She raised her arms and did a few flamenco steps, whooping happily. Kendall Learner, ever the suave, calm Englishman, simply raised an imaginary glass in a toast to victory. Even Sister Lavine, the velvet and steel receptionist who made sure that Section 89 ran like a well-oiled machine, hearing the jubilation, peered around the door frame to give a quick thumbs-up.

Dove's attention was wrested away from the virtual representation of his insides when Corinne grabbed him in an enthusiastic hug. He laughed and returned the squeeze, accepting her congratulations on being "officially off the plague rolls." As she grabbed Kendall, though, Dove looked at Merry. Dr. Galen looked halfway between calmly accepting and thunderstruck. It wouldn't have surprised him to hear her thoughts at the moment; she talked to her husband the way he sometimes made comments to his brother Benny, and for the same reasons.

Chris, we did it! Merry exclaimed silently. She could almost see his look of confident pride.

"Merry," Kendall's soft voice—and the third repetition of her name—startled her back to the mundane reality of the lab. "You should notify Elder Nabil."

"Me?" She blinked, then smiled at him. "But you're the chief researcher around here—and the one who put the final touches on our masterpiece. You should do it."

"Well, one of you had better do it, or I will!" Corinne exclaimed. "This is much too wonderful to keep quiet about for more than a couple more seconds!"

Kendall looked at her, looked at Merry, and shrugged, smiling. "I do hope I'll have a chance to get used to working in a lab with so little devotion to petty politics."

Merry laughed, giddy. "I hope so too! Go ahead, make the call. I'll put a bandage on Dove here."

"Make it a conference call," Corinne ordered, bounding down the hall to pull Sister Lavine into the show.

Taking a deep breath, Merry spent a lot more than strictly necessary concentration on patching the hole in Dove's arm. He and Dr. Resnik, the family doctor who came in to tend to the general health of Section 89's guinea pigs, had joked about installing a faucet there—or at least a doggie door—to make it easier to get blood out and experimental serums in. Corinne's excited voice came clearly from down the hall, mixing with Kendall's more measured tones. Merry smiled, relieved to have a moment of quiet; she still felt breathless, and in dire need of a moment to think, to get her mental and emotional bearings. It felt as if the wall she'd been pushing against with all her strength for the last several months had given way, sending her pitching forward, off balance. All the late nights, all the strange inspirations, Kendall's counterintuitive idea to use a set of junk-DNA sequences, the equipment malfunction that spilled random strands into one of the protocols Corinne had prepared, all looked from this side of the long road like a clearly marked path up a mountainside.

"Your ways are not my ways," she said, the scripture fragment catching in her mind and memory.

"But He does a good job, with His ways, doesn't He?" Dove asked. "You already said thanks?"

"No," Merry admitted, startled at the direct, sincere question. "No, not yet. I don't quite know what to say."

"How about this? Thank you, God, for showing us what we needed to do here so we can get on with the rest of your work," Dove suggested.

"Amen to that!" The sincerity in his voice—and in the simple, direct words—made her smile, but she also completely agreed with the sentiment. They'd found the cure, but the race wasn't over yet. Now, they had to get the word, and the serum, out to all those who needed it.

Dove stretched, flinging his arms out as if shackles had fallen from his wrists. "Man, I feel good now that the AllSafe stuff's gone! Felt like I had a bandito creeping around my veins, looking for an opening to bushwhack me."

"Well, in this case, sending a thief to catch a thief worked out well," Merry observed, checking the screen one more time. The results still scrolled by, showing that the detached strands of AllSafe and the snipper strands that cut it apart were both dissolving into random proteins in Dove's cells as his body's garbage-cleanup procedures ran their natural course. "You'll just need to keep that spigot open for another couple of weeks, so we can take a look at you every day to make sure there's no recurrence."

"Is that the only reason?" Dove asked, giving her a sideways look and a teasing smile. "You're not trying to keep me around here longer?"

"Of course that's the only reason," Merry informed him, raising her eyebrows. "It's just protocol. We can't just assume our cure works, without waiting a decent amount of time to see if our guinea pig turns toes up on us."

Dove's shoulders slumped, his head bowed; he looked utterly crushed.

"What's wrong?" For a moment, the act got her. *Had she been too blunt with the guinea-pig comment?* and then she snorted and lightly punched his unbandaged arm when he looked up with a broad grin on his face.

"Just disappointed that you're not using good science as an excuse to keep me around longer," he told her. "You give me a little come-on, I could get a serious Florence Nightingale crush on you."

"Oh, please," Merry rolled her eyes. "Cute kid like you? You've just been deprived of other female company for too long."

Cute kid? He mentally pegged that as her strategy to put more distance between them than their actual ages deserved (he was eighteen, and she couldn't be more than thirty—and they'd both be dead in fifty years anyway, right?), but he decided to respect the implications. She was a doctor, he was a border rat—besides, she'd already found her one true love, and he had things to do. What's more, he already had a crush on Renata Begay, and there were just so many noble ladies a knight errant could swear allegiance to, right?

"I don't think that's all," he said, giving her a sincere smile. "But I'm going stir-crazy around here."

"Well, it appears that you may have your walking papers now, young man." Elder Nabil came almost bounding into the examination room and smiled at both the physician and her experimental subject before shaking both their hands warmly. "I got the call from our excitable Corinne and imperturbable Kendall as I drove from the office, and I had to come to see you immediately. Congratulations, my dear Meredith!" With a brilliant smile on his handsome face, he abandoned the formal handshake for a grandfatherly embrace.

He swept Dove up in a hug as well, to the young Navajo's surprise. "And to you too, Salvatore!"

Corinne, who'd come in with Elder Nabil, claimed her hug too. Kendall settled for another handshake. Elder Nabil beamed at them, rubbing his hands together. "Oh, yes, you have tied up this particular camel well indeed. Now, with Allah's help, we'll start on the rest of the herd. Can your genetic manipulations defeat this unpleasant disease wasting the flesh away from so many unfortunates?"

The medical discussion got too deep and technical for Dove to follow; he knew more medical jargon now than he'd ever imagined, but he knew the limits of his vocabulary. He also knew the limits of his interest, and the bits and pieces of doctor talk reminded him of Dr. Joe—which led to the reservation, the Begays, and his long-neglected Santos.

"Sir?" he said, catching Elder Nabil's eye.

The Apostle had been a practicing physician before he quit his practice to accept his call to full-time Church service, but his specialty lay in areas other than genetic manipulations, so his attention did wander slightly when Kendall expounded on the intricacies of protein sequences. He nodded, subtly gesturing for Dove to lead the way.

Stepping outside the door, Dove apologized, "I'm sorry for pulling you away, but I need to ask a favor."

"No trouble—we'll let the bright minds play with the new problem for a while, and then tell me how they intend to tackle the solution." Elder Nabil smiled. "I'm sure it will be interesting. Now, what can I do for you?"

Encouraged, Dove plunged on. "Now that I'm clean, would it be all right if I went home—just for a visit? Calls just aren't the same, even when the Church lines don't have static on them."

Elder Nabil considered, his dark eyes seeming to see through Dove's skin to the ultimate truth beyond. He frowned slightly, as if processing a new and possibly suspicious idea, then slowly nodded. "I believe that would be a good thing," he said, gesturing gracefully to Merry, who left the intense medical discussion to join one she suspected would be just as intense, but on a different subject entirely. "With your doctor's permission, of course. Dr. Galen, in your considered medical opinion, is this gentleman fit for a desert trip?"

She could see Dove was angling to go back home for a visit. In a way, she couldn't blame him; hanging around Section 89 couldn't be interesting for an active young man, and Dove was used to a much more—exciting—life than she could imagine dealing with. That and the fact that he was missing the Begays and the crazy friends she'd heard so much about. Calvin she could almost imagine meeting; Perro, well she'd just as soon hear funny stories about him from a safe distance. How would she feel, separated from everything she knew and loved? That train of thought threatened to dump her at a stop she didn't want to get off on. She missed Carmen something fierce, and Chris—okay, enough of that, so she brought it to a sharp halt.

"Doc Resnik says I'm healthy as an ox," Dove wheedled. "Except for the AllSafe stuff, and you just said that looks like it's on its way out. I haven't coughed in months!"

That was true; AllSafe had eliminated the plague he'd caught from Slick's infected blood, and he'd healed quickly. Technically, there was no health-based reason he couldn't mount a one-man expedition to the North Pole. The only variable came with the SemiSafe. It should isolate the AllSafe DNA, chop it out of his immune cells, and form a self-contained knot of loose DNA that would flush out of his system without attaching to anything else. It looked good so far, but there was the risk that it would develop unexpected side effects over time. On the other hand, having him kicking around Section 89, bored and pining for his adopted family, wouldn't do anyone any good. The SemiSafe would do its work whether he was here or in New Mexico, and he'd earned a furlough. If it came to that, she sometimes wished she could take a vacation too; fascinating as the work here was, she'd been hard at it since Chris died, and sometimes her brain felt as exhausted as the rest of her psyche felt lonely. Carmen had already invited her out to Nauvoo to see the new house, but she'd put that off, due to the wild weather—and the excited press of being just *this close* to an AllSafe antidote.

She gave the eager young man a calculating look, but empathy won out. "Will you promise to take care of yourself? Pay attention to how you're feeling, and remember to get back in a week?"

"I always pay attention to how I'm feeling," Dove assured her.

"You didn't pay careful attention before," Merry reminded him. "By the time you got here, we were worried about pulling you through, even with the AllSafe."

"Oh, I knew I was sick." Dove brushed off the implication that he hadn't paid attention. "I figured I'd caught Slick's blood poison. It's just that I had more important things to do."

"Sometimes you sound so reasonable." Merry shook her head, grinning in spite of herself. "And then I listen to what you're saying, and I just despair." She caught his shoulders, shaking him slightly as if that could help her capture his full attention. "Hasbídí, you don't have Slick's poison in your blood anymore, or AllSafe either, but you do have an experimental vaccine in its place." Her smile sparkled a bit more as she added, "We need you back so we can make sure it's working the way it ought to. You signed on as a guinea pig, and we're not going to let you disappear back into the wilds of Amexica without getting our money's worth."

He gently placed his own hands over hers. He half considered kissing her hands as he removed them from his shoulders, but a combination of embarrassment and propriety, especially with Elder Nabil right there, kept him from going that far. Thanks to Benny's firm-handed upbringing, he was much more a fighter than a lover. He definitely appreciated Dr. Galen's ironic sense of humor, though. With a careless shrug, he let her hands go, observing, "Yeah, well—you're probably right. Figure I've got a couple grocery loads of room and board to make up, even though you've been taking blood out of me all this time." More seriously, he said, "I'll be back outside a week. And I'll pay attention to how I'm feeling too."

"You do that," Merry told him. To her surprise, she found herself tearing up. Her watch chimed, rescuing her. "Okay, that's my signal to pick up Missy. You be good. I'll see you when you get back." She shook hands with Elder Nabil again. "I'll see you soon?"

"Oh, yes—we have your next assignment to discuss in more detail," Elder Nabil assured her, smiling as she practically sprinted for the door. Good-byes were not Meredith Galen's forte.

Nor did a certain young Navajo have a talent for gracious leave-taking. After a few hasty good-byes and before Dove could sprint off to gather his duffel and disappear into the desert, the Apostle caught his shoulder. "Be careful, Salvatore. Dangers lie on the roads these days, some of them more dire than gangs or weather or earthquakes. Visit Jonathan before you go."

"Sure will." Dove stopped at the door, looking over his shoulder. "Why?"

"Did you intend to walk to New Mexico?" Elder Nabil asked, raising his eyebrows.

"Oh." Dove shrugged nonchalantly. "No, I figured I'd hop a bus, or find somebody going that way and hitch a ride."

Elder Nabil shook his head. "There are easier ways, Brother Nakai. Jonathan will get you a car to borrow for your journey. I hope we can trust you with it—and to take care of yourself as well as the vehicle?"

"Sure you can," Dove assured him. "Thank you, sir."

He repeated the same assurances to Jonathan Crow, who handed him the keys to a discreetly sleek sedan. "Don't worry so much, John Boy. I won't crash it anywhere."

"You'd better not! You also better not get yourself hijacked or avalanched, or anything else that can happen out there in the wilds, because if we lose you, Merry Galen will be using us as guinea pigs next," Jonathan warned.

Jonathan's comment did make Dove pause—not the guinea-pig part, but the warning about "the wilds." It had gotten worse out there; between towns that could defend themselves, worse threats than a flat tire or empty gas tank lurked along the long stretches of desert highway. True, the odds of banditos or drug runners lying in wait for a single car were long, but not vanishingly small. His hand drifted to the knife he always kept in its sheath at his belt, but what he asked was, "Jonathan, where can I get a gun? Just in case?"

Jonathan shook his head. "I wouldn't know. I'm not into that kind of thing. Maybe Ramon would know." The security guard had admired Dove's knife, and had the look Jonathan associated with Wild West types—like Dove himself. Jonathan knew that violence was necessary in some situations; he also knew that he didn't ever want to find himself in one of them. But Dove had grown up rough and seemed to take potentially lethal risks in stride. Sometimes Jonathan suspected that part of his cabin-fever boredom here in Salt Lake City came from the fact that nobody was shooting at him. "Actually, I think you should go talk to Maynard and Juliet."

"Fox and Socks?" Dove asked, surprised. Socks hardly ever left his electronic cave, and Fox didn't strike him as the sort of girl who kept a shooting-range pass in her purse. "Why?"

"I think it would be a good opportunity to test the precision of our satellite tracking and communication system," Jonathan said. "They've been talking about it for a couple of weeks now, hooking all the satellites together in one network so we get visual coverage of most of North and South America. They've got safeguards in place to fight off the sunspot activity, and Juliet told me that they can reposition the sky eyes slightly, enough to overlap scanning fields. They could give you a transceiver, then monitor your progress."

"Hook me up with a radio collar?" Dove cut to the heart of the matter.

That made Elder Nabil's assistant laugh. "Well, kind of. It'd let them talk to you as well as find you—but more importantly, they could scan the road ahead of you for any suspicious activity. You know, dust storms or cricket swarms—or those banditos you mentioned." He didn't add that Elder Nabil had already considered using the young Navajo's overflowing energy to test the system. That would give both Socks and Dove something useful to do. "Keeping an eye on our Dove as he flies" was how Elder Nabil had put it.

"Well, I guess they could do that." Dove considered it. He didn't know anyone else to tap as a wing man; all the people he'd made friends with in this civilized town were doctors or Churchmen, not exactly a road-toughened bunch of coyotes. He didn't think anyone would mess with him, or that he couldn't handle it if they did, once he found something with more reach than a knife, but backup would come in handy, just in case.

"I think Elder Nabil would recommend it," Jonathan pointed out, playing his hole card. Dove practically worshipped the senior Apostle; for that matter, Jonathan did too.

Dove shot him a suspicious look, then grinned and saluted. "As you wish, sir." Even if Jonathan was invoking Elder Nabil's name in vain, and he probably wasn't, since Jonathan didn't do that kind of name-dropping casually, an Apostle's advice was nothing to take lightly. Dove fell into step with Jonathan as they headed for the elevators, resisting the urge to roll his eyes at the thought of having a pair of cloistered computer geeks looking over his shoulder, literally, from orbit—especially the one who treated the real world like some kind of giant, multiplayer virtual game.

* * *

"So what's it look like from the first-person shooter angle?" Socks's voice came clearly through the tiny receiver in Dove's ear. It wrapped around like a tiny silver snake, its own audio pickup snug against Dove's skull to pick up his voice in return.

"Like New Mexico," Dove said shortly. "You ought to come out and see it sometime."

He said that only partly to tweak Socks about his unwavering devotion to the dim cave that contained all his precious electronic gadgets. Outside the windshield, the amber, olive, gray, and rust landscape rolled slowly by, the speed-blur of the cheatgrass and sagebrush near the roadway slowing to the eternal stillness of the high desert hills beyond. Above the earth tones, the sky shone with a brilliant series of blues, pale at the horizon and darkening to brilliant depths at the apex, where the sun shone between the high streaks of white cloud. The scene raised Dove's spirits; while he didn't have the love affair with the desert that traditional Navajos supposedly did, the desert meant freedom after months of city streets and medical restrictions.

Physical freedom in this case, if not freedom from observation. Above the clouds, the bright lens of the Church's satellite gazed steadily downward, splashing the picture of Dove's progress onto the computer specialist's console screen. From the high-altitude view, the bumps in the road smoothed out, leaving a single silver ribbon through the dirt-colored landscape. A single vehicle blazed down the long stretch of empty desert highway, lacking only a trail of dust and maybe some pursuing Apaches to fit Socks's image of the perfect Western scene. Then again, Dove was a Navajo, so maybe he should be pursuing cowboys instead.

A change in the landscape caught Socks's eye. "Hey, check out what's coming up to your left there."

Dove glanced that direction as he topped a slight rise between two hills. The rainstorm that had momentarily washed the clouds out of the sky had washed a lot more than clouds out of the gully. Mud and boulders fanned out from the ragged edges of the cut in the earth, forming a dry delta that looked as if a raging river had deposited it. He'd seen traces of the gully-washer floods that had washed out roads, stranded travelers, and in two cases buried small towns in the Southwest. The weather alternated between vicious droughts and pouring rainstorms. There was so much time and heat between showers that the desperately thirsty soil couldn't absorb the water it needed, so the liquid flowed over the surface, collected, and blasted its own channels through the parched hills. He'd passed a line of cliffs whose sandstone and limestone layers showed the signs of a recent torrential waterfall, the impromptu river already melted into the cracked desert floor.

This was the first flood debris that he'd driven across, however. The trails of dried soil bumped under the wheels, the layer of loose dust on top of the mudflow making the wheels waffle slightly as they lost full traction. That gave Dove a nerve jag as he steered around a large rock that the flash flood had managed to roll into the roadway. The back wheel hit the rock and rolled over it with a jolt. Dove muttered a Navajo word that would've earned him a warning look from Renata Begay.

"Rough road?" Socks asked.

"Duh," Dove shot back. He scanned the horizon. Floods came out of side canyons—and so could banditos, as he knew from personal experience.

"Thought all you tough guys knew how to drive," the computer geek persisted.

"Calvin does the serious driving." Dove righted the car, leaving the rough behind. "Perro does the nonserious driving—and all the yakking about it. Kind of like you, Maynard. How about you concentrate on watching the road—especially the sides of the road—and let me listen to the radio music for a while?"

"Hey, I'm a fan of country too," Socks assured Dove. "Especially the new stuff, you know, with the old-fashioned lyrics, kind of folk music, but more modern—"

Dove tuned him out and turned up the car's radio. Navajo voices came over the channel, talking through the reservation chat/news broadcast. He understood about half of it, enough to know that they were talking about the destruction, both natural and man-made, that devastated the area around the Rez. Locusts had come up from the south and down from the north, the two-legged ones infesting the roads and little towns, robbing and killing anyone vulnerable, stealing everything they could carry, while the six-legged ones swarmed out of the dust so thickly that their airborne swarms blocked the sunlight and ate everything that survived the drought.

"Even animals now," the caller on the radio told the host. "I found rat bones, just bones, all chewed on the edges, bug teeth marks. They're out of plants, and they're coming for things that move."

"A real plague of locusts, huh?" the host asked. He didn't sound as skeptical as Dove expected.

"Whoa—hey, Tonto!" Socks's urgent tone broke through Dove's mental soundproofing. "Something coming up here—it's either the lowest storm I've ever seen, or some kind of desert fog, or—"

The glittering black shadow overlying the road resolved itself into millions of tiny, chitinous bodies. They filled the air on whirring wings and crawled over the surface of the road. The tires hit them like a pile of crunchy slush, sending fountains of pulverized insect goop splattering behind the car. Locusts crunched and splattered against the windshield and grille, then bounced off as Dove slowed cautiously, wishing Calvin were driving. Rain was bad enough—bug blizzards were worse.

Abruptly, the crunching noise stopped. The sun shone again, bright through the high clouds. In the rearview mirror, the wall of locusts rose like a wall of heavy smoke, slowly writhing and swirling against an invisible barrier. "What just happened, Socks?" Dove asked, staring at the amazing scene in the mirror.

"You just entered Navajo Temple territory," Socks informed him. The computer geek sounded smug. "Welcome to God's own country."

The next welcome Dove received wasn't as warm—but it was more efficient. A pair of smiling but watchful Navajo Tribal Police officers stopped him at a roadblock, chatting easily as they double-checked his ID against the information from the satellite computer hookup. One handed him back the laminated driver's license and grinned. "Hey, Nakai. Bishop Yazzie says *ya ta hey* from back at Command."

"*Ya ta* back at him," Dove returned. "My Begays still out at their place?"

"Sam and Renata?" the cop nodded recognition. Yazzie said Nakai would ask after them. "Nah, they moved into town—with everybody else who didn't pull a skip and disappear. Your country-loving computer nut's turned townie. Go on straight down there, and ask at the gate. You can't miss it."

"So everybody's inside now, or out permanently?" Dove asked, shading his eyes as he looked down the long slope. In the distance, the glitter of sun on glass and a slight change in the heat shimmer told him that the town lay beyond the next rise.

"That's the way it's gone down," the officer looked back as well, a thoughtful expression crossing the part of his face visible around his sunglasses. "We lost a lot of good guys—and some bad ones too."

"What happened to old Gordo?" Dove vividly remembered the heavy, cruel face of Sheriff Pizarro. He'd joined the town council's efforts at securing their people against Garza's attacks, but he'd never warmed up to the idea of putting himself in the line of fire for actual public good.

The cop grinned, tight and sharp. "He's a lot thinner now. Down to pretty much bones. Turns out he started taking bribes to let the Dust Devils run their meth trade across the border territory when Travell Capshaw took over the California route. Señor Martel found out about it and threw him out, along with the deputies who'd gone along with him. The Devils strung him up just the other side of Navajo Route 3, to show us all how disappointed they were."

"Bad end for a bad man," Dove observed. He knew he shouldn't feel a swell of nasty satisfaction, forgiveness being important and all, but he did. It just fit that Pizarro ended up as crow bait because he'd bet on the wrong horse.

"It's just too bad that Escobedo ended up going the same way." The cop shook his head. "We've lost a lot of people. I guess it's not all bad, though. We've picked up a lot of new recruits out of White Sands and the other military bases who come back here to sleep, then head for the base to work; the rest have shut their gates and hunkered down. They're on edge and don't know what to think, got all their ears on for rumors from down south."

"You two done with your powwow? Turns out we need your parlor here for a road." The other officer came out of the booth, gesturing down the road. A cloud of dust spiked with hard metallic gleams announced the arrival of a convoy of large trucks. "We got houses and stuff to build, if you can move your lazy tails outta the way."

"Can't they go 'round?" Dove suggested. He returned an equally blue shot to the cop's bawdy response but obediently got back into his locust-splattered car to get out of the way.

The first officer leaned over as Dove drove by. "Hey—your friends are still knocking around Mama Rosa's, if you want to pick up with the suspicious crowd you used to run with."

"Think I'd do that?" Dove grinned and tossed him a salute. The new town that sprang out of what had been a dusty desert surprised him. It looked like an idealized piece of Salt Lake City, transported magically to the New Mexico desert. Unlike the actual Salt Lake City and the other temple towns, however, no refugee camps had sprung up around the outposts of Zion in the desert. The weather and the incursions of outlaws from both sides of the border made it much too dangerous to squat at the edges. As the officer at the border had said, here the choice was stark: get into Zion and behave yourself, join the outlaws, or leave for safer shores somewhere else. It pleased Dove to see how many had chosen to become part of Zion, even if the precise street grids and tidy yards of the neighborhoods, purposely engineered for minimum environmental impact and maximum beauty and utility, made him feel like a scruffy outsider. He found the Begays' neat, new-smelling house easily, following the directions from the kindly, chatty *abuelas* at the town's gate, more of a ranch marker than barrier, declaring the town Navajo Temple City.

* * *

"It's amazing, isn't it?" Sam Begay stood at the top of a long ridge-line, looking out over the rough country. Not so rough at the moment, and getting softer every day as a slow but steady wash of green crept over the desert floor. Sam gestured toward the newly flourishing farms and foraging pastures. "Look at that. You know the old quote about the desert blooming? It's happening right here."

"Like a rose, wasn't it?" Dove asked. "This looks more like an alfalfa field and tomato patch."

"Which would you rather have?" Sam asked, grinning. "I'll take tomatoes. Roses don't make good chili."

"Mama Rosa does," Dove returned the grin with a bad pun. "But so does Renata, though her mutton stew's better. Never thought I'd see you two move into an actual city. Thought you were a sunrise and pollen kind of guy—when you weren't chasing code bugs."

Sam looked toward the hills, where his and Renata's house nestled in the lee of a rocky hill. He did miss the space and the silence. His ancestors had been shepherds, and he still had the need for open skies deep in his bones. "We'll get back there. This is just an emergency measure, temporary until things cool down. Until the real kingdom comes, and we can do what we want to without worrying about raiders spreading bullets or rogue germs."

"That's the way it goes, isn't it?" Dove asked. "Gather everybody in to hunker down until the Gadiantons overextend themselves and we can smash them back to the Stone Age." The thought brought a hard smile to his face, showing the tips of his teeth. As long as he kept breathing, nobody, not Garza, not Pizarro, not the Brujos or Slick, were going to put down his people, broadly defined as anybody who tried to do right, narrowly defined as the Mormons, and especially the Navajo Mormons who'd saved his life. "Those that don't know history are doomed to repeat it—or just doomed, however that goes."

He sobered, thinking about the seriousness of the situation. It was all well and good to get excited about kicking the bad guys' tails, but doing it cost blood, sweat, and usually tears. "How's it going down here, Sam? Really? Perro's gone between telling me about imaginary shootouts and claiming he's bored 'cause the Mormons have taken over and there's no good gang fights anymore. Calvin's just said he's reading the Book of Mormon and keeping an eye out and that I shouldn't worry. Which makes me worry. The news doesn't say much about Amexica except that we're all outlaws fighting each other while Homeland Security threatens to send in enough troops to shoot everybody that moves—as soon as they take care of California, Florida, and the AllSafe problem to get Garlick reelected."

"Shows you can't trust the news, unless you're getting the report off the Church satellite." Sam shook his head. "That's what Channel 8 wants people to hear, all right. It's a lot better around than they're saying. The Santos have grown and got organized—I'll take you around tomorrow. Everybody's going to love seeing you."

"But there's worse than locusts out there, huh?" Dove didn't let Sam change the subject. He appreciated everybody trying not to worry him, because it meant they loved him, but it also made him crazy. Dr. Galen declared him healed, he was healed. For crying out loud, if it came down to cases, he was healed months ago when they hit him up with AllSafe and zapped the damage out of his lungs! He'd hung around as a guinea pig because they wanted to see if SemiSafe finally worked, not because he didn't feel good. "What's up with General Garza? Seen a lot of his soldiers? Seen any more mystery viruses?"

"No," Sam said with a silent sigh. Renata told him not to let Dove get involved in the war again right off, but he'd known there was no way to keep the kid out of it—and he didn't think Dove should stay out of it. Without him and his persuading the citizens of the border towns to stand against Slick, and the Santos' duel with the General's soldiers at Blanca Hacienda, they'd be in a lot worse spot. Standing up to the General's incursions meant they didn't have to run with only the clothes on their backs when the word came to gather at the temples. They already had safe communities set up.

Giving Dove a look that he hoped expressed the need for circum-spection, he continued, "No new viruses, and no organized pushes, like Slick tried. Mainly we're dealing with unaffiliated outlaws, plus a few gangs spreading out from Ciudad Juárez and Tijuana. There's rumors about bigger moves down south, though."

Dove nodded thoughtfully. "That's what I've heard too. We've got Mercury down there—you remember him, the little street-rat truant kid? Turns out he's the son of that rebel chief, Major Zamora, who's running around causing headaches for Garza. He's wormed his way right into the enemy's comm system now. He says there's doings, but he isn't seeing much of anything about the borderlands. Mainly, the General's tightening his fist around what he's got. Brindermann, this German majordomo Garza brought in, thinks he's got the Mormons bottled up, most of them 'confined' to Zion areas, or in outside ghettos and work camps where they couldn't make the temples. He thinks they're cooperating, so he hasn't started any pogroms."

"Pogroms," Sam repeated. The kid's vocabulary still amazed him—this from a rough-edged border rat?

"You know, persecutions meant to confine and kill a minority? Like the Trail of Tears or Bosque Redondo?" Dove explained, then ducked as Sam thumped his shoulder. "Okay, you know already. I've had a lot of time to read lately." He sobered, looking south. "Garza's going to move again soon."

Sam nodded, following his friend's gaze. "Yup. We're hearing nasty rumors from our own sources. We don't have to have Mercury's inside information to figure that Mexico's next—and then us."

"Eagle Eye to Inchworm. Come in, Inchworm!" Socks's transmission made Dove wince—out of inanity, not for volume. Socks was having way too much fun with this controller/field agent scenario.

"What?" Sam asked, noticing Dove's sudden flinch.

"Got a bug in my ear thinking he's cute," Dove told him, touching the minuscule button to turn on the audio transmission so Socks could hear his comment. The computer geek laughed.

Sam just stared at him. "I wondered what kind of wacky jewelry they were wearing up north these days, and why you took it up. What is it really?"

Dove turned his head, brushing his hair back to show Sam the little device. "It's a two-way radio transmitter, connected to a satellite channel. Socks, Maynard Stockton, a computer communications tech in Salt Lake, can talk to me through it. He's watching us too through the spy satellite. Go ahead, give him a wave."

With a glance upward, Sam caught Dove's shoulder and examined the device closely. "I think I'll pass on that one. This is remarkable. Got to be the best application of hard-wired circuitry I've seen."

"What is this guy, unfriendly or something?" Socks asked.

"He's particular about who he talks to," Dove informed him, then twitched out of his friend's hold. "Okay, Sam, enough. If I want somebody playing with my ears, she's going to be a lot prettier than you are."

Sam grinned. "No loss there—who'd want you, when Renata's around?"

"Yeah, rub it in," Dove growled. He'd pretty much had a crush on Renata since he first saw her. Renata, Meredith Galen, Fox and her big eyes at sky-lab boy Hideyoshi—he had to meet a single girl.

"Renata's the wife, right?" Socks asked. "I saw her before—wow, nice!"

"Keep your sky eyes on me, and lay off the outside observations." Good thing Socks was a good guy at heart; Dove certainly wouldn't trust Perro at the other end of a satellite camera that powerful! "What do you want, Socks? Or you just bored, hanging out at work on a Saturday all by yourself?"

"Just proves my dedication. I'm here for you, guy," Socks said virtuously. Even he couldn't keep a straight face (or voice) on that one, though. "Seriously, I just got a note from our favorite Chilean molé." He laughed at Dove's groan at the pun; Socks had a hard time keeping anything serious. "Okay, anyway, Mercury says that they've sent a package up, something interesting for Dr. Joe. He didn't stay on long—he says the Net's getting more haunted every day, some kind of cracker security going on. To get around it, he's spoofing his transmissions to look like the CIA's tapped into one of Garza's legacy networks, the one the Chilean government was using, I think. Really surprised me, first time I got a buzz from the CIA, before I figured out who it was by that Santos logo he hid in the header. He's sending the messages in English too, bouncing them around half a dozen switches and ports—"

"Did Mercury say anything about the package that I need to know?" Dove interrupted. Socks, for all his reclusive hacker tendencies, loved to tell people all about his electronic universe. It got even worse when Fox wasn't there to be his amused or annoyed audience. Weren't all computer geeks supposed to be shy, monosyllabic introverts? If they were, Socks was definitely the exception that proved the rule, and Dove would rather talk to people he hadn't seen in months than listen to the intricacies of smuggling electronic bits out of Garza's HQ.

"Well, just that it was interesting, and that Dr. Vasquez—who is a real looker too, by the way—thought Dr. Joe would be interested in the actual blood samples or viruses or whatever it is, and maybe so would Dr. Galen. So if you get time, swing by and pick some up on your way home." Socks made it sound like dropping by the store for a dozen eggs and a gallon of milk. Which it probably was, for him—not that he commonly carried top-secret, stolen viruses, but that venturing into the real world for eggs and milk was about as unusual.

"Got it," Dove clicked off the audio transmitter. He didn't bother to click off the receiver, though he could if he wanted to; he figured he'd let Socks listen as well as look, give him a sense of normal human interaction. As it happened, Dove's intentions proved a bit optimistic on that score.

* * *

"So, how's the breathing?" Dr. Joe didn't even bother with "hello" before he lifted Dove's loose shirt and stuck a stethoscope against his back.

"Better than your manners!" Dove couldn't help laughing, even as he submitted to the blatant invasion of personal space. In his previous life, something like that could have gotten the perpetrator killed—or at least earned him a broken bone or two, just to maintain Dove's status and reputation with the other thugs. "Doc, you need a vacation—or a wife to teach you about interacting with people."

"I do just fine with people. You're a patient, and a recalcitrant one at that, not coming in until those friends of yours had to carry you." Dr. Joseph Gee listened intently to the sound of air pumping in and out of a whole pair of lungs. Modern medicine didn't know everything, but what it did know—what it could do when necessary—still elated him. Between the antiviral agent and the rebuilding proteins that helped the kid's system repair the pulmonary damage, it sounded like Dove would have many years of getting into scrapes ahead of him. "Okay, I concur with Dr. Galen's diagnosis: you're clean. Congratulations, chico. Welcome back to the land of the living."

"Hey, doc, I never left," Dove reminded him. "Thanks to you."

"So you admit that now?" Dr. Joe asked lightly. He wasn't much of a one for praise, but he had worried about giving Dove that shot, when the kid was so violently opposed to it.

"I never didn't admit it. I just didn't figure it mattered much." Dove sighed at the naivete of doctors. "Anyway, I'm clean now all the way through—the AllSafe you stuck me with killed Slick's poison, and

Dr. Galen's miracle serum killed the AllSafe. I'm grade A now." He flexed his arms, hitting a bodybuilder pose for just a second before it felt too stupid and he laughed.

Dr. Joe grinned back. "I'd say you were strong as an ox and almost as smart as a mule. Which reminds me." Walking over to the small medical cooler in the corner of his personal office, he extracted a padded case, which he unzipped to show its contents.

The row of vials glittered in the light, sending a tight, nervous rush through Dove's gut. It looked like the contents of the package he'd delivered for Abuelo last year, vials of viruses that killed a bunch of banditos Slick had fooled into playing guinea pigs to test. They'd thought it was an antidote that would save their lives when the General unleashed his bioweapons on the unsuspecting Amexicans; it turned out to be lethal.

"What is it?" he asked.

"They're variants on the same virus Slick had, the one he gave you." Dr. Joe's serious tone matched Dove's. He glared at the sparkling bottles with cold hate, amazed that human beings could deliberately come up with such a vicious idea. "According to the data that came with them, smuggled out of the research lab in Bogotá, General Garza's trying to create a paired weapons system: on one side, a virus that causes total physical and mental breakdown in a matter of a few days; on the other, a vaccine that keeps the virus from infecting the host cells."

"Still on that sickness kick," Dove growled. "So, what do we do about it?"

"I can identify it, with what we've got here, but I can't go further. This needs to go to Section 89, for professional treatment." Dr. Joe glanced at Dove, gauging his reaction.

"Only fair." Dove nodded easily. "I ran the General's first poison out to Blanca Hacienda, I'll run his second—or third through sixth, looks like—up to Salt Lake. He doesn't even have to pay me this time."

"Generous of you." Dr. Joe smiled at Dove's unconscious bravado. Was he ever that young? Tucking the case back into the cooler, he said, "It can wait a couple of days. When you're ready to go, come over, and we'll set it up to move. It's pretty secure now, but it wasn't traveling over bandit-infested roads until it got to Mexico."

"Then how did it go?" Dove asked, interested. He'd done a few runs into Mexico with Benny, negotiating with Abuelo's rivals and potential allies south of the border, helping to add some firepower when one of those allies called on the gang to return a favor by joining a battle. "They take the old Coyote Highway up from Chiapas?"

"Coyote Highway?" Dr. Joe frowned. "I'm not familiar with that one. The agents in Colombia handed it off to another outfit that got it as far as Guatemala, and then it got buried in a load of illegally traveling Mayan antiquities. The 'art distributor' takes extra packages for a small consideration, as long as they're not drugs, because he likes Mormons—and he's got enough firepower to discourage would-be thieves."

"Coyote Highway's not really the name, it's just what we called it when we went down there," Dove explained. "It's a series of roads and trails, kind of out of the way, that the coyotes and gunrunners used—still do, I guess, or did until that Aztec Liberation outfit started causing all the problems."

"The Aztec Liberation Front won't cause you any trouble moving these, but somebody else might." Dr. Joe turned the subject back to the vials. "Be careful, Hasbídí."

"Got it covered, Doc." Dove watched the doctor stow the vials back in the safe. "I've got a guardian angel watching over me." He tossed that bone to Socks, grinning as the programmer tuned back into the conversation abruptly with "Huh? Oh, thank you, thank you very much!"

"I figure I'll haul along a couple extra hands for protection too—not a big posse to attract a lot of attention, but enough to discourage anybody looking for easy pickings or back them off if they get uppity." Dove's hand automatically brushed across his hip at the thought, feeling for a holster that wasn't there. He'd have to rectify that situation too, now that he'd left the civilized confines of the Church's former capital city.

* * *

"I can't believe you drove all the way down here without a security blanket." Calvin shook his head sadly at this dire evidence of Dove's losing his mind. He expertly racked the pistol in his hand, cycling a bullet into the chamber, and offered it butt-first to Dove. "I've been keeping it warm for you."

"Thanks." Dove took the gun, feeling the familiar, reassuring weight of it, looking down the matte-black barrel and across the front sights. Even through his enlightened outlook on life, things just looked a lot clearer through a gun sight sometimes. He'd keep it under his coat at the Begays' for dinner tonight, though; Renata acknowledged the necessity for such weapons, and had willingly learned enough about handling Sam's rifle to defend herself and the girls if necessary, but she didn't like to think about them. Abish, on the other hand, had happily showed him her ability with her .22 auto to punch a tight pattern in a target at a respectable distance. Not bad for a ten-year-old.

He pulled the sights up abruptly as Perro danced across his line of vision, waving wildly and pretending to dance around the barrage of bullets Dove didn't fire. "Get out of the way, you clown!" Dove yelled. "We got serious firepower over here!"

"Oh, yeah, you're always serious." Perro made a face, coming over to flop down beside Dove at the less unsteady of the two tables outside Mama Rosa's Mexican restaurant, or "diner," or possibly "taquerita"—Franklin's efforts went toward the food, not the decor. He took a long swallow from the bottle he held—cola, not beer, Dove noted, shooting Calvin an approving look—and belched happily. He gestured with the bottle toward the filthy but high-quality car sitting in the dusty parking area in front of the building. "That's some serious ride you got there too. What you do, sell a kidney or something up there?"

"Nah, that's a rental. Asked for a rusty pickup, but they were all out, so they had to give me that instead." Dove shrugged casually. The ticket for the rental, prepaid, had come from Sister Lavine, who hugged him and told him, like everybody else in the universe, to be careful.

"Poor chiquito," Perro snorted. He flexed his hands greedily, affecting a mad-scientist voice. "So, when do I get my claws on the little darling? We can put her through her paces, see when she screams!"

"Maybe I'll let you drive on the straight stretches, if it's not too windy." Dove looked him over doubtfully, as if he were concerned about Perro's ability to see over the steering wheel—or to know what to do with a steering wheel at all. "Calvin's going to be doing most of the navigation—especially through those locust storms."

Calvin looked up from nimbly stocking clips with tight, neat rows of bullets. "Yeah? Where are we driving to through locust storms?"

"Salt Lake City," Dove informed him, then glanced at Perro to include him in the oblique invitation, more of an offhanded command; Dove assumed leadership roles easily. "I'm heading back Tuesday. Figured you could do with a change of scenery."

"What we hauling?" Calvin asked. He knew that Dove liked their company—who'd hang with Perro if he didn't?—but he could also read the handwriting on the wall when Dove called not just to say hi and tell them he'd meet them at Mama Rosa's but to ask them to bring the Nakai family guns and all their metallic cousins with them.

"Don't tell me; let me guess," Perro exclaimed brightly. He'd been following Dove's long-distance orders to improve his mind by reading and saw the opportunity to get in a couple of digs in return. "We're carrying a sinister piece of jewelry to Oregon, fighting our way through zombie armies to drop it into that big volcano!"

Dove grinned and smacked him upside the head. "No. We're carrying a sinister case of vials containing a collection of deadly viruses up to Section 89, where we'll carefully place it in the hands of Dr. Galen and then run for it before you break something valuable—or contagious." He easily deflected Perro's playful return punch, adding, "But the vials are sparkly, so you can think of them as jewels if it'll help you get your head around the idea."

"Playing courier for deadly viruses, trying to avoid half a dozen bandit gangs, flash floods, and locust storms while driving through the high desert with only these for protection." Calvin gestured at the array of firearms spread on the rickety table in front of him and looked at Perro.

"Sounds like a sure bet for trouble." Perro looked from Calvin to the guns to Dove and took another pull from his bottle. Wiping his mouth, he nodded and said, "Sounds fun. I'll check my calendar. Tuesday, you said?"

"Tuesday," Dove affirmed, his expression as serious as theirs.

Perro riffled through an imaginary appointment calendar. "Nope, the big gala ball's on Friday, and the polo match isn't till Sunday afternoon. Looks like I'm clear. What you got, Mr. Calvin?"

Calvin slipped a shell into the chamber of a lever-action 30-30 and smiled. "No gigs for me either. Looks like we're a go—I'll even bring my violin case."

Dove nodded, pleased, and sat back, spreading his arms to embrace the dusty parking strip, the weathered boards, the blood-tinged sun setting amid streaks of black clouds. "A road trip with a noble aim, good friends, cold steel, hot lead, and a fully insured rental car. Who could ask for more?"

"I think y'all did," Franklin answered, shoving aside Calvin's collection of fire iron to thump down plates of beans, rice, sauce, tortillas, and slices of carne-heavy heaven onto the table.

"That's a spread to give thanks over," Dove said, smiling at the cook. "Thanks, Franklin. Good to see you."

"Good to see you too, in spite of the damage you always do to my kitchen stock." Franklin's dark face wrinkled around his smile. "You and these reprobates done good, Dove. You just be careful, y'hear?"

Dove gave him a wide-eyed expression of innocence, liberally mingled with exasperation. "I *am* careful! I'm always careful! Why do people keep telling me to be careful?"

* * *

The day had started peacefully enough, with everybody telling him to be careful and Renata giving Calvin a box of goodies for their lunch on the road. Dove, Perro, and Calvin had tooled along the road with nothing more exciting than running into a swarm of locusts at seventy miles per hour. The crunching noises reminded Perro of an explosion in a potato-chip factory, not that it stopped him from happily crunching potato chips out of Renata's snack supply while watching the bugs splat on the windshield. The radio pumped out road-trip music, Dove caught up on the borderlands gossip, he and Calvin debated the finer points of tactics in the Book of Mormon (should Moroni have told Ammoron off like that, or just agreed to exchange prisoners?), and Perro practiced his comedy routine on both of them.

That's when Socks chimed in over Dove's headset. "Hey, Crazy Horse, there's a school bus up ahead of you, just inside the canyon."

"There's a bus ahead, on the canyon road," Dove repeated for Calvin's sake. "So what?"

"So there's also a big-monster SUV up there, only the SUV's off in one of the side gullies," Socks told him. "Looks like it's lurking to me."

"An SUV lurking in a gully?" Dove asked that aloud, but as much for his own information as the others'.

"Is lurking a normal thing for SUVs to do? I mean, guzzling fuel, cutting in front of you in traffic, running over smaller cars, but lurking?" Perro asked. Calvin shushed him.

"Looks like one of those wolf packs out to get itself a nice, fat sheep," Socks opined.

"A wolf pack? Banditos going to ambush the bus?" Dove asked aloud. "You sure it's a school bus?"

Calvin and Perro exchanged glances through the rearview mirror. "Here we go with the heroics," Perro muttered. Calvin just grinned.

"It does look like that, but it might not be a bus full of kids. Maybe it's one of those decommissioned Bluebirds." Fox's voice came through the link, backing up Socks's melodramatic prediction. She sounded interested, and slightly unbelieving, as if she couldn't quite get her head around seeing it. "Looks like two men on the rim of the gully, one with binoculars. They're looking toward the bus. Now one of them is hustling down the edge of the cliff, waving at the men at the bottom. They're pulling the truck out into the road."

"Right across it," Socks added. "Looks like a roadblock ambush, all right."

"Well, Socks, you said you wondered what a real firefight was like," Dove said aloud. "Here's your chance to find out without getting that pasty white tail of yours shot off. Think you can keep up with us?"

"Sure I can! You don't move all that fast from up here." Socks's voice practically vibrated with excitement.

Calvin glanced at Dove, got the nod, and hit the accelerator. The desert blurred around them, the canyon mouth rushing toward the car. Perro muttered his standard litany of prayers to whatever saint might be listening, and pulled the arsenal out of its box on the backseat. He missed the security of the Dogmobile's heavy frame and sheet-metal sides. A chichi vehicle like this one was probably made of all the latest polymer super panels, all ready to crumple into safety zones in a crash, utterly useless for stopping bullets.

"We're with you. There's a curve up ahead, a fairly sharp one, and then the back of the bus. They'll see you as soon as you come around the curve," Fox said calmly, but there was an edge to her voice as she narrated what was happening. "The bus is slowing, stopping. The driver's gesturing for them to get out of the way, but he can't get through. Looks like six—no, seven men, standing in a semicircle around the front of the bus. They've pulled their weapons, looks like rifles and pistols, nothing heavier."

She didn't need to add that; the sound of shouts, followed almost immediately by the heavy pop of gunfire, came clearly through the still air. Calvin pulled to a halt just around the turn. They could see the hard orange-yellow of the bus through the meager branches of the bushes and stunted trees holding onto their perches on the gully walls.

"If you're fast, you could probably make it around the turn and take cover behind the bus before they see you and start shooting," Socks advised. His fingers itched; he had to stop himself from reaching for a joystick.

"One more turn, then the bus," Dove told Perro and Calvin as all three of them piled out of the car. Dove had considered using it in a full-frontal charge, but with the bulk of the bus between them and the wolf pack, it wouldn't give them any advantage. Better to keep it out of the way, in case they had to get out in a hurry. "Seven banditos, and maybe a driver or two." He hefted his pistol. "They got what we got arms-wise."

"Any reason to be discreet about it?" Calvin asked.

Dove matched his wolf grin. "Nope."

"As General Custer said, bring on the Indians!" Perro exclaimed.

"I think he said it this way," Dove corrected. "Charge!"

Which they did, with no further ado or planning. Much to Socks's and Fox's surprise, the three Santos tore around the curve in the road and hit the scene with a whoop, guns blazing. Two of the banditos went down immediately; a shotgun blast from the bus driver's window leveled another who'd hesitated a moment too long. The outlaws, while ready for at least token resistance from the primary target, hadn't expected to become targets themselves. They had plenty of experience in the Amexican badlands, however, and took cover behind the heavy bulk of the bus on the side next to the canyon wall and returned fire. Fortunately for the Santos, the bandits' initial volley was more enthusiastic than completely effective.

Dove, running bent over for the other side, fired low and parallel to the ground. The shots whined beneath the bus's chassis, puncturing the legs of a bandito. The others scurried for cover behind the big dual tires, and returned fire underneath the bus. Dove avoided the shots by springing up onto the guardrail next to the sharp drop-off into the canyon bottom. Perro and Calvin threw themselves to the ground just behind the rail, using the sharp drop itself as cover. "Nothing," as Perro often said, "stops bullets as well as dirt."

Another bandit wormed out of the front door of the SUV, hitting the ground and aiming upward.

"Watch out!" Fox's sudden warning and the whine of the bullet that hit his shoulder brought the memory of Benny and his first fire-fight into Dove's mind.

"Watch out!" Benny had shouted, just before he threw a can at Dove's head. The sparkle of it still shone vividly in his memory, arcing toward him to make him duck. He'd raised his gun and blown it off course instead—and the bullet Benny had tried to force him to evade flamed into his leg. It hadn't been a total failure, since the lead slug only bit a chunk out of his calf instead of breaking his bones, but it hurt like blue blazes. The wound had taught him two important lessons: that pain didn't have to kill you, and that it was better not to get shot. At least Benny hadn't told him to be careful!

The impact nearly sent him toppling into the canyon. With less grace than inspired flailing, he managed to crash into the bush just behind the guardrail, lying there for a vital couple of seconds, while he figured out that his arm was just creased, not seriously injured. Dove took a deep breath, banished the memory, clenching his teeth against the fiery hurt burning down his arm from the nick out of his shoulder. He rolled back onto the hard surface of the road and plunged back into the fray without rising from the horizontal, though he did roll enough to put a rock between himself and the lead flying around. The bottoms of the boots on the bandit who'd shot him showed under the vehicle's door; Calvin whistled encouragement and gave him a thumbs-up before turning his aim on keeping their enemies pinned between the bus and canyon wall.

A bandit popped out from around the corner of the bus, blasting away from the cover of the big, metal vehicle. He jerked right back as Dove's expert returning shot drew blood—now they had matching notches out of their jackets. Screams from inside the bus said that most of the outlaws' intended victims still had enough breath to invoke the wrath of God down on their attackers' heads. That and luggage; a couple of heavy carry-on bags tumbled out of the high windows, knocking one of the banditos over. The passengers' chants and prayers, mingled with the occasional decorous but heartfelt curse, rose like a choir score soaring over the hard beat of gunfire.

"Two bandits coming around the front of the bus—looks like they're trying to get back to their SUV," Socks said in Dove's ear.

"Perro!" he shouted, hoping Perro would get the last-minute code and that the bandits wouldn't. "Clients at the box office!"

Perro, looking around the juniper he'd adopted as temporary and, with all the bullet holes in its trunk and branches, increasingly sticky cover, gave Dove a look of total incomprehension. Dove gestured toward the front of the bus, sparking an "Oh, that's what you mean!" expression and a grin. Perro obediently rose to his knees, ready to sprint. Dove rose as well, from his own position behind a washed-down boulder, and blasted a line of bullets at about shoulder height. Perro ran along right behind, throwing himself into the fire shadow of the bandits' big four-wheel SUV. Dove slapped another clip into his gun and walked the line of fire back along its original path, catching one of the banditos by surprise. He fired automatically and the man staggered, falling heavily beside the bus's big front wheels.

"How many left?" Dove demanded.

"Four down—no, now five," Socks told him. "That quiet friend of yours is a mean shot."

"Two left," Fox did the subtraction for them. "They're just at the front of the bus, on the driver's side, looking at their getaway car. Looks like the driver's out of ammunition, so they're safe."

Dove stood up, holding his gun at the ready. "You're skinned," he shouted toward the front of the bus. "Give up now, and we'll see if any of your buddies are worth scraping off the road."

The shouted reply was as emphatic as it was unprintable, and a barrage of bullets followed instantly.

"What do you bet that's wolf for 'you'll never take me alive'?" Socks asked.

Dove moved out of the direct line of fire but didn't retreat, starting to zigzag closer to the front of the bus. Perro covered him from the side of the SUV, shooting at any bandit parts he could see. The two remaining wolves took turns popping up to shoot at the two Santos.

"Calvin's gone around the far side of the bus," Fox said. "What is he do—" Two gunshots answered her question. "Seven down," she said, swallowing hard. The tiny, sprawled bodies on the screen, in the tight-focus shot that let them see into the canyon, looked like abandoned dolls. To her surprise, that thought made the cold reality of death more stark and sickening rather than less.

Socks's reaction was considerably less subdued. He flung his arms up, his chair whirling around a full circle on its wheels. "Wahoo! We won!" he exclaimed.

"Whoa!" Dove exclaimed and raised his arms too, but for a much different reason.

The driver of the bus glowered menacingly out of the smashed window, the gray barrel of the shotgun ready when the young man came around the bus.

"Hey, papa, we're friends, right? The ones who came to your rescue?" Dove smiled reassuringly as he gingerly moved aside the muzzle of the shotgun so that it didn't point at his head anymore.

"Yeah, you don't need to shoot at us. Besides," Perro pointed out practically, "you're out of shells." He glanced down at the lead-peppered body of the bandit who'd crashed into the canyon wall, and then back at the driver. "Good shot, though. And shotguns make for good clubs, in a pinch."

"Thank the good Lord!" the driver exclaimed. "We're rescued!" he shouted back into the bus. Faces appeared all along the sides, peering out of the broken windows. When his passengers saw the bandits dead and their three rescuers relatively unharmed, a cheer broke out— along with an enthusiastic impromptu prayer of thanksgiving for the miraculous rescue.

The prayer—and the hymns that accompanied it—continued through the rest of the long drive through the twisting canyon. Behind them, a column of black smoke rose to cliff level, then flattened and streamed southward in the wind, marking the burning SUV that they'd used as a makeshift crematorium for the ill-fated wolf pack. Reverend Clearwater, the driver and spiritual leader of this group of pilgrims, said a few words on behalf of the deceased before

Perro and Calvin doused the vehicle with the gas canisters it carried to power its old-fashioned engine and set it alight. Dove watched the whole thing from the front seat of the bus, where Mrs. Meriwether used the contents of the industrial-sized first-aid kit to patch his creased shoulder. She'd done a good, professional job, telling him she'd worked as an ER nurse in Mesa for fifteen years, then, noticing the scars on his chest, patted his good shoulder and let him go with, "You should be more careful, young man."

Perro and Calvin, with Socks chiming in through the link, teased him about it all the way to Monticello, where they delivered their busload of hymn-singing Christians to safety at the Monticello Stake of Zion. The guys' playful banter faded, however, as they watched half of Reverend Clearwater's people cross the line into Zion. The others, much to the reverend's and Mrs. Meriwether's disappointment, balked at the invisible barrier. Deciding they simply couldn't abide the requirements for living inside the sphere of divine protection, they turned away, wandering into the small refugee camp clinging to the edges of safety around Monticello.

Dove grabbed Perro, catching his face and glowering at him. "You'd better never do that to me," he growled. "You better follow right along wherever I lead."

"Hey, chill, Hasbídí." Perro caught his wrist, but to Dove's surprise didn't pull away. Instead, he pulled Dove into an awkward hug, then let go, embarrassed. His usual goofy grin didn't hide the flush in his cheeks, or the shine in his eyes. "Wherever you go, there I go too—even if it's easier to get me to follow you to hell than heaven."

Calvin punched his arm and gave him a quick, sweet smile.

Perro punched him back, the old bravado returning. "You chill too, copycat boy. Don't go running for the holy water yet."

"We'll get you dunked sooner or later," Dove promised him.

That gave them a new topic of argument to keep things interesting until they got to Salt Lake City. Perro not only followed Dove and Calvin into Mormonville, as he called it, without developing more than a put-on case of the twitches, but he even managed to keep from saying anything egregious when they met the medical team and Elder Nabil at Section 89, though he flirted outrageously with Corinne, who found him "funny."

"So this is the latest mischief that the General is cooking up," the Apostle sighed, looking at the sparkling glass vials in their dusty case. He nodded to Kendall, who picked up the case carefully but eagerly, whisking it off to the lab facility's high-powered analyzers. Turning back to the trio of Santos, the smile returned to his face. "And you rescued a group of refugee Baptists as well. An eventful trip indeed. I have heard one version of the tale—Maynard is quite proud of his excellent performance in an actual battle."

Dove couldn't stifle the involuntary snort of laughter that remark provoked; he could just imagine Socks, rumple-shirted and wild-haired, pounding out a wildly colored e-mail account of his first gunfight. Perro, unacquainted with Socks as anything but a theoretical ghost in a spy satellite, rolled his eyes impatiently at this evidence of civilian naiveté.

Elder Nabil looked from one to the other, then at Calvin, who smiled serenely, and laughed. "Clearly, there is much more to this story than I know. Come along, boys. I'll feed you dinner, and you can tell me all that our electronic eyes missed."

"Thank you, sir," Dove said promptly. The other two nodded. Food always made Perro feel better. "Have you heard anything more about the General's move into Chiapas? That's the rumor coming through Amexica."

"Nothing so specific, though that does tally with what our sources have told us." Elder Nabil frowned. "In fact, your young friend Mercury sent a coded message from Elder Molina, hinting that Garza's organization is massing men and matériel at Mexico's southern border. Publicly, he says he stands ready to assist the Mexican government against the Aztec Liberation Front."

"And privately?" Dove asked. He didn't need an answer and didn't wait for one. Glancing back at the lab as they walked into the parking lot, he added, "I wonder how long it will take him to make his move."

"Whenever he does it, we'll be ready for him," Perro said confidently.

"We will be prepared," Elder Nabil agreed, but his tone was sober. "But I fear many will not be."

* * *

"This village was completely unprepared for the guerillas' sudden attack." Rosa del Torres stood in front of the charred remains of the antique church that had once graced the small plaza. "The Aztec Liberation Front forces moved through this area 'like a swarm of locusts,' in one eyewitness description. The death toll in this village is 136 killed, and almost twice that number is injured." Stunned survivors haunted the edges of the screen, too wounded to acknowledge the camera's bright light or the reporter's subdued glamour as she told the world about their plight.

"The insurgency is ripping through Mexico," Rosa continued, walking slowly along the ruined street, past the burned-out shells of homes. "The violence has spread all the way from Chiapas to Mexico City itself. Amazingly, many Mexicans have expressed sympathy with the rebels' aims, if not with their tactics." File footage of the perennial peasant protests underscored her statement. "The militants, and a significant minority of other citizens, are demanding restoration of Indian land and property rights, the overthrow of the corrupt government in Mexico City, and mandated profit sharing by all foreign businesses operating in Mexico."

Plus anything else that would buy them a few seconds on the news broadcasts, but Rosa didn't add that. She didn't need to—she simply waited silently until the rebels, speaking during previously taped interviews just outside General Garza's headquarters in Bogotá, finished their rants about the loftiness of their goals and how much they regretted having to use extreme measures against the stubborn and untrustworthy government forces. The smoke that blew around her, and the blood-stain still visible on the plastered wall, burned her eyes and plucked at the deeply buried strand of her conscience, but she brushed both discomforts away as the price of getting what she wanted: an audience even larger than Channel 8 would give her. As chief reporter for the United States of South America's newly formed national media establishment, she finally had the audience she craved. A few dead peasants weren't going to overshadow that.

"The rebels have also clashed with the army in several open battles, and reports point to something even more dire on the horizon," Rosa continued, expertly playing her role. "What will the Aztec Liberation Front do next? And will the Mexican president accept General Garza's offer of assistance in quelling the rebel threat? Only time will tell—and time, it seems, is running out. This is Rosa del Torres, for USSA National News, in Chiapas."

* * *

"She's doing well," Brindermann observed, glancing up at the monitor relaying the newscast in Garza's headquarters. "I wondered if she could at first, but she is a most accomplished actress."

A jagged hole appeared in the center of Rosa's forehead. Tiny streaks of lightning followed, then the mortally wounded screen went dark. The thin trail of smoke that rose from it matched the curl from the muzzle of the General's gun.

"A comment on the report rather than the reporter, I assume," Brindermann said. He rechecked the figures on his own personal communicator. A hundred thousand troops at least, his contact promised, able to secure their own provisions, well motivated for a fast-moving campaign, if he could provide air support. He sent an acknowledgment before putting the tiny machine back into his pocket.

Garza glared at him but finally holstered the pistol. Pacing like a caged predator, he glowered at the other three screens, where the Mexican president claimed that his administration could handle the rebel threat as he promised a return of law and order without having to resort to the assistance of an "opportunistic jackal" like Garza.

"Jackal," Garza repeated. He did not shoot another screen; he closed his eyes, as if hoping the stillness would calm him. It failed. He began pacing again, but smiled. "Perhaps I am a jackal, impatient to the chase." Turning back to fix his second in command with a long stare, he continued, "And for good reasons. The longer we wait, the more restless the men become, the more likely the threat of discovery, and the more likely the opposition will be prepared."

"True," Brindermann conceded. "But we still need more time to finish preparing for a major invasion. The Aztecs are softening up the Mexicans—and providing an alibi that only grows stronger with time. In another month, we will be ready to sweep into Mexico City at the head of a victorious army."

"As we did with Santiago, and Quito, and too many other capitals to name." Garza shrugged. The thrill of those victories had paled as it had come; he needed more, a bigger win, a greater show of strength. The entire world should cower on its collective knees before him, and thus far, he had subdued only a mere continent and a half. And even that hadn't proved a total success. His eyes darkened. "Even without success from that whining skeleton Twilley, we have the weapons we need to take Mexico."

"We need more, and a secure supply line for them," Brindermann said. He didn't need victories; he needed peace, order, and the absence of chaos. Speed made waste, increased the chance that random factors would ruin the best-laid plans.

"A secure supply line," Garza repeated. "Yes, that would be helpful, especially since we lost four shipments of those precious weapons in the last week, all due to that sneak thief Zamora. Setbacks we cannot afford—and I do not like his ability to divine which of your convoys carry corn and which carry bullets, Johann."

The fist dipped to his waist, rose with the pistol ready in it. The gun's round, black mouth pointed at Brindermann, then at the large computer console behind him. "And I do not like that blasted pile of electronic junk that spreads my secrets over the airwaves for anyone to read!"

The German looked more concerned when the gun pointed at the computer than at his own head. He rose from his seat, meeting the General's eyes directly, as he would confront a snarling wolf. "Your secrets are safer with that pile of electronic junk than with the couriers we initially used. How many times did you have to execute them for betraying you? How many dogfights did you arrange to punish those who used your secrets against you?"

"Too many," Garza growled, staring back into the German's cold, gray eyes. "Shall we find out how well your computer protects you against fangs?"

"No," Brindermann said, dismissing the possibility with finality he didn't feel. "We will isolate the leak and stop it—permanently." He raised his own personal communicator, showing Garza the data on the possible break-ins. "From the information left by the invaders, we believe that the Americans, probably the CIA, have located a minor security breach in the matériel supply database. It contains nothing of great value besides the transport schedules, which the Americans have fed to Zamora to harass us. In fact, it would not surprise me to find that Secretary Garlick is behind these counter-intelligence maneuvers. He recently had one of his allies assassinated; he may intend to build up political capital by appearing to oppose you."

As he'd hoped, presenting Garza with a more tempting target drew the immediate heat in another direction. "The secretary is an ambitious fool," he said, "as is Zamora, and President Aguilera, and our disappointing friend Serrey. I am surrounded by ambitious fools." He looked at Brindermann. "What shall I do about that?"

"You will give me approval to tell Serrey to find and plug the leak in his organization, and to commission Medea and her Ten Tribes minions to trap and unmask the American agents in the system," Brindermann told him. The set of the General's shoulders made him nervous. Garza had come to a decision that he would not like.

"I approve." Garza nodded. "Do that, Johann; secure my supply lines and my computer system by whatever means you deem necessary. And do it quickly, or I will kill you."

"Understood." Brindermann did understand; the wind had risen around his delicate high-wire act. The heat behind the order he mentally composed to Serrey and Medea went up several notches.

"I knew you would. And now, we will defeat all those who spy and mutter, stealing our plans from their insecure resting places." Garza strode to the door of the command tent.

Brindermann walked after him. They stopped outside the primary hangar, techs and junior officers hastening to stand to attention.

"Bring out the standby Velociraptor," the General ordered the senior tech, "and load it with one of the special warheads we procured from our Georgian friends."

"General," Brindermann began as the techs saluted and moved to comply.

Garza held up a hand, pointing a threatening finger at Brindermann. "No, Johann. Don't tempt me to hurt myself by shooting you. You are still valuable, though sometimes I wonder why."

The Velociraptor rolled out of the hangar, its deadly payload in its munitions bay. It slid efficiently onto the short airstrip without a human hand guiding it. With its stealth technology, no one would even see it coming.

With a flourish, the General flicked open his personal comm, keying the code that established a connection with the lethal flying machine. "You see, the only way to keep my plans from leaking out the holes in your supposedly secure system is not to put it into any system. Act before they expect, and you gain the element of surprise. And so I stop waiting; as the impulse strikes, so do I."

One more touch, and the Velociraptor's engines whined, carrying it down the field and up into the cloudy sky. It rode the air currents, its onboard computer compensating for the rough winds. In a few seconds, it disappeared, heading northwest.

"Now we'll have something worth watching the news for," Garza said, turning to Brindermann, who stood still, staring after the auto-piloted plane carrying the weapon he had always wondered if Garza would use.

Hundreds of miles to the north, the rumors of an escalation in the never-ending Mexican rebellion came abruptly to life, as a large sector of Mexico City disappeared in a huge burst of incandescent flame, smoke, and radiation. The blast, rising up and out from a precise target in the most sensitive part of the sprawling megalopolis, wiped out the recalcitrant president of Mexico and his contentious, corrupt legislators. The force of the explosion blasted through the downtown office buildings and swept across a wide swath of the slums built up on the dumps. In the heat, secondary explosions rippled through the methane pockets and toxic-waste swamps. The cloud of corrosive chemicals blew outward in turn, wiping out those who survived the explosion, but even the blistering vapors did not travel so far or so efficiently as the invisible poison of radiation.

Both clouds rolled from the central pillar of fire toward the temple on the outskirts of the city, boiling toward the line of Saints waiting just inside the line of divine power, praying for protection, calling to those who lingered outside to come in. The clouds swept around in a huge, harmless arc, sparing everything inside Zion.

Everything outside the boundaries, however, crisped, bubbled, and burned.

With images of a mushroom cloud, a palm tree of smoke and flame, rising against a bloody, crimson and scarlet sunset, the Aztec Liberation Front announced, through Rosa del Torres, that it took responsibility for the nuclear blast that killed over a million in Mexico City and promised more to come. Including, if their demands were not met, strikes across the border into Mexico's imperialist oppressor, the United States.

* * *

"Once again, a mushroom cloud rises into the sky, and all of humanity wonders if the nuclear nightmare will ever stop." Images of the atomic blast in Mexico City flashed again and again as Clara read the quasi-profound commentary from the prompter. A list of previous nuclear explosions scrolled underneath the dramatic images (Hiroshima, Nagasaki, Chernobyl, Bangalore, Ho Chi Minh City) along with the latest casualty figures and damage reports, which mounted almost by the minute.

"The devastation from the suitcase nuke that exploded in the heart of the country is unmatched in modern times, due to the density of the population there. As the few remaining authorities in Mexico City desperately mobilize to treat the wounded and set up aid stations for the millions fleeing the fallout from the explosion, the toxic cloud has spread on the prevailing winds." Now a map appeared, showing a huge splash of red slowly creeping outward from the initial blast site to envelop a wide strip of the suburbs and countryside. "Radiation, particulate contamination, and chemical smoke has continued the devastation of the initial explosion."

The scene changed again, picturing that devastation: a wall, like that preserved in Hiroshima, blackened and blistered, with the silhouettes of a half dozen people burned into its surface; gutted tenements and office buildings, their floors sagging and open to the sky; an overwhelmed, dust-covered rescue worker collapsed on the curb in his bright-yellow haz-mat suit, crying; tin shack roofs melted and pitted from the acid rain that fell through the chemical vapor clogging the sky; trees in a park ripped out by the roots and flattened like matchsticks; the wide, stunned eyes of a child with radiation burns on her face, dying in a makeshift hospital. The tumbled stones of the walls around the Mexico City Temple received extra attention, as Channel 8 implied that the Zion community there suffered as much as others;

only on the Church's news briefs did footage of the clouds' miraculous dissipation at the gates get any airplay.

"These are good, but we need more," Monk muttered. The ratings bars were high—everybody loved a good disaster—but the USSA National News bar rose perilously high to Channel 8's own score. Grabbing the phone that spread his commands to the outside world from his dark cave, he talked to half a dozen apologetic or brusque reporters, cameramen, and political pundits. They all had the same response. Furious, he threw the phone across the room. "USSA National News? Rosa del Torres? Who ever even heard of that outfit until a month ago, and now they've got the exclusive track on the Aztec Liberation Front? I want an interview with those guys, and I want it now!"

Kim, silent as ever, retrieved the phone so her boss could continue making calls, trying to find someone to beg, borrow, or steal an interview with the culprits. Settling back into her own chair, she watched Clara's broadcast, expertly queuing up the heartbreaking scenes—and the perfectly placed ads that went with them.

Aerial photos of the blast site showed glimpses of the crater through the slowly dissipating clouds of smoke from the fires still burning in the wake of the explosion. "But how did this happen, and where did the bomb come from?" Clara asked. "Channel 8's expert commentator, Darren McInnes, has some answers."

"Not as many answers as questions, unfortunately, Clara." Darren appeared from the safe vantage of a media station in El Paso. "But we do have some clues as to what happened here—and the answers are even more troubling than the questions. It appears that someone has finally solved the technical challenge of creating a small, transportable nuclear device—a 'suitcase nuke' in military parlance." As he spoke, diagrams showing the bomb fitted into a passenger truck or van illustrated the concepts the news team had researched from Channel 8's military contacts.

"We've never seen this kind of device before, and some experts even doubted it was possible, until yesterday. More troubling is the question of where the device came from in the first place, especially since Mexico itself is not a nuclear power and experts doubt that the guerilla movement has the ability to create a bomb from raw materials." Maps of possible sources for the device appeared, location points spotted throughout the old USSR and down into the Middle and Far East. "Some sources look more likely than others. Speaking on conditions of anonymity, one high-placed Pentagon official said, 'Looks like we just found some of that missing Soviet firepower.' We all hope that they find the rest of it before it goes off. Stay tuned for my in-depth report, *Nuclear Nightmare*, tonight on Channel 8. This is Darren McInnes, reporting live. Back to you, Clara."

"Thank you, Darren. I'm sure your report will help us all understand what happened here—and when and where it will happen again." Clara turned back to the camera. "The Aztec Liberation Front has claimed responsibility for the blast. However, unverified intelligence reports also implicate General Andrea Garza, now president of the newly established United States of South America, in the attacks. Unverified reports coming out of Mexico seem to imply that General Garza has begun moving troops into some areas to provide peacekeeping services without being invited." Grainy footage, taken from Channel 8's shaky spy satellite connections, seemed to show an armored column on the southern plains.

"Homeland Security secretary Howard Garlick is scheduled to address the public concerning the Aztec Liberation Front's threats of further nuclear incidents aimed at the United States. Right now, the Office of Homeland Security advises all Americans to remain calm and to report any suspicious activity—especially heavy trucks parked in unusual or public places. Stay tuned to Channel 8 for more in-depth coverage of the nuclear terrorism in Mexico City." Clara shifted gears as the graphics around her changed from maps of nuclear fallout and potential targets in the United States and Canada to maps of wider weather patterns. "We've heard a lot about the prevailing winds over the Yucatan Peninsula in the last twenty-four hours. What's up with the rest of the weather, Cal?"

"Well, weather's the one bright spot in the news," Cal said, his professional weatherman's smile stuck firmly to his face, denying the stress wrinkles that threatened to crack it. He pointed out the lack of clouds, hurricanes, tsunamis, tropical storms, blizzards, and pouring rains on his weather map. "It looks like Mother Nature's decided to give us a break for a couple of weeks. Clara, it's a great weekend for a picnic—or taking that flight you've been putting off."

"Sounds great. I haven't had a picnic in, well, it seems like years. I'm sure we'll all appreciate some good weather." Clara smiled at the viewers. "And whatever your plans are, we hope they include Channel 8 News."

* * *

"Sunny afternoon," Hideyoshi repeated, rolling the words around his memory. Sunlight, grass, a light breeze, enough room to run around—opening his eyes to the gray, metallic confines of the ISS was a definite letdown. The globe swirling through space below showed far fewer bands of storm clouds, though the gray streak of ash from the Big Sister volcano still marred the Northern Hemisphere.

On the communications screen beside the main tectonic displays, chatter over the Church's channels told him that the Saints were busy taking advantage of the momentary calm to step up their last-ditch efforts to pull as many to salvation as would make an effort. Encoded personal messages sped through the network, carrying instructions and encouragement to the Gatherers in every corner of the world. The notice for a live broadcast of a Seraph concert caught his eye, along with reports from every continent about the Church's more conventional outreach programs—supplying humanitarian aid and feeding and providing shelter for thousands of refugees, both outside Mexico City and everywhere else in the world. The work on the huge farms and new factories pumped out much-needed supplies, while divine protection descended over the Zion settlements and the specially called agents providing safe passage to those strongholds. Other chatter, much closer to him, told a less optimistic story.

"I don't care if it's three in the morning down there! Get him out of bed!" Mir shouted. Her voice sounded hoarse; she'd been burning up the airwaves for three hours, ever since her own projections finally confirmed that the weather had settled. "What? Don't you dare—you hang up, and I'll—"

A particularly empty threat, Hideyoshi reflected, since she couldn't stop them from hanging up, and stuck in orbit as she was, she couldn't do anything to them after they did. "Hey, hey, Ivana, they're gone," he said, rescuing the receiver she pounded on the communications console.

"Let it go. Breaking the equipment isn't going to get them back—or speed them up."

"They can't just hang up on me," she said again, in the face of all evidence to the contrary.

He risked a quick pat on her shoulder, testing to see whether she would accept it or hit him with the phone or some other piece of abused equipment. When she didn't explode, the light touch turned into a comforting rub. "They're trying. It's not that they don't want to get us out of here. You know that."

She did, but it didn't make her feel any better. Every ground-based control center she'd talked to started off sympathetic. Unfortunately for the stranded and increasingly stir-crazy ISS crew, however, the insane weather of the last six months was just one of the obstacles the various Mission Control offices faced in mounting any kind of space mission, full-blown crew replacement, or even just a rescue flight. The problems they faced ranged from the standard difficulties that came with the territory of space exploration—inexplicable gremlin attacks, or gross negligence and incompetence, in Mir's hotheaded assessment, causing catastrophic equipment failures—plus the widespread loss of funding due to the general economic avalanche engulfing just about every world market, and total military lockdowns of all sensitive areas, including space-station launch facilities, due to the nuclear strike in Mexico City and the threat of further attacks throughout North America.

The trail of sound caught Hideyoshi's ear over the incessant hum of the ventilation system. He sometimes dreamed that it had shut off, and his first reaction was always relief that the oppressive noise was gone—before the implications of silence occurred to him and panic kicked in. "At least up here we aren't contributing to the overpopulation of the world, right?" He tried for a light tone, waving at her weather monitor and the cloud-streaked, blue planet it displayed. "Really, Ivana, do you want to go back down there now, go back to a world with actual nuclear bombs going off?"

To his surprise, she burst into tears, thumping her head against his chest as deep sobs racked her. That wasn't supposed to happen. Gingerly, then more confidently, he put his arms around her, stroking her hair, rocking them both as they floated in free fall. Gradually, the sobs lessened, until just the tears remained. "It'll be okay, Ivana," he said at last. "It'll all be okay."

Instantly, she pulled away with such force that both of them spun into opposite walls. Her eyes, still wet in her tearstained face, blazed. "It'll be okay? You are as totally delusional as the rest of the loony tunes down there! How in any sense at all will any of this be okay? And don't give me any of that faith crap! If God existed at all, there wouldn't be a baby dying of radiation burns in a ratty field hospital while we slowly rot away from ultraviolet poisoning up here! Wake up to reality, James!" She swirled away down the cramped corridor, blindly righting herself when she rebounded off a tight curve.

"Faith is all we have left, Ivana," Hideyoshi said to the empty space where she'd been.

The noise of the ventilation system, the incessantly blinking lights, the cold darkness outside the view ports, the stale memory of every member of the crew in the air all crashed in on him, tightening his muscles so hard that he thought for a moment that he would vomit or suffocate at the pressure. Forcing a deep breath into his viselike ribcage, he prayed, a wordless plea for help, for courage, and for faith, the strength to endure. From somewhere beyond the tight confines of the fragile shell around him, a breath of light blew through his soul, bringing with it the clear scent of mountain pine and cold sunlight. The pressure relented; the air in his lungs was still stale, scented with artificial lemon and plastic, but it moved out more easily.

"Thank you," he whispered, brushing a shaking hand through his hair. Best to keep busy, not let himself dwell on things. Breathing slowly and forcing himself to relax, he turned back to his monitors. A glitter of brilliant blue caught his eye and even brought a slight smile to his face as he leaned forward, checking the statistics on the new water sources gushing through the Sinai.

* * *

"Well, Brother Hassan, how goes the work today?" Benjamin Cohen approached the chief foreman with a smile, disentangling his hand from its mess of blueprints, charts, sketches, and receipts to stretch it out toward the man who had practically become family in the last months. His wife, Hannah, initially suspicious of the Hassans, now shared more confidences with Sariha Hassan than she did with her own sister. Which meant that both Benjamin and his Palestinian colleague got doses of Hannah's ruthless logic and Sariha's warm-hearted practicality from both sides.

Mohammed Hassan shook the chief architect's hand, smiling through his black beard. "It goes well, Brother Cohen." He gestured upward, where a crane delicately laid a massive limestone block into place in the temple's brilliant facade. "Just the north face to go, and the exterior is finished."

The final touches, gilded accents, and sweeping, graceful carvings hand cut by devoted Saints encased the sturdy, perfectly engineered core of the building. The Cohens and Hassans, guiding their teams of workers, had built the new Jerusalem Temple to withstand any force nature could throw at it, from earthquakes to lightning strikes—and most forces man could muster, short of an atomic blast—but the white building rising into the mountain blue of the sky would give viewers the impression not of massive, earthbound solidity but heaven-reaching hope and beauty.

Even unfinished, the temple's bright spire drew the eyes of every-one in Jerusalem. Some vocal opponents resented it bitterly, declaiming on the floor of the Knesset that the Mormons' abomination represented a slap in the face to Jews and Muslims alike, a modern crusaders' castle casting its dark shadow over the recently healed wounds of the twin states of Israel and Palestine. Those voices also decried the growing presence of the Children of Light in the neighboring states of Egypt, Syria, and Jordan, criticizing the sight of Brother Light's portrait in a once-abandoned mosque in Tel Aviv. In their own like-minded groups, they even muttered maledictions against the new order that paired Israeli and Palestinian peacekeeping forces, the treaty that forced them to treat each other as equals.

Other voices, however, cried hosannas at the long-awaited appear-ance of the Lord's temple in the Holy City, calling all who would listen to come to the walls of the house of the Lord. Observers and com-mentators, long steeped in cynicism about the interaction, and more frequently, clashing of East, West, Muslim, Jew, and Christian in the ancient crossroads of Judea, watched in amazement as literally hundreds of people flocked to the Mormons' ice-white spires. In those shadows, all Saints, whether coming from Jewish or Muslim ancestry, bowed to give thanks to the same God and rose to work alongside each other in peaceful brotherhood. Or at least mostly peaceful; the shared gospel didn't cool culturally hot tempers, but it did help the arguments to resolve more quickly and the tearful reconciliation to bring harmony more completely.

Cohen smiled, remembering the clash between the interior decorator and the carpet layer who felt he knew exactly what the design lacked to make it utterly perfect. The two had screamed imprecations and threats at each other until Hannah had arrived on the scene and reminded them that they stood in the house of the Lord, each abusing one of the Lord's children. Tears and apologies followed, so many apologies that Hannah had stepped in again to quell an incipient argument over who had been most at fault—with each claiming that black mark for herself. But the result of cooperation had indeed made the brides' room that much closer to a celestial vision.

All the architect said aloud, however, was, "The interior work is progressing as well. And the gardeners have arranged the delivery of the plantings."

"As soon as we get our bulldozers out of the way so they can do the important work, Sariha says. She plans almost a full replica of the Garden of Eden." Hassan laughed, but his face grew sober as he leaned in close to Cohen. "It will be ready in two weeks, on schedule. Is it true, the rumor?"

"Yes," Cohen said, also lowering his voice. "President Smith and Associate President Rojas are coming at the end of the month to dedicate this temple."

"Here in Jerusalem. It is a dream," Hassan breathed. He looked up toward the spire, where a golden angel would take its place as the crowning touch. "I hope it does not turn into a nightmare."

Cohen shook his head, not denying, simply indicating his ignorance. "I don't know, Mohammed; the voices of the ancient prophets through the scriptures have dire things to tell. And Hannah found out from her friend Connie at Elder Nabil's office in Salt Lake City that the Presidents are coming against the initial urgings of several Apostles, and not only for the health concerns Elder Nabil raised for President Smith." He sighed. "Still, they must have come to a consensus."

Hassan nodded, the worry on his face smoothing away. "So it goes. Allah provides clear skies for their flight; He means for them to come here to us. And He will protect His people, here and everywhere. We will see great things, Benjamin. We will see the triumph of God."

"I know we will, and that part of me that will always be twenty-one and fearless is thrilled at the thought." Cohen half smiled at the vision of the young man Hannah married hidden inside the middle-aged form she saw now. That young man had seen the beginning of the peace here, and it appeared that the older man would see it shatter. "It's just ironic, isn't it, that at this moment this place, the site destined to see Armageddon, is one of the more stable countries on the planet?"

CHAPTER 14

"So who else wants to destabilize Mexico?" Senator Holly Cox stared at the intelligence reports spread over her desk and the three monitors in the room. She already knew one answer: General Andrea Garza. She also had the creeping suspicion that she could make a more than educated guess about who might be helping him.

One of the screens showed an interview between USSA National News's star reporter Rosa del Torres and the Aztec Liberation Front's cutely named leader, Montezuma. Cox evaluated the guerilla leader with a narrow-eyed stare as he told Rosa that he regretted having to nuke Mexico City, but that they had to "slash the snakebite and get the poison out." He didn't look like a desperate liberator to her; he looked like a scruffy, young thug with enough low-class sex appeal to fit the public's internalized stereotype of a desperate liberator. And that name—Montezuma, for crying out loud! They weren't dealing with a brilliant populist leader here, or even a wild-eyed terrorist; they were dealing with a figurehead puppet taking orders from someone else.

Her eyes strayed to the top corner of the desk, where a publicity photo of General Garza dominated another pile of reports. Visible under the corner of the General's portrait, another face glowered out of a spy-camera telephoto shot: El Jaguar, another romantically named rebel who'd converted to Garza with suspicious speed. That one wasn't a pretty boy or a puppet, she figured; he was a nasty gunrunner who did the General's dirty work firsthand—like running down Major Zamora in Chile—but he wasn't having a lot of luck at it. A faint smile crossed her face at that thought, which also turned her attention to the much thinner but much more useful pile of reports on the other corner of the desk.

This pile was smaller because it came with all the fat cut out of it, direct reports on conditions all over the world, gathered through the Church's uninterrupted satellite network and sent to her, as well as a few other highly placed Mormon politicians and administrators in several countries, in strict confidence. The messages didn't contain orders to her from the First Presidency, as her opponents, Secretary Garlick chief among them, claimed. Instead, they contained the vital information that she needed to do her job of representing the people of her state and the United States Senate. The Church needed freedom—true freedom—to spread the gospel, and she had come to Washington, D.C., to promote and protect that freedom.

Which meant she felt a duty to go through the entire contents of the stacks with a fine-toothed comb, looking for the real threat. She figured Garza was the puppet master behind both El Jaguar and Montezuma; so did most of the U.S. intelligence community, but they couldn't be bothered to care much about the perennial problems in South America—especially if her speculations about ties between Secretary Garlick and Garza held water. If Garza promised to help Garlick by chilling the drug trade across the southern borderlands, which had happened in the last year or so, why wouldn't the ex-senator be willing to throw in a few good words for the South American caudillo? In fact, the exact words involved praise for the "leader who had at last brought peace to the suffering people of Colombia," which Garlick said in a speech only a few months ago.

The question was what else had Garza gotten out of the deal, besides a few verbal bouquets. Maybe the biggest prize of all: American noninterference as he gathered all of Central and South America into his iron fist. The pattern stood out in all the reports from Church teams in those areas, even if it didn't come through so clearly in Channel 8's news broadcasts. The General used local insurgents or drug runners to stir things up with the local, sometimes corrupt military, then swept in to offer his help to the besieged governments to handle their "rebel" problem. Once he folded the nation's military into his own machine, the rebels disappeared—or gave up and joined the conquering army, like El Jaguar. And the rest of the world, tired of images of burning villages, wounded peasants, and crying children, applauded apathetically, sent congratulations, and went back to their own concerns. Until something happened to stir them out of their apathetic acceptance, that is. And nothing did that with quite the panache of a nuclear explosion.

Cox shuffled the reports about the Mexico City bombing on the smooth surface of her desk, laying them all out in order. According to the official story, repeated ad nauseam in the TV, radio, and Net coverage, the Aztec Liberation Front set off three suitcase nukes in the center of the downtown political district, nuclear bombs they bought on the black market from underground dealers in a former Russian republic. That explanation had the official endorsement of the Office of Homeland Security, and when she tried to contact the CIA directly, they told her in no uncertain terms that any official Senate inquiry into their findings should come through official Senate channels. Garlick had locked them up (she could just hear Senator White's broad accent here) as tight as a clam. Which to Senator Cox's suspicious mind smelled like he had something to hide. She figured that a closer, cold-eyed examination of the data could punch several holes in Homeland Security's public theory—and she had the contacts to put her own hypothesis to the test, even without Garlick's cooperation. Looking at her watch—1:30 A.M., just about right—she punched another number into the phone.

After just one buzz, the voice on the other end answered with a simple, "Greg here."

"Hi! It's Holly," she said conversationally. Introducing herself as Sister Cox might be more appropriate, but it would also be a dead give-away that she'd gone around Garlick's jurisdiction by sending the data she'd gathered to a contact in the FBI for an off-the-books analysis—a contact who happened to be both LDS and uncorrupted, which meant he hadn't risen far in the Homeland Security hierarchy. He was also a cousin, which made their conversation slightly less suspicious, just in case any eavesdroppers lurked in the electronic loop. She'd become accustomed to an entirely new level of security, but she hadn't dabbled in any actual cloak-and-dagger maneuvers before, and she felt totally unsuited to the task. Weren't top-flight female spies all young, lithe, and drop-dead gorgeous? Having to repress a giggle at the image of herself, middle-aged, well padded, and maternal, Mata Hari added an extra note of bubbly charm to her voice. "I figured I'd catch you still hard at work. How's the baby?"

"Hey, Holly." Greg's voice didn't include any bubbles, just the routine weariness of an analyst working way too late. "The baby's fine—just keeping me up all night. Good thing babies are cute, huh? You want to see the latest pictures?"

"Sure would," she agreed. Sure enough, a photo of an adorable baby girl appeared on her monitor when she opened the attachment to his transmission. "Oh, she's just gorgeous. What's her name again?"

"Eleanor," Greg said, stifling a yawn. In the background, she heard a door open, and another man's voice. "Hey, Tom. Okay, gotta go, Holly. Say hi to Grandma for me—oh, and check out the captions on the pics."

She did, as soon as the open connection closed. Clicking the activator Greg had sent her previously, she watched as the adorable baby pictures dissolved into the footage of the explosion site gathered from the Church's clear-eyed spy satellites. The captions changed too, from innocuously clever comments about the photos to short but telling analysis of the satellite data. As she read, a dark frown settled between her eyebrows. Greg's findings suggested a high probability that a missile rather than a suitcase bomb hit Mexico City, specifically, an American stealth missile armed with the core of a stray Russian nuke. No amount of nuclear material of any kind, packed into any number of trucks, could have caused that blast pattern. The bomb had detonated just above the ground, in one central place calculated to do the most damage to the communications and government centers—which all had tight ground security arranged intentionally to discourage truck bombs.

"So where did they get the missile, and how did they deliver it?" Cox said aloud. Her gaze strayed to a small stack of pictures, sent anonymously over e-mail, showing men in Garza's uniforms tinkering with cutting-edge American weapons, the same weapons Greg wrote about when he identified the photos as legitimate, undoctored representations of reality. She suspected she wouldn't like the answer.

Arriving at that unpleasant answer, however, proved even more complicated than securing trustworthy analysis of the blast data itself. Nothing in the reports suggested that any ICBMs had gone astray. Something as big as that would have made it into the news as well as the secret files, which was reassuring. Not so reassuring was the small plane that appeared on the edges of the satellite-sweep footage, like a black bird hovering almost out of sight. The satellites hadn't caught a high-resolution image of the phantom flyer, because the operators hadn't known to focus on it, as they had on the wreckage of the bombing site. That silhouette, plus cautious reports in the Church intelligence summaries of high-tech codes squirreled away in General Garza's tactical database, courtesy of Mercury, dictated the next place the senator knew she had to look.

"How's the search coming?" she asked the next day, stopping by her assistant's desk. She'd given him the somewhat daunting task of running down the identities and descriptions of the weapons in the anonymous e-mail. Using Charlie had two advantages: it saved her time she didn't have, and it looked less suspicious to have an enthusiastic young man researching the intimate details of military gadgets. Washington had its share of military-history buffs and hardware aficionados, and having Charlie pose as one of their number let him investigate without drawing Garlick's suspicions about what Senator Cox was up to now.

"We don't have many service-oriented people over at the Pentagon, ma'am." Charlie hid a huge yawn and shook his head. "They pretty much blew me off. One secretary did tell me I should check Jane's, if I'm so interested in identifying military hardware. So I did, even though the catalog's a year behind, due to intelligence and top-secret considerations." He opened a heavy book, extracting several pages of printout from the back. Handing them to her for inspection, he added, "It looks like all the stuff in the pictures—and that strange little plane in the aerial shot—are ours, and I think they're newer than the ones in the book."

"My word, even newer." Her tone stayed light, but foreboding dropped into her chest. "Well, thank you very much, Charlie. I appreciate the research. You've done well."

"That's what I'm here for, ma'am," he said, happy at the praise. "You need me to lock horns with any more snotty bureaucrats, you just let me know."

"Will do," she promised, saluting him with the printouts. The next round of calls, however, she didn't delegate to a harmless-sounding assistant. It was time to use the power inherent in the title of senator— even if it raised suspicions. She didn't think she had a lot of time to waste sneaking around.

After spending just fifteen minutes making the front-door effort at extracting information directly from the top—and getting more politely but just as firmly blown off as Charlie had, she switched to plan B: taking advantage of the momentary lull in solar and earthly storms to contact actual commanders in the field, asking what high-tech equipment they requested and what they received. The military men gave her less static than she'd expected. They felt stranded on battlefields they had little hope of securing or escaping, and they seized the chance to lobby her for increased support for their overstretched operations, requesting additional manpower, weapons, and other matériel. She promised to do what she could for them.

Getting the latest manufacturing and inventory reports from various military contractors proved more difficult because they felt fat and sassy rather than thin and overextended. "You don't sit on our advisory board, Senator Cox," one particularly oily executive pointed out.

"Indeed I do not," she agreed. "But I believe that Senator Benyanny does. Shall I call her office and have her ask the question for me—as well as more pointed questions about your financial status?" An hour of sniffing the political wind melted his confidence and elicited the report she wanted.

* * *

"As you say so often, Senator White," Cox reminded him, laying out the final summary of her findings over the gleaming mahogany surface of his desk, "success in politics came down to a matter of exerting the right kind of pressure." She surveyed the results, nodded with satisfaction, and looked at him. "What kind of pressure do you see here?"

The senior senator grunted as he flipped through the evidence. "What I see is that Garlick hasn't been as smart about General Garza's intentions as he should've been—but also that you don't have a lock on the hard evidence that Howard's been doing more than shutting his eyes to a situation because he's made a couple of bargains under the table, let alone shipping our gadgets to some crazy banana-republic dictator. Those are dead-serious charges, Holly. It goes way beyond a little tampering with the First Amendment."

"I know they're serious, William," she told him, her voice level and confident. "I investigated all of this information carefully before I brought it here. This isn't petty politics—and I don't think there's any such thing as a 'little' tampering with the First Amendment."

White gave her a look under his wildly thatched brows, reminding himself that he was dealing with a real Girl Scout here. Returning his attention to her evidence, he added, "Still, I also see discrepancies between the weapons inventories at the stateside bases, the orders for the military, and the shipments to the divisions out there fighting losing battles against the chaos of the world, which might be useful."

"I think you'll find this last piece of the puzzle even more useful," Cox said, looking so sorrowful that White expected the next set of papers she set down to contain information that torpedoed the fragile web of implied guilt the rest of her evidence built around Garlick.

Instead, it brought him out of his chair, staring at the pictures in his hands. "By thunder, Holly, you've found it! With this, we can barbecue that bull!" He waved the photos of Garza's men with American weapons over the rest of the report as if fanning the flames that would engulf his hated rival.

"I'd say it's enough to open a full investigation at least," Cox said more cautiously. A thrill of excitement buzzed through the genuine sadness and concern she felt. There might be a way to stop the cancer eating out the heart of the country she loved so much after all! "Howard is going to hit the ceiling."

* * *

Garlick did more than hit the ceiling. When he received the official notice that the Senate, at the request of Senators Cox, White, and Benyanny, had moved to open an official inquiry into the practices of the Office of Homeland Security and the actions of Secretary Howard W. Garlick personally, he hit his desk, the chair, and the door, roaring curses on all their heads. Ms. Lincoln, who knew exactly when to duck, escaped decapitation by paperweight, then emerged from her bolt-hole in the outer office to take a memo when the storm had passed.

"Secretary Howard W. Garlick of the Office of Homeland Security absolutely decries the idea of a Senate committee investigation," read the statement, after she had edited the most colorful metaphors out of it. "In this time of turmoil, with enemies domestic and foreign threatening the fabric of American society, it is the height of arrogance and the depth of treason for a group of un-American operatives to attempt to hamstring the public's last defense against the nightmare threatening to engulf the country. Secretary Garlick categorically and unreservedly expresses deep contempt for this petty political maneuvering, but expresses his intention to cooperate as fully as possible with the ethical members of the panel to assure a speedy and satisfactory conclusion to this ridiculous exercise."

Getting that out of his system, and repeating it on every news broadcast for six hours, went a long way toward lowering Garlick's blood pressure. It spiked right back up, however, when underling after underling appeared on those same news broadcasts to announce their intentions to testify for the prosecution.

"So Cox wants to play girl detective, does she?" Garlick glared at the soft-looking, iron-spined woman on the screen, brushing past reporters with a brief "No comment," his face flushed to crimson. Cox infuriated him even more than White, who'd sparred with him since they both entered the Senate, and even that traitor Benyanny. She'd even turned his own subordinates against him before he could hang Homeland Security's failures around the smarmy traitors' necks!

Spitting the words as if they were nails, he dictated another memo to Ms. Lincoln, this one for immediate publication not to the press but to his allies in the Senate. Because it was an internal document, she took it down word for word, including the senator's vivid and entirely inaccurate description of Senator Cox's ancestry, sexual preferences, and personal habits. Boiled down to its essentials, which would also receive wide release the next day, the notice acted as the second volley in the battle, launching another investigation, this one against Senator Cox herself.

Within forty-eight hours, both impeachment hearings plunged into full swing.

* * *

"So, as senior members of the Senate go *mano a mano* with a former colleague, the question all over Washington is who will win the heavyweight bout," Clara summarized, making the statement a neat segue into the evening's sports coverage. The ticker not only gave odds on the boxing match in Las Vegas, but handicapped the various senators as well. At the moment, Holly Cox had the underdog spot, with close odds on whether her political career would survive a hot war with Secretary Garlick. William White, with his long history of brilliant maneuvers and narrow escapes added to Garlick's dropping poll numbers due to the seemingly impossible AllSafe situation, had long odds in his favor.

"Looking over the odds, there's times when I want to switch which horse I'm backing," Johnny Mack said, flipping a golden coin from knuckle to knuckle down his hand. He'd seen the trick in an old gangster movie and thought it looked cool. He glanced at Augosto, angling for a response that would help him gauge his boss's mood.

Augosto generally didn't spend much time watching the TV news, unlike Johnny Mack, who liked to see reports about the more spectacular rubouts he participated in. Augosto knew it was all smoke and mirrors, illusions bought and paid for; he'd done enough of that himself. Unusually, he'd sat quietly for a couple of hours now, paying close attention to the reports on every channel he could find to confirm Channel 8's official line, checking the Net and radio reports against the in-depth report on the Senate investigation. He'd made a few phone calls early on, confirming some piece of information or the other with his contacts in other government offices, but that stopped pretty quickly. Text messages flashed back and forth on the screen in his hand—as did the strange photographs Virginia Diamante had sent, images that morphed from salacious publicity shots of her to pictures of military men and machines when he used the encryption key she sent with a different message. The more he heard and saw, the quieter and more intent he became. By the time Johnny Mack made his comment about changing his bets, Augosto had come to an unpleasant conclusion.

"Sometimes that's a good idea," Augosto finally said. His voice sounded as flat as the unreadable expression on his face; he didn't look at his bodyguard as he added, "Especially when the horse you bet on turns out to be a donkey."

That gave Johnny Mack all the clue he needed to Augosto's mental state—and the probable consequences. He stowed the coin and rose to his feet, adjusting his flashy jacket. "I'll call Smokey, tell him he's off stable duty."

"No." Augosto's hand rose, stopping the younger man. He doused the screen's glow with a decisive snap. "No, tell Smokey that he's still on stable duty until tomorrow afternoon. Tell him to get out the blinders."

"You know Smokey—he's a simple guy. He's not going to understand that," Johnny Mack hinted, hoping for an explanation himself.

Augosto finally looked at him, and Johnny Mack, hardened as he was, nearly recoiled at the fury he saw in the crime boss's eyes. The Senate investigation of Garlick's operation was bad enough news to demand instant, effective action. He'd supplied Garlick with enough money, backroom alliances, and strong-arm security services to keep the FBI off his back, not to bring an entire avalanche of Justice Department investigators down on them both. The doubts that had grown in the back of his mind since Travell Capshaw's dramatic execution flowered into absolute certainty in the hot light of the news cameras; he had no doubt that the former senator would sell all his allies down the river in a split second if it would save his sorry hide, and the last thing the Mob boss wanted was to see his own dealings with Garlick splashed over Channel 8's news banners. That kind of betrayal didn't surprise Augosto—he'd never shared the delusional belief in honor among thieves—but what the senator had done went far beyond the usual, and often expected, double-cross maneuver. Caesar Augosto was a lifelong Mafia man, an unrepentant and open-eyed criminal who harbored no illusions about the exact nature of the business he engaged in. However, he also, delusional or not, believed himself to be a good, loyal, and red-blooded American.

He surged to his feet, the heat and energy of his anger erupting. "How's this for simple, Johnny? This horse hasn't pulled up lame—he's a traitor, pure and simple. Howard W. Garlick, secretary of Homeland Security for the United States of America," he practically spat the words, "sold us out—not just us as in the organization, not just us as in the family, but us, the entire United States of America—to a greasy South American warlord!" Taking a deep breath, he forcibly composed himself. Running on emotion never yielded good results. "And the Senate's pit bulls will dig up everything Garlick's ever done—sticking their noses in our business while they're looking for every scrap of evidence that proves he's in bed with Garza."

"Guess that explains Virginia's little birthday present, huh?" Johnny Mack's quip earned him a sharp look, which quelled his attempt at witticism.

"For once, Ms. Diamante struck a real vein instead of fool's gold," Augosto admitted. He silently thanked Saint Anthony that he'd opened her message instead of deleting it as he'd almost done. He preferred classier women, and found Virginia's blatant sexiness overdone, but if he could use her, he wouldn't hesitate to do it. "She might be useful after all, to wipe out the rest of the vipers." The image appealed to him; he appreciated the image of Garlick as a massive rattler that had reared up to strike at him. "Tomorrow, we cut the head off the biggest snake, to show the others they'd better keep their fangs to themselves."

A sharp smile spread over Johnny Mack's face as his employer laid out the ingredients of the antidote in the flat, unemotional tones that always meant Johnny Mack would get to use his knives on another victim. In this case, the weapons of choice also included an office computer, an ancient torture technique, an open microphone, and a van with dark-tinted windows.

* * *

The van slipped easily through the streets of Washington, its Homeland Security plates reassuring the nervous officers on patrol. Johnny Mack, his hair tucked under an innocuous policeman's cap, saluted them and drove through the security cordon.

"What are you going to do about AllSafe?" shouted a red-faced woman.

"Bring our troops home to protect us!" yelled a man dressed in his veteran's fatigues.

A chain of Whole Earth Alliance disciples linked arms through the crowd and chanted "Save Earth now! Save Earth now!"

A mass of protesters filled the wide space in front of the memorial to Terrorism's Victims, hundreds of people gathered to vent their anger and frustration in front of the podium that Secretary Garlick had set up for his press conference. He hadn't meant for his address to provide an opportunity for a public rally, but fate, and Senator White, had conspired against him. Even as the secretary cussed out the Homeland Security flunky who'd had the bad luck to break the news to him that the crowd they'd hired would have to compete for standing room with an actual herd of citizens, he knew it was too late to change venues. The reporters who'd come to document his public affirmation of innocence and competence were already filing into the space inside a tight cordon of Garlick's security guards, and if he backed out now, it would look like he was intimidated—or guilty.

Growling to the slab of meat Augosto assigned as his backup bodyguard to keep his eyes open, Garlick straightened his lapels, submitted to a last-minute dab of powder and spritz of hair-hold, and briskly mounted the steps of the podium. The secretary's private security agents, all on loan from Augosto as a sign of goodwill to a valued ally in troubled and insecure times, closed in, separating Garlick from his Homeland Security squad.

"Ladies and gentlemen," Garlick intoned, sweeping the knot of reporters with the intense, charismatic look that, in conjunction with massive amounts of money, had won countless political battles, "thank you for coming today to hear not the protests of an innocent man accused, but the denunciations of a true patriot against traitors—"

The sea of protesters shouted and screamed from the background, trying to get their points through to the secretary—or at least to the reporters and cameras inside the tight wall of riot-control officers. A couple of the cameramen inside the circle turned their lenses outward, capturing the sea of vocally discontented humanity surrounding the podium on three sides. One camera caught a glimpse of the dark-windowed white van pulling to a stop before moving slowly away for a few feet. He hesitated turning back to the senator in response to some specialized journalistic instinct for incipient disaster.

The van's doors opened, spilling a woman onto the hard cement of the Mall. She hit the ground and lay there, moaning, for a long moment, then held her head as she struggled to her knees. Picking herself up at last, she staggered toward the people nearest the vehicle, hands outstretched, pleading for help. The woman waving the poster caught one glimpse of her explosives-laden vest and screamed. Lurching violently backward, away from the suicide bomber stumbling toward her, she crashed into her fellow protesters, drawing their attention to the danger at their backs.

Like a ripple passing over a pond or a wave through a stand of tightly packed dominoes, panic swept through the gathering. In an instant, a semiorderly throng of protesters morphed into a frantic mob stampeding in all directions. Some shoved to escape the explosion, others moved violently simply to avoid getting trampled. Slogans and complaints changed to cries of fear and pleas for help. The wave sped on, throwing a massive surge of human bodies against the ring of police holding them back from the podium. Amazingly, the blue and black line held firm, repulsing the first rush, even as the staggering form behind the wave disappeared in a vicious explosion.

The police line collapsed completely, however, as shots rang out through the smoke, completing the transformation from bedlam to pandemonium. Johnny Mack, from the cover of the van's front seat, blasted a line of lead across the front of the podium. A suited, sunglassed member of the FBI security team jerked and spun to the ground, his body swallowed in the second wave of the stampede.

The remaining Homeland Security agents, reacting instantly, took up defensive positions, a second line of defense, pistols pointing outward, seeking the source of the shots. Two agents, frantic and disoriented, thinking they were under close-order attack, fired into the crowd. The Mob-provided security officers on the platform fired as well, the barrage of gunfire only exacerbating the panic, causing the crowd to surge backward again.

Garlick, staring in frozen fascination at the tsunami of panicked humanity bearing down on him, found himself thrown to the carpeted platform. The heavy hand on his back pressed the breath out of his lungs. Above and behind him, sounding miles away in the roar of the stampede, he heard Smokey's deep voice roar, "The secretary's been shot!"

"But I'm not," he managed.

"Mr. Augosto says you are," Smokey told him. The bullet that tore into Garlick's head came with the one last word he heard: "Traitor."

The same word splashed across headlines, banners, and radio broadcasts, as FBI and Justice Department agents checking Secretary Garlick's office found damning photographs of American weapons in the hands of foreigners, files of messages between Garlick and Johann Brindermann, and mysterious gaps in the electronic record that hinted at the deletion of further evidence. Ms. Lincoln, Garlick's own secretary and keeper of the keys to his information system, had vanished as well. An APB crackled through the Homeland Security apparatus, sending her name, photo, and vital statistics to every office in the nation as a "person of interest" in the investigation into the secretary's dramatic death and his shady dealings in office. No one in the medical examiner's office thought to connect the ragged, trampled remains of a suicide bomber to the cool, level-headed keeper of Garlick's schedule, memorandums, and passwords.

* * *

"It seems as inescapable as it is unbelievable. Howard W. Garlick, secretary of Homeland Security, was gunned down in broad daylight by agents of the terrorist elements to whom he was selling American military hardware." Darren McInnes frowned magisterially. The running commentary under his handsome face reduced the tragedy to a series of headline sound bites: Howard W. Garlick assassinated by suspected foreign terrorists; General Garza denies complicity in the attack but admits to "assisting" the secretary by testing new designs of military hardware; computer files in Garlick's office point to deals with foreign nationals to sell state secrets; CIA director to resign over implications that he knew about the deals and failed to report them; FBI director refusing comment, saying the "investigation is proceeding"; international expressions of condolence—or accusation of complicity with terror, depending on the source of the statement; Senator Holly Cox expressing shock and sorrow that a trusted official would betray his office; Senator William White calling on the president to appoint a new secretary of Homeland Security to head the investigation and clean up the administration; rumors that Garlick had used his influence to do favors for those who contributed to his campaign for Homeland Security, including manipulating the FDA to approve MedaGen's new AllSafe vaccine, seemed confirmed.

* * *

"It's just like the lights are going out, one by one, just leaving all of us in the dark!" A volunteer at the Crusaders for Jesus revival rally dabbed at her eyes with a tissue, staring at the endlessly repeated footage of Secretary Garlick falling to the press-conference platform, dead despite the valiant efforts of the men who threw themselves on top of him.

"There's still lights out there," Sally Mae assured her, giving the woman's shoulders a quick squeeze. "Why, that's why we're here, isn't it? To help spread the dear Lord's light through Reverend Gibbs's revivals. You're doing a great job. Here." She gently but firmly tucked a large handful of programs into the volunteer's hands. "You just take these out there and talk to people as you collect the donations. They're scared too, and they need to see a smile. You just tell them that the good Lord is watching out for them, and He's glad they're here. All they need to do is put their money where their mouth is, help the Crusade gather up more of our brothers and sisters, and they'll be just fine. And so will you."

The woman gave her a watery smile, which she returned confidently before gently herding all of her charges on their mission of selling programs to the attendees, who'd already paid once to get in the stadium door. Her supervisor watched them leave the cavernous backstage area for the stands, giving them a quick wave of encouragement as they plunged into the vast throng of people seeking spiritual comfort, reassurance that nothing bad would happen to them, and a chance to spend a little worldly wealth to ensure their reservation for the Rapture.

Though Sally Mae's smile never wavered—projecting a happy, confident image was a must for all Crusade workers—the comment about the lights going out struck an uneasy chord in her. Images from her dreams rose in the back of her mind: Tommy Gibbs, standing at the altar in his gold and blue glory, seemed to glow from within as he preached the power of grace without works to the darkness that closed around him. Sally Mae gazed worshipfully up at him from where she huddled with other volunteers, Crusade workers, and audience members, looking to him for protection, guidance, and safe passage through the devil's storm. But the thickening shadows fell like heavy fog from storm clouds; the vapor blurred his shining form, dulled his ringing voice, rolled toward him threateningly. He raised his hands against it, ordering it to disperse, to get behind him, to trouble the faithful no more. And the darkness—laughed. Its laughter rang out like the clash of iron, and Tommy Gibbs fell, bleeding, into the void in front of the altar, where the shadows ate him, quenching his light forever. Then the blackness rolled over Sally Mae and the other believers, icy cold and roiling with all the cacophony of war. Far away, through the endless night, another light gleamed, a light that Tommy Gibbs could have led them toward, if only the spotlights hadn't blinded him to its existence.

A treacherous thought niggled in the back of her mind, added acid regret to the fear that woke her, sweating and shaking, in the night: her beloved Reverend Gibbs had gone off course, he'd lost the true path, and he didn't even know it. She tried to push the thought away, but no matter how much she prayed, it only got stronger. What if it were true? What if these dreams were like the visions she'd had of the tornado, of the jealous boyfriend's anger—not merely nightmares, but divine messages?

The crowd's roar as a few eager fans glimpsed Tommy Gibbs himself entering the stadium blasted through the echo of the dream's horrific sounds. Sally Mae blinked, trying to shake the horrible premonition away, to deny that her dreams came from anything but stress and too many hours of watching the news on the buses and long waits backstage. As her head cleared, she realized she was standing in the path of the swiftly moving group of executive Crusade workers, bodyguards, and special guests pouring out of the long tunnel from the high-security vans in the VIP parking garage to the greenroom. And there, detaching himself from the center of the entourage for a quick word with Michael Romanoff, was Tommy Gibbs himself.

Sally Mae hesitated for just a moment, before the fleeting feeling of divine pressure transformed into utter conviction that the good Lord had arranged circumstances for His own purposes. The dreams had to be true warnings, and Reverend Gibbs would listen to her, if she only had the faith and courage to follow dear Jesus' promptings to testify. A sudden feeling of total inadequacy swept over her, threatening to push her away, keep her silent, but, ironically, her native humility pushed her forward. If a donkey could talk to Balaam, a prophet in the

Old Testament, then she could talk to the great Reverend Tommy Gibbs. She'd better hurry, though; he had finished his strategy session and moved easily to catch up with the rest of the group at the entrance to the backstage lounge, where only the inner circle could set foot.

"Reverend Gibbs!" she exclaimed, hurrying forward with more speed than dignity and drawing stares from the backstage crews. "Reverend Gibbs! Just a moment, please, a minute of your time!"

Gibbs, surprised at being accosted by a plump, pink-cheeked, sweet-looking woman wearing the blue ribbon of a volunteer wrangler, hesitated then stopped. He made a show of glancing at his watch, then smiled. "The podium calls, but I think I have a minute to spare. What can I do for you, Ms.—"

"Loftus," Sally Mae filled in, slightly out of breath as she lifted the ribbon on her sweater slightly to let him read the name across the center tag. "Sally Mae Loftus. I'm a volunteer here—well, a volunteer coordinator. I—" She shook her head, stopping the nervous flow of words before she poured out her entire employment history. Jesus hadn't sent her to talk about herself. "Reverend Gibbs, I believe so much in what you're trying to do, bring people into the arms of sweet Lord Jesus in these horrible end times. The adversary's out there, trying to pull us away from the light. But, Reverend Gibbs, I have a message for you: you're going the wrong way."

The warm smile froze on the popular preacher's face.

Sally Mae's voice, instead of wavering into uncertainty, grew at once gentler and more confident and firm. "You know what is right, and you know what message these people need to hear. Tell them the truth, even if the truth is hard for the natural man to hear. Feed my sheep, Tommy. Lead them to the fold of the true Shepherd before the final night falls."

"What?" he asked, stunned by both her words and the way they sank into his heart, chilling and warming at the same time. "Why are you saying this?"

"I've seen it," Sally Mae said. "You have such a great work to do, if you will make the sacrifice."

The darkness and hope of her visions shone in her eyes, a conviction that spoke to him through the blinding glare of the spotlight and his own rationalizations. He had studied the Bible thoroughly, paid the high price to understand the historical and cultural underpinnings, devoted long hours to building reasoned arguments for Christianity as well as blood-stirring sermons promoting the gospel of Christ. The words of the ancient Apostles and their meanings rose in his mind: the ultimate necessity of Christ's grace balanced with the necessity of obeying His commandments, even if imperfectly, and enduring to the end; the hard truth that wickedness never was happiness and that no money or reassurance could change that cold fact. His own words rose as well, pale ghosts of the truth shining through the window of the scriptures, cutting corners and obscuring responsibility, glossing over the need for repentance and charity, making the edges softer and easier for busy, materialistic people to swallow. For an eternal instant, the glare of the spotlight lifted enough to let him see himself darkly in the shadowy glass, a poor shepherd letting the sheep run where they would because he wanted them to love him.

"Oh, I see you've met Ms. Loftus." Michael Romanoff, who'd glanced over in time to see his meal ticket accosted by a mere volunteer herder, put a hand on Gibbs's shoulder and smiled professionally at Sally Mae. "She's one of our dedicated workers, just joined the Crusaders full-time from a job as a *phone psychic*." He gave the last two words the same inflection as *mental patient*.

The promoter's words broke Gibbs's stunned physical and spiritual immobility. A phone psychic. He shook himself, logic and self-interest reasserting themselves. A phone psychic—and yakking about visions! The vast sound of the crowd singing hymns as they waited for their spiritual leader to appear swelled in his mind. The faces and the beautifully tailored, richly textured clothes and sparkling jewelry of the affluent, influential men and women waiting for him beside the stage door came into sharp focus. His hands rose to accept the velvety weight of the gilded blue robe that Romanoff put into his arms. He took it almost eagerly, holding it between himself and Sally Mae as if it were a shield.

What was he thinking? He must be tired. Had he almost considered changing his sermon tonight from the enlightened, compassionate realism that drew so many eager listeners to his Crusades? If he thundered away at the pulpit like some fundamentalist throwback, they would disappear, and any hope of reaching them would disappear too.

No, better to take it gradually, to ease them into Christian behaviors. Milk before meat. Romanoff had the right idea—build the kingdom one brick at a time, or risk losing it all. He had far too much power, too much influence, to throw it all away on a fleeting feeling. Of course he wanted to preach repentance, the meat of the gospel—but he simply couldn't do that right now.

"We all do what we can, Sally Mae. You help with volunteers, and I'll take care of the sermons. I think that would be best for all of us," he said, verbally pushing away her comment about sacrifice as he physically brushed past her, utterly polite and as distant as the stars. "Thank you for your dedication and enthusiasm."

Sally Mae watched him go, her head and nerves still buzzing from the feeling that had washed through her. They had both felt it—she knew that. But something had happened, something cold had come between them, and the light that poured through her hit a wall it couldn't breach. Now the flood shrank to a trickle and all but disappeared, leaving her chilled and filled with a sadness beyond anything she had ever felt. The desolate sorrow slowly dissipated, but worry grew to take its place, the conviction that she was in the wrong place, that she needed to be some-where else. She walked back to the volunteers' area, wondering what to do, wondering if she could be so wrong about her dreams, about the feelings that burst out of her. Where should she go? Where could she find safety, someone to explain what had happened to her?

* * *

"The Unity holds the answers to all the problems in the world." The attractive, soothing voice of Brother Light drew Sally Mae's atten-tion. On the small screen set up at the volunteers' table, a commercial for the Children of Light advertised the easy way to enlightenment and prosperity, its Prophet extolling the virtues of sharing wealth, accepting all who professed belief in the One God, minimizing pain and maxi-mizing pleasure. She realized it was a news item, not a commercial—though it was difficult to tell the difference. The commentator outlined the amazing growth of Rashi Janjalani's mystic but pragmatic religion, the attractiveness of its charismatic leader, and its success in pacifying areas of the world historically torn by sectarian feuds, mostly by killing anyone who didn't convert; but Channel 8's editorial policy, well-greased with Janjalani's money and support, dictated silence or soft-pedaling on such unfavorable items. She watched the smiling faces on the screen promising safety and certainty—and a feeling of revulsion, as if someone had screamed a warning at her, made her stumble. Catching the edge of the table, she steadied herself, reaching for the button to turn the console off. Halfway there, however, her hand slowed.

Anne O'Neal appeared on-screen, an African savannah replacing the green lushness of Manila. "Thank you, Clara. While it is true that the explosive growth of the Children of Light has surpassed the growth of The Church of Jesus Christ of Latter-day Saints in the last few years, the Mormons' achievements are still impressive. From its humble beginnings in the eastern United States, the Church has grown to a vital presence on every continent and in almost every country on the globe. The Church's financial holdings, while privately owned and undisclosed, are rumored to be in the billions of dollars. Its membership includes prominent members of governments, businesses, and charities. Here in West Africa, the Mormons' villages are islands of peace and stability in a war- and disease-ravaged landscape."

* * *

Far from both Anne and Sally Mae, Monk sat in his dim control room and growled. "Keep it neutral, Annie," he ordered through the audio link. "They're not paying us to sing the Mormons' praises."

"They're paying me to give accurate reports," Anne shot back, as footage from a previously filed interview with an Ivory Coast stake president rolled onto the airwaves. "And to earn bigger ratings—which the Mormon stories always do. People like to hear about them."

Monk sighed and settled for reminding her that Channel 8 determined what people liked, but he didn't push too hard. Yes, Channel 8 had taken money from MedaGen, the Children of Light, the late secretary of Homeland Security, the Crusaders for Jesus, and half a dozen others to put a negative spin on the Mormons. What did money matter, stacked up against ratings? Not much, for Monk. Anne had it right—people were interested in the Mormons, which tickled the ratings numbers up. The only thing he did say aloud was a sour, "They've got their own channel too. Why don't you let them defend themselves?" He didn't add that even non-Mormons all over the world tuned into it with alarming frequency, looking for facts about world events, a stark lack of advertising hype, and a crystal-clear signal. In a short time they had risen to the number-ten spot and would easily go even higher.

The video feed came back to Anne, the wind ruffling her hair. She began slowly walking, as if closing in on her quarry. "The question lingering in many people's minds is simple: is the Mormon Church in the midst of building an empire? During my next series of live reports, I'll look into that question, from its headquarters in Independence, Missouri, to its newly built, controversial temple in Jerusalem."

* * *

Mormons. The word evoked a tangle of emotions and thoughts in Sally Mae's mind. Negative rumors and stereotypes swirled, but the memory of Donna Callatta broke through the muddle. Donna, the sweet girl whose friendliness made work more bearable, and whose Book of Mormon Sally Mae still had, sitting like an unopened gift in the oversized purse she hauled around every day. Donna, whose family had been chased out of Lake Creek by crazy men with guns. Somehow, she'd never believed that the Mormons deserved that, though others told her they did. But hadn't they gone to another town, the one with the funny name—Nauvoo? Yes, that was it. The town that the tornado couldn't blow down. The town where you could be safe . . .

"Ms. Loftus!" Romanoff's harsh tone startled her. She turned to see the producer bearing down on her, a thunderous frown replacing the professional smile on his face.

He stopped close to her, glaring. "I don't know what kinds of stunts those psychic people put up with, but we absolutely cannot tolerate such disrespect as you showed to Reverend Gibbs. You are an employee—and an unnecessary, low-ranking employee at that. You will do your job, and you will keep quiet about things that are not your concern, or you won't have a job!"

"I'm sorry to offend, but I said what I knew I had to say." Sally Mae drew herself up, facing his glare without flinching. "And I'd say it again, if I thought it would do any good."

For a split second, Romanoff just stood there, nonplussed at her unexpected defiance. Anger swiftly replaced the surprise. This *nothing* woman had almost thrown Tommy off his stride before the biggest sermon of his career so far! "I'm sorry to hear that. Ms. Loftus, you are fired."

"That's just as well," she shot back, surprising herself. "I don't think I have time to give two weeks' notice." With that, she removed the blue ribbon from her sweater, picked up her purse, and walked briskly out of the long tunnel to the stadium parking lot.

It wasn't until she reached the pavement that she realized she was going to Zion—and the realization, strange as it was, came as a great relief. A warm feeling of heavenly reassurance that she had done what Jesus wanted her to competed with the cold knot in her stomach. She was unemployed, far from home, in a town where she knew no one at all, and her noble leader had just proved that he had feet of clay. Maybe she was supposed to bring a message to the Mormons, like Donna's family, to help set them on the right path.

"All right, Lord Jesus, I'm in your hands now. You just put me where you want me to go." She sat down on the bench beside the bus stop outside the stadium portals, pulled the Book of Mormon out of her bag, and began to read as she waited for the sign that would tell her what to do next. Over her head, the moon hung full, low, pale, and blood red.

* * *

Dear Chisom,

As I sit here tonight preparing to write to you, I am once again impressed that prophecy is being fulfilled. From the window of my den, a red moon peeks out between clouds, basking the dusty air and earth in bloody hues. Thus, this sign, as predicted in D&C 29, has come again, hailing the host of ills that cause it. The result is "weeping and wailing among the hosts of men." D&C 45 states clearly, "In that day when they shall see all these things, then shall they know that the hour is nigh. And it shall come to pass that he that feareth me shall be looking forth for the great day of the Lord to come, even for the signs of the coming of the Son of Man."

As we watch the inhabitants of the earth brutalize themselves with all nature helping, we do look forward to the signs because they promise relief, peace, and rest. The sign we wait for more than any other is the great and last sign promised by the Lord. He told His disciples that it would be like "the light of the morning coming out of the east" and covering the whole earth. The appearance of this "sign of the Son of Man," as He called it, shall cause the tribes of the earth to mourn, but the Saints will rejoice. For more on this, see Joseph Smith—Matthew 1:26, 36. Joseph Smith spoke of this sign, saying, "The dawning of the morning makes its appearance in the east and moves along gradually. So also will the coming of the Son of Man be. It will be small at its first appearance and gradually become larger until every eye shall see it. Shall the Saints understand it? Oh yes. Paul says so (1 Thes. 5:4–5). Shall the wicked understand? Oh no. They will attribute it to a natural cause. They will probably suppose it is two comets coming in contact with each other. It will be small at first and will grow larger and larger until it will be all in a blaze, so that every eye will see it.

The Church, the bride of the Lord, will know what it means—the sign that she is to prepare to meet her Bridegroom. It signals that the wedding feast has come. John, in Revelation 19, put it this way: "The marriage of the Lamb is come, and his wife hath made herself ready. And to her was granted that she should be arrayed in fine linen, clean and white: for the fine linen is the righteousness of the saints." And, "Blessed are they which are called unto the marriage supper of the Lamb."

Interestingly, as the Saints go to banquet, so, too, another feast takes place. This feast, according to Revelation 19, is called "the supper of the great God." Its invited guests are "all the fowls that fly in the midst of heaven." And upon what do they feast? "The flesh of all men, both free and bond, both small and great." And where is the feast served? At Armageddon.

I am amazed how this period of time mirrors that of the prophet Enoch's day, when the world feared because the glory of God was upon His people. That fear did not, however, prevent the wicked from warring with one another. Yet in the midst of this man-made fury, the Saints dwelt in peace and flourished (see

Moses 7:16–17). That is exactly what we are seeing. Take, for example, our Church farms. Through careful management and multiuse agriculture, they are producing abundantly. In some of the harder-hit areas, the farms are not all they could be. Nonetheless, they do produce, and some even miraculously. The result has been both envy and hatred. Our enemies use this as the sure sign that we are guarded by the powers of Beelzebub.

The result has also been, as I mentioned before, that we are able to feed not only our people and keep them employed, but also those who have joined with us. One of the places this condition is obvious is Africa. Our people there are running the farms efficiently, and it is making a difference.

Our success has caused us problems in another area. The Church has for decades been engaged in humanitarian aid. Now with conditions so bad, many are calling upon us for help. The Church is willing to give, but only on condition. The people must cease fighting, give up their sordid lifestyles, agree to live by our civil standards, and gather to us. What amazes me is how many feel that we are asking too much. They claim that we are using food as a means of forced conversion. How foolish. We are not asking anyone to be baptized, only to be civil. The prophet has promised us that if they join us on our terms, the Lord will increase our yield and we will be able to include them. We cannot, however, support them in their debauchery. They have chosen sin, and they must face its consequences, or they must repent and enjoy the rewards of righteousness.

Well, here I go again, preaching to the choir, and my poor dear Chisom is a choir of one. Take comfort in this: you don't stand alone. Adaure and your brothers and sisters must also endure my ranting. I'm just grateful that all of you are not only patient with me but also on my side.

I must close, but with one observation. Lest you think I have forgotten or grown less curious, I still want to know about the young woman in those pictures you sent a while ago. I notice a loud silence on that subject in your Vids. Should I consider this a sign?

With love and respect,
Your father,
Chinedu

* * *

"Is it blasphemous to consider this a sign?" Merry asked, her face bathed in a cool, blue glow.

"Do mice bite?" Missy's question only partly distracted her mother from the slide show of microscans that flicked across her screen in rapid succession.

"Mice can bite if they get scared, but usually they don't," she answered, belatedly adding, "Why?" when she realized that Missy had left her "hut" on the floor underneath Merry's desk.

Missy, already halfway to the door, looked over her shoulder, her eyebrows arched innocently. "Oh, just making sure." She had Corinne's inflection down perfectly.

Merry sighed. "No, Missy—the mice in Corinne's lab cages don't bite, but you can't get them out to play with them. They're important scientific mice, not pets like at preschool."

"Oh, rats." Missy pouted, then laughed. "I mean mice!" She wandered over to lean against Merry's legs, looking up at the monitor. "What are we doing again?"

"We're playing with computer simulations of the virus that Dove brought us from New Mexico, trying to find the antidote to General Garza's latest try at creating his own personal bioweapon, based on the information a gospel sister named Dr. Vasquez smuggled out of a hidden jungle lab. That's this side of the screen," Merry pointed to the morphing, twisting genetic patterns mixing and matching in completely unrealistic vivid colors. "Super spy stuff."

"Super spy stuff," Missy echoed, regarding the monitors with slightly more interest. It looked like the same old thing to her, the same thing her mommy had done since her Dadadad had gone to heaven to wait for them.

"And we're also checking the results of the expanded human trials for SemiSafe—or whatever we're going to call it for real," Merry told her. "That's these pictures, the ones showing blood cells and viruses."

"Dove's viruses?" Missy asked. She liked Dove; he called her "Little Doctor," due to her readiness with bandages after Dr. Resnik took yet another blood sample, and he listened to her.

Merry said something like, "Mm-hm," and patted her head.

"I wish Dove was here," she sighed, when she realized that she'd lost Merry's attention.

That was the thing Missy hated about the lab—too many things for her mother to do. Playing at the lab was more fun than playing at Tasha's, though—the desks here made good huts, and Corinne usually had crackers in her desk. And being with her mom made her happy, even when her mom was always looking at those silly computer screens. She retired to her hut, singing about mice, and watched the colors on the monitor.

So did Merry, but Merry wasn't singing. A trace of a repeating genetic sequence showed in the virus from Dr. Twilley's Bogotá lab, triggering a ripple of recognition in the back of her mind. Guanine, cytosine, C, G, T, A, telomerase, enzyme blockers, receptor points—the patterns of the simulation flickered past. She sat down in her chair, gently toeing Missy out of the way, and activated her own high-powered terminal, the one that fed the rack of display monitors. She touched the screen, tracing this, tapping that, manipulating the tiniest details, her fingers almost seeming to know what to do before she consciously directed them; it almost felt as if someone else were guiding her hands.

The picture of Chris, smiling from the shelf above the row of screens, caught her eye, bringing a mischievous smile to her face in answer. "You know something I don't?" she asked. As if in answer, the final manipulation twisted one tangled string of protein around another on the screen, the two wrapping together like pieces of a puzzle ring. Every lock had its proper key, every receptor its corresponding protein—and there on the monitor, the antidote agent wrapped around the white blood cells' receptors, barring the nasty virus's entrance point.

With a feeling of irrational but complete confidence, as if she were dreaming and knew exactly what to expect, Merry looked from the simulation monitor to the rapid-fire analysis of the blood samples from the AllSafe volunteers. In slide after slide, the SemiSafe-modified DNA had completely detached and replaced the AllSafe alteration, snipping away the genetic code that made the immune system run amok. Her hands shook slightly as she reran the scans one more time, pulling the blood work on every volunteer, cross-checking and double-checking the results of the in-depth genetic scan. Every one came out exactly the same way—the AllSafe had utterly, completely disappeared from their blood.

The brilliant colors of the screens shone in her eyes as she stared, wide-eyed, realizing what it meant. They had the antidote to both AllSafe and the General's virus now. They were absolutely, totally, utterly prepared to fight off both MedaGen's and Garza's weapons!

She leapt out of her chair, kissed Chris's picture, swept up Missy, who giggled as Merry shouted, "Hosanna" out of excitement. She tore like a maniac down the hall, yelling, "We've got it! We've got it! We got 'em both!"

That announcement, in more carefully crafted, precise words, spread like wildfire throughout the Church's communications network, and then on to the wider world beyond. Section 89 sent the recipe for the antidote, which used biotech ingredients and techniques available in genetics labs all over the world, over the free channels of the Net to anyone and everyone who wanted it. The actual serum could not spread over the wires, but soon the medical professionals among the Saints were dispensing the St. Paul antidote to all in need. The name came thanks to Merry's sense of humor—she thought it appropriate, since the original MedaGen code name for AllSafe was Corinth. The shots went first to all the inhabitants of Zion who had taken AllSafe—and, as the supplies of the antidote became available, to those outside the circle of divine protection. The numbers of non-Zionites waiting outside the towns swelled by the day as desperate people, unable to pay for the boosters that would keep them and their children alive, flocked to the gates.

"It's an absolute madhouse here, as thousands of people come to beg, borrow, or even steal the St. Paul serum from the Mormons!" Behind the reporter, a local stringer hoping to step into Anne's shoes, a shouting mob flowed around the littered streets of the refugee camp at Independence. People pleading, offering bribes, and shouting threats collided with each other and with the protesters claiming the "right" to get into heaven with their sins. Merry's mother, Sidney, seized the opportunity to use her daughter's renewed notoriety to both claim the spotlight and deplore the methods the Church used to distribute the St. Paul serum, methods she considered bigoted and misogynistic.

Channel 8 also covered the riot that broke out on the borders of Salt Lake City among those who had come for the antidote and found the supply depleted for another few days. The coverage took a far more sensationalistic tone than usual, with Anne thousands of miles away in Africa, but the basic facts didn't change: the Church, and Meredith Galen, had discovered the way to disarm the AllSafe bomb. MedaGen's stock price took an abrupt plunge toward the basement. Official interest in Meredith Galen, on the other hand, rose on an equally stark trajectory.

CHAPTER 15

"Senator Cox?" Merry blinked, staring at the screen that had switched from pictures of bloody rioters getting first aid, if not antidote shots, from Mormon medics to shots of grim-faced politicians glaring over high desks at a succession of witnesses in the belated investigation of the late Secretary Garlick's involvement with the AllSafe fiasco. The investigation into the missing weapons had also grown, reaching from Bogotá to MedaGen's corporate headquarters and beyond. All of that meant that Senator Holly Cox found herself in the hot glare of a spotlight she had always tried to avoid. Personal publicity got in the way of the people's business. And now the senator was on the other end of the line, speaking to another reluctant celebrity.

"Yes, Dr. Galen," she said. "Congratulations on your amazing discovery."

"It wasn't just me," Merry corrected. "The entire team at Section 89, Dr. Learner, Dr. De la Guardia, Dr. Resnik—they all contributed to the St. Paul serum as much as I did—"

"I'm sure they did," Senator Cox broke in gently. "Meredith, I don't mean to diminish their achievements at all, but if genius is ten percent inspiration and ninety percent perspiration—"

"In this case, the percentages are probably closer to fifty-fifty." Merry couldn't help correcting her, thinking of the way things fell into place so perfectly. Even if Chris weren't involved, someone had been.

Cox laughed. "Well, I can tell you that unlike what you've been doing, politics is one percent truth and ninety-nine percent perception. That's why I need your help, instead of Dr. Learner's or Dr. De la Guardia's." She sighed, looking at the news summaries in their tidy folder on her desk. "I know it's hard, but you're the one with the name, the one who the public knows. Your story made quite a splash out here, the brave young woman standing up to the evil corporate giant to save the world from a self-serving poison—and then coming up with the antidote for that poison, all without a lawyer or movie deal in sight."

"Corinne told me there was a movie in the works," Merry said darkly. "Did someone suggest that Virginia Diamante could play me?"

"I'm sure someone did, and I'm sure someone else shot down the idea—not because she's nothing like you, but because there's some other up-and-coming actor whose publicist is angling to step up with movie roles." Cox laughed again, though there was a weary note behind her amusement. "We're in the midst of an economic crash, there are wars all over the world, the Second Coming is imminent, and people still pay more attention to celebrities and lavish fantasies than getting their own lives in order."

"You have to admit, it's a lot easier," Merry pointed out. She caught Missy's hand, giving her a stern look. Missy blinked innocently, but when Merry released her hand, she went back to cutting construction paper into pieces and kept the scissors away from her hair.

"True. And sometimes it works to our advantage as well as to the opposition's. As in your case." The senator smiled, thinking about how unusual Merry's aversion to celebrity would be in the three-ring circus of the capital. "Which brings me back to why I called. People will hear you, listen to you, and I need to ask you to lend that weight to our cause. Dr. Galen, I would like to extend a formal invitation to you to come to Washington. We need you to testify before the committee about AllSafe—specifically, what MedaGen's officers knew about its potential effects and when they knew it."

* * *

"So they ask you to come to Washington, D.C., to testify before a Congressional committee about the AllSafe data they all wanted to ignore last year." Carmen's voice came through the line from Nauvoo so clearly that Merry could hear the impatient click of her tongue. "Talk about a turnaround. Babylon the Great is falling for sure!"

"Well, it's hardly Babylon that asked me," Merry reminded her, smiling at her friend's dramatic way of putting things. "Since Senator Cox is one of ours. I know there's still a lot of work to do at Section 89, but I think I can help her team out there. It shouldn't take me away from work for too long. What do you think?"

"I think you need to get out of that lab and get to Washington to put a big old nail in MedaGen's coffin is what I think!" Carmen exclaimed.

"Not that you have any personal feelings about it," Merry laughed. She looked out the window, where the sun set in a wash of red and gold. High clouds, volcanic vapors mixed with water droplets, still hung in the atmosphere, but the storms had not returned. Meteorologists and forecasters warned nervously of the return of wild weather, speaking in terms of "Indian summer" and the calm before the storm. If she was going to go, now was the time. All over the world, people were taking advantage of what everyone seemed to know was a temporary lull to fly to anywhere they thought they wanted to be when the storms came back.

Carmen's thoughts had run along the same lines. "Actually, it almost looks like you've got divine intervention on your side again, with the weather finally behaving itself. Maybe this is what you're supposed to do. Finish up what you and Chris started." That idea led to another. "What did Elder Nabil say?"

"He asked if I thought I could do it, if I could take the pressure MedaGen and its allies would put on me," Merry told her. "He said that it was my decision and that he'd support me in the answer I chose. Of course, he also said it was my chance to 'testify to the world of the wickedness they embraced, give them another chance to redeem themselves and repent,' which is important to him. And he said that if I did go, he would make sure I had people with me, just in case MedaGen did try something nasty."

"So what I'm hearing between the lines here is 'Carmen, tell me you can babysit Missy for me for a week while I flit off to Washington, D.C., with an entourage of dashing bodyguards, and dazzle the capital at the trial of the century," Carmen summarized.

"Carmen, it's—" Merry began, shaking her head at the absurd image of her with an entourage of anything.

"And I say, 'Of course I will!'" Carmen exclaimed, overriding her friend's incipient objections. She preferred her own highly colored version of events. "Meredith Galen, you get on a plane immediately and get you and that cute girl of yours out here to Nauvoo. I'll even make my famous lasagna for you and all your bodyguards."

"Thank you, Carmen." Merry gave up trying to talk herself out of the feeling that she should go to Washington. The lab could take care of itself for a couple of weeks, her country called, in the person of Senator Cox, and MedaGen deserved everything nasty but true she could say about them and their business practices. Besides, it had been a long time since she'd had good lasagna.

* * *

"It has been a long time, Mr. Abbott, since such a sorry example of corporate corruption has come before this investigative committee," Senator Benyanny intoned, as much for the cameras as for MedaGen's CEO, who sat behind the table in front of the committee's high-fronted dais. "Not only has MedaGen willfully deceived the FDA about the dire dangers of AllSafe, creating a health crisis like none this country has ever seen before and placing an unbelievable burden on the already ailing health-care system, but allegations have arisen that your company, with full knowledge and malice aforethought, has gone so far as to aid and abet a ruthless dictator in creating biological weapons to enforce his reign of terror on the people of South America and even extend his reach into the United States itself through stealth attacks. What do you have to say in the face of these shameful facts?"

Other than you should've cut that gout of self-righteous blather into about six separate sentences? Abbott thought acidly. The thought didn't show through his confident yet contrite expression.

"Your pardon, senator, but those are hardly facts," Mr. Frieze objected coolly. "As we speak, MedaGen is working with representatives from the FDA to pinpoint any flaws that might exist in the approval process for AllSafe—a vaccine, may we remind the distinguished committee, that has saved literally hundreds of thousands of lives in the last year alone."

"And are we to understand that the AllSafe booster does mitigate the unforeseen side effects of the original AllSafe vaccination?" Senator

Inverness asked. As an ally of Garlick's, she had a vested interest in preserving his image and as much of her own prestige as possible.

"Indeed it does," Abbott assured her and the rest of the committee. "In fact, with the booster, AllSafe is absolutely guaranteed to protect the patient against all viral infections. After centuries, if not millennia of searching, we can say with full confidence that we have finally found the cure for the common cold."

Someone in the gallery, with perfect timing, sneezed.

Abbott looked up with a photogenic smile and said, "Gesundheit!"

The spectators laughed.

Senator White shared the moment of amusement, still smiling as he leaned forward to look at the printouts on the desk in front of him and then at MedaGen's CEO. "And we're all grateful for that, Mr. Abbott. We just regret that in many cases, the allergic reaction that AllSafe triggers ends up curing that cold by killing the patient. One of those cases where the cure is worse than the disease, eh? But that's a subject for another day—and perhaps another Senate investigative committee. No, what I'd like you to talk about, Mr. Abbott, is the evidence that your organization colluded with the late Secretary Garlick in supplying arms to General Andrea Garza."

"MedaGen is a biogenetic pharmaceuticals company that specializes in curing disease. We're hardly arms dealers," Abbott averred.

"Really?" White fixed him with an over-the-glasses look of surprise. "Then how do you explain these?" He passed the pile of pictures to an aide, who transferred them to one of Frieze's legal eagles, who put them in front of Abbott and MedaGen's chief counsel.

A white building shone against a lush, green background, sentries in camouflage standing at attention in front of the lab's single door. In another shot, lab techs hauled coffins out and stacked them on a flatbed truck.

The lawyer immediately sprang to his feet. "Senator, I must object!"

Abbott caught his arm. "Relax, Mr. Frieze. We're hardly on trial yet. We're just here to assist the investigative committee in their duty of looking into the shenanigans of the late secretary of Homeland Security. I understand my colleague's surprise at seeing these pictures, since we haven't seen them. I assume that building is a medical facility, and it appears to be in a warm location, but certainly neither of those two things says 'MedaGen' to me. I still don't know where these out-of-the-blue accusations against MedaGen come from."

He certainly recognized both the lab building in the pictures and the report they belonged to, but he didn't know that the pictures had come to Senator Cox from Humphrey, by way of Virginia. She'd sent follow-up messages as soon as Garlick was gone, to make sure that no one overlooked Abbott and Zelik in the confusion. She wanted to see them crawl, and the snail's pace of a full senatorial inquisition had already worn her patience thin. The fact that he didn't know where the leak sprang from sent a colder chill down his back than merely seeing the pictures in Senator White's hands. If these could get out, what else might? Clearly, the time had come to implement damage-control measures.

"Does the name Erwin Twilley help bring them down to earth?" Senator White asked. "I believe that's him, in the last photo."

Sure enough, Dr. Twilley's long, thin face glared out of the final page, caught midtirade and at an angle that suggested the photographer had perched atop a roof to catch the unflattering portrait. Once Senator Cox sent a request to Fox telling her what to look for, she easily focused on Garza's bioweapons lab—and its senior scientist.

"Twilley," Abbott frowned, scribbling "Tell Zelik to assemble the evidence" on the pad in front of him and shoving the note over to Frieze. "Of course I know Erwin Twilley. He was the second team lead for the production of AllSafe—he replaced the original lead, Gregor Christoff, when Dr. Christoff died in a car accident. A brilliant researcher, if a hard man to like."

"I'd say that's an understatement," White said, earning titters from the onlookers.

"I'd say it's completely irrelevant!" Senator Benyanny broke in, eager to keep the conversation on track and recapture the spotlight. "The real question is, why did MedaGen send Dr. Twilley to Bogotá to develop bioweapons for General Garza, a known enemy of the United States?"

"He's hardly a known enemy," Inverness spoke up. "General Garza and the president have had several high-level meetings, and the General has brought stability to—"

"MedaGen didn't send Dr. Twilley to Bogotá to develop anything for anyone," Abbott said easily, shooting Inverness an apologetic look but regaining the floor. "In fact, Dr. Twilley left our company a few months ago."

"Are you saying that Dr. Twilley is a renegade agent?" Benyanny demanded.

"I don't know if I would put it in quite those—colorful—terms, Senator," Abbott said. "But I will tell you that this sad news helps solve a mystery that our internal investigators have been working on. Shortly before Dr. Twilley left, we found evidence that someone within the company had gained access to some sensitive corporate intelligence data. Unfortunately, that data had to do with bioterrorism."

A gasp rippled through the room. Abbott held up his hands. "To be more precise, that data had to do with countering bioterror attacks. Dr. Twilley, after his success leading the AllSafe team, was promoted to lead the Pacifica project. MedaGen undertook this project in cooperation with the Office of Homeland Security, in an attempt to identify potential biological weapons and develop antidotes for them. Obviously, Dr. Twilley took advantage of his position to reap personal profits from the work."

"So now you're saying that Erwin Twilley took top-secret information from your company and used it to create bioweapons for General Garza?" White summarized.

"Yes—only I believe that he used it to gain probably lucrative employment with General Garza, and, as a disgruntled former employee, probably hoped to embarrass MedaGen as well," Abbott amplified.

"Still, the information came from MedaGen's connection with Secretary Garlick," Benyanny persisted. "How do we know that the entire project wasn't a cover for Garlick's intention to sell the weapons to General Garza along with the other missiles and drones we know he sent? A deal MedaGen would profit handsomely from?"

"Please, it's one thing to investigate a possible security breach," Inverness exclaimed. "It's quite another to assume that Secretary Garlick was guilty. That's needlessly smearing a dead man!"

"MedaGen never had any intention of profiting by illegal sales of potentially hazardous biochemical materials!" Frieze protested—utterly falsely, since AllSafe was certainly a potentially hazardous biochemical material that they definitely intended to profit from.

Fortunately for him, MedaGen had bought enough senators, lawyers, and judges, either outright or through Zelik's impressive cache of personal and political dirt, that it wasn't too difficult for Frieze's legal team to twist the argument about whether MedaGen was or had been involved in developing bioweapons for Garza into an intricate argument over just how much control MedaGen could legally be expected to exert over a former employee with whom the company had held only an annually renewable employment contract.

The cameras lost interest in the ensuing floor debate and followed Abbott outside. Sunlight glinting from his hair and gold suit coat buttons, Abbott confidently assured reporters that it was all Twilley's idea, the deplorable actions of a renegade MedaGen ex-employee who took private corporate intellectual property and vanished. The rest of the scandal led right back to Secretary Garlick, who had, for reasons Abbott wouldn't speculate on out of respect for the dead, seen fit to sell weapons to an outside force. He even worked in a chance to tout AllSafe and promised that MedaGen was on the verge of releasing a neutralizer for AllSafe for those nervous about allergic reactions.

MedaGen, eager to show its cooperative attitude toward the Senate investigation, promptly released all the information from its own internal investigation of Twilley's fictional break-in. Zelik arrived in Washington with three large boxes full of discs, printouts, bank transfers, and other evidence to deposit on the committee's doorstep, nearly ninety pounds of black-and-white testimony against Garlick and Twilley, his ally in crime. The e-mails, transfers, and other information came with all the right dates, times, places, and data—because Sean, under Zelik's watchful eye, had manipulated the correspondence between Abbott and Twilley to look as if it had passed between Garlick and Twilley. With the late secretary well beyond defending himself and Sean under threat of both judicial action (from the Senate's committee) and death (from Zelik), no one could definitively disprove any of it.

That annoyed and troubled many people, but the one with the most fragrant reaction was Virginia Diamante. Watching Abbott and Zelik stride confidently from a follow-up hearing in which they maintained MedaGen's innocence and subtly blackened Garlick's already charcoal-colored name, she screamed and threw the bottle in her hand at the screen. Glass hit the edge of the gilded frame and shattered, spattering the wall, screen, and Julian with shards and several ounces of extremely expensive perfume. "No!" she shrieked. "He's dead. They should be dead too! Who do they think they are, God?"

* * *

"All hail the One God and the Prophet!" The chant rose from thousands of worshippers swaying in the packed stands of a soccer stadium in Lahore. The Children of Light had gathered to sing the praises of their spiritual leader, spread their message of unity, and watch the execution of three ayatollahs who had opposed the new religion in the name of Islam. The white tide had swept out of India in an unstoppable wave of singing, proselyting, looting, and pillaging. Anyone who was not with them was, by definition, against them and therefore deserving of death, either immediate under the guns and knives of the Hands of the Prophet or of starvation or disease in the chaos the horde of human locusts left behind as it swept on.

Brother Light stood on the vast stage, his arms upraised, and surveyed the crowd, feeling their belief and devotion like a huge wind, bearing him forward and upward. He could call them from all the ends of the earth if he chose, send them marching through deserts and mountains to any destination he desired. They would die or kill at his command. They had left their former gods to fling themselves at his feet and embrace the minor deities of wealth, lust, and violence that he preached so convincingly. And still, the vast power he wielded didn't satisfy him—it just whetted his appetite for more.

Stalking offstage, he shoved away the young women who immediately rushed to his side, in no mood for their cooing stupidity. He always had a ready harem of beauties at hand to suit his moods; in an exquisite twist, he had appointed Sepphira to look after them. His black-robed soldiers closed around him, cutting through the multitude without compunction or compassion as the wave of humanity threatened to roll over the Prophet. The bloody wounds would turn to scars that the young men who bore them would show proudly, as evidence of their willingness to suffer for the One God. The object of all this activity took no notice of the screaming chaos around him; he threw himself into the waiting limousine and glared into nothing. The small screen embedded in the mahogany panels showed the breathless news reports of the unprecedented gathering—and the equally unprecedented executions. The Hands formed a square around the vehicle, trotting along with it as it rolled slowly away to the luxurious hotel the Children of Light had co-opted to house their Prophet.

"Rashi." Sepphira, huddled on the seat in front of him, finally broke the brooding silence inside the car. "Rashi, what's wrong? Lahore is yours now. Soon Kandahar will rise as well, under the Unity."

Her voice broke through his reverie. "Stupid woman," he snapped, kicking her leg hard enough to send her sprawling over onto the seat. "Lahore is mine, and Delhi, and Manila; Mecca belongs to Allah no more. But only a third of the world has seen the ultimate Truth. The entire world must see, must admit and profess, that I am the only One, the Unity, the God of this earth!"

"You?" The word slipped out before Sepphira could catch it. Always before, Rashi had spoken of the One God with himself as that god's prophet.

"Yes, Sepphira." He looked at her, and the old light was back in his eyes and face, the electric charisma that let him exert such incredible control over those looking for leadership and inspiration. His voice gentled as he explained, "I have only realized it lately myself, a conviction that has grown until I cannot deny it. At first, I saw the reality of the One God; then I saw the reflection of the One God in my own countenance. And now, I realize I am the mirror, not the reflection. I am the living avatar of the Unity itself, and now I must discover the full extent of the power I must wield in this world."

Sepphira's eyes flickered to one side, where one of the ever-present shadows clung, spiderlike, to the roof of the car, hanging like smoke beside Rashi's head, whispering into his ear. The shadow looked back at her with eyes like flaming coals—and it laughed. "Are you sure?" she asked. "What about the shadows, Rashi? Where do they come from, if you are the One God?"

For a second, it looked as if he might kick her again, his eyes flaming almost like the demon's, but then he relaxed and smiled. "They are evil, Sepphira, as you know. They have power because I grant them power, because I have not gathered all existence into myself. I let them exist because they are useful. When they have served their purposes, I will summon them back into the Unity." He reached over, tenderly stroking her cheek. "When the world bows to me, little Sepphira, the shadows won't trouble you anymore. I promise that." Discontent filled his face once more. "There is too much disbelief. The world is not ready for that day, when the Unity reveals itself." His fist struck the panel beside her. Sepphira flinched back automatically.

The scene on that panel caught his attention before his irritation at her jumpiness earned her a slap, however. Anne O'Neal stood in front of a lovely, white building in Ghana, promising a report on the Mormon renaissance there. The scene switched to Clara, who smiled as she introduced another religious renaissance: Tommy Gibbs's planned Crusade in Houston, billed as the largest one-day revival meeting ever conducted in North America.

"It is time for all true Christians to step forward," the evangelist said earnestly, gazing out of the screen as ticket prices and event information for the Crusade scrolled under his image. "It's time to for all of the true believers to take a stand for Lord Jesus, to show Him that we're ready to take His hand when He comes to sweep all the faithful up into His kingdom while the wicked world burns behind them."

Sepphira, seeing the way Rashi's eyes fastened on the screen, risked a glance at it herself. The American preacher reminded her of Rashi in a lot of ways—except that he lacked the fire and drive that had driven her once-husband to conquer a third of the world with nothing but his message of Unity. Of course, the armed assassins, mob fury, ruthless will to power, expedient gospel, and demonic intervention helped as well, but Sepphira had conditioned herself—with Rashi's conscious assistance—not to think in those terms.

A slow smile spread over Rashi's face. "Yes, it is time for all Christians to step forward," he said. "Step forward out of their chains, abandon their stupid faith in a dead religion. I will show them the truth of the Unity, force them to acknowledge my power and supreme leadership by proving that the Christians' God is dead." He laughed. "Though that may not be too difficult, since their own philosophers came to that conclusion long ago." His smile grew sharper, the glint of blood in his eyes.

"We—you—do well in the West, and punishing the infidels on our own lands," Sepphira assured him, deliberately not mentioning the Mormons' ability to turn back the attacks of the Hands. That would only make matters worse. She didn't like this mood; she had seen enough of death and suffering to last her all eternity, and that look in his eyes only promised more blood. "We have many Children of Light in Europe now, and the number in the United States grows every day."

"Europe." He shrugged carelessly. "I have given up on the Europeans altogether; they're an old, weary society crumbling away into dust and ennui, too dry even to have children anymore. We will sweep over them easily, with the Children of Light already gathering in the Balkans. No, the ones who need to hear the clash of iron bells are the Americans— not the fat, wealthy cattle who stand there like idiots while their leaders are murdered in front of them, but the ones with enough fire in their hearts to do the murders. I want them," he spread his hand over the screen, as if he extended his control over the thousands of people the report showed gathering for Tommy Gibbs's world-record Crusade, "the ones who believe, the ones who will follow their prophet to death and beyond. I will show them that their pathetic dead god cannot protect them, they will join the Unity, and I will gather the wealth of the West into my treasuries." Flipping open his phone, he ordered, "Get me the Hand in Houston."

* * *

"We've got the satellite up," Romanoff announced. He gave Tommy Gibbs a thumbs-up gesture from the communications box, where the techs were warming up the satellite feed.

An electrician went past him, rolling a large spool of wires, making last-minute adjustments to the stage and set. Befitting the largest revival in American history, tonight's show included more lights, moving platforms, and exciting stage effects than ever before. Romanoff kept getting little jags of déjà vu from his stint as a concert promoter for pop extravaganzas. Visually, it meant that this sermon would hit new heights of appeal. Practically, it meant that Romanoff now had to deal with about twice as many crew members as usual, since the stadium's usual crew didn't handle the kinds of specialized setup the show required—and it had been a long time since Romanoff's clients traveled with their own roadies. Good thing his local contacts had come through, sending him an experienced wire-monkey crew to take care of last-minute technological details.

Gibbs adjusted his blue robe, breathing deeply. Usually, the pre-show jitters only energized him more, pumping him up for the sermon that would bring his evangelical audience to their feet. Today, he felt oddly off his stride, as if something was holding him back. Probably the amount of hype Romanoff had pulled for this revival, he told himself. Billing it as the largest gathering of Christians in the world had seemed a little much, but Romanoff had assured him that it was the right strategy. "Standing-room-only always sells more tickets. People like to be part of something big. It makes them feel important, gives them something to remember to their grandkids."

They'd remember this one, if only for the heat that pounded down out of the almost clear sky. Maybe the temperature would drain some of the enthusiasm from the masses of white-robed Children of Light who had gathered outside the stadium to stage their own devotional service near the entrance. Rumor had it they were calling on that pagan god of theirs to show the Christians who was boss. He hoped their bullhorns melted in the incandescent sunlight pouring over everything.

If his sermon was half as hot as the afternoon outside, he'd have them dancing in the aisles before the first hymn break. Of course it would be—he had it all lined up: the world going to hell in a hand-basket; the need to stand up in opposition to the anti-Christian forces massing in the world (the Children of Light finally taking over from the Mormons as the threat du jour); the assurance that their presence here, their trust in the good Lord Jesus, would make up for any sins they still committed. God was, first, last, and always, a God of love, which meant He would never leave any of His true children, meaning Gibbs's devoted followers, to burn with the wicked when the Final Judgment arrived. Gibbs glanced at the few notes he used as mnemonic devices (he'd long since memorized his presentations, including the specific parts of the scriptures that he quoted during them), then tucked them into the impressively gilded and beribboned Bible that he always laid open on the podium.

With a wave to Romanoff, acknowledging the countdown for broadcast, he strode to the center of the platform, standing behind the podium that would raise him up through the floor and into the massive stadium. "Oh, Jesus," he whispered sincerely, "be with me tonight as I preach Your words."

The lights flashed on, the crowd roared, the screens around the stadium—and all around the country, if not the world—caught the satellite feed, the podium rose on cue, and Tommy Gibbs faced the largest audience of his life. Their roar almost blew his hair back, and he looked out over a vast sea of faces all turned toward him, begging him to tell them what to do, what to believe, how to feel. He bestowed that famous smile on them and raised his hands to acknowledge their enthusiasm. "Brothers, sisters, dear friends, fellow believers— welcome to the true Crusade for Jesus! Get ready, because we're going to hear the true word of God tonight!"

With that, he dramatically opened the huge Bible. He always opened it near the middle—it looked better on camera that way. Usually, he did so without even realizing what page it had landed on. Tonight, however, the glittering edge of gilding caught his eye, drawing his gaze down to the page. Out of the blur of black letters, one verse stood out as clearly as if it were printed in neon: "No man can serve two masters: for either he will hate the one, and love the other; or else he will hold to the one, and despise the other. Ye cannot serve God and mammon."

The words hit him like a thunderbolt. His cue cards, tucked beside the scripture, the gold braid on the sleeve overlaying the edge of the page, both seemed dingy, stained with greed and compromise. "Repent"— the word swam up out of the blur in front of his eyes. "Feed my sheep"—the phrase echoed in his head, in Sally Mae Loftus's voice, in his old teacher's voice. "Sell all that thou hast, take up thy cross, and follow me," whispered a still, soft voice that he couldn't identify. The crowd resolved before his eyes into individuals, frightened, lost on the wrong path, paying money to hear him speak easy platitudes that required no hard changes—and led them no closer to true salvation.

Panic rose in his throat, choking his golden voice. Grabbing the glass of water on the podium for a hasty sip as cover, he felt as if his entire life balanced on a pinpoint, tilting either direction from this moment. He could either take this moment to recant the easy promises on which he'd built his career, irrevocably ruining his chances of ever speaking to an audience this large again, or he could continue with the presentation he had planned, knowing by spiritual witness what he said was not the word of God but the teachings of a well-meaning man. Eternity stretched out before him—and then the glint of the gold braid on his sleeve caught his eye again. Surely, now that he realized what he needed to say, it would be better to ease into it? Coming over with fire and brimstone would just alienate these people, he rationalized, and completely ruin his marketability. Romanoff would say that it would be better to lead them gently to the truth. He'd begin slowly, and by the end of the year, he'd have spread the gospel of repentance far and wide. The panic receded, leaving what he told himself was icy calm in its place.

Gibbs smiled, back in control once again, setting the glass down. "Just a little choked up there, to see so many of you here tonight to listen to the message that Jesus is sending to each of you personally." Oddly, at that, several people got up quietly and headed for the exits. Behind them, the crowd surged to its feet, calling hallelujahs as Tommy Gibbs swung into one of his most masterful sermons yet. Without breaking stride, he swung through an hour of high-energy preaching, as the sky above the stadium gradually darkened into evening.

"And it's all because Jesus is the one true Healer, the one true Shepherd, the one true Light of the World!" Gibbs exclaimed, raising his arms high.

Light crashed down from the high ceiling of the stadium, enveloping the evangelist in its blinding flash. For an instant, he stood silhouetted there, a black form in the midst of evanescent glory. Then the furious light disappeared, leaving only a charred, smoking figure that slowly fell backward as more lightning bolts slashed into the stage. The electrical storm, released through cables carefully placed and sabotaged by Children of Light masquerading and, in two cases, working as stage technicians, crackled across the huge screens mounted around the stadium.

When the static cleared, the face of Rashi Janjalani, Brother Light, looked out over the stunned multitude, beamed over the satellite broadcast link that had carried Gibbs's sermon—and his spectacular death—to the world. The two red-masked men in the control booth stood over the broadcast controls—and the bodies of the communications technicians. "There is but one true god," Brother Light intoned. "But that is not the god of the Christians. Jesus Christ died for your sins—and He is still dead. The only true power, the only force that can save you, is the One God, the god of this world. Come to the

Unity and live!" Another stray bolt of lightning crackled around the podium. "Join the Children of Light that await you outside the spiritual prison you have made for yourselves. Choose life, choose love, choose to unite with the One God, or choose death!"

With that, bolts of electricity began again, striking into the stands themselves this time. The stampede began immediately. Some ran to join the Children of Light, their trust in their formerly beloved Savior extinguished in the same flash of lightning that killed Tommy Gibbs. Others ran simply to get away from danger, mindlessly fleeing into the night. Romanoff ran because he saw a half dozen, no, just five men in black robes emerge from the control booth he'd left to get another cup of coffee. As he ran, however, he wondered if Brother Light could use a producer. The thought was utterly disloyal, and the shreds of his conscience told him to feel guilty about it, but it persisted—right up to the point that a red-masked assassin, recognizing the man as Tommy Gibbs's right hand, settled the question with the gleaming edge of a sharp knife.

* * *

Dear Chisom,

Thank you for telling us, at last, about your "friend," Wei Wei Ming, and her family. The story of their escape from northern China, being found by our Gatherers, and finally their conversion to the gospel is truly breathtaking and amazing. They are people of great faith and I am glad you shared their experience with us. I suspected Miss Ming was from up north due to her height. I might add that, from what I can see in two or three of the pictures you sent, the "friendship" seems to be coming along nicely. Okay, I won't pester you anymore on the subject, and I'll take your word for it that you didn't say anything because you two were just getting to know each other and seeing if things worked out. I certainly don't want you to rush into things, but just keep in mind, you're not getting any younger and I'm getting a lot older and don't have near enough grandchildren.

On to other matters. I must mention the work of U.S. Senator Holly Cox and her allies. Her untiring service has proved an unimaginable boon to Zion and to the United States. She has taken the heat in Washington for her opposition to AllSafe and Senator Howard Garlick's machinations, not to mention being barbecued for being a devout Latter-day Saint. Her determination, example, and efforts have rallied a lot of support for law, order, and the safeguards of the Bill of Rights. She has not worked alone. The other three LDS senators and eleven congressmen (well, nine congressmen and two congresswomen), along with quite a number of their upright colleagues, have served this nation and our church well. As a result, our nation is in better shape than it would have been. I can't help reflect on another prophecy Joseph Smith made. This one is not in any of our scriptures, but many Saints know about it and, from time to time, I hear it quoted but most often inaccurately. Somewhere people got the idea that the Prophet said the time would come when the Constitution would hang by a thread and, if it were saved, it would be the elders who would do it. That's wrong. We have the contemporary account made by one of Joseph Smith's clerks, and the Prophet said nothing about the Constitution hanging by a thread. He did say that "this Nation will be on the verge of crumbling to pieces and tumbling to the ground and when the constitution is upon the brink of ruin this people will be the staff upon which the Nation shall lean and they shall bear the constitution away from the verge of destruction." Well, Senator Cox and her colleagues have gone a long way in rallying "this people" and others into doing that thing. The Brethren are pleased with the hard work and success of this righteous, bright, courageous, and tenacious woman.

Securing the Constitution has not come a moment too soon. President Smith has told the Saints that we should now get ready for the Second Coming in earnest, for the day is at hand. Of course, our detractors have gleefully pointed out that this is more evidence that the Mormons are guided by a false prophet. Matthew 24:36 clearly states, they argue, that neither man nor angel shall know the day or hour. Those who know us well also say that our prophet has contradicted our own scriptures and cite D&C 39:21 and 49:7 that confirm Matthew to prove the point. The problem is that they don't know us well enough. Joseph Smith addressed this issue in a conference talk he gave on April 6, 1843. Joseph had stood against a prevailing millennial fervor that had swept much of the United States. He said that the Second Coming was at least decades away. His critics said that, based on the Bible, he could not know that the day was not about to happen. Joseph explained that when Jesus made the statement He did not speak it as a general principle through all time. Jesus, Joseph Smith taught, "spoke in the present tense. No man that was then living upon the footstool of God knew the day or the hour. But he did not say that there was no man throughout all generations that should know the day or the hour. No, for that would be in flat contradiction with other scripture, for the prophet says that God will do nothing but what he will reveal to his servants the prophets." In just weeks, history will prove Joseph Smith right and our critics wrong.

The Lord told the Saints that His Second Coming would overtake the world as a thief in the night. In D&C 106, He went on to say, "Therefore, gird up your loins, that you may be the children of light, and that day shall not overtake you as a thief." Well, the Saints are aware, but the world, in spite of all the signs, doesn't have a clue. Of course, even that was prophesied. The Lord told his ancient Apostles, as recorded in Joseph Smith—Matthew, that "as it was in the days of Noah, so it shall be also at the coming of the Son of Man; for it shall be with them, as it was in the days which were before the flood; for until the day that Noah entered into the ark they were eating and drinking, marrying and giving in marriage; and knew not until the flood came, and took them all away." Jesus prophesied the exact condition we are seeing today. The signs abound, yet the vast majority of people is oblivious to the warning and will continue to be until the end comes.

And I hope the end comes that all this horror may stop. I can clearly see why the angels in Revelation proclaimed, "Just and true are thy ways, thou King of saints," and, "In righteousness he doth judge and make war." The angels know that God's destruction of the wicked is a totally righteous act, because His enemies will not repent. They will continue to make a hell of this earth in their mad rush for power and, in the end, they will destroy all unless God stops them. And He will, shortly.

In response to your question on my take on Tommy Gibbs and his horrible death, let me just say that I felt he was a sincere man but too taken up with fame to tell the hard truth about our Lord and His demands. Sad as I am that a good, if foolish, man is dead, what troubles me is that Janjalani had him killed. Though some claim Gibbs is a martyr to the Christian cause and hold more firmly to the faith, many have abandoned it and turned to the Unity. I wrote you some months ago that in Revelation 13, John saw a lamb with two horns that brought people to worship the dragon by its power to call down devouring fire. One aspect of that lamb is certainly Janjalani. The pyrotechnics he caused in Houston are a sure sign to all who can see that he is a beast.

What a time to live, my son. Our eyes are seeing unimaginable horrors, and yet we will soon see glories only dreamed about by the Saints of old. I can only raise my voice with those in the book of Revelation and say, "Lord, Come."

But, even though the time grows short, we still have our work to do. Let's do it with fervor, for we are close to the edge.

With love,
Your father,
Chinedu

* * *

"You have no idea how close you are to the edge." Brindermann's voice, as controlled and precise as ever, came clearly through the speaker in Abbott's office. His image, wavering only slightly around the edges from sunspot interference, showed a face as expressionless as his voice. The white walls and shaded observation window of Dr. Twilley's lab office formed the backdrop.

"Now, Johann," Abbott said soothingly, "you know this is all just a matter of politics. I have nothing but the highest respect for General Garza—and for you, of course. I say what I have to say in front of the cameras for MedaGen's sake. We can't help you if we're tied up with federal investigations—or behind bars."

Zelik thought Brindermann didn't need soothing. In fact, he didn't look or act like a man who felt his allies had betrayed him; he held the reins, and he knew it. That concerned her.

"You would never end up behind bars, Herr Abbott." Brindermann brushed off Abbott's conciliatory tone and his words. "As the General says, your fate seems to have reserved you for a more fitting end. You have played your hand well on the news and in the political hearings. Congratulations. You will probably escape prosecution through your own corrupt system. But no matter what you have told the judges you bought and paid for, and no matter what political points you score by using the General as a sword over the heads of your enemies, you still owe him a bioweapon, as you contracted. One without a free antidote."

That dig made Zelik's jaw set hard and brought a deep frown to Abbott's face.

"That's why you have Dr. Twilley down there in Bogotá," Zelik reminded Brindermann with a poisonous glare at the dig, remembering the bloody conference with MedaGen's board after Meredith's announcement. They'd threatened to fire her and Abbott for incompetence, unless profits and stock prices rose dramatically. It would do no good to point out how unrealistic those demands were, in a period of dramatic economic slump and worldwide chaos; the board didn't care about realities—they just wanted their money to shield them against the effects of exactly those financial conditions.

Brindermann smiled at their reactions to his snide comment, and in anticipation of their reaction to his next revelation. "Oh, yes, Dr. Twilley. Unfortunately, though Twilley proved a useful scapegoat for you, he was less useful for General Garza. In fact, your statements to the illustrious investigators about his unauthorized use of your corporate intellectual property were not so wrong—though in this case, the use was literal, not merely figurative." He stepped aside, touching the button that opened the viewing panel behind him. Through the opening, Abbott and Zelik saw a tiny, bare room, its walls grotesquely stained, and a writhing, moaning figure thrashing on the floor.

"Twilley?" Abbott stared, the horror of it hitting him even through his hardened self-interest.

"The disease is in its beginning stages now, just four hours into the infection, just starting to eat away the lining of the lungs and stomach, its attack on the brain causing the first of many convulsions.

As you see, the search for an equally fast-acting, dependable bioagent antidote has been unsuccessful thus far." Brindermann sounded as calm as the narrator of one of MedaGen's popular medical documentaries. "Even though we can see that Dr. Twilley has given his all to the program."

A slight smile crossed Zelik's face as the initial shock wore off. How fitting a fate for the doctor, winding up on the sharp end of one of his own experiments.

"General Garza does not view this as an acceptable level of performance. He expects far more competence—especially given the generous fee you have already received as an advance on the full price." Brindermann turned away from the window but did not close the view port. "In fact, the General is so displeased with your performance that he asked me to remind you that while you wriggled out of the trap your enemies in the Senate set for you, you will not so easily escape him. He can send evidence to the investigative committee that you will not find so easy to alter to preserve your innocence—if he chooses such a relatively innocuous method of expressing his dissatisfaction. Dr. Twilley, as incompetent as he was, left an entire lockbox full of alternatives to legal measures."

"Please, Herr Brindermann." Abbott pulled himself together. "We share your disappointment with Dr. Twilley's performance. I thought he would be just the right person to give you everything we promised. I admit we were wrong, and I assure you that I have every intention of honoring our agreement."

"The General will be glad to know that. So you will send us a top-flight researcher, someone with no direct loyalty to MedaGen, someone we can trust to carry out the assignment," Brindermann ordered.

"Someone like Meredith Galen," Zelik suggested. Competent, obviously; no loyalty to MedaGen, equally obvious; and, even better, joyfully expendable.

Abbott shot her a look, then caught the vision.

So did Brindermann. If they could get her, Galen would fit their needs perfectly. She had already proved adept at discovering antidotes to MedaGen's engineered viruses, and she was Mormon as well—which meant she had weak spots. Could she refuse to work for them if they shot one of their Mormon workers for every hour or minute she chose to be stubborn? "Very well. You collect and deliver Dr. Galen into our hands, and you will receive the payment that the incompetent Dr. Twilley put in jeopardy. We will expect a report tomorrow, with details of exactly how you intend to secure her presence. We'll take care of securing her cooperation."

He leaned forward, looming on the screen above the polished conference table. "Remember that we will hold you both personally responsible. As we did Dr. Twilley." The screen went dark, leaving the shadow of the threat hanging in the silence, along with Twilley's last moan.

Abbott exploded out of his chair, cursing Brindermann, Twilley, Garza, his own bad luck in getting involved with any of them, and Zelik for her harebrained ideas.

"Calm down and get a grip on yourself," Zelik advised. "He wants you upset, lashing out at me instead of thinking clearly. That's why he's treating you like his errand boy."

Brindermann was treating them both as lackeys, which irritated her even more than it did Abbott, but she recognized that he also held the upper hand at the moment. When the time came, she would take it out of his hide, but for now, they had to swallow the insult and smile.

"Oh, is that it? You should run workshops on corporate psych warfare tactics," Abbott snapped. "How exactly do you plan to get hold of Meredith Anthony?"

"You sent me to fence with the Senate committee today, handing over the evidence of Twilley's defection," she reminded him. "While I was there, Frieze told me that Cox has invited Dr. Galen to Washington to testify about the AllSafe FDA approval that Garlick pushed through."

"She's going to Washington?" Abbott asked, unholy glee spreading across his face.

"She's going to Washington," Zelik affirmed. "Into the Senate lion's den, not just to that Mormon bomb-shelter camp outside the city."

"They'll have her guarded," Abbott pointed out, glee abating. "Either she'll have a bunch of Church goons or Cox's security guys all over her."

"But we have something up our sleeves as well," Zelik assured him. "I'll take care of securing Dr. Galen. You take care of arranging our stay in Washington—and our quick getaway."

* * *

"How did she get away?" Brindermann demanded of a pale-faced sentry. The man had come to report that they couldn't find Yazna Vasquez anywhere in the lab building and that no one had seen her leave. She had inexplicably disappeared right after the General's men had come through the lab and taken Dr. Twilley to his last, fatal progress interview. It appeared that she had guessed they would come after her next, which annoyed Brindermann even more. He'd planned on presenting her as exhibit A when Meredith Galen arrived, to persuade the American doctor to cooperate with the General.

"Look again!" he barked. "And make sure that nothing else is missing."

The lab techs confirmed that all the top-secret sample materials were accounted for. The doctor's clothes and toiletries were still in her cell-like sleeping quarters—in fact, it looked as if *all* her clothes were still there, both of the outfits she wore beneath her lab coat. Brindermann threw a skirt onto the cot, glaring around the room. She hadn't walked out naked. "How many security agents came from Santiago?" he asked the sentry.

"Two," the man said. "They had their papers in order—signed by President Aguilera, countersigned by Security Chief Serrey. There's no way they were forged. I checked."

"No, there were three of them," the other sentry corrected, staring at his comrade. "I came on duty right as they left. I saw them leave, and I could've sworn there were three of them."

"You saw two of them and me leaving, you blind idiot," the first growled. "There were only two."

One of the assistants, checking computer files for evidence of unauthorized downloading, finally exclaimed, "I think I've got something!"

Cached conversations scrolled across her screen, messages between Vasquez and Serrey. The security chief sent thinly veiled threats against the Mormons in Chile to keep the doctor in line—and added edged innuendo hinting at what she could do for him personally to make their lives, and her own, more pleasant. She responded coldly at first, delivering only the required reports to prove that she was doing the work within the terms of her conscription duties, giving him no excuse to carry out his threats. As the days passed, however, her messages gradually took on a different tone, including a few statements that an egomaniac psychopath like Serrey could read as flirtatious. The last, delivered only that day, ended with the teasing suggestion, "If you're in Bogotá, you could come inspect the lab. I'll give you a *personal* tour."

"Serrey," Brindermann hissed. It would be a simple thing to bring a spare uniform, time a visit to coincide with sentry change, and sneak Vasquez out of the lab to continue the online flirtation in person. Serrey's reputation only strengthened Brindermann's suspicion.

Serrey was indeed with a long-haired woman when Brindermann's security guards broke into his luxury hotel room a half hour later—but she wasn't Yazna Vasquez, and she'd never been to the bio-weapons lab.

"The witch sent this back when I told her I would come to see her this afternoon," Serrey snarled at Brindermann, dressed again and furiously confronting Garza's second in command. He threw a crumpled sheet of paper onto the table, continuing as the German read the blunt rejection written on it. "You think I would take her out of there? Against the General's orders? *Estupido!*" The slow, lazy smile appeared on his face as he realized the full extent of what had happened. "But now she's run away? From you? Embarrassing, with all the *presidentes* in town for the General's big meeting."

That earned him a cold look. "She will be found. Dismissed."

She wasn't found—because nobody thought to look in the sealed coffins containing the sad remains of the other lab experiments; vivid memories of exactly how those pitiful creatures died made them give the sealed containers a wide berth, even though they were completely sealed. Nobody, that is, but Neruda, who obediently packed them up for disposal as the debate over Vasquez's disappearance raged through the lab and its environs. He checked each one carefully—and opened the one with a double set of biohazard stickers once the truck stopped behind the hill of garbage that hid the incinerator.

The lid lifted away, revealing Vasquez's oxygen-masked face. She opened her eyes, saw Neruda silhouetted against the blue sky, and removed the mask. Taking a deep breath of free, if incredibly odiferous, air, she exclaimed, "Brother Neruda, I've never been so glad to see anyone in my life!"

"Don't say that too fast," he advised her, grinning. Neruda, as befit a man married twenty years, was an incurable romantic.

"Are you all right?" Zamora asked, extending a hand to help her out of the box.

Vasquez shot Neruda a smile and took the major's hand, rising out of the coffin. "Hardly a Sleeping Beauty moment," she told the recently commissioned garbage man/intelligence operative, pulling the hospital gown she wore more closely around her. Zamora offered her his camouflage jacket, which she accepted gratefully.

"How did you escape?" Zamora asked. Before she could answer, he shook his head, waving away the stupid question. "You got into a coffin and had Neruda pick it up, as you'd told him to. I mean, how did you arrange the distraction for Brindermann?"

"I carried on an absolutely shameful flirtation with that unspeakable Jorge Serrey," Vasquez admitted. "I'd definitely have to go to confession for that one—both what I implied and the fact that I was lying all the way." The hours hidden in the coffin, the stress of waiting to find out if friend or foe would open the box, or if no one ever would, and the relief of getting out of the lab combined to make her eyes brighter and closer to laughter or tears than usual.

"Good thing," Zamora agreed, returning the smile, impressed with her tactics—and the guts it took to carry them out. He still vividly remembered Serrey's cold eyes and wanted to blacken both, but he forced himself to concentrate on what he needed to do on each step of the way to getting to that point. "Let's get you out of here."

"Let's get you out of here too," Vasquez said, following him to the battered long-haul truck that had brought a small contingent of rebels so deep into Garza's home territory. Neruda strode easily along behind them. "What are you doing in Bogotá? It's incredibly dangerous for you to be here. Talk about walking into the jaguar's den!"

"El Jaguar's looking for me outside Santa Lucia," Zamora assured her. "I came to give the codes for the last set of locked munitions boxes to the depot commander." He smiled. "Mercury managed to get into the system and pull the combinations for the Keepsakes locks. He took a copy for us and scrambled the records in the database. When the order comes, we will be able to arm every Saint in every capital city with the arms the General has extorted from us to give to his armies."

"I hope that comes soon." She looked from one man to the other, her face deadly serious. "They don't have the antidote they're looking for yet, but they have at least a dozen vicious diseases, and I don't think Garza will wait much longer before he starts spreading them anyway. He doesn't care about killing his own people." Her eyes darkened. "I'm pretty sure that Dr. Twilley, the head of the lab, is going to be next—if he isn't dead already. Garza's been impatient lately, and he kills people who disappoint him."

"We'll have to avoid disappointing him then," Zamora said lightly, hiding a flash of concern for Mercury.

"Too bad he wasn't disappointed with Serrey." Neruda settled into the driver's seat, glancing back to make sure that Zamora, Vasquez, and the two rebel roustabouts had found their places in the small sleeping space at the back of the cab. A smile crossed the trucker's face, and he winked at Vasquez. "You embarrassed old Serrey, though. They busted in on him in a way he won't soon forget. Which reminds me—how did you end up in a coffin, when word had it that you'd slipped out of the lab with a couple of Serrey's agents, disguised as a soldier yourself?"

"Word had it?" Vasquez asked, puzzled. "I don't know. All I did was try to set up enough pointers that they'd think Serrey came to get me—or at least that he'd know where I was. I admit I figured it would be pretty thin, but it would give them somewhere to look besides into the coffins, just in case. How did they get the idea I'd dressed up as a soldier to leave?"

"When we came to get the garbage, I heard the sentries arguing about how many Chileans came and went today," Neruda explained. "One says two, one says three—and handily enough, it was three leaving."

"Interesting." She shook her head. "The disappearing soldier. It's like a ghost story."

"I think it was a spirit all right, but not a soldier's ghost." Zamora thought about the strange occurrences in his running war with El Jaguar, the moments when he and his men seemed to be invisible at exactly the right moment, or a prompting directed them down an unexpected path just before an ambush could catch them. His eyes refocused, meeting Vasquez's steady gaze.

"Holy Spirit, right?" She managed a smile, feeling distinctly odd about the situation. "I meant to tell you that you're not the only one who makes miraculous escapes. I've had a couple myself."

"You're worth it," Zamora said quietly, then blushed. He hit the back of Neruda's seat. "Get moving."

They disappeared, like phantoms themselves, back into the jungle roads that led to Santiago.

CHAPTER 16

"It's a jungle out there—you'd better be careful, Doc." Dove leaned against the doorway of Merry's office.

Missy, with a delighted shout, flung herself at his knees. "Hey, Little Doctor." He caught her, swinging her easily up to perch on his shoulder.

"Thanks, Dove. I'll keep that in mind." She looked up from the disc popping out of the console's drive bay and smiled at him. "We'll be all right. Senator Cox said she'd arrange to have people meet us in Washington. And," she nodded toward her purse, "Fox even gave me one of those interesting little ring transceivers, just so she could keep an eye on me, she said. The chance to test the signal at long range is a bonus, of course."

"Watch out—those computer geeks will talk your ear off, if you let them," he warned, patting Missy and ducking out of her enthusiastic head hug. "You sure you don't want me coming along, just in case? We could ditch Perro, if you think he'd be too embarrassing in Washington."

"Like I'd embarrass her more than you would!" Perro poked Dove in the back, tweaking Missy's knee as he pushed past to look around at the office. He whistled. "So this is the place where you beat out the General."

"Hey, Perro. You too, Calvin." Merry looked around him to include their quieter friend, who gave her a shy grin from behind Dove—and then caught Missy when she launched herself off Dove's shoulder at him.

"Please, Mamamam? Take the boys with us?" Missy wheedled from her new perch. "It would be fun!"

"I'm sure it would be," Merry agreed. "But you'll have Gianni to play with, and the boys have important things to do here, sweetie."

"Oh?" Dove looked interested. "What things?" The trip to New Mexico had helped cure his cabin fever, and showing Perro and Calvin around the city had kept him happily occupied for a few days. Running practice missions in the mountains and deserts around Salt Lake, pushing Socks's spy-eye abilities, kept them occupied too, but having something new, and hopefully real, to do sounded good indeed.

"I don't know exactly," Merry admitted, tucking the disc into her purse and picking up her overnight case.

Dove took the case from her and punched Perro's arm. He punched back, but obediently picked up the garment bag slung across the back of the chair.

"But?" Dove prompted, following her through the corridor. He caught Dr. Resnik's eye and waved. So did Perro, who assumed that he knew everybody Dove knew. Calvin, his arms full of Missy, just smiled politely.

"But Tasha and Jonathan have been talking about all the planning and counterplanning going on at Elder Nabil's office—and in Independence," Merry continued. "With the big announcement that President Smith and President Rojas are going to Jerusalem, and all the Gatherers out there doing all kinds of things, there's a lot of bustle. Jonathan said that Elder Nabil may have to go to Independence himself soon and that they might have to pull the Apostles in from all over the world for a general quorum meeting."

"Which means what for us?" Dove asked, tucking the case into the trunk of Merry's car.

"Besides if we want to get Elder Nabil's autograph, we'd better do it soon?" Perro added.

Merry grinned as both Dove and Calvin poked Perro. She double-checked Missy's seat belt, but Calvin had buckled her in securely. "Well, let's just say that if I needed someone to escort an Apostle through the badlands, I know three guys I wouldn't want hung up outside a committee meeting in Washington. You take care. We'll see you soon." She got into the car. Missy waved wildly until they couldn't see her anymore.

"Seriously? They'd want us to pull watchdog duty for an Apostle?" Perro asked.

Dove snorted. "She's teasing us, man. That's one of the scenarios we've played with Socks, remember? Elder Nabil's using us to keep him busy—and him to keep us busy, so we don't go back home and start stirring up trouble Amexica way. Any Apostles need to get back to Independence, they'll come on a plane, like anybody else."

"Unless the big winds come back and the planes can't fly," Calvin said quietly.

* * *

No winds interfered with the regular flight from Salt Lake City to points east, including Independence, Nauvoo, Harmony, New York City, and Washington, D.C., on the outbound leg. Merry and Missy looked out the round window on a strangely calm day, flying between the thin chiffon of lower-lying clouds and the envelope of volcanic ash that spread through the upper atmosphere to darken the daylight over most of the Northern Hemisphere. Missy knelt on the seat, singing random snatches of melody as she stared at the ever-changing cloud patterns until she finally fell asleep. Merry spent the flight reviewing her notes on the AllSafe trials and side effects, reducing the intricate medical detail to "short, simple sentences that even senators can understand," as Senator Cox had suggested. She was only half kidding. The captain's announcement that Nauvoo was the next stop came as a relief.

"There's my favorite little girl!" Carmen exclaimed, sweeping Missy up the moment she ran out of the disembarkation area.

Missy hesitated for a moment, but Carmen's familiar scent and unmistakable mommyness reassured her; she enthusiastically hugged back. Then she caught sight of Gianni and squealed. Carmen put her down and watched indulgently as the two three-year-olds got reacquainted by arguing over who got to hold the bag of cookies Carmen had brought to keep them occupied on the drive back home.

"And one of our favorite big ones," Tony added, smiling warmly at Merry. He took her overnight case and Missy's backpack and gave her a one-armed hug before Carmen practically tackled her.

"Honey, you look like you've been spending way too much time locked up in the lab," Carmen announced.

Merry ran a hand through her hair and laughed. "Well, thank you. Are you going to say I look tired too? That's just what I need to hear."

Carmen pulled a semicontrite face and gave her a big hug. "Just a lead-in to saying that you look like you could use a good, hot dinner and a chance to put your feet up. How was the flight?"

"It was fine—even though it felt a lot like cramming for comps again, trying to get all the AllSafe and FDA data straight in my head so I'll be ready when they grill me about it. I keep telling myself it can't be worse than my doctoral defense, but it doesn't make for a restful flight." Merry returned the hug. "A good, hot dinner and some time with my feet up sounds great."

"Then come this way, m'ladies." Tony made a graceful gesture with both hands. "Your carriage awaits."

"And so do the girls, back home." Carmen caught both little kids by the hand and swept them along. "Getting dinner on the table to be ready when we walk in the door, if they know what's good for them."

They did—and dinner was good too; it felt almost as if the past months had never happened. Only Chris's absence—and the slight catch in her voice as Carmen said Giovanni's name—reminded them of all that lay between them and the old days in San Diego. Merry listened, holding Carmen's hand, as her friend told her how much she missed her eldest boy, how proud she was that he'd fulfilled his mission so honorably, and how confident she was that he was still carrying on that mission beyond the veil. "Maybe they've got him working with Chris," Carmen said, smiling through her tears. Merry managed to smile back, picturing her gentle, scientific husband paired with Carmen's exuberant, athletic son. If Chris couldn't reason spirit prison's inmates into seeing the truth, Giovanni could probably joke and tease them into it.

Merry also hugged both Lucrezia and Donna, amazed at how much they had changed in what felt like so short a time. Donna told war stories about teaching junior high students; though conditions in Zion were certainly better than those in the outside world, adolescents still had their own, uniquely unhinged (as Donna put it) way of looking at the world. Lucrezia threw in a few stories of her own about high school life in Nauvoo and the adventures her friends had in the few hours of free time they had between classes, gardening, and construction projects—nearly losing Imre Sarkesian to an avalanche of feed corn, for instance.

"Which just goes to show that junior high kids aren't the only uniquely unhinged folks around here," Tony observed, then laughed as Lucrezia rolled her eyes at him.

"It also sounds like you're all keeping busy," Merry said, after helping Missy and Gianni clear the table and bundling them into the bath and into bed. Missy had declared herself content to stay with Gianni and "my Callattas" until Merry returned from her meetings.

"Understatement of the century," Lucrezia muttered.

Carmen squeezed her and handed her a dishcloth. "Better busy than bored, hon."

"Which they definitely are," Donna assured Merry, proud of her parents. "Mom and Dad have been up to their elbows getting the community going. I don't think the ward here could get on without them."

Tony kissed his daughter's head, then temporized, "Well, nobody's indispensable. They could spare us if the Church needed us to do something else."

"Oh, I think we're doing just what we're supposed to be doing right here," Carmen told him, giving him a quick squeeze and handing him a dishcloth too. "He's disappointed we didn't get tapped as Gatherers," she explained to Merry. "Me, I'm just as glad we didn't. We've got enough to do with all the Baptists pouring into Zion. That poor Tommy Gibbs's dying seems to either drive people to absolute despair—"

"The suicide rate after that night in Houston skyrocketed," Donna said. "Literally went up about 600 percent. People just can't cope anymore."

"Idiots," Lucrezia growled. "They shouldn't be killing themselves— they should be going after that slimy Brother Light creep. He's the one who's the real threat. Where does he get off saying God is dead? And where do they get off believing him?" She waved a hand around, taking in Nauvoo, the Church, and the curtain of undeniable divine protection over Zion. "Can't they see what's going on?"

"Some of them can," Carmen pointed out. "That's why we've got so many coming into Zion now. Believers have to believe something, so it's a good thing that they're choosing the right way at last."

"That'd be more comforting if a whole other gob of them didn't run right out of the stadium and convert to the Children of Light," Lucrezia shot back.

"Even more of them turned *against* the cult," Tony said. "Whatever Brother Light wanted to prove in Houston—and in these suicide attacks his people keep pulling in the South Seas and Asia against Zion—he's not convincing everybody." He smiled grimly. "There's quite the back-lash against the Children of Light. A whole lot of people have decided that whether or not Mr. Rashi Janjalani is a prophet, he's definitely a terrorist."

* * *

Figures ran wildly through the streets, their white robes flowing; this time, however, they were the hunted, not the hunters. A mob of shouting men pursued them, throwing rocks, bottles, and dire threats after them. A reporter appeared, shouting over the noise of curses, screams, and breaking glass, as the riot spread to opportunistic looting and destruction. Police, overwhelmed, underequipped, and more sympathetic to the pursuers than the pursued, hung back, protecting the businesses on the edges of the clash. "The backlash against the Children of Light and their self-proclaimed prophet has resulted in riots in six American cities, including Houston, where the cult's members have been accused of arranging the accident that killed well-known evangelist Tommy Gibbs." Images of the evangelist's dramatic demise replaced the riot footage.

"Get 'em," muttered an old man, taking a deep drag on his pipe. "Kill every last one of those blasted bohos. Drive 'em back to the desert they came from."

"The jungle," his wife corrected. "Those Children of Light, they came from the jungle. Out in the Philippines. They've just been spreading into the Middle East lately. Haven't you been watching the news?"

"Watching the news is all we do around here anymore," her husband complained, waving one arthritis-crabbed hand around at the shabby Red Cross shelter.

Mr. and Mrs. Grumman had come to the shelter when the last hurricane leveled their home—and had never left, for lack of anywhere else to go. They'd arrived at the former bus station with most of their possessions packed into an ancient sedan, including the screen they set up in a corner of the big room, where they sat watching Channel 8's endless broadcasts with other homeless and frightened people seeking refuge from the storms, violence, and disease flooding the world outside. The Grummans stayed on even when the frazzled, apologetic Red Cross volunteers told them that they had no more funds for supplies, food, or even lights. They just kept sitting there, powering the screen with the batteries from their defunct car, lending out spaces to sleep under a solid roof in return for new power sources. Mrs. Grumman had an uncanny ability to make enough stew to feed them all and to maintain order among the ragged wanderers who came into her sphere. At the moment, sixteen people sat or lay on the benches in the big room, most of them staring at the screen, all at loose ends.

For the last two days, that included Sally Mae, who had ended up at the end of the line when the bus she'd selected evaporated halfway to Nauvoo. The driver shooed everyone off, saying he needed to fix a flat—and then drove off, taking the bus and all the luggage they'd left on board.

"Hijacker," Mrs. Grumman snorted. "Happens more and more. Goes to show that parents just aren't teaching their kids responsibility these days."

"Good thing we got old Betsy here." Mr. Grumman patted the shotgun lying across the arms of his chair.

"More like good thing nobody here has anything worth taking," his wife corrected, "which is a darn good thing, in the circumstances."

Those circumstances definitely applied to Sally Mae, left with only her large purse, a small bag of clothes, a credit card that didn't work, and no cash. And a lingering sense of urgency pushing her toward Zion, which seemed farther away now than ever. It warred at the moment with a lingering sense of guilt. She looked from the screen to the elderly couple, swallowing hard against the tears that rose in her throat. If she'd only tried harder to warn Reverend Gibbs, would he still be alive? "Poor Reverend Gibbs," she said, half out loud, then sobbed.

"Don't cry, honey." With a brisk pat on Sally Mae's hand, the elderly lady heaved herself to her feet. "Everybody's gotta go sometime. Just most of us don't get electrocuted on live TV. I'll go check on dinner."

As she bustled away, the news report shifted. Garrett de Long appeared, touting a special on the lives of the rich and famous who left the economic collapse to play in the hot sands of Waikiki.

"It's still not Zion," Sally Mae said.

One of the boarders looked at her, surprised. "Zion. Is that where you're headed?"

"I was. I don't know how I'm going to get there now, though," Sally Mae told him, a half-smile tugging at her mouth. "Unless Jesus decides to step in and lend a hand."

"Jesus, huh?" The man snorted. "Ma'am, I'd settle for a regular bus."

Moments later, the brilliant beams of two high-riding headlights bloomed through the old terminal's windows. Outside the doors, the silver gleam of a huge vehicle sparkled. The roar of the engine dropped to a basso hum. Through the windows, the word *Zion* shone in the front of the bus. The terminal door opened, and Mia Valados stood in the doorway, shining in the brilliant light. "Anybody here looking to go home?" she asked.

Sally Mae leapt to her feet, warmth flowing through her. "Thank you, Jesus!" she exclaimed.

"Guess that's my ride too," the man muttered, picking up his computer and briefcase.

Several other refugees followed his example, hoisting their packs and gathering their belongings as Brother Valados, with the help of four passengers, hauled out two large grocery boxes of supplies. "Looks like you could use these, ma'am—unless you're planning to come on the road," he said to Mrs. Grumman.

"Well, thank you," she said, trading a glance with her husband. "But no, you go on. We're just fine here. Though if you want to stop by, once in a while, to pick up anybody who needs a ride . . ."

"We surely will," Sister Valados promised. She smiled at Sally Mae, who smiled eagerly back, and at the man, who nodded gruffly, and at the others. As usual, she'd managed to sweep up a baby. "We're heading east, but we'll be back by when we're needed."

"Well, that's something different," Mr. Grumman observed. He watched the lights of the bus until they disappeared into the darkness, then turned back to the glowing screen and its vivid displays of chaos and violence.

* * *

Sepphira watched the rout of the Children of Light in Houston, hearing the simultaneous chatter on their satellite channel that Rashi had paid one of the space-station workers to set up for them. As she thought of the woman, Mir, Sepphira suppressed a flash of jealousy. Killing Tommy Gibbs hadn't had the effect Rashi had hoped. That thought set off a rapid-fire chain reaction in her mind: Rashi had miscalculated, which meant he was not infallible, which meant that his inspirations did not come from an omniscient Unity, which meant that his guise as the Prophet—or, as he claimed more and more, as the One God himself—rested on the mists of a grandiose dream rather than the hard rock of reality. She looked at that conclusion looming in the distance, then at the invisible shadows clustered around the far end of the ornate room, where Rashi was deep in conversation with someone thousands of miles away, and deliberately closed her eyes. Rashi had to be right, because he was her whole existence, her love and her life and her one thin thread to sanity. And someday, when he didn't need them anymore, he would make the shadows go away.

So what had happened in Houston? She concentrated on the reports, untangling the threads of reality from the propaganda and lies of the Western infidels. They said the Hands' actions were terrorist attacks meant to further destabilize their Office of Homeland Security while the Senate investigations were continuing, but she knew better. The real reason Rashi had stretched forth his Hands to destroy Gibbs was to prove the Unity's superiority over the dead god of the Christians. However, the evangelical congregation had the wrong reaction. Some of the American Christians had lost faith in a god who couldn't stretch out his hand to protect his anointed messenger, but it seemed that more had decided that they would act as the hands of that god in wreaking vengeance on Gibbs's killers—and still more ignored the entire demonstration. They already possessed the wealth and ease that so many looked to Brother Light to provide, so they had nothing to gain by adopting a creed that told them they could freely take what they needed or wanted from the infidels. And they certainly had no need for Rashi's approval of sensual freedoms. What could Rashi do with a society so wrapped up in itself that there was no room left for the One God or any other?

A laugh from the far end of the room drew her attention. Subconsciously, she dissected that laugh, looking for clues that would tell her whether to brace for a blow or expect a caress. Rashi swirled away from the communications console, gracefully rose from the chair, and danced a few steps toward her. When he held out his hands, she eagerly rose to take them, whirling to his lead.

"What's happened, Rashi?" she asked, laughing and bright-eyed at his obvious pleasure.

"We have just made a new friend," he told her. "A valuable new friend. An infidel, true, but a useful one, a man looking carefully for advantages in an uncertain world, one with the power of wind and fire at his fingertips, which we will put to the service of the One God. My will rolls on, Sepphira. Did they disbelieve when lightning struck down the false servant of their dead god? Do they say that the walls of their so-called Zion can repel the forces of hell? Do they say that Islam will withstand the assault of the angels of light? We will see what they say when I stand across the holiest city in the world, one foot on the Dome of the Rock, the other crushing their Church of the Holy Sepulchre!"

He spread his arms, laughing again, and whirled to command his Hands to gather the Children from every land. "We march," he declared, "to a final battle against the enemies of the One God, offering them the only choice: Unity or death!"

Sepphira joined the cheer that the Hands set up, but the laughter of the demons around Rashi chilled her even more than the thought of driving their believing but disorganized mobs of followers into a battle against the sleek weapons and heavy armor that Israel and Palestine could summon. The gleam of metal caught her eye, images of bombs, guns, and strangely thin airplanes flashing across the screen as if to confirm her fears.

* * *

"The list of weapons Secretary Garlick unofficially loaned to General Garza for testing is finally complete," Clara announced. "They range from high-tech independent drones capable of unmanned flight to state-of-the art targeting systems for smart bombs. In high-level talks with administration officials, Garza has confirmed that he received the weapons systems from Garlick, but he also says the secretary provided them for field tests against the drug-dealing rebel cartels in South America, and denies allegations of bioterror involvement."

Vivid images of smart bombs striking their satellite-painted targets alternated with footage of full-uniform drills in the new capital of the USSA and troop trains carrying cheering men through the rail yards. "Garza also characterizes the movements of thousands of soldiers toward Mexico's southern border as military exercises to train the combined militaries to work in conjunction with the high-tech weapons systems in eradicating terrorists, drug cartels, and other rebel groups."

The vast, fiery column and cap of the nuclear explosion that destroyed Mexico City replayed in slow motion. "General Garza said in a prepared statement that the government of the United States of South America was unaware that Secretary Garlick had not received clearance for the loan program."

"The weapons loan program gives us an unprecedented opportunity to test our mechanized weapons systems in real-time combat activities without risking American troops," a uniformed military spokesman pointed out. "And because the safeguards against unauthorized use are still in place, we feel fully confident that these weapons would be useless if they happened to fall into the wrong hands."

"Secretary Garlick may have made a mistake in his methods, but his intentions were completely honorable," Senator Inverness argued for the benefit of the camera and her continued political survival. "Knowing how overburdened our military infrastructure is now, he used an unconventional tactic, recruiting a friendly ally to test the weapons that would keep American interests safe in the future."

"A surprising development in the Senate investigation of the late Secretary Howard Garlick," Clara noted. The scene behind her changed, from a visual catalog of the weapons in question, sprinkled with images of General Garza waving to flag-waving crowds, to the front of the Senate and its own crowds of sign-waving protesters. "That investigation has spawned other inquiries, however, including the investigation into the role Secretary Garlick played in the botched FDA approval process for MedaGen's revolutionary AllSafe vaccine. MedaGen's chief executive officer and chief operations officer came to Washington, D.C., today to testify before the investigative committee—and to confront evidence given by Dr. Meredith Galen, the Mormon researcher who first discovered the potential side effects of the AllSafe vaccine."

"It became quite clear when we analyzed the data from the simulations that AllSafe would cause permanent changes to the immune system." Merry appeared, speaking clearly and calmly to the senators on their high platform. "And those changes, if left unchecked, would push the immune system into overdrive—essentially, the patients would become allergic to their own blood and tissues."

"And is this something that the FDA trials would have uncovered?" Senator Cox asked.

"Yes, they would have, if they had done the trials themselves." Merry touched a button, and the data from MedaGen's human trials appeared on the screen behind her and beamed to the senators' own computers. "But, as you can see here, MedaGen arranged to have its own research team conduct the trials outside of the United States, where the laws governing drug protocols aren't so strict. They sent on the initial findings, which proved that AllSafe successfully destroyed a wide variety of viral diseases without immediate side effects."

Merry touched another button, to bring up the files that had made her cry when she found them that night at MedaGen. "However, they intentionally hid the rest of the story, the part about what would happen a year or so later, even though they had run studies to not only suspect but confirm the need for a booster shot." The sad face of Xavier Chaudry, one of the volunteers who had died during the tests for the Corinth project, accompanied the dry numbers and summaries of twenty people who had died as Dr. Twilley's team watched to see if the immune system could readjust itself without the booster.

"This is the material that you obtained through deceptive means, is it not?" Senator Inverness asked. "In fact, through corporate espionage?"

"According to the federal grand jury that evaluated the accusations MedaGen brought against me," Merry said carefully, "my actions were legal, acceptable under federal whistle-blower statutes. My husband, Christopher Galen, discovered irregularities in MedaGen's records of the tests and made every effort to bring those irregularities to the attention of his superiors through regular channels. When he died in a car accident, I took a job at MedaGen to confirm our interpretation of the data. When I knew that the vaccine could be deadly and that the MedaGen officers were fully aware of that fact and had no intention of stopping production, I took the steps necessary to warn the public about the potential danger."

"So, you're saying that because the grand jury didn't indict, what you did was right?" Inverness's question stabbed at Merry—and the camera cut away before capturing Merry's reply—but neither the rhetoric nor the quick editing could diminish the implications of the data, or the power of the melancholy picture of the dead man who had gazed out of the screen.

Footage of Abbott and Zelik walking down the Senate steps replaced the scene inside. They reached the sidewalk, and Abbott stopped, facing the flock of shouting reporters with an easy smile. "Of course, we've heard all of this before. We acknowledge that there were mistakes made in the initial FDA approval process for AllSafe, but those mistakes have been thoroughly corrected now. Full information on the vaccine and its necessary booster shots is available—and with the free neutralizer, anyone who doesn't want to take advantage of AllSafe's revolutionary antiviral properties is completely free not to."

"A dramatic announcement from MedaGen, the embattled but still industry-leading biotech firm," Clara reappeared, with a ticker across the bottom of the screen showing MedaGen's approval ratings climbing dramatically. A Web site and phone number flashed, inviting investors to pick up MedaGen stock. "Predictably, however, MedaGen's announcement was not met with universal acclaim."

* * *

Virginia stared at the screen without seeing the disastrous numbers, the afterimage of a smiling Abbott and cool Zelik burning in her eyes. "They're going to get away with it," she said, her voice rising. "They're going to walk away scot-free!"

"No, they're not," Julian said soothingly, carefully pinning the end of a braid with a jeweled clip. "They're in deep trouble, and it's all thanks to you."

"No." Virginia shrugged that off. "That ice-man lawyer of theirs is going to put a lock on the judges and totally hash Senator Cox's push to get them investigated. That Inverness woman is pushing it all away, and White doesn't care about MedaGen. Did you hear that? Abbott's all but threatening not to release their AllSafe booster unless the government drops the suit!"

She slapped at Julian, snatching her phone. "They think they're going to get away with it. They're going to think that they can just dump me like last night's party favor and walk away. Well, that's just not going to happen. They absolutely will pay for what they did to me! They are going to take me seriously this time!" A pause, then, "Errol, darling. It's Virginia. I want to talk to you. No, not socially—this is business. I want more sugar. But this time, how about double the whipped cream?"

Humphrey paused, looking at the office speaker. "Double?"

"Absolutely. Double." Virginia nodded. "And this time, I want to use it in a recipe that nobody can alter. Just like a computer, if you understand me, what comes in comes back out. No fakes."

"No fakes," Humphrey repeated. She'd caught him late, in the midst of packing his personal belongings and rearranging the rest of the office to look like its owner didn't have every intention of disappearing into the sunset, contract or no contract. He'd seen the broadcast too, but he wasn't as confident as Virginia in MedaGen's ability to skunk their stockholders, even if they did wriggle out of a federal indictment.

He'd done enough deals to build up a tidy sum in his well-hidden personal bank account. Technically it was illegal, since he still owed MedaGen's board rights to all profits he as an incorporated entity made. Originally he had thought to use it to pay off his contract, but now it was simply to finance his escape to a life of simple luxury on some far-off, third-world beach. He considered telling the former spokesmodel to shove off, but greed got the better of him. "All right, you want more sugar? I can give you the rest of that bag tonight."

"No." Virginia's flat refusal startled him. "No, I don't want the rest of that bag. I want something else, a brand-new flavor. Something—" She paused, and he heard Julian's voice prompt her. "Something more sweet, less savory. Something that'll put the cream filling in a couple of cupcakes."

He gritted his teeth. While he appreciated her not coming right out on a possibly tapped phone line and asking for dirt on Abbott and Zelik because the Pacifica plot with Garlick hadn't worked out, the metaphor she'd chosen was getting ridiculous. He also suspected that assistant of hers had a real sarcastic streak that Virginia didn't understand. "All right, I'll drop by the bakery and see what I can come up with."

"Oh, you're a sweetie," she cooed. "You get that and wrap it up for me, and let Julian know when it's ready. I may be out, finding somebody to share it with."

"Got it." Humphrey clicked off the speaker, irritated at Virginia for using him as a delivery boy. Double the original check went a long way toward soothing his suffering ego, however. Good timing for one last raid into hostile territory. Abbott and Zelik were both in Washington, so nobody was using Abbott's office.

Turning to the console, he sent a chunk of virtual platinum and a message to Sean: "I'm going to the gents'—appreciate some privacy." The cameras would record nothing more than an empty hall as he slipped out of his office; he took no other precautions. By the time they checked the recordings, he'd be lying on a beach. He was still smiling as he slipped into the conference room, heading for Abbott's office and its electronic gold mine—or sugar factory, to continue that obnoxious metaphor.

The screen lit obediently—but so did the ambient lights around the room. Stifling a curse, Humphrey forced his muscles to relax. He swiveled the chair around, trying to look innocent.

"Surprised?" Zelik asked, standing in the doorway, her hand on the light controls.

"To say the least." He tried a broad smile but dropped it when it felt brittle at the edges. "I thought you were in Washington until Sunday."

"That was what I told everyone." Her eyes were as cold as the sample freezers downstairs. "I've come back every other day, just to make sure things are moving along smoothly. It appears that we just can't trust anyone these days."

"Too true," Humphrey agreed. Like Sean, who'd been acting squirrelly lately. Maybe Sean had more to feel guilty about than lending a hand in Humphrey's little schemes. "But it helps to run into somebody who's willing to tell the truth."

"Really?" She hadn't moved, regarding him like a snake watching a rabbit. "And where would I find someone like that?"

"Right here." He lifted his hands. "Okay, you caught me dead to rights, getting into the network. I even corrupted a network administrator to help me get a skeleton key. And this isn't the first time. I've used it before, specifically to look at Abbott's personal project files."

"You sold the Pacifica pictures to Senator Cox." Zelik leapt to a solid conclusion. "And now you've come back for more. What is it this time? The Corinth data? No, that's already public."

Humphrey shrugged. "Actually, it was just a fishing expedition, looking for whatever might come in handy. The skeleton key only opens semishared files, not the deep-cover stuff. I found out about Pacifica because Abbott had to open a network space to share the data with you and Twilley."

"And now it doesn't do that much," she said. "Try it."

He typed in the password. Instead of open access, a message directed him to another connection. When he opened it, the feed from the parking-garage camera came through, showing a pair of burly security guards muscling a struggling network technician into a company van. One of them slapped an anesthetic mask on Sean before the van's doors closed.

"We thought that as a reward for his faithful service, your friend Sean could give us a hand with our research," Zelik told Humphrey. Her cold fingertips touched his neck. "An idea we shared with our Pacifica collaborators. Is there any reason you shouldn't take one last trip to the islands, Errol?"

The irony of the phrasing nearly choked him, but he rallied under pressure. "Mainly, because I would be a lot more useful to you here than disintegrating in some lab. I know what happened with Pacifica. And now I know what's going to happen to Sean. And I suspect that the same kind of thing happened to Whittier."

"Yes, you did get a battlefield promotion of sorts," Zelik said. "Mr. Whittier had the opportunity to join Mr. Abbott and myself in a profitable but highly confidential venture. Unfortunately, he had an attack of conscience."

"I've got an advantage over him there, then," Humphrey assured her. "I have no conscience. I'll do anything to save my hide. So make me an offer better than the lab-rat position, and I'll prove how well my self-interest can work for you."

She realized she was smiling. He was a sneaky creature, but a capable one when sufficiently motivated. "All right, Mr. Humphrey. How is this for an offer? You come to Washington and help us kidnap Meredith Galen. When we deliver her to Johann Brindermann, you'll get 10 percent of five million dollars and walk away with an intact skin."

His silence surprised her, given his blithe denial of conscience. She raised a hand, one nail poised over the button that would summon security. "Why the hesitation, Errol?"

He sighed. "Just trying to figure out which approach would work best, the old-friend routine or the terrified cry for help. In the circumstances, I think the latter. We just weren't that close."

Zelik removed her hand from the alarm and motioned for him to follow her.

"Kidnapping, though—that's a pretty big step," Humphrey observed. "Federal offense, in fact. Grabbing a well-known scientist and hauling her off to a South American dictator ought to be worth more than 10 percent, don't you think?"

"No, I do not," Zelik snapped, pressing the elevator button. "All you have to do is lure her out to where our security men can catch her. No more. You will not be going to Bogotá for the delivery."

"How are you going to get her there?" Humphrey persisted. "It'll be pretty hard to smuggle a struggling or unconscious woman through security onto a commercial plane. Especially one with her face on all the news reports. Hey, the more I know, the better I can help you. Don't hamstring me here."

"Abbott has arranged transportation—a private corporate helicopter to come to our hotel tomorrow night," Zelik told him. "So don't lay any elaborate plans. You have only tomorrow to catch her. And if I tell you any more, I will have to kill you."

"I don't need to know any more then," he assured her as he followed her into the elevator.

"And neither do I," whispered Virginia Diamante. Impatient as ever, she had come to see if Humphrey had her sugar yet. While Julian kept security busy with demands that they inspect Virginia's former office for lost jewelry, she announced that she was going to see Humphrey and flounced upstairs. When he wasn't in his office, she'd headed for Abbott's, just in case she could do a little profitable snooping herself—

luckily, the security guards had hustled Sean away so quickly he hadn't had time to reset the cameras to real-time display.

She waited until the elevator traveled several floors down before clattering down the stairs. "We're leaving—now," she informed Julian, heading for the garage and her convertible.

"Where do you want to go?" Julian finally asked, slowing to a stop at an intersection. Distant gunfire added a crackling undercurrent to the night; from the sound of it, the police were fighting the gangs over disputed turf.

Virginia stared forward, then nodded. "The airport."

Julian swung the car into the correct street. "Why?"

"Because I'm going to catch a plane to New York," Virginia announced.

"Why New York?" Julian asked.

Virginia giggled. "Because that's where Caesar Augosto lives. I'm going to New York, and I'm going to give him all the pictures and data we got from Humphrey about Garlick, and I'm going to tell him that Abbott and that witch Zelik have something else up their sleeves, and he's going to rub them out. And I'm going to watch."

Julian brought the car to a hard stop. "You are *not*."

Virginia glared. "Oh yes I am, and don't you take that tone with me!"

"I'm sorry. I didn't mean to be pushy." Realizing the tactical error, Julian tried to change approaches. "Augosto's dangerous. Way too dangerous for us to mess with. Think about it. He *killed* Secretary Garlick."

"I know." A feline smile flicked over Virginia's full lips. "And he'll kill Zelik and Abbott too. I already called him and told him I was coming and that I was the one who told Senator Cox about Garlick."

"You told him? Yourself? How dumb can you be?" Julian yipped, too upset to be tactful. "After all the circus we went through to make sure Cox got them anonymously? What if he comes after you?"

"What if he does?" Virginia tossed her head. "I like men who aren't afraid to use their power to get what they want."

"He's hot all right—get too close to that heat, and it'll burn you too." Julian regained control. For someone so smart about manipulating people, Virginia never could grasp the limits of her charm.

"We finally have Kama Records lined up—they're even willing to fight MedaGen's noncompetition clause. This is our chance to make it on our own, without having to depend on anybody else—especially anybody frightening like Zelik or Augosto. This is what we've always wanted. Let's stay and get that record deal. Then we can kick back and laugh while we watch karma catch up with the whole lot of them."

"I don't want karma to catch up with them," Virginia snarled. "*I* want to catch up with them. Another record deal—another bunch of stuffed suits telling me that I'm getting too old! It's too late, Julian. Your bright ideas about doing 'real music' are totally backfiring. My last album *tanked*, you idiot!" Her hand hit the dash. "I am not going to let anybody tell me what to do anymore. This is my ticket, and I'm taking it, no matter what you say. I know Augosto is dangerous—that's why I want him. You think Abbott and Zelik aren't dangerous? They are—I just heard her telling Humphrey they're going to kidnap that Meredith Galen doctor. What if I'm next? I'll wrap Augosto around my little finger, and he'll take care of Abbott and Zelik before they can get me. They'll get to dance to my tune for once."

"Everybody danced to your tune, and they will again, if you get that insane idea out of your head. I'll write music for you that you can sell, like you do so well—you don't need some Mob boss who won't help you anyway," Julian tried again, anger, fear, and jealousy fueling a lash of hard truth. "He doesn't like you. You won't wrap him around your finger, and you won't seduce him."

That earned her assistant a backhand slap. Julian stared at her, stunned. "I've done everything for you, given up everything for you—even my own songs. All for you to throw everything away to get mixed up with the Mob? What about me?"

"What about you?" Virginia shrugged. "It's not about you. It's never about you. It's about me."

"I thought it was at least a little about us," Julian whispered. All the years of standing in the shadows, the abuse, and the betrayal joined the stinging from the slap and hardened into cold fury.

She snickered nastily. "Us? There's never been an 'us.' It's my career; I just let you come along for the ride because you do a decent enough job writing dance music. You're my assistant, Julian."

Watching Julian's face, Virginia realized that she had pushed it too far. "Oh, come on. Sorry I lost my temper with you. We've had some good times, right? You let me handle Augosto, and maybe we'll finally get you that songwriting award you want so much." Satisfied that a few kind words would melt the ice in her assistant's eyes, she leaned back. "Now, get me to the airport, Julian. We've got places to go."

CHAPTER 17

"Nobody goes anywhere quickly in Washington. All these stairs—it's quite a climb, isn't it? I bet it feels a lot better coming down than going up too," observed Agent Ettinger lightly, his eyes scanning the surroundings with vision-enhancing sunglasses as he escorted Meredith Galen down the long flight of steps. The ever-present crowds of protesters roared in the distance, but the police hadn't had to pull out the tear gas today. Reporters lurked at the edges of the security cordon, but the other two bodyguards closed in, muscling their charge through with no more than a curt, "No comment."

Merry glanced at the agent Senator Cox had introduced to her when she arrived in Washington. Apart from the fresh scars on his face, he fit her mental stereotype of the straitlaced government operative: tall, fit, and alert to the point of reminding her of an otter. They told her he was on loan from the FBI, temporarily assigned to assist Senator Cox's security detail during the investigation. "Late of Homeland Security," he'd added, touching a scar on his cheek. "Very nearly permanently late."

He held the door open for her, slipping in right after. In the quiet of the car's interior, the actual content of his remark finally got through the weary relief spinning in her head, and she smiled. "Yes, much better coming down those stairs than going up—for all kinds of reasons." She blew out a quick breath. "I'm glad that's over."

"Well, mostly over," Ettinger told her, looking apologetic.

"Mostly over?" Merry asked, looking pitiful.

"We can't let you go quite yet," the agent explained. "There are a couple of follow-up questions Senator Cox's team wants to ask you tomorrow—the technical stuff that doesn't play well on the news. And we can't let you go back home without treating you to at least one six-star dinner."

"That's generous," Merry said ambivalently. She nodded outside, where the writhing mass of protesters became visible between a pair of buildings before vanishing again. "Are the restaurants still running, with all that going on?"

Ettinger glanced that direction and shrugged. "Oh, sure. That's the thing about Washington—the proles riot, the pols order another plate of caviar. The city and the government don't relate to each other. For years, Washington had the highest murder rate and worst educational system in the country. Could still, for all I know. And still the gears of government grind on." A flash of bitterness crossed his face. "Money can't buy happiness, but it can buy power—and power can buy security."

Merry looked out the tinted window, noting the general run-down air of the streets just outside the halls of power. The sight depressed her, especially compared to the order and care evident in Salt Lake City and Nauvoo. Shrugging off the dark mood that threatened to settle over her, she smiled. "Well, thank you much for providing me security—because I surely don't have the power to buy it."

"Senator Cox is the one with the power to pay for it." He shot her a quick smile. "But seriously, it's no problem. In fact, it's kind of nice to be with a doctor who's not poking stitches into me. You've been an easy mark to guard. I mean client."

"I should hope so." The ring of her phone interrupted Merry's playful remonstrance. Carmen had her number, and so did the team at Section 89, but no one else did. She told herself that just because the phone rang didn't automatically mean that Missy had broken her arm or something had gone direly wrong with the St. Paul serum. Maybe they were calling to tell her she looked cute on TV. That didn't sound plausible, but amusement at the thought did reduce her initial jag of anxiety. "Just a sec," she said, clicking it on and tucking the earpiece into place. "Merry here."

"Hey, Merry." The voice, low and hurried, sounded almost familiar. "Listen, I'm going to send you a data file. Are you alone?"

"Who is this?" Merry asked, looking at the phone's tiny screen. Figures scrolled across it—medical notes, formulae, dosage amounts. "What are you sending?"

"It's Errol Humphrey." The moment he said his name, recognition clicked into place.

"Humphrey!" she exclaimed. "How did you get this number?"

"I didn't," he said. "I called that lab outfit you work for, and they transferred me. Did you get the file?"

"Yes, I've got it, but I don't know what I've got," she answered, her mind spinning. Suspicion danced with total confusion. Why would Errol Humphrey, MedaGen's indentured servant, Chris's coworker, and her sometime boss, be calling her out of the blue, let alone sending her files?

"It's part of Twilley's work—part you haven't seen yet," Humphrey told her. It sounded like he was walking, city noises rushing through the background, his breathing slightly rough. "Merry, it's scary stuff. Too scary even for me. Listen, I'll admit it—I was the one who sent those pictures to Senator Cox, the ones that started the whole investigation. Since then, I've found out about something even worse."

"So send the rest to Senator Cox," Merry advised. "Quickly, before Zelik realizes you sent the first batch."

"That's the problem." Humphrey's voice sounded stressed. "I was too scared to turn whistle-blower right off, like you did. I thought the senator's investigation would take care of it without me having to come out, but they were too slick for me. And I think they've figured it out. I need help, Meredith. Serious help."

A faint shout came through the line, then the sound of rapid foot-steps. When Humphrey spoke again, his breath came harder and echoed slightly, as if he were in an alley. "They're after me. If I come in, if I tell Senator Cox what I know, can you arrange protection for me?"

"Humphrey, I—I don't know." Merry hesitated, looking up at Ettinger. Urgency, compassion, suspicion, and a strong sense of revul-sion played tug-of-war in her head.

The agent looked back, raising an eyebrow. "Am I going to have to take back my comment about you being an easy client to guard?"

"Come on—they're closing in!" Humphrey pleaded. "Can you come get me? Please? I'm just off Indiana."

"It's a man from MedaGen," Merry explained to Ettinger, muting the phone's audio pickup. "He says he's got more information about the project Twilley was working on—much more dire information. He also says that Zelik's security agents are after him. Can we pick him up?"

Ettinger hesitated, considering the options. "You know this guy?"

"I used to work with him." Merry shook her head. "He's a weasel, but he did help me escape, in a way. He certainly has no love for MedaGen—and he sounds frantic."

"They could be using him as bait, trying to lure you out into the open," the agent pointed out.

"To do what to me?" Merry asked. "Seriously. If MedaGen wanted to stop me from testifying, they would've tried something before I testified. Would they be stupid enough to try to hurt me just for revenge? Ms. Zelik may be that nasty, but she's not stupid. Look at what she did to Carmen—well, anyway, she punished my friend Carmen's family for helping me, but she did it through blackballing Carmen's husband, putting a lien on their house, turning their neighbors against them, that kind of thing. Wouldn't ambushing us look completely obvious?"

"It might." Ettinger frowned, not liking the taste of the situation.

Merry didn't either, but through the phone she could still hear Humphrey's rapid, frightened breathing and the random noises of footsteps and shouts around him. She repeated her arguments to herself, trying to diminish the weird feeling of warning that kept knocking the rational line of thinking off its tracks.

"Merry, please, are you still there?" Humphrey begged.

"Give it to me," Ettinger ordered. He took the phone Merry disentangled from herself, using the pickup himself. "This is Agent Ettinger, Dr. Galen's security detail. Where are you?" Nodding, he relayed the information to the driver, who took the car into a wide turn. "Keep moving. We'll come up alongside you and slow down. When the door opens, get in." He waited for Humphrey's hurried and grateful acknowledgment, then clicked off the phone. "Watch out for him, so you can point him out—he'll be on that side of the road."

"Right," Merry agreed. She leaned forward, scanning the sidewalks, but her hand drifted toward her purse. Obeying what felt like an exasperated impulse, she slipped the sparkling oval of the satellite-transceiver unit over her fingers. Before her fingers could find the tiny button to turn it on, however, she spotted Humphrey. The MedaGen manager walked swiftly along the uneven sidewalk, looking unshaven, worried, and rumpled. "There he is," she told Ettinger, pointing him out.

"The one in the black suit," Ettinger called to the driver. "Slow down. Pickup maneuver." He braced his hand against the door handle, and as the sedan pulled just in front of Humphrey, he popped the door open.

Merry slid swiftly back along the seat to make room—and, almost unconsciously, tucked the transceiver into the pocket of her blouse. Then she needed both hands to fend off Humphrey, who leapt into the backseat on a nearly horizontal trajectory.

"Go!" shouted Ettinger, and the driver obediently picked up speed, merging into traffic.

Humphrey sat up, giving Merry a smile. "Hmm, close quarters here. The last year's been good to you."

"You don't look so good," she shot back. "Now, what's the big emergency?"

"Well, about that," Humphrey began. His hand came out of his pocket holding something shiny.

Ettinger already had his gun halfway out of its holster, hampered by the tight fit of three adults in the backseat of the car, when a thin mist poured out of the lighter-sized container. The driver, glancing back, brought the car to a rolling stop, as the other bodyguard in the front seat reached back toward Humphrey through the thickening air. Merry recognized the effects of the mist as a combination of muscle relaxant and anesthetic before reality went hazy and swam away.

* * *

The long, gray shape swam through the water, cutting away just before its pointed snout hit the side of the tank. With a flick of its tail, the shark turned and flowed through the water of the huge tank, a curtain of brilliantly colored tropical fish parting to let it pass. Virginia looked from the tank to Johnny Mack standing at casual attention beside one of the marble pillars in the large foyer off of Augosto's study. The bodyguard's scale-patterned coat and tattoos echoed the colors of the smaller fish in the aquamarine water.

"Your boss ever feed anybody to those sharks?" she asked playfully.

Johnny Mack didn't bother to remove his eyes from the neckline of her plunging jacket. "No, those are just makos. They couldn't eat a human fast enough to keep the body from making a mess in the tank. We did throw a guy's kid in there once, though."

Virginia's eyes went wide, her skin paling under her perfect makeup. She shot a glance at Julian, but her assistant didn't meet her eyes or offer any reassurance. "A kid?"

Her reaction made Johnny Mack grin. "Well, not a kid. But the fool treated that Chihuahua like it was a baby or something. You should've seen him when the sharks fastened on that dog. Mr. Augosto didn't even have to say anything to get his point down. Dude never skimmed off the profits again."

"Ms. Diamante isn't interested in our business, Johnny." Augosto himself stood in the double doors across from his bodyguard, the wavering light from the aquarium reflecting off the silver-gray suit he wore.

Virginia thought it made him look like a shark himself, sleek, cool, and dangerous. She smiled and extended a glittering hand. "Mr. Augosto. Thank you so much for seeing me on such short notice."

He took her hand. True, he only shook it briefly, rather than kissing the back of it as she'd hoped he would, but it was a step forward. She put it down to her charm. He did it because the message she'd beamed to him en route had caught his attention, confirming his suspicion that she could provide valuable information.

"Come and tell me the details you promised in your message," he commanded, leading the way into the rich, leather-scented study.

"That was a long trip," she sighed, settling onto a chaise and stretching her elegant legs along the velvety fabric. Augosto would have to be dead not to look. He wasn't dead. He looked. "I don't suppose you have anything here to drink, do you?"

A faint, predatory smile crossed Augosto's face as he settled on the end of the chaise beside her feet. Reaching out to encircle one of her ankles with his hand, he examined her diamond-studded anklet, like she was a mannequin in a jeweler's display, and observed, "You haven't done anything to earn a drink yet. What did you come here thinking to get?"

"I came to give you something," she breathed.

To her disappointment, he let her ankle go and motioned with one hand. "So give."

"It's about MedaGen—Abbott and Zelik." Virginia sat up, foregoing the attempts at seduction for now, though not altogether—she did lean forward more than necessary. "And Secretary Garlick, and selling bioweapons."

Augosto's eyebrow rose. "So you said in your message. And you said you were the one who sent those interesting pictures to Senator Cox. Congratulations. You spawned a Senate investigation—one that caused me some effort to avoid inconvenience. Is that what you intended to give me? A headache?"

"No. I don't give people like you headaches," Virginia assured him, her mind sorting through the possibilities. "I just came to warn you that you might be getting a bigger headache soon. Abbott and Zelik are planning to buy their way out of the FDA investigation by selling you out to Senator Cox."

"What?" Augosto came to full attention, his eyes fastening on hers. Paranoia, suspicion, and the premonition of danger that had dogged him since Garlick's death bloomed in his mind.

"I went to MedaGen today to find my contact there, because I'd heard rumors that they were in deep trouble and looking for any way out," she explained. "What I heard was Zelik talking to Errol Humphrey, their marketing manager, about how they'd be staging a big PR push. He wanted to know what they would do about Senator Cox, and she said that they had the perfect bait to get the senator to give them a 'get out of jail free' pass, because Garlick told them all about you, and the business he was in with you. She even said they knew about your ambitions in California."

Virginia hid a smug smile as Augosto rose to his feet, jaw clenched. When the truth wouldn't get you where you wanted to go, invent a lie that would. And the critics said she couldn't act!

"When did you hear this?" he ground out. It fit perfectly—Abbott, the backstabbing poisoner, and his ice-queen lieutenant had always acted too comfortable around him, too smugly self-assured. They thought they had the advantage over him, thanks to that traitor Garlick's loose mouth!

"Last night—just before I hopped the jet here." She rose as well, catching his arm. Stroking the elegant cloth, and the arm underneath, she moved close enough to whisper, "I heard them making other plans too. They'll have a helicopter landing on the roof of their hotel tonight, for important company business. That'll tell them whether they need to sell you out to Senator Cox or not."

"Their hotel tonight," Augosto muttered, then shouted, "Johnny!"

"Yes, sir?" Johnny Mack appeared in the doorway.

"Find out what hotel Mr. Abbott and Ms. Zelik are staying at, and whether it has a helipad," Augosto instructed. "Call the D.C. branch of the office, and tell them to heat up a riot downtown to provide cover. Then get the boys together. We have a visit to pay to our friends from MedaGen tonight."

"Yes, sir." Johnny Mack's gold, canine grin sparkled in the soft light.

The glint from Virginia's jewelry caught Augosto's attention through his dark thoughts. "And have Luisa show Ms. Diamante to the guest room. No doubt you'll want to rest after your long flight."

"I would," Virginia agreed. She smiled playfully, tapping his chest with one finger. "But don't you dare even think of leaving without me. I want to be there when you show Abbott and Zelik the error of their ways, thinking they could sell you out to save their hides."

A spark of grim amusement lit in Augosto's eyes. Of course— they'd dropped her, hadn't they? The worst insult they could throw at a vain woman, telling her she was too old and unattractive to flaunt their merchandise. "So this is why you haven't told me what you want in return for the information. You just want to watch?"

The fire in Virginia's eyes matched the gleam in his. "That's right, Caesar. I want to watch."

"All right. We'll call you when we are ready." He nodded.

"I'm ready whenever you are," Virginia assured him, her vamp smile returning. "Just call and I'm there."

Augosto hid a grimace at the blatant proposition, simply nodding before he returned to his study to make a couple of calls to his contacts on the police force.

"Luisa will come get you," Johnny Mack told her. He leered. "You want to wait in my room?"

Virginia gave him a disdainful look. She didn't want the lackey; she wanted the lord. "You'll be busy." Another thought struck her. She looked around the foyer, but it was empty in the wavering light. "Where's Julian?"

"Ms. Diamante?" A woman in a sober, black dress appeared across the foyer and picked up Virginia's new suitcase. Julian had bought it, and the few necessities in it, at the airport shops. "This way, please."

Virginia followed the maid, leaving the bodyguard to do something useful, and mentally chastising Julian for leaving her alone like this.

Much to Virginia's surprise, however, her assistant hadn't returned by the time she woke from her nap. Luisa tapped on the door, informing her, "Mr. Augosto and the others are leaving in a half hour. He says you should be ready if you want to go." Luisa found herself drafted to assist an annoyed, petulant Virginia into her costume for the night's activities. Fortunately for the maid, the pop queen didn't demand that she accompany the hunting expedition to Washington.

Instead, Virginia gazed out the window of Augosto's limousine, mentally berating her assistant for such a petty display of selfish inconsideration. True, now that she had Augosto to play with, she wouldn't be bored. But what if she needed something done? *Julian, where are you?*

* * *

The phone rang on Senator Cox's desk, startling her. She looked at Ettinger to see if he'd finished.

The agent sat slumped in the guest chair beside the senator's desk, his shirt torn, new bruises covering the healing scars, Meredith Galen's purse on his lap. Ettinger had come running, limping slightly, but still moving at a respectable rate of speed, to her office just an hour before, to report that Errol Humphrey had kidnapped Meredith Galen. He'd told her the story, leaving out no extraneous detail: Humphrey must've taken a counteragent beforehand, he informed the senator. When he woke, he and the other two bodyguards had to fight their way through a wolf-pack gang that had come out to grab the car. He'd gotten that far—and far enough to apologize to Senator Cox—before the phone rang.

"It may be Humphrey, calling to give us ransom demands," Ettinger nodded, motioning that he'd come to the end of his report. "Or to tell me how stupid I was." So far, his illustrious career hadn't been all he hoped.

"Holly Cox," the senator said briskly.

"Hi, Holly," Julian's voice came over the connection from a borrowed phone in a telecom shop. Virginia had finally pushed her loyal assistant too far, and this time she was going to pay for it. "I'm glad I caught you. Can you see the picture I'm sending?"

Cox could, and it grabbed her attention. The first showed a tech working on a sleek, matte-finished plane in a hangar. A lab building, white against the jungle green, with camouflaged soldiers guarding it, appeared in the second. They were both part of the package she'd received from the anonymous source—but neither of these had been part of the set released to the press or the public. "Yes, I see them. Do you want to explain them?"

Writing on a piece of paper on her desk, she held up a sign to Ettinger. "Trace this!"

"I think you know the explanation," Julian said. "I'm one of the people who sent the originals to you. I'm sending these so you'll know I'm serious, because I have something else to tell you now."

"Something about MedaGen and General Garza?" Senator Cox asked, getting the okay signal from Ettinger, on another line with the communications security team.

"Oh, I think you already know that Twilley was working for General Garza under Abbott's orders; you just can't quite prove it," Julian said. "I think the more important part is that Errol Humphrey is going to kidnap Meredith Galen under Abbott's orders—if he hasn't done it already."

"What do you know about it? Where is she? Is she safe?" Cox asked.

"I only know that Ms. Zelik ordered him to do it and that a helicopter will come to their hotel sometime tonight to take her away to Bogotá. And that Mr. Caesar Augosto will probably show up there too." Julian looked out the window. No sign of pursuit yet, but this call had gone on too long already.

"Augosto? Why?" Cox blinked in surprise. Why would a New York–based crime boss be involved?

"Let's just say there are personal factors involved. Good luck, senator. I hope you can rescue Dr. Galen." Bitterness filled Julian's voice. "And when your agents pick up Virginia Diamante, tell them to tell her that she was right—it's all about her."

* * *

"Oh, Merry, didn't you see that coming?" Chris stroked her hair, shaking his head sadly. Light gleamed through the emerald and gold leaves that waved gently overhead, sending dappled light over his shoulders.

"Of course I didn't see that coming," Merry protested. "I was supposed to see that Humphrey was going to jump into the car and gas us all, like some kind of super spy? Real life isn't like that!"

"Well, maybe other people's real life," Chris gently pointed out. "Yours certainly has been lately."

"Well, maybe if you had stayed around to protect me from my own stupidity," she began, then remembered the nagging feeling of revulsion that hit her when he called. "Okay, sorry. I guess you tried. But why would he do that? I don't understand."

Partial understanding hit her as reality came flooding back with a stinging slap across her cheek. Groggy, Merry looked up through the haze to see the cold face of Ms. Zelik above her. "Wake up. How many fingers am I holding up?"

"Three," Merry answered automatically. She shook her head, breathing deeply against the lingering dizziness. "But more importantly, what do you think you're doing?" Looking around at the gray walls of what had to be a boiler room, she spotted Humphrey, sitting on the floor with his arms crossed over his knees. He met her glance and gave her an ironic little wave.

"I think I'm making an investment in my future," Zelik told her. She caught Merry's hair in a hard grip, looking into her eyes. "And paying off a personal debt. And I'm right on both counts."

The stare lasted a long moment, Merry refusing to blink as she met the other woman's reptilian glare. How could anything so cold walk around in a human skin? She felt a faint flutter of fear in her stomach, but it stayed faint; she felt much more angry, embarrassed, and strangely apologetic than scared. *Sorry, Chris,* she thought.

Zelik, disappointed at the lack of fright in Merry's face, let her go. "Sit up," she ordered coldly, standing above her captive.

Merry, surprised that she hadn't felt one of those sharp-toed shoes in her ribs yet, pushed herself upright. Realizing that her hands were free surprised her even more. She glanced at Zelik, folding her arms across her chest. "What, did you forget the handcuffs?"

"Oh, shut up!" Zelik snapped. "As if you pose any threat at all. You're hardly a martial-arts expert, Ms. Galen. Besides," a frozen smile flicked across her face, "handcuffs can cut off the circulation—and you're going to need those hands of yours where you're going." With that, she walked out of the small room, closing the door securely behind her.

"Which would be where?" Merry asked, looking at Humphrey.

"Why would I know?" He looked at his fingers, twisting the heavy gold class ring around, watching the gem glitter in the low light.

"Because you make sure you know everything." Walking over to stand in front of him, she put her hands on her hips and looked down at him. She resisted the urge to kick him. "And because you feel terrible about what you just did." A flash of real concern hit her. "What did you do? And what happened to Agent Ettinger and the others? Humphrey, tell me what's going on!"

He came to his feet, spreading his hands; she backed off several steps. "Okay, I'll tell you. Ettinger and the other two are probably waking up with headaches like you've got if they haven't already—because I couldn't stand to shoot them up with poison like I was supposed to. Maybe they won't wake up, if the wolf pack on the street where I left them takes a liking to their car. That better happen, because if Zelik finds out, she's going to use the poison on me instead, unless I can convince her not to. I'm still working on that one."

"But not killing them yourself is so much better," Merry said sarcastically, but feeling distinctly relieved that Humphrey's cold blood hadn't extended to outright murder. "So you knock us out and bring me here and Zelik gives me the cold shudders and then what?"

"And then they're going to helicopter you off to Bogotá to work for General Garza, because you're so smart he figures you can finish the job Twilley started."

"And he thinks I'd do something like that why?" Merry demanded.

"Oh, they'll think of something," Humphrey assured her. He began to pace, keeping away from her as much as possible in the tight space. "They always do. Maybe they'll threaten your daughter."

"She's safe in Nauvoo." The total confidence that suffused her on that score even surprised Merry.

"So they'll try something else. This is General Garza we're talking about, not just some biotech executive." Humphrey shrugged. "Maybe they'll try brainwashing—or threatening to use you as a guinea pig."

"They wouldn't do that, because they need me to experiment on the guinea pigs," Merry argued.

He threw his hands up, exasperated. "Don't tell me that! Tell them! It's not my problem."

"But it is your fault," Merry informed him. It wasn't fair, but she jabbed at the soft spot of guilt she thought she detected in his weasel armor.

"It is not my fault," Humphrey nearly shouted back.

She'd poked a soft spot, all right; before, he'd been able to carry out all his machinations and manipulations at least a step removed from their unpleasant consequences, let alone lethal ones. Contemplating kidnapping Dr. Galen and sending her to General Garza for a share in five million dollars sounded like a good plan in the abstract, but facing Merry in the dank boiler room of Abbott's hotel and having to answer her questions definitely bothered him. His conscience didn't bother him, as the poor thing had long ago expired of disuse; what he objected to was being put in a situation where he had to take responsibility for his actions, if only to himself and the person most directly affected by what he'd done. A person for whom he felt no particular malice was a lot harder to stab in the back than an enemy—especially when she kept standing there *looking* at him.

"Listen, Meredith." His voice took on a tone halfway between apologetic and wheedling. "You just don't know how tough it is to be in my situation. Those people—MedaGen, Abbott, Zelik—they literally own me. Oh, sure, slavery's illegal, but they still own me professionally. People complain all the time about being unemployed—I would love to be unemployed! And this was my big chance, my chance to get the cash I need to disappear, to make a new life for myself somewhere else, away from the people who've taken advantage of me all this time." His eyes darkened as he warmed to the subject of all the abuses the uncaring world had perpetrated on him. "Zelik caught me trying to pick up some more data to sell—I did sell those pictures that Senator

Cox had, I did make a difference there—and she threatened to kill me if I didn't help. What could I say? No? And I knew they weren't going to hurt you. This could even be your big chance, if you do a good job for Garza."

Merry just stared at him in amazement, listening to him not only absolve himself of wrongdoing and paint himself as a victim, but even convince himself that he'd done her a favor by helping Abbott and Zelik sell her to General Garza. Absolutely unbelievable—but as long as he was talking and pacing, he wasn't paying close attention to her. They'd taken her purse (no surprise), but they hadn't bothered to search her. As Zelik said, she wasn't exactly known for her tendency to carry weapons. Folding her arms tight across her chest, she felt for the hard ring of the transceiver, ran her fingertips along its curve, hoping she could make out the button through the pocket of her blouse. At last, her nail slipped into a shallow groove. She pressed the button, feeling it click into place. The hard concrete around her dampened the initial surge of triumph at getting the tiny unit turned on; the signal probably couldn't punch through that much interference. But they'd have to move her sometime, if Humphrey was right about the helicopter. Now, the battery better last long enough. She sent a quick, silent prayer through the concrete. Heaven had better receivers than even the Church did.

The door opened again, revealing Zelik and two beefy security guards. "Come on," she commanded. "Quickly." It was probably the first time MedaGen's COO had ever been an answer to a prayer.

* * *

"It's a sad statement about the state of affairs in the nation's capital that even a distinguished visitor can be the victim of a carjacking," Clara observed soberly. Behind her, images of Merry from the day's Senate hearings flashed, along with her printed description, last whereabouts, and invitation for anyone who knew her current whereabouts to please call the D.C. police with information. "This is just the latest in a long sequence of disturbing incidents that have raised questions about the breakdown of civil society."

The news report went on, analysis from social commentators speaking from the safety of their ivory towers alternating with complaints from the citizens who had to live and work in the streets that got crazier every day. Vivid footage of protests, riots, continued FEV outbreaks, and exclusive parties accompanied it all, with the inevitable ads hawking everything from the latest street fashions to the drugs that would let anybody escape from it all.

Ettinger found the musical chime pulsing through his comm unit much more interesting. "We've got a signal!" he exclaimed, passing the word along. "Downtown—Imperial Hotel."

* * *

Hotel service areas all looked the same, Merry decided, following Zelik through the back-corridor labyrinths. Peeling paint, scuffed tile, threadbare carpet, and battered freight elevators seemed to be the standard, no matter how fancy the guests' areas. She assumed this hotel would be upscale indeed, both because the floor numbers on the elevator went to thirty, and because Abbott had the reputation of a dedicated luxury hound. MedaGen's elegant CEO would look as completely out of place in these surroundings as his ice-cold COO did at the moment. As the scratched and dented elevator door opened, revealing a weary maid pushing an overloaded laundry cart, Merry considered making a break for it, asking the maid for help, even screaming that they were kidnapping her.

Zelik must have thought she was capable of such a move, because she stepped back, between Merry and the laundry cart, shooting a warning look at her captive.

Humphrey took Merry's arm, leaning over to whisper, "Don't try anything. You don't want to find out what she'll do if she gets angry."

Merry shrugged off his hand, irritated at his weasel behavior. She stared at the numbers as they climbed, her mind spinning through possibilities. Did she want to start a fight? She was in better shape now than she had been the last time MedaGen's goons had chased her through Channel 8's San Diego office, thanks to her daily jog around Section 89's grounds—but she'd known where to run then. Dang— time to add karate lessons to her schedule. The thought brought a wry half-smile to her face. Who would've believed that she'd still need karate lessons in the well and truly last days? Christ had come to His temple, for crying out loud; Zion was established! And here she was, in some hotel in Washington, getting hijacked off to Bogotá to straighten out a madman's bioweapons program. It felt unreal, so silly that she had a hard time believing it was happening. The set of Zelik's shoulders and the cold triumph on her hard face, however, told Merry that she, at least, wasn't kidding.

Humphrey just steadily avoided Merry's gaze, doing as little as he could for either of them.

Please, Heavenly Father, tell me what to do to get away, she thought—almost demanded. Modifying her mental tone, she added, *Or at least help somebody else help me. And please let Missy know I love her, just in case you have other plans for me.* As hard as she listened, nothing came but the smooth hiss of the lift and the chime as it passed floor after floor. She couldn't even tell if the transceiver next to her heart was working.

The doors opened, revealing the immaculately dressed form of Mr. Abbott. His famous smile spread across his face as he looked Merry up and down. "Well, Dr. Galen! This is an honor. Ready for your trip to greater things?"

Merry looked beyond him to where a set of metal stairs ascended toward the roof. "Actually, no," she heard herself say. "I understand it's a helicopter ride. I'm afraid I get airsick, so I'd better not go."

Abbott, Zelik, and Humphrey all stared at her. For an instant, she stared at herself too, seeing the scene from outside, as if it were a dream. Then Abbott laughed.

"Airsick! They say you're a brilliant researcher, Dr. Galen. They didn't say you were a comedian as well." He motioned toward the stairs. "Go with Ms. Zelik, and don't worry about airsickness. I'm sure we can secure some motion-sickness pills for you—or even a complete tranquilizer, if you make that necessary. We are officers for the world's leading bioceutical firm, after all. Mr. Humphrey, if you would?"

This time, Zelik caught Merry's arm, propelling her up the stairs, as Humphrey reluctantly led the way. They emerged onto the roof, under bright spotlights below a cloud-heavy sky. Waist-high safety railings ran around the edge of the roof, and a boxy formation of vents and air-conditioning towers rose on the far side of the landing pad, a mass of silver and shadows. The large, black, insectoid shape of the helicopter squatted in the center of the harshly lit expanse, its pilot waiting beside the door. A rumbling hum from its warmed and ready engine came through the stiff breeze. Black-uniformed MedaGen security guards stood at attention on the four points of the compass around it, eyeing Merry with deep suspicion.

Abbott brought up the rear, still chortling—not so much at Merry's unexpected answer as out of pleasure at a plan coming off perfectly. Law enforcement thought Dr. Galen was dead or at least missing, General Garza would deliver the entire five million dollars once they sent him proof that she was safely on her way to Bogotá, and Mr. Frieze assured him that MedaGen would beat any rap connected with the FDA investigation. Add the FEV antibiotic to the mix, and this week's work saved his job and put a nice pile of feathers in his personal financial mattress. Maybe it would even lighten Zelik's mood enough that he could finally locate a chink in her ice armor.

Abbott's smile instantly changed to a frown, then to a snarl, as they all heard the frantic message crackling over the security guards' radios: "Intruders! We've got intruders in the hotel! They're coming up—"

The broadcast went dead at the same time that the firecracker noise of distant gunshots rose from the street. Augosto's men, positioned outside the hotel, started their boss's riot, throwing Molotov cocktails, smoke grenades, and flash bombs on the street in front of the massive building. Outside the diversion, the strike team ran into the hotel's back entrance, easily blasting their way through the locks and securing the elevators and stairs. They burst out of the elevator just then, raking the roof with gunfire.

To Merry, the sudden explosion of noise only increased the nightmarelike atmosphere. She watched as the security guard at the top of the stairs jerked and fell backward, landing hard on the rough surface of the landing pad. "Get to the copter," Zelik shouted at her, pushing her hard toward the middle of the roof. Both women began to run, Humphrey outdistancing them as Abbott brought up the rear, shouting for the pilot to open the other doors.

The intruders smashed through MedaGen's security squad; though Zelik's men were tough and well trained for securing office buildings and transporting unwilling lab rats, they proved no match for the professional mobsters who came up the stairs with all guns blazing. Two of Augosto's soldiers went down as the security team returned fire, but within seconds, six bodies lay sprawled like black shadows in the stark light. A bullet whined over Zelik's head as she reached for the door of the helicopter, leaving an ugly mark on the metal finish. Merry ducked, looking back toward the roof-access hatch. A dozen gun-toting, suited men spread out from the door in a half circle.

"Raise your hands high and back away from the chopper, or we'll shoot you where you stand." Augosto appeared at the top of the stairs, as sleek and calm as ever as he shouted the order. "Walk over to the railing there."

"Move!" Johnny Mack shouted.

Behind Augosto, the brilliant spotlights glittered from the diamonds Virginia wore as she emerged from the depths of the stairwell and picked her way gingerly around the dead MedaGen guards. Gaining clean ground, she smiled, watching as her enemies obediently backed away from the black machine. This would teach them to fire her!

Abbott tried his confident smile, trying to look casual as he leaned against the indicated railing and watched the man walk toward him. "Augosto! What are you doing? There's no need for all this."

"Isn't there?" the Mob boss asked, stopping a few paces away from Abbott. Hate gleamed in his eyes. "I should just let you sell me to Senator Cox? Spend time in a federal lockup so you can save your precious company?"

"What?" Abbott stared at him. Had the man gone completely mad?

Virginia walked around Augosto, trailing one hand over his sleeve, to confront the two MedaGen officers. "That's right. Try to deny it. Caesar's too smart for you. He figured out that you were going to throw him to the wolves so nobody would find out about you sending Twilley to help Garza."

The wind whipped Zelik's hair out of its tidy arrangement, waving strands of it around her face. The lashing tendrils accentuated the disgust and derision in her expression as she growled, "You mean you told him that. You set him up to hit us. You cheap, lying, *ugly* tramp!"

With a shriek, Virginia lunged forward and, for the second time in her life, slapped Zelik across the face.

This time, however, Zelik didn't just promise retribution. She caught Virginia's bangle-bedecked arm in one hand, the other clawing deeply into the other woman's piled, braided hair. Pulling Virginia close, she hissed, "I have hated you and your kind since I could walk. And you just turned from asset to liability." Then, with all the malice that created the frozen acid in her blood, she wrenched around and threw Virginia from the roof.

Merry cried out and lurched toward the rail and the falling woman, but Humphrey blocked her hard, sending them both sprawling to the ground.

The others rushed the rail, watching the flailing body fall, the building lights still striking glints of pale fire from her jewels. She landed at terminal velocity, with a dull thud and an impact that collapsed the hardened cover of one of the huge rubbish bins at the back of the hotel.

Abbott turned to look at Zelik, his face pale. "That was completely unnecessary."

"But deeply satisfying." She returned his look and turned her sub-zero eyes on Augosto.

The Mob boss raised his gun, covering the poisoner and his psycho-pathic harpy. He hadn't cared for Virginia and could easily give the order to eliminate her if she became inconvenient, but Zelik's conscience-less murder rattled him. "What are—" He didn't finish the question.

"Freeze! FBI!" a voice bellowed. Agents and police swarmed onto the roof, out of the access stairway and from the huge stacks of climate-control machines.

No one did. Augosto's men instantly spread out, seeking cover or throwing themselves to the ground, firing as they did so. Zelik grabbed for Merry, but her erstwhile prisoner was already crawling for the thin shelter of a bank of roof-mounted lights.

"Leave her!" Abbott shouted. "We're blown!"

Throwing caution to the winds—he'd rather get shot than arrested—he sprinted toward the helicopter. Zelik snarled and ran after him. They threw themselves into the open door even as the helicopter began to rise, the pilot having used the momentary distraction with Virginia to get himself into his machine and his machine ready to go. The helicopter heaved skyward, its engines thudding heavily, the roar of the wind through its rotors momentarily drowning the noise of the firefight. A few bullets pursued them, but the mobsters and FBI saved most of their fire for each other. Abbott and Zelik shared a quick look of relief at their escape as the hot, white top of the hotel fell behind them, despite the buffeting as the wind hit the helicopter.

Merry ducked behind the bank of lights, praying wordlessly for reassurance more than anything concrete. She felt a hard tug on her sleeve, saw the hole the bullet left, then turned her head away from the blast of wind the chopper left behind. Humphrey cowered next to her, not praying but carrying on a running commentary on the treachery of Abbott and Zelik for leaving him.

"Would you rather go with them?" Merry shouted at him.

"I'd rather be with them than shot!" he yelled back.

"Hold still and show me your hands," commanded another voice. Another shot rang out, followed by the sound of another body hitting the hard roof, and then silence descended under the noise of the wind.

Merry looked up, taking her arms away from her head, to see Agent Ettinger. Recognizing her, he lowered his gun. "Dr. Galen! Are you all right?"

"Yes," she whispered, then swallowed hard and repeated more loudly, "Yes. Yes, I'm all right." She took the hand he offered and stood, brushing uselessly at her skirt.

The agent's smile faded as Humphrey rose—Ettinger's pistol did as well. "Mr. Humphrey."

Humphrey smiled apologetically. "Hello. Again." He spread his hands innocently. "No tricks up my sleeve this time. I'm sorry about that." Looking at the other two law-enforcement types who came up behind Ettinger, one with handcuffs ready, he hastened to explain, "But listen, I didn't have any choice. I didn't want to do it, but I had to follow orders. You can't arrest me for following orders. Check my records—I'm only property."

"Well, Errol, consider yourself confiscated." Ettinger nodded to the agent with the handcuffs.

"Dr. Galen—Meredith," Humphrey pleaded, as the man cuffed him, "you've got to help me here!"

"I can't help you out of this," Merry told him, feeling as much exasperation at him as pity for his utter lack of spine. "You should've come with us when you pretended you wanted to. You told Chris you'd jump the fence anytime the advantage looked better on the other side—it looks like your fence jumping landed you behind bars."

"Oh, very funny," Humphrey snarled. Once again, the world conspired to mess him up. "God's out to get me," he complained to the stone-faced agent who hauled him away. As if in agreement, lightning flashed in the distance. The basso rumble of thunder rolled under the noise of the wind.

Around the roof, the FBI squad cuffed the survivors. Blood covered Johnny Mack's gaudy tattoos and Augosto's silver-gray suit. Neither of them earned handcuffs; they got body bags instead. Smokey sobbed heavily, muttering Hail Marys for his boss's soul.

"What say we get you out of here?" Ettinger suggested to Merry, gesturing toward the back stairwell. "You're a popular girl; I'd like to leave before any of your other old acquaintances come calling."

"Calling!" Merry exclaimed, stopping on the steps. "Does anyone know what happened? Do they know I was gone—or that I'm all right now?"

Ettinger gently urged her on and handed her his phone. "Everybody knows you were gone, but the official story is that it was a carjacking. We didn't want to put the wind up on Abbott and Zelik. Go ahead. You've got a worried friend to reassure. And Senator Cox promised to tell a Dr. Nabil as soon as we had you back too."

He half listened to the conversation as he led her down the long stairwell—the evidence guys had the elevator taped off already—from the roof utilities and then into the guests' elevator. They emerged into the lobby as she finished, clicking the phone shut and handing it back to him.

"Well, did you reassure your friend that everything was all right? It sounded more like she was reassuring you," he observed.

"Oh, yes—Carmen told me that the minute they saw the news reports, they all started praying for me, and that they knew I'd be just fine. Even Missy—my daughter—told me that she knew the bad guys couldn't get me." Merry laughed, a little shakily. "Well, not permanently, anyway."

"I never knew doctors had such exciting lives," Ettinger said. "I may have to try that if the whole FBI thing doesn't work out."

"I think it's working out well," Merry assured him. She smiled, offering her hand. "Thank you for the miraculous rescue, Agent Ettinger."

He took her hand, shaking it solemnly. "All in a day's work, ma'am. Now, let's get you back to Senator Cox's office, with no unscheduled stops this time."

"Actually, Elder Nabil—Dr. Nabil—told me that he already had the wheels moving to get me back home. He'll let Senator Cox know that he's arranged secure transportation back to the airport for me," Merry told him.

"Really?" Ettinger looked around at the debris-strewn street, listening to the noises of the D.C. police battling off the protest riot that had so conveniently sprung up in front of the hotel. The unexpected gleam and brightly lit windows of a city bus caught his eye. He stared, his next question forgotten.

The silver behemoth drove up to the loading area of the hotel and stopped in front of them. Its doors opened with a hiss. Mia Valados appeared on the steps, smiling broadly. "Well, Meredith Galen! You've had some adventures, young lady!" She dismounted and gave Merry an enthusiastic hug. "It's good to see you again." Turning to the FBI agent beside her new passenger, she gave him a grandmotherly peck on the cheek and said, "We'll take over from here, thank you, young man."

Ettinger opened his mouth to protest, then shut it again. "All right. Great. You have a good trip. Call me and tell me when you get home safe."

Merry, pausing on the steps of the bus to look at him, asked, "Would you like to come?"

The words hit a chord in him, a chime that resonated with something much deeper than the mere offer of a ride. He felt a strange tug, but duty pulled in a different direction. He shook his head. "No—but thanks. I'd better get back to Senator Cox." An odd feeling of warmth replaced the momentary indecision.

Sister Valados smiled at him. "If you follow where Senator Cox leads, you'll be just fine."

He watched the bus doors close and the silver vehicle with its blue "Zion" destination panel disappear, then headed for the front of the building, flicking out his phone. "Senator? Ettinger. She's on her way. On a city bus." Thunder rumbled in the distance, as the storm moved closer.

* * *

The thudding rumble of helicopter blades rose to a roar as the sleek, black machine came in for a landing on the airfield outside of Garza's Bogotá headquarters. The moment its runners touched down, the door opened and two rumpled, harried-looking figures got out.

Garza, waiting at the edge of the strip, tilted his head to one side, then looked over his sunglasses. A slight frown crossed his face as the man and woman ducked under the rotating blades and ran through the localized windstorm toward the General.

"Well, Mr. Brindermann, what have we here?" he asked, moving forward to meet them.

"It appears we have Mr. Abbott and Ms. Zelik of MedaGen," Brindermann said, absolutely deadpan.

"And it appears that we do not have Dr. Galen," Garza added.

"No, sir," Brindermann agreed.

"We had to leave, or get arrested by the FBI. Not a tenable position!" Abbott snapped, stabbing a finger at Zelik to emphasize his point.

"So now we're fugitives, in Bogotá, of all the uncivilized pestholes!" Zelik snarled back. "We ran, so we look guilty. We should've stayed, blamed the whole thing on Humphrey."

They stopped in front of the two military men. Abbott extended a hand. "General. What an honor to meet you in person."

The General did not bow back—nor take the proffered hand. His own hand dropped to his side, his fingers playing with the butt of his pistol. "Where is Dr. Galen?"

"We ran into a small problem," Abbott began.

"We had her in custody, when a mobster and the FBI staged a firefight right before we put her into the helicopter," Zelik said flatly. "Too bad you melted Twilley's brain—he may have been the best bet for finishing the project."

"Oh, I wouldn't go that far," Abbott protested.

A bullet between the eyes ended his explanation. Another caught Zelik through the temple as she whirled to escape. Both bodies hit the ground, raising dust clouds from the airfield.

Garza reholstered his weapon. "So, it appears we will not have Dr. Galen to complete the Pacifica project," he observed, walking back toward his command tent.

Brindermann fell into step beside him. Neither man looked back as sentries dragged the former rulers of MedaGen off through the dust.

"Johann," Garza announced, throwing open the entrance to his command center and striding through, "I am weary of waiting for the stars to align in that perfect order you lust after."

He gestured at the glowing electronic map in the center of the room. South and Central America glowed soft green. Crimson flared from Mexico, golden spots dotting paths up the coasts, then inward toward the black hole that marked the ruined moonscape of Mexico City. Shining green shapes showed the forward deployment of the thousands of troops who had moved north at Garza's orders, waiting to sweep into Mexico when their general sent the word.

Garza's fingertips tapped the forward positions on the battle plan, the golden spots marking the primary weapons targets. "Watch carefully, Johann. Now we test the rest of the heavy weapons, wiping out the cartels' strongholds like gods throwing thunderbolts. Then I send the order to charge, and we loose all of those troops of thugs, drug runners, outlaws, and rebels massing under your nursery-room discipline to overrun and overwhelm what resistance remains."

"I will issue the mobilization order now." Brindermann knew when to fasten his seat belt, hold on for the ride—and make sure a backup plan was in place.

"Mobilize the pharmaceutical factories as well," Garza ordered.

"Why?" Brindermann paused at the door.

"To formulate several hundred thousand doses of the virus we used to ensure the loyalty of the late, lamented Slick," Garza told him. "Since we cannot obtain Dr. Galen's services, we will unleash the disease we already have. The management medicines will keep the troops healthy long enough."

"And then they will die," Brindermann pointed out.

Garza shrugged. "They will last long enough to wipe out any resistance that remains in North America after our thunderbolts strike, and that is all they need to do. We will have other troops for the next phase of conquest. You have made progress on that front, I trust."

"Some," Brindermann said. "I will report when negotiations are more concrete."

"What a pair we make, eh, Johann?" Garza smiled. "Each with his secrets. I am sure you will. And I will eventually tell you of my own success in preparing the Old World for its first invasion from the New."

Within minutes, his junior lieutenants scattered to bring the entire spread of tactical weapons online, targeted on Mexico, then the United States, then Europe. On Brindermann's order, the entire bureaucracy converted with astonishing speed from gathering men and matériel to shipping them northward. As they left, an invisible but no less powerful web of commands rippled through the computerized heart of Garza's mechanized force. The men were necessary, but primarily as mop-up scavengers and cannon fodder; the General's real trust lay in the cold electronics and explosives of his begged, borrowed, and stolen high-technology weapons.

CHAPTER 18

"Whoa." Mercury stared at his screen as the previously serene tactical area of the invaders' network lit up like a fireworks display. Commands raced back and forth from node to node, carrying instructions for men and machines alike. He tapped into the streams of urgent messages, bringing up a deployment order here, a sequence of activation codes there. Maps flashed, satellite telemetry glowed, columns of vital statistics scrolled. He'd not only finally found the way to worm deeper into the secure communications streams in the tactical area, he now had access to more activity than he ever expected.

Gaining that vital initial access had proved comically easy. Ironically, the Santiago team, as the most competent team farthest removed from Bogotá or the U.S., had received the order to help debug the communications network to eliminate the CIA spies that the system's watchdogs had detected when Mercury didn't get out of the way quite fast enough. The code rats had struggled to stifle their laughter when the recently elevated General Archuleta appeared to inform them, with many portentous pauses and self-important glares, that the debugging operation would prove their loyalty to the General and the USSA. Señor Colón had kept a straight face as he saluted and assured Archuleta that it would indeed.

Raul, the same data streams reflecting in his eyes, looked up at Mercury over the top of the monitors they'd used to run diagnostics on the system. "What's going on?"

"They're moving," Mercury whispered. "Looks like the General's ready for the next big push."

Previously closed and locked files came online, opening data-transfer channels from the central computers to a series of addresses that made no sense—until the satellite telemetry pictures caught Mercury's eye and reminded him of the illicit news reports coming in from the Church's network, as well as the corporate-controlled feed from Channel 8. These codes had to be the control numbers that activated the drones Garlick "loaned" to Garza, the keys that aimed and armed their bombs, the instructions that let them "think" for themselves as they flew without direct human guidance.

"What do we do?" Raul stared at the screen, watching Brindermann order the warehouses to ready their stocks of supplies, ammunition, and arms for rapid transit to the impending front line in Mexico. "Stop them?"

"No." Both boys started as Señor Colón walked up behind them. He looked at the screens, sadness crossing his face. "Elder Molina told us to watch and pray, gather intelligence but not interfere. Look," he indicated the crisscrossing communication paths, "every order is digitally signed and countersigned. If we interfere, we will succeed only in telling them that we can see what they say."

"But they're going to invade Mexico!" Raul objected.

"As they did Peru, Ecuador, Argentina—and Chile," Señor Colón reminded him. "We have infiltrated their networks, factories, transports, and now we watch and wait until God sends us the order to strike."

"As young lions among the flocks, that tear evildoers in pieces and none can defeat or escape," Mercury muttered, paraphrasing one of Dove's favorite scriptures.

Señor Colón patted his shoulder, a warning as the perennially bored military watchdog assigned to keep tabs on the network engineers sauntered through the door. The senior tech moved off to assure their nominal superior that he could tell Señor Serrey that the debugging was proceeding apace.

Mercury glanced back, stifled a completely fake yawn, and slipped a disc into his console. Using the debugging account, generously enhanced with several layers of privileges he'd added himself, he slid into the system hiding the secrets of the drone ships and their companion bombs. It lay beside the electronic strongboxes he'd already plundered for the digital keys to the Keepsakes Ltd. weapons caskets, storing its vital information in a tidy database. One looked as if someone had modified it, he noticed, looking at the file logs and profiles.

Whoever the Net watchdogs were, they'd had a go at altering the drone ships' original programming as well. Fine—he'd get their modifications as well as the originals. The codes streamed through the ether and dropped, like rows of tiny black or white diamonds, onto the surface of the disc waiting for them.

He watched the progress of the copy with one eye out for the lieutenant who, in the tradition of jocks everywhere, liked to show his supposed superiority over geeks by various juvenile and obnoxious means. Mercury tried to puzzle out what the modifications might have been. The name "Zamora" crackling over the wide-open flow of communications brought him to attention. Something about having found Zamora?

Tuning in to a tight-band comm channel, he heard a man's voice. Even through the faint hum of the powered amplifier that threw the voice to the satellites and back, he could hear the triumph in it. "Rebel base camp located, empty outside of three sentries. Strike force arrival time fifteen minutes. Rebel column arrival time twenty minutes. Say goodbye to Major Zamora, General."

"We'll celebrate when you finish the kill." With a start, Mercury recognized the voice of the General himself. "Don't disappoint us."

"I won't." And that one had to be El Jaguar. Did they think they had found the rebels' base camp? Abandoning the rest of the information flow, he zeroed in on the bright line that led from the satellite to the high slopes of the Andes. What he saw sent a chill through his gut. The coordinates for El Jaguar's transmission almost perfectly matched the coordinates he'd used to send the last transmission on weapons shipments to his father.

But how had they managed to track Zamora back to his hiding place? The soft chime of the computer telling him it had finished downloading the files hit his ears like a fire-alarm bell. Cursing himself for being an idiot, he pulled the debugging files on his CIA alter-ego. If he could surf the sealed communications channels of the tactical system, why couldn't someone else? Even if they couldn't get into the armored thread that contained the actual transmission, thanks to the Church's unbeatable encryption, they could track it. A discreetly named log file gleamed from the screen, tucked away inside the same debugging program he was using. Sure enough, the watchdogs had set their own tiny spider to watch the spaghetti branches, patiently tracing each connection, eliminating the calls that went to known destinations, isolating the ones that seemed to go off on tangents to unknown and unauthorized destinations. The spider had finally found the four unauthorized satellite-channel connections Mercury had opened along the communications backbone of Garza's computer system. And one of those connections led, with some extrapolation and number crunching, to Zamora's base camp deep in the mountain forests.

He'd led El Jaguar straight to his father, Captain Guerra, Señor Olivares—the entire "rebel" movement that provided cover for the more subtle Mormon infiltration. Another soft chime told him that another entity had entered the same Net space he virtually occupied. The watchdogs had put a bell on their spider, to tell them when someone else discovered it. He was well and truly blown. For a split second, he froze, staring at the monitor, picking up the visual feed from El Jaguar's shoulder-mounted camera, turned on for the General's benefit. No, he couldn't stop Garza's gathering invasion, and he couldn't stop the watchdogs from realizing that the CIA agent's account came from the Santiago node, but he could stop El Jaguar from ambushing his father.

"Raul," Mercury said, "we're blown. They found our outside line."

"Señor Colón?" Raul asked, already extracting his virtual presence from the network, clicking off the safeguarding self-destructs they'd installed just in case. One by one, the accounts they'd jerry-rigged into the system closed and deleted themselves. He rose, stretching casually, waiting for the answer.

"Tell him—scapegoat time," Mercury whispered. With those code words Señor Colón would "discover" the off-code shenanigans of the code monkeys supposedly set to watch him and his fellow Mormon techs to prevent sabotage; the files they'd prepared showed that the monkeys had used the General's network to funnel low-level secrets to the CIA, arrange drug transfers, and skim money off the top of Brindermann's tightly wound civilian bureaucracy. He would try to wait long enough to give the boys a head start to escape out to the temple community—where, supposedly, no one would look for a bunch of non-Mormon cyber criminals. Especially non-Mormon cyber criminals who'd used Serrey's personal credit account to book a charter boat for friendlier climes.

His fingers flying, Mercury changed accounts, slipping out of the debugging mask the watchdogs were closing in on, putting on another persona—the elusive CIA agent. At the same time, he pulled open another communication channel, blasting open a direct feed to Zamora across the network's powerful transmitters. "You've got company," he spelled out, foregoing the less secure voice stream for encrypted text. "El Jaguar. Fifteen—now thirteen minutes ETA. Ambush at base camp."

From deep in the green maze of the forest, an answer streamed back: "They won't get us, but send any details."

* * *

Zamora raised his hand, bringing the line of rebels to a halt on the undergrowth-choked game trail. The men moved together, clustering and dropping to their haunches, waiting for orders. "We've got a cat waiting for us at home," Zamora said. "Planning an ambush."

"Like we did way back when. They got away from us that time." Guerra's grin resembled a jaguar's.

So did Zamora's. "Not this time." He watched the shorthand descriptions appear on the tiny screen he held, as Mercury relayed the information from El Jaguar's video feed. The main force, approximately twenty soldiers, waited on the northeast side of the camp, ready to charge when the rebels sprang their trap, while El Jaguar and his men ghosted through the empty installation to hide inside each tent. Zamora blinked, concerned, when the transmission cut off in midsentence. It resumed again, but under a different sender's name.

Zamora didn't share his son's hacker tendencies, but he knew enough to know what that meant. "Get out of there *now*," he ordered through the link.

"In a minute," Mercury fired back. "El Jaguar inside command tent. Blow-by-blow coming."

Zamora sent an exasperated prayer heavenward for his stubborn son—and for the rebel troop about to face the forces that had pursued them through the mountain passes in a series of running battles that had inflicted more frustration than casualties. The war was about to go from shooting at figures at a distance to close-quarters combat. A tight, ringing feeling shot through his nerves, fear and eagerness fused into an electric thrill.

"God be with us," he said. "Guide our hands to do Thy will and help Thee preserve Thy people."

"Amen," the rebels responded, a few adding their own prayers, a couple crossing themselves.

They rose, falling into the stealthy marching order they'd drilled on for so many raids on Garza's sentry posts, and melted into the green and brown of the trees around them. On the ridge that hid the rebels' bolt-hole from spying eyes, the troop split in two; the smaller group headed down toward the seemingly deserted camp, while the larger slipped through the undergrowth along the game trail that led away from the tents. Zamora paused just long enough to reconfirm with Mercury that El Jaguar's troops hadn't moved, then signaled just once, pointing toward their base.

With a roar, the smaller force erupted out of the jungle, riddling the tents with bullets. Tent walls torn to rags fluttered like leaves into the air; two tents burst into flames as the rebels threw incendiary grenades into them. Answering shouts, surprised and fearful rather than bloodcurdling, came from inside the cloth structures, and El Jaguar's men scrambled free of the hiding places that had transformed into blinding barriers. El Jaguar himself, emerging from the flaming ruins of Zamora's own quarters, caught sight of the rebel major and bared his teeth in a snarl. When he realized he faced a mere handful of rebels, his face lit with fury and bloodlust. He shouted an order to his men, collecting them and driving them toward Zamora's rebels.

"Reserves coming in," Mercury warned Zamora, switching to voice—and another user account. He was running out of keys into the communications system, as the watchdogs savaged one after the other and Raul's track-hiding program deleted the rest. Seeing the walls closing in, he sent one last message: "I love you." The channel slammed closed.

"I love you," Zamora said, blasting a series of shots at the snarling commando chief bearing down on him. The man in front of him represented everything Zamora had to save his son from, all the darkness and terror and cruelty in a Godless world.

As Mercury had warned, the troops hiding outside the camp came charging in, driving Zamora's smaller group before them. The major turned and ran a few steps, stopping to shoot back along the game trail. El Jaguar ducked behind the thick trunk of a hardwood tree, whirling away from cover to blast away at Zamora—who had already taken to his heels again, racing down the curving game trail, bringing up the rear. Heavy undergrowth on either side channeled the men into an emerald and ebony tunnel, leading deeper into the ravine. At last, the trail bottomed out in a dead-end canyon, a waterfall sprinkling over the far edge to fill a pool at the bottom of the cut.

The rebels climbed into the rocks around the tiny box canyon, but Zamora himself was still on the wrong side of the pool as El Jaguar leapt into the opening. His men spread out behind him, forming a half circle facing the back of the canyon and their trapped prey. With a triumphant roar, the General's chief raised his gun, leveling it at the major who had humiliated him so many times, and pulled the trigger.

Zamora's pistol ripped out of his hand as a bullet hit it, then he fell backward himself into the water.

El Jaguar raised his arms and shouted a triumphant curse at the sky, at his enemy, and at their god. He jerked forward, half turning, blood spraying from his shoulder—and saw Captain Guerra in the ravine's mouth, already realigning for a second shot.

Above, all along the canyon's rim, the rest of the rebels appeared, shooting down into the open bowl below. Their comrades emerged from their hiding places in the rocks on the other side of the pool and added another layer to the deadly web of crossfire.

The guerilla chief whirled in a circle, spraying the walls with gunfire, stumbling backward as his men fell around him. His boots hit the water, the smooth rocks in the pool—and a hand, which wrapped around his ankle and pulled. With a titanic splash, El Jaguar fell into the pool, grappling with a shadowy shape who caught his gun hand and wrenched at the weapon. Lead drove into the water all around them, the hot ripples of the bullets' passing barely registering as El Jaguar and Zamora thrashed in the depths. Lurching toward the shore, Zamora half dragged the guerilla out of the water, then tripped as El Jaguar kicked his legs out from under him. His lungs burning, Zamora punched his enemy's wounded shoulder, once, twice, feeling the man's hand spasm and lose its grip on the pistol. Pulling the weapon free, he shot through the dark water, pulling the trigger until the clip emptied. Darker shadows flowed up around him, a dead weight attached to the gripping hands dragging him down; even in death, El Jaguar would not let him go.

Panic threatened to choke him; he caught a half mouthful of water. The flat-iron taste of the blood in it, coming through the salt and bile, brought a vivid, if disjointed, memory of the words "this is my blood." Calm spread through him, and he stopped struggling, utterly still. The dead hands loosened and fell away; he floated gently upward toward the rippling light.

"Major!" Guerra caught him, yanking him out of the water, slamming him with more force than intent against the hard rocks of the pond's bank. "Zamora! Breathe!"

Zamora coughed, batting away the man's hands, and rolled to his side, coughing again.

"Are you all right, sir?" the captain asked, catching his shoulder.

"I'm getting there," Zamora finally said. The lack of gunfire finally penetrated the whirl in his head. He looked up, seeing his men walking around the box canyon, gathering weapons and bodies into two separate piles. One more body floated facedown in the pond, surrounded by a dissipating cloud of crimson. A slow smile crossed his face, despite the pain in his lungs—and his hip, where El Jaguar's bullet scored his bone. "Yes, I think I'm all right. Thank God." Struggling to his knees, with Guerra's help, he watched as his men fell to their knees as well. For a few minutes, silence reigned in the canyon, the sparkle of light off water the only movement.

* * *

"Order for all stop, quick quiet!" Flame-haired Medea relayed the command to her watchdogs as the Net spiders sent the message that they'd finally isolated the last user sending unauthorized files over the secure communications network. All three Net rangers in Bogotá set their own cascading safeguards in motion.

In Santiago's data center, the cascade of images, files, codes, statistics, and text, glowing like a preternaturally orderly swarm of fireflies in the monitors, went abruptly dark. So did the lights, as Raul hit the last switch to set off the final stage in the plan to cover the code rats' tracks through the system. The emergency blinkers came on, the sirens howling distress.

"It's the Mormons!" Mercury shouted, springing up, the disc with the weapon codes snugly hidden inside the tongue of his shoe. "Sabotage!"

He advanced menacingly on Señor Colón, Raul, and the others spreading out to "cover" the other senior network administrators.

The lieutenant, taken by surprise, shouted to them to make sure no one got away, grabbing his comm unit to summon additional security police. Right on cue, the overhead sprinklers came on, drenching the entire room and all its occupants. Bright flares erupted from several computer boxes, acrid smoke filled the room under the haze of airborne water droplets.

"The computers!" Raul yelled. "Turn off the sprinklers!"

Leaving the lieutenant and falsely accused senior techs to do what they could to unplug and protect the equipment still running from the uninterruptible power source, the junior techs scattered, some out one door, others out the second. Meeting the military police pounding up the stairs, Mercury waved a sopping arm at them and shouted something incoherent about finding the shut-off switch for the fire sprinklers. One of them looked at him suspiciously, but the shouts of the lieutenant drew them on. In another fifteen minutes, the entire team of code rats had completely disappeared, melting into the random flow of aimless refugees in Santiago's streets.

Señor Colón, with the matter-of-fact cool of a true network guru, faced the frantic lieutenant through the indoor downpour, his hands raised to shoulder height in the face of the soldier's wavering pistol. "It seems they can't find the shutoff," he said simply after a few moments, turning slightly to show the newly arrived security backup team that he was completely harmless. "If you will let me try, before the boxes are completely ruined?"

"You'd better turn it off," the lieutenant snapped, waving his pistol, "or we'll turn you off!"

Hiding his ironic reaction to that idiotic statement, Señor Colón strode to the far wall, opened the fire-alarm hatch, and pulled the emergency release. The cloudburst from the ceiling slowed, drained, and then fell to a mere trickle. Immediately, the other senior techs began inspecting the equipment.

"What are you doing?" the lieutenant demanded, waving his gun again.

"Checking the computers to see which ones shut off in time not to short out," Señor Colón said reasonably.

"You're sabotaging the system," snapped the lieutenant, having completely forgotten, for the moment, exactly where that accusation had come from.

"No, we didn't." Another of Señor Colón's colleagues spoke up. "That bunch of code monkeys you brought in to spy on us did the sabotaging. You notice they haven't bothered to come back?"

The lieutenant shouted at the security police to find them. The thugs spread out on a fruitless search through the streets. The most vocal reaction they elicited with their questioning came from an old lady, a Señora Ulloa, who told them that she hoped those boys they were looking for had already joined the rebels and would come back to shoot them later. Only the fact that an impressively large and disconcertingly calm crowd formed around both the elderly woman and the security police saved her from the harsh consequences of her words; the press subtly but inexorably moved the two sides apart. By the time the security police had pushed themselves free, the old lady had disappeared.

* * *

"They're gone. Whoever they were." Medea sat back in her low-slung chair.

"You have no idea?" the German asked.

"I have some idea." She flicked her fingers toward the screens. "We were chasing a CIA agent who was using the tactical comm system to piggyback encrypted transmissions on our bandwidth. Turns out some of those signals were going out to the rebels who toasted your late, lamented cat man." The last transmission from El Jaguar's camera glowed, the ambush frozen, on the center screen. "Thing is, the CIA boy didn't do it alone. He had inside help down in Santiago. You know, the crew you put on debug detail with us?"

Brindermann frowned. The tattooed Amazon slouched against a console, tensed, ready to defend Medea if the big man made any suspicious moves. Medea decided to drop the needling and save them the trouble. She'd dealt with scary creatures at a distance before; having Brindermann and Garza in the same room was a new and unwelcome experience.

"Okay, well, it turns out that those code monkeys were better at it than they let on during their exams." At her command, more data scrolled across the screens, pinpointing the holes Mercury had exploited to slide into the system, outlining how far the corruption had spread into the General's system. So did the details of what he and his friends had supposedly done with their access: calls to Zamora showed up clearly, as did the eavesdropping posts Mercury had set up along the secure communications lines. As planned, however, the watchdogs had also discovered a plethora of planted information: bank transfers from Brindermann's banking programs, caches of valuable military data for later sale, even an electronic boxful of Dr. Twilley's reports back to MedaGen.

"So this is how that Senator Cox female found out about our deal with Garlick." Brindermann's glare deepened.

"Maybe. Turns out our little crackers were in bed with a whole crew of people." Under Medea's fingers, another set of data points lit. "Either that, or they managed to crack the unhackable. They used the Mormon network at least twice. We haven't even been able to get in there to monitor transmissions, and we've been trying to crack their system for three years now."

"They said the Mormons were the ones who sabotaged the system," Brindermann noted.

"Nah—you look at this, you can see the fingerprints. Those Mormons were on the system as themselves, doing heavy coding or admin, while the code boys and their CIA agent were messing around," Medea pointed out. "Classic diversion—and your idiot guards fell for it. Good thing they didn't shoot the real administrators by mistake. No, the real question is, did the Mormons holed up in Santiago know they were using the system? Either way, it looks like somebody down there can use the old parochial lines to get word in and out of your tight little universe."

"Then shut it down." All five of the room's occupants turned as Garza walked into the electronics-packed room.

"We can't shut down the entire system," Brindermann protested. "The deployment logistics, communication systems, even the weapons codes, are all in the computers—"

"Not the entire system," Garza growled. "The Mormons' communication system. I want them deeply, completely, permanently incommunicado. You can do that, I trust, even if you cannot get into it?"

"We can do that," Medea answered. "You want them completely out, or just cut off from the satellite?"

"The difference is?" Garza demanded.

"Taking them out completely will take all of Santiago out with them," Medea said. "It's like cutting a main phone line. Cutting their satellite connection is just a question of deploying a jamming signal. It'll black out all wireless calls out to orbit and shut them up."

"It will also black out our own wireless calls to orbit from Santiago," Brindermann said. "Mr. Serrey will no longer be able to use the direct line—nor will President Aguilera. We will lose contact with Argentina as well."

"So they have to make do with the land lines." Medea shrugged. "A little skin off their noses, big boost in security for us. What do you want?"

"Cut them off," Garza directed. "Both Santiago and Osorno. Send a message telling them they have lost communication privileges, and we will punish them."

"You got it." Medea saluted. A curtain of impenetrable silence fell over most of the southern half of South America.

* * *

"Sir!" The thunder of footsteps along the subterranean hallway leading to the communications headquarters in the maintenance area of the Santiago Temple grounds heralded Mercury's sudden arrival. He burst into the quiet room, Raul on his heels, and skidded to a halt in front of Elder Molina, who sat thoughtfully in front of the flickering terminals. Both young men looked much the worse for wear, dressed in the cast-off pieces of uniform that Aguilera's least-qualified recruits favored, their faces smudged, a few bruises showing on their exposed arms.

"What happened to you?" Major Zamora asked, noting the blood-crusted welt on his son's cheek.

Mercury looked into the corner, saw his father settled uncomfortably in a chair, and threw himself to his knees to give Zamora an enthusiastic (but embarrassingly gentle) hug. "What do you mean, what happened to me? You're the one with the crutches, Papa," he teased gently.

"A cat scratch, no more." Zamora couldn't help smiling as he ruffled Mercury's hair. "Thanks to you. But now we have a more urgent problem to solve."

"How did you know?" A flicker of surprise crossed Mercury's face. He untied his shoe, bringing out the opalescently gleaming disc. Holding it up, he continued, "When they cut all wireless transmissions—nasty, using a feedback loop on the broadcast bands like that—I couldn't send this to you here, or get it out. But we have to find some way of getting these codes to somebody who can deal with them. It looks like Garza's had somebody, probably the watchdogs he's got tracking his comm system, mess with those American weapons. I don't know what he's tricked them out to do, but I'll bet we won't like it when we find out. I wish we did have a CIA agent on the line—he might be able to tell us how to disable the long-range bombs, at least. If . . ."

The dead silence in the room finally got through his rapid-fire monologue. Looking from his father to Elder Molina to Raul, who shrugged slightly, indicating his own puzzlement, Mercury trailed off. "What else happened?"

"Plenty, from the sound of it." Señor Olivares emerged from the doorway behind them. Mercury started, wishing the spy would make some kind of noise when he walked. He gently detached the disc from Mercury's fingers, tossing it into the air and catching it. "It appears we have two vital entities to smuggle out of Santiago physically rather than virtually." He glanced at the Apostle, raising an eyebrow.

Mercury and Raul just stared at the quiet, older man, waiting for some kind of explanation; Zamora looked thoughtfully into the middle distance.

"The other would be me." Elder Molina sighed. "Just before the curtain came down, we received an urgent message from Independence. With Presidents Smith and Rojas flying to Jerusalem, the President of the Twelve sent word that all the Apostles must gather to headquarters. As third-ranked in seniority, this means I must find my way to Missouri." He looked worried about more than the journey, hard as it would be, but said nothing more about that; instead, he smiled. "So it appears we have a courier for that important disc. I can take it with me, make sure it gets to Senator Cox, who, I am confident, will get it into the proper hands."

"Which just leaves the question of how you're going to get there," Zamora said, frustrated. He glared at the crutches next to his chair, angry at the twist of fate that put him out of the running to escort Elder and Sister Molina.

Elder Molina smiled, laying a hand on the major's shoulder. "Don't worry, Manuel. Brother Neruda will bring us out from under the General's curtain. Our brothers in Quito still have communications with the satellites. Even without your strategic planning, I think God will provide a way." For a moment, his eyes shone, as if he looked beyond Zamora's face into the soul beyond, seeing his potential—and destiny. His hand tightened. "Watch out for this little flock, Manuel. Do what you need to do. Listen to the Spirit and all will be well. The Lord will prevail, though all the hosts and fires of hell bar the way."

* * *

Dear Chisom,

It sounds like things are as hectic over there as they are here. I am sorry to hear that your biggest challenge comes from the emissaries of Brother Light. His doctrine of heaven on earth appeals to so many, and his teaching that the souls of those who die in his cause simply cycle into the next baby to be born among his followers does promote a kind of fearlessness among his more fanatical followers. You are fortunate that the South Chinese government does not put up with the terror tactics he has used elsewhere. I am pleased to report that our members in the Philippines, who have received the brunt of much of his abuse, are now safe in our temple cities and the work of the Gatherers is moving apace over there.

Our biggest challenge here is one that brings us joy. It is the success of the work of the Gatherers. People are coming into our temple communities and secure stakes all over the Americas. In some areas, President Smith has had to designate additional places of safety due to population pressures. Many do not wish to become members, but they do respect us and are anxious to live our civil law. In that light, I might add, we have had our first non-LDS chapel dedicated here in Independence. A group of devout Evangelicals have been working hard for some time to get their chapel up. With the help of a stake full of elders, it was completed a couple of weeks ago and dedicated by their pastor last Sunday. I rejoice that we can live with our Christian brothers and sisters, even with strong differences of opinion, in unity and peace. I also rejoice that they are pure enough to enjoy living in Zion.

I am also pleased to say that our baptisms have skyrocketed. Over and over again people are drawn almost irresistibly to the Gatherers. These missionaries radiate a light so bright, intense, and beautiful that it reaches far afield. That light, the light of Christ, unseen but deeply felt, touches people, drawing them to Him. As He said, "My sheep hear my voice, and I know them, and they follow me." Right now the Gatherers are the Lord's voice, and they are surely doing a good job.

I find it interesting that I can open the prophetic portion of my scriptures and say, "That's where we are right now." It's thrilling to see how long ago God revealed to His faithful Saints how history would move and, thus, had them prepared. For example, we are now seeing the fulfillment of Revelation 14. There John saw the time when the "Lamb stood on mount Sion" directing the work of the 144,000. Then the scene shifted and the seer beheld "the Son of Man, having on his head a golden crown, and in his hand a sharp sickle." He "thrust in his sickle on the earth; and the earth was reaped." Thus did John symbolize the gathering of the righteous.

John's vision did not end there. I wish it could have, but latter-day conditions would not let that happen. He saw another harvest, performed by one of the destroying angels. He, too, had a sharp sickle that he thrust "into the earth, and gathered the vine of the earth, and cast it into the great winepress of the wrath of God." Certainly conditions are moving toward those two ends.

Frankly, I fear for the Americas. We see General Garza's massive army that he plans to turn loose on North America if he is able. However, I am most doubtful that it will happen. There is a great unrest among the most righteous inhabitants in

Central and South America, especially among our people. It is as though they are wound up like a spring prepared to be loosed. When they are, for all his power, Garza will fall. I say this in light of a Book of Mormon prophecy the Lord made not just once, but three times when he appeared at the Bountiful temple (if you want to check them out, see 3 Nephi 16:15–20; 20:15–22; 21:11–25). In short, He promised the Lamanites that if the Gentiles did not repent, "Then shall ye, who are a remnant of the house of Jacob, go forth among them; and ye shall be in the midst of them who shall be many; and ye shall be among them as a lion among the beasts of the forest, and as a young lion among the flocks of sheep, who, if he goeth through both treadeth down and teareth in pieces, and none can deliver. Thy hand shall be lifted up upon thine adversaries, and all thine enemies shall be cut off." I pity Garza and anyone else who opposes the righteous wrath of the Lord's people once it is cut loose.

I find it most interesting that we are on the brink of war while your area remains at peace. I am pleased about that because it is allowing the work to continue among some of the Chinese people. I wish the whole country were at peace. I fear we will never be able to send any missionaries into most of that vast and war-torn land before the end comes. Still, we will have prepared the base in that land, as we have in so many others, for the great millennial missionary work.

I am glad that we are a part of it, though I must admit, I did not see the added boon of you finding a lovely lady over there to court. I am pleased that things are going well between you and Miss Ming. I would not be overly concerned about cultural differences if the relationship blossoms further. Your concern is somewhat justified. I am sure, however, that your training and experience will go a long way in overcoming potential problems. Love, righteousness, communication skills, maturity, and a willingness to give and take always lead to the oneness God designed marriage to create. Besides, we are rapidly moving toward the millennial world, and I think the cultural shock we will have to go through during those early months will far surpass any faced by you and Wei Wei alone.

I send my love with that of your mother (she'll send you a Vid in a couple of days).
Your father,
Chinedu

* * *

Twisting columns of fire rose high above crumbling tenements, their tops spreading into vast canopies of smoke and flame. Beneath the nightmare trees, uniformed and civilian figures ran frantically, pursued and pursuing, carrying on their own firefight even as the bombs and infernos reduced the city to debris and ashes.

Rosa del Torres appeared in front of the scene, the camera pulling back from its focus on the destruction. "Chaos has utterly enveloped southern Mexico, as the forces of the Aztec Liberation Front clash with the peacekeepers sent from the USSA to restore order and safeguard civilians. In the wake of the catastrophic bombing of Mexico City, which crippled the central government, independent warlords have taken over the outlying areas, declaring themselves the rulers of their own small states. The rebels have allied with several of the most vicious of these warlords, making common cause with the drug and smugglers' cartels to target civilians—and any foreigners still in Mexico." Previously recorded video replaced the live-action war footage—a spectacular explosion in Cancun that reduced the elegant tourist trap to a maze of smoldering, jagged-edged ruins. Bodies sprawled lifelessly on the lush beaches.

"Reports of massacres and bombings come from refugees streaming south toward the rescuing forces. Even more frightening, some refugees tell tales of fast-acting, unfamiliar diseases that seem to spring up wherever the rebels have encountered resistance from local residents. Montezuma, leader of the Aztec Liberation Front, appears to have acted on his threat to use bioweapons as well as nuclear bombs," Rosa observed over footage of frightened, weary, stunned people carrying their valuables on their backs or in a few broken-down cars or trucks.

"However, the citizens of Mexico do not face this horrendous threat alone. General Garza, acting independently, has offered assistance to the loyal Mexican military leaders. Garza's troops have advanced north, first securing the border, then setting up aid stations for the civilians caught in the crossfire," Rosa explained, over the requisite images of ragged, dirty-faced children lining up for their rations of tortillas and beans.

She didn't explain that Garza commanded both Montezuma's rebels and his own Pan-American armies, which were currently acting in concert to smash any local resistance to their inexorable advance. The resistance her cameras caught, rather than coming from rebels disloyally attacking Mexico, represented the Mexicans' own efforts to resist the conquest of their country. The reporter finished her dramatic update and instantly ran to the well-armored and heavily guarded news van to check her international ratings. Monk had finally acknowledged the importance of the news coming out of South America, and she saw to her great satisfaction that her news broadcasts not only beamed over Channel 8 to the entire world but drew millions of eager eyes.

"We're due in Oaxaca for the next rebel bombing," the PR coordinator, also a member of Garza's elite cadre, told her, opening the van's doors and motioning the USSA's official spokesperson to take her seat.

"Let's go get them." Rosa climbed into the back of the vehicle, settling eagerly into place to review her notes—and the upfront narration of events that her PR man provided. "But we need more action. Battles catch eyeballs. Humanitarian efforts only work as report closers."

Thousands of miles away, Clara acknowledged Rosa's update and turned to the next report. "The fallout from the shocking incident in Washington, D.C., continues to affect markets all over the world today," Clara noted. Recorded footage appeared on the screen, white lights delineating a rectangular rooftop, the black helicopter squatting in the center like an enormous cricket while mobsters shot it out with the FBI and D.C. police.

"The involvement of MedaGen's CEO and COO in the dramatic attempt to kidnap Dr. Meredith Galen drew denunciations from the corporation's board of directors, who denied any knowledge of the plot or the current whereabouts of Abbott and Zelik, who have so far evaded the police and FBI." Their faces appeared next, publicity stills doing the work of mug shots. "MedaGen is offering a substantial reward for information leading to their apprehension. One member of the board was quoted as saying that he would shoot Abbott himself when they finally found him. Shooting the fugitives may not be enough to save MedaGen, however." Stock-exchange charts showed MedaGen's once-elevated share prices tumbling toward junk-bond territory while BritPharm's climbed. "Investors have deserted the once-powerful biomedical company in droves, despite the board's announcement that the release of the AllSafe neutralizer would proceed on schedule."

Financial experts and graphs disappeared as Clara shifted gears. "And speaking of on schedule, The Church of Jesus Christ of Latter-day Saints has announced the completion of their unprecedented building efforts in Jerusalem." A lovely, white-stone building rose majestically into the cloudy sky, the Old City of Jerusalem spreading out behind it. "The Church has completed the construction of one of its temples in the city that three of the world's religions regard as a holy site." Turbaned Muslims bowing in prayer, black-coated Jews rocking back and forth as they read the Torah, and neatly dressed Mormons flickered past in rapid succession.

"Despite protests by Jews, Muslims, and conservative Christian groups just outside the new temple's grounds, which the cooperative governments of Israel and Palestine deeded to the Church, the Mormons have continued with plans for a formal dedication," Clara noted. "The Church's President and Associate President have both arrived in Israel, where they will stay through the dedication ceremony." Shots of shouting, angry, even weeping protesters filled the other half of the screen, seeming to direct their opposition at the figures of President Rojas, President Smith, and others disembarking from a sleek jet at Tel Aviv's airport.

"The objections to the Mormons' presence come from untraditional sources as well." A vast throng of white- and black-robed worshippers erupted on the screen, chanting and waving their fists in unsettling unity. Brother Light's face smiled down from huge signs and banners. "The Children of Light, obeying orders from their Prophet, the former Rashi Janjalani, have gathered by the thousands, preparing for what the Prophet describes as a 'holy pilgrimage in honor of the Unity of the One God.' This pilgrimage, according to the man known as Brother Light, will cleanse the historic Holy Land from the contamination of competing faiths and restore it to all true believers." Clara turned to face the camera as the troubling footage of assembling believers disappeared. "Stay tuned as Channel 8's own religion specialist, Anne O'Neal, brings you exclusive reports from Jerusalem as the theological drama unfolds."

Monk nodded approval, sending Clara a swift green-light message; she'd struck just the right tone to hype their broadcast while making the religious fanatics involved look like unsophisticated rubes. Well, maybe not so unsophisticated. He read through the latest memo again, then passed it to Kim. "Looks like that Brother Light wasn't born yesterday, even if he does believe God speaks to him directly."

As part of his campaign to bring all the faithful to proper devotion to the One God, Brother Light had convinced Channel 8's own powers that be that it would be to their advantage to cover the coming showdown between him and the Mormons with a strong pro-Light slant. Not only would he buy advertising time at double the current rate, but he would also guarantee Channel 8 the exclusive media rights in the vast theocratic empire he had built in Southeast Asia, the Pacific, and India—an empire that was expanding into Turkey, the Middle East, and the Balkans. The board had granted Brother Light a worldwide microphone and platform to spread his propaganda.

* * *

"That is such total—" Perro coughed as Corinne elbowed him in the ribs. He caught Dove's glare at the same time and obediently modified his protest as he flailed a hand at the monitor relaying Channel 8's broadcast to the world—and in this case, Section 89's lab lounge. "Bananas. Such a load of bananas."

"Gotta keep up on what the enemy's saying," Dove told him.

"And we did get to see our Merry get away from those horrible MedaGen people," Corinne pointed out.

"Yeah, go Dr. G!" Perro's buoyant mood reasserted itself. He elbowed Dove. "You got to teach her to shoot. She coulda grabbed a gun off one of those dead gangsters and taken the kidnappers right out. Bang! Whoo!"

"How is she doing?" Calvin asked the post-doc researcher. "She get back to Missy in Nauvoo okay?"

"She's fine." Corinne smiled warmly at him. She'd taken quite a liking to Calvin; he was quiet, polite, and less rough edged and wild than the other two. Of course, she'd never seen him drive through a firefight. "She called a half hour ago, said she'd made it to Callattas' without any further incidents and that Carmen was insisting she stay for at least a week, until she stopped shaking, Carmen said."

"Carmen." Perro savored the name. "Love the sound of that. She single?"

"She's married," Corinne told him, rolling her eyes. "And she's old enough to be your mother."

"She does have a daughter. Donna. Bella Donna. Just about our age, too," Dove pointed out. When Perro perked up again, he added, "She'd look at you just long enough to avoid running into you. She's a class act."

"Like I'm not?" Perro demanded.

Kendall Learner's arrival cut short the incipient ego massacre, pre-empting Dove and Calvin's opportunity to tell Perro just exactly how he wasn't. The expert researcher looked worried. "Corinne," he began, then stopped when he realized they had company.

"Keep going," Dove said with an encouraging gesture. "Maybe we can help."

"Yeah," Perro added. "What's up, Doc?"

Calvin grinned at Corinne's wince.

Kendall didn't seem to notice—a sure sign that he had something important on his mind. "Oh, I doubt—" Abruptly, he cut off his own denial, looking from one Santo to the next. His frown deepened, then began to clear. "Or maybe, just perhaps, you can." He turned to Corinne. "The tests on the vaccine for the Bogotá viruses have finished, and they look good. While they can't completely knock out the virus in all cases, it looks like they can reduce its effects from lethal to flulike at worst."

"That's great!" Corinne exclaimed. "So there's got to be something else that's got you worried. Though you don't look so down now as you did a couple of seconds ago."

"I'm not," Kendall assured her, with another puzzling look at the young men lounging on the battered napping couches. "I think we can get around the problem that had me worried. We have the anti-dote, and we have the means to produce it in large quantities—but the people in the way of the virus don't have either."

"So we broadcast the formula for it, like we did with St. Paul," Corinne suggested. Even as she said it, however, she saw the problem. They could broadcast the formula and directions for producing the vaccine to every Zion community in Mexico, but if the people didn't have access to a state-of-the-art biomedical lab, the formula and directions for creating the vaccine would do them as much good as detailed explanations of how to fly to the moon.

"Or we take it to them." Dove stood up, his eyes shining. "You said we can make enough, right? So we make it here and send runners out to all the Zion towns out there, delivering enough to keep the people safe."

"Takes drug running in a completely different direction," Calvin observed with a smile.

"And hey, we've got experience," Perro pointed out. "Plus, we know the back ways down the western side into Chiapas. And we're bored right out of our skulls."

Corinne and Kendall exchanged a look. Perro bored was enough to drive them out of their skulls too.

Sister Lavine poked her head through the doorway. "Dr. Learner? Jonathan Crow just called. Elder Nabil has received several reports, confirmed through local authorities, of what looks like General Garza's virus being used against the resistance in Mexico. He'd like you to come to his office to brief him on the status of the vaccine project, as soon as possible."

Kendall smiled. "I'll be right there. And for once, I think we've anticipated Elder Nabil's needs." Turning to look at the Santos, he hesitated for just a second, then remembered that Elder Nabil seemed unfazed by the wild boys' unorthodox ways. "Why don't you come too? You can explain your idea for making deliveries."

They did, using the drawing board in Elder Nabil's elegant office to outline a strategy for carrying shipments of the vaccine along the old coyote trails to the Zion communities scattered throughout Mexico. Fortunately, Perro let Dove do most of the talking.

"It's a seven-day run, here to there and back," Dove finished, tapping the spots on the surprisingly accurate map he'd drawn. "Benny and me did a couple runs for Abuelo, hauling ammunition for another señor further south. With Fox and Socks watching out upstairs, plus keeping to the back ways, we should be able to hit the targets without running into Garza's men—either the ones in uniform or those fake rebels. If we do run into them, we've automatically got surprise on our side, anyway; with enough hardware stowed in the back, we can take out anybody who stands in our way." He surveyed his plan, pleased with it—or at least the part of it he could handle himself. "Of course, we'd need to find another couple of teams at least, to cover the central and eastern sides."

Elder Nabil, settled in his chair, regarded them all over his steepled fingers: Kendall sitting elegantly as he waited for official approval or disapproval, Jonathan hovering attentively near the door, Perro perched on the edge of his desk, Calvin leaning against the wall beside the board, Dove standing straight and confident in the center of the circle. Finally, he sat forward, spreading his hands. A smile lit his handsome, dark face. "Our Father created the heavens and the earth, and all things that in them are—tigers as well as lambs, lions as well as sheep. I believe we can let His wisdom guide us in this."

"So what did he mean about lions?" Perro asked Dove, relaxing slightly as they left the amazingly—well, *holy*—confines of the Apostle's office. Sure, everything in Zion had this weird smell of sanctity around it, and he had to tread a tighter line than he ever thought he would, to keep guilt from climbing right into his gut, but being around Nabil made the hair on his arms rise.

"It means there's a place for macho gunslingers in Zion, just like there's a place for tall, smart PR men," Dove said, nodding toward the tall, elegant man coming down the hall toward them. "Hello, Brother Ojukwu," he said, offering his hand to the man. "I heard you'd come back for another visit."

The man took his hand warmly and firmly, saying, "Dove, it is good to see you. I understand our guinea pig is completely healthy."

"More like a border rat," Perro corrected, grinning. "They're real hard to kill."

"Yes, thank you," Dove responded, punching Perro without looking at him. "Thanks to Dr. Galen too, I'm fit to run with these losers again. Brother Ojukwu, this is Calvin, that's Perro, from down Amexica way. This is Brother Chinedu Ojukwu, head of the Church's public relations team."

Chinedu shook each boy's hand in turn, a sparkle in his dark brown eyes as he asked, "More border rats? Or, as rumor has it, Soldier Saints who are even harder to kill?"

That image appealed to Perro's macho self-image; he unconsciously flexed. Chinedu's sharp eyes didn't miss the move; he smiled broadly and shared a knowing look with Dove. "So, I suspect you were visiting with Elder Nabil, probably about our antidote?" he more observed than asked.

"Yeah," Dove confirmed. "We're going to help get it to those who need it most."

"So am I," Chinedu said. "That's what I'm here for, in fact. To lay the groundwork for a huge publicity push that will tell the world what we have."

"Bet when you took this job, you never thought you were going to be a drug pusher," Perro quipped.

That brought a laugh to Chinedu's already warm face. "A drug pusher," he mused. "Never thought of it that way. Well I guess I better go meet with my supplier," he said, nodding to each boy and moving off down the hall still chuckling. "Drug pusher. Oh my."

"Drug pusher, right." Dove punched Perro again, glad that the churchman had taken Perro's flip comment so graciously. Excitement buried the momentary embarrassment, though; he shoved open the last set of doors and ran a couple of paces, leaping down the short set of steps to land a handspring and come up facing his two friends. "They need us, amigos! The Rez got it under control, and now the Santos can move into Mexico, spreading medicine to the Saints who need it."

"A little like the gift of healing," Calvin said quietly.

"We'll get a truck—something beat up. Then we'll make it bullet-proof—load it up with the good medicine, then just blend in," Dove continued, his eyes bright with plotting and planning.

"Man, it sounds good, getting back on the road," Perro grinned. His face fell as the blending-in comment penetrated. "It might be tough, not standing out as Americans, though. I don't speak Spanish all that well."

Calvin punched his shoulder. "Don't worry, Puppy—you can just play dumb. Shouldn't be that hard for you." He laughed and ducked Perro's return swing. "Watch the arm—you're going to need me to drive, remember."

Perro laughed back—and hit him. It didn't seem to impair Calvin's abilities later, however, as he spun the wheel of the big, rusty, deceptively battered truck with the padded cases of securely packed vials of antidote resting under its peeling shell top. They all waved to Jonathan and Tasha Crow and rumbled out of Zion toward the south, the Saints in need, and Garza's oncoming army.

* * *

The short line of uniformed soldiers formed a tight, menacing semicircle just outside the gates of the Santiago Temple community. They stood at attention, their weapons poised to take aim at the Mormons standing within the gates. Directly in front of the unarmed sentinels calmly watching the show of military might, Serrey walked through the security line and surveyed the opposition with cold, sardonic eyes. Major Archuleta, now promoted to general but still moving with the crisp uncertainty of a man whose career depends on the favor of his patron, came to a halt beside the security chief.

"I want to speak to somebody with the authority to carry a message," Serrey told the Mormons.

One man stepped forward. "My name is Reyes. I can answer your questions—and relay your message."

"Reyes." Serrey's lazy glance swept him from head to foot. "The former 'mission president' here."

"Mission president?" Archuleta snorted, glowering at the man. "We want Molina. Go get him, or we'll shoot you where you stand."

Serrey didn't even look at Archuleta as he overrode the paper general. "Tell Molina this. We know that the Mormons in this ghetto have been using government connections to communicate with your leaders in the north. The conscript network team has already determined that their measures to cover your illicit use of General Garza's computer system aided the efforts of a CIA spy and his criminal associates to break into the system as well. What they did earned the jamming signal that shut down our entire section of the grid—and yours."

"The team." Reyes paled involuntarily, thinking of Señor Colón and the others. "Are they—"

"They are fine, if sore and sorry for their role in playing the Bogotá network administrators for fools." Serrey didn't wait for him to finish his question about the team's fate. A vicious wisp of smile crossed the security chief's face. "I should say they are fine for the moment. If you do not surrender Molina—"

"We'll start shooting Mormon conscripts, two an hour, starting with that precious network team," Archuleta interrupted this time, delivering the threat with relish. "Right here in front of the gates. You go tell Molina that, and get him out here. You have two hours until we start shooting."

Reyes automatically looked at Serrey, recognizing the true source of the threat. Serrey nodded coolly.

* * *

"Just as cold as you can imagine," Reyes finished his quick summary of the situation, looking across the table in the communications room at Major Zamora and Señor Olivares. The other brethren, the Area Authority Seventy, the stake presidents, the select few who ran the Santiago Branch of Zion in Elder Molina's absence, listened intently, a soft rustle of comment going around the table at the news. "He's going to do it, just start shooting people—people outside the gates, outside the protection. What do we do?"

"First, there is no such thing as a place outside God's protection," Zamora said, earning an abashed nod from the mission president— and smiles from a few of the others around the table. "Second, we can't deliver Elder Molina, because he's gone—even if we would do something like that, which we wouldn't. Which means we have to find some other way to stop Serrey."

"Given your previous comment, I'm surprised that you feel the need to do that," Olivares said smoothly. "Won't your God stop the killings?"

"Dying is nothing to God; He sees the other side, remember?" Zamora rose painfully, resenting the wound that kept him limping on crutches when he wanted to pace. The spymaster's tone grated on him.

"And you believe there is another side. So why worry about a few sacrificed pawns?" Olivares persisted, speaking without allowing interruption from anyone else.

"Because they're not pawns—in the fight we're facing, they're bishops. Some of them literally," Zamora added, forcing a smile. "And we need all the men we can get to fight the General's forces when the time comes."

Olivares nodded, unwilling to let it go; he could sense that Zamora was about to do something militarily brave, honorable, and utterly foolish. "Do you need so many? Remember Gideon's army?"

Gideon, who defeated a huge opposing force with a bare handful of men. A nice parable, but long years of actual combat had amply demonstrated the value of superior numbers, planning, and luck—along with the occasional lift of divine assistance. Never trust solely in the arm of the flesh, but never fail to do everything possible to take advantage of God's arm when He chooses to reveal it. Zamora began to answer, but stopped and smiled, substituting an equally platitudinous answer instead of the hot-blooded one that sprang to his tongue. "God will do what He will do, but it behooves us mere mortals to do what we can to bring to pass His will."

He eased to his other foot, looking at the rosters of conscripts, duty stations, and messages from their rebel army throughout Chile (in the communications blackout, the word-of-mouth network through the wards and stakes had become absolutely necessary to supplement Olivares's spy networks). "The infiltration is complete. Serrey and his monsters don't know that they can't hurt us within the walls—and I don't want them to find that out until the last moment, when we have no alternative but to run. We need time to spring our trap, drive Garza and all his minions into the sea permanently."

"And what do you suggest that we do to keep them from pre-empting that plan?" Olivares asked. "Especially given our inability to deliver the man they are demanding we surrender?"

"We don't have Molina, but we do have someone they want even more, though they didn't think to ask," Zamora said, that strange flicker of smile still playing around his face. "I think they would accept me instead."

Olivares watched, amazed, as the Mormons conferred, consulted, prayed—and finally agreed to let Major Manuel Rafaelo Rivera Zamora, dubbed public enemy number one to Garza's and Aguilera's forces in Chile, walk out of the gates and turn himself in to Serrey and Archuleta.

"You have lost your mind," the spymaster assured Zamora, as Mercury helped his father fasten the last buttons on his uniform jacket. "He'll shoot you the moment you set foot outside the gates."

Zamora smoothed down his lapels. "No. If he were smart, he would just shoot me. But he and Archuleta aren't smart—they're vindictive as well as vicious. Besides, Aguilera will want to make a big splash, put me on trial to legitimize their governorship of Chile."

"And make the General look good, like he's finally winning the war here," Mercury added.

Olivares looked from father to son, then shook his head. He had never understood heroism. Pragmatism, the politics of power, the necessity of personal sacrifice, yes. Blind faith, however, was as alien to him as was sentimentality. Offering his hand, he said, "I won't try to dissuade you again. Good luck, Major. If you survive, be assured that I stand ready to assist you when we spring the trap for the General's forces."

Mercury waited until the gray man had disappeared, then hugged his father tightly. "Do you have to go?" he whispered, tears choking his voice.

Zamora hugged him back, hard enough to make the boy's ribs creak. He had so much of his mother in him—Isabel's laughing eyes, her slender frame. He loved them both so much. "Yes," he said, releasing his hard grip to touch his son's cheek. "It's the right thing to do. I know this because the Spirit tells me to go. I will trust Him and follow His commands wherever they lead. Sometimes it's better to sacrifice one to save others. Remember, Michael Angel, that no matter what happens, you will always be mine. And your mother's."

"And you'll always be mine." Mercury blinked hard, banishing the tears that mirrored those in his father's eyes. "You just be careful. Come back and raise me right."

"Amazing as it is," Zamora told him, smiling despite the situation, "I think we already have."

The major didn't smile when he limped through the gates—but Serrey did, and so did Archuleta. Rosa del Torres's expression remained suitably grave as she reported the apprehension of Major Zamora, the Chilean rebel and traitor responsible for President Quintana's assassination and numerous terrorist attacks aimed at unseating President Aguilera. "The major's trial promises to put the final nail in the coffin of Chilean resistance," she assured the watching world. "And we'll all be watching as events unfold in Santiago. This is Rosa del Torres, reporting live from Chiapas for USSA National News."

* * *

"We've got a live one around the corner!" Perro hissed in a stage whisper, motioning to the end of the fuchsia-colored wall he crouched against.

Dove nodded, slapping another clip into his gun. Through the dusty streets of the tiny village, the sounds of shouts and shots collided, a composition in percussion and vocal with no discernible melody.

A band of Aztec Liberation Front soldiers had roared up the dusty road between the cornfields and garden plots to demand that the town's inhabitants surrender to their rule—and eventually General Garza's, once he'd tricked the world into believing that there were two armies running rampant in Mexico instead of just one. Much to their surprise, the "rebels" found that the farmers were not only ready for them but completely unwilling to submit. The alcalde had politely but firmly rejected their ultimatum and given his own in return: they could turn themselves around and leave town under their own power, or they'd be carried out and buried in the small cemetery over the next hill. Of course, they'd completely underestimated the chances that the farmers not only weren't joking but were both determined and capable of resisting—and figuratively adding the rebels' footwear to the local equivalent of Boot Hill.

Especially when they had the enthusiastic assistance of a trio of Santos Soldados, who had come to deliver the antidote to General Garza's nasty virus and had stayed to mobilize local residents to fight off the soldiers who came to spread that disease. A volley of shots blasted around the corner when Dove flashed his hand past the wall. Sure enough, at least one of the Aztecs had holed up between the fuchsia house and its neighbor, an equally small but tidy house colored an eye-wateringly enthusiastic turquoise. What the farmers' community lacked in material wealth it more than made up for in an enthusiastic color scheme.

Like shooting out of a tunnel, Dove thought, with the house walls preventing attack from either side and the shed at the end of the short alleyway to guard against approach from the back. Not a bad strategy for someone who found himself outgunned, on the run, and surrounded. A long string of chilies hanging from the awning over the door brushed his shoulder. He reached up to push them away, and grinned at Perro. It was a good strategy as long as your opponents didn't think to look up.

Perro caught the idea as soon as he saw Dove's glance at the chilies. Returning the grin, he dashed forward, throwing himself into a tight roll as he passed the mouth of the short alley. His speed and unexpected trajectory worked as he'd planned; the opposition's shots went wild. Landing on his feet in front of the turquoise house, he gave Dove the thumbs-up. Instantly, both Santos shinned up the walls, using the awnings to swing themselves onto the roofs. Running across the flat surfaces, they arrived at the opposite sides at the same time, throwing themselves down to peer into the roofless tunnel between the houses.

A group of three Aztecs crouched there, two watching the mouth of the alley, guns at the ready, the other readying something shiny, light bedecked, and lethal looking.

Dove didn't bother to try to figure out what the device would do; he simply took aim and shot it out of the Aztec's hands. The shiny globe spun away as the man who had held it shrieked and held his bloody hands. His two companions looked wildly around, trying to figure out where that shot had come from.

A whistle from Perro drew their attention to the roofline. They saw the two young men instantly—and more importantly, they saw the muzzles of the guns trained at their heads from above. At the same moment, three farmers appeared in the mouth of the alley, three more firearms drawn tightly on the rebel targets. One of the rebels, probably the commander, though it was always intentionally difficult to tell ranks with Garza's rebel forces, muttered a curse, taking a firmer grip on his own gun. He didn't raise it, however, and his unwounded companion hesitated only briefly before dropping his own weapon and putting his hands up. The bomb expert had already stopped paying attention to anything but the pain throbbing in his bone-splintered hand.

"That's the toughest thing about training a new dog," Perro observed to Dove, as the farmers led away their Aztec prisoners. "Teaching them to look up. The smart ones catch on after the first time."

"How long did it take you to catch on?" Calvin asked, coming up to his fellow Santos.

"Ha, ha," Perro snorted sarcastically. "Mr. Smart Guy, huh? How many Aztecs did you bag?"

"Four," Calvin told him complacently. "One more than you—two and a half, if you split these three between you and Dove."

"I'll let the alcalde take my share," Dove told them, nodding toward the bloody but unbowed village leader.

That worthy came over to them, smiling broadly under the bandage that covered his forehead. "Bueno, muchachos. So we show these southerners how much we like invaders here in Chiapas." He chuckled dryly. "We have enough rebels of our own—we don't need any imports."

"They're just the first," Dove warned. "Until someone stops the General, he'll keep sending his coyotes."

"Until someone stops him, yes." The alcalde nodded solemnly, but a bright spark lit in his dark eyes. He patted Dove's shoulder. "But don't worry. We don't need the Americans to save us this time. When the Gentiles' wickedness reaches full ripeness, the Lamanites will drive them out of the promised land." A wink accompanied that dramatic pronouncement but in no way diminished the confidence behind it.

Dove grinned, the thought of standing against the creeping evil in the world lifting his spirits. He had never felt connected to any culture other than the rough hierarchy of the borderlands gang he and Benny had adopted as a surrogate family after their grandfather's death— until he read the Book of Mormon. The heroes and even villains in its pages not only spoke to him but settled into the empty niches in his soul where images of ancestors, so important to a Navajo, had lain empty. "We surely will, Señor."

The alcalde sent them on their way with fresh tortillas, tomatoes, and several more boxes of ammunition tucked into the tight space in the front of the battered, rusty truck. They left a stock of vaccine behind and drove toward the next town. They'd made their way along the circuitous trails that drug and people smugglers had blazed through the desert, forests, and hills, stopping at the settlements Fox and Socks directed them toward, Mormon towns that had small satellite transceivers. In those towns, they delivered the vaccine, shared news of the invasion, and received suggestions about the next place to stop.

"That's it for the southern route," Dove announced, looking at a well-creased map scribbled with hand-drawn trails too obscure and names of towns and settlements too small to make the cut for inclusion in the USGS official atlas. "Looks like it's time to turn north again. We can cut through that way, hit Toro Negro to pump up the fuel cells and trade some of those tomatoes for ammunition."

Calvin nodded and turned down the track Dove indicated. Perro leaned forward to turn up the radio. At least one station, probably coming out of one of the Mormon towns, was still playing upbeat salsa.

"Where's Toro Negro?" another voice whispered into Dove's ear and through the speaker jacked into the dashboard. Socks watched the rust-colored truck from his orbit-eye view, seeing it as a boxy beetle making its way through a green and tan landscape flattened by distance and perspective. He could zoom in closer, as he had during the sporadic battles that blew up, but whenever the team was on the move, he kept a wider view. "The better to see you with, my dear," as he said to Dove.

"Hey, Grandma," Dove responded, grinning as he imagined Socks's pained expression.

Actually, the computer geek had gotten over his pique at such a girly nickname quite early; it tickled his ego that he had a nickname at all—it made him feel part of the macho culture he'd read about but never had the credentials or opportunity to join himself. He grinned. "Hey, Tonto. All that shooting make you deaf?"

"No, I hear just fine—I was ignoring an unworthy question," Dove informed him. That drew a laugh from Perro, but Dove relented. "Toro Negro's a smuggler's burg, a village the coyotes set up as a way station. It's just about thirty miles from here, if it's still there."

"Small place, just one main street—a church on one end, and what looks like a cat house on the other?" Socks asked, looking at one of his many screens.

"That's the one," Dove affirmed. He sounded impressed—and was. "You got that in the Church database?" You never knew, he'd found, how much information flowed through the Church's information network.

"Not until just recently. It just came up," Socks told him, scanning the communications associated with the town's name. "Whoa."

"You mean stop?" Dove's sharp tone brought Calvin to full attention; he began to slow the truck.

"Oh, no," Socks said hurriedly. His tone changed, going from hastily reassuring to speculative to excited. "I just found out why we've got Toro Negro in the DB. That's where Elder Molina is right now!"

"Elder Molina—the old guy coming up from Chile?" Perro blinked.

"The Apostle coming up from Chile," Dove corrected.

"Sure enough," Socks confirmed. "Looks like Elder Molina's made it all the way up to southern Mexico—fella named Neruda did most of the smuggling on him."

"The same one who arranged to deliver the virus samples," Dove filled in the blanks. "He knew about Toro? I thought he was a legit businessman before he turned James Bond."

"Right, he was—maybe he's got some guys working for him who used to be gunrunners. Sometimes those guys can go straight, you know." They could all hear the grin in Socks's voice.

"Not likely," Dove snorted. "Those guys are bad all the way through." The idea that someone had brought Elder Molina to Toro Negro did worry him, though; while he was kidding about all runners being evil by nature, he also knew the kinds of men who passed through the outlaws' way station, and their probable reaction to an outsider. *Maybe Elder Molina's escorts are some of Elder Nabil's wolves too,* he thought. *But maybe they're not,* whispered the little voice underneath his unquestioning faith in Mormon leadership. *Maybe they don't know what they're walking him into. Or, even worse, maybe they do.*

"Oh, hey, I agree," the voice of their eye in the sky said blithely. "Anyway, looks like Elder Molina's come with another special delivery, courtesy of your friend Mercury." Socks whistled, scanning over the latest transmissions. Elder Nabil had expanded his security clearance, so he—and therefore the Santos—would know as much as possible about what was happening in Mexico. "Looks like they've found the codes for those weapons Garlick sold to Garza, and Elder Molina wants to get them to Senator Cox in person. He got out from under Garza's thumb, but he's just barely ahead of the army."

"An Apostle's in Toro Negro?" Perro asked again. He was experiencing the same kind of psychic dissonance as Dove as he tried to place Elder Nabil, the only Apostle he'd met, in the dusty streets of Toro Negro, walking around with the banditos, runners, outlaws, and gang enforcers who used the tiny settlement as a hideout.

So was Calvin. "Think he could use some help?" he asked, glancing at Dove.

"You know it." Dove didn't even need to wait for the warm certainty that welled up in his chest. Duty called, or at least vaguely hinted that it might possibly be interested in his assistance, and he was more than ready to spring into action. "Right place, right time, right chicos. To Toro Negro, Calvin—and don't spare the horses!"

* * *

The white horse curvetted prettily, tossing its handsome head and flicking its long, shining tail. Brother Light smiled, pulling the beast into a dramatic rearing pose. He pointed forward, and the entire line of riders broke into a gallop, the Hands of the Prophet on black horses to match their black robes, crimson harness decorations and saddle cloths matching their deep-red hoods. Behind the cavalry charge, a vast horde of white-robed Children of Light surged forward as well, shouting their devotion to the Unity, the One God now embodied in the Prophet, the messiah come to save them all.

"We are seeing the largest religious mass movement in history, as the followers of Brother Light gather by the thousands," Clara narrated over the images coming out of the hotly contested borderlands between India and Pakistan. "An estimated thirty thousand Children of Light poured into Kashmir today, moving north and west through Pakistan." More marchers appeared, carrying flowers, banners of Brother Light's face, and weapons of all descriptions, from ceremonial belt knives to shoulder-mounted grenade launchers. Among the foot traffic, trucks, cars, and even the occasional tank appeared, carving out a mechanized path through the mob.

"While the exact objective of the march remains unclear, it is obvious that the unprecedented migration poses a threat to the stability of the entire region." The United Nations headquarters appeared next, delegates from all over the world rushing in and out, conferring, arguing, staring bemusedly into space. "The UN Council is split on the topic; proposals for sanctions against the new governments formed in the wake of the religious takeover have directly collided with other calls for official recognition of those governments."

"Rashi Janjalani is the most dangerous popular demagogue and messianic pretender the world has ever seen!" cried the ambassador sent by India's exiled government, now taking refuge in Tibet. "The world must move to stop this madman before he plunges all the countries in the Fertile Crescent into a devastating war!"

"Brother Light is the embodiment of the divine will to Unity," the ambassador from Pakistan said confidently. He represented the new government in Lahore—the one Brother Light put into place. "The Children of Light welcome all believers—Muslim, Jew, Hindu, Buddhist, and Christian—into one great fold. The crusade is a march of peace on an unprecedented scale. Only a warmonger would oppose such a benevolent purpose."

"Charges that the Children of Light are a marauding army laying waste to the countries they pass through were met by official denials," Clara noted. While the images behind her showed Children of Light looting shops, setting fire to opulent palaces, and flagging down transports at makeshift checkpoints, she continued, "A spokesman for Brother Light explained that one of the central tenets of the Unity is the equal sharing of all wealth, which should 'flow like love between all true believers, unbounded and unrestrained.'"

"What we see here is another manifestation of the central tenets of Marxism," a bearded, jacketed social historian intoned, gazing intently through his glasses. "As Karl Marx preached, the Children of Light believe that each should give his efforts to the community, and each member of the community should receive a share of the material goods the community produces."

"Marxism or modern Messianism, what are the underlying foundations of the Children of Light?" Clara asked. "Stay tuned for Channel 8's special report on the origins, current activities, and possible future of the Children of Light and their charismatic prophet." The Web site for official information about the Children of Light scrolled through the ticker—as did advertisements for special discount rates for traveling to join the pilgrims' crusade, Brother Light memorabilia, and BritPharm's travelers' vaccination program.

Turning to face another camera, Clara continued, "And speaking of religious events, Anne O'Neal is in Jerusalem, where another unprecedented event is taking place. Anne?"

"Thank you, Clara." Anne O'Neal appeared, standing on a hill with the entire city spread out behind her. "I am in Jerusalem, where the President and Associate President of The Church of Jesus Christ of Latter-day Saints have just concluded a weeklong dedication ceremony for the newly built Mormon temple in this historic city."

Images from the dedication rolled past as she briefly described the momentous events: President Smith and President Rojas, dressed in white, conferring with the political and religious leaders of both the Palestinian and Jewish communities; a colorful throng of thousands of Saints dressed in their best clothes, come from all over the world in the momentary lull between storms to attend the dedication services; little children smiling as they reached out to shake hands with the bowed but bright President Smith; President Rojas standing in the gilded, marble doorway of the great temple itself; the brilliance of sunlight flashing from the golden statue of the Angel Moroni as a crane lowered it to its place on the highest spire.

"While most of the crowds have gone now, dispersed on their leaders' order to the far corners of the world once again, the native Mormons are still here in Jerusalem busily carrying on the Church's work," Anne noted. Leon's footage of Mormon volunteers working to clean up storm damage, give safe havens to refugees pouring in from all over the Near East as they ran from the oncoming tide of Children of Light and the chaos enveloping their own countries, working on plantations that fed thousands who would otherwise starve, smiling as they waved to the Western cameraman on the streets of Jerusalem.

"Unfortunately, the Mormons have had to expand their activities beyond the traditional humanitarian aid," Anne said. "While a bubble of calm still persists around this area, the neighboring states are feeling the pressure of the religious revolution spreading out of Southeast Asia to engulf the traditionally Muslim areas of the Middle East." More images of the Children of Light appeared, documenting their progress along the highways and easiest paths leading from India to Pakistan and onward toward the Tigris and Euphrates Rivers. Anne had chosen footage captured from locals, filming the scenes of looting, pillaging, and burning even as they ran from the marauders. They took everything they could carry and swept on, leaving the weak to starve. The harsh logic of the march applied to their own members as well; white-robed bodies often fainted by the way, left behind in the wake of the tide sweeping forward. Other images came from the Church's network, passed along to Anne through private channels, documenting the desperate plight of those whose devotion to God, Allah, or Yahweh would not let them profess devotion to Brother Light. Vast torches with human bodies at their centers often lit the way for the advancing hordes of Rashi Janjalani's human locusts.

"What's she doing?" Monk growled, watching the preview footage that streamed past on Kim's monitor. "We can't show that kind of thing. The board would have kittens. Cut that. Go to the second reel, the stock footage of the march from the European office."

Kim's nimble fingers hesitated, then touched the controls, shunting the visuals from Anne's live feed into the archive bins, queuing up the standard images of Rashi Janjalani's crusade—the ones with the flowers and cheers rather than the dead bodies and rifles.

Unaware that Monk had preempted her visuals, Anne continued, "The clashes between Muslims, Jews, and the Children of Light have escalated to violence even within the borders of the combined state. In a nightmarish situation of déjà vu, mobs throwing rocks, guerillas staging shootouts, and even two suicide bombers on a road leading into Jerusalem have shattered the peace and security so many residents here had finally begun to enjoy. In this situation, the Mormons have increased their efforts to provide for the physical as well as spiritual needs of the people on all sides of the religious lines." President Rojas appeared again, walking up the steps of the Knesset with Israeli leaders and meeting with Muslim imams.

Anne reappeared, the sun setting slowly over the city behind her, glinting from the metallic Dome of the Rock, shining like gold from the white spires of the newly dedicated temple. "So far, the religious communities have held together against the outside threat, thanks in no small part to the evenhanded leadership President Rojas has provided. But can there truly be any peace in a city that all the world's religions seem eager to claim as their own? With the Children of Light advancing yet another claim that they seem to be willing to back up with violence, can the Mormons keep the longest cease-fire in Middle Eastern history from dissolving into bloodshed once again? We'll be here, watching as the situation unfolds, keeping you up to date on these momentous events. This is Anne O'Neal, from Jerusalem."

"Nice," Leon told her, after the ruby glow disappeared from the top of his camera. He glanced at the sky, where clouds had begun to pile up, reaching to blot out the setting sun. They shone as red as the "on air" light, replacing the golden light across the city with blood-colored shadows. Frowning, he muttered, "Red sky at night might be a sailor's delight, but I don't like the look of those clouds."

Anne shivered, though the rising wind was merely cool. "I don't either. Looks like we're in for a storm."

"In more ways than one," Leon agreed. "What's the odds we can get out of here before those typhoons Cal Weathers keeps talking about come back and we're grounded?"

"I'd give it about a million to one," Anne told him.

* * *

"What's it looking like?" Perro whispered.

Dove peered into the broken window of Toro Negro's single, brawl-battered saloon. "Ten to one." He evaluated the situation, giving his friends the rundown. "Two up—looks like Elder Molina and his wife—two down. I can see their boots behind another table, but that's it. Don't know if they're still breathing. Looks like Badger's trying to shake down the Molinas, but nobody's tenderized them yet." The scene in the middle of the bar had the total attention of the room's inhabitants; nobody noticed Dove's reconnaissance.

"Oh, no problem, then." Calvin grinned. "Go get 'em, Perro. Straighten it all out."

"You both just shut up and look nasty," Dove ordered. "Be ready, but don't draw off until it's bad." With that, he straightened up, eased his shoulders, and sauntered through the battered door of the nameless saloon like he owned the place. All eyes immediately turned to him, glinting darkly in the bright light that came in with him. The older couple in the center of the ring of banditos practically glowed as they looked toward the silhouetted newcomer.

"Abuelita!" he exclaimed. Without a pause, he strode over to the classy-looking woman sitting at a scratched, unsteady table. Brushing aside the large man standing beside the woman's chair, he bent to kiss her cheek. Her dark eyes met his as he pulled away, and he saw a sudden glint in them.

She patted his cheek. "Ah, chiquito. Good to see you."

Dove looked at the distinguished man in the other seat, hoping he was as quick on the uptake as his wife. Elder Molina, confirming Dove's high opinion of Apostles, simply smiled and nodded a familiar greeting.

"Nakai?" The bearlike man Dove had pushed away grabbed his shoulder and pulled him around.

"Oso." Dove caught the man's wrist and threw his hand back at him, stepping forward to catch the damp-stained front of his shirt too. "You met my grandparents yet?" His voice carried more menace than the mere words could possibly convey; it made the only correct answer excruciatingly obvious. The other two banditos standing around the table glanced at each other.

Oso glowered, especially since Dove had a few short hairs in his grip as well as the shirt. Before he could answer, however, another voice cut across the confrontation. "Little Salvatore Nakai? Thought you were an orphan, chiquito. Come here, let me see you."

Dove let Oso go, wiping his hand on the bouncer's slightly less damp sleeve, and turned to face the owner of Toro Negro's only bar— and the bandit chief of the gang that ran the outlaws' hideout. Badger leaned against the bar, favoring the stump of his leg, his massive forearms easily supporting the weight of his correspondingly broad shoulders. His small eyes, set deep in a face with incongruously sharp features, scanned Dove.

"Hey, Badger. Yeah, it's Nakai." Dove walked forward, the other two bouncers making way. Calvin and Perro slid in behind Dove, hovering beside the Molinas.

Silence descended, broken only by a screech of high, drunken laughter from the tiny brothel across the dusty street and the scratch of boots on the uneven floor as a bandito shifted his weight, as Dove met Badger's stare. They both knew that Sister Molina was no more Dove's grandmother than Badger was; what they had to determine was how far either of them would push the claim if pressed. Badger hadn't survived as long as he had without developing an almost supernatural ability to judge, if not the character of his guests, their potential, talents, and taste for violence. What he read in the serene but steady gaze of the half-breed border rat finally earned a slow nod. "So how's Benny these days? Still chasing all the wrong women?"

A ripple of relaxation, mixed with both relief and disappointment, spread through the room. The banditos who'd watched the shake-down of the possibly wealthy southerners lost interest and turned back to their own plans for profiting from the chaos they hoped that Garza's army would leave in its wake. Oso shot Dove another hard look, then faded back to take his place by the door, the other two bouncers trailing in his wake.

"He's good; he's just not around anymore," Dove answered, accepting the tacit truce. "Garza's man ambushed us. Benny took a couple of bullets."

"Heard about that Slick hombre." Badger nodded. "Paco told me. Hard case. Told me you punched his ticket for him. Hard case yourself." The barman glanced from Dove to Perro and Calvin, then looked at the Molinas. "My boys figured Garza would throw some silver their way for those two."

"Maybe he would, but he'd gut shoot them right after," Dove said flatly.

"Yeah, probably so." Badger nodded again. "Take your family reunion on the road." One of his shovel-shaped hands came up from behind the bar, a shotgun resting easily in his grip. He laid it on the bar, just to emphasize his invitation. "Sayonara, Nakai."

"Adios, Badger," Dove replied casually.

Behind him, Elder and Sister Molina stood up, Perro and Calvin falling in behind them as they walked to the door. Sister Molina glanced back at the unmoving bodies of their former escorts, but kept moving. No one stopped until all five had piled into the truck, Calvin and Perro in front, Dove handing the Molinas into the back, where they settled among the provisions stowed beside the large cooler of vaccine.

"So that's another Apostle," Perro mused aloud, as Calvin pulled away from Toro Negro. "And his wife." He clicked the transceiver. "Hey, Sock Boy—we got 'em, in the back with the dope. Spread the word." Leaning back again, grinning at Socks's whoop of delight, he continued, "Smart people. Wonder why they smell like onions."

"We came the last sixty miles in a produce truck," Elder Molina told Dove.

Sister Molina sighed as she leaned against the sleeping bag at her back, stretching subtly, enjoying the relative roominess of the truck.

"And before that, they had us stowed away in weapons crates, of all things. There we were, bumping along with General Garza's supply train, disguised as bombs or rockets or something."

"I'd say you were secret weapons, all right." Dove smiled, then grew sober. "What happened with the guys ferrying you? It didn't look like they made it."

That comment struck a spark in Sister Molina's eyes. Elder Molina shook his head sadly. "Unfortunately, Brother Neruda's contacts in Mexico weren't all we'd hoped. He warned us that he'd primarily worked with smugglers on this side of the border—any port in a storm, he said—which meant we might not be able to trust them completely. Still, we had a good feeling that we should go with the plan. And they did get us as far as Toro Negro, as they promised."

"Even though it turned out that we couldn't trust them at all once we got there," Sister Molina added. "They hid us in their onion truck, all right, and got us through the first few miles, but when we stopped in Toro Negro, they decided to sell us to Garza's agents, as soon as they could find one. The reward offer has been all over the General's radio broadcasts. Just as they'd decided that, the big bouncer came over and started asking questions. When they tried to hide who we were—afraid that the men in the bar would take us away to get the reward money themselves—they both got shot. It would almost be funny, if it weren't so pitiful."

"Pitiful, all right," Dove agreed. "Sounds like the sooner we get you out of here, the less chance that somebody else will see you as a big payday. Good thing we were in the area. Good thing you were so fast on the uptake there in the bar too." He grinned at Sister Molina. "You could've blown my whole entrance."

She smiled back. "Oh, I'd never do that. It's not often I would pass up a kiss from a handsome young man."

Elder Molina cleared his throat meaningfully, which made her laugh. "And I'd never pass up a kiss from a handsome older man," she assured her husband, who took the opportunity to test the veracity of her statement.

Dove glanced away, both surprised and unexpectedly cheered by the display of affection between the Apostle and his wife. He still had a hard time believing that the Church leaders were human, rather than walking statues of perfection. That thought led to another, which prompted him to ask, "Why did you go with those banditos, when—" He stopped abruptly, wondering belatedly if the question would offend Elder Molina.

"When they weren't trustworthy?" Elder Molina finished for him.

"Right." The rest of Dove's question rushed out. "Wouldn't God tell you, warn you not to go? He does talk to you, right? Why would He let you go into danger like that?"

The Apostle smiled slightly, reassuring the young man. "Well, first, remember that He sees more of the picture than we do; if I could do Him more good by falling into the enemy's hands, so it would be. Remember that no angels came to rescue Elder Stacy." He patted his wife's hand, as if apologizing for bringing up a distressing incident; she squeezed his hand and nodded, sorrowful but fearless. "But in this case, I felt sure that the Lord would provide a way for us to continue our journey—by whatever means came to His hand."

That fit; God always got His way, even if He did use methods that any smart gang leader would blink at. Dove nodded, relieved. "Good thing we came along. We've been delivering vaccines to the towns around here, down the smugglers' trails from Amexica. We were just turning around when Socks gave us the word you'd headed for Toro Negro. Guess we turned up right in time."

"Oh, I think that God had a hand in that too," Sister Molina told him, a twinkle in her eye.

Dove smiled back, pleased at the thought. "Let's hope He clears the way for us to get to the airport in Tuxtla Gutiérrez too. We're surfing the wave coming out from the South as it is—Garza's troops are coming up fast. With a price on your heads, we're going to have to hit the back roads at high speed." He knocked on the cab's back window, which Perro obediently slid open. "You two may want to get some sleep, if you can—it's going to be a long night," he advised before sliding through the window and into the front seat.

Perro grinned, waved at their passengers, and closed the window. The syncopated beat of salsa music tangoed through the back of the truck. Elder Molina gently stroked his wife's hair as the two of them settled down on the boys' dusty bedrolls. A few minutes later, both had fallen asleep in the swaying, bumping truck bed, secure in their faith in God's plans—and the capabilities of three of His lions, or more like cougars—to bring them safely through the General's forces.

* * *

"The combined army of the USSA continues to move into Mexico, routing the Aztec Liberation Front's rebel brigades," Rosa del Torres announced. Behind her, enthusiastic crowds waved handkerchiefs and cheered as General Garza's soldiers marched through the streets of a newly "liberated" town. They knew better than to try to run or shout anything but cheers; outside the camera's viewfinder, other troops stood behind the crowds, their weapons at the ready to quell any "rebel" activity that might crop up.

Maps showing Garza's unstoppable advance appeared next; neither they nor Rosa acknowledged that local forces in many areas had mobilized to stand against the invaders—with surprising success in many small villages, where the people utterly failed to succumb to the infections Garza's troops spread over resistant areas. "As they face certain defeat, the rebel forces are retreating northward. Montezuma has issued a call for the United States to come to the aid of the people of Mexico."

Montezuma's face replaced Rosa's, giving an impassioned plea for the Americans to intervene, to save the rebels from Garza's army. "And if you do not help us," he finished, his face darkening dramatically, "we will consider you enemies of the revolution, and we will punish you as traitors. *Viva la revolución!*"

Rosa took center stage again, frowning with concern. "The rebels' threats have reached General Garza, who expressed concern that their next target may be the United States. In a direct call to the American president, the General urged that the Americans mobilize their forces along the Mexican border to prevent any of the Aztec Liberation Front forces from crossing over. He also urges increased vigilance for possible terrorist activity and has formally extended an offer of assistance in quelling the threat if it does pass the border."

"I bet he did," Perro muttered, glancing at the monitors flickering above the airport's security counter. Around them, crowds of frantic, numb, or simply determined people waited or shoved forward, all eager to get out of Chiapas before Garza's troops, or the Aztecs—though most Mexicans had long since realized they were the same thing—secured the airport and cut off their lifeline to the outside world.

Dove scanned the chaotic scene, looking for someone with the authority to get the Molinas on one of the last planes heading north. The sparkle of epaulets on a uniform caught his attention; gently taking Elder Molina's arm, he pulled the Apostle to the side, out of the mess, toward a man whose gold braid matched his officious attitude. Perro and Calvin closed in on either side of Sister Molina, muscling her through the press.

"Señor!" Dove called.

The airport official, realizing that he'd been spotted, went to duck back into his office, then hesitated when he saw Elder Molina. After many years of providing customer service in exchange for additional considerations, he'd developed a good sense for relative importance. Elder Molina, travel-rumpled, unshaven, and weary, still exuded an unmistakable air of authority, which usually meant both a desire for special treatment and the willingness to pay for it. Motioning for a pair of well-armed and equally well-muscled guards to bring them in, the airport's security chief did go into his office. He arranged himself behind his desk, ready to negotiate the highest price possible for his services.

"We need to get these people to the United States on the next plane," Dove informed him, cutting through the customary pleasantries with border-rat bluntness.

"Well, we'll see what we can do," the airport official huffed, irritated at the lack of manners that the notables' bodyguard displayed. He waved a hand toward the door. "As you can see, we have far more passengers than we have seats."

"I can see that," Dove snapped. "How much do you want?"

Again, the rudeness! The official glared at him. "Well, perhaps if I knew who I was dealing with . . ." Even as he said it, however, the screen of the antiquated computer on his desk drew his attention. There they were: a man and a woman, middle-aged, distinguished looking, and wanted for a handsome reward by General Garza.

Dove saw his gaze shift and shifted himself, his hand diving toward the gun concealed in its holster under his arm.

Elder Molina gently caught his elbow, keeping the gun where it was, and stepped forward. "We are servants of the Lord who need your assistance to reach Washington, D.C. Do not think that you can gain from betraying us." When the man hesitated, staring at him, Elder Molina raised one hand and said, "I command you in the name of the Lord and Savior Jesus Christ to help us."

CHAPTER 19

"Just like that!" Perro blinked, still stunned. "The Apostle just raised his hand and, bang! Just like that." He waved his hands, bonking the seat backs in front of him.

That would've earned glares from the occupants of those seats—if he hadn't looked like such a dangerous creature, and if they weren't just glad to have a seat on the plane out of Tuxtla Gutiérrez. Even the pilot and copilot had looked stressed when the five of them rushed onto the plane at the last minute. They'd barely strapped in before he gunned it down the runway and into the air, headed for Miami and safety. It wasn't the most direct path to Washington, D.C., but it was the next plane out of Chiapas.

"They want a bribe, then they want to turn him in, and then they just give in when he comes over and lays a command on them! He's like one of those Shaolin masters—all calm," Perro went on, "like he could deflect bullets with one wave of his hand. I keep thinking he's going to start calling me Cricket or something."

"Grasshopper," Calvin corrected. He was impressed too, but not as stunned as Perro; like Dove, he practically expected Apostles to do magic.

"What?" Perro blinked, thinking he'd misheard over the roar of the plane's engine.

"It was Grasshopper, not Cricket," Calvin said louder.

Perro snorted. "Okay, sorry—forgot you're the man on antique movie references."

"It was a TV show, not a movie," Calvin informed him, dropping his gaze as Elder Molina looked across the aisle to catch the boys looking at him. Calvin managed a smile despite the blush that burned his ears. "And he's a lot more than a Shaolin master."

A crackle from the intercom interrupted the debate. "This is your captain." The man's voice cracked. His deep breath was audible over the open channel—and so was the catch in it. "I regret to inform you that the city of Miami has just been hit by a nuclear bomb. A suitcase bomb," he continued, his voice gaining strength as shouts of horror rang through the passenger compartment. "Reports say it was the Aztec Liberation Front, because the president wouldn't send the army into Mexico to fight General Garza."

"Go to the cockpit," Elder Molina told Dove. "Now!"

Dove instantly rose, almost running down the narrow aisle. As he drew near the sealed door, he stopped. What could he do? Over the intercom he could hear the pilot's professional reserve breaking down. "I'm sorry. I'm so sorry. It's just so awful—the whole world is awful. It's just too hard to live anymore." The plane lurched, its nose shifting downward at a noticeable angle. "I'm sorry. It's best that nobody suffer anymore." The intercom switched off.

From inside the cockpit Dove could hear shouting. The copilot yelled, "What are you doing? Are you nuts?" The plane swayed, suggesting there was a fight over the controls. Then there was a gunshot, and the plane banked down.

The flight attendant screamed and grabbed the key opening the door. Dove muscled her out of the way. The gun came up, but Dove was ready; he caught the pilot's wrist and wrenched the muzzle away from a second shot. They wrestled for the weapon, the plane diving at an ever-steeper angle toward the blue water that the pilot believed would spare them all unnecessary pain. The pilot's arms relaxed—he no longer tried to point the gun at his opponent. The sudden lack of resistance and the tilt of the floor threw Dove off balance; he pitched forward, still pushing the gun away from his own face. Using that momentum, the pilot twisted the gun, brought it against his own head, and pulled the trigger. Snarling in disgust and fury, Dove shoved away from the bloody mess, the gun finally coming away from the dead fingers.

A weak moan from the copilot's chair instantly brought Dove's attention from the clouds whipping by the windscreen. The flight attendant, standing wide-eyed in the doorway, rushed forward. "Luis!"

"Careful." Dove caught her arm before she flung herself on the wounded man. Bending over the copilot, he could hear the sucking sound of a lung wound even through the roar of the engines. "Oh, no," he said. That earned another shriek from the flight attendant. Dove caught her shoulders, shaking her slightly. "Señorita—señorita, listen to me," he ordered. "Get Elder Molina. The man in 10A. Get Elder Molina!"

With a shove in the right direction to get her going, he turned back to the controls, wondering how to stop the shallow dive before the plane hit the water. Buttons, dials, levers, sticks all blinked and gleamed back at him, unhelpful. The bloody streaks and spatters on the windscreen dripped sickeningly. "Oh, man, Benny. I don't want to buy out in a plane crash! We got things to do!" He reached across the pilot and gently pulled back on the stick, easing the plane to a more horizontal position, without having the slightest idea what to do next.

"Dove." The sound of his name jerked him back into awareness of his surroundings. Elder Molina stood in the cramped space over the fatally wounded man. "Dove, have you been ordained an elder?"

Dove blinked. "Just barely. Sam and Bishop Yazzie did it, before I left—" He cut off the ramble of unnecessary detail as the Apostle brought a tiny bottle of oil out of his pocket. The keys on the same ring jingled.

"We need to give this man a blessing," Elder Molina told him. "Right now."

Dove let go of the stick, only to find that the plane began descending again. "Tell me what to do." Dove moved closer, instantly following the instructions on anointing with oil.

He wasn't ready for what happened as the Apostle pronounced the sealing blessing, calling Luis (the flight attendant couldn't remember his last name) back from the edge of death. Under Elder Molina's hands, and Dove's, though he felt only a tingle of the divine power pouring through the older man, the bright blood pumping from the wound stopped, the organs, tissue, bones, and skin pulling together. Luis's breathing began again with a gasp, then settled into a slower, steadier rhythm. As Elder Molina finished the blessing, Luis's eyes opened, focused.

"No time," Elder Molina said authoritatively, as the copilot's mouth opened as well. "Luis, we need you to pull this plane out of the dive we're in and land us somewhere safe."

With a crisp nod, Luis turned to the panel, his fingers flying over the controls that had baffled Dove. The plane leveled out, streaking above the waves. Dove held on to the headrest of the pilot's seat, stunned. Outside the windshield, the gray dimness of clouds gave way to brilliant sunlight as the plane regained altitude. The light seemed to fill Dove's eyes, his head, his heart with a testimony too deep for words.

"Hey!" The sharp exclamation finally punched through the wonder filling the young border rat. He blinked, looking down at Luis.

"You know left from right?" the copilot (*pilot,* Dove thought— *battlefield promotion*) asked again.

"Left from—yeah," Dove shook his head. "You need some unskilled help?"

Luis grinned. "A monkey could fly one of these planes, so long as he had a good copilot. Which you do." His face darkened slightly as he touched the front of his blue shirt, the blood already stiffening. "Peel him out of that seat," he said, nodding to the late pilot, "and sit down."

"For what we hope isn't a crash course, right?" Dove asked, black humor getting the better of him.

While Elder and Sister Molina reassured the frantic passengers and Dove learned more than he'd ever wanted to about flying jetliners, the plane streaked across the sky over gathering clouds and through screaming winds. They landed on emergency clearance—without crashing, but just ahead of the gathering storm—in Charleston, South Carolina, where they joined the swarm of people trying to escape the waking nightmare of nuclear attacks on American soil.

* * *

"Who says having a bomb shelter in the basement is crazy now?" asked a hard-faced man with the cynical smile of one who has finally been able to tell the world "I told you so!" and make it stick.

"For thousands in downtown Miami, no bomb shelter would have been enough to save them," the Channel 8 stringer at a safe distance from the scene intoned, plunging into a commentary as poetically scripted as it was inane in the face of a catastrophe of that magnitude. The footage of the explosion scrolled endlessly, a huge column of smoke and flame caught by professional crews, amateurs making home videos, national weather satellites, and the International Space Station.

"There's lots of bombs," Gianni told Missy solemnly, pointing at the screen.

"No, sweeties, only one," Merry said, turning away from Channel 8's sensational coverage to the sober announcement on the Church's satellite stations.

She still tuned in to Channel 8's broadcast out of morbid fascination with how the world tried to assure itself that all was well while profiting from people's terror at watching disasters unfold in their living rooms—or the courtrooms, for that matter. At least Sidney's lawsuit had stalled out in court, since the Mormons had readily complied with the judge's order to let both Sidney and Samuel Lebaron walk into Salt Lake City. The court was still grappling with the fact that both had walked right back out again with no visible coercion. Watching an exasperated judge tell Sidney to "Make up your mind—do you want to stay there or not?" was almost worth the annoyance.

Watching their coverage of the mind-boggling events in Jerusalem, however, and realizing how much the network put their own spin on even Anne O'Neal's fair reports, made her feel infuriatingly helpless and weakly amused. They were determined to paint the Children of Light as the "good" religion, against the repressive backdrop of seemingly every other major religion in the world. How did they so consistently miss the real import of everything that was happening? Did it come down to lack of faith or a willful disregard of the truth?

Either way, it had the same result, a result altogether too evident in the way the reporters squeezed every last drop of pathos out of the plight of the people killed, wounded, and displaced in the horrific explosion, while ads continued to scroll along beneath the images, suitably sobered up, of course. And why did they feel the need to point out that "the entertainment world, already reeling after the loss of one of its brightest stars, Virginia Diamante," (she would be one of its brightest stars until her image or memory no longer sold broadcasts and products) "has turned out to pay tribute to the heroes of Miami."

Monk watched the ratings numbers, the glowing bar of the Mormon satellite channel, whose jump to number 8 he took as a personal affront.

He promised himself he'd find a way to torpedo those noncommercial upstarts somehow, and nodded at Kim to cue up the next round of commentators.

* * *

Senator Cox turned away from the endless replays of the disaster in Mexico, rubbing her eyes. The official memo lay on her desk, drawing her gaze even more magnetically than the strident coverage. General Andrea Garza, savior of the United States of South America, had repeated his formal offer of assistance to his neighbor to the north, offering to help them locate, apprehend, and eliminate the terrorists planning more biological and nuclear attacks against American targets. He had done as much for the governments of South America, his statement read; how could he do less for the land that stood as a beacon of liberty and protector to the entire world? He asked only that they let him know within the next day, because he already had intelligence that suggested more attacks were imminent. A few senators still thought of Garza as a hero, if a "colorful" one, a man whose methods, though regretfully barbaric, had at last broken the cartels' and corrupt militaries' grip on South America. Most of the senior legislators, however, recognized Garza's message as the veiled threat it was.

The administration faced a vicious dilemma, caught between a stunned, angry population demanding action and a man who wanted nothing more than an excuse to unleash the rest of his arsenal. An arsenal that, in large part, had come from the country's own weapons store. The press still jabbered about a "suitcase" nuke, but even preliminary investigations dovetailed with the senator's previous data about the Mexico City bombing, pointing convincingly at airborne delivery. The pictures of the UCAVs in the Bogotá hangars came vividly to Cox's mind. Garza had the weapons from his contacts in Europe, and he had the codes and vehicles from the Americans.

As Senator White observed dryly, "Garlick's chickens have finally come home to roost, but now they look a lot more like buzzards."

Rumors and riots exploded in Washington as protesters called for government action to save them from nuclear, biological, and social threats. The president's announcement that the people of the United

States thanked General Garza for his concern and lauded his efforts at pacifying the rebels in Mexico but would not accept his offer of assistance got barely more airtime. General Garza's expressions of stern sorrow at the "unilateral" decision and his warnings of further attacks played enough to thoroughly panic the few citizens who watched the news for serious coverage.

Within the walls of Zion, no one panicked, but the sober word spread that the world was about to get a dose of divine justice that would go down bitterly indeed. From the communication headquarters in Independence, Elder Nabil watched with Fox and Socks, whom the Apostle had taken with him, as the messages from the Saints' South American outposts flared into a virtual hurricane of questions and suggestions—before one tightly coded, perfectly worded message over the satellite link from Jerusalem answered them all. It ended with the simple injunction: "Do what you must do for your God, your religion, and freedom, and your peace, your wives, and your children." With that, all traffic on the South American links went silent, leaving the lines humming with anticipation—and determination.

* * *

Dear Chisom,

What a delight it was to visit with you and Wei Wei over the NAT. As I say so often, technology is both deadly and wonderful. Using the new equipment shows how wonderful it is. However, I wish someone would get busy and invent a teleporter. That way we could have both of you right here with us. Even so, with the NAT system, it was like sitting across the table from you. I find it truly amazing. Thank you for setting it up. I know that this is how the Twelve communicate with the First Presidency weekly, but I did not know how real it feels.

I agree with your assessment of Miss Ming—she truly is a remarkable young woman. Your mother found her quite adorable. Wei Wei was certainly gracious and appears intelligent and loving. I was impressed with her English as well. I am not surprised you feel deeply about her. May her family give you their blessing. You certainly have ours.

I reviewed your Vid on the activities and methods of Brother Light's people in your area. I am impressed with the degree of their devotion and relieved that you do not have to put up with the fanaticism of the Hands of the Prophet. Brother Light and his Hands revealed their unbelievable viciousness when they sabotaged the gathering of Reverend Tommy Gibbs and his followers. And to think that, for the time being, they got away with it. Even more stunning was the positive interest the attack generated for Brother Light in many overseas countries. That stunt, as I'm sure he anticipated, bought him a lot of disciples. The South Chinese government was wise in not allowing the Hands into their area. I understand, however, that Brother Light is recruiting heavily in the Middle East and also moving many of his followers there, especially the Hands of the Prophet. One would have to be blind not to see forces moving irresistibly toward Armageddon. I can't help but feel that Brother Light is aware of the Bible and staging this whole thing. Pushed by an unimaginable ego and satanic influence, he has deliberately set his course to prove prophecy wrong. In other words, he is challenging God. The three frogs of Revelation are driving him. You watch, my son—his ego will prove his downfall.

Over here, I fear, we could have a kind of Armageddon of our own. Even as I write, fear grips many people. The Latin American conqueror, Andrea Garza, has made veiled threats against the U.S. that promise the use of weapons of mass destruction unless it capitulates.

Oh, how well did John foresee this time period. In Revelation 9, he saw the amassing of a great army like locusts ready to swarm across the land. Interestingly, the army's first assignment was not to kill, but to torment "those men [and women] which have not the seal of God in their foreheads." John goes on to say that "in those days shall men seek death, and shall not find it; and shall desire to die, and death shall flee from them." That is exactly what we are seeing among a large segment of society. Existential angst and nihilistic hopelessness force many to consider death, but their consciences are so guilt ridden that they fear the other side. Thus, they vacillate between fears with paralyzing results. They wish to die, but stand in fear of death. To my sorrow and dismay, they refuse the hope and promise we extend. They are only, so to speak, a step away from enjoying peace and security, yet they will not join us. It fascinates me that for some, a worldly hell is far more attractive than an earthly paradise.

If conditions keep moving as they are, they will yet find death in man-made hellfire. A few months ago, I mentioned that Joel 2 speaks of the horrors of the last times being blood, fire, and, to translate literally, "palm trees of smoke." We may see that prophecy fulfilled to an extent I had not imagined. Only time will tell. Still, there is calm among the Saints. President Smith has assured our people all over the world that we have nothing to fear. It is my hope that something can be done to stop those "palm trees of smoke" from spreading too far.

I have hope about that because President Smith has given the signal to the Central and South American Saints to arise. Jesus' prophecies that I mentioned in a letter some time ago are about to be fulfilled. The Lamanites are going to move through the wicked Gentiles as lions among sheep. Nothing will stop them now, and their enemies will fall. Mark my words, Chisom.

What a world we live in. Blood and carnage cover most lands, and yet the gospel continues to spread. Pockets of temporary peace show up in this or that area just as the Gatherers are ready to go in. They circulate among the people, gather out those who will come, and, after they leave, the peace evaporates. I have been quite delighted that peace has lasted for so long in your area and certainly pray it may continue to do so. The Church still has much to do in the Far East and in other parts of the world, and I know the time is short. It looks like we'll be pushing not just until the Lord comes but for a long time after. I am so pleased that we are both working together, albeit on opposite sides of the earth.

Please keep us posted of any developments. Especially on the interpersonal front (yes, you know what I'm talking about).

With love,
Your father,
Chinedu

* * *

"So the Americans refuse my help," Garza observed, looking at his map. Each target glittered, gold against a background of red. The plan it outlined was simple: bomb ten population centers to break the back of the Americans' will to resist, then sweep over them with a ground attack using the combined South and Central American armies as cannon fodder, forcing the few military installations to waste their weapons on masses of troops.

"Now we take the next step, the ultimate step. The Americans will choke on the irradiated dust from their own weapons, and I will be master of the entire New World!" His eyes strayed to the other maps, unlit as yet—the step beyond the next one, the conquest of the entire world. His agents in the Balkans and Eastern Europe were watching closely, knowing that their mobilization would come as soon as North America fell. Turning to the woman who sat motionless under the guns of four of Garza's personal troops, the General ordered, "Begin the attack."

Medea's eyes flicked from the guns to her Ten Tribes hackers to the map of the United States glowing in the dimness of the command tent.

Brindermann noticed her hesitation. He drew his own gun, pressing its muzzle against the shaved skull of Medea's sister. "Now is not the time for doubts."

Medea spat a Net-ranger curse at him.

"Such a small thing, but so revealing," Garza patted Medea's flame-red hair. "I wondered if you had finished altering the codes on all the Velociraptors, or if you had cut corners. Thank you for finishing the job—and for your reluctance to unleash the flight of dragons you created, which proved it." He pressed the control that sent the specialized codes Medea's team had programmed sizzling through the broadcast frequency into the electronic brains of the automated flying machines.

One by one, they purred down the runway and roared into the air, heading for the United States and the major cities that were the programmed targets for the bombs they carried in their bellies. As they flew, they automatically adjusted for the winds that screamed out of the sky. Still not detectable by radar, they were seen by spy satellites that the military had programmed to look for them. They adjusted to the sudden appearance of a squadron of fighters too, nimbly maneuvering in and out of weapons lock. One Velociraptor, moving too slowly, disappeared in a sudden ball of flame. The rest scattered, accelerating into the billowing clouds. Screaming after them, the fighters hit the cloud banks, their pilots switching to instrument flight—but not as easily as the Velociraptors. Another vivid fireball lit the inside of the cloud, but this time the radar image of a fighter blinked out on the officers' command screens. One by one, the Velociraptors evaded or destroyed their human pursuers, sweeping and turning as they learned from their mates' and the fighters' mistakes, but always circling back to their programmed courses.

* * *

"They're coming, Senator," Ettinger announced, opening the door to Cox's office. "Just got word from Defense. Looks like two dozen last-generation UCAVs are still in the air and closing fast. Whoever's piloting them is a flight-simulator champion. They've evaded two flights of fighters. We lost seven planes."

"They're unmanned, driven by computers. What about the override codes? Has anybody been able to send the overrides?" Cox asked, pulling on her coat. The FBI agent turned personal security assistant moved to help her, hurrying her along even though he suspected that it was already too late for either of them to get to safety.

The capital city had dissolved into almost complete chaos; only the discipline of the National Guard troops kept the Capitol itself secure. It seemed like those who weren't fleeing Washington, or trying to, had decided to demolish it before the bomb had a chance to do it for them. Thank God, she sent a wordless prayer heavenward, her husband (and Charles and, with any luck, Greg) had been able to get to the temple community before the streets filled with desperate, despairing anarchists. Everyone who could leave already had; she'd stayed to offer her assistance to the president—or rather, to his military advisers, since the president himself had boarded Air Force One and was on his way to a secured location far from the likely impact zones. They had appreciated her insights into the exact numbers and types of weapons Garlick had "lent" to Garza, but they eventually dismissed her, advising her to get out of town, which she was at last going to do—or try to do.

As the senator snatched up her purse, the phone on her desk rang, startling them both. Shooting Ettinger an apologetic glance, she darted back to grab it before joining him at the door. Just the fact that a call came through the packed circuits was enough to make it sufficiently important to take, even if it did delay them slightly. When she heard the voice on the other end, she nearly dropped the small handset.

"Senator Cox, this is Elder Molina of the Quorum of the Twelve," he said.

"I know who you are, sir," Cox exclaimed. "But what—where— I thought you were in—"

"I am in Washington now," he interrupted gently, the smile clearly audible in his voice. He was in Washington, but more specifically he was sitting on the front seat of a huge, silver city bus with the word *Zion* shining across its destination sign. "We have some important information for you, Senator. General Garza employed a group of computer specialists to reprogram the drones sent by the late Secretary Garlick. We have the new codes, which we must get to you."

"Where exactly are you?" Cox asked. If she'd thought about it, she might have stopped to wonder how an Apostle came by illegal variants of top-secret military codes, but the confidence in his voice and the warm confirmation she felt came through so strongly that the question didn't even register at the time.

"As I said, we are coming to you," Elder Molina said. Brother Valados gave him a confident nod, pulling through lanes that miraculously opened in the traffic-jammed streets. "We are on the street east of the Capitol building now. I am sending three young men to help you through the fighting. Can you get to a door they can reach and tell your guards to stand down?"

"Yes." She rattled off directions, practically running through the eerily deserted halls. Staffers and other senators who had waited too long to escape huddled in their offices, afraid to leave a building that had become both a refuge and a deadly trap. They cowered, afraid of the incoming bombs, but more afraid of the seething mob of people outside the gates who blamed them for the situation. It boiled down to a choice between an immediate, messy death or a delayed but relatively clean demise—and most people, when given the option, choose to delay the inevitable for as long as possible.

Elder Molina repeated the senator's directions aloud, his voice precise. Just twice, he asked for clarifications, seeing confusion on Perro's face. Finally, he said, "Thank you, Senator," and clicked off the connection. "She will be waiting for you in two minutes," he told the three Santos. "Go and get her. Have faith. The Lord will help you."

With that, Brother Valados opened the door. Dove hit the ground first, Calvin and Perro right after him, spreading slightly to either side. Like an abstract arrowhead, they drove into the chaos surrounding the Capitol. Vaulting over the heavy concrete barriers, the three young men cut through a shouting mass of people throwing rocks and debris at the building and the guards surrounding it. Perro bounced heavily off the shoulder of one huge man, who whirled to swing a haymaker blow at his head. He ducked, rebounded into another body, and found himself surrounded by furious, fist-waving people. Drawing back his own fists, he braced to take a stand and give as good as he got—when Dove broke through the ring and grabbed him.

"Keep moving!" Dove shouted. "Just have faith they'll get out of your way!"

Muttering what else he'd be glad to have enough faith to make them do, Perro fell in behind Dove again. This time, he just kept moving, no matter what loomed in front of them. So did Calvin, feeling as if he were surfing the thin curl on the edge of a miracle, refusing to look down or think about it, lest he begin to sink into the water under his feet.

The vast, gray wall of the building loomed in front of them, cut at regular intervals with windows, columns, and doors. A shout sounded from somewhere above, accompanied by a sharp whistle—and the sharper whine of bullets. The belated cracks of gunfire hit at the same time that chips of concrete sprayed up in front of Dove, announcing that the National Guardsmen had finally seen the three supernaturally successful intruders.

"Stop! Friendlies!" Ettinger dove out of a small entrance, waving toward the snipers on the roof. "Senator Cox!" he shouted, trying any words that he thought might penetrate the military panic on the upper balcony. "Senator! Friendlies! Cease fire!" His suit coat, belling out behind him in the stiff wind, acquired a pair of new, ragged buttonholes.

"Ma'am, you need to come now," Dove called, dodging around the gesticulating agent. He extended a hand to Senator Cox as another bullet spanged off the iron railing beside Calvin. "Elder Molina's waiting for us."

"Coming," she said, taking his hand.

He swept her around, taking her arm. Calvin took the other, with a quick, shy smile, and the two of them took off, moving her at a faster pace than she would've thought possible. Perro, adding his own vivid phrase to Ettinger's yip of surprise, grabbed the FBI agent's jacket shoulder and hauled him along too. They aimed directly at what looked like the tide of writhing humanity, pushing through the barriers and dashing through the eddies in the crowd.

"Don't look back, and don't look sideways," Perro advised Ettinger as they pounded through the clear spaces. "Just keep watching Dove, and don't think about it." He caught the agent's shocked expression and looked up at the silver front of the bus that loomed in front of them, somehow within the outer ring of concrete barriers and, with a shrug, added, "Don't think about that either."

The door hissed open. "Next stop, the Pentagon," Brother Valados announced, as Dove and Calvin literally tossed Senator Cox up the stairs before rushing in themselves. She managed to keep her feet long enough to redirect her momentum, with quick assistance from Sister Valados and Sister Molina, into a semidignified collapse on the front bench.

"Unless you think we should go somewhere else," the driver added, closing the door behind Ettinger and Perro and pulling into the divinely provided space that let the bus travel through any traffic obstacle without even seeming to do anything unusual.

"The Pentagon will be just perfect," she gasped, out of breath after her run.

Dove handed her purse to her, half smiling apologetically. "Sorry about the rough dash, ma'am, but we needed to hurry."

"We surely do," Cox agreed, pulling out her phone and punching in a top-secret number that Greg had ferreted out for her. "I haven't run so far or so fast in ages. But thanks to you two boys, I think I'll be just fine." At the tone, she added her authorization code and heard the call signal sound on the other end. Unable to resist, she added, "You both must be good dancers."

As the two Santos traded a puzzled glance, and the two sisters exchanged an amused one, she amended, "No, not you, Lieutenant.

This is Senator Holly Cox. I must speak to the secretary of defense immediately. Tell him I know why his codes aren't working on those UCAVs—and I have the codes that will."

* * *

"I hope you're right," a gruff general informed the senator as he hurried her—and her strange entourage—down a bustling hallway. The military contingent wasn't huddling or cowering, though they may have wanted to; they all exuded hard-faced, purposeful focus.

In a glass-and-LED room that reminded Dove strongly of Fox and Socks's lair but tripled in size, they came to a halt in front of a bank of monitors. Harried techs slammed code after code into the ether, trying to make connection with the oncoming UCAVs, to break their connection with their ground-based controllers. The automated planes refused to acknowledge the codes or allow communication with the Pentagon command center—or any of the other military bases that bombarded them with orders to stop, retreat, land, or self-destruct.

The secretary of defense, pacing as he watched the satellite and radar images of the planes drawing closer, looked up. A thin smile crossed his face. "The Senate rides to the rescue, eh? Well, what do you have?" He gestured at the techs. "Show us what we're doing wrong."

Cox didn't bother to answer the sarcasm. Instead, she nodded at Elder Molina, who handed the glittering disc to the chief tech. "Garza changed the UCAVs' programming. They're not tied to human operators anymore," she told them. "These are the new codes—and the new command channel, courtesy of our agents in Chile."

With a slight shrug, the secretary of defense indicated that he was willing to try anything at this point. The general nodded to the tech. "Implement the new codes, lieutenant."

"Looks like we've got a comm lock," the lieutenant announced, as the communications channel finally glowed on the screen. He expertly read the codes scrolling across the bottom. "Looks like we've got one code for each plane, and they're either self-destruct sequences or abort orders."

"Destroy the UCAVs?" the secretary of defense yipped. Catching glares from both Senator Cox and the military men in the room, he waved his hands. "Fine. We've already lost the budget on them anyway."

"Send the order," the general told the lieutenant, who saluted and hit the button.

"Communication established," the lieutenant said tensely. A grin spread across his face as he followed it with, "Orders accepted. Program changes underway!"

Dove caught Calvin's eye and grinned, exchanging a subtle handclasp. Perro wasn't so discreet, whooping, "Yes, Mercury! Viva Santos!"

The techs' and officers' incredulous looks changed gradually to amazement, then to sheer delight, as one by one the planes' trajectories slowed and curved away as they received the abort order. Like gigantic, metal homing pigeons, they turned back toward Bogotá.

* * *

"We've got interference on the channel. Something's in the system—they're coming back!" Medea shouted. She stared at the screen, which showed the same scene that caused rejoicing in the Pentagon. It caused utter consternation in Garza's headquarters tent.

"Cut the outside access," Brindermann snarled. "Get them back on course."

"I can't." Medea's hands flashed over the controls. Beside her, the two other hackers did the same, with identical results. "They're using the same connection I am—there's got to be a splice somewhere in our system. We don't have time to find it and wrangle planes at the same time. I can override the abort order, but the intruder just puts in another one. We keep doing this, the planes' processors are going to lock into a loop."

"They're turning back toward us," Brindermann reminded her.

"Are they sending them back at us?" Garza demanded.

"No—they can't. They've just got the abort codes, not the whole range of commands. I—we kept them separate to increase security," Medea said. "The leak only got the comm channel and abort code."

"They wouldn't send the bombs back armed, in any case." Brindermann's voice dripped contempt when he realized that the planes, though stymied, were still under control and not mindlessly reversing course to deliver their bombs to their point of origin. "They do not know for certain that you are here in Bogotá, and they would not risk destroying civilians."

"What happens if they lock?" Garza watched defeat coming at him.

"The planes lose control—basically, they ditch into the ocean or ground or whatever," Medea told him. "Instant metal pancakes, and you've lost all your bombs."

Silence lasted for five long minutes, as the hackers' efforts vainly attempted to persuade the Velociraptors to continue their mission. On the screen, twenty-one unmanned planes switched back and forth, engines straining as they tried to obey conflicting orders. Only a single plane escaped the fate of its cousins. Rogue and not responding to commands from either Washington or Bogotá, it drove forward, flying northward in huge sweeps over ocean and land. With mechanical precision, it kept to its course, even as towering thunderheads rose in its path, boiling out of clear skies. Lightning crackled along the tops of the cloud mountains, glowing from deep inside the vast storm. The Velociraptor slowed to attack speed when it detected the strings of glowing jewels that marked the city sprawled across the desert. The plane's orders didn't tell it to attack Albuquerque, but its off-kilter automatic brain settled for any large settlement to fulfill the lost parameters and triggered the ignition switches, sending the bombs rolling forward in their deployment bays. Before the bombs could drop, two massive lightning strikes reached up from the ground toward the clouds, enveloping the plane in blinding, searing energy that shorted every circuit, fused every board, and melted the delicate fuselage into a ruined hulk that began the long fall toward the ground and final destruction.

Far below, Sam and Renata Begay watched a sudden, brilliant light flare in the sky, then fall flaming to the earth. Around them, cheers rose from the Saints gathered on the hilltop. Channel 8 was already relaying word that a freak electrical storm had destroyed one incoming bomb. The Mormons knew better.

The fireballs on the screens reflected in the General's eyes as he said, "Bring them home." He couldn't afford to lose the planes; his entire plan depended on technological superiority. His iron certainty wobbled for a split second, before his insatiable pride and anger reasserted itself. He could salvage the situation and punish those responsible for this humiliating defeat.

Medea let the planes accept the abort order and turned her attention to pulling the unauthorized splice out of the communications network.

Thousands of miles away, Sister Molina caught Dove's arm, pointing at the screen as the channel icon went dark.

"Looks like they pulled the plug on their end." Ettinger leaned over to look at it too.

Around them, jubilant celebration broke out as the UCAVs disappeared from the screens, dropping out of range, pulling evasive maneuvers that no flesh-and-blood pilot could imitate and live. The pursuing fighter pilots tracked them—until live antiaircraft fire from Garza's forces in Mexico augmented the Velociraptors' own aggressive maneuvers. The pilots' commanders called them back, recognizing that the stealth-skinned automatic planes could easily evade their men over distances.

"They found Mercury's splice," Dove told Sister Molina and Ettinger through the noise. He frowned, recalling the lonely antenna in the New Mexico desert, the tiny box Mercury had jacked into the General's transmitter—and the body of the man Garza had hired to put up the antenna in the first place.

"So, do they break out the champagne, give everybody medals, and party until dawn?" Perro pounded Dove's back, grinning.

Calvin poked him. "You better ask for milk with your medal, juvie boy."

"Let 'em keep the medals." Dove shrugged. Looking at Senator Cox, deep in conversation with the military men, he decided she had the political side well in hand. He'd had enough of a taste of doing that kind of inspirational nagging back in Amexica; he'd let her mobilize the military and civilian forces to defend themselves. The Capitol was safe, and now it was up to her to finish securing the Constitution. "We got other things to do. Come on, Santos, let's mount up."

"What? Already?" Perro protested. "There's a cute little army officer over there giving me the eye."

"Yeah, already. Save you from getting your butt kicked by a chiquita in a uniform skirt." Dove smiled at Sister Molina. "We've got an Apostle and a lady to deliver to Independence, and then we've got to get back to Amexica. Garza's going down, hard, and I want to be there to get my licks in with all those banditos he's sent to harass my family."

"Good for you, Brother Nakai." Sister Molina nodded firmly, extending her hand for Dove to help her up. They collected Elder

Molina on their way to the door, slipping away from the politicking and negotiating.

Senator Cox and a contingent of hard-faced military police caught up with them at the doorway they'd used on their way into the massive building. The MPs spread out in a protective perimeter against whatever threats might spring out of the crackling darkness around the Pentagon. Cox shook hands with all of them—and then hugged them all. "Thank you. Your country is deeply appreciative of your efforts today," she announced, then laughed, rubbing her eyes. "I'm sorry. I am deeply appreciative of your efforts, and I'm sure that other people would be too, if they realized what you'd done. Are you sure you have to go so quickly? I would love to have you stay . . . if only Washington weren't such a mess right now."

"Thank you, Sister Cox." Elder Molina pressed her hands between his, smiling at the American politician. "We should much like to visit you again, when conditions are better. For now, we have delivered our message, and we must go on. Other duties call."

"Of course they do," she agreed. With President Smith and President Rojas keeping Jerusalem from the same kind of panic that produced the smoky, orange glow rising above Washington's skyline, Elder Molina did indeed need to rejoin the other members of the Twelve. And she had a long day—many long days—ahead of her, trying to patch the damage Secretary Garlick's shortsighted selfishness had caused. Then she would have to arrange for proper thanks, medals—and sparkling cider, for Perro. Graciously, she released the Apostle's hand and smiled at them, her eyes lingering on the unusual figures of the three Santos. "Thank you again."

"Glad to help," Dove told her. "I'll tell Mercury to call you. He's the one who hacked those codes. His dad's Major Zamora."

"The Chilean rebel," she supplied instantly, impressed with this Mercury's pedigree.

"Freedom fighter," Calvin corrected, a mischievous glint in his eyes.

"Freedom fighter," she conceded, laughing. "And you three, take good care of the Molinas."

"We will—between us and Brother and Sister Valados," Dove amended. "Then we're back to Amexica. Come on, chicos. Us lions have got some sheep to protect."

"Domesticated," Perro grumbled, climbing the bus stairs. "That's what lions are that herd sheep."

"Hey, ease up, blue boy," Calvin advised, then grinned teasingly. "Sure, you missed the cute Army chiquita, but you also had a U.S. senator in your arms! How many border rats can say that?"

"Just us three," Dove answered. A deep glint flashed in his eye as he looked westward, remembering the UCAVs' flight. "But plenty more are going to be able to say they took a piece out of Garza's hide tonight." A strange feeling of pride filled him, not in himself but in the hardscrabble border rats' will to fight for the right. Their people had been hunted, killed, ground down, just as Moroni had prophesied—but, as he'd also prophesied, they'd risen at the last, to drive evil out of the promised land. And he, Salvatore Hasbídí Nakai, was part of it, part of God's army! Their Captain had come, and they would ride to victory as long as they proved faithful. Which they would, until they won the last battle. Unashamed of the tears that filled his eyes, he cried, "Viva Santos!"

Even Elder and Sister Molina joined in the answering shout, "Viva Santos!"

* * *

By sunrise, Channel 8 had reported the failure of the "latest Aztec Liberation Front terror attack," the president of the United States had emerged from his secure location to declare the USSA and its commander guilty of "aiding and supporting terrorist activities," and Garza's temper had transformed from deep-space chill to a fury that made the blazing orb rising over the treetops look cool in comparison.

Medea gave him a concise summary of what she'd found during the long night. "Somebody with internal access put a virtual splice in our communication line, then used a debugging account to break into tactical and steal the first code and command file for the UCAVs. We've pulled the splice out. We'll have to modify the hard coding on the Velociraptors to change the abort codes."

"Do it," the General commanded. "I want it done by tonight."

The hacker knew better than to argue for more time.

"All but one." Garza's words ground out between set teeth. "I want one armed right now and programmed to drop its payload directly on that obscenity of a temple in Santiago."

"Santiago is one of the most productive cities in South—" Brindermann's protest died as Garza's hand shot out to wrap around the German's throat.

Garza pulled his lieutenant's face down to his own. "The Mormons in Chile hacked your network, stole those codes, and hijacked my planes. They fooled that idiot Serrey—and you—into believing that a band of code rats did it. I tolerated your fetish for Mormons because I thought it wouldn't matter to my plans and might help move the mobilization forward. I now know I was wrong. The world knows I was wrong, and they are laughing, making jokes at my expense." Gazing into the blue eyes inches from his own, he asked, "Do you want to make a comment?"

Brindermann stared back, hearing Rosa del Torres's voice alternating with that of Clara Cortez as the USSA spokeswoman tried vainly to salvage the reputation and status of her president and employer. With every word, the fire in Garza's eyes flamed higher. "No," Brindermann said at last.

"Good." Garza let him go and turned his attention back to Medea.

Brindermann straightened, his iron self-discipline stopping his hands from reaching up to touch the bruises darkening on his throat. He watched as a single Velociraptor flew into the gathering clouds, aiming for Santiago, its self-contained guidance system safe from any outside interference.

Other communication channels sprang to life, however. As the intelligent flying machine battled the fierce winds over the Andes and oriented on the shining building at the outskirts of Santiago, signals poured out of the sky to every receiver in Central and South America, bearing just one message: "The lion wakes." Conscripted computer techs throughout Brindermann's perfect bureaucracy sent acknowledgments and passed the message through the computer and human networks. Locked boxes appeared from under stacks of potatoes and toilet paper, springing open as eager fingers keyed in the codes that popped their high-tech locks. Heavy packages passed swiftly from hand to hand; workers took oddly sequential bathroom breaks and came back to their posts with heavy folds in their coats. Inside the communications system, virtual switches opened, electrons flowed, and the curtain of silence that had covered Chile tore apart.

Mercury, dozing in the command center beneath the Santiago Temple, woke to the sudden hum and whistle of reactivated communications links. He read the message pouring across the screen and ran, shouting with excitement, up the stairs to find Captain Guerra, President Reyes, and anyone else to share the good news. "We're back! The Molinas are safe! And we're on the march!"

* * *

The elder Zamora emerged from a subterranean room as well, but with considerably less excitement. Military police closed around him, escorting him from his cell. They pushed the pace, purposely forcing Zamora to limp painfully on his wounded leg. Only President Aguilera's orders that Zamora appear unharmed for his trial and, Zamora suspected, a thin slice of divine intervention, had kept Serrey from doing much more than simply denying him food and any more than the barest medical care during the last two weeks. The security chief had visited almost daily, however, telling him that they had captured Captain Guerra or begun shooting Mormon conscripts. The major's calm in the face of these statements infuriated Serrey, but he had to content himself with describing in vivid and vicious detail what he planned to do to Zamora, and Vasquez, if he caught her, and the rest of the Mormons in Chile, once Aguilera's precious trial had convicted Zamora of assassinating President Quintana and vindicated Aguilera's presidency. Now it appeared that the promised but vague court date might have arrived at last.

The major's famously calm expression showed no sign of the pain he felt, even when he stumbled on La Moneda's sweeping staircase. He came to a halt at last in the office that Aguilera had stolen from President Quintana. The bloodstained carpet, he noted with the shadow of a sardonic grin, had been replaced. The beautiful ebony desk had not. To his surprise, however, none of the men in the room paid him any attention initially. Their eyes were fixed on the screen that dominated one wall of the familiar office. The comm tech monitoring the feed made an adjustment, and the picture flickered between a satellite shot of the city and tracking telemetry from the computer installation where Mercury had worked his magic.

"Unidentified intruder sighted above Santiago," a crisp voice narrated. "Suspected drone. Bogotá orders stand-down on all defensive measures."

At the same moment the Velociraptor reached the apex of its flight and released Garza's revenge from its munitions bay, a long-dormant camera mounted on the temple's satellite transceiver sprang to life, broadcasting the image of a shining star in a blue sky. All over the Church network, Saints, and others, watched as the bomb's guidance engine flamed into brilliant life. The rocket soared, following its course perfectly, aiming exactly for the temple's spire. It grew larger, the lethal power of a nuclear reactor hidden in its silver nose, the embodiment of Garza's destructive fury—and then it wobbled, the engine flamed out, and the sleek agent of destruction fell into the dormant flower bed in front of the temple, punching out a deep crater and spraying dirt over a wide area. It lay there, smoking slightly, completely harmless. A vast cheer rose from Zion communities all over the world, a roar of praise to the God who protected His faithful people.

Watching the unbelievable sight of the missile deflected and deactivated, Garza heard the Mormons' jubilation only in his mind, and it turned his rage into madness. "Kill them!" he screamed. "Kill them all!" The scream echoed in official communications all over Garza's vast, unstable empire.

"Bogotá orders all Mormon traitors terminated," said the same crisp voice over the open channel that had carried the General's humiliating defeat.

Serrey, however, was more interested in the orders as given than in wondering why the communications officer didn't repeat them. He looked at Zamora and smiled. "Well, turns out we won't have to waste effort on a trial after all. We'll just take you out in the public square and shoot you to prove to the rest of the Mormon scum that they can't get away with not getting burned up when the General bombs them."

"What will you do to prove to the non-Mormon scum that they can't get away with not getting burned up when the General bombs them?" Zamora asked, his voice still calm and utterly reasonable. "That bomb would have incinerated all of us if it had hit the temple."

"Oh, nonsense!" Aguilera brushed off the implication. "Garza wouldn't send a nuke. That was just a bunker buster. A defective one. Rather like you, Manuel—a defective weapon."

Archuleta, however, went a bit pale as the implication of Zamora's suggestion hit him.

"What does it matter?" Serrey shrugged off the entire topic, pulling his gun from its holster in one smooth, practiced motion. "Whether you escaped the bomb or not, you're going to die now." He glanced around at the office and laughed as his lazy, psychotic eyes passed over Aguilera, Archuleta, Fresno, the nervous guards, the impassive comm tech at the console, Zamora standing in front of the desk. "Looks like the same old scene again. Will you jump out the window like you did last time, Manuel? But this time we've got you surrounded."

Zamora, who had watched the darkened monitor all the while Serrey threatened him, was the first to see the comm tech rise from his chair and turn to face the assembled officers and president—with a leveled gun held in his steady fist. A soft noise from the corridor made the already nervous Archuleta slew around, only to see another group of men stride into the room. Señor Colón tossed a salute and a smile at Zamora. At the same time, every conscripted technician, bureaucrat, gardener, cook, and driver in Santiago had stepped forward to confront Aguilera's and Garza's forces, armed to the teeth and determined to drive the invaders out.

"Are you sure about that, Jorge?" Zamora said.

Something clicked inside Serrey's head, the sadistic viciousness that lurked there abruptly snuffing out the logical calculation that held it in check. With a weirdly feline hiss, Serrey stepped away from the presidential desk, giving himself room to maneuver, and leveled his pistol at Zamora. It wavered as the first bullet hit Serrey, sending him stumbling backward, but he moved inexorably back to aim again. Zamora caught the gun that Colón threw to him, blasting a second hole in Serrey's chest. Once again, the security chief howled, trying for another shot—and once again, Zamora shot him. The force of the final bullet, combined with his own momentum, sent him crashing into the glass behind the silken curtains. This time, it was Serrey who pitched out of the office windows, but he landed lifeless on the grass below with three bullet holes in him.

Aguilera, shouting with terror and fury for his guards to kill the impostors, took cover behind the heavy desk where his predecessor had died. Fresno, as stupid as he was big and loyal, went down hard, a bullet from Zamora's next shot in his head. Another guard died as well, pulling his pistol on Colón's grim-faced techs. Archuleta looked at the bodies, at the Mormons surrounding him, and held up his hands, dropping his own weapon. Aguilera called him a coward; the Mormons forcibly separated the two and cuffed them.

"La Moneda secure," Señor Colón reported through the console to the resistance at large. Glancing at Zamora, who had sunk wearily into the president's chair, he added, "Major Zamora is in our custody as well."

All over Garza's empire, the supposedly humble, meek Mormons pulled out the weapons they had held back, hidden, and appropriated. The *mayores* and other opportunists who had turned a blind eye to the conscripts' long hours and depended on their frightened obedience found themselves staring into the determined faces and menacing gun barrels of their erstwhile slaves. Far to the north, in the borderlands and throughout Mexico, men wearing the sword-bearing angel logo of the Santos Soldados led their comrades on lightning-strike raids against Garza's agents and armies. The General's cannon-fodder forces, made up of bullies who preyed on the weak, panicked and ran, only to be hunted down and rounded up by the people they had thought of as easy marks. Without their leader's technological superiority to back them, they lost ground to the wave of fathers, brothers, and sons that rose to defend their homes, families, freedom, and religion. The militias, gangs, thugs, rebels, corrupt military officers, and all other oppressors crumbled under the prophesied onslaught of the "remnant of Jacob" and their allies that rose out of the stakes of Zion "as a lion among the beasts of the forest, and as a young lion among the flocks of sheep" to destroy the enemies whose actions set in motion the divine promise of defeat for those who disregarded God's commandments in the promised land. For weeks, battles raged all over Central and South America. Though some put up valiant fights, Garza's forces succumbed to the fury of righteousness. But mostly, the opposition simply collapsed, because the fighters either didn't have the heart for the job or ceased to kick against the pricks.

CHAPTER 20

General Garza stared in blank disbelief as, one by one, the lights on his maps winked out. The horrified announcements from his elite staff rang in his ears: "We've lost Quito!" "Tierra del Fuego is gone!" "All of Bolivia just disconnected from the command net!" "Belize has fallen!" His entire empire dissolved before his eyes, the grandly and ironically named United States of South America coming apart like the beads of a broken necklace. No, not quite like that; as the would-be conqueror watched, a new pattern began to form. The countries were not breaking apart into the ruthless nationalistic anarchy that had kept Latin America divided, torn, and wounded for centuries. They were emerging under a new leadership, a philosophy of equality and charity that was as foreign to Garza as the divine power motivating and supporting the new leadership. Garza did not believe in God, and he had not wanted to believe in defeat, but he recognized it when he saw it marching toward him. On the leather shoes of computer techs and bureaucrats, of all things!

"Pull out." The two words struck the frantic techs and junior lieutenants dumb. Their blank faces turned toward their leader, who shouted, "Pull out!" His voice settled, crisp and clear. "Emergency evac, all top-level troops. Get the weapons loaded. Implement retreat plans." Turning on his heel, he stalked out. If only El Jaguar had lived, the idiot—the crackle of weapons fire at the headquarters' fences interrupted his mourning for lost tools that might have pulled victory from defeat.

General Garza didn't wait to hear that even his sabotage plans had failed. Pausing just long enough to oversee the flight of the Velociraptors into the wild sky, he ran to his own emergency transport. A knot of officers ran with him, thinking to accompany him to safety, only to stare in horror as the plane's staircase rose without them. "Die fighting," Garza advised them from the portal, as the plane began to pull away. "Make me proud."

Closing the door, he threw himself into a crash seat, buckling in as the plane screamed down the runway, scattering panicking guerillas and hardened soldiers. A hard bump said that one hadn't moved fast enough, but the jar didn't have enough force to slow the plane. Reaching the far end of the runway, it followed the automated planes into the sky. Immediately, the wind seized it, shaking the frail machine until it stabilized, banking around to streak out over the ocean. The storm boiled and roared behind it, thunder rumbling threats and lightning flashing. It grew, reaching out, nipping at the plane's heels as it began the long journey to North Africa. Garza had intended to use the bases there as the initial staging area of the next phase of his conquest; now, they were just the first stop on a headlong retreat across two continents. The thought burned in his brain.

Brindermann turned from the window to see Garza staring at him over the muzzle of a gun. His face as impassive as ever, he asked, "Are you sure you want to lose another vital asset today?"

"And what makes you so vital, after today's events?" Garza asked.

"You need someone to bring order and discipline to Brother Light's crazed fanatics," Brindermann said.

"And why would I need that?" A flicker of suspicion—and amusement—appeared in the General's eyes. Trust Johann to play a trump card at the last moment. It was almost a pity that they'd looked at each others' decks so often.

"Because you and I have both approached the so-called Prophet about using his forces to take the Middle East." Brindermann shrugged. "It amused him that we each had the same idea. But he was willing to ally with us to further his own plans. The man intends to prove his god supreme by taking Jerusalem."

"And I intend to take the land bridge between Asia, Europe, and Africa—with its oil reserves as a convenient fallback," Garza shrugged back. "We have the Velociraptors and the weapons stockpiles our Balkan friends have prepared for us to handle any major fighting. My negotiations with Brother Light were perfunctory, merely an agreement that he will stay out of my way. Why would we provide order and discipline?"

"Because your high-tech weapons are only part of the puzzle. You have the Velociraptors," he paused as a hard jolt of turbulence shook the plane, then continued, "or at least as many as make it through the storm, and our Balkan friends can supply the smart bombs and heavy equipment, but you need bodies, and Light can supply them. My own negotiations were considerably more detailed. The Children of Light are already swarming like bees, badly disrupting the military efforts of the already tottering governments in that area, but their leader has no head for tactics. When I asked his plans, he laughed and said that he had 'as many children as the Muslims had bullets'—hardly a logical strategy for permanent conquest. But a useful one for us, if we control when and where the Children of Light meet those bullets. Our double-edged strategy in Mexico worked—until the Mormons betrayed us. There will be no Mormon underground this time."

Garza considered, noting the acid edges to Brindermann's tone. The German felt the sudden reversal as strongly as he did, perhaps more, since he wanted to put an end to the chaos, warfare, destruction, and waste that he had seen as a child in Eastern Europe. Brindermann's obsession with order made a convenient leash.

At last, the General nodded, holstering his gun. (Neither of the men paid attention to Medea's hacker crew, huddled at the far end of the compartment, so they didn't see the Net rangers' disappointment.) The German would never make the same mistake twice, and perhaps he was just treacherous enough to trust. For now. "Very well, Johann. You have charge of the bodies. What will you do with them?"

Brindermann smiled back, the expression wintry. "That depends on where you want them. As the tactical genius and world conqueror, you should know best where to deploy your cannon fodder. As a good bureaucrat, I will simply arrange for the best ways to follow your commands."

"Good. I'll give you the first one right now." Garza's smile broadened. "We will take Palestine and Israel, Johann—and I want you to personally supervise the complete extermination of every Mormon between the borders of Iran and Egypt."

"Shall I add the Jews to the list as well?" Brindermann asked, a trace of bitterness in his voice at Garza's reference to the old Nazi stereotype.

"I think our friend Brother Light will take care of most of that for us," Garza admitted. He lit a cigar, leaning back to watch the wild clouds scudding along beside the plane. Another whirl of turbulence rattled their teeth. "But just in case he doesn't, I want you to prevent any possibility of Mormon resistance. Make sure they will never steal from me again—and we both know that dead men carry neither tales nor stolen command codes. Nor do they stage amusing little rivalries or place bets. I will miss our American fighting dogs, Johann."

* * *

Garza's fighting dogs, the elite officers and command crew, missed him as well—though they expressed it in panted curses as they ran to fight or escape the oncoming resistance forces. Far from headquarters, specially picked crews carried out their own emergency orders, spreading out to sabotage charges that would destroy railroads, transmitter stations, and power plants. To their amazement and horror, however, they found the opposition waiting for them when they moved in to set off the bombs laid around the Mormons' ghettos.

"Thank you, Ricky," Brother Neruda said with a smile, removing a heavy plastique bomb from the shaking hands of a would-be saboteur whose orders sent him to destroy the gates of the temple in Bogotá. Though the attacks on the government infrastructure succeeded— segments of oil pipeline burst into flames, railroad lines like the one over a steep mountain pass in Peru vanished in man-made avalanches, the power grid flickered and went out—the same scene of failure played out all over the occupied territories when the saboteurs tried to wound the Saints.

In the city of Santiago, with the roar of the sporadic fighting between the last holdouts of Aguilera's army and the insurgents some- times drowning out her words, Rosa del Torres stood in the fresh- ening rain under the thunderstorm, trying to salvage the situation, turn the reversal to her advantage somehow. She'd come to cover the trial of Major Zamora; instead, she saw Aguilera's government crum- bling and heard rumors that Garza himself had been routed.

"In a surprise coup against the legitimate government of the United States of South America, rebel forces have risen and taken control of capital cities all over the young country," she shouted. "Reports confirm that General Garza was able to avoid assassination by the terrorists surrounding the General's Bogotá headquarters. Highly placed sources assert that Garza was able to secure the command codes for the American weapons before his retreat . . ." So intent was she on her explanation that she didn't notice the red light on the camera's top flicker and die as Channel 8 cut her feed.

Major Zamora, emerging haltingly from La Moneda with Captain Guerra, heard the reporter before he saw her. With a sigh and a prayer for patience, he limped over to her and caught her arm. "Ms. Del Torres, you should get under cover. It's raining." When that statement failed to penetrate the blank stare she gave him, he added, "And the fighting isn't quite over yet. If you stay here, someone may shoot you." He sounded like he could thoroughly sympathize with whoever that might be.

She tried to pull away. "You can't interrupt a live broadcast like this! You can't accost me before a worldwide audience . . ." Her voice trailed off as he shook his head.

"I'm sorry, Ms. Del Torres. No one is watching." He pointed to the camera, now lying on the ground where the cameraman had left it when the major distracted her. Unlike the reporter, the cameraman had a well-developed sense of self-preservation—though he feared Zamora more than any random gunfire.

Rosa stared at the abandoned camera, seeing in its inert silver shape the ruin of all her schemes and dreams, the end of the career she'd sold her soul for—and that vision broke the nerve that a hundred bloody murder scenes, jungle fights, and interviews with vicious terrorists couldn't shake. She fainted dead away.

Zamora more or less caught her. Mercury, tearing up to his father, helped lower the woman the last few inches to the ground. After figuring out that she'd just fainted—rain on her face would be just the thing—he didn't waste any more time on her. He touched his father's shoulder. His last couple of weeks of wondering if he would ever see his papa again vanished in a cessation of tension so sharp it almost hurt, like the disappearance of a wall he'd spent his strength pushing against. The lack of resistance nearly toppled him into tears. "Are you all right?"

Zamora grabbed his son and hugged him. "I'm fine. Tired of this hip, hungry as a horse. Better for seeing you." He waved Captain Guerra over, directing him to take Rosa into protective custody. With the look in her eyes, he feared what she might do when she woke. Then he leaned against Mercury's shoulder, as the two of them staggered to the car that Señor Olivares once more sent to pick them up.

Reassured that the major would hold out until they reached the temple community, Mercury plunged into the more important news he had to deliver. "The Church satellite network is back online, but it looks like everything else has collapsed. Brindermann's crews toasted their own network before they left. A bunch more blew up all the power plants they could reach. One outfit even tried to overload a nuclear reactor, but our people caught them before they got in. Now, the only power anywhere in South America comes from the Church stations."

Zamora whispered a prayer of thanks, hugging Mercury's shoulder again in love and support. The car door opened, and Dr. Vasquez jumped out, hurrying over to take charge of her patient. Zamora smiled, feeling a huge weight lift. "All the power anywhere came from the Church stations. That's the way it's always been. It's just more obvious now."

* * *

"Power comes to those willing to reach out and take it," Rashi Janjalani observed to the man thousands of miles away in a harsh Moroccan desert, hastening to meet him in yet another desert. "You will be a powerful man, Herr Brindermann."

"Power is a means to an end for me," Brindermann said. "A tool only. For General Garza, however, it is an end in itself, which is the reason for this conversation. Garza agrees to assist the success of your religious crusade in return for your followers' assistance in pacifying the populations of the occupied territories. Do you accept the General's offer of alliance?"

"In the name of the One God and the Unity of all creation, we accept," Janjalani intoned. "Thus may we be bound, for all time."

Brindermann either missed or refused to acknowledge the liturgical slant that Brother Light had put on their gentlemen's agreement. "Noted. Also accepted. Is this channel secure?"

"Absolutely." Janjalani covered a yawn. The connection came through the satellite link that he secured through Ivana Mir, paying her in funds she still fiercely hoped to spend back on Earth someday. It had even better reception than Channel 8's ubiquitous signal, and certainly better encryption.

"You will receive further communications in one hour, outlining strategy considerations and operations timetables. I am sending the initial outline now." Watching the data flit through the ether, Brindermann added, "It is absolutely confidential and must remain that way. Do you understand?"

"We will burn the tongue from the mouth of any who whisper your secrets. Rest on your faith," the Prophet and Incarnation of the One God assured his new ally in the great battle against the infidel. "Control freak," he added after clicking off the connection.

"So the Western infidels will help us?" Sepphira asked, knowing that Rashi didn't want to deal with forming up an army; he was God, not a military planner.

Janjalani stretched. "The high and mighty General Andrea Garza will be a tool in Our divine hand to prove to the world that We are the one true God."

He says it so casually, Sepphira thought. *Why do I fear so much that General Garza is a weapon that will turn on its master?* Rashi also considered the devils, the almost man-shaped shadows hovering in ever-growing numbers around him, as tools. She suspected that he would be surprised to learn they saw him exactly the same way. She only hoped that he was strong enough to prove them wrong.

Brother Light opened the embroidered flap of his tent and looked out at the vast camp of Children of Light. The white-robed soldiers had joined his crusade from the sheep camps, opium fields, oil refineries, battlefields, and slums of India, Pakistan, Afghanistan, Iran, Iraq, Kharagizstan, Turkey—everywhere corrupt governments and intolerant clergymen preached fanaticism that led their followers into Janjalani's clutches. They would help him prove to the world that he was the only true deity, the One God of the earth against whom none could stand. Jerusalem beckoned him; once he took it, none could cling to their dead gods or deny their whole-souled devotion to the Unity. Miracles, like the blasting of Tommy Gibbs and the destruction of the Aswan Dam, which he prophesied as well as lent his Hands to arrange, gained attention but could not convince by themselves. No, the world understood violence, power, and wealth—with this vast army, he had all of those, and with Garza behind him, he had the technological power to stage miracles of destruction unmatched in any age.

Even without technology, the Children of Light already left destruction and devastation in their wake. They swarmed like iron locusts across the most fertile and livable routes to their destination, looting and pillaging their way through India, the Levant, and the Middle East. Another contingent, smaller but even more voracious, spread across North Africa and through the western wastes of Egypt, moving across the deserts in a fleet of commandeered vehicles, stripping the oases bare. They seized food, water, vehicles, weapons, fuel, and even people, supplying themselves by stripping their surroundings bare as they rolled through the countryside. What they couldn't use or carry, they ruined, blew up, and burned; pillars of smoke and fire marked their passage.

The locals, caught in the path of what seemed to them like a human hurricane of immense and pitiless proportions, had a simple choice, if they survived long enough to make it: accept the Unity, profess faith in the One God, and join his crusade, or die. Most threw their hands in the air and loudly proclaimed that they had found the one true religion. That profession didn't save them all, however; though Brother Light assured the starry-eyed European reporters that his camps were outposts of safety and security in the godforsaken world, every morning bodies (sometimes white robed, more often naked, because the dead don't need clothes and the living do) lay in the wake of the night's camp, exhausted by the hard march, dehydrated, and starving. In the Unity, all property was owned in common, but the strong could claim and keep more of the common wealth than the weak could.

Forces sent to stop the swarming advance found themselves looking through their rifle sights at children who ran in advance of the vast army. The children, ranging from near teenage to barely old enough to follow orders, scouted, spied, and reported back to their black-robed, crimson-hooded masters, earning the rations of rice and water that kept them alive, the treats of candy that kept them hoping for more. And sometimes they carried gifts for the soldiers across the ridges, gifts that exploded in their backpacks, sending them to heaven and the soldiers to hell.

* * *

Benjamin Cohen watched the screen, as if from a cloud, as a tiny figure ran forward toward battalions of guards ranged along the Jordanian border. Others appeared out of the desert scrub, following the first. They drew nearer, the burdens on their backs clear. And then the first fell, spinning almost entirely around, before hitting the ground in a small cloud of dust. The others followed, mowed down in a hail of bullets as the soldiers at the front finally obeyed their commanders' orders to shoot. Fires blossomed from several of the small bodies, as the bombs they carried ticked off their last second.

Tears streaming down his face, the architect turned away from the feed coming from the Church's satellite cameras, broadcasting the hard truth to all who would see it and listen to the reality of Brother Light's crusade. Many refused; they had their own problems, and the cynical even proclaimed that if anyone could bring peace to the region and stabilize fuel prices, they said more power to him. "Oh, Hannah, how could anyone do such a horrible thing?"

Hannah put her arms around him, holding him close. "They do it to break the will of the soldiers," she said. "They know that good men cannot easily shoot children and keep fighting. So they use the babies the way the Americans used cluster bombs—to soften the resistance for a later, harder blow." She knew he didn't need to hear the tactics behind it, but she needed to say it; putting words to the pictures made her feel there might be a rational reason behind the insanity they saw, a logic, even a cold logic, that she could understand, if not relate to.

All over Jerusalem, Mormons, Jews, and Muslims watched the same horrible pictures, all made worse by a deepening realization that the entire demonic horde drew nearer day by day to the city that Brother Light still claimed to want to enter only "as a peaceful pilgrim." That story did not square particularly well with the fact that his followers drew up in a siege all along the borders of the states neighboring Israel/Palestine.

"We seek only peaceful passage," Brother Light protested for the hundredth time, his remarkable eyes limpid and compelling as he addressed the world through his satellite link. "All who worship God worship a facet of the One God. The center of that worship for half the world's population rests in Jerusalem. All we ask is the simple freedom to pay our respects at that holy city."

"Though Brother Light's allies in the United Nations and on corporate boards are pushing for the official recognition of religious liberties in the huge crusade stopped in the desert miles from here, others are not convinced that a movement that has produced so many casualties could ever be a peaceful one. Spokesmen for the Children of Light dismiss the reported attacks on border guards, saying that the incidents are the wholly understandable reactions of frustrated pilgrims kept from their divine goals," Anne O'Neal reported, standing on the ancient fortifications of the Golan Heights. Behind her, the Syrian landscape stretched toward the east and the siege simmering there. Brother Light had not ordered an all-out attack. Apart from the constant, daily and nightly incursions of bomb-rigged women and children, and the occasional berserker charges of the demon-possessed Hands of the Prophet, whose murderous ruthlessness and supernatural stamina frightened their opponents more than any massed charge would, the Children of Light seemed to wait as patiently as their Prophet claimed for permission to freely pass the borders.

"So far, Syria, Jordan, and Egypt have resolutely refused Rashi Janjalani's request to allow the Children of Light free passage through their nations. In a historic agreement, Israel and Palestine have both pledged their support to their Arab neighbors, sending troops and matériel to a front no one expected to have to defend." Footage of Israeli and Palestinian fighter planes, soldiers, and convoys flashed past, grim-faced men and women preparing to defend the territory of the nations that stood between them and the vast horde that many had begun to realize represented their utter destruction.

"Along with traditional war preparations," Anne continued, as the scene shifted to the lovely, flower-bordered square outside the shining Jerusalem Temple, "religious leaders have gathered to ask for their own type of protection. President Smith of The Church of Jesus Christ of Latter-day Saints conducted a closed devotional meeting, to which all Mormons were invited. Unfortunately, Channel 8 could not obtain copies of that broadcast."

The media blackout in that case was intentional; President Smith had gathered all the Saints in Israel and Palestine together for a meeting that lifted their spirits with song, prayer, and reassurances in the true prophet's gentle voice and brilliant eyes that the Savior, who had come to His people once already, still extended His hand over them. "We watch the forces of the adversary gather, we see the horrors that evil will wreak on even the innocent, but we do not bend. Our fear does not overcome our faith. Rest assured, brothers and sisters, fellow Saints, believers in the justice and the mercy of the Most High God, that He will protect His own. Keep your heads high and your faith bright. Though we walk through the valley of the shadow of death, as the psalmist said, we fear no evil."

His eyes twinkled, and a gentle smile crossed his face. "Remember, there can only be shadows when there is light to cast them. Even the devil himself cannot exist without our Father and His glorious Son. Stand fast; do what must be done, no matter what happens. Strengthen your testimonies and your families. Move forward in love, and trust in the One who created the earth and all things in it, who atoned for the Fall that all His creation could be made perfect again. He broke the bands of death and hell, and they have no more power over Him, or over His children."

President Rojas, speaking to Anne O'Neal and the world in general as well as the Saints, repeated the prophet's basic message. "We absolutely stand with the brave men and women on the front lines, and we also stand firm in our faith that the forces of evil will never win the day. And be assured, the man who calls himself Brother Light has aligned himself and his followers with those forces. We call upon them all, with all the energy of our souls, to repent and come back to the true light of God. If they continue in their course, if they continue to use violence and fear to destroy all who do not swear allegiance to the darkness sweeping the world, they will pay a heavy price. Not only death in this world, but the eternal death of separation from the light of Christ."

* * *

"The infidel threatens *us*?" Brother Light sprang from his throne, his face crimson with fury. He threw down the letter President Smith had sent, urging what was left of good in Rashi Janjalani to come to his senses and disband his army or face the consequences of his actions. "He threatens *us* with death? I will see his blood on the streets of Jerusalem!" He stormed out of the tent, his phone already connecting to General Garza's lieutenant.

Sepphira, watching out of the corner of her eye until she was sure he had gone, slipped forward and picked up the paper Rashi had crushed. She smoothed it against the carpet, reading the words. It contained no threat, no anger, but a pervasive sorrow seemed to spread from it, through her fingertips and deep into her wounded heart. It felt as if she caught a glimpse of a light and warmth that would stay forever out of her reach. For a moment, a dizzying impulse rushed over her; she couldn't reach that light if she still clung to Rashi. But what if she let go of him, dropped the weight that pulled her down? Possibility opened before her, a vast sky studded with stars giving way to a glimmer of sunrise.

But what would that sunrise reveal? whispered a demon voice in her ear. She shuddered, as the shadows wreathed around her. *Can you face the light? Or will it burn you so completely that nothing is left? You are filthy, Sepphira, unworthy. God hates the filthy, the unworthy. He has already damned you. Your only hope is in Rashi, in the one who can defeat the judgmental God who waits to destroy you.*

Sobbing bitterly as she turned fearfully away from the light on her spiritual horizon, Sepphira ran to hide in the deepest hole she could find. She found him deep in conversation with the most vicious of his Hands, preparing for the greatest miracle of his career. Collapsing in the corner of the tent, pulling her veil across her face, she soundlessly cried until her tears ran out.

* * *

"If the infidels continue to bar the way," Brother Light said, his tone pouring godly sorrow and divine judgment on those who stood between him and his goal, "they will suffer a wrath so great that it will leave their palaces and great places in ruins, their men dead in the dust, their women prey for jackals, their children food for eagles, their bones the spoil of wild dogs." He raised his hands, preaching to the huge congregation of crusaders hungry for spoils. "We call the power of the One God down on the heads of those who seek to bar the way of the Children of Light! Go, take your places, and prepare to taste the blood of the enemy as the sun rises!"

Standing at the back of his army, the Prophet of the One God issued the order for them to rise and stand to see the destruction of their enemies. As one, the white-robed horde turned to face the long line where their enemies lay waiting for yet another day of siege. A low hum began, seeming to come from everywhere at once as it reflected from the clouds, rocks, and low hills. Brother Light held his pose, then slowly brought his hands down to point dramatically at the lines of soldiers guarding the border.

A trio of red lights flashed from the sky. A split second later, metallic thunderbolts screamed from the sky. Huge explosions threw flame, sand, rock, and bodies into the dust-choked air. Again and again, pillars of fire sprang up along the lines, hitting artillery emplacements, massed troops, and heavy armor. The heavy weapons utterly annihilated their targets, precisely aimed to hit the border guards and leave the Children of Light completely untouched. Frantic commanders issued orders across the few communications sets that remained intact through the barrage, telling their men to retreat, using all available cover. The line collapsed in a vast cyclone of sand and blood.

Fighters scrambled in the black-clouded sky, belatedly providing cover for their routed and badly wounded comrades. They found themselves chasing phantoms through banks of electrified mist, as the Velociraptors, their mission completed, winged their way back to the aerie Garza had established for them.

At a word from their Prophet, the Children of Light surged forward, overrunning the ruined fortifications. Singing praises and shouting hatred for the infidels, they streamed into the countries that stood between them and their goal. Thousands of civilians, joining those who had already retreated to Israel/Palestine in a desperate quest for safety, ran before the onrushing horde. Those who could not run fast enough were swept up in the human tide and, more often than not, spat out behind it, broken and dead. Their killers left nothing but trash, fire, and rubble behind, scooping up all the wealth they could lay their hands on. Even the livestock weren't spared; bonfires doubled as barbecues, as the human locusts ate up every living thing that couldn't get away from them.

The sorties the defenders sent against the flanks of the horde met the same fate. Syrian, Jordanian, Egyptian, Israeli, and Palestinian commanders, as well as officers and diplomats from half a dozen other countries, gathered to throw their best punches at the oncoming army of bloodthirsty pilgrims. None succeeded. The shadows told Sepphira exactly where the special-forces troops would emerge through the landscape, and she relayed their messages to the grim-faced enforcers. Brother Light smiled as he dispatched his Hands to destroy them. The next day, the Children of Light laughed and threw obscene salutes at their bodies, strung up along the line of march.

Demons, inner or outer, were not the only reasons the coalition's counterinvasion measures failed time and again. Every fighter plane that scrambled to fight the almost-invisible shapes flitting through the clouds fell to the ground as a chunk of burning wreckage or limped back to its starting point, battered and barely flying, the pilots bearing tales of perfectly targeted missiles flashing through the polluted sky like sharks through clear water. Far above the ground-based invasion, flights of automated drones hovered, laying a withering hail of fire that pushed the defenders ever farther toward the far borders of the countries that had stood between the Children of Light and the object of their crusade. Amman and Damascus disappeared in a wave of flame and smoke, the vast shapes of the explosions mirroring the shapes of the palm trees burning in the streets and courtyards.

"It seems that nothing can stop the advance of the Children of Light," Anne announced, the glow of fires lighting the Syrian horizon far behind her. "Coalition forces have fallen back to positions behind the Israel/Palestine border where they wait, forming a last line of defense against what has proved to be a literal crusade. All of us hope that this one won't end as the medieval Crusades so often did, with the sacking of Jerusalem." As she spoke, pictures of tense soldiers waiting behind banks of sandbags, checking their equipment and watching the sky, flickered across the screens of Channel 8 viewers.

"This time, however, Muslims and Christians find themselves on the same side of the battlefield." The scene changed to show the grim faces of the leaders gathered in Jerusalem, arguing tactics over the floor of the Knesset, proclaiming their determination to withstand the onslaught, decrying the "invasion in the name of God." "And this time, the mortal defenders are calling upon their shared God to defend them in public prayer ceremonies and private meetings." Another clip replaced them, this one showing President Rojas striding into the venerable building among a small group of religious leaders. The Mormon leader was barely identifiable through the interference that garbled Leon's transmission.

"Can't we get that blue-streaking image cleaned up?" Monk demanded, paying scant attention to the actual content of the broadcast he wanted to improve. "Get on the wire to the space station—tell Wong to deploy those baby satellites of his and relay our signal or whatever they do! This is the biggest story of the century, and we've got the worst reception of the century!"

Kim nodded, opening a channel to the ISS and shouting through the crackling sunspot static.

Wong reluctantly woke from a nap that had lasted twelve hours. The station's doctor had more cases of depression, panic disorder, and, in Mir's case, dramatic mood swings than NASA training had ever prepared him for; Captain Nakima asked only that he make sure that everyone stayed sane enough not to commit suicide or kill anybody else. He listened to Kim's laconic request and Monk's considerably more verbose threats and pleas, then groggily made his way to the darkened communications center. He nodded to Hideyoshi, who floated upside down, watching another broadcast beaming up from the earth. That channel, inexplicably, looked crystal clear. Tethering himself to the console, the communications expert began to nudge the controls on the fleet of tiny sheepdog satellites whose small magnetic fields swept the worst of the interference away from the communications satellites relaying Channel 8's signal. He watched until the image of Anne O'Neal steadied on the screen. She wasn't totally clear, but at least the picture didn't buck like the deck of a freighter in a typhoon. He nodded to Hideyoshi and went back to his hammock and his uneasy dreams.

Hideyoshi nodded back, watching the forces of evil cross the desert toward the temple and the Saints its underground honeycombs protected, and praying that something, anything would stop their advance. The water of the river he'd helped free from its underground aquifers gleamed in the few breaks between the clouds. Mir's neglected atmospheric sensors painted brilliant abstracts, patiently recording and tracking the swirling storms pouring from the deserts to scream across the Mediterranean. To Hideyoshi's weary eyes, the skyborne storms seemed to embody the unstoppable fury of the human storm rolling beneath them.

In the path of that storm, good-hearted people gathered, speaking, supporting each other with outward calm to mask inward tension, presenting a serene face to the millions of people watching them from all over the world. Those millions also faced violence, terror, chaos, and fear, whether from the iron fists of the Hands of the Prophet scattered throughout Asia and the Pacific to guard Brother Light's wealth or from the corrupt governments and warlords that needed no megalomaniac delusions to oppress their people. The people of Jerusalem, of Tel Aviv, of Nazareth, of Jericho, of Hebron, of Haifa, of all the towns and farms scattered throughout the Holy Land, held their heads high, for their own sakes and for the sakes of the people suffering evil's torment in every country. And as they showed their defiance through their care for each other and the refugees who belatedly streamed into their fortresses, they clung to the hope that by some miracle, their enemies would turn aside. The storms could not last forever; the sun had to come out.

"We ask Thee, O God our Father, to extend Thy hand over this land and Thy people, to protect us from the power of the adversary approaching," President Rojas prayed. All around him, in the huge conference room under the temple's foundations, faithful Saints added their faith and silent prayers.

And then the winds turned. The clouds that had streamed out of the deserts at Brother Light's back slowed in the face of the freshening sea wind, piling up in huge thunderheads above the massed army of the Children of Light. They sensed the literal change in the air— and the more subtle, unnerving change in the spiritual flavor of it.

"Holy One—the storm comes toward us!" The black-robed man paled under his crimson hood, raising the flapping doorway of Brother

Light's tent. A thin stream of dust poured in around his legs, throwing a sparkling trail across the rich carpets. Behind him, stars shone briefly through the gaps in the clouds, then disappeared.

"Let it come!" Rashi Janjalani strode out of the pavilion to stand on the high ridge above his vast army of followers. In the distance, over the Judean hills, streaks of lightning flashed. He looked at the sky, his eyes blazing with defiance. "Let it come!" he shouted. Raising his arms, he roared, "We defy you! We defy your power! You are dead and power-less! The Unity and the One God of this earth will throw your sanctuaries down into the dust! We damn you and all those who worship you to eternal hell!"

On his order, boomed over the vast communication network that connected Brother Light to his disciples, the Children of Light shrieked and shouted their own defiance, raising their weapons high. Lightning flashed on the glittering blades and ebony muzzles. They ran forward, shaking the ground with the weight of their advance. A few drops of rain fell from the towering clouds, as if the sky wept for what would follow.

The rain thickened, from sprinkles to a shower to a downpour so dense that the Children of Light saw it as a silver curtain pouring toward them. In an instant, it seemed that water had replaced the air itself. The sheets of rain fell so hard that each drop hit the ground and threw a dozen more tiny droplets into the air. Choking on their shouts of defiance in the saturated air, as wet from below as from above in the violence of the pounding water, blinded with the violence of the storm, their charge faltered and came to a ragged halt along the entire miles-long line. The whips of the Hands of the Prophet could not force them forward against the impossible storm; Brother Light finally sent the word through the ranks that they would "let the shower pass by" before they continued their march toward the Holy City to free it from the grip of the infidels.

Gratefully, the Children of Light took cover wherever they could find it. Not that they could find much of it, and what they did find proved horribly insecure. Wind howled and shrieked around the camps, driving the sheets of rain sideways into every nook and cranny. Tents shook, flapped against humming ropes, and took off like huge, ungainly bats, flopping their way through the growling sky. Hundreds crammed into the motley caravan of hijacked vehicles, huddling in cabs and truck beds, watching the storm with wide eyes that reflected the lightning.

That lightning struck the ground in and around the camp, so close and so fast that the noise of thunder drowned every other sound, every thought disappeared in the unending reverberation. The supercharged air crackled despite the pervasive soaking, smelling of ozone and power. Lightning struck hundreds, leaving charred and smoking bodies along the full line of the stalled advance. Fingers of white light reached up to the clouds, meeting their companions lashing down; the surges of energy swirled across the surfaces of the huge, foam-churned puddles, electrocuting thousands who were out of the direct path of the original bolts.

Terrified, the Children of Light prayed to their One God, pleading with the Unity to restore calm to the elements. In his own tent, secured on hawsers that twanged with the forces pulling at them, Brother Light heard the prayers—and cursed them for signs of weakness, shouting at the Hands to somehow get the army moving again. Nothing, and especially not a show of strength from a useless, dying god, would stop his victory!

Dawn came, somewhere beyond the clouds, bringing with it a fresher wind and a barely perceptible slackening in the torrents of rain. The lightning, however, at last drew off, crackling into the desert hills. Far to the west, a dim line of brightness appeared, marking the border of Israel/Palestine, where the rain had fallen in a refreshing shower, soaking but not flooding the plants in the newly farmed desert plantations.

The battered Children of Light sent up a cry, equal parts thanksgiving and defiance. The distant light drew them, inspiring equal parts hate and avarice. Slowly, they reassembled into marching formation—and found that where dry land had lain the day before, they now faced vast mud plains. The mud sucked at their feet, fouled the axles of the trucks, pulled tanks into impossible quagmires. Exhausted stragglers dropped ever further behind, unable to push on through the thick puddles, sinking into the wet desert soil.

They were the first to hear a new rumble coming from the hills. The torrents of water from the clouds fell incessantly on the parched dirt—and eventually ran off it in gathering cascades. From every gully, every ravine, every slope, water rushed, collecting into ever-growing rivers taking the easiest path downhill. Those paths, also the easiest roads for humans and animals, were filled with the slogging columns of the Children of Light. By the time the rearmost sounded the alarm, the flash floods had grown to devastating proportions. The walls of whitewater ripped through the narrow places, lifting even the heaviest trucks, throwing them aside like battered and broken toys. Those who escaped death by drowning and battering in the ravines lost their footing in the wave that spread from the mouths of the cuts. Bodies slowly rolled to a halt in the mud as the surge passed.

And still the rain fell.

* * *

"This is unbelievable," Cal Weathers exclaimed, his pointer tapping over the massive storm front that hovered just east of the Mediterranean Sea. "We haven't seen a persistent storm like this since—well, ever. The average rainfall for Damascus for the last ten years has been three inches. That's three inches, total. We've seen nearly two weeks of constant precipitation over this entire area, with totals in some areas nearing two feet. Just for comparison, the wettest place in the world, an island in the South Pacific, gets three feet a year."

"You want to know why the weather does something?" Ivana Mir rolled her eyes impatiently at the Channel 8 weatherman's question. Static fuzzed out her expression, though the contempt came through in her voice. "Yeah, a two-week storm like this is unusual. But we've got a whole lot of unusual factors to consider here too. For example, we've had another eruption from the Big Sister volcano in Oregon. Maybe what we're seeing here is due to greenhouse effects from all the volcanic gases in the atmosphere. Or maybe it's coming from the after-effects of the tsunamis that hit after the asteroids."

"Or maybe it's just bad karma," Cal Weathers suggested.

"Oh, yeah, that's scientific," Mir snarled, breaking the connection.

"Very professional, too," Hideyoshi observed.

Mir shrugged. "What are they going to do, fire me? If they get mad enough to bring me home to take my head off, good!"

"So, what is causing this amazingly focused rainstorm?" he asked, idly adjusting the settings on the tectonic receptors buried all through the Sinai. Even they showed rumblings from the weight of the water blasting to the sea, much of it flowing through the channels he and Becker had helped lay out, he noted.

"I'm still running analysis and simulations. The same kind of thing's going on in a few other places—Sichuan Province in China, for instance—and over a big slice of Botswana." She glared at the twinkle in his eye. "If you tell me it's some kind of divine protection, I'll ask Doc to put you on psychotropics with the rest of us, whether you think you need them or not!" A wry smile crossed her face. "Tell you what, we've got the best seat in the house for this show—whether it's just sad bad luck or crummy karma."

"The saddest thing is that it doesn't need to happen," Hideyoshi said. "If they'd just go home." If he thought about what he could see through his tight-focus monitors when the clouds briefly parted, his heart hurt so much it was almost physical. Bodies littered the muddy plains of Syria, Jordan, and Egypt, pitiful sacrifices to their leader's insatiable pride and appetite for destruction. The great horde of the Children of Light had ground to almost a complete halt under the vicious downpour, making perhaps a mile a day, losing vehicles, supplies, and soldiers, and yet their Prophet drove them mercilessly on.

"That Brother Light might be rich, but that doesn't mean he's sane— or any of the rest of them, either," Mir snorted. "I don't think they've got the sense to come in out of the rain."

A sudden change in the colors on her monitor drew the attention of them both. The greens of the rain had lightened into an icy blue that swirled through the upper levels of the storm. The whirling tightened as they watched.

"What does that mean?" Hideyoshi asked, a feeling of foreboding managing to sink into his stomach.

"Usually, it means snow," Mir explained, absorbed in the readings. "That far south, that far into the desert—it's got to be hail."

Absorbed with their own emotional stress and what was happening on the earth, and without their astronomer, no one thought to monitor the astrophysics lab or set the alarms on its monitors. Thus, none saw the blips signaling new meteors that appeared on the computer screens. The computer, however, did note the heavenly bodies and quietly projected their path right into the earth.

"With winds that high, those hailstones are going to weigh a ton before they fall," Mir projected. "They're going to be deadly." Little did she know that the astrophysics lab showed worse would follow.

* * *

Far below, the winds threw rain droplets high into the clouds, where they hit the flow of cold air spreading down from the north. They fell again, gathering more droplets around them, freezing, gathering, freezing, gaining weight and mass with each circulation. When even the winds couldn't support them, they fell.

The cold wind blew into the faces of the Children of Light, but for once it didn't bring suffocating gushes of water with it. A murmur of relief slowly spread through the immense army. "At last," they said to each other, "the One God has mercy on us!"

A black-robed member of one of the Hands splashed forward, raising his sword to point to the still distant but palpably nearer line of light that marked their goal. "Onward!" he shouted. "The One God defeats the dead god of the infidels as we shall crush their cities!"

A fist-sized chunk of ice, born in the freezing winds far above, hurtled out of the sky and struck the man's crimson hood. Instantly dead, he toppled backward, landing with a splash in the mud. More splashes followed, accompanied by screams, groans, and curses as hailstones blasted like bullets from the clouds. Replacing the needles of rain, the chunks of ice left bruises, broken bones, and dead bodies in their wake. The trucks and cars still managing to slog along the ridgelines to avoid the worst of the mud came under a different kind of fire as huge hailstones bashed out windshields and deeply dented hoods and roofs. The smaller particles fell like stinging snow, piling up under feet and wheels, sending the unwary and unprepared sliding into mud holes, down ravines, and off cliff sides. The momentary respite disappeared into a worse natural assault than any of the desperate people suffering beneath it had ever imagined.

"The line buckles, Holy One," a panting messenger announced, bedraggled and bloodied from the beating he had taken on his run between the communications truck and the trailer Brother Light had commandeered. "The Children cry for salvation from the ice that falls from the sky."

Fury reddened Brother Light's face. He had tried to stop the storms, exerting all the divine power he could summon, shrieking curses and threats at the clouds and the power he knew lay behind them, promising eternal destruction to the devotees of the entity opposing him—all to no avail. He had beaten Sepphira unconscious when she told him that the shadows laughed and danced around him, mocking his efforts. Now, he lashed out, knocking the shaking messenger into the mud outside the trailer's dented metal shell.

"They suffer because they lack faith!" he bellowed. "If they were truly faithful, the skies would clear. Until all put their trust in the Unity, Nature is not one with them. Kill any who murmur; drive out any who lack faith!"

The order spread through the horde. More bodies joined the drowned and broken ones already left as testaments to the storm's fury; these, however, bore silent witness to the viciousness of man. Some died as they stood to defend themselves against their mates' frantic accusations of faithlessness; others met their ends as they tried to leave the ranks. And with every one who died, the rest cursed their lives—but, more fearful of death, struggled forward in the face of all the fury of heaven.

* * *

"Please, Father, if it be Thy will, touch the hearts of those who come across the desert," President Rojas prayed, when it came to his turn during the prayer rally held in the courtyard of the Dome of the Rock. "Persuade them to turn away, to no longer continue in the face of Thy wrath, to abandon the wickedness that destroys them. We pray that Thou wouldst keep the hand of Thy protection over this, the ancient promised land, inspiring the hearts of the people within these holy borders with faith and courage." As he ended the prayer, a single ray of light stole through the clouds that had covered Jerusalem as well for the last month. It slid across the golden dome and white marble, lit the faces of the people, and touched gently on President Rojas's dark head.

"Oh, please let them listen," Carmen breathed, tears running down her face as she watched the devotional service broadcast over the

Church's network. All over the world, Saints prayed with their Associate President, watching the events in the Middle East unfold with both joy at the evidence of God's care and presence, and sorrow at the destruction the wicked had brought upon themselves.

"It'll be okay, Mom." Lucrezia squeezed her mother's shoulders, pressing her own wet cheek against Carmen's. Snuffing impatiently, she rubbed her hand over her face. "Come on—Dad's waiting. We've got everything packed up to take down to the Lius. Man, I'm glad I'll never have to have a baby on a bus!"

Carmen took a deep breath, composing herself. Her familiar, sweet, mischievous smile crossed her face. "Well, we hope you won't have to. You never know—other than you should never say never."

"Oh, come on," Lucrezia rolled her eyes. "There aren't going to be buses after the Second Coming."

"Why not?" Carmen teased, getting up and grabbing the packet of baby blankets and clothes that she and the girls had gathered for the new parents. The work went on, saving souls, redeeming the dead, taking care of the Saints—even while Armageddon gathered around Jerusalem.

Incongruous as it seemed, Carmen took great comfort from the sheer mundanity of the details of taking care of the refugees who still poured into Zion from the chaos outside its borders. Heavenly Father knew what He was doing, she and Tony had decided. The world needed the big showdown, the last battle to prove that He did hold the reins. The faithful already knew that and so could get on with the more important things. Charity, when given half a chance, never failed. They would do their part here, Giovanni would do his part on the other side, and through Christ's grace, they would all be reunited for the next great adventure. She had no idea what that might be. The uncertainty irritated Lucrezia and Tony, but Carmen and Donna accepted it with the good humor of people who had enough everyday details to worry about. Carmen, however, knew the future was in good hands. She paused to flick off the screen before following Lucrezia into the warm afternoon, so she didn't see the announcement that Homeland Security was in new hands now.

Merry did, looking up from her research on diabetes (Chris's old nemesis, and her project whenever she had a moment) to watch

Senator Holly Cox be sworn in as secretary of Homeland Security. The Church newscasters didn't describe her appointment as a "surprise move" or a "controversial decision," but Channel 8 did. Darren McInnes's expert panel dismissed Cox's appointment as an attempt by a weakened administration to score political points by appointing Garlick's nemesis to the post—and to snatch back some of the power he'd usurped by selecting a new secretary without the political backing to be a threat to its authority. They were all in for a surprise.

"Good luck, Holly," Merry said aloud.

"Good luck," Missy echoed, vrooming her trucks around the intricate set of roads she'd built under the desk. "Mamamam, is Dove coming back soon?"

Merry glanced at the screen, where a report on the stabilization of the Southwest and Mexico had appeared, prompting Missy's question. They both watched, hoping for a glimpse of their favorite border rat in the images of determined, good-hearted folk rooting out the last nests of Garza's defunct army and other criminals. For a split second, the dramatic image of a Santos logo gleamed, but Dove, as always, managed to duck the limelight. He led from the front, and always seemed to move too fast for any cameras but Socks's spy eyes to catch him.

He did stop long enough to peer over Perro's shoulder at the dramatic pictures out of Jerusalem as the broadcast update came on. A freak asteroid shower, unexpected even according to the simulations on the International Space Station, had begun over the Middle East. The streaks of light glowing on the monitor reflected in Dove's dark eyes, lighting fires deep inside them.

"These unbelievable disasters haven't stopped the huge army of self-proclaimed crusaders still marching toward Jerusalem," Anne O'Neal said. She stood on a bluff under a cloud-clotted sky, lurid light playing around her. "Even their spokespeople have finally dropped the line that the movement is a peaceful pilgrimage, acknowledging publicly that Rashi Janjalani plans to conquer all of the Middle East. One spokesman described the city as the 'crowning jewel' for the victory of the One God."

"Those who oppose the march of the Children of Light will fall to divine thunderbolts, just as their predecessors did. However, the enlightened shall be spared. The Holy City will welcome its Lord and King with open arms," proclaimed the Pakistani ambassador, his immaculate white robes glittering with golden embroidery as he addressed the press.

"It seems more likely that the city will experience the same fate as Damascus and Amman," Anne observed. Images of the ruins of those cities flashed across the screen, vividly showing the devastation the Children of Light left behind them. "Now, however, we have learned enough to shed light on the dramatic attacks that routed the coalition forces on the Syrian and Jordanian borders."

Another set of images appeared, crystal clear underneath the snow that fouled Channel 8's broadcast. They showed perfectly, however, on the Church's satellite channel, sent through an offshoot feed from Leon's camera. A neat, heavily armed camp appeared, well to the north of the action. The focus zoomed in, click by click, until the men standing beside the sleek form of a Velociraptor became clear.

"General Andrea Garza, after being routed from the Americas, has appeared in the crisis zone," Anne announced. "It was the contribution of his forces, and specifically their long-range weapons, including stolen American bomber drones, that destroyed the resistance and let the Children of Light proceed through the borders."

Monk tuned out the reporter's words, staring at the spy-satellite images. "Where did she get those?"

Kim glanced over, shrugged almost imperceptibly, and pressed another button. A report appeared on Monk's screen. The producer's eyes narrowed as he read a standard media-cooperation agreement, signed by Anne, that gave her and Channel 8 a right to broadcast the Mormons' exclusive footage of Garza's camp—in exchange for a secondary feed from her reports from the front lines. For the first, nearly unbelievable time, the Church's satellite channel and Channel 8 were broadcasting in tandem. And to his horror, Monk saw the Mormons' ratings flicker and climb up another laborious point.

His fist hit the console. "I want that agreement ended now!" he shouted. Clicking open the channel that connected him to his rogue reporter, he snarled, "If you're thinking it's easier to ask forgiveness than permission, you're dead wrong!"

Anne managed not to wince as Monk's voice blared in her ear (static and all). "The question now is whether what looks to many like the wrath of an angry God will discourage the Children of Light or persuade

Rashi Janjalani to order his followers to retreat to save their lives. Live from the battle several commentators have termed incipient Armageddon, this is Anne O'Neal for Channel 8 News."

Leon did wince, sending a quick apology to the Church controllers before he cut their line. The Church's able techs replaced the shot of Anne with dramatic footage of the asteroids streaking through the clouds to explode like bombs on the drowned, battered plain below.

* * *

"Garza," Dove growled. "So that's where he's got off to." A faint smile crossed his face. "Looks like the General walked right into a real dose of the Old Testament. I hope he chokes on it."

"Rain, hail, and now fire," Calvin said as his hands, busy sharpening a knife, slowly came to a halt. "He's going to do more than choke. Brimstone's next."

"What?" Perro couldn't drag his gaze from the horrific scene, half on the screen and half in his imagination, as he watched projectiles of partially molten space rocks smash into the massed and battered hordes of the Children of Light.

"It's what happens to the armies of Gog and Magog," Calvin explained. "I've been talking about Revelation with Sam Begay. God hits them with rain, hail, fire, and brimstone, trying to get them to turn back."

"Do they?" Perro asked. His brain reeled; for a moment, life felt like a movie Calvin had seen and he hadn't. He wondered if it was cheating to ask what happened at the end.

"No," Calvin sighed. "The idiots just keep on coming. And things get worse before they get better."

"Poor dogs," Perro muttered.

"Pray for them," Dove advised, slapping his shoulder. "And get your lazy butt up. We've got the old Blanca Hacienda road to run. Socks says he saw banditos out that way. Garza got away from us, but they won't."

"Is God going to hit them with meteors, like He's hitting their boss?" Perro asked, reluctantly standing up.

Dove grinned. "Nah—he's going to hit them with us instead. Meteors are just for the second string."

CHAPTER 21

Brother Light stared at the wreckage left behind by the meteor shower: craters studded the muddy plains, the smoking ruins of the last of the tanks embedded in them; trails of flame spread into the sky from the direct hits on the tanker trucks that had carried the fuel for the vehicles; a scattering of the crusaders struck dead by the molten hail lay staring sightlessly at the roiling sky.

"Why haven't you already cleared their defenses?" he demanded, turning his attention to the crackling but momentarily open communications channel.

Miles to the north, General Garza set his jaw in annoyance. "I told you—it does no good to blast open the border defenses before the infantry force is in place to occupy the country. Your march is taking too long. If you do not reach the Golan Heights at least by the end of this week, we're going on without you."

With an irritated snap, he shut the communication channel on Brother Light's enraged protest. The Prophet didn't want him using one of his last three nuclear bombs on Jerusalem, but without the infantry to back up the conventional bombs, the city would still stand between him and total domination. "Blast the man," Garza muttered. "And blast Brindermann for pushing this insane alliance!"

He stalked away, intent on his own plans. His Balkan associates had upheld their side of the bargain, bringing the bombs and heavy artillery to join the Velociraptors' lethal cargo of weapons. Now, he needed a victory, a big one, to secure the land bridge he would use to launch invasions into every continent in the Old World. Jerusalem represented that victory to him, the act that would prove to the world that nothing—not even seemingly divine intervention—could defeat him again.

"Janjalani did handily overwhelm every government between here and Thailand," Brindermann observed, falling in step with the General. He'd heard the curse on his head—and occasionally agreed with it. Neither of them had foreseen being held down on the last march like this. "And his forces are still making progress, however small." He glanced at Garza, a subtly malicious light in his eyes, as he added, "Which can't be said for your independent attempts. How many bombs did we lose to that 'electromagnetic interference' over the Golan?"

Garza whirled on his lieutenant, his face distorted in rage. "Jerusalem will fall by the end of the week, or it will disappear in a radioactive cloud!"

* * *

"Jerusalem will fall, or the One God will strike you all down as the faithless traitors you are!" Brother Light's declaration rolled majestically out of the speakers his tenacious Hands had salvaged from the broken caravan and powered with scavenged fuel cells. He looked over what remained of his army—still immense, but less than a quarter of the numbers he had started with. The others lay moldering in a grisly trail strung for miles behind them. Only the strongest, most determined, and most ruthless survived, those whose hate, greed, and pride pushed them forward through every obstacle.

Their leader smiled, his remarkable voice instantly modulating to the seductive promise that lured them to him in the first place. "Only ten more miles, and the green lands of Palestine will be yours," he purred. "The wine will flow freely. You will have meat to waste, and women to take as you wish." Weaving a vision of plunder and power perfectly tailored to the hungry, weary, dangerous men, he stoked their inner fires to a fever pitch.

The chants began, then rose in volume as the remaining crusaders, beginning with the Hands, took up the rhythm of praises for the One God of the earth and the One Prophet.

Brother Light pointed at the hills now clearly visible in the distance, all rain, hail, and even meteors gone, as if heaven had spent its last bolts. "Your plunder awaits. Go, strike the infidel in the name of the One God!"

With a roar that echoed from the distant hills, audible for miles down the long lines of the militant army, the Children of Light moved forward on their last, long charge. The ground trembled under the massed assault.

From high above, on the cliffs, the defenders watched the onrushing horde. For some of them, the wave of blade-waving barbarians represented the final nail in the coffin containing their last shred of faith, proof that nothing could hold back the forces of evil. For others, still trusting in God and better versed in the prophecies of scripture, the charge told them that the end was truly nigh—but they also knew what that end would entail. Many had joined the prayer service that morning, deep under the Jerusalem Temple, and heard President Smith ask that God grant their enemies one last chance to give up their evil designs and turn away.

A faint tremor that quivered through ancient rock barely jarred those faithful soldiers and their comrades. It did more than jar the sensors scattered throughout the tectonically active points Hideyoshi monitored. Alarm bells jangled—unnecessarily, since the tectonic specialist was already hovering in front of the monitors, watching in astonishment as long-quiet faults shifted, slipped, and slid.

The earth heaved, throwing the onrushing army to their knees or headlong. A deep wave rolled through the ground, the surface heaving like the ocean. With a rending crack, huge fissures appeared, steam and hot smoke boiling skyward. A band of the Children of Light, caught in the confluence of two steam vents, died even as they screamed, instantly flash cooked. Others scrambled back from rock slides that sent boulders bounding down the hillsides, crushing and mangling any human in their way. And then, with a violent stench of sulfur, the trenches opened to the deepest pits, sending gouts of magma erupting into the air and gushing along the ground. The heat and poisonous vapors of brimstone rolled over the invaders, killing and searing.

"Keep them moving!" screamed Brother Light into the communication channel that, with the insidious presence of the shadows, all of the Hands tuned to. He held desperately to the side of the trailer on its higher vantage above the battlefield, trying to shove his army through the earthquakes and volcanic explosions through sheer force of will.

Sepphira, huddling behind him, barely saw the shadow that slipped up to her, throwing itself into her, blanking out her consciousness. "Run to the northeast ravine." Her voice, dragged out of her protesting throat, caught Rashi's attention. He listened to the plans from the shadow inside her, a slow smile spreading over his face as he relayed the directions to the Hands. They obediently gathered every man they could, marshaling them to follow the demonic advice in avoiding the worst of the earthquake's power.

Slowly, the aftershocks died away; the earth seemed to groan as the remaining Children of Light at last reached the borders of the Holy Land. After the upheavals of the planet, the mere weapons fire that met them seemed barely noticeable, like the buzzing of insects after eagles' attacks. They swarmed toward the defenses, shooting and shouting.

Far above their heads, the Velociraptors swooped, throwing bomb after bomb down onto the long lines of allied forces desperately holding off the badly decimated but still huge army. To Garza's fury, the rate of misfires was staggering; several "smart" bombs even careened off course to detonate in the midst of the Children of Light. Gradually, however, those that did get through destroyed weapons emplacements, ammunition caches, communication centers. And just as gradually at first, then more rapidly, the most frightened defenders, the ones who lacked faith or fortitude, those who valued their lives above their liberty, began to drop their weapons and run. Some ran away, deeper into the country they were abandoning. Others surrendered to the black-robed Hands, throwing their lots in with the force that they believed would sweep all before it. Even the forces of heaven hadn't stopped the Children of Light, they reasoned; perhaps the One God did represent their only hope of survival. As the lines crumbled, another message came through, this one a combination of the standard order to retreat and the silent but powerful voice of the Spirit, calling the faithful home to safety.

The Children of Light at last crossed the borders of Israel/Palestine, to find the country stretching before them practically undefended. Brother Light and General Garza shared one giddy moment of absolute victory, their minions raising a triumphant shout to the cloudy skies.

* * *

"The day has finally come that all dreaded," a haggard Palestinian captain said, too weary even for fear. "We cannot stop them. We come to Jerusalem to make our last stand and die with those we love."

Anne turned to face the camera as he led his bedraggled troops on their final stand on the city walls. In the distance, columns of flame and smoke marked the sites of the smart-bomb explosions that destroyed the last few tanks among the desperate coalition army. "Tel Aviv has fallen to the Children of Light, as has Haifa. All over Israel/ Palestine, the resistance is being overrun. I'm standing on the main road into Jerusalem now, where thousands of refugees are making a last mad dash for the city—or even the Mediterranean beyond."

Behind her, heavily laden family cars rolled slowly along battered pavement, weaving among throngs of equally heavily laden pedestrians. Leon's camera caught a tiny, sobbing baby, held close to its shock-worn mother. Anne suppressed a sob of her own. She had never wanted to be a war correspondent, and now she found herself in the middle of Armageddon. Flickers of faith from her long-lost Catholic childhood kept flaring up, making her heart hurt because it seemed to offer hope that all the suffering would end in a burst of glory. She tried to stop them, to take a rational view of the conflict.

"The last hope of the thousands here in Jerusalem seems to be negotiation of a peaceful surrender," Anne continued. "And the men most likely to conduct those negotiations are the two Mormon presidents, who have proved a source of strength to Jews, Muslims, and Christians alike during this last month."

"That'd be a good tagline—Prophet vs. Prophet." Monk smiled nastily as Anne's summary went on. "We'll have to get a camera in there when it happens. The Knesset's wired for broadcast—" He stopped abruptly, as the static on the screen grew opaque, then began to clear.

Brother Light's form shone from the clearing screen. His eyes shining, his white robes immaculate, he walked sedately beneath arches of palm branches held by adoring disciples to face the camera. Holding out his hands in an inviting, seductive gesture, he announced, "The Unity has at last come to the Holy Land. The One God treads the ground all revere as sacred, and claims the kingdom that was ever divine. Oh,

Earth, your God has come to you at last!" Every channel transmitted through the International Space Station transmitted the scene, as Rashi Janjalani proclaimed himself the Prophet of the World, the God who came to the earth to dwell with His people, the ultimate embodiment of the Unity, appearing "as the sun rises in the east" to all the world at the same time.

And then the broadcast went dark. As the pirated channels regained control of their broadcast frequencies, Mir burst into the communications module of the ISS, shouting, "Hey! What do you think you're doing?"

Hideyoshi turned his head, his face nearly white beneath its space-darkened tan. His hands still rested on Wong's communication controls, holding down the last command that had interrupted the timer system and undone the universal transmission override links.

"What do I think I'm doing?" he managed to whisper. Crimson rushed into his cheeks, replacing the pale shock. "What do you think you've done?" He swallowed hard, choking down fury and tears as he stared at her.

"I think I just made a million dollars with a stupid prank. Remember? Nakima said I could have some broadcasting bandwidth, since he was letting you use it. So I did. I made a million dollars letting some wacko in a white bathrobe make a total fool of himself on worldwide TV." A manic grin spread across her face even as her stomach felt queasy at his expression. "Oh, come on, Jim—it's funny!"

His hands left the controls in a blur, grabbing her shoulders hard. Through superhuman effort, he managed not to shake her. "No, it's not funny," he told her but with molten heat that penetrated the fog of antidepressants in her brain. "It's *blasphemy*, you idiot!"

Regaining enough control to let her go, he turned away to stare at the broadcast; only the Church's channel hadn't been hijacked.

"Jim—Jamie, I'm sorry," Mir said, her own tears flowing.

"Don't tell me, Ivana. You'd better start praying." Hours later, he was still there, huddled in the communications module with Mir wept out and sleeping as she floated beside him. A feeling of calm finally came through the hurt as he looked at the face of President Rojas.

* * *

The Associate President appeared at Anne's side, reassuring the hurting, terrified world that the real God still cared for them and would achieve the final victory. His dark eyes serene, Rojas said, "President Smith and I will do everything we can to bring this situation to a peaceful conclusion. We are ready to make any necessary sacrifice. The Savior truly does extend His protective hand over those who trust in Him."

Leon's camera followed President Rojas into the Knesset, Anne hurrying alongside as they walked through the packed corridors into the main chamber. President Rojas paused now and again to touch a hand or shoulder, whisper a comforting word. He left the reporters at the door, moving to join President Smith on the dais. The assembled dignitaries quieted, taking their seats with grim faces and weary eyes.

"Ladies and gentlemen." President Rojas stood at the speaker's podium, looking over the assembly. "President Smith and I thank you for your confidence in selecting us to head the negotiation team—"

A sudden scream interrupted him. Both Presidents turned toward the disturbance along with everyone else, but the camera caught a fleeting glimpse of resignation on President Smith's gentle face.

Four black-robed assassins burst out of a service entrance. The shadows' guidance and a few cowards' help had brought them through the back alleys and underground tunnels of the city to do their master's bidding. Three spread out, shooting into the crowd, forcing a clearing. Terrified people fled in all directions, leaving the wide, littered floor empty. The last, a monster of a man, strode forward like Goliath, his eyes glowing with demonic power behind his crimson hood.

President Smith, bent but unwavering, and President Rojas, tall and immovable, remained where they were as the giant moved toward them.

"We see thee, emissary of Satan." President Smith's voice was gentle, but with a power that made it clear over the pandemonium filling the room. "Your dark master will not win the victory."

"Our Master sends us to remove the last pretenders," the man growled back, all hell howling in his voice. "He sends this, and bids you take it to your dead god."

With that, he threw a glittering sphere that seemed to grow into a huge ball of white-hot sunlight. It engulfed the two prophets and blinded the cameras as a crescendo of screams rose. When the light faded, the two men lay lifeless on the floor. The light had hidden the assassin who crept up behind them to stab them through the hearts; the giant shouted that the divine wrath of the One God had struck them down.

Anne jerked forward, her hands out; Leon held her back, somehow managing to balance the camera while stopping her. Through its lens, he saw the Hands converge on the two bodies, hoisting them up with obscene shouts of triumph.

The black-robed servants of Brother Light paraded the two dead prophets through the battered halls, shooting all who opposed them. When they reached the street outside, hundreds of refugees whipped off kaffiyehs and skullcaps, shrugged off jackets and garments that had hidden their filthy white robes. The revealed Children of Light shouted praises to their One God, proclaimed curses on the souls of the dead infidels, and bellowed threats against all who opposed the Unity. As the real refugees screamed in terror and scattered away from the knives and guns of the invaders, the Hands lashed their hated, murdered victims to light poles as trophies for all to see.

And the world saw them. Even Clara Cortez went pale as she replayed Anne's footage of the assassination. For a single moment, the world blanched as one, feeling a loss greater than they could explain. All eyes turned toward the Mormons, whose beloved leaders had died in such a brutal, public execution. The response stunned them.

"We mourn for our brethren in Jerusalem," Elder Molina said for the world to hear, his face sorrowful but composed. "We mourn for the hate and pride that brought so many low enough to commit such horrendous acts. But we look with confidence and serenity toward the blessed coming of the Son of Man in glory. The time has come."

* * *

"The time of victory has come at last. The last barriers to the complete domination of the One God have fallen at last," exulted Brother Light, standing in the rubble-strewn Jerusalem street, surveying the lifeless forms hanging against the ropes. Turning to the Children of Light who filled the street—and all the streets beyond, and massed outside the city, waiting on his word to begin the last great slaughter—he raised his hands and shouted, "The Holy Land is one with Unity! It belongs to the Children of Light now and forever! Cleanse its streets and stones with fire and with the blood of every infidel within its borders!"

The order blasted outward, carried to the Hands, who passed it to their cadres. Civilians and soldiers alike fell under the bullets and blades of Brother Light's army—unless they forswore their God and joined the slaughter. And the butchers laughed, throwing each other flowers, raising toasts with stolen wine, celebrating the deaths of those who had thwarted their advance for so long. General Garza's forces joined in, setting off a fireworks show over the city that was as impressive as it was devastating. High on drugs, wine, and the heady rush of victory, the Children of Light advanced slowly through the city, driving the remaining fighters inexorably into the walls of the Old City and toward the outskirts—and the beautiful, white building on the hill where thousands huddled inside rock-hewn chambers, singing praises that echoed to heaven and caring for the wounded. Outside those alabaster walls, the grotesque songs and braggadocio of the invaders drowned out the sound of their hymns.

Far away from the bloody streets, others celebrated as well, if less barbarically; calls flitted through the ether as corrupt politicians, warlords, and criminal businessmen paused for a moment to mutter that the Mormons had finally gotten what they deserved. "That'll show them. Nothing cures a religious fanatic like meeting a religious fanatic with a bigger gun," went one coldhearted phrase, usually followed by, "Now, maybe they'll shut up."

By the second day of celebrations, however, Garza had grown impatient. "You've proved your point," he informed Brother Light over the static infesting their communications channel. Brindermann had ordered Medea's hackers to thoroughly prepare it this time; no one listened in on the two commanders' conversations. "We've got Jerusalem, and now's the time to move on to the next phase." The light of megalomania filled Garza's face as he glanced from the monitor showing his ally's luxurious new headquarters to the map spread out before him. The world spread out before him. "Europe lies open for the taking; our forces have already pacified Egypt. Brindermann can help you set up the supply lines for the next push, and I have more forces waiting in the Balkans—"

Brother Light yawned, interrupting the General's eager plans. "The world is already ours."

Garza's eyes came up, narrowing dangerously. "Don't play with me, Janjalani. You have Jerusalem, and a quarter of the army you promised. Do not push your luck again."

"Or what?" Brother Light sat up, meeting Garza's eyes. The hate they felt for each other—for every living creature that did not bow to their will—reflected in both their faces. "We have Jerusalem. We have no more need of you or your petty technology. You are nothing—a toy to cast aside. The power of the One God cannot be defeated!"

Brindermann stared at the screen, thinking that the man had finally gone completely mad. When he caught sight of the General's face, he knew it. And he knew that Garza had joined the self-proclaimed Prophet in a netherworld of berserker rage. Neither could bear to be defied—or defeated.

"You will swear allegiance to the Unity," Brother Light continued, "and give over your weapons to the Hands of the Prophet." A slow smile crossed his face. "And we may let you live."

Garza returned the smile—and with a gesture sent a bomb hurtling into the Knesset. It destroyed half the building, killed the collaborators who had agreed (out of cowardice, greed, or heedless self-preservation) to accept the Unity and set up a provisional government. It was also the first shot of a battle royale that raged over, around, and through Jerusalem, a final contest between Brother Light and General Garza, Gog and Magog. Massed infantry charges and guerilla attacks pushed against smart bombs and Velociraptors; fanatic hate for all infidels and hunger for their wealth shoved against cold contempt for the enemy and determination to exterminate all opposition.

Buildings toppled, fires raged, towns disintegrated, blood flowed on both sides—and through it all, the white walls of the temple stood shining and invincible. No bomb, aimed or flying wildly, could strike it; no Hand of the Prophet, or the demons raging in him, could break through. It became a secondary target in the titanic struggle, the target for either side when they spared a moment from blasting at each other. Inside its walls, the Saints and the faithful of all religions waited with bated breath for the final act.

Except for two figures, dressed in gray to blend into the shadows, who slipped out of the mouth of the tunnel connecting the deep catacombs with the streets of the city.

"This is nuts," Leon whispered as they emerged from the tunnel, casting wary glances around the ruins standing stark against the huge flares of light in the sky, filling the street with rubble. "How did you find out about this, anyway?"

Anne avoided another body. They lay thick as cordwood in some places, bundles of bloody rags that only the flies profited from. Her face set in determination as she slipped from one shadow to another. "Brother Cohen told me about it. I remembered it, from when I interviewed him before he left. He's the architect. And Brother Hassan is the builder. Between them, they knew which tunnel to take."

"So we can follow up a crazy tip from that same *Mr.* Cohen." Leon caught her hand, helping her over a jagged pile of rock.

"No, more than that," Anne said. "He only told me what would happen, not when. But somehow, I know it's now. I can't explain it— I just know it."

"Your journalistic instincts again?" Leon sighed. "Listen, we're just going to get ourselves killed, and for what? If they believe it, they don't need to see it."

"But everybody else does," Anne shot back. The shattered bulk of the Knesset rose across the square, only a few black-clad figures in sight. Most of the fighting had drifted northward for the moment, as the Children of Light made a concerted rush for Garza's camp. "And I do," she added, her voice thickening. They positioned themselves where they could see the bodies of the two prophets.

"I still—" Leon began, then choked himself. "Oh, my God." It was the first prayer he'd said in years.

Around the two battered bodies of the prophets, still lashed to the light poles, a soft light had begun to glow. Leon scrambled for his camera, raising it and turning it on. Anne reached over and clicked another switch, sending the dual signal through the ether to the transmission station deep under the temple's foundations. As they watched— as the world watched—the light grew, cool and pure, gold and green and white as sunlight. Shining figures appeared, gently untying the two prophets, laying their bodies down with the tender care of parents. Bright hands rested on the ruined flesh and bones, sending flows of life-giving fire into the empty shells. Power poured through those hands, breath filled the transformed lungs, the stilled hearts beat back to life. The angels raised the two prophets to their feet.

"Holy Mary, Mother of God," Anne whispered, tears streaming down her cheeks as she recited the rosary, the only prayer she could remember. Movement at the side of the incredible tableau caught her eye. Tearing her gaze away, she saw the black figures of the Hands running forward. *Would they attack even angels?* she wondered.

She raised a hand to catch Leon's shoulder, warn him as the assassins came closer, and felt a sharp blow to her chest, a shattering feeling, searing pain, and a sudden rush as if she were drowning. The force of the bullet threw her backward into the pile of rubble. *No, but they would attack mere mortals,* the thought wandered through her spinning mind.

Leon, his face a mask of horror as he saw her fall, turned back to see the four assassins converging on him, drawn like deadly moths to the ruby light of his camera—and behind them, the figures of President Smith and President Rojas. The two prophets still carried a residual glow, standing out from the darkness as they walked forward. President Smith raised a hand, calling out words that seemed to echo through the cameraman's skull and pass through without leaving more than echoes of themselves.

The four assassins halted, standing stiff and still as dead trees. With a scream that spiraled up into the heights of agony, four shadows ripped free of their hosts, vanishing as a bolt of divine power banished them. The bodies they had inhabited fell, their own spirits unable to withstand the unadulterated presence of the Spirit.

The camera fell as they did, catching the image of Leon kneeling to catch up Anne—and the shoes of the two prophets as they walked over to the two journalists.

President Smith laid a hand on Leon's shoulder, gently pulling the young man away. "Let us take care of this," he suggested, in his sweet voice that still retained the authority of thunder.

Anne opened her eyes to see President Rojas kneeling over her, the pressure of his hands lifting from her head. He smiled, offering her a hand. She took it, sitting up, the reflected light of eternity slowly fading from her eyes along with the memory of the pain. "Thank you," she whispered, as her eyes flooded with tears. "I used to know, and then I—I forgot. Oh, Jesus, how could I forget you? I am so sorry—I was so wrong! We were all so wrong!"

"Leon," President Smith asked, "could we use you and your camera to make an announcement?"

"Uh, sure," Leon said slowly, still stunned by what he had witnessed. Then professionalism took over and he picked up his camera. Expertly framing the prophet, he said, "Whenever you're ready."

"Brothers and sisters," President Smith began, "the great lights in the sky you are seeing through the thinning clouds are the foretold sign of the coming of the Son of Man. Prepare, my brothers and sisters, to meet our Lord."

* * *

"What is this?" Monk demanded, staring not at the screen, where one of the most amazing sights the world had ever seen had played out, but at the line of ratings bars. One bar—the bar for the Church's satellite broadcast, the bar he hated with a passion—rose steadily, overtaking the other competitors one by one, until it stood equal to Channel 8's. And then passed it. "What's happening?" he demanded. "This is an exclusive! What are they showing?"

Kim tapped another control—and the feed from the Church's broadcast filled the large screen. It showed President Rojas and President Smith helping Anne to her feet.

"They've turned the back feed on again!" Monk stared, livid with fury and fear and thwarted pride. This could not happen—he would not lose the ratings war he'd fought his entire life, the battle he'd built his entire identity on, to a reporter leaking exclusive footage to a rival!

"Turn it off!" he screamed at Kim. "Hit the auto-kill switch on that camera! I want that gone *now!*"

Kim's head slowly turned, her eyes reflecting the glowing figures on the screen. She slowly stood, removing the headset that had been practically part of her. Setting the set on the console, she gave Monk an almost pitying look. "I can't do that," she said, and walked out.

The door closed behind her. Every monitor on the wall glowed sunbright, as what he guessed was a massive surge of sunspot energy wiped out Channel 8's satellite relays, then blew out its screens, leaving the producer in total darkness.

* * *

Triumph danced in Brother Light's eyes, blinding him to the sign in the sky the rest of the world could see. His officers reported that his shock troops were about to breach the centuries-old but well-defended walls around the Old City of Jerusalem, even as he and the bulk of his forces drew near Garza's besieged encampment. Victory fluttered in his grasp, like the failing heartbeat of his former ally. With a wolfish smile, he sent word for his troops to charge. As one they moved, the overwhelming numbers blasting through the General's perimeter defenses, the mob pouring in to fight for control of the camp and the technological control center in its heart.

A huge, crimson-hooded figure burst out of the darkness, striding into the low, amber lights of Garza's command post like the shadow he carried inside him. All around the camp, the last charge of the Children of Light had broken through the General's elite troops. The officers around him scattered to defensive positions, firing desperately. Garza whirled away from his command console, instantly drawing his pistol from its holster. He fired shot after shot into the oncoming giant, each heavy bullet staggering the man. He fell at last, but two more appeared, their long-bladed knives flashing. A wild grin spread over Garza's face as he dropped one clip and snapped another into the gun. He paused just long enough to touch a single control, then charged toward the demon-possessed hordes. He roared defiance as first one giant, then another toppled into the dust. The roar choked on a gush of blood as the last crimson-hooded assassin drove his knife through the General's chest. Looking at the blade, Garza managed a last curse, bringing his pistol up. The single shot tore through General Andrea Garza's own skull.

Johann Brindermann heard the shots and slowly rose from his post at the command console in the next tent to face the mob of Children of Light bearing down on him. Under his delirious gaze, they transformed into the forces of chaos he had always hated and feared, the sadistic criminals in soldiers' uniforms who had come out of the darkness to destroy any shred of security he had ever known. He faced them with blank and empty eyes, firing again and again until the tide washed over him. As he died, the actinic flash of the self-destruct he'd set on the command post seared into his eyes; he, his attackers, and the communications techs disappeared in a brilliant ball of fire.

The fires reflected in Brother Light's eyes as he stared hungrily toward the ridgeline battle. When he saw the white-hot flash, he raised his arms and crowed, "So dies the infidel!" Laughing, giddy with his own power, he stabbed his hands toward the battle. "So We unleash all the powers of hell on all those who oppose us!"

"You've won," Sepphira said from where she stood in the back of the room. Shadows played around her, around him. She stepped forward, holding out her hands in supplication. "Rashi, you've won. Can you please call them back now? Can we please stop the fighting now?"

His fluid movements froze. Glancing at her over his shoulder, he said coldly, "They will fight until the last infidel's last breath is spent."

"But what about the Unity?" Sepphira asked. "Shouldn't we convert them, bring them into the great love of the One God? The love you offer to so many—that you used to offer to me? Isn't that what this is all about, gathering all into His love?"

"*His* love," Brother Light snarled, whirling to face her. She cowered away from his stinging slap. "We are the One God! You are undeserving of our love, as you always have been! Faithless whore!"

The words cut into her, wounding and searing. Sepphira looked up, seeing the shadows gibbering all around him—even in his eyes now, the eyes she used to love, that once showed her love in return. He hit her again, the hard impact against the wall knocking the breath out of her.

A high scream rose over the curses that rained on Sepphira. An explosion rocked the ground, shattering the far side of the building they had taken as a field headquarters. High above, the last of Garza's missiles, the ones he spent his last few seconds guiding, bore down on Janjalani's position.

Brother Light whirled, staring up at the fiery death coming from the sky. Raising his hands, he shouted, "None can defy the power of the One! We command the forces of the Unity to blast the weapon from the sky!"

One of the Hands, watching fires spring up just yards from him while Brother Light called upon the powers of darkness to stop the next volley, began to laugh. Others simply ran, caring more for their lives at the end than for their spiritual leader. The sound of his laughter echoed, harsh and demonic. "The forces of Unity thank you, Rashi" he said, drawing his long knife. "But we no longer need you. You have delivered us all the souls we hungered for." The shadows swirled around him, their ember-red mouths soundlessly echoing his laugh as he lunged at Brother Light.

The lunge ended in a sudden plunge to the floor, as a bullet destroyed the brain the shadows needed to control the hijacked body.

Their would-be victim looked over the body at Sepphira, standing with another Hand's discarded gun. Disregarding both the assassin and the savior, Brother Light turned back to command the missiles to turn back. He jerked hard, blinked at the holes exploding through his chest, and fell forward, dead. One more shot rang through the shriek of the incoming bombs; Sepphira crashed to the floor beside the body of the man she had loved, killed, and died for. A second later, the bombs blew apart the remnants of Brother Light's army in a wave of ground-shaking fire. The blasts continued to shake the ground as the last of the armies destroyed themselves.

At Jerusalem, unaware that their leader had been killed, Hands of the Prophet led the Children of Light through the gap that finally breached the east end of the Old City's walls. The Israeli military bravely laid down cover fire as the civilians moved toward the western side of the city. The frantic crowds behind the thin protective line knew they had nowhere to run, but pressed on, driven by a hope they did not fully understand.

More self-propelled rockets slammed into the walls of the Old City, causing the earth to quake. Under the man-made earthquakes, however, another, deeper vibration grew. The vibrations reached far into the ancient rock surrounding the battered city, setting loose tiny rock falls that grew into avalanches. With a groan that reverberated even through the unmoving rock under the temple's foundations, the Mount of Olives split in half. Those behind the beleaguered walls of Jerusalem abandoned the city and fled into the opening and to the safety it promised. Some recognized they were compelled by more than fear and desire for safety. Indeed, they felt the promise of something more than physical salvation.

As the last of the Jews and their allies fled, the earthquake ripped again, this time taking full vengeance on the enemies swarming though the city. As the ground buckled, the buildings and now useless walls crashed down upon Brother Light's minions, stopping the advance and destroying many.

The titanic heave rocked the tectonic sensors, setting off the InSAR alarms that clanged through the tiny room where Hideyoshi watched the seismographs record the quieting of the earthquake. Then light pulsated through the tiny cabin. His eyes rose from the readouts as the Spirit filled his soul, his heart leaping as he looked out of the port to see a brilliance like the first light of dawn appear through the darkness, a dawn coming at midnight. The divine radiance swept over the globe like the most incredible sunrise since the first one, the coming of the Son of Man arriving like dawn from the east, rising for the final time over all His creation.

* * *

My dear Chisom,

I am jubilant. In just three days, we will, at last, see you in person. What is more, we will be able to meet your bride-to-be. How we look forward to that. My heart is nearly ready to burst with happiness. Considering that the earth is now experiencing joy upon joy, it does not seem possible I could hold any more, yet it is so. Who would have thought that we could have joy to the point that it is almost painful? Contributing, of course, is the flood of calm, peace, and love that has covered the earth since the coming of the Lord.

To think that in almost an instant, He changed the world from an infernal hell into an Edenic paradise. And His coming literally saved the world. This poor old earth has clearly taught the cosmos the self-destructive nature of sin run rampant. Had the Lord not interfered, no one could doubt that all would now lie in ashes. But sin did not win; evil was not victorious. Both lost to Him who, in His own way, destroyed the destroyers of the earth.

I shall never forget the moment when all saw Him, red in his apparel. Silence reigned for many minutes as even Nature herself held her breath. His majesty captured every eye and stayed every hand. None moved, terror gripping many, awe gripping all. Then He released His glory and it blasted across this earth, changing everything in an instant. He spoke, and His voice came as it were from Zion and Jerusalem, like great thunder breaking down the mountains and filling up the valleys. With a command, the great deep moved back into the north countries, and the islands became one with the land, leaving the earth as it was before the great division (just as it says in D&C 133).

What a wonder that we have lived not only to see but to participate in His Second Coming. Our feelings and experience here were so much like the ones you described. The wonder of being caught up to Him in the air—rapture is the best word to describe the overpowering feeling and wonder of it all. His glory suffused everything. Because they were sufficiently pure, terrestrial souls were safe in Zion or in their innocence. Because they were not, telestial souls were burned. Indeed, as the scriptures prophesied, "every corruptible thing, both of man, or of the beasts of the field, or of the fowls of the heavens, or of the fish of the sea, that dwells upon all the face of the earth" were consumed, and also the elements melted with fervent heat such that all things have become new. What was the result? Just what the scriptures said: God's glory and knowledge now dwell everywhere upon the earth (see D&C 101:24–25).

The irony of the event overwhelms me. The exact same glory with the exact same intensity that brings us so much joy destroyed the telestial souls in an instant. They simply could not withstand the glory and attendant love that He manifested. It overwhelmed them; they resisted and died. Mercifully, He allowed their spirits to escape, for the moment, into spirit prison. The memory of the pain and heat caused by God's glory and love will remain with them while they wait for the final judgment. That memory will prove to be a great motivator as they prepare for the time when they will once again have to face the fullness of that love. You can bet that all but the most hardened will be ready.

You asked about the return of Enoch and his people. That was something. Just a few days before the Lord came, the Brethren told us to prepare for another great moment. Another influx of the righteous would be coming, but unlike so many, these would come bringing strength and assistance. It was shortly after noon the next day when we saw a light streaming as it were from heaven and covering the temple area. We rushed out of our offices and others from their homes to see it more clearly. As it lifted, there they were with the Lord, the people who had built the former Zion. Love and appreciation for these early Saints burst upon us. The same thing happened to them at the same moment. We rushed together, hugging, crying, praising God, dancing—for quite a while there was a tumult of ecstasy until the Lord called us to order. He then had us kneel with Him as He prayed to the Father in thanksgiving and gratitude. The moment was overwhelming, and we cried great tears of joy. Since then, they have been working with us as we prepare to take the gospel to the "heathen nations."

One more item impresses me. For a couple of days after the Lord came, I kept feeling like something was missing. It was as if a great load had been lifted, but one I had become used to carrying. Only then, with it gone, did I become aware of it. As I searched for an explanation for my ease and lightness, it dawned on me. What was missing was the ever-present pressure from Satan and his temptations. I am now amazed at how much energy it took to continually resist him, energy I am now free to turn to my Lord's service. I am so glad that the devil and his angels have been shut up for a millennium. Now the earth can rest for a season, and we can all devote our services to the Lord and His children. In that regard, I find it interesting that there is no difference in our mission between the telestial world we came from and the terrestrial one we now live in.

It will, however, be good to have you here helping me with that mission and working on my team. Adaure and I believe that this Thursday will never come. You can bet we will be at the airport on time. We just hope the plane is not late. We so look forward to having all our family together, and we include Wei Wei, for the first time in over four years. I am humbled and pleased that through all the temptation and strife, we have lost none of our five children, their mates (or mates-to-be, in your case), or grandchildren. Family means everything.

With love, highest respect, and deepest anticipation,
Your father,
Chinedu

Epilogue

"Was it really like that? Like the sun coming up in the middle of the night?" Eager little faces and bright eyes looked up, six great-grandchildren waiting for the final confirmation to cap the best bedtime story ever.

Merry laughed and gave it to them. "Oh, yes, just like the sun coming up in the middle of the night—and in the day, too—so bright that He made the sun look dim."

"And did you and Tio Dove, and Uncle Calvin and Aunt Donna, and Grandma Carmen, and everybody really do all those things, fighting the dark at the end?" asked Bella, taking the lead as she always did. She took after her grandfather Gianni with all the dark curls, but that smile came directly from Missy.

"Oh, yes, we did." Merry leaned forward, wincing slightly at the creak in her back, and fixed each of them with a long look. "But it wasn't the end—it was just the beginning." Touching each one lightly on the head, she continued, "And I expect you all to train your own kids to fight valiantly when the real last battle does happen. There's going to be one more, you know, and I expect all of you to meet me and Grandpa Chris on the other side when you've won it."

"Oh, we will!" Bella assured her. The others nodded happily.

"All right, who's up past their bedtime?" Missy came in and shooed the laughing kids off to their parents and bed. Leaning over to kiss her mother's cheek, she gently stroked Merry's hair. "You look tired, Mamamam."

"I am tired," Merry agreed. "Time for me to go to bed too. Good night, sweetie. Love you." She watched Missy bustle out after returning the good-night wish, then leaned back against the chair cushion.

Maybe just a quick rest, to get up the energy to move into the bedroom.

She shut her eyes, feeling herself drift off—and then drift weightlessly, as if she floated in water, or in air, bodiless. No, not bodiless; she felt herself present, but without the weight of years pressing on her. A surge of energy flickered through her, as if restraints had come loose. Through her eyelids, a gleam of gold light shone, warm and welcoming.

"Merry?" a voice called.

Her eyes flew open, and she flew into his arms, warm, solid—and real! "Chris!"

ABOUT THE AUTHORS

JESSICA DRAPER is unaccustomed to writing about herself in the third person. She is also an avid reader, big sister, trained librarian, amateur needleworker, cat owner, and possessor of a rich fantasy life (obviously). She currently works at the Center for Instructional Design at Brigham Young University, after spending many years writing software documentation (which often qualifies as speculative fiction).

RICHARD D. DRAPER is a professor of ancient scripture at BYU and the director of the Religious Studies Center. He holds a PhD in ancient history. Brother Draper is a best-selling author of several books and talk tapes, and has written numerous articles for the *Ensign* and other publications. He has been a popular lecturer at Know Your Religion and Education Week for many years.

Richard and his wife, Barbara, are the parents of six children and reside in Lindon, Utah. Outside of the fact that he is the only one in his family who dislikes cats, Richard's kids think he's all right.